The Dream Chaser

Morgan True Blum

First Printing, 2021

ISBN 978-0-9980429-2-3

www.MorganTrueBlum.com

The Dream Chaser

To my son, Magnus.

To Granddad, who really did get a bunch of Eskimo boots with his friends, paint them with polka dots, and go downtown so that people would make fun of them and they could get into fights. To Granddad, who was placed in an orphanage, and had to grow up moving from foster home to foster home. To Granddad, whose favorite Elvis song was *In the Ghetto*. To Grandad, who was all too acquainted with the pressure to be tough to survive.

To Mr. Schultz, and Our Savior Lutheran School where I always felt safe.

Trigger Warning

Chapter one depicts a fictionalized mass shooting that takes place at the hands of the Red Army. If you are triggered by such things please feel free to skip chapter one.

The Dream Chaser
Prologue:
December 1917
The Proposition

It was clear as Staccato stood before the Warden that she was aware of his surprise at finding her so young. He fidgeted with his hands, something he was not accustomed to doing. It was not the best way to begin things. There was nothing in her expression to suggest his presence inspired any sort of reaction beyond a vague sense of annoyance. But then why should she recognize this strange older man with the shaved head and short, scruffy goatee? He'd retired from government service fifteen years ago, and this young woman was barely twenty-five, not much younger than his daughter.

"I'm here to see Mr. Anomaly," he explained in his smooth, grandiose voice.

The Warden's eyes glazed over. "And you are?"

"Sir Staccato Nimbus. Friend of the family."

She crossed her arms and leaned back in her chair. Her eyes rested upon his staff with pernicious hatred. Such attitudes towards Fay were not uncommon these days in Capricorn, but it was still rude.

Staccato sighed and retrieved the note from his pocket. "The Head of Security said to give this to you when I arrived."

The Warden snatched the note from his hands and scanned over the writing with impatient eyes. Staccato raised an elegant eyebrow. Twenty years ago, the Warden's behavior would've been met with severe repercussions, but that was before Sultana Charmion came to power, when her sister ruled the kingdom.

When the Warden finished reading the note, she crumpled the paper in her fist and glared at Staccato with new significance. By now she had probably figured out Staccato was here to arrange for Pyro's release, and unlike Pyro's parents or King Thayer, he was quite capable of pulling it off. Staccato threw back his shoulders, showcasing his full height. The Warden was unimpressed.

"You'll need to hand over your staff."

Staccato could have laughed aloud, but of course to do so would've made matters worse. As he turned in his staff, he wondered if it wasn't a blessing the Warden was so young and knew nothing about him. She clearly wasn't aware that he didn't need his staff to wield his powers. She made him sign a piece of paper on a clipboard, and led him towards the heavy steel doors with the caution tape. A sign read, "Warning: High-Risk Prisoners."

Staccato knew as he passed over the threshold that the cells would be overcrowded with Fay rebels from Aquila and Delphinus, but he wasn't prepared for the inmates' horrible living conditions. Capricorn always found loopholes in the international law, but Staccato didn't fully realize the extent until he looked into the faces of the emaciated prisoners rotting in their beds. Of the countless seraphs all had their wings in vices, even though there was nowhere to fly to. Mermaids sat in tanks hardly bigger than an aquarium. The most any sylph had was a bucket's worth of soil on a stone floor.

There was no telling what they had done to Pyro. Staccato knew from the papers that Pyro had grown up to be an incredibly athletic young man in top physical condition. But whenever he thought of Pyro it was hard to imagine him as anything but a fiery-haired little boy of nine or ten. He hadn't seen Pyro in person since his parents sent him off to boarding school in the Pan.

Staccato followed the Warden around the corner. When his eyes registered what lay at the end of the hall, he let out an audible gasp.

"You've been keeping him inside a water tank?" He could not mask his outrage. "How is he still alive?"

"We monitor his vitals and take him out before any permanent damage is done."

But Staccato was hardly listening. "That's a violation of international law! Capricorn could be expelled from the Ecliptic Council for keeping such a monstrosity!"

The Warden pursed her lips. "Technically we're not breaking any rules. The water is sterile, the temperature is regulated, and as I stated before, we're not allowed to confine him any longer than what's safe."

Clearly aggravated, she picked up her pace, making Staccato work to keep up with her. When they reached the door of Pyro's cell, Staccato could fully appreciate what the boy had been made to suffer. His head leaned back against the side of the tank in sleep. His chest rose and fell rapidly. He struggled to breathe. A muzzle covered his face below his nose, and he was now sporting a beard.

The Warden unlocked the door and ushered Staccato inside. It would have been easy to mistake Pyro for his brother, with how thin he had grown. The thought was quite disturbing when one considered how differently the two boys had been built. Arson had taken after their mother, tall, thin, and statuesque. As for Pyro, despite being muscular and fit, he was always short and stocky. Now the bones in his chest were visible.

Staccato jumped as the Warden banged on the glass. Pyro screwed his eyebrows together and awoke with a start. He met the Warden's eyes begrudgingly.

"You have a visitor." She crossed to the back and ascended a small set of stairs leading to the tank.

Pyro eyed Staccato with foggy scrutiny. Considering Staccato and Pyro were both spies employed by King Thayer, he had expected Pyro to recognize him. But the unfamiliarity in his countenance did not fade away.

The Warden unbuckled Pyro's muzzle and deposited it on a hook beside the machine. Pyro groaned and tried to sit up straight.

"Can I have some water?"

Staccato was surprised at the lack of cheek in his voice. The Warden eyed him over.

"That depends, are you going to spit it at me?"

That was more like it. Pyro's eyes were dull. "Are you gonna punch me if I do?"

"Yes."

Pyro yawned, then coughed and shook his head. "Then no. I'll save that for later."

The Warden went to the sink, filled up a glass of water, and—much to Staccato's astonishment—actually fed it to him. When Pyro finished, he threw back his head in a fit of hacking.

The Warden tapped her foot. "What do you say?"

Pyro wrinkled his nose. "Thanks, Nettie."

The Warden looked as though she might smash the glass over his head. Pyro rolled his eyes.

"Thank you, Ms. Green."

The Warden descended the stairs and pulled out a chair for Staccato.

"If he tries anything funny, just press that button on the wall and the guards will come and assist you."

She left the door unlocked behind her and retreated into her office. Staccato sat down. He and Pyro stared at each other in silence as they listened for the noise of her clinking footsteps to die away. Finally, Pyro blinked.

"Who are you?"

"Staccato Nimbus."

"Never heard of you." He closed his eyes and leaned his head back again.

Staccato kept his voice steady, bearing in mind that Pyro had been inside this tank nearly every day for the past two months. Furthermore, Pyro had been a child when last Staccato saw him, and Staccato was merely another boring dignitary his parents were acquainted with.

"You don't remember me?"

"Should I?" He turned his shoulders and winced. Exasperated, he opened his eyes again and sat up. "Look, did my parents send you or something?"

"They did."

For some reason this annoyed Pyro. "I suppose it was too inconvenient for them to show up themselves."

"Capricorn wouldn't permit them to enter the country."

"Well, why are you here? I don't know you. It's not like you can bust me out of here or anything."

"Actually I can."

Pyro's eyes widened. Staccato leaned forward with his elbows on his knees.

"It just so happens that I have a proposition for you. To be honest, I'm surprised you aren't more familiar with me. You and I happen to work for the same person."

"Are you Thayer's valet or something?"

Pyro was going out of his way to be rude now, and Staccato wasn't sure how much longer he could tolerate it.

"I do undercover work."

But Pyro wasn't listening. "Wait a second, Staccato Nimbus … I remember you!" He threw back his head and laughed. "Oh, they used to talk about you all the time in the Saighdeoir!"

Staccato sat tall and straightened his cravat.

"You're the chap who knocked up the queen!"

Staccato's hands dropped. A great power surged beneath the skin of his palms. He instinctively reached for his staff, forgetting he'd left it at the front desk. Pyro continued his guffawing.

"She'd been hauling your ashes how long? Three months? And ol' Bruin still thought the baby was his!" He could hardly contain himself.

Staccato flew at Pyro, knocking over his chair in the process. Pyro's skull banged against the back of the tank. Staccato never had to lift a finger.

"Here's a history lesson for you," Staccato hissed. "I happen to be the most powerful miraculous in history, one of only three who don't need a staff to wield their powers. In fact, it only makes me weak. I've been fighting the C.O.N. since before you had the motor skills to wipe your nose. I've served the second-most-powerful kingdom in Voiler under two different monarchs, and held a seat on the Ecliptic Council. I've been knighted in three different countries. I was awarded a Scarlet Scale when I was ten years old for rescuing Queen Calliope from a fury. King Javaid, whom I am on a first name basis with, made me godfather to his daughter. Suffice to say, Mr. Anomaly, I am an important person. Important enough to kill you and have it swept under the carpet."

He flattened his hand against the glass and willed the water to claw at Pyro's throat. He lowered his voice further still.

"If you ever speak disrespectfully of my wife again, if any foul remark falls out of that stupid, inebriated mouth of yours, I will see to it that you have a federal warrant in every country that matters! And the moment they arrest you I will be there to execute you myself!"

Pyro looked as though he were just short of a panic attack as he nodded his head up and down, craning away from the ghostly waves. Staccato removed his hand from the glass. The water fell tame.

"I'm sorry." Pyro took a deep breath, or at least he tried. "S— sorry. I've been here so long I've forgotten my manners."

Staccato reached out his hand and summoned the chair right-side up again.

"According to the papers—and your parents—you forgot them a long time ago."

"Look, Mr. Nimbus. I mean *Sir* Mr. Nimbus! Should I call you Sir Mr. Nimbus? You said you can get me out of here, right?"

Staccato made himself sound uninterested. "I can, however, there's a catch. Are you familiar with the Cirque De Fay?"

Pyro arched his neck. "Way back in history, when the Fay were still nomadic, they put on performances for ordinary folk using their powers. I wasn't half bad at history."

"As you're probably aware, the art form has made quite a comeback in the past decade."

Pyro bowed his head and groaned. "Oh no, don't tell me Thayer's got you manning that whole undercover circus thing? I told him it was a silly idea!"

"It's panned out far better than I anticipated."

"How does it work exactly?"

"There are several uses. Traveling undercover enables a group of highly trained professional spies to travel places without looking suspicious. We can hunt down ophidians in the Other without drawing much attention. Best of all, we're frequently hired by well-to-do ophidians and C.O.N. members who like to dabble in Fay arts for the publicity."

"So what do you do?" Pyro inquired. "What's your act?"

Staccato drew back, frowning with dignity. A flicker of fear flashed through Pyro's eyes, no doubt afraid he had insulted him once more.

"I'm the manager! I do *not* perform."

Pyro appeared genuinely surprised. "Well, why not? I mean, you are the most powerful miraculous in history, aren't you? I'll bet you can do all sorts of amazing things."

Staccato tossed his head to one side. "Well, I do provide illusions for the scenery, and … well, at this point half the performers are hallucinations. There aren't many of us. Which brings me to my next point. If you agree to come and work for me as a performer I'll bail you out of here."

Pyro's head fell forward as he laughed aloud. "Me? A spangly circus performer?"

"You are a gymnast, aren't you?"

Pyro's face fell. "Well … yeah, but—"

"And a powerful igneous."

Pyro glanced from one side of the room to the other. "Yes, but—"

"I'm afraid you've got two choices: spangly circus performer, or half-starved prisoner. Which is it going to be?"

Pyro looked down at the water. Staccato crossed his arms.

"I should inform you that if you decide to come and work for me, a certain code of conduct is expected of you. You see, not only would your parents like your freedom but they'd like to see you straighten out as well. There will be no drinking, at least until you've proven you're responsible enough to handle alcohol. There will be no late-night partying. No dalliances with cabaret dancers. Foul language is prohibited."

Pyro lifted an eyebrow. "Blazes, do I have to attend Sunday school as well?"

Staccato slipped him a wry smile. "That won't be necessary. Our strongman is a former reverend."

Pyro smirked. "Sounds like a pretty square deal so far. Alright, Mr. Nimbus. I'll come work for you under one condition."

Staccato looked Pyro over, taking note of the overgrown beard, the bruised veins, the open blisters, and scoffed. "*You* have a condition?"

"Hear me out, it's only one, a small one … I think. See that fella in the cell behind you?"

Staccato looked over his shoulder at the underfed prisoner lying dismally on his cot. He was a young man, maybe even younger than Pyro—who was only twenty-five.

"Yes, I see him."

"He comes too."

Staccato stretched his eyebrows. "You want me to bail two high-security prisoners out of Kilgoree?"

If Pyro could've crossed his arms he would've. "It's either both of us or neither of us."

Staccato turned and eyed the prisoner. Only a baby could have been less harmful looking. His brown arms and legs were long and thin. Any lean muscle had eroded away with starvation. He had a broad mouth and thick hair that curled like an expensive china doll's.

Staccato got the feeling from looking at him that if it weren't for his present circumstances he would've been very lively. His eyes scanned up and down the long passage of chained innocents. Freeing a prisoner in Algedi wasn't the same as freeing a prisoner in a place like Pisces, or Taurus.

Staccato stroked his beard. "What's he in for?"

"He tried to strangle Senator Sobek."

Staccato was so startled he almost knocked over his chair a second time. "He what?!"

Pyro lowered his eyebrows. "Do you have any idea the sheer amount of deaths Sobek is responsible for? It's a shame Skelter didn't kill him!"

Staccato rubbed his temples. "I'm not disapproving!" He sighed impatiently, then stole another glance at the prisoner called Skelter who was now drawing a butterfly with his finger in the grime on the wall. He was almost cartoonish.

"Him? *He* broke into Vega Hall and physically assaulted Sobek?"

Pyro was grinning as though they were discussing a character like Robin Hood or Sinbad.

"Turns out he's an amazing acrobat! That's how he was able to get close to Sobek in the first place. He even slipped through the bars when the Warden was withholding my meals."

"She withheld your meals?"

"Yeah, she does that sometimes. But Skelter fed me. He doesn't deserve to be here! I mean, nobody does really, but look at him! How long do you think a fella like him can last in a place like this?"

Staccato cradled his head in his hands. "It's not that simple. Skelter tried to assassinate a government official. Wars have been started over such instances! Great Northern Star! The whole of the Other has been fighting for the past three years because an archduke was gunned down by radicals!"

Pyro glowered at Staccato with a hard, stubborn stare. "*Oi*, if you're as important as you say you are, Mr. Knighted-in-Three-Countries, you can bust my friend out of Kilgoree for trying to assassinate a murderer—not an archduke, but a man who wiped out an entire kingdom of innocents."

Chapter 1:
Seeing Red

"Faina!" Faina's fifteen-year-old brother Leo came jogging across the snow. "There you are! What are you doing?"

Faina stood with her freckled, nine-year-old face turned up to the night sky. "Looking at the stars."

Leo grabbed her by the chin and examined the sticky crumbs staining her cheeks. "Just how many gingerbread cookies have you eaten?"

Faina looked down at her hands thoughtfully and began tallying on each finger. "Um, five?"

"You better hope Father Christmas isn't watching. You wouldn't want to land yourself on the naughty list the night before Christmas!" He grabbed her by the hand and towed her towards the church. "Come on. Service is gonna start soon."

"But Father Christmas can't come this year, or else the Reds will shoot him down! You heard what Papa said, the Bolsheviks want to ban Christmas."

"Don't you start worrying about that again. Everything will be fine."

"That's what you said when we left the Urals because the Red Army took over the city, and now we're having to leave again! Just last week I heard Mr. Bagrov telling Papa of the executions in Yekaterinburg. Next they'll be coming here!"

"Well, we'll be long gone by then so there's no use thinking about it." He stopped to hold open the heavy oak door, but Faina remained staring up at the sky.

"Mama says that in New York City you cannot see the stars because the lights are so bright. Aren't you going to miss them?"

Leo shrugged. "We might not live in the city, you know."

"But that's where Uncle Matvei lives, and he has his own business!"

"The city isn't the only place to have a business, Faina." He waved her inside. "Now, come on. We're letting in a draft."

Faina sighed and reluctantly tore herself away from the silver lights. The atrium of the church was perfumed with evergreen and citrus garlands. On the far side of the room was the long banquet table where Faina had gotten her cookies. The trays were stacked with colorful cakes, aromatic pies, and shiny braids of bread with crust that scintillated with a subtle egg-wash shimmer. Two young ladies passed in front of them. They had sprigs of mistletoe pinned to their collars. They glanced up at Leo and burst into a peal of flighty giggles.

Leo was always getting noticed, and it was no wonder, for he was a handsome boy with a charismatic personality to match. He had floppy auburn hair, a short, compact build, and a proud, smirking mouth. He had a habit of gazing out at people from the corner of his blue eyes so that he always appeared to be scheming or flirting. His hands were always callused from climbing trees, and he had a sprinkling of red freckles across his nose and cheeks.

Mama and Papa were situated at the far end of the atrium. Their father, Adrian Spichkin, stood like a long, red advent candle over the crowd, his lean face the tapering wick. Like Leo he was handsome, but slightly more on the harried side. He was a tall, slender man with wild waves of strawberry blonde hair, coke bottle glasses, and a bushy beard.

Their mother, Ariadne, served as the perfect model for what Faina would look like when she was grown up. She had a broad forehead with full apple cheeks, and a pointed chin. Like Faina, the high bridge of her aquiline nose descended down her profile like a queen's, and her hair was like a dense, black veil that trailed behind her.

"There's my little spitfire," exclaimed her father when they spotted the pair coming towards them. His voice was littered with the biases of his own Celtic tongue. Once they were eye level, he dropped his head closer to her mouth and lowered his voice.

"Do I smell gingerbread cookies?"

Faina curled her hands up by her lips and chewed bashfully at her fingernails.

"Maybe …"

Papa tossed his head like a lively Christmas robin, and laughed his merry laugh.

"Well, it'd be an awful shame if there weren't any left for Father Christmas."

His nose touched hers so when she looked up, his smile seemed to have stretched to an impossible degree, and she could not help giggling.

"Where were you, darling?" Mama pushed a stray hair back from Faina's forehead. "We were looking for you everywhere."

"I was outside looking at the stars."

Leo rolled his eyes playfully. "She acts like we're never going to see them again after we leave for America."

Papa chuckled. "You're like your papa, a country girl through and through."

"Now how can you say that when she's never even been to the city?" Mama hugged Faina to her hip. "Really, Adrian, you will throw her off New York before we even get there. Do not spoil it for her."

"I just don't see why we're so settled on New York. We could go anywhere in America! Why not settle out in the country? I hear there is an entire community of Russian immigrants in Washington state."

"Matvei says the future of America lies in cities like New York."

"Matvei would say that, he lives there."

"And owns a thriving business!"

"Ariadne, I'm a geologist, not a businessman. Our future lies out west with the trees and the mountains, a place where you can still see the stars."

Faina's head dropped down towards the floor with a sigh. What would a starless sky even look like? Her mother bent down and lovingly laid her lips against Faina's forehead.

"New York City was made of stars, my *ogonya*," little fire, "and if you look hard enough you can find them in the strangest places." She cupped Faina's cheeks, beaming at her as though she were admiring a perfectly shaped apple. "Don't you worry about a thing, my wild girl."

The pipe organ heaved a sonorous bellow from inside the sanctuary, signaling the start of the Christmas Eve service. Papa took Faina's hand and, with his arm around Mama's waist, shepherded the family through the enormous wood doors.

Faina flinched as she passed the candle at the edge of the pew. Papa laid a heavy but comforting hand on her shoulder.

"It's alright, Faina darling. It won't hurt you."

Once they had settled into place, they joined in the joyous singing of *Hark the Herald*. Mama's hymnal was open needlessly, for they all knew the words by heart. Faina focused her attention on the precious detail around her, determined to remember her last Christmas in Russia: the onion-domed ornaments tucked into the greenery; the sleepy aroma of the Christmas feast outside the sanctuary; the white paper stars the children had decorated the tree with.

Beside Mama, Leo was making eyes at Maria Antipova. Mama swatted Leo with her Bible.

"Leontiy Adrianovich!"

Faina pressed her fingers over her lips in a failed attempt to stifle her laughter. Feeling sorry, Mama winked and ran her fingers through Leo's hair in a conciliatory gesture. Papa gave Faina's fingers a kiss. When she looked up at him she realized just how long his pale gold eyelashes were.

A loud bang cut through the music as the sanctuary doors were kicked aside. The parishioners turned their heads like dominoes. The pipe organ let out a horrified scream as the player's fingers tripped over the keys.

Faina rose up on her toes and craned her head around. She could just make out the tip of a pointy hat with a red star on the front. Papa shoved her protectively behind his back. The Red Army had invaded. From her new vantage point, Faina could see the tip of the rifle aimed threateningly at the priest, and the endless flood of soldiers assembled at the door.

"Man," Father Ilya sputtered desperately, "this is a house of God!"

"The State is God, and you will all bow. Down with the Bourgeois!"

Faina's ears ripped with a horrible popping noise, and she instinctively shielded her eyes. Shrieks whistled through the gathering like an out-of-tune calliope. Blood stenciled the white robes of the cleric. He fell dead upon the altar. Everything crescendoed into one simultaneous nightmare. Bullets sizzled indiscriminately through chests with a caustic blare. Bodies dropped lifelessly like scarecrows.

Pleas. Shrieks. Blood fell upon them like raindrops as the soldiers fired at random into the fold. Papa had one hand on Faina's shoulder, and the other extended like an umbrella over Mama and Leo as he struggled to herd them out the aisle.

Faina yelped as blood splashed the side of Leo's face. Mama dropped down between them, her hand trailing over Leo's shoulder.

"Ariadne!" roared their father.

Faina let out a scream that seemed endless, pouring over her mother's blanching cheeks as she lay in the pew. Papa lifted her into his arms and ordered Leo to keep moving. A force threw their father's head back. Blood blossomed over his shirtfront.

"Papa!" shouted Faina.

Papa went limp and slid to the floor, dropping their mother on the ground in front of him. His eyes struggled to stay fixed on Faina as he fell back in his own blood, dead. Faina felt the roar winding itself inside her lungs again, but Leo seized her around the waist and slammed a hand over her mouth. Faina bucked and kicked, clawed at the pews, straining to remain with their parents.

"Faina, we have to go!"

"Mama, Papa—"

"They're gone, Faina! There's nothing we can do! We have to go!"

The clamor was dying down now as the final remnants of life began to dwindle. The torrent of motion slowed to a sickening pace, punctuated every now and then by the loud popping of a gun. Leo froze. His eyes darted wildly around the sanctuary. With his arms locked into a vice around Faina he wrestled them into a laying position and smuggled them halfway beneath a pew. He lowered his lips close to Faina's ear, and his breath felt hot and shrill.

"Act dead."

Faina made herself as motionless as possible and lay her cheek in the still warm blood upon the floor. Her eyes scanned the endless clutter of hands thrown over the ground and hanging from the backs of seats. As her gaze crossed to the adjacent row she found herself staring into the lifeless blue eyes of Maria Antipova, her arm thrown out in front of her as though she had fallen, her mouth partially open. Faina's shoulders trembled with shock as she wrenched her head away.

Leo's hand clenched around her forearm in warning. From her place beneath the seat she could see one of the white paper stars lying on the floor, the tide of blood leaking onto the parchment until the whole thing was colored red. Every now and then a whimper would make its way up from an unfinished throat only to be silenced by another shot. In her mind, Faina kept telling herself she was dead, as though she could reason her body into a convincing corpse.

Two wet boots paced up the aisle and stopped in front of their pew. The soldier was so close Faina could see the ice stuck to his shoelaces. She shut her eyes.

"All clear," barked the official. There was a noise like an empty can being tossed aside. The brassy aroma of gasoline filled Faina's nostrils.

"Move out!"

They listened as the troops filed out of the sanctuary. There was a clatter as a soldier kicked over one of the candle stands. The flame became an orange smear of light as it fell to the floor. The doors slammed and bolted shut. Fire spread across the pews. Faina gave a cry.

"Shhh!" Leo squeezed her hand. "It's alright, Faina, it's alright!"

But there was nothing to indicate Leo was right. He scuttled out from under the pew and hauled Faina up by her waist. Blood soaked through their clothes. Flames clawed up the walls. Leo hoisted Faina into his arms and headed for the corridor behind the altar where communion was kept. He ducked beneath the flames spreading over the doorway.

"Where are we going?" Faina cried.

"I'm going to get us out of here." Leo wrenched the handle of the side door. It did not budge. He reared back and kicked it down. A bottomless stairwell was laid out before them. Too afraid to look, Faina buried her face in Leo's neck, bouncing as he rushed down the stairs. The air felt icy and dank on her bare fingers.

She could hear Leo's shoes echoing on the stone. The wood creaked overhead as the flames ate away at the floor above. Faina's nose knocked against the edge of Leo's shoulder. They were running up the steps to the cellar hatch. Leo stopped and listened. The lintels gave another groan.

"The cellar door should be hidden beneath the snow." It was almost as if Leo was talking to himself rather than to her. She felt him reaching up with his free hand and turning the lock.

"Whatever you do, don't scream. Don't make any noise. We're going to run."

"*Da*, Leo." Yes, Leo.

The soft curl of his hair brushed against her cheek as he nodded his head and drew a deep breath.

"Alright, here we go."

Leo threw open the door, sprinkling them with a shower of wet crystals, and shot out of the cellar, tripping with Faina still in his arms. Faina felt her hair being dragged through the wet powder as Leo struggled to his feet and carried her off into the woods.

The burning wind whipped frosted scars through their tears. Brittle pine boughs smacked at their backs as though urging them forward. *Run! Run away!* they seemed to whisper before clasping their branches in a chain of defense behind them. In the distance men were shouting like wild dogs.

When the smell of smoke had faded considerably, when the light of the inferno ceased to cast shadows through the branches, and when the woods had gone mute again, Leo collapsed at the foot of an enormous tree and at last gave vent to his tears. Faina gathered his shirtfront in her fists and wept for their mother and father. Leo pressed her head into his chest and cried out in agonizing grief.

"Bastards! Murderers!"

Faina looked up at her brother. Leo's eyes were digging for a word they'd never find. Hopeless and tired, Faina wrung her hair and threw herself prostrate in the snow, letting it bleed into her lips and eyes as she wailed tirelessly. Their parents were gone.

Chapter 2:

The Lamp Beside the Golden Door

The thick, crowded air of the steerage was a ceaseless clamor of countless languages Faina could not comprehend set adrift in a sea of limitless hope that bordered on delusional. The worn mattress of her barrack seemed to be the only stable thing she could cling to, and so she did not move from it. She kept her cheek pressed resolutely to the moldering threads and her eyes pasted closed. They had one destination, and yet her life felt directionless.

She resisted food and water because it meant she'd inevitably have to get up off the mattress to relieve herself. When Leo ordered her to come eat she ignored him. She told herself again and again that she was dead, just like she had in the sanctuary.

Finally, after two days of refusing to eat, she felt herself being hauled over Leo's shoulder like a sack of flour. Having been seized so unceremoniously from her little raft, Faina turned rabid. She would not form conceivable words, but screamed and cried as though she had forgotten how to communicate any other way. Leo struggled against her.

"You have to eat, Faina! You can't just lay there the entire voyage!"

Faina threw back her head and, with an anger she herself could not comprehend, kicked and screamed at her brother until he was forced to drop her on the icy, metal floor. Eyes stared down at her from the other bunks and crowded doorways, so she forced her eyes closed and groped her way back to the mattress where she threw herself facedown and cried as quietly as she could manage. Leo's footsteps died away and for a moment she was left alone with a chorus of clucking tongues and foreign chattering. Now and then a motherly voice crooned beside her. A sympathetic hand patted her back.

Minutes passed and soon she felt the mattress sink with Leo's weight. He forced her onto her back with strength she could not fight, her head on his knees. Something wet and cold poked at her mouth. She pushed it away blindly. Leo's hands seized her roughly by the chin as she writhed, and a spoon was jammed between her lips. Cold potatoes with wet, papery skin tumbled into her throat and made her cough.

"*Nyet!*" she shrieked, spraying Leo with a shower of half-chewed food. Leo neither retaliated nor relented, but, pinching her chin harder, shoved another spoonful into her mouth. After the second bite she could feel the potatoes settling into her stomach and filling her cheeks with color. Slowly, she allowed her body to curl towards Leo like an infant as he fed her and lifted her head to a cup of milk. When she'd eaten her fill, Leo lay back against the wall still holding her in his arms.

For a brief moment Faina decided to open her eyes. Leo's head was thrown back in exhaustion, and she was surprised to find him looking slightly pale. She focused in on his features: the light sprinkling of freckles across his nose, the proud chin. His eyes were shaped like their mother's. It was then that Faina realized he was the only sight on the entire ship that held any familiarity for her, a face that she could not remember having seen for the first time, a face that had always been there. Now he was the only person to have that distinction in her life. The only person left who had been there from the very beginning.

When he caught her staring, he attempted a weak smile and said in a tired voice, "Hey, Domino-Face."

With great affection, she rested her head against his chest. Leo's hand slid up her back and pressed her closer in a protective embrace. His lips pressed against the top of her head.

After that encounter, Faina became slightly more compliant, though the monotony of the trip quickly began to buff the edges of her spirit. When the days stretched to the point where she felt she could take it no longer, the moment finally arrived.

***

Leo did not even bother to shake Faina awake when he plucked her from the bunk, still wrapped in her covers.

"Faina, you have to see this!"

As Faina let out a groan she could see her breath rolling into an opaque cloud at the tip of her nose.

"See what? Where are you taking me?"

"Up on deck before we miss it."

Faina let her eyes fall shut again as they passed up the hallway. "It's already cold enough inside."

"Says the Siberian! Where is your sense of adventure?"

"I left it back in Russia."

Leo pushed open the door. A flood of frigid harbor air slapped their cheeks.

"Oh, I think all that will change when you look outside."

The sky was a carapace of whey-faced clouds oscillating with white seagulls in indistinct patterns. The morning breathed a heavy fog upon the deck, ceremoniously swathing the passengers in thin white mantles. Everyone had gathered in a commotion of heavy anticipation, heads craned towards the sky, waiting for something to emerge.

After an innumerable tally of self-imposed comas, the collective promise of whatever mystery lay behind that fog destroyed the last of Faina's apathy. She opened her eyes to their fullest extent, the first time in twelve days. The Statue of Liberty appeared, her skin like pale grass breaking through the frost in spring. Her presence was heralded by shouts of laughter and tears of joy, and neither Leo nor Faina were exempt. So enraptured were they, they did not notice the boat leaning forward where the passengers had gathered to catch a glimpse of the statue. Crew members hollered for everyone to step back, but no one stirred. This was the moment they had been waiting for. This was America.

As they drifted closer, Faina could make out a series of geometric shadows climbing endlessly towards the sky.

"Are they trees?" she asked, tilting her head and screwing up her eyes.

Leo's mouth fell open in absolute awe. "Those aren't trees, Faina. Those are buildings!"

"Buildings?" She could not believe it. How could someone build something that tall without it falling over? Even if they had managed to do so without it breaking in the process it would certainly be in danger of tumbling down. Surely, it was just a trick of the fog.

Between them and their new lives lay an island with a red brick building. Its four spires had rusted to a shade Faina dubbed "Liberty Green." It was Ellis Island, and its appearance on the horizon ushered a new barrage of fears into Faina's mind.

"What if we get turned away?"

Leo arched his neck and groaned. "Don't start that."

"But everyone has been talking about it!"

"Look, remember what Uncle Matvei wrote? Less than one in fifty get turned away. Now," he brushed a curl behind her ear, "you remember your English?"

Faina sighed worriedly and bent her head. When Leo was born Papa had been good about making sure his son knew English in addition to Russian. As a result, Leo was fairly fluent. But by the time Faina rolled around, an unprecedented six years later, he had lost steam, and though Faina was somewhat skilled at speaking English, she was not at all fluent.

* * *

To say Faina's fears were put aside when they reached customs would be a terrible lie. Uncle Matvei had failed to mention that men, women, and children were separated for inspection once they reached the top of the winding staircase. Faina was herded into a line between two little girls, one Polish, one Hungarian. Neither spoke Russian. There they waited to be inspected by the doctor.

When her turn came she stood before a balding man in a white lab coat armed with a flashlight and a stick of white chalk. The light was shined into her eyes, her mouth, her ears. The translator sitting nearby interceded when necessary, but for the most part the examination was straightforward. They checked her head for lice and her nails for mold. All the while Faina stared at the chalk, her shoulders rigid. She knew from Uncle Matvei's letters that those who did not pass the examination were marked with chalk symbols on their sleeve. But the doctor did not reach for the chalk. Instead he waved her ahead.

A deafening roar of human voices speaking in a hundred tongues ushered her into the unbelievably enormous space that was the registry room. To Faina's eyes the domed ceilings were lofty enough to contain their own solar system, and as the volume of foreign vocabularies filled the cavernous void she thought to herself, *This must be what it is like to be God and hear the prayers of the world.*

Tall metal rails sketched boxes around the numerous lines of people crowded on wooden benches. After only an hour of sitting in the stuffed queue Faina began to feel as desperately hot as she had been cold that morning in the frigid January harbor. Two and a half hours passed before Faina finally got to the front of the line, time she spent in silence with only the visual chaos surrounding her to entertain her. She was escorted to a room with a dark polished desk and seated across from a man in a uniform with a folder of papers. With the help of an interpreter, Faina was asked to confirm the information on her paperwork.

"You came here with your brother?"

"*Da*, yes."

"What is your brother's name?"

Faina hesitated for a moment as she deciphered the two words she recognized. Brother, *brat*. Name, *imya*. Just as the interpreter was leaning forward to translate, Faina hastily answered.

"Leontiy Adrianovich Spichkin." She folded her hands in her lap and swung her legs back and forth, feeling proud of herself.

"And how old is your brother?"

Again the translator edged forward. "*Skol'ko let tvoy—*"

But Faina cut her off, eager to impress. "Fifteen."

The man asking the questions started to say something, then stopped. He flipped a page back, looked over one of the lines, then back to Faina.

"Fifteen?"

"*Da*. Fifteen."

The translator looked over the inspector's shoulder and, leaning closer to Faina, asked in Russian, "Are you sure you don't mean sixteen?"

Faina stopped swinging her legs and stared back at her innocently.

"Fifteen. His birthday is November twenty-seventh, 1902," she managed to reply in somewhat broken English which sounded more like, "He born twenty-seven, November. 1902."

The inspector and the translator exchanged wary glances that made Faina's chest cold. The inspector waved for the guard at the door.

"Go find Leontiy Spichkin and bring him here, please. Came over on *The Nasovia*."

Faina looked helplessly to the translator, having only understood her brother's name and the name of the ship. The translator smiled consolingly and patted her knee.

"They're fetching your brother. They only want to ask him a question."

Faina nodded distractedly, somewhat pacified but still nervous. A few minutes passed and the guard returned with Leo. Faina turned in her seat and gave an excited bounce.

"Leo!"

Leo's smile seemed forced as he reached out and patted her on the head. Something was wrong. There was a slight frown to his lips as he sat down in the seat beside her, an expression Faina rarely saw her brother wearing. The guard handed the inspector Leo's file. The inspector opened to the front page and looked up at Leo sternly, but curiously.

"You're not sixteen, are you?"

Leo shook his head gently. "No, sir. I'm fifteen."

"Why did you lie and say you were sixteen?"

Leo drew a tired breath and pushed his hair back from his forehead. Before he could answer the inspector cut in.

"Do you realize no one under sixteen is allowed to travel without a parent?"

"We were supposed to be traveling with our parents, but they were killed before we left the city. We saw our mother and father shot right in front of our eyes. We couldn't wait another year! They would've tried to place us in an orphanage. There isn't even any space left in the orphanages! Children are being forced out into the street! They would've separated us—"

The inspector held up a hand for Leo to stop.

"Do you have any relatives here in the United States?"

"Yes! Our uncle. He's waiting for us. Matvei Dalka. He lives on Orchard Street, and owns the Dalka Brewery."

The inspector pinched the space between his eyebrows with his fingers.

"Alright, son, alright. Calm down." He closed the file. "We're not going to send you back. You and your sister can go through." He stamped each permit and slid it across the desk towards Leo. "Welcome to America, kid."

At last Leo and Faina made their way to the first floor where passengers they had traveled with were running with open arms to the loved ones awaiting them. There were shouts of joy and tears of laughter. As they descended down the stairs with their luggage Faina couldn't help but wonder, would Uncle Matvei cry too? What about her cousin, Anya? Leo pointed to a tall mustached man standing near the exit, a small child clinging to his hand.

"Uncle Matvei!" Leo shot his hand in the air and waved.

The man turned. His arms spread wide with rejoicing.

"*Leonya! Fainya!*" He threw back his head and laughed out loud as he ran towards the stairs to meet them.

In photographs, Uncle Matvei and their mother were a perfect example of twin likeness, but outside the frame their differences colored them the way beet juice stains a potato. Mama had stampeded about in a flurry of passion and intensity; she burned with life. Uncle Matvei, on the other hand, glowed with an amiable warmth. He had a friendly face, one that could never be intimidating even if it tried. He was the type of person that if he'd met you once and saw you on the street he would shake hands with both his clasping yours, then hold them there as he inquired with unquestionable sincerity as to how you were doing. And you would know from the meaningful, soul-searching glance of his eyes that he really hoped you were well.

Uncle Matvei had moved to New York City before Faina was born, and the last time he had visited Russia was shortly before the war broke out when Faina was five. She recalled that she had liked him very much, that he had a sense of humor like Mama, and was always making her laugh when the grown-ups were being boring. He'd kept in close correspondence with them over the years, sending them pictures, and regaling them with florid descriptions of what life was like in New York. Through his letters, Mama had fallen in love with the place and had longed to move there for years, but for some reason Papa was always hesitant.

Uncle Matvei's long arms were large enough to gather both of them tightly into his embrace. As he held them close to his chest, Faina could feel his tears falling onto her head.

"Oh, *moi deti*," my dear children, "we have waited for so long and worried so much!"

He took turns kissing both sides of their cheeks. He pinched Leo's chin and lifted it towards his gaze.

"Look at you, Leontiy! How you have grown! A young man now, *da*?"

Leo smiled and Faina could tell he was truly happy and relieved to see Uncle Matvei. When Uncle Matvei turned to face Faina he stopped abruptly. His bushy, black eyebrows drew together almost painfully. But the shock was sloughed away by an expression of gentle fondness as he cupped a hand to her face and stroked his thumb across her cheek.

"*Obaldét'*," my goodness, "you are even more a perfect replica of your mother than I remembered."

Faina smiled. "Not as perfect as you."

Uncle Matvei chuckled. "I don't know about that. You see, I have a mustache." He tapped a finger to his upper lip and Faina giggled.

From behind her father's lanky shadow, out shuffled Anya, which was short for Annabelle, twisting her foot bashfully and smiling from Faina to her shoes. Unlike Faina, Anya was petite in stature and rather on the thin side. She was slightly pigeon-toed, and her hands were always gathered close to her body. She never looked anyone in the eye for very long, letting her gaze wander to the floor with a timid simper. It was a week before Faina caught a glimpse of her eyes long enough to determine their color, which hung somewhere between blue and green, much like her hair which was somewhere between blonde and brown.

Faina had never met Anya in person. She had been born in America, a first-generation New Yorker. Faina was not shy and did not hesitate to lasso her cousin into a tight hug. It would be nice to have another little girl to play with for once, even if they didn't speak the same language.

Uncle Matvei and Anya each took a part of Leo and Faina's luggage and, with happy tears trailing down their faces, made their way out of the building and towards the ferry that would usher them into the legendary place known as America.

Even after years of growing up in the Siberian countryside, New York was by far the wildest territory Faina had ever beheld. There was a ceaseless energy circulating in the very pavement beneath her feet. People were everywhere. Not only were they crammed at her elbows, but stacked on top of each other in steel buildings, and sardined into trains that raced underground through dark tunnels. It could easily have been a fantasy world erected from the pages of a wonderful book.

And the motorcars! At most, Faina had probably seen two, maybe three motorcars in one place at one time, and they had most often been a truck or van of some kind. But here the roads were congested with fancy black Model Ts and Roadsters, their shiny metal spokes weaving webs in the spinning wheels.

When Faina was seated in the subway car, she was given an opportunity to turn her attention upon the New Yorkers themselves. Her eyes lingered admiringly on a pair of two-toned, heeled, leather boots with pearl buttons. Scanning the crowd of pointed and squared toes peeking beneath skirt hems, she realized nearly every woman in the car was sporting a pair of high-heeled shoes, and their fluffy heads were capped in wide-brimmed hats with boxy crowns to accommodate their hairstyles.

Glancing to her left, Faina took a moment to observe Anya's style of dress. Uncle Matvei had done well for himself in New York City, and it was clear his daughter was well assimilated into Western culture with her clean pinafore, wool coat, and matching hat. It had been a long time since Faina's coat had looked that fine. Her gaze washed down her own dress front, taking note of the fraying ribbon on her collar, and the place where her sole was detaching itself from the shoe.

When their subway ride was over they made their way up the dark green staircase and into the jungled mosaic of the Lower East Side. Here was an odd marriage of the novel and the familiar. The long streets, flanked by tight rows of storied tenement buildings, were carpeted with stalls, shawled women selling eggs from wheelbarrows and fruit from truck beds. It was all an open-air market. To Faina's surprise not all the children were dressed as nicely as Anya. Many were clothed in a mixture of old world and new, here a worn linen tolstoy, there a crisp sailor dress.

On Orchard Street, Uncle Matvei shepherded the gathering towards the widest building on the block, a russet structure of bold red brick and earthy terra-cotta with checkered panels beneath the projected bay windows. A courtyard thirty feet or so in length split the building directly down the middle.

Uncle Matvei's liquor shop, *Opa!* was on the left-hand side of the courtyard. It was a small but handsome establishment looking out over Orchard Street. It had freshly painted gold letters on the window in both Russian and English. A little gold bell hung quaintly over a door that, like many things in New York, was a cozy, dark green. Uncle Matvei lived in the flat overhead.

The liquor store was furnished with a private staircase in the back which led directly into the apartment. Unlocking the door, Uncle Matvei ushered them inside. From what Faina understood, Matvei's tenement was nicer than what most people could afford on the Lower East Side, and though Faina had nothing to compare it to so far, she could easily believe it. The creamy wallpaper was unsullied with nary a tear or wrinkle. There were photographs and artwork hanging over the dining table. A spinet piano was set against the wall, slightly worn, but still in working order.

In the corner nearest the doorway sat a polished mahogany cabinet with hand-carved trim, and a crank jutting out from the side. Faina's mouth fell open in awe. It was a Victrola, the latest model.

Outside the kitchen hung a framed article taken from the *New York Daily* featuring a picture of Uncle Matvei standing in front of his shop with her late Aunt Margaret and baby Anya. Though Faina could not understand most of the article, she did recognize one word repeated over and over again: *Kvass*.

Kvass, a drink made from fermented rye bread and sweetened with fruit, was responsible for making *Opa!* a local treasure. With all Uncle Matvei's good fortune it was easy to forget he had once peddled his product from a pushcart on the street. His rise to fame was gradual, beginning on Orchard Street, then slowly germinating through lower

Manhattan. Sooner or later Matvei's brew was a staple in the working immigrant's répertoire.

But it wasn't until Governor Al Smith (who was just a Tammany Hall politician at the time) paid a visit to Matvei's humble kiosk that the name *Kvass* was carried above East Fourteenth Street. Soon the champion of the Lower East Side was passing the word onto his fellow members of the New York State Assembly. Massive orders sprang up from all over the city: six cases for a Fourth of July picnic on Long Island, ten cases for a bachelor party on Fifth Avenue, twenty cases for a yachting get-together thrown by Florence Ziegfeld!

With all New York salivating for a taste of his Slavic ambrosia, Matvei earned enough for an apartment and storefront in one of the brand new, multi-lot tenement buildings on Orchard Street. Operating from a permanent residence only increased his popularity, and before he knew it, Uncle Matvei had enough money to buy the entire building—or at least half of it, specifically the left half. The other side belonged to an elderly Polish widow, Mrs. Borsuk, who was always keeping a competitive eye out for her neighbor.

And it didn't stop there. To meet frequent demands, Uncle Matvei had to open a small but busy distillery which only helped bring in more money. With his newfound wealth, many had expected Matvei to move out of the Lower East Side, but Matvei took pride in being a self-made man. Not wishing to forget his humble beginnings, he remained in the Lower East Side so he could share his wealth with those who needed it most: poor immigrant families who didn't speak English, struggling artists and musicians, poor widows with mouths to feed. These were the sorts of people who made up Matvei's tenants and paid far less than the average rent cost, and when they couldn't pay, kind Uncle Matvei would ask instead for a song on the piano, or a famous homemade pie, or a flower from the window box. He was a pillar of the community, both beloved and respected.

Faina's and Leo's luggage were put off to the side and soon they were gathered around the table enjoying a warm dinner. As Faina shoveled a spoonful of potatoes into her mouth, she thought about how nice it was to have them hot and seasoned as opposed to the cold, shriveled tubers they were fed on the ship. When she politely asked if Uncle Matvei could pass her the milk, she noticed for the first time he wasn't eating.

"Aren't you hungry, Uncle Matvei?"

For a moment it looked as though Uncle Matvei had gone pale, but he quickly smiled and, getting up from his seat, poured the heavy pitcher of milk for her.

"Oh no, darling, I am still very full from lunch."

Faina wondered what would compel Uncle Matvei to skip such a delicious meal after having to wait for them in the cold harbor all day. But with such luxury, perhaps he really was full.

When dinner had been consumed, Faina and Leo were comfortably sleepy, and after such a long day, Uncle Matvei thought it best they turn in early. To make room for his niece and nephew, Uncle Matvei had moved his bed to the back room of the shop downstairs, and added a second twin bed to Anya's room.

"*Fainya*, you will be sharing a room with Anya." Uncle Matvei turned down the covers. "And look, we put you right beneath the window so you could see out into the courtyard."

Faina could feel her face turning red as she retreated bashfully behind her brother. Leo put his arm around her and scooted her forward again.

"What's wrong?" Uncle Matvei glanced her over with a worried eye.

Faina fumbled for an answer. She looked desperately back at Leo, then down at her shoes. Uncle Matvei had been so kind, and it was so thoughtful of him to place the bed underneath the window where he thought she might enjoy it. The last thing she wanted was to hurt Uncle Matvei's feelings, but … Faina thrust her hands over her eyes and began to cry.

Anya cast a sympathetic look towards Faina and addressed her papa. Faina did not completely understand what Anya was saying, but she did pick out a few familiar words such as "afraid," "away," and "Leo." Leo shrugged his shoulders apologetically and spoke in Russian so Faina could understand.

"For now, it might be best if you let her stay with me. Ever since the incident, she's been struggling with nightmares. She often wakes in the middle of the night screaming. I can put her at ease."

Faina peeked out from behind her hands and glanced at Uncle Matvei. He didn't look insulted at all, instead he was lifting her lovingly into his arms.

"Of course, I understand completely."

Anya tugged at her father's shoulder and squeaked something in English.

"Thank you, *Annushka*," Uncle Matvei nodded his head. "I think that would be best." He wiped the tears from Faina's eyes. "It's alright, *malyutka*," little one, "you and Leo can share a room for as long as you want. Anya doesn't mind. There's no need to cry."

Faina laid her head on his shoulder. As he kissed her cheek it felt so much like Mama that Faina thought her heart might tear itself apart.

Chapter 3:
The American Way

Leo stood behind the cash register as he watched his uncle flip the sign on the door from open to closed. Uncle Matvei dusted his hands and, smiling, strode back towards the counter and patted Leo on the shoulder.

"You've done a good job today, Leontiy. Go ahead and start counting the cash." He jerked his thumb over his shoulder. "I will just be a moment. If I don't finish filling out that order form tonight I know I will have forgotten it by tomorrow."

Leo propped his elbow upon the cash register with pride, as though it were a brand new Model T, and Leo a trusted mechanic. "Don't you worry, Uncle Matvei. I got everything taken care of."

Uncle Matvei chuckled as he pattered off down the hall towards the back room. "I can always count on you, Leo."

Slipping off his apron, Leo opened the drawer and carefully dealt out the cash. The little bell hanging over the door gave a ring. A man pushed his way into the store. Uncle Matvei must have forgotten to lock the door.

"I am sorry, sir, we are closed."

The man, who was broad shouldered and fairly muscled, paused over the threshold to glare at Leo in an unimpressed manner. He ignored him, and shut the door behind him.

"I am here to speak with Matvei Dalka on personal business. He knows me." With stocky, dust-covered hands, he removed his brown bowler hat, showing off the receding line of coarse, mousy hair. The muscles of his brow seemed permanently fixed into a slight scowl over sour eyes which were almost mournful.

Leo studied him with caution. The condescending manner in which he spoke to Leo, the way he forced himself inside with little explanation and no apology, and the general sense of unease accompanying his presence warned Leo this was not a man with good intentions. He set his hands firmly on the register and steeled his jaw.

"He's finishing up an order in the back, if you could kindly wait just one moment—"

"I am afraid he has kept me waiting too long as it is."

The man stormed past the counter, but Leo sidestepped him. "Please, sir," he insisted with false politeness and genuine warning, "it shouldn't be more than a minute. Is there anything I can help you with until he gets back?"

The man's lips twitched angrily beneath his bushy beard as he reached across his jacket and peeled back the opening, disclosing the presence of a revolver in his inner pocket.

"You can help me by kindly stepping out of the way."

"Leontiy!" Uncle Matvei barked as he suddenly appeared, frantic looking in the doorway. With hurried strides, he grabbed Leo by the shoulder and drew him back.

"I'll handle this, son."

But Leo resisted. "Uncle Matvei, this man has a gun—"

"I know, Leo! I know. Just stay back. I will take care of this."

The strange man smirked as he ran his fingers through his beard and watched the exchange with amusement. "I have come to collect my money, Dalka. You are two weeks behind, and your last payment came up short. I am afraid I will have to charge you interest."

Uncle Matvei held out a shaking hand. "Please, Viktor—"

"Mr. Volkov," the man corrected him over his shoulder as he browsed the nearest shelf. He paused to address Leo. "It is custom in America to address each other by one's surname. As a sign of respect, no?" He selected a bottle of Pabst from the shelf and, taking advantage of the bottle opener fixed to the counter, snapped off the cap.

Uncle Matvei's already exhausted eyes were looking heavier by the second. "Forgive me, Mr. Volkov. I know I have been a bit behind on payments lately, but can you please just give me one more week? My niece and nephew arrived just a month ago from Russia, barely escaping the Bolsheviks. My little niece, she had holes in her shoes, her coat was so worn it could not keep her warm enough. They are still getting settled, still getting their strength back. For their sake, I am afraid I cannot pay you the interest right now."

Mr. Volkov's thin nose seemed to twist and his nostrils flared as he set his beer aside and drew out his revolver.

"If your niece and nephew are a hindrance then I can gladly get rid of them for you." The barrel slid in Leo's direction. "Or how about just one? The boy seems like a good choice."

Uncle Matvei hurled himself in front of Leo with his arms outstretched.

"*Nyet*! No! Please, take whatever you like, just don't touch my family. Don't involve my children. This is between us."

With his arms wrapped securely around Leo's shoulders, Uncle Matvei stepped back from the cash register, and indicated for Volkov to have his fill. Volkov smiled coolly as he strode behind the counter and opened the drawer.

"I knew you would see reason, Dalka. After all, you are a clever business man. I am sure you can come up with the extra money. I mean, what are all those tenants for? Eh? If you are struggling, why not raise the rent a little?"

Uncle Matvei drew a heavy sigh. "There are enough immigrants struggling to find housing in this city without me raising their rent."

"Perspective." Volkov tapped the corner of his eye. "This is what I like about you, Matvei. You may sit here watching me take your hard-earned money and be tempted to lament your position in life. But there are many here in New York who are much worse off than you, Matvei Dalka, especially here in the Lower East Side."

Leo could feel his nostrils flaring as he watched Volkov empty the register of every last penny and tuck it away inside his jacket pocket. When Volkov was at last finished, he made for the door. He stopped with his fist enclosed around the handle and stared pointedly at Leo.

"I expect better treatment from this boy in the future, Dalka, unless you want to reconsider my offer." And, doffing his bowler hat, he left and disappeared beyond the glow of the nearest lamppost.

The moment Volkov shut the door, Leo turned round to face his uncle. "Who was that man? Why did he threaten you? Why did he steal our money?"

Uncle Matvei shushed Leo and bent his head low as he steadied himself against the counter.

"He is with the Bowery Butchers, a street gang running out of the Lower East Side. About a year ago they expanded their territory up Orchard Street."

Leo tossed his shoulders, his lower lip shoved out in defiance. "So? What does that mean?"

"Any licensed business owner without Butcher affiliation on Butcher territory is forced to make payment."

"B—but that's illegal! Uncle Matvei, that man is dangerous! We need to call the police!" He reached for the phone, but Uncle Matvei drew him back.

"I have already tried, Leontiy. It's no use. The Butchers have gotten to the authorities as well. Paid them off, or something. For now, this is how it has to be." He made a weak attempt to straighten himself and lifted Leo's chin in his hand. "And don't you go standing up to any more armed thugs, is that understood? It is my job to take care of you and keep you safe. If you see that man come in again you do exactly as he says or come get me. Don't waste your time trying to defend me, *Leonka*."

He pressed his lips against Leo's forehead. With his back hunched like an old man's, and one hand covering his eye, he shooed Leo towards the stairwell.

"Go on up to bed, Leo. I will lock up for the night."

But Leo did not go to bed immediately; he stayed hidden at the top of the stairwell in case Uncle Matvei faced any further trouble. From the landing Leo could just make out the labored noise of his uncle's sobs, and the whisper of his prayers.

Chapter 4:

Like Robin Hood

Because Faina was not yet fluent in English she could not immediately begin her education. The school Leo and Anya attended offered classes for teaching immigrant children English, but considering they spoke chiefly English at home (Anya did not know Russian, and Aunt Margaret had been Irish) Matvei was in no rush to enroll her, thinking she would pick it up naturally. So for the first few weeks in New York, Faina was able to stay home and help Uncle Matvei in the shop.

Meanwhile, Leo had been enrolled in school for three weeks now. The first day he had come home with a bruise or two, but according to Anya it wasn't unusual for a new boy to get beat up once or twice, and Leo had quickly proven he could hold his own.

So far, he seemed to enjoy school. Faina knew he would. He had already been recruited to the gymnastics team, and was thinking of joining the school paper. With his good looks, sense of humor, and natural charisma, Leo could fit in anywhere. He had been born with that enviable ability to thrive wherever he was planted.

As Faina was returning to the shop one day after delivering a bottle of wine to a neighbor, she spied Leo's satchel lying on the counter. Faina shed her coat and raced excitedly to the storeroom, hoping to get in some playtime before he started work. But the moment she rounded the corner she halted at the door. Tall, lean shadows fell across the opposite wall from the curtained threshold as Leo and Uncle Matvei argued in harsh tones.

"My friends at school were telling me about this rival street gang of the Butchers'. They call themselves the Breadwinners. Everyone says they're the defenders of lower Manhattan."

Uncle Matvei's shadow was shaking his head. "No, no, no, Leo—"

"People say they help struggling immigrants achieve the American Dream. They help men find ways to support their family. People go to them all the time—"

"Enough, Leo! The American Dream does not involve crime! In this family we are honest, upright citizens who obey and respect the law."

"But the law isn't protecting us!"

"This isn't Russia, Leontiy, we don't have to become deviants to survive! That is why we came to America, so we could have opportunities and justice."

"Then where is our justice? Why won't the police help us? We're enslaved to this man, Uncle! Playing by the rules has led us nowhere. Why not beat Victor Volkov at his own game?"

"By enlisting the help of other criminals and barbarians?" Uncle Matvei threw up his hands and scoffed.

"They're not like other criminals, Uncle Matvei. They live by a code, like Robin Hood, or something. They believe it's a man's duty to protect those who can't protect themselves. The widow and the orphan, the sick and the invalid. The Butchers make their money off prostitution, extortion, and arming radicals. But the Breadwinners do protection racketeering, operate a black market, host street fights, that kind of stuff. They say street fighting is one of the most lucrative positions in the entire ladder. Maybe I could—"

"You could what?" he snapped. "Become a street fighter?"

Leo's voice wound in a submissive circle. "Well, yes."

"You know how boys become street fighters, Leontiy? Did they tell you about that at school? You must first become a member, and to become a member you have to pass an initiation. I have seen boys as young as thirteen with stripes on their backs, hiding their limps from their mothers. And then those very same mothers go sobbing to Klokov, the head of the Breadwinners, pleading for their son's release. But it is no use. Once you are a Breadwinner you are a Breadwinner for life. Desertion is punishable by death. You think I don't know about the Breadwinners, Leo? I have lived here a lot longer than you. There are boys in this very tenement with hands like old men, wasting away their childhood by punching and kicking day after day. Go to the Breadwinners, you say?" Uncle Matvei turned and spat on the ground. "Better we go bankrupt first. Better we end up on the streets."

Faina was pasted against the wall, her chest heavy. What kind of trouble were they in? Who was this man, Victor Volkov, whom, according to Leo, they were enslaved to? Leo spoke again, softer this time.

"What will you do when Faina starts school? You've had to let go of all your store employees because of this man. Faina helps run the shop and does errands while Anya and I are at school, but what will you do come September? You can't run the store by yourself, and you can't pay anyone to work for you."

What was Leo saying? Uncle Matvei ran the most popular liquor store in all of lower Manhattan. He had his own brewery in Brooklyn! He owned half the building! His apartments were so popular that Mrs. Borsuk next door felt threatened by his success! How could Uncle Matvei be having money trouble?

"We will pray, Leontiy," sighed Uncle Matvei. "We will pray."

Chapter 5:
Detained

Pasha watched, enraptured, as Mama rubbed a kopeck back and forth on her elbow with a mischievous smile. Her hat was crooked on her billow of chocolate brown hair and it somehow added to the playful glint in her eyes. Beside him, his three-year-old little sister, Katya, furrowed her brows in a very serious manner and narrowed her pale blue eyes on the hand covering the coin.

Suddenly, Mama stopped. Her eyes grew wide and her mouth dropped as she turned out her palm, revealing that the kopeck had vanished into thin air. Pasha laughed as his little sister's jaw fell open in amazement. Her spongey yellow curls bounced as he nudged her with his elbow.

"Where did it go, Katya?"

Katya swiveled around in her seat, dumbfounded, her plump lips puckered in confusion. Mama gasped and pointed to Katya's collar.

"Katya, look!"

Mama reached into the neck of Katya's dress, and when she drew away she was holding the kopeck between her fingers.

"It was in your collar the whole time!"

Katya slapped her chubby cheeks with both hands. "It was?"

"It was, *Katenka*," she insisted.

A uniformed man standing in front of one of the legal examination rooms called out their names from a list.

"Lydia Davidovich Chevalsky, Pavlo Ruslanovitch Chevalsky, and Katerina Ruslanova Chevalsky!"

Mama hastened them to their feet. "Come along, children."

Pasha reached behind his head and smoothed down the stubborn ducktail cowlick at the nape of his neck. He grabbed his little sister's hand and towed her towards the door.

"I speeg English," she was saying to the guard as he held open the door for them, and she began reciting botched lines from *The Tale of Peter Rabbit*. "'Flobsy, Mobsy, and Cottontail who ver good leetle bunnies had meelk and blagberries for supper!'"

Pasha covered his mouth with the back of his hand and tried not to laugh. Katya was always making friends wherever she went. People adored her because she was friendly and cute. Her enormous eyes were fringed with gold lashes so that every blink was more of a bat. All she had to do was smile and say something in her dreamy, cloud-wandering voice and people opened their wings to her like butterflies.

The guard could not help but smile as he bent down to pat her forward into the room.

"Well, you're already on your way then, aren't you?"

Katya stared at him uncomprehendingly. She did not really speak English, but she was very proud of the few phrases she could recite. Pasha squeezed her hand.

"Say 'yes, thank you.'"

Katya swiveled back around to face the guard, her cheeks swelling with a ginormous grin.

"Yez, thangyoo!"

Pasha, on the other hand, was an aloof but well-mannered child who had mastered the role of the wise older sibling quite beautifully. His face was leaner and paler than Katya's, and he had thick, dark hair with large, brown eyes that always appeared to be daydreaming. He was tall for his age and already somewhat lanky.

They took their seats at a large desk. To help Mama, Pasha made Katya sit in his lap and put a hand over her mouth when she began singing to herself. The official on the other side of the desk had three files open beneath a table lamp, and was scanning down the first page. The questions were simple.

"You are Baroness Lydia Davidovich Chevalsky?"

"Yes, sir, that is correct."

"Your birthday?"

"March twentieth, 1890."

Pasha watched as the guard glanced up from his paperwork to look her over. He knew what he was thinking. Mama did not quite look like a third-class passenger. In addition to her fine clothes, she was a poised, confident young woman who gave no indication of anxiety or fear. She spoke eloquently, never once stumbling over her English, even though her accent was decidedly Russian. Furthermore, she had a title stamped in front of her name. What was this woman doing on Ellis Island?

"I must say, ma'am, your English is excellent."

Mama smiled bashfully and tilted her head in an appealing, mannered way.

"Thank you, sir. My father was English. I have been speaking it since before I can remember."

He smiled and brushed a finger over the corner of his mustache. At last he leaned forward and folded his hands on the desk.

"If you don't mind my asking, ma'am, why are you here?"

Mama's smile shrank. She fiddled with the fingers of her gloves, pulling them past her knuckle and twisting the ends.

"My husband was killed by invading Soviet forces after Crimea declared itself independent. He was an aristocrat, you see, a baron, and a White Army sympathizer. So we were labeled as enemies of the state."

"And your husband, he is here now?"

Mama drew back slightly. Had the guard been listening?

"Well, no, he was hanged, right in front of us."

The guard furrowed his bushy, gray eyebrows. He opened the file back up and ran his finger down the page.

"He died?"

Mama's forehead gathered in a pucker. "Yes."

"So you're single?"

Mama ducked her chin to her collar as though the suggestion had offended her. "Widowed."

"But you haven't remarried?"

Mama shook her head back and forth in confusion. "Of course not, he was killed two days before our ship departed."

The man stared at her incredulously for a moment, then turned his eyes pitifully upon Pasha and Katya. Breathing a heavy sigh, he dragged his hand across his face and rubbed at his temples as though something truly distressing had occurred.

"Ma'am, I'm afraid we don't allow single women to enter the United States unless they're accompanied by a relative or have someone waiting to receive them. I'm sorry, truly, I am."

Pasha felt his throat stiffen, his breathing accelerate. Were they to be sent back? A hand wrapped around his wrist.

"Pasha!"

It was as though his mother had jerked him back to the present by a long tether. He hadn't realized he had begun to shake. He stared in bewilderment at his surroundings, testing to see if they were real. Lydia reached under his chin and stroked his face.

"*Vse dobre.*" It's alright.

Pasha forced himself to exhale. He could feel the color draining from his face.

His mother's shoulders stiffened as she faced the official a second time. "It just so happens we do have someone waiting for us."

For a moment the man looked hopeful. "Really?"

Pasha was no longer listening. What was Mama up to? They didn't know anyone in America! Had the stress of being turned away after losing Papa been too much for her to handle?

***

The echo of the door was still fresh in the cement walls of the third-floor dormitory as Mama hung her head against the doorframe in shock. It wasn't locked, and they were free to go down to the cafeteria, but Pasha wasn't sure his mother understood that. Her hair had come undone and was sticking out in several different directions. Tears drew parabolas down the height of her cheekbones. Slowly, Pasha approached her from behind and tugged at her skirt.

"Mama, I don't understand. If they don't allow single women to enter America without a relative, why did you write you were married?"

His mother's lips opened, but she was silenced by her own sob. Inwardly, Pasha admonished himself for the stupidity of his question.

"It's alright, Mama." He wrapped his arms around her and leaned affectionately against her. "Y—you were upset. Papa's death was so sudden, you didn't think to write single." He was fighting against his own tears now.

Lydia reached around to squeeze Pasha's hand, but kept her forehead pinned to the wall.

"We are not going back," she repeated softly to herself. "We are not going back."

"But Mama, we don't know anyone in America. They won't let us in."

She shook her head. "We are not going back."

Pasha was silent for a moment. When at last he spoke there was a measure of composure to his voice again. "Who did you tell them was waiting for us?"

"Papa," she whispered.

"You told them Papa was waiting for us here?"

Mama shook her head. When she could not open her mouth without crying, she pointed to herself.

"Your papa?"

His mother nodded.

"But Mama, you said your father died when you were sixteen."

"Maybe he is still alive. Maybe he came to America. Maybe he is waiting for us."

Pasha took a step back. His mother was in shock. He had to remember that. Making his way over to the mattress on the lower bunk, he laid down beside Katya, who was sleeping, and buried his slim nose against her plump cheek.

Chapter 6:

The Kissing Cat Burglar

The window of Matvei's fogged at uneven intervals as Leo struggled to steady his breathing. He was pasting Valentine's Day decorations Anya and Faina had made against the glass in an attempt to distract his nerves.

When he'd first gone to Klokov and offered himself as an associate in payment for protection, he was hoping to get assigned to a car dealership like the cousin his friend Roman worked for, or perhaps someone who watched over one of the numerous warehouses where goods were kept. Unfortunately for Leo, he wasn't the only desperate young man looking to become a Breadwinner associate, and the only available positions were thieves, or what Klokov euphemistically called "suppliers."

When he wasn't working with the school paper, or attending gymnastics, Leo spent his time thieving from shipyards and delivery trucks. There was an endless list as to what items were valuable: car parts, jewelry, gasoline, silverware … With a catalog that long, it wasn't exactly a difficult job, but it was still degrading, and Leo couldn't help his feelings. He was a good kid, and he didn't like stealing things that people worked hard for.

In the end, Leo had been surprised by Klokov's generosity. Though Leo had offered his services as an associate in exchange for Breadwinner protection, Klokov had insisted on paying him. All Breadwinner associates received free protection in addition to a salary. Were Leo to receive protection without money, Klokov would have been cheating him out of what he earned.

Everyone said the Breadwinners were different from other street gangs. Little boys looked up to them, girls swooned over them, and mothers and old women were always wanting to bestow them with little gifts whenever they crossed paths.

"You are a good boy, Leontiy," she would extol, stern faced, but sincere.

Leo didn't know what to think. Unsure of what to do with the extra money, he decided to stick it in the cash register in hopes that Uncle Matvei wouldn't notice.

Just as Uncle Matvei was coming through the front door with a new shipment, a chain of paper hearts came unglued from the window and fluttered to the floor.

"Ah, Leo, my boy! Home from school finally?"

As Leo bent to pick up the fallen paper chain, he jumped and hit his head on the windowsill.

"Hey, Uncle Matvei."

His chest surged with adrenaline. Perhaps he shouldn't have put the money in the cash register. Maybe it would've been better to hide it in Uncle Matvei's wallet, or his pocket. Uncle Matvei placed the shipment on the counter and dusted the snow from his gloves.

"How is the school paper going?"

"Uh, great! I'm learning to use the printer this week."

"Wonderful." Uncle Matvei hung his coat on the hook. "I am so glad you are getting involved in school. Your parents would be so proud!"

Leo's head lowered slightly as he thought about what his parents might think of his theft and involvement with a street gang.

"Mr. Volkov hasn't come by recently, has he?"

Leo's forehead began to sweat. "Uh, no. No, Uncle, I haven't seen him."

Uncle Matvei scratched at his mustache. "That is strange. Not that I am complaining."

The bell rang as Uncle Matvei opened the cash drawer. Even though there wasn't really a good reason for anyone to say anything, the room felt uncomfortably quiet. Taking up the box of decorations, Leo began power walking towards the back, but Uncle Matvei stopped him.

"Leo!"

Leo froze. He forced himself to turn around. Uncle Matvei was hunched over the cash register, his head hanging low, his hands steadying himself against the counter.

"Come here, son."

Leo swallowed the lump of fear rising in the back of his esophagus and, setting aside the box, approached his uncle with his eyes fixed on the floor and his hands folded behind his back.

"Yes, Uncle?"

Uncle Matvei rubbed the space between his eyebrows.

"Where did this extra money come from?"

Leo opened his mouth to say something but the words would not come out.

"I …" He rocked back on his heels. Leo gasped as Uncle Matvei seized him by the arm and shoved his sleeves back.

"Take off your jacket," he commanded, trying to sound authoritative, but the tremor in his voice betrayed his underlying fear.

Leo did as told. Uncle Matvei twisted him around by the shoulders. He lifted Leo's shirt up with such force that Leo feared for a moment he might rip it. When Uncle Matvei saw that there were no lash marks on his back, he heaved a sigh of relief. He turned Leo back around with his finger pointed firmly at the drawer.

"Where did you get it? I know you put it in here."

Shame flooded Leo's spine as Uncle Matvei's words, uttered just moments ago, echoed back in his ears. *"Your parents would be so proud!"* He saw himself hiding in the shipyard with a crowbar, waiting for his opportunity to attack the crate furthest from the lamp. He felt his lower lip force its way out and his nose wrinkle as tears burned down his cheeks.

"I got a job working as an associate for the Breadwinners for the next three years. I'm sorry, Uncle!"

Uncle Matvei's mouth fell open as he put his arms around Leo and pulled him close to his chest, shedding tears of his own now.

"Oh, my boy!" He cupped the back of Leo's head in his hand and pressed his face into his shoulder. "They didn't hurt you, did they?"

Leo sniffed and shook his head. "No. I didn't have to become a member. They said they would make me an associate which guaranteed automatic protection and that way I could still get paid. I'm sorry, Uncle Matvei, I'm so sorry. I know you're disappointed. I didn't want you to lose everything you worked so hard for. And I didn't want to lose any more of my family."

"It is I who should be sorry, *Leonka*." Matvei's hands passed over his eyes as though his head had become physically heavy with grief. "You should never have had to worry about the security of this family. That was my job. That was a burden you were never meant to bear. I could have gone to the Breadwinners. I could have tried to relocate us somewhere else, but I was cowardly. And you children have had to suffer for it. I should be ashamed, Leontiy."

"*Nyet*, Uncle. You've been so good to us!" He felt Uncle Matvei lifting his chin upwards to look into his eyes.

"I want you to know that I am always proud of you, Leontiy. And I am proud of your courage." He reached into the cashbox and pulled out the money Leo had stowed away. "And this, this is your money. You keep it. You earned it." He patted Leo's shoulder. "I realize I can't negotiate you out of the situation. But I still want to speak with Klokov."

Leo rubbed at the space behind his collar. "I know it's not an ideal setup, but I want to honor the arrangement that was made. They showed me great kindness, Uncle. They're not bad people. Not truly. It really is like everyone says; they do good things."

Uncle Matvei massaged his jaw thoughtfully. "You said you have to serve three years?"

Leo nodded.

"Well, we will see if we can't get that reduced to two years or less." He prodded him towards the stairwell. "Go on up and relax, Leontiy. With the weather like it is, I doubt I will be getting more than I can handle." He kissed Leo on the head. "Get some rest, my boy."

Leo made his way to the top of the stairwell and entered the warm flush of the apartment. Anya was laid out in front of the radiator tending to her homework. When she saw Leo, she drew up her shoulders in a shy little coil. At first Leo didn't think much of it. Anya suffered bouts of bashful spells from time to time, even amongst those she was comfortable with. Ordinarily, he could coax her out of it by making her laugh. But lately these cures seemed short-lived, which meant Anya was harboring a secret she did not want to keep.

"What are you up to, *Annushka*?"

"Nothing," she replied in a barely audible voice, a timid little smile fastened to her lips. "Just homework."

Leo rolled onto the floor beside her and scratched playfully at her nose.

"Just homework?"

Anya hid her face behind her hands as she grinned.

"What about Faina? What's she up to?"

Anya's cheeks sank as her grin evaporated. So it was Faina's secret.

"Nothing. She isn't up to anything. I don't know. She's in her room. She's probably reading. You should go check."

Leo strived to appear as though he didn't suspect anything.

"Alright. I'll do that."

He ruffled her curls and headed off to the room he and Faina were still sharing. As usual, he found her buried in another book, just as Anya had predicted. When the door shut behind him she looked up and smiled as though she had nothing to hide.

"Alright." He tossed his book bag onto the bed. "What secrets are you forcing Anya to keep?"

Faina did not drop her smile but coolly set aside the book and began rummaging beneath her bed.

"I might ask the same of you, Mr. Sneaky-Associate-Person. Anya told me about the rumors that have been flying around school. Everyone is saying you've become an associate for the Breadwinners."

Leo rolled his eyes. "Well, the cat's out of the bag now. Uncle Matvei knows everything. We won't have to worry about money trouble anymore, which means Uncle Matvei can hire help again, and you can go to English lessons."

Faina tugged a box out from underneath the dust ruffle. "Good, in that case I suppose it is time for me to reveal my secret as well."

Leo plopped down on the bed and massaged his temples. She was so dramatic! Faina pattered over to the mattress and dumped the contents of the box upside down. It was an assortment of peculiar objects. There was a pair of boy's oxfords, a Woolworth brooch, a fountain pen, a pair of fur gloves, silverware, and candlesticks. Leo's eyes widened.

"Where did you get all this?"

Faina set her elbows firmly on the edge of the bed. "I want to help Uncle Matvei, like you. So, I collected things I thought you could sell to the Breadwinners."

Leo squinted his eyes. "By collected, do you mean stole?"

Faina threw her hands on her hips. "Another's cow can moo, yours had best stay silent." Which is a Russian way of saying, "Look who's talking."

"Who did you steal it from?"

"Different people."

"Different people where?"

"Up and down the street. I don't see what you are getting so upset about." She crawled onto the bed. "I'm only doing what you're doing to help Uncle Matvei. Anya said he was in a lot of trouble, that a bad man was coming around and threatening him for money!"

In her face Leo saw his own fear reflected back at him. He pinched the bridge of his nose and shut his eyes.

"I don't need your help, and it's wrong to steal from our neighbors."

"Where do you steal your stuff?"

"In shipyards and—" Leo stopped, throwing himself back on the pillows. "Why am I telling you this? How long has this been going on?"

Faina fiddled with the hem of her dress. "A couple of weeks."

Leo stared at her in silence.

"You're not going to make me give it back, are you?"

Leo sifted through the pile and frowned. "You never got caught?"

Faina shook her head.

"Giving it back would mean you'd have to confess, which would make Uncle Matvei look bad." Leo picked up the brooch. "I suppose I could give these to Klokov." He pondered once more at the sheer number of loot. "You seriously never got caught?"

She shrugged. "Have you ever got caught?"

"Not yet." He swept the contents into the box and handed it back to her. "Alright, I'll take this to Klokov, but don't do it again! I mean it!"

Faina returned the container to its hiding place below the bed. "Have they printed the school paper yet? I want to see the article you wrote about Wheatless Wednesdays and war rationing."

Leo removed the paper from the inner pocket of his satchel. "I haven't even looked at it yet."

Faina clapped her hands together excitedly and leapt back onto the bed. Leo snickered as he slipped his arm around her and opened to the first section.

"Let's see." He was just about to scan down to his story when a different headline caught his eye. *The Kissing Cat Burglar: The Lower East Side's New Bandit.* Leo narrowed his eyes as he skimmed over the article.

The Lower East Side is never short on crime these days, and trades in criminality seem to be trickling their way down to the local youth. A flood of reports are germinating throughout the lower grades claiming that a little girl has been breaking into apartments and stealing valuables, with a signature twist. It appears she's been targeting the homes of little boys between the ages of eight and eleven, and kissing her would-be-tattlers to keep them quiet. Like any good bandit, it seems this little heartbreaker knows the value of a good trademark. As for any clues to the identity of this little burglar, these boys say their lips are sealed.

Leo's hands dropped to his lap. His mouth fell open.

"You have got to be kidding me."

Faina didn't seem to understand. "What? What happened?"

Leo covered his eyes. "Faina, you didn't! Tell me you didn't!"

"Didn't what? What did I do?"

Leo sat up with such force he nearly knocked her off the bed. "This is you, isn't it?"

He thrust the article in her face. Faina squinted her eyes.

"*Keess ... Kissing ... Cat ... Burglar ...*" Her eyes lit up with pride. "Oh, yes, that is me!"

Leo tossed the paper into the air. "Faina! You can't just go around kissing every little boy in town! People will think—" His voice began to sputter. "People will … that just doesn't look good! That is not how proper young ladies behave! Oh my gosh, this is so embarrassing! Don't do this again!" He waved the newspaper in her face as though she were a misbehaving puppy. "Do not do it again! I mean it! I'm serious!"

And with that he threw himself down on the bed and covered his face with his pillow. After a couple of moments, he could feel Faina bouncing beside him with the newspaper in hand.

"You're still going to read me the article, right?"

Chapter 7:

A Miracle

Pasha awoke shivering to a rimy sunrise as a fist pounded outside the icy metal door. Mama gave a start as she rolled up from the mattress. They had slept in their clothes.

"Mrs. Chevalsky?"

Pasha had asked his mother before why she was letting people call her "Mrs. Chevalsky" as opposed to "Chevalskaya," as in Russia females always add a suffix ending in "a" at the end of their surname. His mother explained that in English, surnames were never gendered, and thus it was just easier to go by "Chevalsky."

Mama rose from the bed, straightened her skirt and walked over to the small square of window in the door.

"Yes, sir?"

"Your brother stopped by this morning asking if your ship had come in yet."

Pasha brought himself to a sitting position. Mama seemed just as stunned as he was.

"My … my brother?"

"He mentioned our names?" Pasha hastily cut in. He knew it was bad manners, but he could scarcely believe what was happening, and as badly as he wanted off the island he would've hated to accidentally take the place of another Mrs. Chevalsky, who might perhaps be waiting in another detention dormitory with her own family. The guard pulled back to squint at a piece of paper.

"Baroness Lydia Sylvia Davidovich Chevalsky …"

Pasha's eyes gave a solid blink. Mama never bothered to write her middle name on anything, for it was a foreign custom to have a middle name in addition to one's patronymic, and incredibly rare in Russia. She had not even bothered to include it in her paperwork.

"Pavlo Ruslanovitch Chevalsky, and Katerina Ruslanova Chevalsky." The guard drew a heavy breath as though his tongue had just run a marathon.

"What did he look like?" interrupted Pasha again. His mother shot him a warning glance over her shoulder.

"You will have to excuse him," his mother lied through a saccharine grin. "He has never met his uncle before. He is very excited."

The man nodded his head accordingly and looked past her to address Pasha.

"He's a tall fella with a goatee. Bald, late forties, gentlemanly type. Carried an ebony walking stick with a silver head."

Pasha and his mother exchanged curious glances before she forced the grin back onto her lips and clapped her hands together.

"That is him!"

Pasha could feel his palms beginning to sweat. He just knew the guard would ask his mother for her brother's name. But he didn't. In fact, he smiled and tipped his cap.

"In that case, Mrs. Chevalsky, you may proceed down to registration when you're ready, and we'll get you taken care of from there."

Mama pressed both hands over her heart. "Thank you, sir! We appreciate it so much!"

Pasha stared absentmindedly at the now vacant window. Something was not right.

"Do you have a brother?"

Mama was smiling so brightly it was almost frightening. "Nope." She clapped her hands together and reached over to shake his sister. "Alright now, time to get up, my darlings. We are leaving the island. Come, come, Katya! Wake up."

Still reeling, Pasha slid his feet into his shoes and followed his mother's orders through their morning routine. What remained passed by in a blur. A guard escorted them straight past the hearing room where detainees' cases were reviewed before being granted permission to leave the island, either for New York or somewhere else entirely. It was almost as if the guard hadn't even known it existed. They were taken through the legal inspection one last time, and again no one asked Mama about her brother.

Pasha eyed the pockets of the guards suspiciously. Was it possible they had been paid off? But who would have paid them? Mama's fictional brother? In less than two minutes the legal inspection came to a close. Their files were stamped. They were handed passes. Finally, they burst through the heavy doors at the top of the staircase and made their way down the left aisle. They were now Americans.

***

When the Chevalskys made their way into the wild, open-air bazar that was Orchard Street, Pasha knew he had now officially seen more human beings in the past month than he had in his entire life.

First there had been the swarms of refugees traveling through Crimea on broken and bare feet; then there was the mass of passengers packed into the steerage; and after that was the kaleidoscopic hive droning through Ellis Island. Now there was the Lower East Side: a bulging mass of haggling tongues, wagging fingers, and hands crossing their hearts. It was a flood of chickens, pushcarts, fish mongers, and dairymen. It was a sea of fiddler caps, *yarmulkes*, *mitcaphat*, and *hijabs*.

Children of varying nationalities whipped past them like a snapping ribbon, laughing, and not nearly bundled up enough for the frigid weather. Pasha shivered.

"It is not supposed to be this cold in March."

His mother slipped an arm around his shoulder and squeezed him close to her hip.

"We are not in Crimea anymore, *moya Patulya*. You will get used to it in time. When I was a little girl growing up in Lake Baikal, the lake stayed frozen from January to June. Just think, you will finally have the experience of seeing snow for the first time."

Katya clapped her hands excitedly, but Pasha was secretly hoping his first snow would be a long way off.

Mama plowed them ahead through the crowded street without intimidation. She stormed towards the first tenement building to boast a vacancy sign, a place called the Frasier. Mama did not shy away from the smells, or the manure puddles, or the pushy old women with their carts. She marched up the front steps with her shoulders thrown back, and knocked on the door.

An emaciated older woman with lean, wrinkled eyes like a badger appeared at the doorway in a cloud of cigarette smoke. Her nose was short and snubbed like a hook to hang your hat on. In fact, the deep creases of her frown lines made it look as though she had hung her sagging mouth there to keep it from falling to the floor.

"Can I help you?"

A shorter woman of similar age was bobbing at her elbow for a better look.

Mama cleared her throat, trying not to cough on the thick layer of tobacco smoke. "Yes, I see you have a vacancy in your tenement. How much do you want?"

The old woman looked her over unsmilingly from head to toe, then took another drag on her cigarette. "What kind of room are you looking for?"

A horrified exclamation poured from a window on the second floor, across the courtyard.

"What is the matter with you?" It sounded like the angry voice of an older boy. "Crazy, evil, horrible little sister!"

Pasha and Katya craned their heads to get a better look into the passage. The old woman rolled her eyes.

"Don't mind them. That's just the niece and nephew of the landlord next door. The man lets them run wild. Anyway, as I was saying, what kind of apartment are you looking for?"

Mama closed her eyes and stammered as she tried to think. "Uh, furnished? Anything, really, it doesn't matter. Look, I have money."

"Hold your horses now. I'm not in such a desperate situation that I'd lease you the place without letting you take a look first."

She beckoned them inside. The halls were thin and stuffy, barely wide enough to allow more than one person to pass at a time. The woman walked with her cigarette between two fingers.

"So, fresh off the boat, huh?"

As they passed, young mothers craned their heads out their open doors to eye the newcomers with suspicion. Pasha watched his mother brush gracefully by as though she hadn't noticed them at all.

"Yes, we arrived yesterday."

With a pair of jangling old keys, the woman unlocked the door of number seventeen. A wall with a broad, four-paned window divided the kitchen from the sitting room. To the right was a hall with two rooms that Pasha would have mistaken for closets, were it not for the beds pushed up against the wall. The landlady pointed to a little door between them.

"Here's something you won't find most places in lower Manhattan." She wrenched open the handle with her bony hands. "A private washroom complete with tub"—the tub being a washbasin sitting on top of a drain beneath a lonely faucet on the wall.

She was just ushering them into one of the bedrooms when a feminine shriek pierced the thin walls.

"He going to kill me!"

"Faina, come back," whined a second little girl. "Leo's not going to kill you!"

"What are you talking about, Anya?" hollered the boy who had been fussing at his sister. "Of course I am!"

Next thing they knew, a slightly chubby little girl in a soft dress was leaping out the window of the apartment directly across the courtyard. Her plump, rosy cheeks, littered with freckles, reminded Pasha of a strawberry, and her waist-length raven hair, which was tied off with the fluffiest ribbon he'd ever seen, whipped around like a wild colt's tail. It was funny to see such a frilly little girl running around in the cold with no shoes, climbing down the fire escape with little regard for modesty, screaming at the top of her lungs. Funnier still, she seemed to know what she was doing.

Dashing out the window behind her was the source of the threat: a short-statured boy of about sixteen with shiny auburn hair who looked as though he could've starred in pictures. To see him vaulting down the fire escape was like watching an Olympic gymnast. He swung from bars, leapt over railings, and scaled down walls.

The landlady heaved an aggressive sigh through her teeth. She plowed through them and stuck her head out the window.

"Will both of you shut your mouths?"

But the warring siblings paid her no mind. A third child, the little girl who had tried to smooth things over, approached the window, but at the sight of the old woman she immediately drew back and shut the curtains.

"Anya! Miss Anya, you get back here this instant. I want to speak with your papa, now!"

Pasha and Katya could hardly contain their giggles. The landlady whipped around, stunning the pair into silence. The floor creaked, and a woman balancing a toddler on her hip found her way into the apartment.

"What is all that noise?"

The landlady tossed a bitter glare towards the window. "What do you think? It's Matvei's brats again!" She returned her attention to Pasha's mother. "I don't believe I introduced myself. I'm Mrs. Borsuk. This is Mrs. Novak."

Mama grasped her extended hand. "Lydia Chevalsky, from Crimea."

"Chevalsky?" blurted Mrs. Novak in her thick Polish accent. "Just like the famous wine! I am only teasing, of course. You probably get that all the time, people asking you if you are related to the Baron Chevalsky."

Mama laughed nervously. "Actually, he was my husband."

Mrs. Borsuk choked on her cigarette while Mama crossed her ankles, looking terribly awkward.

"You mean you are the Baroness Chevalsky?"

"A noble …" muttered the young woman in Polish, clearly assuming Lydia would not understand. "I thought they all stayed in Europe."

"Apparently not," rejoined Mrs. Borsuk.

Pasha narrowed his eyes. Mama may not have been able to speak Polish, but Pasha, who had a gift for foreign language, and whose grandparents had been Polish, understood every word. Returning to English, the woman began circling his mother in a mock-friendly fashion.

"I would have thought a place such as this would have been beneath you."

Mrs. Borsuk put her hands high on her hips. "Excuse you, Ada Novak, but this is a very fine establishment! It's certainly been good enough for your highfaluting backside!"

Mama turned down her eyes for a moment or two, but she was not intimidated, no. Pasha had seen her operating under snide comments such as Mrs. Novak's for years; she knew how to handle bullies.

"It may surprise you, but the lifestyle I am accustomed to is quite different from what you are suggesting. I grew up a commoner on the shores of Lake Baikal. When I met my husband I was just a young vineyard worker, far from home."

The woman smiled as though she understood completely. "Ah, I see! A woman with ambition. In that case you will feel right at home in a place like New York."

Lydia glared at her. "It wasn't like that. I loved my husband."

Over Mrs. Borsuk's shoulder the shrieks and shouts of the brother and sister had started up again.

"Uncle Matvei," the boy was hollering, "Uncle Matvei!"

"Slow down, Leo, what seems to be the problem?"

The little girl's voice had grown shriller still as she shouted in Russian, "He is trying to kill me!"

"Faina, quiet down! Hey, hey, *nyet*! Leo, stop trying to grab her! What is the matter with you two?"

"She kissed Roman! She kissed Roman on the lips! She kissed my friend, Uncle Matvei! Do you realize how embarrassing that is?"

"You did what?"

By now Pasha and Katya were running to the window to take a peek at the kerfuffle in the courtyard. A tall, gangly man with a mustache stood between the children, with his left hand pushing back Leo's chest and the right on top of Faina's head.

A second youth, also about sixteen, vaulted over the sill and made his way rather quickly down the fire escape with his book satchel thrown over his shoulder. The mustached man called out.

"Roman, where are you going?"

"Oh, uh, gee, Mr. Dalka, I gotta run. I'm late for Sabbath."

Leo threw out his hands in exasperation. "You're Catholic! And it's Monday!"

But Roman was already disappearing around the corner. "Catch ya at school, Leo!"

Katya and Pasha were forced to move aside as Mrs. Borsuk elbowed her way to the window.

"Matvei Dalka, will you please keep your children under control?"

The man turned his face up and gave a friendly wave. "Oh, hello, Mrs. Borsuk!"

"I am trying to show a vacant apartment to a potential tenant, and as usual your children are causing a disturbance!"

Veering around Pasha, Mama leaned forward to get a peek out the window.

"Are you the potential tenant, ma'am?" hollered Mr. Dalka amiably.

"Yes, that is me." Mama appeared somewhat amused by the whole affair.

"Well, let me know if she doesn't offer you a fair price. I can get you something cheaper on my side of the building."

Mrs. Borsuk beat her fist on the windowsill. "How dare you, Matvei Dalka!"

A merry laugh echoed through the courtyard. "It was only a joke, Mrs. Borsuk."

Pasha peered his head over the edge once more in hopes of catching another glimpse of the pretty girl in the frilly dress. He found her still hiding behind her uncle, but she was looking up at him with curious, sparkling brown eyes. Pasha gave a timid wave. The corners of her lips turned up slightly, and she waved back.

"If you don't mind my asking, ma'am," proceeded Mr. Dalka, "it is just, your accent. Are you new to this country?"

Leo reached around and snatched at Faina's hair, causing her to cry out, and the whole affair started over again. Mr. Dalka pushed Leo back a second time.

"Leo! Leo, that is enough!"

"But Uncle Matvei, she completely humiliated me!"

Uncle Matvei looked up apologetically at the party leaning out the window.

"Welcome to the neighborhood, ma'am!" And with that, Mr. Dalka squeezed his niece and nephew firmly by the shoulders and shooed them back inside. Mrs. Borsuk hissed under her breath and snapped the window shut, nearly catching Pasha's fingers, and turned a pleading eye upon his mother.

"I am so sorry, ma'am. Please, I implore you, do not let those nasty children, especially that little hussy, persuade you to turn down what could be your first real American home!"

But Mama was doubled over in hysterical laughter, so much so that she had to steady herself upon the dresser. Though Katya did not understand English, she too began to titter. Pasha felt a little spark of happiness inside his chest. It was the first time he had heard his mother laugh since Papa had died. And then Pasha was laughing too.

Mrs. Borsuk and Mrs. Novak stared at them as though the three had turned into birds. When Mama finally caught her breath, she straightened herself and brushed the front of her skirt.

"Don't be silly, Mrs. Borsuk, we will take it! How much do you want?"

Hiding behind the baby in her arms, Mrs. Novak leaned close to Mrs. Borsuk and began muttering Polish once more.

"Surely, you are not going to let her off that easy? She is a former baroness, after all."

"Are you kidding? If I'm going to have to put up with all her airs and graces I'd at least like to make a profit off of it. What do you think? A dollar extra?"

"A dollar fifty."

Pasha had heard enough. Pushing past the two women, he threw open the window and cupped a hand over his mouth.

"Mr. Dalka!"

Pasha's mother looked alarmed. "Pasha, what are you doing?"

It just so happened that at that moment, Mr. Dalka had stepped outside to sweep off the sidewalk.

"Yes, my boy, how can I help you?"

"You wouldn't happen to have any available rooms on your side of the building, would you? Mrs. Borsuk is trying to take advantage of my mother because she is a former baroness."

Mrs. Borsuk made a noise like an upset hen.

Mr. Dalka set aside his broom. "That is a very serious accusation you are making, son. What makes you think she would do such a thing?"

"Because she said so just now, only she said it in Polish to her friend here. She said it thinking my mother would not understand Polish, and well, she doesn't, but I do, and I heard every word of it."

Below them in the street, a couple of ladies who happened to have been passing by and heard the whole thing pressed their hands against their lips and stopped to watch the scene unfold. Pasha looked back at Mrs. Borsuk, who was standing horrified in the center of the room with her tobacco-stained mouth hanging wide open.

"Shall I continue, Mrs. Borsuk?" he said, loud enough for the crowd gathering outside to hear. "I am sure all of New York would love to hear how you tried to take advantage of a potential client by charging her unfairly. I hear the housing market is pretty competitive here, and it is valuable information. Don't you think so, Mr. Dalka?"

By now Mr. Dalka had come into the courtyard and was staring up at him with a look of impressed satisfaction.

"I certainly would, my boy. In fact, my offer still stands. I just had a vacancy open up yesterday. I'll even take a dollar off."

Mrs. Borsuk flapped her skinny arms. "No, no! That won't be necessary! Four dollars a week!"

Pasha rubbed thoughtfully at his narrow chin. "Make it three-forty."

"Done!" Mrs. Borsuk shook her head, realizing she was haggling with a child, then turned to Pasha's mother, who smiled complacently.

"Three-forty a week will be just fine." She ran her fingers affectionately through Pasha's hair as Mrs. Borsuk made her way to the window once more.

"You hear that, Dalka? She's taking it! So hands off!"

Shrugging, Mr. Dalka returned to his sweeping. "Fair enough, Mrs. Borsuk. You win."

It was then that Pasha noticed Faina watching him from her bedroom window, half hidden behind the curtains and beaming behind timid fingers.

Chapter 8:

Out of the Fire and into the Pan

With a cigarette slipped between two fingers, Pyro stood at the ship's railing and watched the snowy planes of Ascella drift into existence. His shearling leather jacket, complete with badges he'd earned in the Saighdeoir, was open at the collar, and he wore a pair of sunglasses over his eyes. Beside him, Skelter stood shivering in a heavy coat with two chunky scarves slung about his throat.

"Well, here we are again," mumbled Pyro between drags. "Right back in the Pan. Good ol' Sagittarius." He looked over his shoulder at his shivering friend. "I went to school here. Parents shipped me off when I was fourteen after I got caught streaking through Piper Scalding's front yard."

Skelter's eyes widened.

"She was two years older than me, and wouldn't give me the time of day. Things you do for love. Am I right?" He chuckled and Skelter couldn't help but shake his head with an amused smile.

The wind picked up and snuffed out Pyro's tiller. He spat and uttered a curse.

"Language, Mr. Anomaly," warned Staccato, as he walked up to join them.

Pyro squeezed the railing. "Tongs and torches, you haven't started my training just yet! We haven't even docked!"

"Are you out of Kilgoree?"

Pyro hunched his shoulders. "Yes."

"Then it doesn't matter." He paused and examined Pyro's appearance. "Are you really going to keep that beard?"

Pyro shrugged. "What can I say? It grew on me."

Skelter snorted and hid his laughter behind his collar. Pyro smiled; it was nice to have someone laugh at his jokes for once.

"Besides, what you got against beards? You have one."

Staccato gave a capitulating grunt. "Yes, well … I suppose I haven't grown accustomed to it yet."

Pyro blew a soft stream of fire from his lips, reigniting the tip of the cigarette.

"Mind where you light that up." Staccato turned up his nose and sneered disdainfully. "We're not all igneous. Not all of our lungs are smoke-resistant. I'd especially appreciate it if you refrained from smoking in my goddaughter's presence."

Pyro gave a delighted chuckle as he recalled his diminutive, curly-haired mermaid admirer from childhood, whom he'd often looked after when the grown-ups were being boring.

"That's right! I forgot Sonny's gonna be there. How is the little mermaid these days?"

"Quite well." Staccato looked out at the horizon and stroked his beard. "Much better than I'd anticipated. But she's overcome quite a lot."

"Ah, that's right, she was separated from her parents during the Land Lock, wasn't she?"

The Land Lock had been going on four years now. The curse, first placed by the secret head of the C.O.N., Cobra Samael, had forced all mermaids in their ocean form at the time of the incident to be stuck in the water, while all mermaids in their land form were bound to the land. Seawater could be fatal for someone in Sonata's position, and the majority of the seven mermaid kingdoms had been forced to evacuate their land cities for their own safety. At times it seemed the entire world had ground to a halt following the Land Lock. Transportation was slower. Several allied kingdoms were left defenseless, exposing them to the C.O.N. Financial accounts housed in underwater vaults were unavailable to land dwellers, crippling the economy. Shortages on mermaid goods inspired rations on a variety of household staples. Separation of families was rampant, even forcing some mermaid children to be placed in foster homes until the curse could be broken. And Sonata was her parents' only child.

"That must've been terrible," concluded Pyro.

Staccato looked as though he had much more to say on the subject, but he stopped and checked his pocket watch. The face had transformed itself into a map of Voiler, and the third hand was pointing at Ascella.

"We should be making land any moment. She'll be waiting for us when we arrive."

Skelter squinted his eyes at the horizon and wandered a few paces off for a better look. Pyro lowered his voice and addressed Staccato.

"How are you going to explain the horse?"

Staccato lowered his chin into his collar. "I'll tell her the truth. Sonata knows everything. There's no point in hiding it from her."

Several weeks ago, as Pyro was finishing up his convalesce in Auriga, Staccato had come to him in the middle of the night with a premonition that his daughter and her family were in danger of being attacked by invading Soviet forces.

"I have reason to fear that she and her family are in immediate danger," he had explained with his staff pointed at Pyro's throat. "There isn't a second to lose! And if for any reason you should hesitate to assist me, or repeat a word of this conversation without my consent, I advise you to recollect the little discussion we had in Kilgoree, for if you do not help me rest assured I will fulfill my threat!"

Staccato had seemed surprised when Pyro willingly agreed and got up to throw on his jacket.

"Before we go any further, let's get something straight." Not one to be bullied, Pyro had pointed a finger in Staccato's face. "Never, ever, threaten me where saving innocents is concerned. It's unnecessary, and I personally find it very offensive. And you wouldn't like me when I'm offended. Saving people is what I do. I may be a scoundrel but I'm not a fiend."

Together, Pyro and Staccato had managed to rescue Staccato's daughter Lydia and her two children, enabling them to escape on the back of his grandson's pet horse, a dappled gray thoroughbred named Harpagos. When the time came for Lydia and the children to board their ship for the United States, the boy, Pasha, had been forced to sell his pet to some travelers. Unable to watch his grandson endure such heartbreak, Staccato bought back the horse, despite Pyro's protestations, and managed to smuggle it back into Voiler.

"I still don't see why you had to bring it here," Pyro sniped again.

"I had to do it, in case there's ever an opportunity where I can return him to the boy." When Pyro stared confusedly at Staccato, he merely smirked. "When you have children of your own someday you'll understand."

"What are you going to do with it?"

"I thought I might teach it to fly, and then perhaps it can travel with us."

Pyro raised his eyebrows in surprise. Turning horses into pegasi was an ancient Fay skill rarely practiced anymore, and from what Pyro understood, it was a difficult art to master.

"And you sorted out the problem with the immigration services in New York?"

Staccato nodded. "I enchanted the guard to let them go without a hearing. Coincidentally, they've settled down in the same tenement building as my aunt. Though she plans to keep her identity hidden through the use of an ambiguous.”

“Does she like it in New York? Your aunt, I mean.”

“She gets by. She’s not lonely. It appears she’s made herself a little friend lately, the landlord’s niece.” He checked his watch again. “If you’ll excuse me for a moment, I believe I left something down in the cafeteria.” He turned and disappeared just as Skelter was returning.

Skelter glanced sideways at the approaching horizon with a nervous expression.

“Nothing to be nervous about, mate,” Pyro reassured him. “Sonny’s a sweetheart. Little bitty thing. You wait and see.” He scratched his beard and smirked. “You know, she always used to say she was gonna marry me when she grew up. Ain’t that something? Kid’s cute as a button.”

***

At the docks, a motorcar was waiting to take them to Feifior, the palace where King Thayer lived, and where Staccato and the other members of his company were staying as his personal guests. As Pyro watched the snow-covered rocks and silvery pines pass outside the window, he felt as though he were returning home. After his parents had sent him off to boarding school in Sagittarius, Pyro had spent more time with his godfather, King Thayer, than he did with his own family. And oftentimes he preferred it that way.

The car ground to a halt outside the front doors. Feifior itself was not a comely castle, but at the very least it was interesting. What it lacked in beauty it made up for in history. The fortress, which was older than antiquity, was a hodgepodge of Scorpion and Sagittarian influences which, despite being a joint rule, could not have been more different in culture. There were places where you could literally see Scorpion roof tiles tacked over traditional Sagittarian slate. Half the towers were ashlar stone, while the other half were cedar wood. Some structures were hip-roofed, others were cone- or dome-shaped.

The outer walls boasted many scars. That is not to imply that the castle merely possessed an abundance of wounds, rather the fortress truly seemed to brag about them. The open lesions left behind in the exterior from generations of enemy attacks were a point of pride for any Sagittarian king to ever wield a bow, and there wasn’t a single monarch worth his spurs who didn’t. And repairing them was forbidden.

According to the Law of No Maintenance, a cosmetic repair was seen as a sin tantamount to vandalism by the Sagittarians.

The grounds were another story entirely. Ascella itself was located on an intermontane plateau, a breathtaking tableland surrounded by mountains. Seated on a shallow hillside in the heart of the prairie, the grounds of Feifior were vast and open, bordered by thick, green woodland. Even in dormancy the frames of the trees sketched full-figured shadows against the backdrop of gray peaks. A glassy lake was laid out at the foot of the palace like a silk carpet.

A flock of swans went gliding past just as Pyro stepped out of the car. He looked longingly out at the landscape. There was a strange sense of security in the thickness of those woods and the heights of those mountains.

Just beyond the property line he could make out the soft, wooly shapes of a nesh herd and its shepherds. Nesh were broad-faced, goat-like creatures with maned humps and flocked, furry horns who grazed on the purple wild wheescht that grew in the meadows. Ascella's abundance of wild wheescht made it an ideal location for the rearing of nesh, whose wool possessed high concentrations of nepenthe, which was used in teas and medicine to ease varying degrees of crippling grief.

While the footmen unloaded their belongings from the vehicle, Staccato disappeared to dictate instructions.

"Careful now! Careful! That's Alberion leather on that valise!"

Skelter stood back in awe, admiring the palace while Pyro lit another cigarette and walked to the end of the parapet overlooking the plains.

"Mr. Anomaly?" a feminine voice called over his shoulder.

Pyro turned, expecting to see a maid, but was gravely mistaken. Pyro's eyes widened. A gorgeous young woman with a familiar face was standing there smiling at him with full lips and dimpled cheeks. His cigarette sagged in his mouth. She had sultry, almost sleepy eyes and carried her minuscule five-foot-one-inch frame as though she were two feet taller. Her dense, dark hair was a veritable tidal wave of various curls and springs that cascaded over her back and shoulders, and her skin was the color of glistening wet sand.

"Sonny?" The cigarette fell out of Pyro's mouth. He fumbled to catch it. "I—I mean Sonata? Is that you?"

She sank her teeth into her lower lip as she giggled, a gesture that made Pyro's knees tingle.

"Don't you recognize me?"

The last time Pyro had seen Sonata, he had been nineteen and she had been eleven, a child who still mooned over him, and rode on his back, and sent him valentines she had pasted together in the nursery. In truth, it seemed as though it were only yesterday. It had never occurred to Pyro, that in all that space of time, she might have grown up.

Pyro reached into the back of his collar. "Well, of course I do! Just ain't used to hearing you call me 'Mr. Anomaly.'"

Sonata brushed a stray curl behind her ear. "It's been so long, I didn't want to make you uncomfortable by sounding too familiar."

"Ah, I'm not much for titles. I'd rather you call me what you've always called me."

He worried that he was looking at her too intensely, for she had one of those faces one could simply not stop staring at.

"Sonata!" Staccato reappeared on the front steps, Skelter in tow. "There you are!" He hastened to catch up with them. "I see you've found Pyro." He roped his arm around his goddaughter's shoulders and hugged her close. "It's been quite some time since you last saw each other."

"I'm afraid it has been."

Staccato beckoned Skelter forward, and turned Sonata's attention to their newest addition, who bowed so low Pyro feared he would fall on his face.

"Come." Sonata corralled them towards the door. "Let's get you boys inside and get you warmed up."

The moment Pyro was sure Staccato and Sonata were out of earshot, he turned to Skelter and muttered, "Blazes, she's a knockout, isn't she?"

Skelter gave a vigorous nod of his head. Pyro paused. He hadn't been expecting Skelter to give such an enthusiastic answer, and he hadn't expected to care.

The inside of the castle was much like the outside in that it was a crooked amalgamation of two contrasting cultures and their storied histories, but there was one feature that had been altered somewhat recently. Under normal circumstances, Feifior boasted a series of watery channels and fully submerged rooms to accommodate mermaids, as many Sagittarian rulers—Thayer included—were mermaids themselves. Now, the watery lanes had either been boarded up or partitioned behind protective glass.

Pyro's chest filled with a heavy sorrow as he was reminded that two of Thayer's sons had been locked into the water while the rest of the family was landbound. They were, of course, incredibly fortunate to have their sons quarantined within the palace as opposed to separated from them in the ocean, where they could've easily been targeted by the C.O.N. during the evacuation, but it was a lonely and depressing life to be limited to seeing one's parents through glass, or fearing to touch them.

A footman helped Sonata out of her coat, allowing Pyro a better view of her feminine figure. She had remained small in height, but her hips now fanned out in a wide, voluptuous curve, and she had plump, sturdy arms with small, dainty wrists. She had a lush beauty, being fuller and rounder in most places. It was all Pyro could do to keep from melting. She was exactly his type.

An orange-and-white cat came running down the stairs towards Sonata, meowing.

"And who's this?" asked Pyro.

"This is my cat, Cello." She reached down and scooped the cat into her arms. "Would you like to pet him? He's quite friendly."

Pyro ran his finger under Cello's chin, and the cat purred contentedly.

"Have you had an opportunity to see your parents yet, Pyro?"

"My parents?" It took him a moment for his brain to register the question.

Sonata returned Cello to the ground and began smoothing her hair over one shoulder. Pyro watched the curls bounce, and fall across the nape of her neck. She always did have lovely hair. Trying to appear casual, Pyro leaned against the grandfather clock.

"Nah, not really sure they're interested in seeing me."

"Pyro, your hand!" Staccato exclaimed.

Pyro turned in time to see the place where his hand was resting crumble away into ash. He jumped back in alarm, swearing profusely. Skelter slammed a hand over his mouth.

Realizing what he'd done, Pyro froze. Staccato was glaring at him with a heat to rival his own. A booming laugh echoed from atop the gallery.

"At it again, eh Pyro?"

A man with a set of armor thrown over a long-sleeved undershirt stood with his arms outstretched. Thayer Takayama may have had a chunk of his finger missing, and his face boasted a variety of scars, but he was an otherwise handsome middle-aged gentleman. Like the Law of No Maintenance, when it came to their own bodies, Sagittarians held much the same principles. Scars were lauded as badges of honor, testaments to strength in hard times, and of survival. Strength of character was valued far more than shallow beauty standards. Thayer was a Scorpius mermaid by birth, and had been appointed to the throne by the former king of Sagittarius after the death of his son.

Thayer hastened down the stairs. "You know, there's still a scorch mark on the tapestry of the Siege of Khan Lau in the Great Hall from when you had a case of the dry bellows! Second-biggest spice trading hub in all Voiler, and Pyro just about destroyed it all." He threw back his head and laughed. "Burned right through Captain Tripp Cortair's head!"

Pyro glanced off to the side and chuckled. "Yeah, sorry about that, Thayer."

The king flung his arms around his godson's neck.

"Ah, it was an ugly clock anyway! Welcome home, you old burn pile!"

Pyro tried not to wince from the pressure. "It's great to be back!"

"So, I hear you've been doing time?" He turned to Skelter, who seemed to be experiencing another wave of awestruck nerves. "This must be the man who took a swing at Senator Sobek. Strength is something we appreciate here in Sagittarius, my friend! And we don't take kindly to C.O.N. members in these parts, especially ophidians who hurt little ones. It's high time someone made him pay for his crimes!" He beckoned them towards the hall. "Come, let's get you boys settled. I'm afraid I've been called away to a meeting, but Staccato here will fill you in on our little undercover experiment."

Pyro's eyes briefly met Sonata's as she turned away. She appeared to hold a sort of secret in her gaze. Pyro could recognize that look anywhere, for he'd seen it on the faces of mermaids a hundred times before: Sonata had sensed Pyro's attraction to her.

Most of the time, a healthy mermaid could tell when a man was interested in her, not that it would've taken a proficient empath to decipher Pyro's behavior. As embarrassing as it was, Pyro reminded himself that it would pass once he had grown accustomed to her presence again. He had already decided that Sonata was off limits. She was young, and they had been friends. The last thing Pyro wanted was to hurt her. Still, there was an inescapable sense of anxiety that accompanied his self-denial, and in that moment he simply could not see his attraction to her fading any time soon.

"I hear it's been quite some time since you two have seen each other," observed Thayer of Sonata and Pyro. "You'll have quite a lot of catching up to do!"

"Indeed," said Sonata, punctuating the sentiment with a sweet smile. "I must say I was quite surprised to hear that Mr. Anomaly would be joining our task force, considering you and Staccato had agreed to hire only experienced performers from now on."

Pyro turned his head up in surprise. Though she could not have expressed herself in a sweeter, friendlier tone, her words seemed to suggest some annoyance with the addition of Pyro. But perhaps he had misunderstood her.

"Oh, Pyro is quite the acrobat," answered Thayer. "In fact, didn't the two of you receive gymnastics lessons from the same instructor as children?"

Staccato nodded his head for Sonata. "They most certainly did. And you forget, Sonata, dear, that you and Melodious are both still amateurs."

Sonata's chin remained high. "That's very true. And what about you, Mr. Skelter? What is your talent?"

Skelter unstrapped his violin from his shoulder and, after a short bow to the princess, dove into a fast-paced, upbeat melody.

Sonata clasped both her hands over her mouth, genuinely pleased. "Oh, how lovely!"

"And that ain't all he can do." Pyro crossed his arms over his chest. "Skelter can climb just about anything. He was a regular flight risk in Kilgoree. Used to shinny over the pipes in the ceiling to stay hidden."

Sonata placed her hands on her hips, satisfied. "Well, I certainly look forward to seeing you try out a tightrope, or perhaps the hoop and silks with me."

Thayer folded his hands behind his back. "Actually, Pyro is going to be your aerial ballet partner."

Sonata's smile sagged into nonexistence. "He is?"

"I am?" Pyro was just as surprised as she was.

Thayer held up a finger. "You haven't seen Pyro out in the field like I have. Running up walls, vaulting over fences, swinging from banisters. He's a natural! Of course, Mr. Skelter is also welcome to give the silks a try."

Sonata placed a thoughtful finger on her chin and turned to Pyro. Her eyes ran him over from top to bottom. It was all Pyro could do to keep from blushing.

"You do have the build for it."

Pyro's eyes brightened. "I do?" He cringed; he hadn't meant to sound so enthusiastic.

Sonata tapped her cheek and stared down at his legs. "Yes … Gymnastics favors short men."

Pyro's eyes glazed over irritably, but Sonata smiled.

"A shorter stature means you have a greater strength-to-weight ratio." She circled him. "Furthermore, you have a lower center of gravity, meaning you have an easier time keeping your balance as well as manipulating your body. People often forget the advantages of a shorter build." She eyed his biceps. "Smaller men are often quite strong as well. You look as though you're pure muscle."

Pyro glowed with astonished pride. His eyes met Sonata's with a playful grin. Skelter threw Pyro an encouraging look while Staccato looked almost appalled at his goddaughter.

"Well," she said at last. "I think it's only fair to warn you that aerial ballet takes a great deal of discipline." She said this last word with such emphasis and intensity, that Pyro instinctively took a step back.

"In that case, you're lucky Thayer did hire a soldier. A Saighdeoir soldier is nothing if not disciplined."

Sonata lowered her lids halfway. "So they say."

"You sound skeptical."

Thayer rocked back on his heels with a wry smile. "You'll find Sonata can be quite particular about her performance."

Sonata wrinkled her nose teasingly at Thayer. "I care a great deal about this circus, therefore I strive for excellence."

"Rest assured, Pyro." Thayer patted his shoulder. "If you do lack any self-restraint, Sonata will be sure to keep you in line."

"I certainly will."

Pyro rubbed his hands and bowed his head respectfully towards Sonata. "I look forward to your discipline."

Skelter smiled awkwardly. It was too late to correct his blunder. Sonata cocked an eyebrow, looking somewhat amused, and flipped her hair over her shoulder. Staccato cleared his throat.

"Sonata, it's nearly noon. Didn't you promise Princess Mai you'd take her out to play in the snow yesterday?" Mai was Thayer's youngest.

"You'll have plenty of time to visit with Mr. Anomaly and Mr. Skelter during practice."

Sonata lowered her chin in an attempt to hide a somewhat resentful glare at Staccato.

"Yes, Staccato." She bowed her head politely to Skelter and Pyro. "I look forward to seeing you two gentlemen at training."

She turned up the nearest staircase. Pyro craned his head as he watched her ascend the steps.

"How—how old is she again?"

The intensity of Staccato's glower could have burnt a hole through Pyro's clothes.

"She's eighteen."

"Eighteen, eh? That explains a lot."

Thayer chuckled and beckoned them onwards. "She certainly keeps her godfather on his toes."

Staccato rolled his eyes in a good-natured manner. "As I would expect from anyone her age."

***

Later that afternoon, after Pyro and Skelter were settled, they went downstairs to meet Staccato who was waiting to escort them to the gymnasium where the company practiced their routines.

"You'll finally have the opportunity to meet our final member, Mr. Krüner," remarked Staccato as he led them through the courtyard.

Pyro ground to a halt. "Wait, final member? You mean there are only four of us?"

"At the moment, I'm afraid so."

"But that would mean before Skelter and I showed up you only had two performers!"

"Well, six actually. Three quit, and one was injured."

They continued walking but Pyro's eyes glazed over with suspicion. "Why did they quit?"

Staccato drew a long sigh and tucked his scarf tighter about his throat. "Keep in mind, the initiative is still in the early stages of development. There were some disagreements between Thayer and the performers."

"What kind of disagreements?" Pyro could see that he was beginning to annoy Staccato, but he couldn't shake the feeling that the miraculous was hiding something from him. Staccato exhaled through his nose and gripped his staff tighter.

"Let's just say the performers decided the initiative was a silly idea, and so they quit."

"Silly? But if they're performers, aren't they used to this sort of circus stuff?"

"Actually, the ones who quit were former members of the Saighdeoir."

Pyro and Skelter exchanged curious glances. "And what about the one who was injured?"

"That would be one of our former aerial ballerinas. She fell off the hoop."

Pyro made a face. With a confused expression, Skelter held up his hand and began gesticulating. Pyro watched closely. He was still learning how to communicate with Skelter at this point, but he was catching on rather quickly.

"Yeah," Pyro agreed. "I thought you said you had carried out successful missions before now. If you were so successful, why did they all quit?"

Staccato halted suddenly in the middle of the path. He threw up his hands and turned to face them.

"Alright, fine! You wish to know what happened with the other performers? Six months ago we carried out a trial run involving three assignments. The goal was to retrieve secret military plans from the C.O.N. for raiding the Eridanus River Valley. We started out with Mr. Krüner, Sonata, and Sonata's aerial ballet instructor, Madame LaBelle DeOddity. However, Thayer decided that the majority of the performers should be experienced soldiers, given the nature of the expedition. Unfortunately, our three men in uniform gave little attention to their performance, instead putting all their emphasis on soldiering. They rarely showed up to practices and when they did, they were so little inclined to do anything that they barely memorized their routines!"

Pyro knit his eyebrows together. "So you didn't pull off the mission."

Staccato held up a finger. "No, we did! Despite everything, we somehow managed to get hold of those tactics so the rebels could surprise the C.O.N. at Lepus Valley. However, the performances of the three soldiers were so pitiful that our last recital managed to earn us a poor reputation!"

Pyro threw up his shoulders as the wind blew the lapels of his jacket open. "So? It's not like you're a real circus anyway."

Staccato's nostrils flared. "In order for the Cirque De Fay initiative to work, it is imperative that we are taken seriously. People have to believe we are the real thing. The goal is to infiltrate affluent Primal circles no other Fay rebel could, to trespass into the Draconian nobility as exclusive, highbrow, avant-garde entertainment. Therefore, it is crucial that we present quality, otherwise no one will hire us."

"So, you really expect us to learn all this circus stuff? It's not just undercover soldiering?"

"A spy is only as good as his disguise, Mr. Anomaly. You wouldn't try to infiltrate the DaPeng with an Ariesian accent and a cardboard quiver, would you? Of course not! So, to answer your question: yes, I expect you to learn this 'circus stuff'! This isn't a game! Just because there's an audience and a tightrope doesn't mean the work my rebels do is any less important than what you do in the Saighdeoir, and I expect your behavior to reflect that. Do I make myself clear?"

Pyro sucked in a mouthful of breath and forced a compliant smile. "As clear as the Eridanus."

Staccato looked him over once, then edged away. "Good." He continued on towards the gymnasium.

Pyro released his breath, and stole a quick glance at Skelter, who was nervously fidgeting with his pockets. Did Thayer really expect him to commit to this role of tights-wearing circus performer? He, Pyro? It would never do! He couldn't help but feel he had been misled.

"Now," Staccato cleared his throat. "There are three types of Cirque De Fay. The first is Uranian dating back to the start of the nomadic period, which employed basic feats of magic and dream interpretation as a means of entertainment. The second is Terpsichorean, first popularized in Cassiopeia under mermaid influence. As you can imagine, terpsichorean puts a heavy emphasis on singing, dancing, and musical performances. The third is Clionean, born out of the scholarly movement during the late epic era when the Fay arts were experiencing their first renaissance. Our performance draws inspiration from the second. Mr. Skelter, as you can imagine, I was most elated to learn of your ability to play the violin, and after hearing you play I am convinced you could not be more suited for our initiative."

Skelter was beaming with pride, but Pyro was still trying to scrape his jaw up off the pavement.

"Woah, woah, woah! You didn't say anything about a musical performance when we were discussing this in Algedi! You know I don't play an instrument, right?"

Staccato glanced back at him with a raised eyebrow. "Yes, I know."

Pyro felt the color of his cheeks deepen. "Staccato, I can't sing."

"I believe the correct phrase is 'won't.' You're Sonata's partner. It wouldn't look right if she sang by herself. But an acrobatic duet? Think how impressive that would be!"

"I'm not going to think about it because I'm not doing it!"

"You do realize that's one of the reasons Thayer recommended you for the job, don't you?"

Pyro's shoulders tensed. If that was true it was news to him. Countless recollections of his parents forcing him to sing in front of their friends at parties as a child flooded into his mind.

"Did he now? Well, I'm afraid he steered you wrong!"

Staccato shrugged. "I thought you sounded more than decent enough."

"When did you—"

"1907. Your parents made you sing at the Soter's banquet in Alveare. You were fifteen."

Pyro groaned. "I nearly jumped into the ocean to avoid having to do that, you know."

They came to the doors of the gymnasium. Staccato turned with his hand resting on the knob.

"We can discuss it later. But first, let's get you acquainted with the basics."

He slid open the door, another Scorpion addition, allowing a warm breeze to flush over the threshold. The first thing which drew Pyro's eye was a humongous, seven-foot-tall man with closely cropped, mousy-brown curls and a thick, bristly mustache to match. He was standing near the center of the gymnasium with the largest weight in the set on his back, and the second-largest tied perpendicular to the first. Pyro watched, completely dumbfounded, as the man repeated squat after squat as though there were no weights on his back at all.

"Good afternoon, Melodious," greeted Staccato the moment they were in earshot.

The man stopped and lifted one bushy eyebrow, though Pyro still could not see the eyes beneath them. The corner of Melodious's mustache twitched upwards, indicating a smile. With ease, he set aside the weights and stood up straight.

"Well, well," he began in a thick German accent. "You must be the Mr. Anomaly I have heard so much about."

Pyro smiled. Already he was liking Melodious. He was one of the few people Pyro had met who, upon introduction, had not bowed, scraped, or referred to him as "your royal highness." He must have read the papers.

"You must be the reverend."

"Indeed. I am Melodious Krüner. But you may call me Melodious." He stuck out his hand, albeit a little off to the side. Pyro eyed it in confusion before shrugging off the eccentricity and shaking it heartily.

"And who else do you have with you?" Melodious asked.

Staccato waved Skelter forward. "This is Mr. Skelter." He hesitated for a moment. "I'm afraid he only communicates nonverbally due to the vow of silence he's taken, so the two of you may have some trouble conversing."

Skelter glanced back at Staccato with an uncomprehending frown.

"Melodious is blind."

"Oh." Pyro's eyes ventured around the mat. He didn't see a walking stick anywhere. Melodious grinned.

"Most people do not realize I am blind thanks to my Moira abilities."

"Ah, you're a Moira?"

Melodious nodded his head proudly. "My brief foresight and heightened senses allow me to navigate without a walking stick or guide. They also help me to find my target."

Pyro blinked as though he hadn't heard Melodious correctly. "Target?"

Melodious turned to Staccato. "Should I show them?"

Staccato stepped aside. "By all means."

As they turned, Pyro noticed for the first time the series of targets set up along the far wall. Melodious approached the nearby table where a set of throwing knives had been laid out.

"I would prefer a bit more of a challenge this time, Staccato, if you don't mind."

"Certainly." Staccato extended his staff and the targets formed a wide, spinning circle around Melodious. Skelter leaned eagerly forward with interest, while Pyro watched with his mouth agape. Melodious picked up the first knife and, bending it over his shoulder, struck the nearest target right in the center.

Hardly a moment passed before he picked up the second and embedded it into a bullseye. Pyro couldn't believe what he was seeing. Not only was Melodious able to hit the mark blind, but his reflexes were superb. The entire display lasted only seven seconds. By the time he was done every knife had been wedged into a bullseye.

Skelter was slapping his large hands together in applause, while Pyro doubled over in awe.

"That was amazing! Tongs and torches, I bet you get all kinds of applause when you perform!"

Melodious smiled and shrugged. "I do enjoy a certain degree of popularity."

"Well done, Melodious!" shouted Sonata from across the room. She had just entered and was approaching the hoop hanging from a three-legged frame. She had exchanged her dress for a leotard, showcasing her plump thighs, and she wore a pair of knee-high boots that looked as though they were made of long strips of satin wrapped around her legs.

"Would you boys like to see my routine?"

Without thinking, Pyro gave an overly vigorous nod of his head, hoping she hadn't noticed him admiring her legs. He tried not to look too bug-eyed as she lifted her leg nearly to her nose and swung it over the edge of the hoop. She braced the sides with both hands and, standing on her tiptoes, was able to climb the rest of the way from there. Staccato raised the hoop for her using his powers, and Melodious turned on the victrola, allowing Sonata to begin her performance.

Pyro and Skelter stood at the edge of the mat with their heads craned back while Sonata performed a series of acrobatic tricks: flipping over the hoop, dangling upside down and spinning with her arms thrown out, and balancing on the axis of her pelvis like the maidenhead of a ship.

Pyro could hardly look away. "She really knows what she's doing, doesn't she?"

Staccato straightened his shoulders with as much pride as if she were his own daughter. "Well, she has been training for almost three years now."

Sonata hung from the hoop by her legs, and draped herself in some elaborate pose. She navigated the air with as much grace and ease as she would have in the water. Her movements were confident and instinctual. She performed not only with her body but with her expressions as well, at times appearing mournful and pensive, only to become empowered and self-assured moments later. When she had finished, she let her legs drop, then hoisted herself back into the hoop by her upper body strength alone.

Pyro flexed his eyebrows. The act of hauling one's bodyweight in such a manner was not always easy, especially for those more heavily muscled like Pyro, as there was more weight to carry. Sonata may have been short but she was not thin. It took a lot of power to lift herself over that hoop.

"No wonder she managed to take on Samael!" Pyro stroked his beard in astonishment. "I reckon she could take me out! What gave her an interest in aerial ballet?"

"Well," Staccato hesitated with an awkward tilt of his head. "It was actually an attempt at rehabilitation."

"Rehabilitation?"

"Staccato," Sonata interrupted them, "do you think you could take a look at my ankle joint?" She turned down the cuff of her left boot, revealing a sort of brace made from leather, and unbuckled the clasp. To Pyro's great astonishment, she grabbed hold of her calf and detached it from her body. The shoe slid to the floor, leaving behind a metal prosthetic leg.

Staccato held up his hand. "Toss it."

Sonata let the leg drop, and Staccato zipped it into his hand telekinetically. The bottom of the shin was attached to the pedal-shaped foot by a sort of ball. Staccato flexed and pointed the pedal, examining the joint.

"Looks as though a screw is coming loose. Can't you slip on one of your other pairs for the time being?"

"Will the ones I was wearing with my tea gown do? I wouldn't want to soil my evening pair before dinner."

Staccato lowered the hoop for her. "Whatever you're most comfortable in." He willed the leg to float back to her, and she went about reattaching it.

"Very well." She hopped down from the hoop and headed for the door. "I'll just be a moment."

As soon as Sonata had disappeared, Pyro wrenched around to look at Staccato.

"What happened to her leg?"

"You didn't know?"

"I had no idea!"

Staccato removed a handkerchief from his pocket and busied himself with a spot on the head of his staff. "Price she paid for retrieving Sea-Splitter, I'm afraid."

Pyro's mouth fell open. The news struck him with such a sinking feeling that he would've liked to have sat down.

"You mean the C.O.N. cut off her leg?"

Staccato's expression grew tense. "Leg*s*. They took both." He lowered his head. "If it's any comfort to you, she was unconscious when it happened."

Pyro raked both hands through his hair, trying to steady himself. He couldn't help but hurt for her. After a moment, he sighed.

"I was curious how she made such a clean getaway. Guess she didn't."

A bitter scoff escaped Staccato's lips. "Far from clean. We barely made it out of Alveare alive."

"You rescued her?"

Staccato grunted in the affirmative. "Didn't you hear about it through the Saighdeoir?"

Pyro shook his head.

"Well, thanks to the Land Lock news does travel slowly these days." Staccato sucked his teeth. "If it travels at all, that is. Thayer didn't mention it?"

"He only mentioned that Sonata had managed to get Sea-Splitter back from Samael, and that she was recovering in Ascella. I assumed he meant from shock."

Skelter merely knit his brows together and frowned, but didn't appear surprised. But such atrocities were common amongst the C.O.N., and he had only just met Sonata.

"Suppose those are a pair of those fancy new prosthetics everyone's been raving about. Seen plenty of Land Lock amputees outfitted with a pair during rescue work. Boy, the chap who came up with those beauties oughta be a saint."

"Well, I do have three knighthoods but I've yet to be made a saint."

Pyro and Skelter turned to stare at him.

"You?" Pyro sputtered. "You patented those prosthetics? The ones that help *double* amputees walk, something that was completely unheard of before now? The ones that use enchantment to help restore natural gait? The ones that have movable ankle joints?"

Staccato rocked back on his heels. "Sonata was the first one to try them out. They worked so well we decided to have them patented, that way everyone suffering from similar disabilities could have a pair."

Pyro stared curiously at Staccato with the slightest trace of an amused smile. Staccato put up quite an icy front, but since their meeting in Kilgoree he'd seen the man rescue his family, smuggle his sobbing grandson's pet out of the Other, and learned he'd invented a special pair of prosthetics just so his goddaughter could walk again.

"What?" Staccato snapped. "What are you smirking about?"

"Just surprised is all."

"Surprised about what?"

"You do have a heart."

Staccato turned on Pyro with an arrogant glower. "Your job is to perform, Mr. Anomaly, not judge my character!" And with that, he swept his nose into the air and walked away.

Chapter 9:

The Anarchists' Boy

Faina made her way out the door of *Opa!*, the little brass bell clanging overhead. Her precious cargo, a rare bottle of wine, was carefully tucked under her arm.

"You must be very careful with this one," Uncle Matvei had said, as he removed the long dark bottle from the crate, littering the counter with curly papers. "I imagine pretty soon this label will be hard to come by."

Curious, she had risen up on her tiptoes for a better look. "Why? What is it?"

Uncle Matvei had held up the bottle for her to observe. It was a Russian label with shiny green paper and a gold embossed image of a tarpan galloping across the Siberian steppe.

"It is a Chevalsky. A 1907 Chardonnay, to be exact."

"It has a name just like our neighbors!"

"That's right, *Solnyshka*," Sunshine.

"Why would it become rare suddenly?"

Uncle Matvei's chest rose and fell as he drew a heavy sigh. "Because Chevalsky is manufactured by the aristocracy, a Polish baron, I believe, living in Crimea. The wine is named after the family. Crimea may have declared themselves independent of Russia a month ago, but I'm afraid the Bolsheviks have already begun to invade."

He tore a long sheet of brown paper from the roll, wrapped the bottle twice, and slid it into a narrow bag.

"This is for Mrs. Waidelich. You remember her address?"

"Eighty-five Delancey Street, apartment fourteen."

He patted her head. "Good girl. Now hurry along. Anya and Leo should be home soon and then you can go play."

Eager to please her uncle, Faina took her job very seriously, and walked slowly to avoid tripping and damaging the bottle.

Piles of snow were crowded against the foundations of the red brick tenement buildings. It was funny how even in the dead of winter Orchard Street buzzed endlessly like an overly congested beehive. Swarms of people hovered in and out of stacked flats, and icicles sucked from awnings and fire escapes like viscous ribbons of slow-moving honey. Already children were returning home from school with book satchels strapped over one shoulder.

She continued on to Delancey Street. On the opposite corner, a young couple in thin, patched clothing was passing out pamphlets and hollering something about the evils of capitalism, and the glory of the revolution overseas. They had been there before. Whenever Faina spied them her eyes burned with hatred. She wanted to run up to them and scream, tear the pamphlets, throw them in the gutter and stomp on them. Didn't they know that it was because of the revolution that her parents were dead?

As she made her way up the street, she spied a familiar face at a distance coming down the street in the opposite direction. She'd seen this boy several times before while making her uncle's deliveries. He was the type one might easily overlook in a crowd, and were it not for the fact that he had a habit of staring doggedly as she passed by, Faina might never have realized he existed.

He appeared to be a year or two older, but even if he were eleven going on twelve and not nine going on ten he seemed a little large for his age, and that is not to say that he was overweight, for he certainly wasn't that, but tall and strapping. And yet for all the vigor in his frame there was something sickly about him. His head was awkward looking, too big for his body. His pale green eyes were wreathed in dark shadows like those of a man who smoked too much, and he hunched slightly when he walked. His skin was sallow like nicotine-stained wallpaper. Even the color of his curly hair, which was ash blonde, seemed like it could have been lighter if he were in his natural, healthier state.

Most days Faina tried to ignore him, for he always wore such an intense look on his face, one that seemed inappropriate to find on a child, and she thought it somewhat intimidating. But after passing him so many times in the street, his attention undeniably glued to her, Faina found herself wondering about him more and more. Why was he always watching her? What had caused such an aura of sadness to cloud his presence? She began thinking. Perhaps it was loneliness. After all, if there was one thing people had in common here, it was a tragedy to escape; war, revolution, any number of hardships. He was young like her, and perhaps new to this city. Maybe he needed a friend. Or perhaps just a smile.

Without thinking, Faina's eyes slid across the road to the passing figure. Her eyes met the boy's severe stare. Blinking once, she flashed him an amiable, close-lipped smile. No sooner had she done this than the boy came speed-walking across the road and down the sidewalk, with such harsh, powerful strides that for a half-second Faina feared he might be coming to beat her up.

She froze anxiously in the middle of the walkway and quickly looked over her shoulder, wondering what to do. But the moment she turned back around, there he was, inches from her, his eyebrows knit so tightly over his eyes they were nearly touching.

"Hi, I'm Anastas Sippenhaft," he said in English.

He jabbed his hand forward in greeting, making her flinch. Faina was stunned. Her eyes darted between his unsmiling face and his massive outstretched hand, trying to connect the two. Reluctantly, she placed her hand softly in his. He gave it one solid shake as though he might wrench her arm off.

"Hello, Anastas. I am Faina. Faina Spichkin." Her English had improved greatly after being immersed in it at home for two months.

"You must be the new girl from Siberia."

Still he did not smile but maintained his overpowering expression, as though he were made of stone and incapable of looking any other way. He had a strange habit of talking uncomfortably close to her, leaning in two hairs past the border of her personal space. She noticed he carried no traces of a European accent, and though he wasn't fast-talking there was a bawdy inflection of New York to his tone. But Anastas was a fairly common name in Russia, though it was Greek in origin. As for Sippenhaft? It sounded German. Before Faina could respond, he was answering the question inside her head.

"My mother is from Russia. Papa is from Germany. They met in Petersburg."

She was almost thankful for his direct way of speaking for it made him much easier to understand.

"Are you from Russia?"

He didn't seem to blink much either. Anastas shook his head.

"I was born here in New York. The first in my family." She must have put him at ease for he finally slid his hands into the pockets of his dingy, baggy coat, making his shoulders relax a little. "So how did you end up here? Ever since the Revolution a lot of Russians stopped coming over."

A familiar voice called out his name. They turned towards the source of the call. It was the woman who had been standing on the corner handing out pamphlets with her husband. Faina could see it now, the same unsmiling face, the heavy garlands of shadows collected under their eyes like layers of dust on a lofty bookshelf. The woman beckoned Anastas towards her.

"Why are you dawdling on the sidewalk? You and your brothers need to sweep out the kitchen. We have company tonight."

Faina wondered if their guests were members of the First International, which, according to Uncle Matvei, was an organization of communists and anarchists. At first Anastas pretended not to hear his mother, keeping his eyes trained on Faina as they had been. But his mother would not have it.

"Anastas!"

Gritting his teeth, he tossed his head over his shoulder and answered her. "Yeah, Ma! I heard you! I'm coming!"

Faina felt her own expression mimicking Anastas's permanent mask of disdain as her lips curled back in a scowl.

"Your mama and papa?"

For the first time, a measure of his flinty exterior softened into something resembling embarrassment, regret, and perhaps even a touch of apology. He rubbed the back of his neck and, chiseling his iron stare away from her, looked bashfully at his shabby shoes.

"Yeah. Those are my parents."

Faina knew she would not be able to form the sentence correctly, but she was determined to spit the words out all the same.

"Bolsheviks shot my parents on Christmas Eve. That why I in New York."

And sweeping her nose into the air, she pushed past him with proud, angry steps, leaving him to watch after her, a slightly injured expression on his face.

Chapter 10:

An Honorable Soldier

Pyro jiggled his foot up and down as he sat in the antechamber of Thayer's study, waiting to be seen. A comforting fragrance of tobacco and old books had stained itself into the leather of the armchair, and Pyro couldn't help but feel nostalgic.

He'd been eager to arrange this meeting ever since he'd learned Staccato expected him to sing. He may have struck a deal with Staccato, but in his own opinion, the famous miraculous hadn't been completely honest with him. More than anything, Pyro wanted to return to the Saighdeoir, and he was sure Thayer could get him out of it.

At length, the cherries on the Scorpion silk wallpaper turned from red to green, a sign that it was now okay to enter.

Pyro rose and swaggered through the open door, where he was greeted by Thayer's jade-colored miniature dragon, Seaweed, who wagged his spiny tail and wound himself around Pyro's legs. Pyro reached down and gave the overly enthusiastic dragon a pat. He was a Scorpion breed, a Dog-Eyed Doragon of the water variety. He had a long, lean body that curled almost like a flag when he moved, and long, flowing whiskers protruding from his nose and eyebrows.

Thayer was standing with his back turned wearing little more than the leather shoulder plates of his armor and his *hakama* pants. Thayer was known for incorporating pieces of armor into his attire, and he oftentimes looked as though he had walked out of his closet half dressed. Pyro waited patiently as his godfather aimed a throwing knife strategically at a dartboard where a newspaper clipping of Samael was pinned to the bullseye.

After several moments of elaborate test throws, Thayer gave a startling war cry and loosed the blade. It pinwheeled through the air with such speed there was hardly enough time to realize he'd thrown it. The knife reached its target and, judging by the holes in the Cobra's face, it had several times before.

"What do you think of that, Pyro my boy?" Thayer offered Pyro a blade.

"I think you need more of a challenge."

Thayer wagged his eyebrows and chuckled. "Oh-ho! You never hold back, do you?"

With one hand in his pocket, Pyro tossed the knife and planted his blade directly beside Thayer's.

"Wouldn't dream of it."

Thayer smiled and retrieved the weapons. "I see your aim is as good as ever."

"I ain't got nothing on Reverend Krüner, but let's just say I can hold my own in a game of Fives."

"A Saighdeoir soldier through and through."

Pyro chuckled and scratched behind his ear. "Yeah, that's exactly what I wanted to talk to you about."

Thayer gestured to an armchair before the fire and together they sat.

"What can I do for you, son?" He removed his pipe from the sash around his waist and set about packing the barrel with tobacco.

"It's about this—"

"Seaweed! Get your head out of the fireplace!" Thayer snapped his fingers at the dragon who had grabbed a hot coal from the hearth as a tasty treat and was now endeavoring to chew it, sprinkling the carpet with hot ash.

"Allow me." Pyro grabbed the dragon gently by the back of the collar and stuck his hand under his mouth. "Drop it!"

Seaweed reluctantly spat the still burning coal into Pyro's palm, who, of course, was not burned by the heat. He tossed the charcoal back into the fire while Seaweed skulked off to his bed.

"You were saying," prompted Thayer.

"It's about this circus business. When Staccato first approached me about the Cirque De Fay, he failed to mention I had to sing."

"When Staccato first approached you, you were twenty pounds underweight and being held prisoner in a water tank." Thayer lit the end of his pipe with a match, then waved the remaining flame out of existence.

"Yes, well—"

"Are you saying if Staccato had mentioned you were required to sing you would have elected to remain in Kilgoree where you certainly would have died a few months later?"

Pyro sighed somewhat irritably and pushed back his bangs. "No."

"Let me guess. You've come to ask me to release you from your obligation to Mr. Nimbus."

"I want to return to the Saighdeoir. Besides, what does it matter? It's really more of an obligation to you, not to Staccato, since you're the one who arranged the whole affair. And I can serve you far better carrying out rescue missions outside the Cauda than I can dangling from a hoop in a pair of sparkly trousers."

Thayer closed his mouth and shook his head. "I'm disappointed in you, Pyro. You made a deal with Staccato to preserve your life and regain your freedom, and the moment you set foot in Sagittarius you began looking for ways to go back on your word. Such dishonor is not becoming of one of my men."

"Blazes, Thayer, that's a little harsh."

"The truth can be harsh at times." He sucked on his pipe and looked away. "It's come to my attention that I've tolerated your behavior for far too long."

"My behavior? Look, Thayer, all I wanted was to see if I could return to rescue and recovery. It's not like I've ever compromised a deal before."

"That wasn't the sort of behavior I was referring to." He paused, stroking his beard before he went on. "When I allowed you to enter the Saighdeoir, I had hoped military life would provide you with the discipline you needed to live a life worthy of respect."

Pyro crossed his legs and stared dully at his godfather. "Oh, you were referring to my social life."

Thayer's nostrils flared as he set aside his pipe and leaned forward. "Is that what you call a life? Carousing with dancers? Getting into bar fights? Drinking yourself into oblivion? If you could step outside of yourself for two minutes, do you realize how incongruous your life would appear? By day you rescue women and children from violent and abusive circumstances, and by night you support the very institutions that encourage such debauchery."

Pyro resisted the urge to wince. Thayer had hit a sore spot, but he refused to appear weak.

"So I go out and party. It ain't illegal. You make it sound as though I'm dining with the Cobra every night!"

Thayer pressed his lips in a thin line and exhaled through his nose. "You don't know what I'm talking about?"

He got up from his chair and moved around to the desk. He ripped open a drawer and removed a folder.

"November twenty-third, 1911," he read from the file. "A year after joining the Saighdeoir, you were caught naked in a broom closet in Tarazed with a dancer named Myrtle Sparks. Do you remember Miss Sparks?"

"Yeah, she was an Aries lass."

"Do you know how she ended up in Tarazed?"

"No."

"She was taken prisoner when the C.O.N. invaded Ewe's Head and was sold as a servant to Colonel Rabdion. After running away from her master, she took up dancing as a way to earn money for a ticket out of Aquila."

Pyro threw up his shoulders. "What does that have to do with me? It's not like I paid her! We were just having fun!"

Thayer continued. "January twenty-fifth, 1913. You were forcibly expelled from a commemoration banquet for being intoxicated." Thayer's mustache bristled. "Yours wasn't the only name dragged through the papers following that scandal. Do you realize how much criticism I received for the way I handled my soldiers after your little stunt?"

Pyro ducked his chin slightly. "You never mentioned it."

Thayer sighed. "I told myself it was just a phase. That your behavior was simply a way for you to process your grief; that eventually you would heal." He slapped the folder on the desk and turned to another page. "I was gravely mistaken. November eleventh, 1915. Two days after a successful mission in Denebola you were found getting your ashes hauled by a one Josephine Wyrm, and two, Hazel Lovelace, who were after top-secret information about the resistance!"

"I didn't know they were liliths, and I didn't say nothing! Once I got wise, I hightailed it outta there!"

"There was nothing wise about what you did, son. And if it weren't for Lieutenant Hearthly I've no doubt you would've remained there until they had cursed you!" He ran his finger down the list. "April third, 1917. You rescued Stella Woodmore from the Maleficum prostitution ring in Aldibain. Three months later you were caught at a club in Tarazed with one of the waitresses. The club was called the Twelve Arrows. Do you know who owns the Twelve Arrows?"

"A stage actor, Percival Haulfrun."

"Do you know who Percival Haulfrun's father is?"

Pyro shrugged as he pulled a name from thin air. "Edward Haulfrun."

"Baron Von Tenebris."

The prideful scowl slipped from Pyro's face like a fallen leaf carried away by a strong wind.

"Baron Von Tenebris?"

"Maleficum's procurer. Where do you think Haulfrun gets those waitresses?"

Pyro lowered his head and blinked several times. The Maleficum was one of the most notorious trafficking syndicates in all Voiler, famous for their use of love potions to lure people into slavery and subsequently control them. Love potion manufacturing itself was a prolific racket in Voiler due to its overwhelming power. There was big money to be made in the brewing of illegal tinctures, and as a powerful substance that essentially coerced the imbiber into nonconsensual behavior, it was highly illegal. That isn't to say Stella Woodmore had been one of these victims, for a love potion would've had to have been tailored to Pyro, and it certainly wouldn't have been free. Still, the association was nothing short of shameful.

"She didn't say nothing about it," Pyro mumbled in a feeble voice.

Thayer took a page from the file with a stern face, and stood before Pyro. "These rules Staccato put in place for you weren't solely the inspiration of your parents. The truth is, arrangements were already being made for your suspension when you returned from Ras Al Akab."

"Suspension? You mean because of the incident at the restaurant? When I was arrested in front of—" He couldn't finish.

"No. It's what happened the night before. One week prior to your deployment to Al Safar."

"I don't remember anything."

Thayer sat on the arm of his chair. "I know you don't."

Pyro's heart throbbed anxiously. What had he done?

Thayer turned his attention to the report. "September fourteenth, 1917. You were reported missing from your barracks. A search went out. General Phlogiston discovered you at the Blood Bone."

Pyro's eyebrows screwed together as he tried to make sense of what Thayer was saying. "The Blood Bone? Wh—what? Me?"

Thayer gave a severe nod of his head. "One of the most prodigious houses of ill repute west of the border."

Pyro gaped. He shook his head. Then, he scoffed. "Thayer, that couldn't have been me! There's no way that could've been me!"

"There are at least a dozen eyewitnesses who can attest to the veracity of this claim."

Pyro felt his mood grow dark. His head sank forward as he swallowed.

"Then how come I don't remember?"

Thayer cast the file at his feet. "Because you were passed-out inebriated!"

Pyro fell on his knees and scrambled for the file. He had to see it for himself. The number of eyewitness reports was somewhere in the teens. He was half tempted to believe it was some sort of collusion, but his suspicions were quelled when he read the description of the brown, pear-shaped stain marring the front of his shirt, a blight which had mystified Pyro for he couldn't remember how he had obtained it. Furthermore, he recalled his fellow soldiers' cold attitudes towards him the week following, how he had been unable to account for it. Pyro cupped his hand over his mouth in an involuntary gesture.

"Do you realize how fortunate you were that no one in that house recognized you?" Thayer loomed authoritatively over him. "The C.O.N. would've had a field day! Picture the headlines of *The Morning Star*!"

Pyro leaned his elbow on the seat of the chair and covered his face with his hand.

"Thayer …" He paused, trying to keep a hold of himself. "What was I doing there?"

Thayer's features softened with rueful pity. He knelt down and placed a hand on Pyro's shoulder.

"Do you remember what event occurred the week prior to your going to the Blood Bone?"

"Obviously not."

"That was the week your mother had written to you about your father."

Pyro's eyes narrowed into a pained glower. A noise somewhere between a groan and a growl escaped his throat.

"You were hurting, Pyro." Thayer squeezed his muscle. "But you have got to find a better way of dealing with your grief. You'll destroy yourself if you don't."

Pyro was silent. After several moments passed, Thayer cleared his throat.

"You may return to the Saighdeoir once you've proven to me you can handle the responsibility. You've got to change, Pyro. Furthermore, I want you to work for Staccato for at least two years. Rest assured, he'll be keeping an eye on you." He patted Pyro's back. "Are you going to be alright, son?"

Pyro nodded his head weakly. Thayer lifted him up by the elbow and set him on his feet.

"Now, I want you to go back to your room and rest until dinner. Ms. Hill's got quite the feast planned in celebration of the recent pheasant kill."

When Pyro reentered the antechamber, he was forced to stop for a moment. With his hand leaning on the doorframe, he covered his eyes and let out an involuntary whimper. Tears of shame gushed down his cheeks. What else could he have done that he didn't know about?

Chapter 11:
First Day of School

"Pasha, am I starting school today?"

Pasha and Katya were strolling towards Henry Street, hand in hand, swinging their arms back and forth. Even though Pasha and Mama had explained everything to Katya before, she still seemed baffled about this school business.

"Not exactly." Pasha stopped them at the corner as they waited for a line of traffic to move past. "You're not old enough to go to school yet. But you need to learn English, and the school offers classes."

Despite being only three years old, Katya had begun speaking at an early age and, as

Pasha would describe her, "hadn't stopped since." For this reason, she was quite eloquent for her age, and was frequently mistaken for being older due to her social skills as often as she was for being younger due to her size.

Once the cars had passed, Katya and Pasha made their way across the avenue.

"Are you starting school today?"

"Yes." He pulled her thumb out of her mouth. "Mama told you not to do that. You will ruin your teeth."

Katya sighed and tried to occupy her hand with the little bows on the hem of her plaid dress. "Do you think you will like it?"

"Of course I will. I have always liked lessons."

But private lessons and school were two entirely different things, and Pasha could not help but feel a slight frisson of nerves at the idea of sitting in a classroom for the first time with other boys his age. Up until then, Pasha and Katya had led fairly solitary lives as the children of a country nobleman; it was one reason Pasha had pined so long for a younger sibling. They were each other's first and closest companions.

At last they came upon a white stone building garlanded with a crowd of children. The school was five stories high with an abundance of wide windows, and the roof was garnished with stately looking parapets. On one side of the structure was a flashy red door with "Boys" carved above the frame, while the other side had a door labeled "Girls."

"Do you think Mr. Dalka's children will be there, Pasha? I didn't see them leaving when we did."

Despite being neighbors, the Chevalskys had yet to receive a formal introduction to the three children living in the apartment across the courtyard. But Pasha had experienced an encounter with Faina their first night in the apartment, when she had seen him crying from her bedroom window. Taking pity on him, the girl had struck up a game of jumping out from behind her curtains in an attempt to make Pasha laugh. The compassionate gesture had so touched Pasha that he had been hoping to get better acquainted with her at school. But so far they'd seen no sign of the Dalka children.

"Maybe they attend a different school."

No sooner had Pasha said this than a clamoring cluster of three children came pounding up the sidewalk in an outright dash.

"This is all your fault, Faina," Leo was complaining.

"Put a sock in it, Leo!"

"If you would have just gotten up when I told you to instead of cowering beneath your blankets we'd all be on time! Thanks to you, Anya and I are gonna be late!"

Anya did not care to state her opinion; she was too busy trying to keep up with her bombastic cousins.

"Wait for me," she panted helplessly, but neither Leo nor Faina seemed to hear her.

Overhead, the first warning bell rang. Putting his arm around his little sister, Pasha decided it was best to ask the school mistress standing guard at the door if she could show Katya where she needed to be. The woman was stern as Pasha approached her, but he quickly won her over with his nice manners. Softening, she herded Katya into the building.

As Pasha was heading to the boys' entrance, Faina came ramming through the cluster of girls like a bowling ball amongst pins. Once she had made it to the door she dug her heels into the pavement and looked around anxiously. Spying her brother sprinting towards his side of the building, she cupped her hand over her mouth.

"Leo! Get Anya!"

Poor Anya had yet to even make it across the street, and appeared to be on the verge of tears. Leo threw up his hands and, cursing, sprinted towards the lagging little girl, stuffed her unceremoniously under his arm, and ran with her like a football back to the girls' entrance. Anya was limp and utterly bewildered. As they passed by in a blur, she looked up at Pasha pleadingly as though to say, "Help me, I have no control over my life."

The second warning bell began to toll. Tearing himself away from the hysterical spectacle, Pasha hurried inside the building and quickly sought out his class.

Inside, boys were sitting at wooden desks, some with their heads resting on their elbows, some fidgeting impatiently, and others leaning back to converse with their peers in the row behind. A few stopped to stare at Pasha as he made his way to a seat in the second row.

After enduring their scrutiny for a minute or two, Pasha felt a tap on his shoulder. He turned around to face a freckly, tow-headed waif with squinty eyes, a triangular head, and a foxlike attitude.

"Hey, ain't you the kid that called out ol' Borsuk on her baloney?"

Pasha could only assume "baloney" meant schemes, or nonsense, or trouble of some kind, so he nodded.

"Uh, yes. That was me."

The boy grinned, showing off his crooked teeth. "Swell!" He swiveled around in his seat and called out to his companions. "Hey, fellas, this is the kid!"

All at once the other boys scooted their desks forward and leaned in to get a load of the new student. The freckled boy stuck out his hand.

"I'm Yuri Mishkin."

Pasha smiled and shook his hand. "Pasha Chevalsky."

A few boys glanced at him curiously, as though there were something familiar about the name.

"Where are you from?"

Pasha felt his palms moistening with sweat. After seeing the way Mrs. Borsuk treated his mother, he wasn't so sure he wanted everyone to know about his upbringing.

"Russia."

Another boy, large and blocky, threw back his head and laughed. "We figured that! You still got the accent. Where in Russia?"

Pasha's eyes circled around the line of eager faces. "I … I am from …"

A towering boy in shabby clothes who had been sitting in the back by himself threw up his hands in exasperation.

"He's from Crimea! Geez! Don't you recognize the name? He told Mrs. Borsuk his mother was a former baroness! They owned the wine label!"

The blocky lad inclined his head slightly. "Mrs. Borsuk *thought* his mother was a baroness. There could be plenty of people with the name 'Chevalsky,' Anastas. An easy mistake."

"Why don't you ask him yourself then, Sergei?" Anastas slumped down in his seat with his arms crossed. "Go on, Chevalsky, is it true?"

"Well," Pasha could feel his cheeks coloring up, "yes."

Some of the boys like Sergei and Yuri leaned back in their chairs with their mouths open, while others, like Anastas, eyed him with disdain.

"You're kidding," exclaimed Yuri. "Wow, my old man loved that stuff!"

Anastas kicked his massive foot at the back of Yuri's chair.

"What are you making such a big deal for? He ain't so high and mighty now. How does it feel, Chevalsky? To be down in the slums like the rest of us?"

Sergei, who was every bit as large as Anastas, and certainly not intimidated by him, waved his hand.

"Pipe down, Sippenhaft." He turned to Pasha. "Don't pay any attention to him. Wanna know how he ended up here? His old man got kicked out of Germany. Then he went on over to Petersburg, met his ma, and got kicked outta there too."

"That's right," sniped Anastas. "My parents believed in something. That's what happens when you have to work for a living, you develop convictions."

***

Lunch was a gritty bull session where the boys crowded along benches in the schoolyard with things called peanut butter sandwiches and casually exchanged insults.

"Here," said Yuri, tearing off a piece of his own sandwich half and giving it to Pasha. "Try it."

Pasha did not take the portion immediately, but stared at it curiously.

"What is it?"

"The best thing about America," insisted Sergei with his mouth full. "They call it peanut butter. You won't find it anywhere else."

Pasha held it up to his nose. "What does it taste like?"

"Kinda sweet. Just try it, you'll like it!"

Pasha thanked Yuri and tentatively took a bite. It was almost buttery, thick, and, as Yuri had described, kind of sweet. Pasha smiled and hummed with satisfaction. Yuri nodded his head enthusiastically.

"What'd I tell ya? It's good, ain't it?"

"It's amazing!"

"Like a real American soldier," said a boy called Daniel. "That's what they all eat in the trenches. Or at least that's what Abe Feldman's older brother says."

"Ah, Abe Feldman's brother is full of beans," snapped his older brother Mikhail.

"So's your old man!"

"We have the same old man, stupid!"

One thing Pasha noticed about American boys—or maybe it was just boys in general, he had no way of knowing after all—was that they were always fighting, then turning around and becoming friends again. In fact, they seemed to enjoy fighting with each other, as though it were a way of bonding. Pasha could no more understand this than he could understand German philosophy.

Across the yard the girls' door thrust open. A flood of white pinafores and stockings paraded onto the playground and congregated on the opposite side. Katya was skipping merrily alongside Faina, her mouth opening and closing continuously as she jabbered on and on.

"So," began Yuri, propping his feet up on the bench as if the playground were a saloon and the benches the brass railing, "anybody get a visit from the Kissing Cat Burglar lately?"

If any of the boys hadn't been paying attention before they certainly were now. They pushed aside their lunch boxes and massed together in a tight little knot.

"Stan did," exclaimed Sergei, pushing forward a lean but handsome boy with a cleft chin. "Go on, Stan, tell us about it!"

"It was a couple of weeks ago," confessed Stan with a wicked grin. "Came in through my bedroom window and took a pair of leather gloves."

"How long did she kiss you?"

Stan rubbed at his chin in a boastful manner which told Pasha he was lying.

"Oh, about a minute."

Yuri threw down his cap. "A whole minute! Are you kidding me? Mine only lasted a second!"

Pasha shook his head. "Who are you guys talking about?"

Yuri slapped the bench. "That's right. You wouldn't know. The Kissing Cat Burglar is a girl who sneaks into boys' apartments, takes a few goods, and kisses 'em to keep 'em from squealing."

Pasha's eyebrows rose to his hairline. "She kisses you? On the lips?"

"On the lips."

"Who is she? What does she look like?"

Anastas stopped eating his sandwich to glare at Pasha. "No one's gonna tell you that, stupid! That's the whole point! If someone squeals they ain't very likely to get a second visit now, are they?"

"Is that what she told you?"

Anastas's face turned scarlet with a mixture of indignation and humiliation.

"No …" Obviously, Anastas had yet to fall prey to the Kissing Cat Burglar.

"But," interjected Yuri, "she has pretty hair. And she's nice."

"Crazy," added Sergei, "but nice."

"And she goes to this school."

At once, every boy who had been a victim of the Kissing Cat Burglar, and there were quite a few, turned his head towards the crowd of little girls across the yard, eyes falling in Faina's direction. When the other girls realized the boys were staring at Faina they immediately began to whisper and slip her nasty looks. Pasha watched as Faina tried to hold her chin high, but her gaze trickled to the ground like water.

The bell rang, and as everyone filed inside, Pasha saw one of the older girls shove Faina backwards as she rose from the bench. Faina stumbled and fell back on her bottom. Her book fell into a mud puddle. The other students were too preoccupied with getting back inside to notice what had happened, and Faina was left to cry by herself.

Pasha rushed over to the place where she was sitting and plucked her book from the dirt.

"Are you alright?" he asked her in English.

Faina stared back at him, bewildered. She appeared too stunned, or perhaps embarrassed, to answer. Pasha wiped the dirt from the cover and helped her to her feet.

"I'm sorry that girl pushed you. That wasn't a very nice thing to do." Taking note of her tears, he reached into his pocket and produced a handkerchief. "Here. You can take mine."

"Thank you." Her voice was timid and barely audible.

"Where are you from?" He had forgotten he had heard her speaking Russian.

Faina gaped at him stupidly, still struggling to get past her hurt feelings.

"Are you Georgian?" He was guessing by her appearance.

She shook her head no and sniffed.

"Russian?"

"*Da.*"

"Mr. Chevalsky!" his teacher, Mr. Schultz, called from the door.

Pasha turned back to her and smiled. "Don't let that girl get to you. Some people are just mean. But you're not. You're really nice." He turned and rushed back towards the door where Mr. Schultz was standing, leaving Faina to stare after him with wide, fascinated eyes.

Chapter 12:

Unlikely Friends

When Faina returned home from her first day of English class, Uncle Matvei was waiting with the usual deliveries. A case of Annheuser-Busch to the Schlabachs, a couple of Pabsts to the Conciennes, and a bottle of vodka to Mrs. Zagorsky. With the enlistment of a little wagon Uncle Matvei had bought especially for Faina and Anya, Faina made her way up Delancey with her beret and fluffy coat.

She was still thinking about her encounter with the Chevalsky boy at recess. To say he had impressed her when he had called out Mrs. Borsuk in front of the entire neighborhood would be an understatement, and then to have received such kindness from him at school! She reached into her pocket and pulled out the handkerchief again to admire it. Faina may have kissed half the boys her age at school, but she'd never felt romantically inclined towards any of them. But this boy? He was like a real-life Nicholas Nickleby, her favorite storybook character, heroic and kind.

The sidewalk on Eldridge was congested with rubberneckers trying to assess the damage of a motorcar accident, so Faina decided to take Allen. When she had made her way down the second block, the wheel of her wagon hit a bump and wedged into a crack in the sidewalk.

Sighing, Faina turned and gave the handle a tug. It wouldn't budge. She looped around to the back and lifted her vehicle from the tight little crevice. It was then that she heard a muffled crying noise coming from the airshaft behind her. She turned around, and peered down the long, narrow passage of puddles and rotten garbage. It was a boy's sobs. Scooping up the bottle of vodka from her wagon, she stuffed it beneath her coat in case anyone should get any ideas, and ventured into the duct.

The building was decidedly run down; in fact, it had hardly been touched for over a decade. There weren't enough windows, and the ones that were there were undersized and often broken. She could hear the sobbing clearly now, but no matter where she looked she could not find the boy. She finally spied him cowering behind a cluster of metal trashcans, hunched over in his thin, floppy coat. It was Anastas. Part of her was tempted to turn away, and yet when she looked at the pitiful scene before her, she couldn't help but feel a little sorry. It was hard not to feel sorry for Anastas really, once you got a good look at him.

Dropping the handle of her wagon, Faina inched silently forward. As she was laying a hand on Anastas's shoulder, he drew back, revealing the deep bruise marring the right side of his face. The blood staining his flesh intensified his already harsh expression, and gave Faina such a scare she jumped back in alarm.

"What do you want?" he demanded, wrenching away so she could not see the tears streaming down his face.

"*Tvoye litso …*"

He lowered his eyebrows even more. "I don't speak Russian."

Faina swallowed, trying to remember the words in English. "Your face …"

"Yeah, what about it?"

"You …" Her mind struggled through an imaginary list of English words, "Hurt?"

Anastas glanced back at her defensively, then softened a measure. Placing her hand on his cheek, Faina turned his head so he was looking at her and examined the blow.

"Your father do this?"

Anastas knit his eyebrows together. "You say that because he's an anarchist. You think because he supports anarchism he must be violent."

Faina rolled her eyes. "No. When boy hit like that, it always father, or … *otchim*," stepfather. "Or mama's lover."

Anastas's head fell slightly, and she thought he looked somewhat apologetic.

"It was my father."

"See!" Faina sucked her teeth as she drew her own handkerchief from her pocket and began wiping away the blood. "What you high and mighty for?"

Anastas's eyes darted towards her in a peculiar, confused manner. She supposed it was her English. She sighed.

"I not finished learning English. You understand me?"

Anastas nodded. "Yeah, I understand you just fine. You just gotta learn grammar, is all. Words like 'is' and 'are.'"

Faina nodded her head. So far articles had been a struggle for her, as there were no articles in Russian, but she would try to find their places so Anastas could understand her. He wiped his eye on his sleeve.

"My parents are not communists, by the way. They supported the revolution, not the Bolsheviks. Communism and anarchism are two different things."

Faina stopped and ran the words back through her head one by one. Anastas saw and understood at once.

"Communism and anarchism are different. You know the word anarchism?"

"I know now. My uncle explain."

There was a moment or two of silence between them, then Anastas spoke.

"Do you hate me because I am an anarchist?"

Faina paused for a moment to think about it.

"No. I have hate for nobody. You hate me because I am white emigre?"

Anastas stared at her for a moment, then said very quietly, "My parents would say I should."

Faina put her hands on her hips. "You wish me death?"

"No!" he insisted somewhat defensively.

"Well, that what it means to hate: wishing people dead, or not caring if harm come to them. Hate not the same thing as disliking or disagreeing."

"I don't hate you."

Faina reached up over his head and broke off an icicle from the ladder leading to the fire escape.

"But you say you …" she hesitated, not sure whether to use an "are" or an "is."

"Are," said Anastas, trying to help her along.

"You say you are anarchist. Anarchists kill people who disagree with them. They must hate the people they want killed, which mean you must hate me." She pressed the icicle against his swollen cheek.

"Anarchists don't kill people! And not all of them believe in violence, you know. Most of them don't."

Faina knelt down beside him and lowered her voice. "But your mama and papa believe this … that what I hear. My uncle say they support Galliani man. Man who write awful newspaper, *The Subversive Chronicle*."

"I am not my parents."

Faina smiled. "Well, that good."

"I'm sorry your parents died. I may be an atheist, but I believe people should have the right to practice whatever religion they want, or celebrate whatever holiday they want. That is part of the anarchist philosophy: individual liberty."

Faina's eyes grew like two large mirrors as she stared back at him in confusion. Anastas pressed his lips together impatiently and repeated himself more slowly, trying to use smaller words, and slipping in the few Russian words he did know.

"It isn't like communism at all. I understand why you're afraid of communism. I would be too if communists killed my parents."

Faina nodded in somber agreement. "Nobody should be persecuted for how they worship. I mean, unless maybe they offering human sacrifices … that probably no good."

This made Anastas laugh. He scratched his chin, as though wanting to ask a question he was afraid to ask.

"But what about Jews? Don't white emigres hate Jews?"

Faina screwed up her mouth. "I do not! And my family do not! And if I did," she gestured to the city around them, "I am in wrong place."

Now Anastas was really laughing, and Faina couldn't help but giggle a little. Their joy was cut short by a tumbling noise from inside the apartment. Faina leapt to her feet as the door swung open and Anastas's severe-looking mother appeared over the threshold.

"I know you," she sneered, pointing her thin finger at Faina. "You are Dalka's girl! The little tart! Anastas, what are you doing talking to this little pig?"

Faina backed away, scuttling for the handle of her wagon. Anastas got to his feet and stepped in front of his mother.

"Ma, it's alright, please don't—"

But Mrs. Sippenhaft had already fetched her broom and was storming past her son, ready to shoo Faina away like a rat in the garbage.

"Go on, get out of here you little slut!"

But Faina didn't need to be told twice; she was already sprinting out of the alley, her wagon flying behind her.

Chapter 13:
The Jar of Elijah

When it came to Pyro's aerial ballet training, he hadn't the slightest idea of where to set his expectations and neither had Sonata. Artistic pursuits did not come naturally to him, though he was a fair dancer when it came to the Foxtrot, and Ariesian Heel Shuffling, a form of step dancing. Furthermore, he was an excellent gymnast and skilled acrobat. But this was different. He could climb the silks, follow instructions, and had the physical strength to perform lifts and maneuvers others could not, and yet Sonata wanted more from him, something he could not seem to grasp.

"Again," she demanded as they began the routine for the fifth time that morning.

Pyro arched his back and drew a deep breath. The gymnasium smelled strongly of worn leather, maplewood floors, and chalk dust. The mat bounced beneath his feet as he made his way back to the starting position. Nearby, Melodious pounded out the notes on the piano keys once more.

It was a darker piece, in which Pyro was supposed to play an ophidian, and Sonata a *saignant,* someone who allowed ophidians and Primals to drink their blood for compensation, usually while unclothed. Under normal circumstances they would never have performed such macabre and sensitive subject material, but the show was designed to appeal to Primals, and they had to gain their trust. The routine required Pyro to get very close to Sonata, making it difficult to mask his attractions. After noticing Pyro's discomfort, Skelter had asked him —in his usual fashion of signing and gesturing— why he didn't just pursue Sonata if he was so attracted to her.

"You kidding? Staccato would kill me if I so much as winked at her!"

The answer had done little to satisfy Skelter, who was convinced Staccato was far too desperate to fire him.

"It's more than that," Pyro had explained. "Sonny is practically family. We grew up together. It would be wrong to lead her on. I don't want her getting hurt."

When Skelter reminded Pyro that he didn't have to have that kind of relationship with Sonata, Pyro had turned to him with a serious expression.

"Skelter, let me teach you something. Some people are meant to fall in love and get married, and some people are just meant to be left. I'm one of the ones who gets left. When you're like me you have to live in the moment. You have to seize every opportunity that comes your way because that's all you get. Happiness doesn't last for people like me. If I tried to carry out a serious, committed relationship, I'd be going against the natural order of things, and it would only end in tears."

Skelter had looked him over with a wry, questioning smile as if to say, "So, in that case, you *do* want a committed relationship with Sonata." When Pyro merely glared at him, Skelter went so far as to suggest that Pyro wasn't pursuing her because he was afraid he *would* fall in love with her.

"It's purely physical! It will pass!" he had insisted. "Besides, she's bossy, fussy, and my complete opposite in every way!"

Now, Sonata stood poised with her arms drawn close to her body, clinging to the collar of an imaginary robe. Pyro circled blandly around her. He paused on her right side. Sonata glanced up, a smirk tucked away in her dimples. She cast her eyes down and extended her arm slowly to him. Pyro took her hand and hastily dipped his head along the curve of her arm.

"Stop right there."

Pyro dropped his arms by his sides. "What?"

"This is exactly what I was referring to last week." She turned and faced him. "You're not dancing, you're going through the motions."

"I thought that's what dancing was."

Skelter, who had been practicing on his tightrope, six feet above the ground, stopped and made a fist, pulling it towards him in a desperate gesture.

"Yes," Sonata agreed. "You have to *feel* the dance!"

"You keep saying that, but I don't know what that means!" They might as well have asked him to tell them what color two o'clock was.

"Put yourself in the shoes of the ophidian," suggested Melodious. "What do you think he is feeling when the *saignant* extends her arm to him?"

"Uh … hungry?"

"Not just hungry." Sonata squeezed her arms in towards her heart. "*Ravenous*." She drew the word out with impassioned inflection. "Filled with desire and temptation!"

Skelter popped his collar up and drew his arm across his face.

"Yes! That's a very good idea, Skelter! Pretend you're Dracula!"

Pyro shook his head. "And what exactly is that supposed to look like?"

She turned to Skelter. "Would you like to show him?"

Skelter sauntered over to the mat with his own awkward grace and a smug grin. He drew a long, slow circle around Sonata, absorbing her with his eyes. He came to a halt at her right side. Again, Sonata extended her arm. Skelter took her hand with all the drama of a seasoned tango dancer and tenderly drew his face across the length of her arm, as though inhaling the scent of her skin. They dropped the act as if on cue and snapped their attention to Pyro.

"Like that," said Sonata.

Pyro stared back at them with an expression that was equal parts squeamish discomfort and embarrassment, sprinkled with a touch of jealousy.

"Shall I give you two some privacy?"

Skelter and Sonata threw back their heads and laughed.

"You really want me drooling over you like some deranged wolf?"

Sonata grabbed him by the hands and pulled him close. "Pyro, it's just acting!"

"I've gotten punched for less!"

"Well, I'm not going to punch you! If it makes you feel any better you have my full permission to act as ridiculously enamored with me as possible, so long as it improves our performance." She held out her arm. "Now, try it again."

Inwardly, Pyro groaned. Melodious started up the music again. Gently, he took her hand in his. He stared down at the soft flesh of her arm and swallowed.

"Don't be embarrassed," she said without looking back at him. "You're a human being. Human beings feel things. In mermaid culture we embrace the human ability to feel, and we honor the feelings of others. Whatever you're feeling, I'm not going to judge you for it. It is a privilege to share in your emotion."

Pyro looked up at her with an innocent expression. The light shone directly on the full upper portion of her cheeks and lips, sending a sort of electric shockwave through Pyro's lower abdomen and up his chest. Sighing, he bent his head and carefully slid his face from the middle of her bicep, past the soft crook of her elbow, and hovered over the tender underside of her wrist. He drew a deep breath, letting the air unravel to the depths of his lungs, then gently exhaled through his mouth, looking as though he might sink his teeth into her arm at any second. The hair on the back of his neck stood.

"Yes! Much, much better! Keep going!"

Pyro sank to one knee. Sonata placed her hands on his shoulders and stepped up on his thigh, extending her other leg back. Pyro grabbed her by the waist. Slowly, he raised her over his head, their bodies working together to transfer her into a handstand position on Pyro's shoulders. It was a delicate process. Though it might have looked as though Pyro were doing all the work, it took Sonata a tremendous amount of strength to balance in a way that would distribute her weight evenly, making it easier for Pyro to lift her.

As their faces turned towards each other, they locked eyes as though their shared gaze were a muscle contributing to the balance. When the time was right, Pyro flipped her over his back and allowed her to roll down his spine like a slide. He extended his leg back, entangling his calf in the silk in a movement known as crocheting, as Sonata lowered herself to her knees and arched her chest up in a backbend.

The gymnasium door swung open with a cool blast of air. Staccato entered staring down at a notepad, flecks of ice trailing at his heels in blustery wisps like some sort of fabric train.

"Alright, everyone, gather around. I have an important announcement." He flicked his eyes up from the paper and stiffened.

Pyro and Sonata were frozen in position, with Pyro hanging from his legs and bracketing Sonata's arched form on the mat. Sonata dropped her spine to the floor.

"We're practicing."

Staccato traced their figures with a cutting gaze. "Practicing what, exactly?"

"Our routine, of course!"

Pyro tried to walk himself backwards with his hands but was in such haste that he slipped and fell directly on top of her. Staccato was affronted.

"Is that so? I was under the impression aerial dance involved spinning through the air, not rolling on the ground." He snapped a page over the spiral edge of his notepad.

Sonata rolled off the floor and dusted herself off. "Oh, Staccato!" She flounced towards him with an almost childish charm, and pulled affectionately on his arm. "It's an expressive art form, you needn't be so defensive."

Staccato put his arm around her and hugged her to his side. "Needn't be defensive?" He scoffed. "I've every reason to be on my guard when you come batting your eyes at me trying to charm your way out of trouble. Now listen up, everyone."

Pyro twisted in the silks, trying to free his foot so he could get closer.

"We've just been given our new assignment." Staccato lowered the notepad. "Thayer's managed to procure us an engagement in Virgo with General Sobek's regiment."

There was a loud thud as Skelter fell from the high wire, landing on his backside on the mat.

"Virgo?" Pyro shook his foot free and stumbled off the pallet. "Alright, but what exactly are we doing? Stealing top-secret information? Rescuing hostages?" He gasped with an excited squeak. "Are we gonna assassinate General Sobek?"

Skelter scrambled to his knees, eagerly nodding his head. Staccato slid his finger under the page with a dry expression and turned the paper over.

"Actually, thanks to Skelter, the general won't be there. Our dealings are with the lieutenant colonel."

Skelter sagged like a wilting sunflower and snapped his fingers. The anticipation was threatening to tear Pyro apart. He bounced up on his toes.

"But what is it we're doing?"

"Have any of you heard of the Jar of Elijah?"

"Of course," exclaimed Sonata and Melodious in unison.

"I think I have." Pyro scratched his face and glanced back at Skelter. There was a withdrawn expression to his eyes, as though his spirit had receded deeper into his body. He gave no indication of a yes or no. Pyro cleared his throat. "Remind us just in case."

"The Jar of Elijah is an enchanted relic located in Virgo, a vessel from which life and abundance never stops flowing. It is what keeps the kingdom of Virgo so fertile and always blossoming. Without it Virgo ceases to be Virgo."

Pyro nodded, his memory catching up with him. "That's that relic the C.O.N. stole that finished off Hydra, isn't it?"

"That's the one."

Hydra, one of the seven mermaid kingdoms, had surprised everyone when it became the only country to have been completely annihilated following the Land Lock. Prior to the Land Lock, Hydra had been an elite military power, made famous by their penchant for chopping off the heads of their enemies. At the start of the onslaught, Hydra had been able to push back their assailants, delaying evacuation. Humiliated by such a defeat, General Sobek later returned to exact revenge, raising the salinity of the sea of Hydra to dangerous levels, wiping out not only the ocean-bound Hydrans, but a large portion of wildlife as well.

"Although I still don't see how a jar that makes plants grow could cause Hydra to become oversalinated," said Pyro.

"Simple." Sonata turned her attention to Pyro. "When the trees cease to grow and the flowers won't blossom there are droughts, and droughts can easily cause oversalination."

"That isn't to say the C.O.N. didn't speed up the process." Staccato folded his arms over his chest and sighed.

Skelter flung out his fingers like a firework, then curled them into a fist and ground it against his palm.

"General Sobek used explosives to trigger landslides from the surrounding karsts, which contain heavy concentrations of feldspar. The C.O.N. then proceeded to dam up the flow from the Eridanus, cutting off any potential source of fresh water."

Pyro nodded. "So … what does that have to do with us?"

"The Jar was displaced from its mount a year ago, causing a severe shortage of produce and grains." Which was nothing to bat an eye at, considering Virgo accounted for the majority of Voiler's fruit and vegetable market, as well as bread. "Hydra has been completely wiped out and Virgo brought to its knees, and yet the troops have yet to leave. Our job is to find out what's keeping the C.O.N. in Spica, and how to restore the Jar."

"When is all this to take place?" asked Sonata.

"A month from now."

"A month?" Sonata gawked at Skelter, and then at Pyro. "Pyro and Skelter have been practicing their routines for only a few weeks! You can't expect them to perform so soon!"

Staccato closed up his notebook. "We may have to lower our expectations somewhat if they're to make it through the show safely. You said you've been working on a routine. How far along are you?"

"Pretty far." She looked back at Pyro as though searching for some sort of confirmation. "As a matter of fact, we already have an original score."

"Do you now?" Staccato gestured to the piano. "Let's hear it!"

Pyro and Sonata joined Melodious at the piano, while Skelter took out his violin. Sonata started them off.

"I burn with longing fire
I sigh away at night
I'm poisoned with desire
A longing I can't fight ..."

Pyro swallowed as his turn came. The constriction in his chest seemed to be squeezing the blood into his face, so that his complexion had taken on a nice shade of scarlet.

"Your blood is singing beneath your flesh
A melody so sweet
Your skin's a veil, soft and fresh
housing primitive beats ..."

They sang together.

"Raise a glass
and drink from me
My lover, drink me in
Time is moving far too fast
I'll be your deadly sin—"

Staccato threw up his hand with an incoherent jumble of words that Pyro took to mean "Stop." He reached his fingers towards the space between his eyebrows.

"Which one of you wrote this?"

Skelter, Pyro, and Sonata pointed a finger at Melodious like children who'd been caught misbehaving. Staccato gaped at the culprit with the shock that often accompanies an older generation.

"Reverend!"

Melodious stammered defensively. "What? It fit the subject matter!"

"And what exactly is the subject matter?" He turned to Sonata. "Just what is this show about, young lady?"

Sonata did not balk or tremble, but stood her ground with Staccato, complete confidence in her position. "An ophidian and his *saignant.*"

Staccato's eyes bulged, the strength in his voice guttered like a faulty lightbulb. "An oph—an ophidian and his—" He shook his head. "What on earth would compel you to choose such a vulgar subject?!"

"Well, you can't expect us to frolic across the stage acting out the dances of Midsummer! Consider our audience. We're performing for the C.O.N.! You have to appeal to their tastes!"

"Oh, well, in that case, I suppose we can choose a volunteer from the audience for Melodious to throw his knives at! And Pyro can light Skelter on fire as he crosses the tightrope! Stars! Why don't we just wheel ourselves out on a silver platter!"

"Staccato, you're not thinking about this in practical terms! As undercover mercenaries, our job is to win the C.O.N.'s trust. Make them believe we are on their side. Several of us have already given them reason to doubt our loyalty: Pyro is a former Saighdeoir member, you've served under two of their greatest enemies, Skelter tried to assassinate General Sobek, Melodious was personally victimized by the C.O.N., and I stole Sea-Splitter." Her eyes bore into him with a pleading intensity. "It's going to take everything we've got to pull this off. We can't take any chances. Besides, it's very tasteful! I am a princess after all!"

Pyro stared at Sonata in silent amazement, stunned by her strategic and self-assured mind. She may have had the charm and sweetness of a princess, but she roared with the authority and tenacity of a seasoned general, or more accurately, a queen.

Staccato passed a hand over his eyes and groaned. He stood for some time, tapping his finger against his chin and glaring irritably at the floorboards.

"You have a point … Alright, fine! But keep in mind, all routines have to pass my approval first."

"I haven't forgotten, but I would appreciate it if you kept an open mind."

"Fair enough." He paused and smirked at his goddaughter. "My dear, if the monarchy ever falls, I'd say you have a promising career in law."

Pyro scoffed. "Or the military."

Staccato stepped back and surveyed them with a lifted chin. "Carry on then." He made his way towards the exit. "You can expect a review from me in a week's time." The door slid shut behind him.

Melodious hung his head over the piano, his shoulders drawn inward. Pyro rested his chin on the back of the instrument.

"What's wrong, preacher man?"

"Nothing." He twiddled with the keys. "It's just … I rather liked my lyrics!"

Chapter 14:

The Thief

That night, the rain lay overtop the clamor of the city like a static sheet, tuning it until it had transformed into a lullaby, and Pasha was able to fall asleep relatively easily. But he did not stay asleep. Somewhere in the middle of the night when the rain had begun to slow, he became aware of footsteps outside on the fire escape. He opened an eye. The first thing his gaze fell upon was Faina's window across the way. It was dark and the curtains were drawn. He shut his eyes once more. He was just beginning to drift off when the window flew open, spraying his cheeks with a sprinkle of cold raindrops. Someone tumbled over his mattress, falling onto the floor. Pasha shot up and found himself face to face with Faina, who slammed her hand over his mouth.

"Shhh! Pretend you are asleep!"

Pasha tried to ask why but his voice was muffled by her palm.

"Just do it! Or else they will find me!"

Releasing him, she quickly shut the window and scuttled beneath the bed.

"Who?" Pasha insisted. A harried rhythm of running footsteps echoed down the fire escape. A sharp white beam of light scanned across the opposite wall. Closing his eyes, Pasha threw himself down on the bed and pulled the covers up to his chin, feigning sleep. Outside the window, two older boys were arguing in hushed tones.

"I saw her go down the fire escape, I know I did!"

"Well, what are we gonna do? We can't just break into someone else's apartment!"

Though his eyes were closed Pasha could not help but wince as he felt the bright light shining into his room.

"Nah, you're right," conceded the first one. "Come on, we better cut our losses."

Their boots squeaked on the metal as they turned away, and Pasha listened as their footsteps died into the night. When he was sure they had left, he leaned upside down over the bed.

"They're gone, you can come out now."

Faina's cheeks swelled with an impish smile. "Perfect."

There was something about the way her eyes pinched when she smiled that Pasha liked. It was a grin that promised mischief, and mirth, and adventure, and Pasha knew immediately that he was going to like Faina.

He rolled off the bed and helped Faina to her feet. Once she was put right, Faina flipped her damp hair over one shoulder and pivoted saliently towards Pasha. Her lively eyes bore into him with a vivacious spark he'd only ever seen in grown women.

"Okay, here is how this works." She placed her hands on Pasha's shoulders and pushed him back against the dresser. "You promise not to tell anyone, and I will kiss you."

Before Pasha could even think of what to say, she was leaning towards him with her lips puckered.

"You don't have to kiss me," he suddenly sputtered.

Faina's eyes snapped open. She drew back at once, looking somewhat offended. Pasha felt his face turn an even deeper shade of red.

"I mean, I don't want you to feel like you *have* to kiss me. I won't tell on you either way. I like you, and I don't want to get you in trouble."

Faina's face softened by degrees until there was a slight smile to her lips.

"You aren't like other boys around here, are you?" She smoothed her hair over one shoulder. "I like you!"

Next thing Pasha knew she was nearly choking him in a vice-like hug.

"I am Faina Adrianovna Spichkin!"

"I know," he wheezed, as she finally let him go. "I am Pavlo Ruslanovitch Chevalsky. But you can call me Pasha."

Faina nodded her head knowingly. "Your name is just like the wine! When my brother heard that Mrs. Borsuk thought your mother was related to the Baron Chevalsky he couldn't stop laughing!"

"He was her husband."

Faina froze. "What? You mean your mother really is a baroness? Your family is the famous wine-making family from Crimea?"

"That's us."

"Wow!" Faina jumped up and down. "Wait until I tell Uncle Matvei!" And as suddenly as she had wound herself up, she stopped, took a deep breath and placed her hands on her hips. She looked him over curiously. "So, you're the future baron of Balalchik."

"Was," he scoffed. "And you're the Kissing Cat Burglar."

Faina batted her eyes as she ran her hand along the top of the dresser. "You have heard of me?"

"You're all the boys could talk about during recess."

"Really?" She seemed genuinely surprised. "I didn't think I was that big of a deal. I mean, I don't do it very often."

"Stan Ivashin says last month you kissed him for a whole minute."

Faina swerved in a perfect arc, her hands making fists, and her mouth dropped open. "I did not! I have never kissed Stan Ivashin!"

Pasha was surprised. Of all the boys in his class, Stan Ivashin was one of the most handsome, as well as the most popular. If Faina was going to kiss anybody, Pasha would've assumed Stan would be the first candidate.

"He seems to think you did," Pasha laughed.

This made Faina laugh too. "In his dreams maybe! Stan must keep his brain where his mother keeps her pickled beets!"

Like most children, Pasha knew things didn't always have to make sense to be funny. Faina's comment was so outrageous Pasha actually snorted, which made Faina giggle even harder. Soon they were laughing so hard they were afraid they'd wake Pasha's mother.

A fist knocked on the window, causing them both to jump. They turned around. Leo had his face pasted against the glass, and was pointing his finger at Faina and mouthing several different threats. Pasha hastened to open the window, and Leo came rolling into the room.

"I knew I'd find you here! I knew it!" he hissed with his finger pointed at the end of Faina's nose. "Just what do you think you're doing? I told you I don't need you to help me do my job!"

Faina shoved her hands high on her hips and leaned forward. "If that is true then why do you keep taking what I give you?"

"To dispose of the evidence so you won't do any more damage to your reputation! You're welcome, by the way!" In one swift move he had thrown her over his shoulder like a sack of flour. "Furthermore, we do not steal from neighbors!"

Pasha cleared his throat. "She wasn't stealing this time, she was just hiding."

Leo lowered his eyelids and raised an eyebrow as he swiveled around to face Pasha.

"Let me guess, she's already kissed you?"

"She offered, but I declined. I would never force a lady to kiss me in exchange for shelter from danger. That would be unthinkable."

Leo's mouth went slack with surprise. "Well, well! Such manners! This one might actually deserve a kiss from you, Faina."

Faina kicked her feet excitedly. "Leo, Pasha's mama really is the Chevalsky baroness!"

Leo stopped and took one step back, Faina still swinging from his shoulder.

"No kidding?"

Pasha folded his hands behind his back. "No kidding."

Leo held out his hand. "Hey, big fan."

Leo looked far too young to have ever had any of his family's wine, but that didn't mean much. Pasha took his hand and gave it a hearty shake.

"Again, sorry about the little sister. She's like a puppy. She finds a hole in the fence now and then and takes off." He crawled back over the windowsill. "But in the future I will try to make sure she doesn't bother you."

"Oh, she doesn't bother me," Pasha insisted. "I like her."

Leo threw back his head and laughed as if it was one of the finest jokes he'd ever heard. "You like her, do you? You don't think she talks too much?"

"I don't mind. I am more of a listener anyway."

"You don't think she's overly affectionate? A tagalong? Overbearing? Dramatic?"

"So are dogs."

Leo thought this very funny indeed. "You don't find her a bit crazy?"

"I think she is funny."

Leo stared back at him, dumbfounded, the boyish pout of his lip pushing out further than usual.

"Alright. In that case, come by anytime. Please, take her off my hands."

Pasha rose up on his toes. "You really mean it?"

Faina waved her hands as she hung upside down. "Of course! You should walk with us to school tomorrow!"

Leo rolled his eyes. "Does that mean you'll be ready on time tomorrow?"

"I will if it means Pasha will walk with us."

Pasha bounced on his mattress. "I would love to walk with you guys!"

Leo threw him a thumbs up. "Swell! We'll meet you in front of the building at seven thirty."

And with that, they bade Pasha good night and disappeared. Pasha snuggled back into his covers feeling at home in New York City for the first time.

Chapter 15:

An Enemy Escort

When Pyro was told they would be making half their journey in a bright yellow caravan, he thought Staccato had been joking. But things became all too real when he saw the thing out in the stables with Staccato one day.

"What in the blazes is that old thing?" It was hauled up in a shadowy corner of the barn, out of sight, but its garish yellow paint made it hard to miss. "Tongs and torches! Is that an authentic Fay caravan?"

Staccato did not look but nodded his head. "It certainly is."

Pyro approached in amazement. "Throw me down on a pyre, thing must be an antique!"

"It is, as a matter of fact. Circa 1692. Now had it been from the nomadic period, that would've been truly remarkable! But how many of those do you think are left lying around?"

"It's yours then?"

Staccato sighed and joined him in staring up at the gaudy façade. "Unfortunately. I inherited it. My ancestors had their own Cirque De Fay as well. It's been passed down through generations of Nimbuses, though no one has ever really used it after the original owners. It's in good condition though, and gets us about without any trouble. Not to mention there's plenty of room for the aerial equipment."

Pyro gazed at him sideways. "Wait … you don't mean you actually use that thing for travel, do you?"

"Why else would I ask to see your pegasus?"

He was referring to Brash, Pyro's Miranian Blue, who remained at Feifior while Pyro was on active duty. He was a lovely, heavily muscled specimen of solid black with flecks of indigo and orange running through his mane like a flickering fire. He had been a gift from Thayer for Pyro's eighteenth birthday.

"I thought perhaps you were going to use him as part of the act."

"I plan to have him help pull the wagon. The more pegasi we have the better. Now that Harpagos has grown his wings we have quite the team."

Pyro circled the caravan, scanning it up and down. "But … there's really no other way to get there?"

"We can get as far as Libra if we take the train, but the rails surrounding Virgo were destroyed during the invasion. Furthermore, the

114

Land Lock has shut down the Subaquatic Rail, the fastest and most widely used transportation in Voiler."

"Can we even all fit in there?"

"Well, of course!" He gestured to the door. "Go in and see for yourself, just remove your galoshes first."

Pyro pulled off his boots and opened the Dutch door in back. Staccato pointed to a lock on the bottom of the door.

"If you pull this one it drops down into a ramp."

"Pretty nifty."

Staccato lit a lantern and shined it on the interior. The inside was not only as bright as the outside but was adorned in rich textures and detail, with ornamented trim, painted tableaus, and velvet curtains. It was much more spacious than Pyro had anticipated with no shortage of sleeping arrangements. There was one bunk bed with a trundle beneath the bottom, and a collapsible Murphy bed towards the back of the wagon. Staccato gestured to an enclosed berth on the far wall.

"That's where Sonata sleeps. And I sleep in the loft." He waved his hand towards a cutout in the ceiling. "It might not look it but it's overall quite comfortable, if you can get used to sleeping in close quarters."

"I'm used to barracks, so you won't be hearing any complaints from me."

And in a way, Pyro remained true to his word, for he never did complain about the space. It was the travel time that bothered him most. On the day they headed out in the caravan he managed to fall asleep on the bottom bunk after the first five hours, but had grown particularly antsy by the time he awoke.

He lifted his head from the pillow and looked around. Skelter was stretched out on the trundle beneath him, his nose buried in a book, while Melodious sat on the Murphy bed whittling away at a figurine he was making.

Pyro sat up and turned around. The doors of Sonata's cabinet were shut, and Cello was stretched out on the top bunk. For some reason, Sonata had insisted on taking him wherever they went. Pyro yawned and stretched his arms over his head. The caravan seemed to be dragging along at an almost sloth-like pace.

"We almost there?"

Without lowering his book, Skelter stuck out his arm and turned his thumb down.

"Then why aren't we flying?" He moved the curtains of his window aside, but the landscape outside was dark beneath the trees.

"No-flying zone," answered Melodious.

"No-flying zone?" Pyro looked down at his watch. "Why not? We can't be that far outside of Spica!"

"It is still technically a war zone. Staccato says it is not safe."

Pyro jumped out of his bunk and pulled down the ladder to the loft. "Isn't safe from what? The C.O.N.'s expecting us with our tail tucked between our legs, aren't they?" He scrambled up the rungs.

Skelter snapped his fingers at Pyro.

"Where am I going?" Pyro scurried over the ledge of the loft and opened the hatch in the ceiling. "To speak to the driver, if you don't mind."

The cool coastal air skimmed Pyro's hair as he poked his head out over the roof. The smell was brinier than he anticipated, with a rotten, almost decaying odor. He rubbed his hands up and down his forearms.

"I thought Virgo was known for nice weather!" He rose out of the trapdoor and got to his feet. A spiny branch struck him in the face.

"Ugh!" Pyro shook his head, spitting what he assumed were red pine needles from his mouth.

"Careful, Pyro," called Staccato from the driver's seat. "Ingesting Sacaporio foliage has been known to lengthen and mold the coccyx into a heliacal pattern."

"Do you mean to say I'll grow a pig's tail?"

"I suppose you could put it like that."

Pyro gave a horrified squeak and, reaching down into the driver's seat, grabbed Staccato's coffee thermos. Staccato watched in horror as Pyro threw back a sip, gargled it, and spit it out over the side of the wagon. Pyro wiped his mouth on his sleeve and handed the thermos back to Staccato.

"Thanks, mate."

Staccato scowled at the half-empty thermos in his hand. "I was joking about the pig's tail."

"Really?"

"Yes, really."

Pyro slid down into the passenger seat headfirst, almost kicking Staccato in the face.

"In that case, you might wanna work on your delivery." He swiveled to an upright position just as the trees were peeling away over a waveless ocean wedged within a dried-up gorge. The scenery was wholly unfamiliar.

"Where are we?"

Staccato sighed. "This is Virgo, or what's left of it anyway."

Pyro stood up in his seat, shocked. It couldn't be. Where were the mossy cliffsides? The renowned fruit trees bowing beneath the weight of their harvest? The vineyards so fertile that the grapes hung like clusters of costume jewelry from vines so hearty and robust you could suspend bridges from them? Where was the rustle of the pale seagrass stitched against a vibrant, blue ocean? Not a single wildflower remained in the valley below.

"You weren't kidding about this whole Jar of Elijah business, were you?"

"I'm afraid not. And this isn't even the worst of it. We'll be coming up on Cereb soon, the capital of Hydra."

Pyro leaned back and kicked his feet up on the dash. "Well, we'd get there a lot faster if you'd just fly." He gestured to the team leading the wagon. "What's the point of having pegasi if you ain't gonna let them stretch their wings?"

Staccato pushed Pyro's legs off the ledge. "This is enemy territory now."

"And who's the enemy? A flock of seagulls? Who can touch us all the way up there? Besides, we're the C.O.N.'s personal guests, aren't we? Surely, they aren't gonna eat the entertainment!"

"These are radical Primals we're dealing with; they are, by definition, lawless. And if my sources are correct we happen to be nearing a settlement of Furies, a demographic considered to be the least in control of their passions. We can fly once we've passed Mount Partinia. Until then, we'll have to watch our backs."

Pyro slumped down in the seat, feeling more restless than ever. Weary of sitting quietly in the caravan, he resolved to stay with Staccato and force him into pleasant conversation.

"Don't you get bored sitting up here all by yourself?"

"No," was Staccato's short reply.

"You don't need someone to talk to?"

"No."

"Someone to keep you company?"

"No."

"Someone to keep you entertained?"

"Let me save you the effort of asking any more questions: I have no needs."

Pyro looked him in the eye with an expression of unimpressed disbelief. "You breathe, right? And eat? And dri—"

"Let me clarify!" By now Staccato looked very much like a disgruntled owl, bristling to such a degree that his beard appeared to stand on end. "I possess no needs that I cannot fill myself! I have no need for entertainment, I don't enjoy talking, and I have no need for company!"

Pyro snorted and removed his cigarette case. "Well, I do!"

"Last I checked there were three other people in the caravan."

"Yeah, and I've talked to them all." He held a finger to his cigarette.

"Put that out this instant!" Staccato snatched the cigarette, dashed it to the floor of the wagon, and ground out the flame with his shoe. "Have you gone mad?"

"What? What'd I do?"

"Does the term 'drought' mean nothing to you? We are driving through a forest of dead pine trees! You so much as sneeze the wrong way and we'll go up like a hydrophobic Christmas tree at a welder's convention!"

"Alright! Alright! Why didn't you say so?"

"Because I didn't think I would have to!"

As a conciliatory gesture, Pyro handed Staccato the cigarette case. Staccato seized it and stuffed it into his pocket.

As they approached the edge of the wood, the road dipped down into the valley at a steep angle. Pyro couldn't help but notice that the horizon seemed significantly darker out in the offing. He stood and narrowed his eyes for a better look.

"Didn't you say there was a drought?"

"Yes." Staccato's voice was a mixture of confusion and irritability.

Pyro pointed his finger towards the place where the sky met the sea. "Then what's that rain cloud doing over the water?"

Staccato looked to the spot where Pyro was pointing. His scowl softened to an expression of curiosity.

"You don't think that could be coming from Mount Partinia, do you?" proposed Pyro.

"No eruption warnings have been issued that I know of. These days experts can predict an eruption weeks in advance."

"But would we receive any warnings? Think about it. If Hydra and Virgo are essentially ghost towns, who's left to raise the alarm?"

An overwhelming gust of sulfurous wind squalled up the crest of the hill. The pegasi ground to an immediate halt. Spooked, Sonata's pegasus, Scheherazade, rose up on her hind legs and whinnied.

"Something's not right," muttered Pyro.

Staccato fooled with the reins. "Alright, steady now!" He reached below the seat and produced a spyglass. "I don't understand! Partinia hasn't erupted in centuries!"

He tossed the viewing apparatus to Pyro who caught it and looked out at the horizon. While Staccato tied up the pegasi, Pyro's eyes wandered through the dense, black shadows until he located a thinning trail of fog, darker than the rest.

"We're too far away for me to make out the volcano, but the shape of those clouds is identical to a fumarole."

He jumped down from the passenger seat and climbed upon a tall rock overlooking the valley. The vantage point made little difference.

"If we knew when all this started we could estimate how much time we had before an eruption." He helped Staccato onto the boulder, and handed him back the spyglass.

The side door of the caravan opened. Melodious appeared, ducking through the archway.

"Ah, just the man we need." Staccato turned and leaned on his staff. "We could use your superior senses right about now, Melodious. It seems our journey might be delayed by a volcanic eruption."

Melodious made his way towards the boulder, sniffing the air. "I've been smelling sulfur for ages now."

"Why didn't you say something?" Staccato reached out his hand to help Melodious, but Melodious nearly yanked him from his perch in the process.

"Didn't you say the C.O.N. had been using explosives to blast away fragments of rock into the ocean?"

"Yes, unfortunately."

Pyro and Staccato each grabbed a hold of Melodious's arm, ready to stop him if he took a step too far.

"Well," began Pyro, looking up at the giant with curiosity, "any impressions?"

Melodious released a long exhale and shut his eyes. "Give it a moment."

The handle turned again, and Skelter stuck his head out the door.

"*Oi*, Skelly!" Pyro beckoned him over. "Come over here, and have a look at this volcano!" He grabbed the spyglass from Staccato and tossed it to Skelter. Skelter's eyes darted suspiciously over their surroundings as he joined them on the boulder.

"Immense pressure." Melodious furrowed his brow. "I see water seeping through cracked earth …"

Staccato shuffled impatiently and shook his head. "I still say it had to have started smoking months ago."

Skelter lowered the spyglass and corrected Staccato with a shake of his head. No one asked Skelter how he knew this, and he did not offer an explanation. Melodious opened a curious eye.

"Did anyone else feel that?"

Pyro turned his head from side to side. "Feel what?"

A thunderous blast issued from across the water, causing a slight tremor beneath their feet. Pyro swore in amazement.

"For the last time," barked Staccato, "language, Mr. Anom—"

A deafening salvo rocked them from their feet with unexpected force, prompting Staccato to repeat Pyro's phrase. Pyro doubled over his knees with hysterical laughter, Melodious and Skelter joining in.

"Alright." Staccato sat up and rubbed at his lower back. "It wasn't that funny."

"Ah, lighten up, Staccato." Pyro wiped a laughter-induced tear with his sleeve. "Even the reverend laughed!"

Staccato said nothing, but lowered his head to hide his amused smile. Nearby, the pegasi continued to whinny and ramp. The door creaked open against the accelerating breeze, and Sonata stuck her head out.

"What's going on?"

Dried needles blustered past them, scratching their faces. Pyro's eyes gave a faint sting. The air was growing smokier and darker. Another blast resounded across the valley. Scheherazade squealed and wrenched her head away, pulling the reins free of their knot, and took off with tremendous speed. Sonata was thrown backwards into the wagon, the door banging behind her.

The pegasi careened down the hill with such speed the wagon flew up from the ground. The men dashed down the road, Pyro leading the way. Halfway down the slope, the pegasi lighted into the air.

Staccato let out a gasp from behind Pyro. "No, no, no, no!"

The wagon turned and ran parallel to the hillside.

"Relax!" said Pyro. "It will take a minute before they can gain altitude in these weather conditions. If we run up the incline, one of us may be able to jump and catch hold of the wheel."

"Yes, good plan. Come on then!"

They each scrambled up the hill as the caravan gradually rose higher and higher. Despite his size and strength, Melodious unfortunately did not possess the grace or lightness of step to make leaping off the hillside very easy. Skelter came the closest by far, but his fingers skimmed the wheel.

"Staccato!" Pyro held out his hand. "Throw me your staff!"

Staccato handed over the rod, no questions asked.

"Now, Mel, give me a boost!"

Melodious hoisted Pyro onto his shoulders while Skelter helped to guide him in a straight line beneath the wagon. Pyro balanced himself in a standing position. The wind was growing wilder and greedier, gathering debris into its arms and chucking it in their pathway. Pyro wound back his arm and aimed the staff like a javelin through a wedge in the wagon wheel.

They each held their breath as the rod tipped precariously forward, looking as though it might fall out, but it tipped in the other direction and settled. Pyro sprang from Melodious's shoulders and grabbed hold of the opposite ends of the stave. The caravan floated higher. Pyro curled his knees to his chest and slipped his leg between the spokes. Letting go of the staff, he dangled from the wheel like a ribbon caught in the billets. He reached under the wagon for the bar adjoining the back wheels.

"Pyro," hollered Staccato from somewhere below, "look out!"

Pyro turned just in time to dodge a huge block of volcanic debris. It collided with the wheel, tearing off a chunk of the wood. He reached for the bar again, this time grabbing hold. The others continued to shrink below him, and soon they were flying alongside the balding cliff face.

"If these pegasi had any sense, they wouldn't be flying in this debris!"

Pyro latched onto the underside of the carriage. The pegasi ripped left, away from the volcano and out over the water. There was a loud bang as the caravan collided with the rock wall, finishing off the right back wheel. Eager to get inside, Pyro reached for the bottom stair at the tail of the wagon and climbed over the ledge. He grabbed the lower handle of the Dutch door, swung it open, and somersaulted inside.

"Don't worry, Sonny!" The door slammed shut behind him. "I'm here to …" Pyro trailed off. Sonata was nowhere to be found. "Sonata?"

Terrified yowling echoed from within Sonata's enclosed berth, indicating that Cello was trapped inside. It was probably the safest place for him at the moment.

"Sonata?" He noticed the ladder dangling from the loft. Pyro shuffled forward until he was standing below the trapdoor. The hatch to the roof was flapping open in the breeze.

"You have got to be kidding me!"

He scurried up the rungs just in time to see Sonata lowering herself over the hem of the roof.

"What are you doing?" The wind ripped through their ears.

"Trying to stop the pegasi!"

"By climbing out on the roof while we're airborne?"

"How were you gonna do it?"

Pyro froze, and pondered her question. "Pretty much like that." He thrust out his arms. "Grab a hold of my hands so you don't slip."

Thrilled not to have someone trying to apprehend her, Sonata smiled and clutched his hands as tightly as possible. Below them the ground thundered, and the volcano released another strident bellow. The caravan was plunged in a filmy, black plume of debris, making it difficult to see.

In a brief moment of clarity, Pyro spotted an enormous man-sized chunk of ash spinning towards them.

"Look out!"

He wrapped his arms around Sonata, pressed her to his chest, and pulled them backwards through the open hatch. The massive rubble skimmed over the portal, tearing a lesion through the ceiling. Pyro and Sonata landed squarely in the center of Skelter's trundle bed.

"Well," Pyro coughed, the wind still knocked out of him, "that couldn't have worked out better."

The caravan flipped forward at a severe right angle, plummeting in a downward descent. Pyro and Sonata threw their arms around each other, screaming like mad. Drawers slid open, spilling their contents into the air. With a snap, the wagon leveled out at a normal angle. The three remaining wheels skipped along solid ground, jostling Pyro and Sonata several times, then dropped to one side as the axle dragged against stone. The pegasi slowed to a stop. Sonata kept her face buried in Pyro's shoulder. He could practically feel her heartbeat drumming against his.

"There," he breathed, placing a hand over his forehead. "We've stopped."

He laid there catching his breath, absentmindedly rubbing his hand up and down Sonata's back until she raised up and flashed him a look. His cheeks coloring, Pyro cleared his throat and stood up.

"I'll just, uh, I'll go check the …" He trailed off and backed out the door.

His foot touched a cobbled road. They had pulled off into a long, stone tunnel. Almost immediately Pyro was struck with an overpowering odor of brine that bordered on sulfuric. Outside the walls, a sloshing noise was competing against the wind. Pyro's chest sank.

"Oh, no."

He bit his lip and tiptoed towards the open mouth of the tunnel. The foaming blue sea was gnawing over the remains of the parapet below. They had landed in the ruins of the city square of Cereb, in a section that had once been under the surface. But the water levels had dropped drastically from the drought, and much of the underwater architecture now sat exposed to the clouds of volcanic ash.

Pyro stared down at the old courtyard. Waves sucked at the bottom stair, whilst all around them the air grew darker and denser. Behind him the caravan door swung open. Pyro threw out his hand.

"Stay where you are!"

Seeing the waves over Pyro's shoulders, Sonata edged back. Pyro was desperate for a solution. A clicking noise froze him in place.

"Freeze!" ordered an authoritative male voice.

Cold, salty brine rinsed over Pyro as he lifted his hands in surrender. He wiped the water from his eyes and looked up. Numerous figures draped in dark blue robes had materialized from the shadowy ruins, armed with an assortment of weapons. An ouroboros seal branded their allegiance on a variety of ornaments; some wore pins at the collar, others displayed their loyalty in the form of belt buckles, others tattoos.

"Well, if it isn't the famous Saighdeoir soldier," exclaimed the man standing at the front, whom Pyro took to be the leader. He lowered his rifle.

He wasn't necessarily a plain man, but common enough to inform Pyro he was not an ophidian. He was too coherent for a Fury, and besides, his skin was not gray nor his eyes red. Had he been a lividium, the male variant of lilith, he would most likely not have bothered to carry a firearm.

"We'd heard you'd been released from Kilgoree. But I would not have expected you to be back on the job so soon."

Pyro smirked sarcastically. "I ain't on the job."

"Why else would you be here? This is C.O.N. territory, and I'm afraid you've been caught trespassing."

"Would you believe me if I said I was invited?"

While several of the militia men laughed, their leader did not appear to have found this amusing. He aimed the gun at Pyro's chest.

"On your knees, Anomaly!"

But his lieutenant held out his hand. "Wait, Captain. Shouldn't we hear his explanation first? It may prove amusing!"

The others nodded in agreement, finding the whole affair rather droll. The captain sniffed, then lowered his weapon.

"Alright. State your business."

"I'm a member of Staccato Nimbus's Singing Circus. We were invited here to perform for General Sobek's regiment."

Even the captain was forced to throw back his head and laugh at this one. He leaned on his firearm and shook his head.

"And I heard you were clever."

"It's true, I swear! Look, we were traveling through Heze when the volcano spooked our pegasi, and they took off with our caravan. I was separated from the group."

The lieutenant pinched the space between his eyebrows and chuckled. "You expect us to believe that you, Pyro Anomaly, favorite of King Thayer, have joined up with the circus?"

"It's true." Sonata had emerged from the tunnel, a cloak now draped over her shoulders to protect her from any moisture that might come off the sea. Rather than expect to be bowed to by a band of ruffians, Sonata herself bowed to her foes.

"I am Princess Sonata Soter. If you really are militia men of the C.O.N. then you'll know that I am a member of Mr. Nimbus's party, and that your masters are expecting us at the Asparona Concert Hall any day now for a performance."

The soldiers looked questioningly at their leader, who rubbed his beard as though deciding how to respond to her.

"I can vouch for Mr. Anomaly." She placed her hand on his shoulder.

The captain nodded his head towards Pyro. "He has an act in your circus?"

"Oh, yes. He's part of my act, as a matter of fact. We're partners, he and I. We perform aerial ballet and sing duets."

This inspired yet another round of hysterical laughter.

The captain slapped his knee in disbelief. "You sing?"

Pyro sighed and glanced irritably off to the side. "Unfortunately, yes."

"Prove it."

A hush fell over the crowd. Pyro stared back at him incredulously. "You—you mean right now?"

The captain raised his rifle yet again. "Did I stutter?"

An indignant glower was fighting for dominance over Sonata's expression, but she dare not speak, not yet. Instead, she began their duet.

"I burn with longing fire
I sigh away at night
I'm poisoned with desire
A longing I can't fight …"
Pyro reluctantly joined in.
"Your blood is singing beneath your flesh
A melody so sweet
Your skin's a veil, soft and fresh
housing primitive beats …"
When they had finished, the soldiers stood back with wide eyes, looking wholly impressed. The captain leaned back on one leg, scratching his beard.

"I underestimated you, Anomaly."

Sonata dared forward with an authoritative sense of urgency and bowed beneath the captain's gaze.

"Sir, I believe we've done more than enough to prove ourselves to you by now." She reached into the inner folds of her cloak and produced an overly perfumed envelope: General Sobek's invitation. She must have grabbed it from inside the caravan when she heard the soldiers. "I believe you'll recognize the seal."

The captain ripped the letter impatiently from the envelope and held it to the light. Pyro watched with satisfaction as the pomp faded from his posture. Sonata stood tall, pressing her lips together.

"At this very moment your superiors are expecting our arrival, and you've done nothing but hinder us. We come on a mission of peace, to serve the C.O.N., and entertain your masters. Our vehicle lies damaged, the remainder of our party is stranded on the opposite shore with no shelter during a volcanic eruption, and I myself am standing here completely defenseless in the midst of an element that would certainly kill me. I cannot imagine your masters would be pleased to discover how you've delayed their entertainment, which I might add has already been generously paid for."

The captain handed the invitation back to Sonata. He turned to two of his privates.

"Escort Princess Sonata and Mr. Anomaly back to camp, and ready the Hermes dragons so we can locate the rest of their party." He returned his attention to Pyro and Sonata. "We'll fetch your caravan. When it's safe to travel we'll personally accompany you to the Asparona Concert Hall to avoid any more hindrances."

Chapter 16:

Finding the Stars

Pasha and Faina's friendship was like the Manhattan gridiron: neither could remember what New York City was like before it, and it was hard to imagine it any other way. To their child minds time had begun with the two of them running wild through the streets of the Lower East Side, chasing baseballs like they were comets, scaling fire escapes like ancient ruins. They were rambunctiously silly together, fogging up the chilly spring air with their peals of breathless laughter.

It was as though they had been cut from the same constellation, patterned after the same galaxy. Time tethered their souls like Pisces's cord. Tragedy and change had unfolded for them in almost identical timelines, each losing a parent, though Faina had lost two, and arriving in New York Harbor within months of each other. And here they had ended up with a bed pushed up against a window, thirty feet apart from each other, heads in the same direction, dreams traveling at a homogenous angle.

Though they were not without their differences, they complemented each other like all good partners in crime. Where Faina was bold, Pasha was cautious. Where Pasha was rigid, Faina was flexible. Where Faina was reckless, Pasha was responsible. Both boasted kind and curious minds that cherished laughter, sought wisdom, and dreamed big.

"What do you want to be when you grow up?" asked Pasha one evening as they were climbing up the fire escape to the roof with backpacks slung over their shoulders, and spyglasses made from paper tubes in their pockets, for they were pretending to be explorers. "Do you really want to be an explorer someday?"

Faina made her way onto the highest platform and looked out over the courtyard with her eyes shielded. "I mean to do many things when I am older, including exploring far-off places. I will ride horses, and drive fast cars, and have fancy parties with champagne and caviar! But I wouldn't say it's what I want to be when I grow up." She pointed to an imaginary star on the darkening horizon. "Ah! Sixty degrees to the right, Galileo! We're almost there!"

Pasha smirked. She didn't really know what she was saying, but it sounded appropriate for their adventure.

"What do you really want to be then?"

She clambered over the edge of the building and onto the cement roof. "An actress, of course!" She stuck out her hand to help him over the side.

"Why am I not surprised?"

They made their way towards the front of the building, which afforded them a clear view of Orchard Street. Faina spread out her arms as though she had just walked onto a stage.

"I am going to be a big star! I will sing in jazz clubs, and make records, and sign autographs!" She had a way about her that made it easy to envision a host of flashing lights all around her, and a chain of heavy diamonds slung about her neck.

"What else will you do?"

The question seemed to genuinely surprise Faina. She turned and faced away from the ledge, letting her backpack slide to the floor.

"Whatever I want, I guess. I'll dance with royalty, and … hunt vampires! Oh, and of course, I'll fall in love and get married, and have lots of babies, at least one set of twins, and then we will go off and have adventures together as a family!"

"Faina, you can't control whether or not you have twins! That's impossible!"

The wind tossed her hair over her shoulders. "No. But my mother was a twin, and my great aunt was a twin. And lots of my cousins were twins. So I'd say I've got a pretty good chance." She unbuckled her satchel and opened a box of animal crackers. "We've had a long journey, Galileo. We have to eat to keep our strength up." She held out the box to Pasha. "What about you? What do you want to be when you grow up?"

Pasha fished a bear-shaped cookie out of the box, and lowered himself to a sitting position. "I am going to remake myself just like the big American giants. One day, I will invest in something and become wealthy again, and I will use all my money to help other people, like Andrew Carnegie. Then I will be able to take care of my family. I will buy Mama big fluffy coats, and I'll pay for Katya's education, and I'll get a big diamond ring and ask you to marry me."

The ram Faina had been gnawing on crumbled and fell from her mouth. "Marry me?"

Pasha thrust out his chin with an innocent but confident smile. "Mhm!" Had it not been for his isolated country upbringing, Pasha might not have possessed the courage to make such a confession. He was too naive to be embarrassed and too sheltered to have developed a fear of rejection yet.

"Well …" Faina hesitated, then snorted. "What do you wanna marry me for?"

"I like you."

Faina stared, waiting for him to go on. "You don't like any other girls?"

Pasha gave it some thought, then shrugged his shoulders. "Not really. Not like I like you. You're different. Other girls would be boring to be married to. But I think we would have fun together." He took another cookie from the box, this time a giraffe, and bit off its head. "Plus, you look different from all the other girls I've seen."

Faina squeezed the hem of her skirt and watched him suspiciously from beneath her lashes. "What do you mean, I look different?"

"You know, you've got all that hair. It's all big, and wavy. I like it. And you've got all those neat freckles. All the other girls at school kinda look the same, but you don't. I never have to worry about getting you mixed up with anyone because you're so much prettier than everyone else."

Faina's hand crept towards her chest. "Prettier?" She was leaning further and further forward.

"Yeah. Like a princess or something. And you're never afraid of anything!"

Faina cast her eyes towards the ground and fiddled with another animal cracker. It was the first time Pasha had seen her blush, and he liked that he had been the one responsible for it. She quickly recovered herself, and looked him over with an arched eyebrow.

"And what makes you think I will marry you?"

Pasha was surprised. Up to this point he had thought Faina liked him too, but she appeared to be putting up a fight. He leaned back against the ledge and stared at the sky.

"I suppose I don't have a lot to offer you, not now that I've lost my title. But I am smart. I make really good grades, you know. Plus I'm one of the tallest boys in my class. Mama says she thinks I'll grow to be at least six feet. I don't know that I'm particularly good looking, but I have had several society ladies say I'm adorable." He scooted a little closer. "And I'd never be mean to you. I would be a good husband. I'd never yell at you, or try to hurt you. We could live in a castle, and read books all the time. And every day I will come home from work and kiss you."

Faina smiled down at her shoes. "You've got a lot of big plans, Pasha Chevalsky." She tapped at her chin with an exceptionally mischievous smirk. "You make a pretty good argument. I'll have to think about it."

Pasha gave a hopeful shrug. "You got plenty of time."

She sighed and gestured to the hazy vault looming over them. "Well, what do you think, Galileo?"

Pasha looked up at the blank cerulean slate of atmosphere as though it were an unfinished canvas, and frowned. "I was hoping I'd see stars once I came up here. I can never see them from the ground. I thought maybe if I was a little higher …" he trailed off. "But I guess not. In Crimea my mother used to lay down in the grass with us and teach us about the constellations."

"You like constellations?"

Faina was sitting on her knees now, facing him with that strange urgency that struck her from time to time in spontaneous bursts.

"Yes, I like constellations."

Faina's smile spread into a catlike grin, and she placed both her hands on his shoulders.

"Do you think you can sneak out after you go to bed tonight?"

Pasha's eyes swelled like big, brown balloons. "Sneak out? As in leave the apartment without permission?"

"Yes! Otherwise it wouldn't be sneaking!" She tugged on his hands. "Please, Pasha, please! I want to take you to see the stars! It will be an adventure!"

Pasha curled his head forward and glanced off to the side. He supposed if it was stars Faina wanted to show him, it would have to be at night.

"Alright fine."

"Excellent." She clapped her hands together. "Meet me down in the courtyard at ten thirty. You don't have to bring anything. Just show up."

***

A few hours later, Pasha found himself sitting beside her on a nearly empty subway car headed towards Grand Central, praying that his mother didn't wake up and decide to take a peek into his bedroom.

The line of bodies swayed to one side as the car ground to a halt. The doors opened. Faina was on her feet before anyone else, tugging Pasha's hand and half-running to get to the concourse.

"Come on, Pasha! Why do you always walk so slow?"

"Why do you always have to run everywhere you go?"

"Because it gets you places faster!"

She led them up the ramp until they reached the main concourse. The endless amount of granite from which the station was built bathed the terminal in a warm, gilded light that permeated every corner. Even the ticket booths appeared to have been crafted with the aesthetic detail of a monument.

Faina seemed to be deriving much pleasure from his astonishment as she swung his hand back and forth.

"Bet you've never seen a train station this fancy, have you?"

"No, never. But what has this got to do with stars?"

Faina lifted her hand under his chin and tilted his head back. Pasha's jaw dropped. High above him in the vaulted recesses of the ceiling was a vast cerulean landscape of dusty yellow stars and the heavenly figures of the ecliptic parading in a long band of constellations.

"Do you see how they are painted backwards?" asked Faina, putting her hands on his shoulders and spinning him around so he could have the full 360-degree view. "That is so you can see it as if you were looking down from Heaven."

"It's amazing." His eyes drew a path through Taurus.

"Coming to New York City is like falling down a rabbit hole and finding yourself in Wonderland. To understand it you have to forget everything you know. If people can live in tiny boxes stacked on top of each other in the sky, then to find the stars you have to go under the ground. Now we can say we have stargazed like real New Yorkers."

And suddenly, the heavenly perspective of the ceiling above them had a new meaning to Pasha. In New York City, the people rose higher and higher into the atmosphere, so when they were looking up through the constellations they were really looking down on civilization. Faina was right, New York City was Wonderland, a city turned upside down. In all that rearranging it made sense that the stars might get knocked down from their perch and end up stuck on the ceiling of a train station, and if anyone could find them, Faina could.

Chapter 17:
Cat's Cradle

The Asparona Concert Hall sat further inland at the top of a hill smothered in tall, yellow grass that had at one point been green. Like most Virgonian infrastructure, there was an earthy appearance to the building, as though it were naturally occurring. It was constructed from clay and boasted all the earmarks of an organically composed edifice.

Pyro was uneasy, to say the least, under the hospitality of Primals. Submitting to the authority of C.O.N. members was difficult to swallow even for a ruse, and yet Pyro soon found himself surprised at how simple it could be. They each had their part to play with little deviation from their habits.

Pyro was a singular person. What you saw was what you got. Rarely did he lie, or even mince words. He was tactless and indelicate. But the Primals translated his cool reservation as embittered defeat, and he quickly became the conquered trophy.

Staccato, on the other hand, was a natural, and could have easily masqueraded as a serpent himself. His existing reputation for being ambitious and ruthless enabled him to play the part of opportunistic self-preservationist: above groveling and flattery, but unapologetically crooked. And he was an excellent liar.

Melodious was the idealistic missionary.

"And what business does a reverend have amongst blood drinkers and pleasure seekers?" a bemused ophidian had inquired.

Melodious simply smiled. "Did our Lord not also keep company with tax collectors and prostitutes?"

The ophidian outright laughed. "I have no lord."

On the whole he remained a point of amusement for most of the C.O.N. Still others regarded him with an unexplained sense of apprehension that Pyro could not seem to place his finger on.

Skelter was stoic, but his mutism excused him from further suspicions. No one seemed to realize it was he who was responsible for their general's absence, but then Skelter had never really given the Capricornian authorities a proper name.

In the end, it was Sonata who struggled the most. No C.O.N. member was ignorant of Sonata's role in the loss of Sea-Splitter, making her presence all the more puzzling.

Upon arriving, they had been received by the colonel, an ophidian named Malfinius Lucien.

"Staccato Nimbus! By my third eye, I had to see it to believe it." His voice was a masculine baritone, and he had a rustic inflection to his words, almost like a cowboy.

Ophidians lived for so long and aged so little that it was uncommon to encounter one with silver hair. But Colonel Lucien was one of these rare breeds, an ancient blood drinker who'd burdened the earth with his existence 117 years, though he didn't look a day over a handsome fifty.

Staccato showed no outward symptom of shame. He merely smirked and raised a haughty eyebrow.

"You wouldn't be the first."

"And here I thought all Fay were so caught up in their own self-righteousness they'd rather die than embrace a new regime."

"Yes, well, it is the superior animal that learns to adapt. Wouldn't you agree?"

Lucien had the pegasi and caravan led away to the stables, and took it upon himself to give them a tour of the camp. A clean-faced youth of an ophidian in highly decorated robes stood sentry at the entrance to the grounds. As the guards issued passes to each member of the company, he beheld them with a befuddled sense of amusement. Colonel Lucien caught him staring and acknowledged him with a somewhat irritable lift of his eyebrows.

"Major."

"Colonel." His eyes wandered across the assemblage with the expectation of an introduction.

The colonel sighed, annoyed at the prospect of anyone slowing their pace, and gestured to the major.

"Major Wynard Periculum." He gestured to Staccato. "Staccato Nimbus and company."

Where Colonel Lucien was able to maintain his decorum, albeit without sacrificing a measure of arrogance, Periculum fidgeted with an excitement that bordered on the vulgar, eager to let the gloating commence.

"A pleasure, I'm sure," recited Staccato.

Perciulum's lip curled over his teeth with a sneering simper as he scrutinized the company from head to toe.

"A bit motley for high-brow entertainment, aren't you?"

Lucien turned towards Periculum with authoritative reproach. "I don't believe you mean that, Major."

Periculum returned his superior's rebuke with haughty defiance. "I hope always to say what I mean, Colonel, were it not so I would say nothing at all."

"Indeed, and the world would be made better for it."

Refusing to award the ajor with any further attention, the colonel led them into the camp. He turned to Staccato with an apologetic smile.

"You'll have to forgive Major Periculum. After having been stationed here for so long I'm afraid my boys are starved for civility, and have grown surly in its absence. Which is precisely the reason you were summoned."

"Indeed, your assignment here has been rather lengthy," agreed Sonata, "considering the degree to which the occupied territory has been subdued. May I ask what delays your return home?"

The colonel narrowed his eyes upon her. "You may not."

Sonata raised her eyebrows and hastily cast her gaze towards the ground. Staccato cleared his throat, eager to smooth over the damage of her faux pas.

"One can only imagine the monotony your soldiers face. Do tell me, are these weather conditions always so abominable? Surely, they must interfere greatly with your recreation."

Pyro had never been to the Asparona Concert Hall before, let alone toured the grounds, but it was easy to get a sense of its former grandeur from the naked tree limbs and bare bushes, like examining cadavers in a specimen lab. Fluid hills traced the horizon line in a series of dried slopes. The trees stood in neat little rows, etched with barriers of river rock.

The camp consisted of a vast number of tents crowned with banners bearing the infamous ouroboros seal. An assortment of people drifted in and out of the canvas flaps, some ophidians, others mere Primals. They congregated in groups, feasting on the open veins of *saignants,* and amusing themselves with dirt-covered dancers who looked as though they'd wandered out of the wilderness in search of a gig.

Pyro lowered his eyebrows. "They don't look starved for entertainment to me."

"*Quality* entertainment, Mr. Anomaly," corrected the colonel. "Our ways may be foreign to you, but we ophidians place a high value on culture. We have our slaves, of course—"

134

Pyro couldn't stop himself. "Slaves?"

Skelter gave his arm a quick swat before the colonel turned around to stare at him.

"Yes, Mr. Anomaly." He nodded towards the filth-laden dancers. "Those are slaves." He smiled, enjoying the discomfort he had inspired. "They won't be the last you'll see on our tour. Just wait until supper."

Staccato, who stood behind the colonel's shoulder, met Pyro's gaze with intensity. *Not another word*, he seemed to be saying. Pyro lowered his head and swallowed.

The tent provided for the company was a large, spacious affair like the ones reserved for the high-ranking officials, and was placed at the top of a small slope, giving them a sweeping view of the camp below.

Dinner was served in the J.S. Dogwood building, an open-air facility which was undoubtedly contributing to the ophidian's crankiness. Without the Jar of Elijah, the weather favored extremes, with uncomfortably cool evenings, and rather stifling afternoons if the sun happened to make an appearance. And always, the black horizon from the volcano, and the toxic-tinged air.

The company crowded on the patio outside the mess hall with the soldiers, waiting for dinner to be announced. Pyro had hauled himself into a corner in one of the rattan chairs, observing the gathering with narrowed eyes. While he was sitting he caught sight of Sonata moving away from the company, weaving through the crowd in pursuit of the colonel. Fearful of what might happen to her outside of Staccato's supervision, Pyro casually got up from his chair and followed her.

She caught up with the colonel on the terrace at the edge of the throng, plucking him from the crowd and pulling him off to the side. Pyro crouched behind a plant, where he could see.

"I'd like to apologize for my forwardness earlier." Her eyes flitted bashfully towards the ground. "I know you must find it difficult to trust me."

Lucien scanned her over as he finished chewing his hors d'oeuvres, and swallowed.

"Indeed. As a matter of fact, I have to wonder what compelled Staccato to allow you to tag along."

"We're alike, he and I. When faced with an obstacle we seek to learn rather than resist."

He looked pointedly at her prosthetic legs. "I would have pegged you as quite resistant."

"If you're referring to the incident with Sea-Splitter, I was young, Colonel. Surely, you cannot fault me for that. As the daughter of a mermaid king, you may see me as a representative for your enemy, but bear in mind that the privilege of my birth has taught me the value of diplomacy. In the face of defeat the wise ruler gains peace by submission." She looked out at the surrounding debauchery and fingered her collar with a feigned sense of wonder. "You embrace all sorts of pleasures here, more than I knew existed!" She bit her lip and made a show of eyeing a young ophidian lustfully. "I'm afraid, Colonel, I've fallen prey to the temptation of your lifestyle."

A smile curled up in the corner of Lucien's mouth like a slimy python. "Primal Instinct has that effect on people." He drew uncomfortably close. "Especially the young and beautiful."

She wore the face of a rebellious teenager having just snuck out of the house for the first time. "As a princess, I'm rather limited in my exposure to the world. There's so much I'd like to experience!"

Lucien looked down at her with a devious grin. "Stick around. You might just get what you're asking for." He winked and departed, leaving to address a band of drunken lividium congregated around one of the waiters.

"In the future, try not to follow me," advised Sonata without looking at Pyro. "It looks suspicious."

Pyro raised an eyebrow. "And here I thought you were a bad liar."

"There are good lies and bad lies. I'm only a bad liar when I feel the lie to be wrong. I dislike keeping unnecessary secrets."

"I was only looking out for you, you know."

"You mean because I'm the most helpless?"

"No, because the C.O.N. sees you as the biggest threat."

The defensive pride fell from her eyes like shed scales.

"You've done more damage to the C.O.N. than anyone else here. You prevented the eradication of an entire people singlehandedly at the age of fifteen. With a single act of bravery you saved six kingdoms from total annihilation. You thwarted their plans. They haven't forgotten that, and I'm not sure they ever will."

Sonata stared at him with foggy eyes and a furrowed brow. She started to say something but stopped, looking as though she had forgotten the words to a familiar song.

Pyro winked. "Can't let anything happen to our most valuable member."

The dinner bell soon rang, and the company was ushered to the table of Colonel Lucien. A sylph in an apple green, satin dress was seated close beside him, her attention fixed pointedly on the table. Pyro could see that she was an incredibly tiny woman with large, sad eyes that took up half her face, and a tiny, pursed mouth like a baby doll. Her skin was a near-perfect shade reminiscent of the clay buildings scattered about the valley, and there was green foliage growing throughout her thick, dark hair.

Lucien roped his arm around her shoulder with masculine pride.

"I haven't yet had the opportunity to introduce you to my mistress. This is the Great Madame Lavanda DeCampanillia Dalia Policarpo Raíz!"

"But you may call me Lavanda," she interrupted with a nervous laugh.

It occurred to Pyro that Madame Raíz must have at one point been a performer, for the moment she looked up her demeanor changed entirely, as though she were a puppet one could activate simply by pulling a string.

"You see, Lavanda herself is a professional dancer," explained Lucien. "Why, she once danced the Padamba for the Maharaja of Qa-Halib!"

Lavanda turned her eyes bashfully towards the ground. "That was a long time ago."

She reached up to brush a stray hair from her eyes, unintentionally exposing a series of injection pricks and bite marks on the inside of her arm.

"The pleasure is ours, Madame Raíz." Staccato gestured to Pyro and Sonata. "Something tells me you and our aerialists will have much to discuss this evening."

"Oh, yes! You must tell me all about your routine! I simply cannot wait to see your performance!"

The uniformed servants were arranging covered dishes on a rolling cart on the other side of the room near the kitchen door. Pyro's stomach simultaneously growled and turned at the thought of what might lay under the cloches.

The tablecloth billowed up in a violent flurry as an imposing gale tore through the pavilion, threatening to disrupt the table setting.

"Cursed weather conditions!" Lucien snapped his fingers at one of the servants. "Bring the girl."

Lavanda's confident charm momentarily waned as she tugged on the colonel's sleeve and lowered her voice.

"Really, I can take care of it, Malfinius—"

"Nonsense! These days you can hardly conjure a weed!"

The head servant stammered anxiously. "Which—which girl do you mean, Colonel?"

The colonel snapped his napkin impatiently. "Which one do you think? The sylph!" He leaned closer and hissed under his breath. "Number seven!"

"He means Miss King," Lavanda explained for him.

Pyro shot a questioning glance at Skelter, but Skelter's eyes urged him to remain silent.

"It always picks up around sunset." The colonel leaned back in his chair, trying to compose himself. "By contrast the day can be abysmally still."

Two underlings brought forth a young woman, forcefully dragging her along by the elbows, though she showed little resistance. She was pixie thin with a diamond-shaped face and diamond eyes, and a sprinkling of freckles across her ochre skin. Her raven hair was cropped short in soft, curling tufts.

"Ah, just the young lady I was looking for." The colonel turned in his chair as she was made to stand before him.

"*¡Oye!*" She jerked her head at the men clinging to her arms. "*¡Puedes soltarme ahora!*" Pyro did not speak Spanish like most native Virgonians, but he assumed she was asking to be let go. The colonel gave a nod of consent.

"Go ahead."

They dropped their hands and stepped away. The woman rolled her shoulders, as though trying to rid her skin of their essence.

"You see we have guests." The colonel gestured to the table with raised eyebrows.

"*Sí.*" The girl gave the company a quick and careless once-over, then returned her attention to the colonel. "What is it you want?"

"One cannot expect to host a proper dinner under such vile conditions."

"Surely, you do not expect me to control the wind."

Lucien leaned back with a smile and stroked his beard. "I am certain someone with your estimable gifts can figure out something."

"Or you could restore the Jar and save yourself the trouble of summoning me every time the weather isn't to your liking."

"You try my patience." He gestured to Staccato. "Go on, show Mr. Nimbus what you're capable of."

The girl cut Staccato a scathing look, then turned and surveyed the direction the wind was coming from. She closed her eyes. A series of green vines began to snake over the archways of the pavilion, growing and weaving themselves together, creating a sort of wind-blocking curtain. She looked back at the colonel.

"Satisfied?"

The colonel nodded to the servants. "You may bring her a chair." He returned his attention to his guests. "Without the Jar, any plant life the sylph conjures cannot be sustained on its own."

Pyro looked up. "Meaning?"

The girl snapped at him. "Meaning without me they will die." Her gaze sliced across the table and stabbed at the colonel. "And my name is Cassia."

One of the officers' comfortable looking armchairs was brought to Cassia, and she was allowed to sit.

"I'm hungry." She was certainly a bold girl, not afraid of making her feelings known.

The colonel exhaled irascibly through his nostrils but conceded. "Bring her food."

Staccato smirked. "No wonder you're so eager to move on."

"Our marching orders can't come soon enough. We've been stationed in this wasteland too long."

A bowl of broth was brought to Cassia, which she drank eagerly while sitting cross-legged in the chair.

When the first course was served, Pyro was relieved to find green soup instead of human blood. His relief did not go unnoticed by the colonel, who regarded him with irritable offense.

"You may relax, Mr. Anomaly. We can be tolerant of our foreign neighbors."

Pyro flashed him a dirty look and dug his spoon into the soup in a most begrudged manner.

After a while, Pyro noticed Cassia was studying him, a fleck of familiarity in her expression. There was no telling what she had read about him in the papers. Pyro hunkered down over his bowl, ashamed and hoping to put her off.

"Tell me, Colonel," Melodious set down his spoon, "once you have finished your tour of Virgo, where do you plan to go next?"

"With any luck we'll be returning home to Draco."

Pyro glanced at Cassia to see if she had stopped gaping at him yet. Instead she was staring intently at the bottom of her bowl. Pyro paused before he could spoon another mouthful past his lips and eyed his own bowl suspiciously. Cassia shifted her focus to Staccato, her contempt replaced by curiosity.

From her pocket, she produced a thick, scarlet woolen thread and wound it about her fingers in a game of Cat's Cradle. She drew her fingers in and out of the loops and tangles in an almost hypnotic manner until she had formed a pattern of seven stars called "the Pleiades." She sat there for some time with her hands extended outwards, admiring her work, until finally she scrapped it and began work on a new one.

Forgetting the peculiar way Cassia had been eyeing her soup, Pyro reached for another spoonful. At the sight of his bowl, he flinched. An invisible force was forming letters in the film of broth lining the lip of his dish.

Stop staring at the thread. Glance only.

Pyro's eyes jumped to Staccato. He was laughing at one of the colonel's jokes, but managed to slip Pyro a swift and meaningful look. Pyro swallowed though there was nothing in his mouth to swallow, and scraped out the message with his spoon.

"How bad do these wind conditions generally get to be this time of day?" Staccato leaned sideways so that the servant could place the main course on the table. "Given that the performance is to take place outside, I fear the weather may interfere with Sonata and Pyro's aerial number. You don't suppose Miss …" He paused. "I'm sorry, dear, what is your family name?"

Cassia poked her head around the high back of her chair, noticeably less hostile than before.

"King."

"Ah, yes, you don't suppose Miss King may be of some assistance, do you?"

The colonel reclined back in his chair and put a finger to his temple. "What do you say, girl? You think you can lend Mr. Nimbus a hand?"

Cassia must have realized she was being too friendly and quickly lowered her eyebrows.

"If I do, will you promise to provide us with some form of heat in our quarters at night so we don't freeze to death?"

Periculum snickered into his plate. "What's the igneous for?"

Cassia flashed him a glower, then looked pleadingly at the colonel. "Must he be permitted to open his mouth when all that comes out are witless jokes?" She shook her head as though frustrated she even acknowledged such a creature. "Or at the very least, will you allow me to take Fuerza out? She needs to stretch her legs! If you continue to keep her cooped up like this she'll—"

The colonel lifted his hand. "I refuse to bargain with you in the presence of guests."

"But—"

"You will assist Mr. Nimbus during the performance. We can discuss the details later."

Cassia flopped back in her chair, defeated, and did not say another word.

"She's right about your jokes." The colonel elbowed Periculum in the side and chuckled. Lavanda edged towards her master with timid glances.

"Perhaps we could allow the girl an opportunity to meet with our guests?" She gave his arm an affectionate squeeze. "What harm would it do? Children love the circus, after all. And if she's enjoying herself she is more likely to behave. Better to do it now and save ourselves the trouble of dealing with her later."

The colonel dabbed at his mouth with his napkin and gave a relenting grunt.

"You do have a point, my dear. Alright." He gestured to the head servant again. "Bring in the little girl."

The conversation dragged on, during which Cassia was able to produce several more patterns, one Pyro recognized as "the Birdhouse." The images were rarely literal, and a knowledge of the game was necessary to interpret the arrangements. This was soon followed by "the Eye of the Cat."

The underlings who had summoned Cassia dragged in a chubby-faced girl who couldn't have been more than six or seven. As they neared, Pyro could see she had recently been doused with water. What's more, the lower half of her face had been fitted with a special fireproof covering. Pyro's heart sank. She was an igneous. It was all Pyro could do to keep from attacking the two servants.

"You may let her go," the colonel instructed. "She will do no harm here."

Cassia swiveled around. "Can they take her mask off?"

The colonel looked as though he were considering it, then slowly gave a nod. The servants unbuckled the girl's muzzle and pushed her forward. The girl staggered forward on her pudgy legs. Pyro's mouth fell open in horror. He knew it would have been prudent to mask his emotions at such a time, but suddenly he couldn't remember how.

"Miss King, kindly see to your charge."

Cassia got up and gathered the girl in her arms, balancing her on her hip.

"This is Fuerza."

Fuerza looked back at Cassia with bashful, brown eyes. "*¿Son estas las personas del circo?*"

"English please," growled Lucien.

Cassia rolled her eyes. "She asked if these were the circus people. She hardly speaks English." She returned her attention to Fuerza and nodded. This seemed to be all Fuerza needed to give full vent to her enthusiasm. She veered round in Cassia's arms and faced the table with a fervent wave.

"*¡Hola!* I am Fuerza!"

A peculiar chemistry of emotions was brewing at the table. Tense smiles tinged with a mixture of adoration and sorrow haunted the faces of the company as they greeted her back.

"*¿Puedes decirles cuántos años tienes?*" She flashed the colonel a look. "I am asking her how old she is."

Fuerza's full cheeks swelled like bubbles as she grinned, and she held up seven fingers.

Lavanda took the liberty of introducing each of the members to Fuerza. When she got to Sonata, Fuerza's eyes swelled with an elation only seven-year-olds can muster. Her lips split open with an enthusiastic gasp, and she grinned uncontrollably.

"*¡Princessa!*" Fuerza wriggled out of Cassia's arms and dashed over to Sonata, her bare feet smacking the floor. She threw her arms around Sonata's waist and leaned her head affectionately against her stomach. A hurricane of emotions warred in Sonata's heart. She pressed the girl close and stroked the back of her hair.

Pyro's eyes fell on Staccato. He had lost all trace of his elegant, snooty composure, and he stared openmouthed at the sight of the sweet child who at any moment would be strapped into a muzzle and dragged away.

Fuerza reached up and fingered one of the spiral curls falling over Sonata's shoulder. "*¡Qué cabella tan hermosa!*"

Sonata kissed the little girl's hand and squeezed it. "*¡Me gusta el tuyo también!*"

It did not surprise Pyro that Sonata spoke Spanish, for it shared some similarities with *Helleta,* a language still spoken in rural Karkinos, and her mother's native tongue.

"Alright!" The colonel checked his pocket watch with an irritable sigh. "I think that's quite enough, Miss King. You may take her back now."

Cassia lowered her eyebrows into a sharp point. "She just got here!"

"I said that's enough! We wouldn't want her getting used to these indulgences, after all."

For a moment Pyro envied the freedom Cassia had to express her temper, but quickly remembered that she had no freedom at all.

"She's a little girl!" Cassia growled. "She needs space, she needs exercise!"

Realizing that their visit was at an end, Sonata began to pull Fuerza in for another hug when a force jerked the girl out of reach, prompting an involuntary cry of surprise from her throat. One of the servants had grabbed hold of her sash and yanked so hard that she fell back on her bottom. Hurt and humiliation colored the whites of her eyes with a faint red.

There was a loud, chalky pop, followed by the sound of rubble sprinkling over the floor. A crowd of Primals flew up from the chairs and backed away from the large stone table they had been sitting at. It had spontaneously split in two.

Pyro turned in time to see Melodious quickly shoving Staccato's staff into his hand. There was a vein trembling in the miraculous's forehead.

"The day we depart from these moldering ruins may yet be the happiest day of my life!" Lucien shook his head. "One can hardly breathe without something falling apart!"

While everyone was distracted, Pyro slipped a flask from his pocket and poured it into his drink.

Chapter 18:
The Fight

"Say, Pasha," hollered Yuri one day at recess, "what size shoe do you wear?"

Pasha looked askance at Yuri as the wind tousled his hair. "About a size seven."

Yuri's mouth split open so that all his crooked teeth showed as he laughed and rubbed his palms together. "Perfect! You're just the right size!"

Pasha still didn't understand. "Right size for what?"

"Someone donated an entire box of Eskimo boots at my synagogue's charity drive, and my Rabbi let me have them seeing as no one was likely to wear them."

Pasha glanced from one side of the courtyard to the other. "And you want me to wear them?"

"Not just you. There's a pair for me, Sergei, Davy, Franklin, and now you!"

At this point Pasha could only assume that wearing Eskimo boots was some strange American custom that he had yet to learn about.

"What are we going to do with them?"

Yuri slid to a seat on the bench and roped one arm around Pasha's shoulder. "Wait 'til you get a load of this! It was Davy's idea! First we're gonna paint 'em white, and then we're gonna stencil in some red polka dots and wear 'em on the Bowery!"

Pasha's mouth hung open. "We can't do that! Everyone will make fun of us!"

Yuri pointed a crooked finger in his face. "Exactly! And then we can beat 'em up!" By now Yuri was grinning so broadly that even the scraggly tips of his strawberry-blonde hair seemed to curl with excitement. He leaned expectantly towards Pasha. "Well, what do ya think? Are you in or what?"

Pasha tried his best to appear interested, but truthfully he couldn't wrap his head around the attraction these boys had to violence. They didn't just beat each other when they were mad; there was a fight for all occasions. Victories on the baseball field were celebrated by jamming each other into headlocks, the grieved were consoled by a hearty punch on the arm, congratulations were expressed by an enthusiastic slap on the back.

What worried Pasha most was that this language seemed universal and not simply an American custom as he had hoped. Other new boys fit in quite nicely. It made no difference if they had come from China, Italy, Ireland, or Poland, they all spoke fluent knockabout. Blood was to a ten-year-old boy what beer was to a grown man.

"When exactly are you planning on doing this?" Pasha managed to churn out.

"This coming Saturday. What do you say, pal?"

Pasha brushed his hair back with one hand and forced himself to look Yuri in the eye.

"Oh, gee, Yuri, that sounds great and all, but I already promised Faina I would play catch with her in the park on Saturday."

Yuri didn't appear to find this surprising at all, but he did look puzzled. He sat back and crossed his arms over his chest.

"Boy, you sure do spend a lot of time with Spichkin."

"Well, she is my neighbor. And we have a lot of fun together."

Sergei, who had been listening to the entire exchange with unmitigated fascination, suddenly spoke up, giving Pasha quite a start.

"But she's a girl! How can you have fun with a girl?"

Gregory Sochinsky, who was quite a bit older than Pasha and the others, piped up from his place beside the tetherball pole. "Wait until you boys get a bit older. You'll find there are plenty of fun things to do with a girl. Chevalsky here is just ahead of the game."

That was when Anastas came charging up to him from across the playground.

"What's the big idea, Chevalsky?" he demanded, dragging Pasha by the collar and throwing him up against the chain-link fence. "You and Spichkin been smooching or something? She hit up your house recently?"

Pasha turned his head as though antlers had sprouted from Anastas's nose.

"*Smooching*? What is smooching?"

"It means kissing," explained Yuri. He shoved the back of Anastas's head. "And leave Pasha alone, he ain't doing you no harm. Spichkin's fair game."

Anastas reluctantly released Pasha's collar. Pasha slid back to his feet.

"To answer your question," retorted Pasha, slightly annoyed, "no, we have not been '*smooching*,' as you say, because I am a gentleman, and the only way I would kiss Faina is if I knew she wanted me to." He wrenched Anastas's fist from his collar.

"That's right, go on!" Anastas hollered after him. "Brag about all those fine aristocratic manners that make you so much better than the rest of us."

Pasha stopped and turned slowly with narrowed eyes. "You don't have to be wealthy to have manners. What is your problem anyway? What have I ever done to you?"

By now their classmates had noticed the mounting tension between the two. Even the girls across the courtyard had taken an interest, and everyone was drawing around them in a circle.

"I don't like you, Chevalsky," declared Anastas. "You think you're so much better than everyone because of your class!"

"What class?" remarked Pasha with a dry wit that transcended his age. "My mother works in a factory."

Many of the boys, including Yuri and Sergei, thought this terribly clever and actually began to laugh. It was clear from the wrathful glare in Anastas's eyes that his humiliation only served to motivate him further. He would not walk away disgraced.

"You're not like us, Chevalsky. You're privileged. You don't belong here."

"You don't know anything about me! I have just as much right to be here as you!"

"Right? What do you know about rights?"

"A lot more than you! What do you know about what goes on in Russia? You were born here! If anyone here is privileged, it's you! So why don't you just shut up and quit making everyone so miserable!"

Half their audience began to clap and cheer. Anastas's lip curled disdainfully over his teeth as he dared closer to Pasha, and the two began circling each other.

"You think it's so great here? The only thing 'great' about America is that it's a great lie!"

"I'd still rather be poor in America than dead in Russia! And if it bothers you that much when people have a different opinion, then maybe you'd be better off there! Then none of us would have to listen to you!"

Sergei began conducting a cheer. "Pasha! Pasha!"

The others quickly joined in, clapping their hands together and hopping up and down. Even Katya, though she did not know what was going on, pumped her fist in the air and chanted her brother's name.

Anastas pounded his fist across Pasha's upper lip. Pasha staggered back, a new pain searing through his mouth. Now the schoolyard was chanting a new word.

"Fight! Fight! Fight!"

Pasha flung himself at Anastas, wrestling him to the ground. The two boys grappled back and forth. With the flood of adrenaline isolating his senses, Pasha did not notice when the cheers died out and were replaced with whistle blowing. Next thing he knew, Mr. Schultz was grabbing them both by the shoulders and pulling them apart.

Chapter 19:

Old Habits Die Hard

"So, have you figured anything else out?" Pyro asked Staccato when the miraculous returned to the tent after a walk through the grounds. A pair of black, silk, Turkish pants smacked Pyro's cheek and landed on his shoulder as Skelter tossed him his costume from a trunk. "Give me a moment!" Pyro folded the trousers over his arm. "I've got plenty of time to get ready!"

Staccato sat down on the end of his cot and wrapped a blanket around his shoulders.

"I suspect the C.O.N. is attempting to transport the Jar of Elijah back to Draco, a rather difficult undertaking I would imagine." He kicked off his shoes and lay back on the bed with his hand covering his eyes.

Sonata ceased rummaging through her trunk. "So that's why they've been here so long!"

Pyro's head was beginning to spin from the alcohol he'd been consuming in secret. He hastily dropped down into a chair. He'd finished off the flask some time ago, and had had to refill it when no one was looking.

"Wait, why would that cause the C.O.N. to be stationed in Virgo for an extended period?"

"The vast majority of powerful enchanted relics have a strict protocol when it comes to handling them," explained Staccato. "You can't just pick them up and move them. There are rules."

"What are the rules for carrying the Jar of Elijah?"

Staccato slid his hand over his mouth and squinted at the ceiling. "I can't be sure, but I have a strong suspicion that the Jar must be carried by seven Fay, one representative for each race."

"What led you to that idea?"

"'The law of seven ambassadors is a common theme when dealing with supernatural paraphernalia.' *Lamps, Swords, and Scales*, chapter seven, page 245, article six. It's textbook. Furthermore, one of the hostages is an igneous."

Pyro shrugged. "I'd reckon they're keeping all kinds of Fay hostages."

"Statistics show that of all the Fay, igneous make up the smallest percentage of the C.O.N.'s prisoners. This is because they are notoriously difficult to contain, especially for ophidians. So, why make the effort? I'll tell you why: because they are in need of one. It would also explain why they've imprisoned a child. Fuerza is less of a threat to them because she's smaller and weaker, furthermore her powers will not have activated yet, making her easy to overpower."

"And yet those hearth-winders muzzle her anyway."

"That couldn't be the only requirement for carrying the Jar, could it?" called Sonata from behind the dressing screen.

Staccato shook his head. "Not likely. We can expect a minimum of three stipulations, but there could be as many as twelve. If we can find out what the rules are for transporting the Jar, then we can use that knowledge to discern the route the C.O.N. will be taking to Draco, providing the resistance with an opportunity to intercept it."

Melodious stepped out from behind his own dressing screen in a glimmering cloak of blue velvet. "You think Miss King will be able to provide us with such insight?"

Staccato stroked his beard and crossed one leg over the other.

"I can't imagine the C.O.N. would be willing to share information with their hostages. Better that they are kept in the dark, lest they resist. However, that does not mean she won't be able to help us figure it out." He checked his pocket watch and looked at Pyro. "You really do need to start getting dressed."

When everyone was ready, they trudged to the amphitheater bracing bits of their costumes against the breeze, and swallowing their nerves. The arena remained an impressive structure even in the midst of ruin. Settled amongst the enormous crags of red rock was a theater unlike anything they had ever seen. Dead trees were sprinkled throughout the aisles, and a series of dirt-covered levels had been dug into the side of the hill. Were it not for the weather conditions, it would have been the perfect spot for stargazing.

The soldiers may have only filled an eighth of the stadium, but they had all the obnoxious volume of a full house. Many had brought their hostages and prisoners, seating their *saignants* between them and sipping from a wrist on either side. Pyro noticed one gathering lending an ankle to a comrade sitting in the row before them.

His head swam with a dizzy fury. *Stay calm*, he kept reminding himself. *You've got to stay calm!* He turned away from the others and drained his flask.

Periculum was waiting behind the backstage partition where various props and equipment had been scattered, keeping a grip on

Cassia's fetters. She had already constructed a curtain of vines on the sides of the stage to block the wind.

"You won't be back here the whole time, will you?" Pyro sneered at the smug-faced ophidian.

Periculum eyed him with another of his signature condescending appraisals.

"Sorry to disappoint you, Mr. Anomaly, but no, I will not be supervising your band of misfits." He tossed Cassia's chain to Pyro, who drew back as though it were a serpent, letting it clatter to the ground. "She won't try to escape … or at least," he surveyed Cassia with cruel amusement, "she would be a fool to attempt it."

Staccato squinted at the girl, his eyes cold with feigned suspicion. "You're certain? I can't waste my time keeping an eye on your slave. I've a show to run."

"You can count on it." Periculum turned and vanished behind the partition.

Pyro surveyed their surroundings with conscious care. Their audience could not have seen over the partition. They were surprisingly secure.

"So," Cassia blurted out. "You are rebels?"

Staccato put a hand up to shush her. "Yes. Don't get ahead of yourself though. We have no shortage of ways to communicate. You need only trust us."

He offered her a seat on one of the large trunks while Skelter took the liberty of removing one of the unused silks from a case and offering it to her as a means of warmth.

"Skelter, you're on first, followed by introductions." Staccato nodded to his goddaughter. "Go ahead and take your place for your solo." He flashed Pyro and Melodious significant looks. "I trust the two of you can take care of Miss King."

Pyro nodded obediently. The others took their places. He could feel his pulse ticking inside his wrists like the machinery of a clock. The roar of the crowd shrank and settled as the first notes poured from Skelter's violin. He looked down at Cassia. She was shivering, but hope brightened her features.

"If you give me your hand I can warm you," Pyro offered.

Cassia looked up at him and slipped her fingers into his grasp.

"You're Pyro Anomaly."

Pyro braced himself for the inevitable pronouncement of his royal title as he let his warmth travel into her veins.

"Yes."

"The soldier responsible for rescuing so many children from the C.O.N."

"Yeah, that's me." He knelt down on the ground. For a moment the world seemed to spin. Pyro pinched his temples. Perhaps he'd gotten carried away with the flask. "Alright, here's the scoop." In a low voice, Pyro shared Staccato's theory of the seven ambassadors. "Do you know if that's true?"

"Yes! Unless it is carried by seven Fay ambassadors, one for every race, the Jar is too heavy to move on its own. That's why they've imprisoned us."

Pyro turned to Melodious. "In that case, why don't we just hightail it with the ambassadors and pack up the Jar in the caravan?"

Cassia looked surprised that he would ask such a question. "You can't. We are cursed, bound to carry the Jar to Draco. If any of us tries to resist, or run away, then we'll all seven of us die. That's what Periculum meant when he said I'd be a fool to try and escape. I'm afraid we are very limited when it comes to lending a hand in rescuing ourselves. Only once we reach Draco will the curse be broken."

Pyro frowned. "Okay, let's just assume we find a way to get our hands on the Jar. I'm guessing there's some silly golden rule on how to carry it, some crazy mumbo-jumbo we have to say while holding the blasted thing?"

Cassia thought this over, biting her lower lip. "All I know is that it must always be carried by either both hands or the dominant hand, never the non-dominant hand alone. There are probably more specific instructions, but none that I'm privy to."

Melodious placed his hand on her shoulder. "Do you know where the C.O.N. might keep such information?"

"No, but I know where they got it. Dr. Desmond, Professor of Antiquities at the Institute for Enchanted Archaeology. Dr. Desmond was the leading expert on the Jar of Elijah. The C.O.N. kidnapped her when they first stole the Jar."

"Is she here now?"

"No. She was removed from the camp not long after the C.O.N. began its occupation of Spica. It's rumored she's being held hostage somewhere. At least, that's what some of the other prisoners are saying."

Pyro started to speak but was forced to cover his mouth as a belch rose up in his throat. He hastily swallowed, praying he wasn't drunk. "They think she's still alive?"

"It wouldn't make sense to kill her." Cassia paused. "At least not yet. If Dr. Desmond is the authority on all things related to the Jar, then it would be foolish to kill her before it reaches Draco."

Melodious nodded. "Miss King is right." He pulled at his mustache with two fingers. "There are any number of reasons to leave her alive."

Cassia sighed. "I wish I could tell you where the C.O.N. might keep any written instructions, but like I said, I don't know anything."

"Is there anyone who you think might know where the C.O.N. would keep such information?"

Cassia hesitated. "Lavanda."

"You mean the colonel's mistress?" said Pyro.

"Pyro!" Staccato was stomping their way. "It's your cue!"

"Is it?"

"Yes! Yes!" Staccato grabbed him by the shoulder and practically dragged him to the partition. "Now hurry up and get out there!" He shoved Pyro unceremoniously onto the stage.

Pyro stumbled forward and found himself squinting through the filmy light in search of Sonata. Mean-spirited laughter leaked into the spotlight as the C.O.N. watched their enemy parade before them in costume. Pyro cleared his throat, his mind settling into the present situation.

Spots formed before his eyes. In the heat of the blinding spotlight, he became painfully aware of the alcohol dousing his veins. Somewhere amongst the fog Sonata had begun to sing.

"I burn with longing fire
I sigh away at night
I'm poisoned with desire
A longing I can't fight ..."

Halfway through the lyrics Pyro's mind was able to dig out her form amongst the spinning shapes. Her eyes cut towards him with an impatient glower. Snickers echoed from the front row. Pyro hastily stumbled behind her and took her hand in his.

"Your blood is singing beneath your flesh
A melody so sweet
Your skin's a veil, soft and fresh

housing primitive beats ..."
Their voices joined together.
"Raise a glass and drink from me
my lover, drink me in
time is moving far too fast
I'll be your deadly sin.
Life's too short to turn away
From pleasure's luring fire
Why abstain and feel the pain
Of curbing true desire?"

As he ran his head along the length of her arm she sniffed the air and squinted at him. Things quickly grew shaky. When Pyro went to lift Sonata, he could hardly balance enough to hold her straight and nearly caused her to fall. It was by sheer force of will alone that he got through his silk routine, though his grace was certainly lacking. At the end of the performance, Pyro and Sonata smiled and bowed just as they had rehearsed, and left the stage holding each other's hands.

Eager to escape Sonata's glare, Pyro grabbed his next costume and hastened behind the dressing screen. He peeled off his black trousers and reached for the green pair folded over the panel, shivering in his underwear. A tremendous force seized the back of Pyro's neck as its source emerged from behind the partition.

"You!" hissed Sonata. She threw Pyro forward with such unexpected strength he went down on his knees. "Where is it?" Her voice had gone husky with rage, something he'd never observed from her before.

"What?"

"Don't you 'what' me! You've been drinking! After you promised Staccato you wouldn't!"

Pyro looked down at his state of undress and flushed scarlet. Sonata narrowed her eyes further.

"You needn't be so modest. I'm a mermaid. I'm accustomed to seeing much less on a man's body."

Somehow this did little to console him. Pyro reached into the pocket of the trousers he'd just removed and slapped the flask in her palm. Sonata's eyes only grew wilder.

"You had it on you the whole time?" When Pyro said nothing she threw her head back in disgust. "Rest assured, I'll be removing all the pockets from your wardrobe!"

"Are you gonna tell Staccato?"

She shut her lips tight and exhaled through her nostrils. "Not at this exact moment." She turned on her heel and departed.

Chapter 20:
Accountability

When the performance was over, Pyro sat on the hillside outside the tent, smoking. Fortunately, everyone had been too wrapped up in interviewing Cassia to watch his performance. Sonata was the only one with any knowledge of what Pyro had been up to.

He focused his concentration on the dried-up scenery before him, his attention drawn to a tent on a lone patch of leafy emerald located on the far side of the valley where two ophidians stood sentry. Pyro exhaled a vaporous cloud. It seemed almost too easy.

"We need to talk." Sonata appeared, looming over him with her hands on her hips. "Do you recall the deal you made with Staccato when he freed you from Kilgoree?"

Pyro spat an ember from the corner of his mouth. "I agreed to cut back on my questionable behavior."

"Why did you break your promise?"

Pyro bent over his knees with an exhale and glared at the trail of moonlight that had settled on the rocky horizon. "I don't wanna talk about it."

"You don't want to talk about it?" The air grew tense and windless. "Then what exactly do you plan to do about it?"

"Forget it ever happened."

"Is that what you told yourself last time?"

Pyro steeled his shoulders. Perhaps if he refused to answer her she'd give up and leave. But his silence only appeared to encourage her. She plopped down in the grass beside him.

"You have to get control of yourself!"

Pyro ripped the cigarette from between his lips and crushed it in his hand. "I am in control! I'm always in control! I know what I'm doing when I make decisions!"

"You're a terrible liar, though you appear to have done a capital job of deceiving yourself!"

Pyro stared at her, feeling more exposed than if she had walked behind that screen and he were wearing no underwear at all.

Her eyes flitted towards the cigarette in his hand. "What you saw tonight upset you, which is understandable. It was hard to watch. So you started drinking. Drinking is the only way you know how to control your feelings."

Pyro opened his hand, allowing the breeze to blow the ash from his palm.

"It's not the only way."

"No, I suppose you're right. But it's the way you chose tonight."

Pyro dug the heels of his hands into his sockets and sighed.

"Look, I really don't wanna talk about it."

Sonata showed no sign of apologizing or leaving. "I'm sure you don't. But you don't really have a choice, do you? If you carry on this way, Staccato is sure to cast you off immediately. You can't return to the Saighdeoir, and your parents won't have you back either, not until you've straightened out."

By now, Pyro had grown quite irritated. "Alright, girly. I've heard quite enough." He put up the collar of his jacket and took off down the hill, his eye on the tent where the Jar was being held.

"Excuse me? Where do you think you're going?"

"To actually do something!"

Sonata leapt to her feet, a warning expression in her eye. "Don't you dare do what I think you're going to do!"

He reached for another cigarette from his pocket. "I don't answer to you or anybody else!"

She pursued him down the hill. "And how's that working for you lately?"

He ground to a halt. "You're awfully cheeky for a princess, you know that?"

"And you're rather vulgar for a prince. I don't hold with stereotypes, and let's not kid ourselves, neither do you. I should warn you, if your plans are to go near that tent, I'm afraid you're about to be greatly disappointed."

Pyro threw back his head with an obnoxious laugh and took a step forward. Sonata stepped in front of him, her hands on her hips. Pyro narrowed his eyes.

"You gonna move?"

"I am not."

"That's where you're wrong." Grabbing her by the wrist, he pulled her around, then seized her shoulders from behind.

"Get your hands off me!"

"Relax, Sonny. You ain't the first girl I've had to shake off, and contrary to my reputation I am able to do it in a manner befitting a gentleman."

As he frogmarched her back towards their tent, Sonata thrust her elbow into his abdomen with such force he was compelled to let go. No sooner had he freed her than he felt the crushing weight of her prosthetic foot smashing his toes. Pyro gave an involuntary cry. Before he could retreat, a shockwave expanded through his sinuses as her fist came into contact with his nose. Finally, she turned and, bringing up her foot, kicked his legs out from under him so that he fell backwards onto the ground, clutching his injuries.

Sonata bent low over Pyro's groaning form. "Do not make the mistake of comparing me to one of your unfortunate cabaret dancers. Let's just agree that I'm my own class of woman altogether."

Pyro sat up, held his hand to his bleeding nose, and voiced his agreement with a rather salacious expression. Sonata was unfazed.

"You could have just said 'no kidding.'" She offered him her hand, but Pyro refused to take it. "You may stamp your feet all you like, but the fact of the matter is this: we're two of a kind, you and I. The one thing you desire above all else is to take down the C.O.N. Well, I want the same thing, and thanks to the advent of Thayer's circus I finally have an opportunity to pursue that desire. Do you have any idea the obstacles I've had to overcome in the pursuit of that dream? Me, a princess, the petted goddaughter of one of the most powerful miraculous in history? And that's to say nothing of my disability, my age, or my size! I've had my desires jeopardized by the selfishness of others once before, and I refuse to let it happen again.

"If you care about the resistance, if you really want to get back to rescuing people, then you can't behave like this! You can't miss practice. You can't hang your head down when you dance like you don't want to be here. And you absolutely cannot be drunk during a performance! You have to take it seriously, and you have to discipline yourself!"

Pyro wiped his blood on his arm. "I'm a soldier, aren't I?"

Sonata knelt down on the ground and tilted his head back with a glowing hand. "Meaning what? You can march in a straight line as you make your way to the local tavern?" She placed her fingers on the bridge of his nose. The throbbing began to subside. "Dance will require another kind of discipline from you, another kind of courage."

"The courage to do what? Wear sparkly tights?"

"To get in touch with your feelings."

Pyro let out a groan and rolled his eyes.

"Listen to me!" She snapped her fingers. "The circus needs performers, dedicated ones, and I'm not about to let you walk away! Besides, you need help."

"Just what is it about me that screams helpless to you?"

Sonata looked at him as though this were a stupid question. "Pyro, you were drunk during our performance! What's more, you're not fooling anyone! It's obvious you want to change! What harm would it do you to talk about it?"

She was looking at him with intense yet considerate eyes. She wasn't going to leave until she got what she wanted so he might as well give in.

He lowered his head and grumbled. "I just wanna be who these kids think I am."

"I'm sorry, what was that?"

Pyro ground his jaw tighter. "I just wanna be who these kids think I am."

"You're mumbling."

Weary of repeating himself, Pyro burst out all at once. "Oh, for the love of shrapnel! I just wanna be the person the kids I rescue think I am! They all think I'm this great hero or something! Then they see me completely blotto at a restaurant getting taken in by the police! Is that what you wanted to hear? Will you quit bullying me now?"

"That really happened?"

He passed his hand over his face. "Look, when I started rescuing kids, I never saw myself as a role model. I didn't think kids would know any better—about the stuff I got up to, I mean." He cringed. "I'll never forget the look on that kid's face when they escorted me out the door."

They sat together in silence for a moment or two.

"I think it's perfectly admirable that you want to do better." Sonata paused. "But you can't do it alone. We can't keep cycling through performers, so I'm willing to help you. And remember, I am an empath so I do know a thing or two about comforting people."

Pyro sneered at her and rolled his eyes.

She looked down at his foot. "How are your toes?"

"Broken probably."

Pyro watched in shock as she began untying his shoe with all the authority of a seasoned nurse. She smirked.

"Let's not be dramatic."

Pyro flinched with surprise as she actually put her hands on his injured foot and healed his pain.

"There. Good as new. Now if you'll just lie back, I'll take a look at your abdomen."

Pyro crossed his arms over his stomach. "It don't need looking at!"

Sonata rolled her eyes and pushed him down. "Oh, for heaven's sake! Just lie back!"

Pyro begrudgingly did as told. The moment she lifted his shirt and put her bare hand against his stomach, every hair on Pyro's body tensed.

"There?" she asked, avoiding his gaze.

Pyro cleared his throat. "Uh, a little higher actually."

"Are you sure? You feel a bit tight there."

Pyro craned his head up. "That would be muscle."

"Oh." Sonata's eyes flicked curiously towards his stomach. He could've sworn she was blushing, but it was difficult to tell in the dark. "You, um … I forget you're quite … muscly."

Her cool fingers wandered up his skin to the bruise. Pyro gave a slight wince.

"There?"

He nodded. "There."

"Now, I'll make a deal with you." She laid her palm flat against his stomach, letting her powers sink into his flesh until the throbbing pain was overpowered. "I won't tell Staccato you've been drinking if you promise to come to me every time you feel the urge to self-medicate."

"And do what exactly?"

"Whatever you like. We'll go for a walk. Play a game. Practice our routine. That doesn't sound so bad, does it?"

Pyro flashed her a look.

"Do you want to make progress or not? Because you're never going to return to the battlefield unless you can prove to everyone you can handle the responsibility."

He took one long look at Sonata and sighed. "Alright, fine."

Sonata gave a curt nod. "Good."

Pyro glanced down at her hand. She had yet to remove it from his abdomen despite having finished quite some time ago.

"Uh, Sonata?"

"Hm?"

He cocked an eyebrow. "You done?"

Sonata's eyes stretched to a new width, as she became aware of herself.

"Oh, um, yes!" She withdrew her hand, but not without letting her fingers "accidentally" trail over the remainder of his muscles.

The grass rolled and bulged beside them as a flowering tree materialized out of nowhere, startling them so much they both gave a shriek. The tree untwisted its trunk, revealing Lavanda in a dark cloak and veil.

"Oh! Oh my! Do forgive me!"

Pyro sat up. "Madame Raíz?"

She peeled back the veil. "My apologies, I did not see you there." Her eyes glided over their bodies huddled together on the ground. "I, uh, I do hope I'm not interrupting anything."

"What?" Sonata wrenched her nose up and instinctively scuttled away from Pyro. "I mean, of course not, Madame!" She rose and dusted herself off. "What brings you to this side of the camp so late at night?"

Pyro checked his watch. "Yeah, it's nearly midnight."

Lavanda's gaze drifted from one side of the valley to the other. "I was just on my way to your tent." She pulled a wrapped package from the inner folds of her shawl. "I have a gift for you, you see, to express my appreciation for your performance."

Pyro leaned over Sonata's shoulder for a better look. Lavanda had tied the twine of the parcel in such a way that she had formed the sign of the Pleiades.

"Let Mr. Nimbus see it before you open it." She lowered her chin, imparting a meaningful look with her eyes. "You understand?"

Sonata returned her gaze with solemnity. "We understand."

"Good, for its care requires very specific … *instruction*." She spoke no further but winked and let her veil fall once more. Pyro and Sonata watched in wonder and caution as she sank into the grass, and became a moving patch of flowers traveling away into the shadows.

"It's the sign of the Pleiades," whispered Pyro.

"I know. It's the symbol of the Fay." She held the package close to her chest. "We should wake Staccato."

Pyro and Sonata dashed back to the tent. Pyro turned the dial on a lamp, while Sonata jostled Staccato's shoulder.

"Staccato! Staccato, wake up! We have something we need you to look at!"

Staccato lifted his head and winced at the glare. "What is it, dearest?"

Skelter and Melodious stirred in their cots at the noise. Sonata handed Staccato the package with the knot side up.

"Madame Raíz came by and delivered this."

Staccato blinked the sleep from his eyes and gave her a baffled look. "Just now?"

"Yes! Just now. She wanted you to look at it before we opened it. I'm sure she wanted you to see this." She indicated to the sign of the Pleiades.

"What is it?" inquired Melodious, sitting up in his bed.

"It's a package," Pyro explained.

Staccato unraveled the twine, peeled back the paper, and opened the box. Inside was a poem framed by an oddly shaped, colorful sketch of various herbs and wildflowers. It was an odd assortment of herbage, and the colors were not well matched.

> *A Recipe for Guidance*
> *Family Proverb*
> *Instruction and knowledge can always be found*
> *Where festivity, substance, and virtue abound*
> *Start with caution at the serpent's knot*
> *And west of truth to hostile thoughts*
> *Humility is a place where trials are sternest*
> *But pursuing wisdom will make you earnest*

Pyro leaned back and scratched his chin. "Well, if that thing's not a bloody clue then that's the ugliest flower sketch and the weirdest poem I've ever seen."

Pyro's remark was all the permission needed for Skelter and Melodious to get up from their cots and begin asking questions. Skelter mimed peering through a magnifying glass.

"Well, of course it's a secret code!" Staccato bristled.

Sonata took the paper and pointed to the sketch. "Think of the poem as just one piece of the puzzle. Lavanda wouldn't just draw an arbitrary arrangement of flowers to go along with it unless they too had meaning." She wrinkled her nose. "Especially not one this ugly."

"Are you certain of this?" inquired Melodious.

"There's an art to codes and hidden messages," said Staccato. "I believe the flowers shown are meant to act as a sort of key to understanding the poem."

Chapter 21:
Summer Vacation

The first day of summer vacation was received with celebratory jubilation as boys ran up and down the sidewalk stripped down to their dirty shirtfronts, and a gathering of little girls danced beneath a busted fire hydrant like an urbanized rendition of a Fragonard painting.

In New York City, the Junes were fresh and light like a crisp linen sheet over a bed of cool grass laid out for stargazing. Even in the steel jungle that was the Lower East Side, children could still enjoy camping. With a few sheets thrown strategically over the top, fire escapes were transformed into tents, sometimes even palaces or fortresses.

Across the street from Pasha, two neighboring platforms were at war with one another, each manned by a high-ranking general heavily decorated with epaulettes of shredded newspaper and various pasteboard medals commemorating the Great Hobby Horse Charge of 1917. Pasha would often watch from his window as one after another the adversaries fired a salvo of pop guns at each other and, clutching their chests, died with grace and dignity, only to resurrect themselves a moment later and fire another round.

When Pasha had washed and dressed, he left Katya playing with her stuffed animals and ventured out to run the morning errands. No sooner had he set foot outside the building than a loud car horn just a few feet away roared in his direction. He jumped and turned around. Parked in front of Uncle Matvei's liquor store was a brand new delivery van, and sitting in the driver's seat was Leo with Faina on his knee. Uncle Matvei and Anya were standing on the sidewalk, all of them giggling.

"Good morning, Pasha," called Faina from the driver's window.

Pasha smiled and shook his head as he made his way over to the front of Uncle Matvei's establishment.

"Don't tell me your uncle is going to let you drive that thing?" he teased Faina.

Leo rolled his eyes comically. "Don't give her any ideas."

Mr. Dalka chuckled as he reached up and ruffled Faina's pigtails. "I don't think driving a delivery truck is a task we need to put you up to anytime soon." He reached into the driver's side and lifted her from underneath her arms.

"But Leo gets to learn," she rejoined as her uncle set her back on the sidewalk.

"I sure do! Business is booming these days, ain't it, Uncle Matvei?" Every day, Leo's accent was growing more and more urbanized, Faina's too—though at a slower pace. He swung himself out of the van and Uncle Matvei patted him on the shoulder.

"That's right, my boy! Not only are we extending our delivery service uptown, but," he turned to Pasha, "wait until you see this!" From his pocket he pulled out a thick, folded piece of paper, and with Anya's help smoothed it out over the hood of the car. Faina hopped up and down beside Pasha.

"Well, what do you think?"

It took Pasha a moment before he realized what he was looking at. "They're blueprints!"

"That's right!" Uncle Matvei rolled the paper up into a neat little coil. "I've finally saved enough money to open a second location in Midtown! *Opa!* is expanding!"

"That's great, Mr. Dalka! I'm sure it will be a great success!"

"From your mouth to God's ear, my boy!" He patted Faina forward. "Well, Faina, you and Pasha better get going on your errands. You don't want to have to fight the crowds."

Pasha held out his arm for Faina and bowed to her like a gentleman. "Shall we, my lady?"

Mimicking an affected accent, Faina took his arm and replied, "We shall."

Leo and Uncle Matvei exchanged amused glances as Leo patted them along.

"Alright, Mr. and Mrs. Goofball, I hope you don't mind me tagging along for a bit." He opened the rear door, reached into the back of the van, and produced a new Kodak Brownie.

"Leo is hoping he can incorporate some photography into the school paper next year," noted Faina.

"And with any luck I'll have had some good practice over the summer." He wiped the lens with the tail of his shirt and motioned them forward. "The camera's easy enough to use. Now all I gotta do is get some talent. Come on you two, let's get a move on."

With their grocery lists in hand, they made their way past various kiosks and little old women hawking goods.

"It sounds like working for the Breadwinners has really worked out for you," observed Pasha.

Leo wound the key on the side of the box. "I'd say so, yeah."

"Do you like working for them?"

Leo glanced nervously at him, and for a moment Pasha feared he may have tread on a sensitive subject, but Leo sighed, then gave something of a smile.

"I appreciate everything Klokov has done for me, and I have a lot to be grateful for. But I can't exactly say that I enjoy stealing. Sometimes it's not so bad if the fella I'm pinching from had it coming. But most of the time they're just regular people trying to earn a buck, like me. I wouldn't mind breaking the law if it was a stupid law that I thought ought to be broken. But that's wishing for a lot." He sighed and drew his hands over his head in a stretch. "It's like the Breadwinners say, sometimes a man has to do hard things to make a better world for his family and his children."

"That's how all the big, successful American giants think."

Leo glanced down at Pasha and smirked. "Oh, yeah, I forgot. Faina tells me you're going to be the next Vanderbilt, or Rockefeller, or whatever."

To think that Faina had referred to him in such a way made Pasha beam. "That's right!"

"In that case, I better stick close to you, huh?" Leo put his eye through the viewer and, making a face, set about cleaning the glass with his shirt cloth again. Pasha took his handkerchief from his pocket and handed it to Leo.

"Here, try this."

"Thanks, kid." As Leo glanced down at the characters on the material, he raised an eyebrow. "Hey, Pasha, what's with all the initials? You got five middle names or something?"

Pasha folded his hands behind his back pleasantly. "No, just two."

Pasha jumped as Faina let out a gasp and hopped excitedly on her toes.

"You mean you have a middle name? Oh, I wish I had a middle name! Anya has a middle name, and I'm so jealous. You're so lucky!"

Leo scratched his head. "Okay, so I get why Anya has a middle name. But if both your parents were from Russia, then how did you get one?"

"Because my mother has one. Her father was English. Anyway, she wanted me to be named after him so she gave me a middle name. After that I guess she liked it so much that she decided to give me another one. But it's not on any of my American records. Mama thought it might complicate the immigration process. She left her's out too."

Faina was nearly bursting. "So, what are they? What are your middle names?"

"David, Nicholas."

Faina sighed as though it were a lovely name and Pasha was the luckiest person on the planet to have been blessed with it.

"If I had a middle name, I would want it to be Mae."

Leo scanned her over with his eyelids half lowered.

"Why Mae? It's not exactly glamorous. Wouldn't you rather be named after some actress or something?"

"Well, what about Mae Dix?"

Leo rubbed the heels of his hands over his temples and groaned. "Of course. Why am I not surprised?"

Pasha glanced curiously between the both of them. "Who is Mae Dix?"

Faina was all too eager to explain. "Mae Dix is a—"

"A dancer!" Leo interjected, slamming a hand over her mouth. "Mae Dix is a dancer." He arched his neck towards the clouds. "God help this child."

"What kind of dancer?"

Leo forced himself between them. "The special kind. She is a very special kind of dancer, and that's all you need to know."

As Leo stopped to say hello to a friend from school, Pasha sidled closer to Faina.

"Do you like dancing, Faina?"

Faina looked at him with wide, innocent eyes as though it were the strangest question she had ever heard. "Doesn't everyone like dancing?"

"I could dance with you if you like."

A sly glimmer slipped into Faina's smile.

"I see, and if I danced with you then I might want to kiss you."

Pasha shrugged as though it had been entirely Faina's suggestion. "Well, if you insist."

He leaned towards her hopefully, but Faina placed her fingers over his lips.

"Listen, doll, I only kiss boys I steal from." And with that she dusted her hands, turned on her heel, and walked on. Leo appeared by his side looking both impressed and somewhat frightened.

165

"Boy, you're one smooth little sap, aren't you?"

Pasha merely shrugged. "I don't get it. When I first met Faina I thought she had a crush on me. But when I told her I liked her she started acting like she didn't."

Leo threw back his head and laughed. "Don't take it so personally, kid. Some girls like playing hard to get. And my sister is one of them."

"So what do I do?"

"Don't make it so easy for her."

"What do you mean?"

"I mean don't try so hard. Pretend you like someone else for a while. Trust me, as soon as Faina thinks you're not paying attention to her, she'll fawn all over you."

Pasha looked sheepishly down at the ground. To him it seemed almost cruel, childish even. "I don't know. I'm not really sure that's my style."

Leo shrugged. "Suit yourself, kid."

They hurried to catch up with Faina, who was making a fuss over an enormous yellow sunflower at a florist cart.

"I love sunflowers! They're my favorite! It's the most beautiful, most ginormous flower I have ever seen in my entire life!"

Leo tugged her along. "Quit lagging, Faina, we gotta get to the butcher's."

"But Leo, look at it! Look how huge it is! It's as big as my face!"

"Yes, I see."

"No you don't, you're not looking!"

"Faina, we don't need flowers!"

The young lady managing the kiosk emerged from behind a pot of hydrangeas. Leo froze like a toy soldier in need of winding up.

She was a slender girl with a brown complexion and such an abundance of thick, brown hair that the humidity of a thousand New York City Julys could not have flattened it a single centimeter. Her protuberant eyes, as black as sunflower seeds, seemed to sink open and take up half her face. And she had a long, elegant neck that looked as though it were fashioned to model expensive diamond necklaces.

"I mean, we don't need flowers that will overwhelm the dinner table!" Leo chuckled awkwardly as he met her self-assured gaze. "But we do need flowers! Lots and lots of flowers!" Leo was grinning now, but unfortunately a customer needed the girl's attention and she turned away. Faina tugged on Leo's sleeve.

"You're wasting your time, Leo."

Leo looked down at her, slightly offended. "Excuse me? What do you mean I'm wasting my time?"

"That is Syreeta Zureiq's older sister, Jazmin. One of their older brothers got caught up with the Bowery Butchers and went to jail. Now the family won't have anything to do with suspected gang members. They won't even enter a tenement if they suspect it's owned by a gang member."

"Yeah? Well, since when am I a gang member?"

"You work for the Breadwinners!"

"As an associate!"

"Were you listening to a thing I just said?"

Leo waved his hand. "I'm surprised at you, Faina, since when are you such a wet blanket?"

"Since I have to smother out the fire of your stupidity."

But Leo was already removing his cap and smoothing back his hair.

"That's, uh, that's quite a big sunflower you got there," he said when Jazmin turned around.

Pasha had to stifle his laughter while Faina rolled her eyes. "Nice opening line, genius."

Jazmin sank her teeth into her bottom lip and glanced down at the sunflower, unsure of what to say. Leo began cracking his knuckles.

"So, uh, how do you get them that big? Is it, like, an old family secret or something?"

Pasha and Faina could hardly keep themselves together as they watched Leo flounder. Jazmin blinked her eyes, then smiled.

"No, not really. In my family we're just good at making things grow, I suppose."

"Ah, I see. Natural talent. You look like someone who has natural talent." He rubbed the back of his neck nervously. "You know, my Ma always said you could tell a gardener by her hands."

Jazmin laughed as she held up her fingers. "Probably because they are always cut up and dirty."

"No, no, you have beautiful hands." He reached out and stopped. "May I?"

Jazmin swiveled her head over her shoulder, fingering the button at her collar. "Um." She forced a smile and tentatively held out her fingers. "Alright."

Gently, Leo took her hand in his. "See? Look at that! Long, beautiful fingers. Picture perfect. Why, you would make a swell hand model!"

Jazmin withdrew her hand, a bemused simper crinkling up her eyes.

"A hand model? They have those?"

"Well, of course! You know, like the girls who hold up perfume in advertisements."

Leo mustered his most comical, feminine expression and pantomimed holding a perfume bottle with his pinky extended daintily outwards. Jazmin threw back her head and laughed. It was clear where Leo's strength lay.

"You're quite the comedian! You should try out for Vaudeville."

He fumbled for his camera. "Actually, I'm more of a photographer myself, or at least I'm trying to be. You should let me take your picture sometime. Your hands would be an excellent subject."

"You would want to photograph my hands?"

Leo's shoulders stiffened as he struggled to maintain an appearance of confidence.

"I—I'd love to photograph any part of your body." His mouth fell open and his cheeks colored as he realized his words had not come out as he'd intended. "That is, uh, I mean you're really pretty."

Jazmin must have understood he meant no harm, for she covered her mouth and laughed into her hand.

"What's your name?"

"Uh—"

"It's Leontiy," Faina reminded him with a swift jab at his toe. Leo smothered her behind his back, pretending he hadn't heard her.

"Leontiy Spichkin, but you can call me Leo."

She reached across the cart and placed her cut hands with the broad palms and long fingers in his once more.

"Jazmin Zureiq."

Faina tugged on Leo's braces.

"Leo, we have to go pick up the beef from the butcher's."

Leo grabbed Faina's wrist so she'd stop pulling on him and gritted his teeth together.

"Alright, alright, I'm coming." He nodded adoringly at Jazmin. "It was lovely to have met you, Jazmin."

Chapter 22:

Earnest

"Oh! Pyro! Pyro! Try *Vance's Volume of Verd Vocabulary*!" hollered Sonata, seated at the desk below which had become overcrowded with books.

Pyro clung to the bookshelf ladder and craned his head back, scanning the spines for any such title. They'd been back in Ascella only a day, but as soon as breakfast was over they had headed to the library to research Lavanda's clue.

Like most rooms in Feifior, the library was chaotic with its own unique hazards. In truth, it was more suited to rock climbing than to reading, with floor-to-ceiling shelves that, for some reason, did not end at the domed ceiling but curled inward at a forty-degree angle, making it so the books had to sit behind a ledge to keep from falling out. The freestanding shelves were no less structurally baffling, some as tall as twenty-five feet with crooked ladders that were often too short.

Pyro snatched the title from the Vs, and scaled his way back down. Meanwhile, Staccato repeated the poem.

> *"Instruction and knowledge can always be found*
> *Where festivity, substance, and virtue abound*
> *Start with caution at the serpent's knot*
> *And west of truth to hostile thoughts*
> *Humility is a place where trials are sternest*
> *But pursuing wisdom will make you earnest."*

"I seem to recall bluebells being used as a symbol for humility in my day," said Melodious, leaning over the table. He wasn't able to do any of the reading, so he made himself useful by offering helpful hints. "However, interpretations may be different outside of Germany."

Skelter, who was seated atop the desk where Sonata was working, turned around the book he was reading to point to a picture of a Lily of the Valley. The caption read, "Humility."

Staccato bent over the poem and stroked his beard.

"One moment. You can put away that book, Pyro. I'm afraid you won't be needing it."

Sonata looked surprised. "Why? What's the harm in checking?"

Staccato shook his finger, never taking his eyes off the illustration. "I'm afraid you've made this far more complicated than necessary. Madame Raíz has already supplied us with the answers we seek." He pointed to the sage. "Here's wisdom." He drew a line to the oleander. "And that's caution. Yes, I'd say one should have plenty of caution indeed when handling this poisonous flower! Festivity … ah! Parsley! Skelter, double check me on that one if you would, please."

Pyro dropped down in a backwards chair and leaned his chin on the backrest. "How do you know all this?"

"*The Language of Flowers* was all the rage when I was young. I'd argue it was almost essential for a man in those days—send your sweetheart an arrangement at random, and you could receive a slap in the face!"

Melodious chuckled. "You must have sent an impressive amount of bouquets to be so knowledgeable!"

Staccato scoffed. "If that were true, I wouldn't be here."

Sonata leaned over the table, biting her lip mischievously.

"Don't be modest, Staccato!" Sonata sank her teeth into her smile as she always did when she teased someone. "I've heard you're quite the expert when it comes to bouquets of the tropical variety."

Staccato glanced up with a warning look that would've made Pyro cower. Sonata, however, merely smiled.

After referencing one or two books, they were able to confirm Staccato's theory. Parsley represented festivity, oregano was substance, mint was virtue. Oleander was caution. Only one translation existed for hostile thoughts and that was tansy. Humility was sweet woodruff, and sage, of course, was wisdom.

Skelter put his hand over his mouth with a wrinkled brow and pointed to the word "earnest."

"He's right." Sonata consulted her notepad where she'd matched a virtue to each flower in the wreath. "Ordinarily earnestness is represented by hyacinth or hydrangea, but there is no such flower present."

"And what about knowledge and instruction?" posed Melodious.

Pyro tipped his chair forward for a better look. "I thought 'serpent's knot' was a flower. Am I wrong?"

Staccato rolled up his sleeves. "Now we come to the real riddle." He paced before the table, tapping the head of his staff to his lips. "Best to take this one word at a time. We'll start with instruction."

Skelter made a face at them, as though the answer were obvious. He curved his hands around an imaginary jar.

"More than likely, yes." Staccato signaled for Sonata to write that down. "For now let's assume instruction means instructions for carrying the Jar."

Sonata looked up from the notepad. "And knowledge?"

Pyro tapped a pencil on the back of the chair. "Could mean the same as instruction. Could mean something different."

"Perhaps knowledge is used to describe the location of the instructions," suggested Melodious.

"So where are all the places knowledge can be found?"

Skelter gestured to the surrounding bookshelves.

"Library!" Sonata added it to the list.

Pyro raised his hand, accidentally knocking over the pencil. "Museum!"

"University," volunteered Staccato.

Melodious began to offer another suggestion, but paused and knit his eyebrows together.

"But what sort of place offers knowledge *and* is also known for its festivity, substance, and virtue?"

Pyro groaned and passed his hands over his face. "None of the places we just mentioned."

While the others continued to brainstorm, Pyro slipped away into his thoughts. There had to be another way to find those instructions! If Lavanda's clue proved useless they would need a backup plan. According to Cassia, the leading expert on the Jar of Elijah was a professor named Dr. Desmond. Perhaps she had written some books that might help them. Careful not to disturb the others, Pyro snuck over to the ancient history section. His eyes scanned the Ds.

Delaney ... DeSirena ... Desellerando ... Desmond! Pyro plucked a book bound in scarlet leather from the shelf and opened to the title page.

Artifacts of the Ancient Hinterlands by Dr. Ernestine Desmond

He flipped to the back of the book where a brief paragraph about the author had been placed.

Dr. Ernestine Desmond received her Master's in archaeology from Elgafar University in Virgo. She currently holds the title of Professor of Antiquities at the Institute for Enchanted Archaeology in Spica.

Pyro slammed the book shut.

"It's Dr. Desmond!" He dashed over to the table. "Lavanda wants us to find Dr. Desmond!"

Staccato raised his head. "What?"

Pyro held up the title page and pointed to Dr. Desmond's first name. "*Earnest* means Ernestine! Dr. Ernestine Desmond! Cassia said she's the leading expert on the Jar of Elijah! That's why the C.O.N. kidnapped her in the first place!"

Staccato grabbed the book and flipped curiously through the pages. "Great northern star, I believe he's right."

"According to Cassia, Dr. Desmond knows the instructions for carrying the Jar."

Staccato placed the book on the table. "We have our object. Now we need only to deduce where they're keeping her. I think it's safe to assume that she's being held in Draconian-occupied territory."

Pyro retrieved the rolled-up map from the edge of the table and unfurled it before the firelight. All the Draconian territories had been shaded in red.

"It's like an entirely new riddle altogether." Sonata stepped away, shaking her head. "How can concepts like truth, festivity, and substance point us to a place on a map?"

Chapter 23:

Aunt Poppy's Bail

"Do you realize how much of an inconvenience your actions have caused me?" Staccato's voice rose, plowing through the thin walls of Aunt Poppy's tenement. "Defacing a sewage truck for dumping in the East River! What did you think would happen?"

Aunt Poppy sat before the window with her arms crossed and her owlish glasses sitting on the end of her curved nose. The stifling August air did little to ease the tension, but it would have been imprudent to leave the window open during such a heated argument.

"We have got to do something to protect our Fay communities! As a volunteer for the Home Sweet Home Society for Volerian Immigrants, I have a duty!" She jabbed a self-righteous finger in the air. "With so many mermaids migrating to New York to escape the C.O.N., it is imperative we keep our waterways clean for their safety and well-being! Do you realize how polluted that water has become?"

Staccato stared back at her in disbelief. "I don't care how polluted the river is! If you're going to live in the Other then you can't interfere!"

It was midmorning, and outside the daylight was fresh and broad. Children darted about the streets savoring the final breaths of summer vacation. Under normal circumstances, Staccato would never have visited Orchard Street at such a crowded time of year. Aunt Poppy was right, Europeans weren't the only immigrants entering New York City. Thousands were fleeing to the Other as the C.O.N. advanced across the River Valley, and they would continue to do so until the resistance could restore the Jar of Elijah.

Several months had passed and no one had been able to decode Lavanda's cryptic message. Thayer had tried to organize a hunt for Dr. Desmond, but there was little to go on. To make matters worse, Sobek's unit had finally received its marching orders. They would be leaving Virgo any day now and no one had any idea which way they were headed.

Staccato was beginning to suspect Pyro was right: the clue could have endless interpretations, whereas a proper code should only have one. Despite her best intentions, Madame Raíz's attempts to assist them had fallen short due to lack of expertise.

"I can't interfere?" echoed Aunt Poppy. "Then what do you call all those years of unicorn conservation in Lake Baikal?"

"That's different, and you know it! This is Manhattan, not Siberia! If you act out here people will notice! And they *have* noticed! This is the second time I've received a letter from the New York Department of Fay Security. One more strike and I'll have to appear in person before the VIPA on your account!" (The VIPA being the Voilerian Immigration Protection Agency.) "You realize they can deport you for this?"

"What kind of person sees something terrible happening but chooses to do nothing?"

Staccato placed his hands on his hips. "You want to help the immigrant community? Stay quiet! You are doing more harm than good when you risk the exposure of the Fay! The Other lives in a post-magic society! Things aren't like they used to be! It's dangerous, it's devious, it's dark, and if you're not careful Voiler will end up just the same way!"

"It's dangerous, it's devious, it's dark, and yet you let your daughter and grandchildren go about their lives in it, never knowing that there's some place better they could be! Do you know what they are being made to suffer?"

Staccato's countenance grew dark. He lowered his voice to a dangerous tone.

"This is not about Lydia—"

"You are right about one thing, Staccato, the Other is a hostile place for Fay! And no one should be made to live here when they don't have to!"

"*I said enough*!" Staccato stabbed his staff upon the floor, causing the frames on the wall to shake. "If things are that bad, then why are you here? Hm?"

Aunt Poppy's shoulders shriveled up around her ears. "I can't afford to live in Voiler. My account is under water."

"Oh, now don't you give me that! You know arrangements could be made!"

Her mouth wrinkled with a proud sneer. "I don't wish to live off your charity!"

"Oh, you don't, do you?" This made Staccato laugh aloud. "Who has repaid Mr. Dalka one hundred forty dollars in bail the past three years? Who is paying for your rent, your medication, medical bills? You are sixty-five years old, single, too old to work, and as you pointed out, you're currently unable to access your retirement due to the Land Lock. You have no choice but to let me take care of you. That being said, *you don't have to live here*! No, Madame. I'm no fool! Things must be awfully bad for a naturalist of all people to haul herself up in a two-room apartment in one of the most overcrowded metropolises in the world with three chickens, two cats, and not a blade of grass to call her own! You're afraid of returning to Voiler, and understandably so, so don't you preach to me about Lydia! But if you want to stay here, you have to follow the rules! I cannot afford to keep bailing you out of jail!"

Aunt Poppy turned away from him, crossing her arms like a petulant child. Staccato sighed and threw out his hands.

"At the very least think of your poor landlord, and how generous he has been to bail you out five times now! And in these troubling times!"

Her eyes darted towards him before hastily retreating back to the window. Staccato folded his arms across his chest with a secret air of triumph. Aunt Poppy exhaled through the corner of her mouth and raised her arms in capitulation.

"Alright, fine! You have me cornered! Are you happy now?"

Staccato sat down in the chair adjacent to hers. "'Happy' is not the word I would have used. Relieved would be a more accurate description." He stopped, making a conscious attempt to soften his tone. "I cannot be called out here again, do you understand? If the resistance can find a way to retrieve that Jar then perhaps the Fay won't feel the need to flee Voiler for their own safety. That's what you want, isn't it? You said you were concerned about the Fay community in New York."

Aunt Poppy craned her head back and removed her glasses. "Things can't possibly get any worse." She dipped her chin forward and spoke in a whisper. "Have you heard the rumors about a gang of Primals showing up in the Bronx a month ago?"

"No."

Aunt Poppy glanced suspiciously out the window before huddling closer. "The police uncovered a minor prostitution ring operating out of an old boardinghouse on Brook Avenue. It was awful! The workers had been sold into slavery by another gang, but no one would say which."

"Those poor women."

"It wasn't just women, it never is. There were men who had been forced into it as well, most very young. They said the victims had surgical-like cuts in various places all over their bodies, in addition to bite marks. It is whispered amongst the Fay that it was really a den of *saignants*."

"Well, what did the victims say? Surely, they would have reported their captors to the underground?"

"That's just it. No one has said anything. It's all being kept very secret, and the victims are too afraid to say anything, as it often goes."

"Whatever happened to the gang?"

"Disappeared without a trace."

Staccato leaned back in his chair with a thoughtful expression. They were just rumors really, but they weren't far-fetched. After all, Primals sought the destruction of all magic; they thrived in a world like the Other. An underground community of Fay immigrants in a post-magic society attracted Primals the way a population of rats would attract snakes.

"All the more reason for you to quit drawing attention to yourself," he at last said.

Aunt Poppy rolled her eyes. "And we're back to the arrest!"

Staccato patted her knee and made his way to the door. "I don't want anything happening to you. You are my favorite aunt, you know."

"Which means nothing when you consider what I have to compete with!"

"My, my! That was catty even for you, Aunt! Did someone forget to take her pills this morning?"

This was enough to get her back on her feet and shooing him out the door. "Oh, go give Matvei his check, and get back to work!"

Staccato chuckled as she pushed him out into the hallway.

"Love you too, Aunt."

He made his way down the stairs and hesitated at the front door. He flicked his eyes towards Pasha's empty bedroom window. There was no easy way of discerning whether or not his grandchildren might pop into Mr. Dalka's shop, not that they would have known him, of course. He stepped out onto the stoop, pulling his hat low over his brow, and made his way out of the courtyard.

From the window he could see Mr. Dalka standing behind the register, polishing the counter while his nephew stocked shelves. There was no one else present. Staccato turned the handle and let himself inside. The bell on the door rang, prompting Mr. Dalka to look up and smile.

"Mr. K.!" He made his way out from behind the counter and approached Staccato. Already he was raising a hand to plant on Staccato's shoulder while the other lunged forward for a heartfelt handshake. "It is so good to see you again! How long has it been?"

177

Staccato tried his best to not appear tense but could only manage a polite smile.

"Quite some time, I'm afraid. Though I do wish it were under different circumstances."

Mr. Dalka gestured to his elbow, a look of concern gathering on his forehead.

"How is your injury? Has it improved any?"

He waited for Staccato's answer with his hands on his hips, leaning slightly forward. Staccato hesitated, caught off guard by the question. Mr. Dalka was one of those rare people who never forgot a face, who listened to every stranger's problem with genuine interest, and who could always be counted upon to ask about it later. In short, the last type of person he wished to run into in a place like New York City when he was trying not to draw attention to himself.

"It's um … much better, actually. Thank you for asking." Staccato cleared his throat. "I hear my aunt has been causing you trouble again."

Uncle Matvei waved his hand and chuckled. "Aunt Poppy is never a trouble, I assure you! Why, she is like family to us! Isn't that right, Leo?"

Leo picked up his empty crate and made his way towards the back room.

"My sister likes to have tea with her practically every week."

"So I've heard." Staccato removed his hat and spun it in his hand. "She appreciates the company." He turned towards the counter. "Now, how much do I owe you?" He reached for his checkbook only to realize he had grabbed his notepad instead. He retrieved his checkbook from his pocket and bent over the counter.

"Eighteen."

Staccato paused with the pen in his hand and looked up at Mr. Dalka with a raised eyebrow.

"Eighteen? Are you sure it wasn't more?"

Mr. Dalka shrugged his shoulders as though he didn't know what Staccato was talking about. "Eighteen was what I was told."

Staccato smiled. "Remember, if you won't tell me my aunt will. Are you certain it was only eighteen?"

"It was eighteen."

Leo reappeared in the doorway with a bottle of lemonade.

"Leo, how much was Ms. Potemkin's bail?"

"Twenty-eight dollars."

Staccato raised his pen triumphantly. "Aha! While I appreciate your generosity, Mr. Dalka, you needn't burden yourself with my aunt's debts."

Leo took a swig of his lemonade and wiped his mouth on his sleeve.

"You know, if you like constellations, I hear upstate is a great place for stargazing."

"Hm?" Staccato finished signing his name and glanced up from the checkbook in confusion. Leo gestured to the open notepad at his elbow.

"Uh, sorry. I don't mean to pry. I just noticed you have Ophiuchus drawn in your notepad. It's a constellation."

Staccato looked back at the notebook where earlier he had jotted down a sketch of the strange shape formed by Madame Raíz's wreath of flowers. Staccato shot up. He held the drawing to the light, turning it this way and that.

"Is that what that is?"

"Yeah, I mean … that's what it looks like anyway."

"Show me."

Leo gestured to the triangular point. "There's the head. That's where the star Rasalhague would be." He traced a line to the second bend on the right side. "There's Marfic, or where his elbow would be."

Staccato lowered the notebook and looked back at the boy in astonishment.

"How do you know all this?"

"My dad was really into astronomy and insisted my sister and I have a knowledge of the constellations. You would have thought knowing the stars was as important as knowing our ABCs."

Staccato studied the drawing in wonder. With a constellation stamped on the flag of every nation in Voiler it seemed impossible that they had missed it, and yet he understood why. While Aries bore the asterism of Aries, and Pisces bore the stars of Pisces, Ophiuchus was not its own nation, it was an exclave of Taurus and thus did not have its own flag. Voilerians had their own asterisms separate from the Other, and only came across their own constellations in matters of geography. Therefore, only a cartographer or a native of Taurus would have been likely to notice. And when hidden in a drawing of flowers? He couldn't beat himself up too badly. He ripped the check from the sheaf and handed it to Mr. Dalka.

"I'm afraid I have to dash." He seized Leo by the hand and tipped his hat. "Young man, you have no idea how grateful I am for your assistance. Thank you once again, Mr. Dalka, and do let me know if she gets up to any more trouble!"

And with that, he headed out the door, leaving Mr. Dalka and his nephew standing bewildered at the counter.

Chapter 24:

The Cat Comes Out of the Bag

Faina already had low expectations when it came to her first day of real school, for the feeling of being an outsider transcends language, knows no race, and holds allegiance to no particular nation. It is decidedly and tragically universal. And Faina knew without ever having spoken a word of English to her classmates, that her troubles would be no different in America than they had been in Russia. Her one semester of English lessons had done little to alter her expectations.

As Faina crossed the narrow threshold of her classroom, a dozen eyes drew from every direction to focus their attention on the girl who had once called herself the Kissing Cat Burglar. Faina swallowed and forced the muscles in her lips to draw up in a smile. A handful of girls returned the gesture. The rest did not.

The cold hard blackboard across the room reminded Faina of a headstone. The seat of her desk was hard and uncomfortable. Her eyes circled around the room, taking in her fellow students who, after a summer apart, had returned to school still looking like little girls, unlike Faina.

She was not the oldest of her class, but already she was on her way to being the tallest. The hair on her arms and upper lip had darkened and thickened. Her nose, though prominent, had never seemed disproportionate until now. Hunching slightly, she decided to drop her books on the desk. No sooner had she done this than whispers and giggles began to materialize in pockets all around her.

The teacher struck the edge of her desk with a thin, wooden rod, commanding their attention to the front of the room. She was a petite, thin-lipped woman of about thirty with a face most would have considered pretty, and yet there was something mean looking about her that was difficult to place, and Faina knew immediately that they were not going to see eye to eye.

"Quiet! Quiet, I say! That's enough whispering from you, Miss Wozniak." She took several stiff steps to the front of her desk and faced the room. "We don't usually bother with introductions, as the majority of you know each other from the previous year. However, we have a new student joining us this semester." Her eyes settled coldly on Faina. "Miss Spichkin."

Faina looked up at her and swallowed.

"Stand. State your name."

Faina did as told, nervously smoothing her skirts over her knees. "Faina Spichkin."

Ms. Ballard—for that was her name, Ms. Ballard—went about studying her in what Faina would learn was her characteristic unsmiling way. "Not many of you know Miss Spichkin, though several of your male classmates are quite familiar with her."

Faina's eyes bulged as several of the other girls snorted and giggled into their hands. Her head dropped to her chest as she felt her cheeks beginning to burn.

"Look up, Miss Spichkin!" Ms. Ballard struck the desk again, startling Faina so she jumped. "It's impolite to stare down at one's feet when someone is talking to you."

Faina did as told, fighting back tears as she stared the teacher down. After a long moment of silence, a look of violent satisfaction eclipsed Ms. Ballard's icy glare.

"Very good. You may sit."

***

Faina welcomed recess with all the jubilation of an escaped prisoner and seriously entertained the idea of running back home and locking herself in her room. But Pasha was there sitting on the bench across the yard, eating his lunch with Yuri and Sergei. Faina sprinted cheerfully towards the other side of the playground, smiling and waving.

"Pasha! Pasha!"

She did not realize that abandoning her fellow female classmates for the company of a boy was, in terms of what her peers deemed good and proper, the absolute worst sin she could have committed to improve her situation. Either Pasha was not aware of Faina's faux-pas by mingling the sexes, or he did not care, for he received her with open arms and hugged her tightly. She thought it very nice to have a friend who was still taller than her, for looking around over Pasha's shoulder she realized her height had surpassed most of the boys their age.

"How's your first day of school so far?" he asked when they let go.

The smile fell from Faina's lips. She blushed heavily. How on earth could she explain to Pasha the trials that had plagued her all morning? As it turned out she wouldn't have to, for next thing she knew, Lena Kuznestov was hurling insults at her from across the playground.

"See? What did I tell you? Flaunting herself in front of the boys like a little floozy!"

Faina stepped back from Pasha with her head hanging low, trying to keep her lip from trembling. Several of the girls began chanting.

"Spichkin is a tart! Spichkin is a tart!"

Faina could feel her cheeks burning. Standing still seemed to make her muscles itch with restless urgency. Her lungs shoved her breath in and out of her nose in a labored drag.

"Spichkin is a tart! Spichkin is a tart!"

Uncontrollable life possessed her extremities as she spun on her heel and marched towards the ringleader. The march became a charge. Faina's mouth forced itself open, and she screamed like a warrior. She tackled Lena to the ground. Her arm drew back like a lance as she javelined her fist into the girl's teeth. Lena's arms were flailing in her fluffy sleeves. Tangling her fingers in Lena's rotten curls, Faina drew her head back and banged it against the asphalt, screaming until the air was scraping her vocal cords. A hand clutched at the back of her dress, but Faina threw it off. It grabbed her skirt, but she resisted. Finally the teacher snapped her hand around the end of Faina's ponytail and drew it back like the reigns of a horse.

***

Faina handed Uncle Matvei the note. They were standing behind the counter of the shop. Faina had been placed in a chair. Anya was standing by her side with a hand on her shoulder. When Uncle Matvei had finished reading the note, he crumpled it up and drew a long, tired sigh. Faina kept her drenched eyes trained on the shiny glare of her uncle's shoes. She would not look up. When a considerable amount of silence had passed between them, Uncle Matvei finally spoke.

"Faina, why did you attack your classmate?"

Faina drew her arms tighter around her; it was all too mortifying. She doubled over in her chair with noiseless sobs. Anya shifted in place. As Faina glanced up at her, Anya was just opening her mouth to offer some explanation. Faina swiftly shook her head. Anya hesitated, then closed her mouth.

"Faina," Uncle Matvei asked again, a little more firmly, but still not intimidating, "why did you do this? You're not in trouble right now, but I need to know what compelled you to hit Lena Kuznestov."

But Faina remained silent, and wept bitter tears. Uncle Matvei got to his knees.

"Darling, I know you. I know you would not have started a fight without reason. Someone provoked you, didn't they? They said something to you."

When Faina said nothing, he turned pleadingly to Anya. Faina grabbed Anya's hand and shook her head violently. Uncle Matvei dragged his fingers across his eyes and massaged the bridge of his nose.

"Alright. Well, until you decide to tell me what happened you are not to get up from this chair, understand?"

Slowly, Faina brought her eyes up to his through a watery mass of tears. She could see the reluctance in his expression. Uncle Matvei was not a good disciplinarian; in fact, he was lucky Anya was such a well-behaved child, for it was obvious he did not like enforcing rules and hated inflicting punishment. Faina managed a short nod as she pressed her lips together, trying to prevent another outburst. He nodded to Anya.

"Get Faina some water, then you go up and start on your homework."

If having to sit on public display behind the counter of her uncle's famous store was not bad enough, the shame of crying would have made it worse. Thus Faina was thankful for the cool glass of water Anya brought her, and the clean handkerchief with which she wiped her tears.

"Why won't you let me tell Papa?" Anya implored her. "It will be less awkward if you let me explain."

"Because then you'll have to explain the Kissing Cat Burglar incident and that would make him so ashamed!"

Anya furrowed her brow. Faina knew she was too bad of a liar to conceal part of the information. If Anya told Uncle Matvei one thing she would be tormented by her conscience until she gave the full story.

"I didn't like stealing, you know," choked Faina. "I didn't really even like kissing those boys. I just wanted to help Leo because I was afraid of something happening to Uncle Matvei." She rubbed her eye. "No one ever thinks they're going to lose their mother and father. At least not when you are young, I think. Maybe that's why it's so hard for the other girls to understand why I did what I did." Her nose stiffened as she fought against another wave of sobs. "Anya, I don't ever want to hurt like that again! Losing Mama and Papa hurt more than anything in the world, and I'll do whatever it takes to keep the family I have left because I never want to feel that again!"

It had been in Faina's head for some time that Anya might resent her for her past behavior, as she derived much pleasure from being proper and ladylike, everything Faina was not. But Anya was also compassionate, and after sitting thoughtfully for a moment she nodded her head.

"I understand, Faina. What Lena and the other girls did to you was awful. Syreeta and Peggy agree too. They think Lena deserved what you gave her."

Faina sniffed as she wiped away a tear. "Really?"

"Of course. Not everyone is mean like Lena. Syreeta and Peggy are nice girls. When we saw Lena's arm fly up around her head we couldn't help but laugh." And putting a hand over her mouth, she struggled to stem a flow of giggles. Faina smiled, and despite her troubles began laughing too.

Chapter 25:
Festivity, Substance, and Virtue

Pyro turned the flower sketch sideways and squinted his eyes. "You're telling me this is supposed to be in the shape of Ophiuchus?"

Staccato crossed his arms over his chest and peered out the library window overlooking the grounds of Feifior. "If you don't believe me, check the map yourself."

"Explains why it's so crooked."

Sonata leaned over his shoulder for a better look.

"Serpent's Knot! It all makes sense!" She pointed to the place on the map near the serpent's head that curled in a loop. "We must start where the Cauda crosses into Ophiuchus."

Skelter jabbed his finger towards the other loop at the tail.

"The Cauda or the Caput?" said Pyro.

They turned their heads expectantly towards Staccato.

"*West of truth to hostile thoughts.*" He crossed to the table where they were all gathered. "May I see the clue, Pyro?" Pyro handed him the sketch. "Here's truth." He pointed to the bittersweet in the illustration. "The Cauda is west of this point. The Caput is east. Therefore we can conclude 'serpent's knot' is referring to the Cauda." He pointed to the bluebell. "*Humility is a place where trials are sternest.*"

Pyro leaned over the table and stroked his beard. "If that's the Cauda then the bluebell marks Diamond Bend, home to some of the most dangerous rapids in the world. That must be the trials she's referring to." He squinted at the trail of sage. "'Pursuing wisdom will make you earnest.' I wonder if sage is referring to a shortcut somewhere near Pilum's Pass." He picked it up and turned it sideways. "Or maybe Fanged Fork. Either way, it looks like it's leading us near Sabik."

"*Instruction and knowledge can always be found, where festivity, substance, and virtue abound,*" recalled Melodious from memory.

Staccato placed a finger to his lips. "Indeed. If we look at the flower sketch, the plants that represent festivity, substance, and virtue are located near the city of Sabik. But where in Sabik?"

Pyro stared back at him with glazed eyes. "You sure this is Ophiuchus? Because I can't think of a single place in Sabik with any festivity, or the rest of it for that matter. Half of it's under Draconian occupation now. The only thing Sabik is known for anymore is historic battlefields and crime."

"Oh, come now." Staccato grabbed one of the books about Ophiuchus from the table. "That's an exaggeration."

"Is it? Quick, without looking at that book, tell me everything you know about Sabik."

Staccato forced a look of confidence onto his face. "Well, I—" his eyes flitted towards the book.

"No peeking!"

"Fine!" He shut the book and set it aside. "Sabik is a city in Ophiuchus, an exclave of Taurus, with the upper half under Draconian occupation. It's a temperate climate located near the Cauda."

"The history! What do you know about the history and culture?"

"They … eat a lot of river prawns."

"1657, the Battle of Rasalhague," interrupted Melodious. "The Herculeans waged war with a tribe of Furies that had come down from the Boötes. The cavalry rode to Sabik and managed to push the Furies back to the Cauda, who shortly thereafter surrendered." He rocked back on his heels, looking very pleased with himself. "I was born in Lake Hercules, you know."

"1789." Pyro handed the sketch back to Sonata. "Siege of Khan Lau. Pirate captain Tripp Cortair raided the second-largest spice trade hub on the outskirts of Sabik and walked away with seven thousand hands worth of contraband. Buried it all on some island."

"The Battle of Zal As Safar, thirteen B.C." Sonata looked as though she were reciting in front of a tutor. "Emperor Zalfique set fire to a settlement on the north bank of the Caput, killing six hundred people."

Pyro was impressed. He had no idea Sonata had an interest in historical battles.

"1843," he continued. "The Defeat of Rasalhague."

"The Trivernia Offensive, 1806." She smirked triumphantly.

"Mar Dunn Campaign, 1883."

"Oh! Battle of Little Pig, 1854!"

"I hear they give tours of that one."

"Do they really?"

"Alright!" Staccato jammed his staff on the wood floor. "You've made your point! Why don't you two take all that energy and put it towards finding something that *is* festive before Sobek's unit advances any further!" He pointed his staff at the stack of books. "Here's what we're going to do." The pile divided itself into three groups and flew towards Pyro, Sonata, and Skelter. "The next few days will be devoted to acquainting ourselves with Ophiuchus's history in hopes that some sort of clue will present itself. Melodious, I'll speak to Thayer and see if we can't find you some volumes in braille."

When Pyro did not immediately grab his stack, the heaviest book nudged him in the head. He let out a groan. "How many days do we have to read this?"

"Come now, Pyro. Who do you think you're fooling? You're obviously more of a reader than you let on. How else could you remember all those battles?"

Chapter 26:
Mermaid Mail

Two days passed. Pyro flipped through the pages of *Ophiuchus: The Land I Love* as he and Skelter made their way to the great hall.

"You don't reckon 'festivity' could mean a victory party, do you? As in, a party following a victory on the battlefield?"

Skelter narrowed his eyes thoughtfully, then wiggled his hand.

"You're right," Pyro agreed. "Even if it did, it doesn't really narrow down the possibilities. There have been loads of successful battles fought in Sabik. You know, a lot of them were navy battles with pirates and mercenaries. Khan Lau was a major trading port back then that attracted a lot of theft. Pretty exciting stuff." They turned the corner. "You think Lavanda anticipated us taking so long to solve her clue?"

Skelter put a finger to his temple and twirled it in a circle. Pyro scoffed.

"Yeah, I'm still not convinced she knew what she was doing either. Would it have killed her to be a little more straightforward? Although, I guess we have no way of knowing how closely Lucien was watching her."

They pushed through the door and bounded down the crooked stairs. It was a winding staircase with two landings. The bottom set had suffered some damage during the battle of Bilderbrass in 1867, and no one had been able to decide whether or not the required maintenance was considered functional or cosmetic. In the end it had been left untouched, but Pyro and Skelter knew to avoid the steps when they could. Pyro hopped atop the bannister and slid down the railing. Skelter followed his example.

"Well done, boys," teased Sonata from the far side of the table. "Excellent dismount."

"Oh, hiya, Sonny." Pyro wheeled around. "Didn't see you there."

An assortment of glass bottles and jars were laid out before her, along with a box of what appeared to be scrapbooking supplies. Cello sat contentedly on the chair beside her.

"What are you up to?" They approached the table.

"Oh, just working on some mail for Mama and Papa, and Aunt Estella." She unscrewed the cap off a bottle of rubber cement, and stroked the brush over the corner of a photograph of her and Cello.

"Looks more like an art project than a letter."

"I suppose you're right." She stuck a little fabric rosette to the corner, and slid the photograph into a jar with a letter strategically placed amongst fake moss. Skelter nudged Pyro's side and signed.

"Ah," Pyro nodded his head. "You're sending messages in a bottle!" He shook his head in self-admonishment. "Obviously."

"I should've said mermaid mail."

He examined a long, clear bottle with a photograph of Sonata and one of Thayer's daughters eating cinnamon muffins. It was weighted down with cloves, nutmeg, and sugar.

"Smell it," she instructed. "I like to make my messages as immersive as possible."

Pyro opened up the jar and inhaled the fragrance of sugar and spices.

"I take it your family has access to some air then." He handed the bottle to Skelter who also sniffed.

The mermaids might not have been able to come to the open surface, but he'd heard they made use of hidden caverns, which were needed when mermaids gave birth anyway.

"Some. Though, it's too dangerous for anyone to visit. They're stuck in Karkinos, of course, which is too close to enemy territory." She slipped a seashell into the jar with a smile both bashful and endearing. "If you've noticed me collecting little tokens and pebbles here and there, now you know why. I like to use them for my letters. All mermaids have a bit of magpie in them, but I often fear I'm the worst."

"That's adorable." Pyro cringed and bit down on his tongue. "I mean funny!"

Skelter slipped him a teasing smile, but Sonata paid him no mind.

"Once I picked up a conch shell that happened to be a very old love letter. Ever since then I've been careful to hold every shell I find up to my ear and listen for music or messages." She inhaled as though she were taking in the fragrance of a giant bouquet of flowers. "It was so lovely though! Dated 1867! I still have it."

Skelter made a questioning sign.

"No." Sonata sighed. "I'm afraid I never did find who it belonged to. I've tried tracing the name but I've yet to have any luck. Perhaps when the Land Lock is over." Her eyes slid mischievously from one side of the room to the other. "I know it's selfish, but a part of me hopes I can keep it, I cherish it so."

Pyro surveyed the bottles and supplies with an impressed air. "Well, I have to hand it to you, Princess. You are quite dedicated to your craft."

"I haven't even shown you the best part yet!" She took a matchbox from her pocket and slid the container out from the sleeve. Three glowing vials were settled neatly inside.

Pyro and Skelter leaned in closer. "What are they?"

She held up the vial containing silvery fibers floating in a substance that shimmered like liquefied pearl.

"A vision. Staccato made it for me. Watch!" Sonata uncorked the vial and poured it into her half-finished bottle. The mist and light flooded the container in a fog of rapidly moving ripples. She quickly capped it. A vision emerged from the clouds. It was Sonata, going through one of her routines on the hoop, complete with glittery costume. Pyro bent down for a better look, completely in awe.

"It's beautiful," he muttered, too distracted to give any attention to his word choice. As the routine came to a close, the image began to fade away. "I think something might be wrong with your vision. It's gone."

"Not at all." She picked it up by the neck. "All one has to do is give it a good shake." The clouds stirred once again, and the image of Sonata dancing returned. "See?"

Pyro leaned against the table and smirked. "Your parents are very lucky to have a daughter like you."

"It isn't easy for us to be apart. I'm sure if they could they would do the same for me." She set down her supplies. "Is this your handiwork by the way?"

As she scooted her chair back, Pyro realized she was in a wheelchair. She rolled towards the tapestry of Khan Lau, its vast ships loaded down with crates of herbs and spices, the junk rigging forming a bold silhouette against the twilight. There was a blackened hole directly where Tripp Cortair's head should have been. She appraised the textile with a dry humor.

"I thought the Feifior custom of no maintenance applied only to damage acquired in battle."

Pyro chuckled. "Clearly, you've never had a case of the dry bellows."

"Clearly."

Skelter was about to indicate something when he suddenly froze. His eyes widened. He stepped back from the tapestry as though trying to take it all in.

"What is it, Skelter?" asked Sonata.

Skelter clapped his hands over his mouth and jumped up and down. He gestured to the tapestry.

Pyro raised an eyebrow. "Yeah, what about it?"

Skelter ran to one side of the tapestry and pointed to a barrel labeled parsley, and a barrel labeled oregano. Then he ran to the other side and pointed to a barrel labeled mint.

Sonata gasped. "*Instruction and knowledge can always be found where festivity, substance, and virtue abound!* Sabik is home to Khan Lau! The—"

"Second-largest spice trading hub in all Voiler," Pyro and Sonata recited together.

Sonata ran her hand along the labels. "Festivity is parsley, substance is oregano, and mint is virtue! Skelter, you did it! You solved the riddle! Dr. Desmond is in Khan Lau!"

:

Chapter 27:
The Wishful
"I had a little bird
her name was Enza
I opened up the door
and in-flew-Enza!"

Pasha's vision bounced as he laid in Mama's bed and watched Katya jump up and down on the mattress in her nightgown singing the latest infernal rhyme, her wet hair smacking her shoulders and splashing water droplets on his cheeks. Pasha winced as one hit his eye. Even with the door shut he could smell the damp wafting from his bedroom where a leak from the apartment above had materialized in the ceiling. He was now forced to join his mother and sister in the narrow excuse for a double bed the pair shared every night until Mrs. Borsuk could be bothered to call a repairman.

Outside there was no moon to line the heavy storm clouds in silver light, and were it not for the artificial hum of electricity throbbing its glow into the heavens, the city would have been lost in the darkness.

Mama sat brushing her long hair before a cracked mirror, the bristles tracing hypnotic patterns through her nearly black tresses.

"Katya, darling, don't sing that," she ordered, wincing at the words.

Pasha was about to remind his sister that people were dying but, not wishing to frighten her, decided not to. Earlier that day he'd heard Uncle Matvei telling his mother that he'd read in the paper that 324 cases of influenza had been reported in New York City alone, and twenty had died.

As Katya made another hop, Pasha's head collided with one of the brass posts. Grabbing Katya around the waist, he yanked her downwards onto the mattress.

"Enough jumping already! It's time for bed."

Katya rolled and flailed in playful protest. She reached up with both hands and squished her brother's cheeks.

"You look like a fish!"

Struggling to fight against his own smile, Pasha took her by the wrists and tried to force her into stillness.

"Shhhh," he hushed in one long note.

"*Katenka*, you have school in the morning," Mama reminded her, turning away from the vanity. She rose in her trailing white nightgown and bent over Katya lovingly. "You need your sleep so you can fill up that restless mind of yours." She rubbed her nose affectionately against her daughter's.

Katya kicked up her legs and heaved a pitiful sigh. "Why must people sleep? Why can't everyone just keep playing? Why do we need to sleep?"

Pasha dragged Katya closer, making room for his mother on the mattress.

"Because if we didn't sleep we'd be too tired to play."

"But I'm not too tired to play yet. How can I go to bed if I am not tired?"

"You are tired, *Rybka*," Pasha insisted. "Once you stop moving you'll realize you are tired and you'll fall asleep."

Like most children, this remark struck Katya as a personal offense, and her face worked itself into an expression of horror as though her inborn rights were in danger of being tread upon.

"But I'm not tired! I'm not tired!" She spun helplessly towards their mother. "I am not tired, Mama!"

"Shhhh, shhhh, I believe you," whispered their mother, pushing Katya's hair away from her forehead. "A grown-up young lady like you mustn't be put to bed before she is ready. So we will do what all proper grown-up people do in the evening. We will talk."

Pasha lay quietly on the pillows, admiring Mama's wily cleverness. When Katya was looking away, she caught his eye and winked at him. Pasha replied with a crooked smile as Mama pulled the covers up to Katya's chin.

"What will we talk about?" inquired Katya, turning her head in an attempt to hide the fact that she was rubbing one eye.

"We will talk about when I was a little girl in Lake Baikal. You always like that, don't you?"

Katya bounced her chin and settled with her head leaning on Pasha's chest, as Mama slid her beautiful ankles beneath the sheet and lay down beside them.

"When I was your age my papa saved me from a Wishful, an evil monster that hides in the water and casts hallucinations of young women to lure little children into their caves."

It was a new invention, one of the few made-up stories of his mother's childhood Pasha had yet to hear, and so rather than allowing himself to nod off, he remained awake and listened to her tale.

Katya sat up and gasped. "Was it going to eat you, Mama?"

"It might have if it weren't for your grandfather. It was a moonless night just like this one, and just like you I could not fall asleep no matter how many times my papa told me to. I was so determined I would not go to bed that Papa fell asleep trying to get me to lie still. I thought to myself, now I can go play and explore until I get sleepy. I put on my coat and shoes and headed down to the lake hoping I might spy a mermaid.

"When I made my way down to the shore I saw the most beautiful woman strolling amongst the rocks. She was wearing a white gown, and had white flowers in her hair and tied in strings around her ankles. Her skin was so pale and fine that it seemed almost transparent, like moonlight. She saw me staring at her and smiled at me. When I waved she threw back her head and laughed, and when she did I could hear a faint twinkling of chimes in her throat, like little bells. She began jogging along the shore and beckoned for me to follow after her.

"I began running as fast as my legs could carry me. When I lagged behind she would stop and wait for me to catch up, but never pausing long enough for me to reach her. She led me through vast thickets, over fallen logs and broken branches."

"Did you ever catch up with her?" asked Katya with wide, stimulated eyes.

Mama nodded, her face grave and full of warning.

"I did. When I caught up with her, she was standing at the mouth of a cave where water from the lake ran in a little whirlpool. She plucked me up from the ground and sat upon a rock at the edge of the cavern. She began cradling me in her arms, and smoothing my hair away from my face. 'Come be my child, Lydia. I want to be your mama. I will take care of you and give you whatever you want.' I began to feel sleepy as she rocked me back and forth.

"Then something terrible happened. The woman opened her mouth and made a low growling noise inside her chest. Her eyes became like hot coals and her fingers grew long and withered like tree branches. Her face grew paler and paler until it had vanished and in its place was the gigantic head of a croaking dragon with a string of bells around its throat like a necklace. It closed its claws tight around me like a cage, and I began to scream.

"Just as the monster was getting up to carry me off to his cave, I heard a gunshot fire in the darkness. The monster squealed and dropped me right there in a pile of thorny branches. I could see Papa by the light of his lantern, see his handsome face pale with terror. He came closer. I tried to get up and run to him, but the Wishful caught me by the ankle and pulled me back towards him. He opened his mouth and another ghost woman floated between us, this time with long golden hair just like yours."

She caught her fingers up in Katya's wavy blonde tresses and tickled her neck until she had retreated under the covers.

"What did Grandfather do?" Katya's voice was partially muffled by the sheets.

"Well, I could see from the way Papa's eyes lit up at the sight of that beautiful woman that the monster was trying to distract him. But Papa was clever. He knew all of the Wishful's tricks and, lifting his gun, he fired straight through the woman, hitting the monster square in the head. The monster released me, rolling over, dragging himself back into his cave as he grew limper and limper. Papa ran to me, plucked me out of the thornbush, and carried me out of the woods as fast as his legs could take him."

Katya was clutching the edge of the sheets. "Did you get in trouble?"

Mama's mouth opened wide as she laughed.

"Oh, I got in very big trouble, let me tell you. I had never seen Papa so angry with anyone, especially me. But what was worse than the punishment was knowing why Papa was so upset. I knew he had been terrified beyond anything he had ever felt before."

"Terrified of the Wishful?"

"No, *radost moya*," my joy. "He was terrified at the thought of losing me, terrified by the idea of my life being threatened, because Papa loved me so much."

Her eyes grew soft and unfocused as she receded back into the memories of her father. Pasha thought she looked childlike, lost even. She had worn that same look on her face when they were detained on Ellis Island. Now it frightened him, and he looked away. He did not want to hear of his grandfather anymore, and the childish stories his mother came up with about him. He turned away from her and shut his eyes.

"Your grandfather was a good man, my darling," she crooned to Katya. "And I know he is looking down on you from Heaven."

"Mama, you don't really believe Grandfather is dead. I know you don't."

Pasha opened his eyes and stared at the opposite wall. His mother was silent. The air grew tense in their lungs like drying cement. When Mama did not answer her, Katya continued. "I don't think he is dead either."

For some reason, this made Pasha even more uncomfortable.

An hour passed after the light had been shut off, and still Pasha could not sleep. He kept thinking about all the fantastical stories his mother had told them of growing up in Siberia. While they were fun to think about and imagine, Pasha was now at the age where he was beginning to wonder what the real story was. Mama had only ever told them fairy tales. He wondered what it could be that she was trying to hide.

Mama's fingers combed suddenly through his hair. He turned in the bed to find her still awake and watching him with her lulling, angelic eyes.

"What is troubling you, *Patulya*?"

Pasha scooted closer and laid his head against the pillow. "How do you know something is troubling me?"

A sleepy but contented smile slipped in at the corners of her lips. "Because I am your mama."

Pasha pulled the blanket closer around his shoulders. "I was just wondering … how come you never talk about what your childhood was really like?"

Mama did not respond immediately but blinked very slowly so that she looked like she might fall asleep. Then she whispered softly. "Can you keep a secret?"

Pasha cuddled closer so that his head was resting beneath her chin. "Always, for you."

He could feel his mother's laughter reverberating through her neck. "I can always count on you, can't I? My sweet boy. What I am about to tell you, I never even shared with your father." She sighed and wrapped her arms around him. "I tell those stories because that *is* what I remember."

Pasha craned his head back to eye her incredulously. "You really remember a cottage surrounded by a giant enchanted hedge?"

"I'm not saying that is what actually happened. It's just … all I can remember."

"But if that's what you remember then it must have really happened, right?"

She shrugged and tried to appear cheerful, but really she just looked tired. "That would be nice, wouldn't it?"

Pasha still did not understand. "But that's what makes sense."

"It makes sense to us. But it wouldn't to other people. I could've just as easily hit my head. That's what a doctor would tell me."

"I would always trust what you say more than what a doctor says, and more than what anyone else says for that matter. Why don't you?"

This time his mother's face lit up with no effort. She hugged him tight and kissed his cheek.

"You are my little hero. Did you know that?"

Chapter 28:

The Widow's Dream

"Ow!" Pyro swatted at a mosquito just as it sank its nose into his flesh. "Torchin' bloodsuckers!"

The company had been fortunate to avoid traveling during the first cold spell of autumn, but the muggy air of late September had caused several spots along the Cauda to grow saturated with pests. Pyro wiped away his blood with a handkerchief and stomped towards the banks.

"Couldn't we have stopped to water the pegasi in a place with less bugs?" He plunged his hands into the water, rinsing away the germs.

"You've seen a place, have you?" Melodious faced him, the mid-afternoon sun having no effect on his eyes.

"Point taken." He splashed some water onto his face. "We'll all be lucky if we don't get Febris! Pests spread disease, you know!"

Since January, Voiler had been plagued with a prolonged outbreak of Febris, a disease with flu-like symptoms. It was a non-lethal malady but was no less unpleasant. Skelter had already had it a couple weeks back, and the rest of the company was holding their breath waiting to see if they would catch it.

"If only the train went as far as Khan Lau," lamented Pyro.

"It used to." Sonata sat down on a rock and unfolded a decorative fan. "The C.O.N. set fire to the trestle over a month ago."

"And no one's fixed it?"

"In these times?" She scoffed. "The trestle is the least of their worries. Last I heard the governor's still trying to come up with the funds to replace the sylph sanctuary they destroyed."

After leaving the train station, Sonata had thrown on a pair of jodhpurs and was wearing her blouse unbuttoned over her camisole, a common style for mermaids. Pyro dried his hands and sat down beside her, hoping that if he were closer he might not have the opportunity to stare so much.

"Here." He held his hand open, revealing a tiny snail shell in his palm.

When Sonata stared down at his hand questioningly, he quickly explained himself. "For your mermaid mail." Before she could take it, he drew back. "Oh, wait. Forgot to check."

He held the shell up to his ear and listened. "Hmm."

"Do you hear anything?"

"It says 'To whomever finds this shell, please note that I, Henry J. Snail, have permanently vacated the premises, having outgrown the property, and shall not be returning. So please feel free to enjoy my former home, there shall be no legal repercussions.'" He placed the shell in her palm.

Sonata beamed up at him. "How very thoughtful of you."

Pyro gave her a mischievous shrug. "What can I say? I'm a thoughtful bloke." He smoothed the knees of his trousers. "Alright, so let's go over the plan again. We're doing a show at the Li Hall—"

"The show at the Li is just an excuse to be closer to Dr. Desmond." She unscrewed the cap of her canteen.

"Yeah, but where's Dr. Desmond locked up?"

Sonata took a swig and held up a finger. "According to the Saighdeoir, Khan Lau has a serious problem with Primal gang activity. They say the Jade Bone practically runs the place." She capped the container and set it down.

"The Jade Bone? As in Kha Fang? The micro-hex dealer?"

"That's the one. So if we find Kha Fang, we find Dr. Desmond."

The branches overhead rustled and scraped together. Pyro and Sonata looked up just in time to see Skelter shinnying across a tree limb and shaking the leaves until a shower of apples rained down around them.

"Thank you, Skelter!" yelled Sonata as she covered her head with her arms. The barrage stopped and Skelter threw them a thumbs up.

"Good idea, Skelly," remarked Pyro. "What with Virgo being out of commission, should save us a fortune on produce."

Sonata plucked up one of the apples rolling at her feet and held it to the light.

"And Kilgoree was never able to figure out where he was from?"

"They tried. Had him in the Nursery for over an hour. All he'd give them was his name."

"The Nursery?"

"That's what they call the interrogation room at Kilgoree, on account of all the crying." Pyro scratched at the mosquito bite on his arm and looked away. "I think he had a family though."

"What makes you say that?"

"Well, he gets down a lot. I don't think anyone could be that sad unless they'd lost something like their family."

Sonata smirked. "He's very lucky to have a friend like you."

"Why particularly?"

"You got him out of Kilgoree, didn't you?"

Pyro rubbed the side of his face and glanced away. "Yeah, well, I owed him."

Sonata gave him a pointed look and leaned back. "It's hard for you to accept compliments, isn't it?"

"Maybe. Why do you have to point it out?"

"Because you're a good man, and I think it's important for you to know that you're worthy of the nice things people say about you."

Pyro said nothing but eyed her curiously. She scooted closer to him, an amused simper filling her lips. Her knees touched his.

"It's normal for people to care about their friends' well-being. Quit looking so suspicious all the time."

Pyro swallowed. Something about the way she was smiling at him made his insides feel like applesauce. They jumped as Skelter began playing his violin from the treetops.

Melodious looked up with an amused smile. "I know this one!" He began singing along.

"Sweet Adeline!

My Adeline!

At night, dear heart, for you I pine

In all my dreams

Your fair face beams

You're the flower of my heart, sweet Adeline!"

Pyro flashed Skelter a warning look while the violinist lay out on his back with a mischievous smile as though he were Cupid himself.

Pyro hastily hopped off the rock. "It's, uh … getting a little too buggy out here. I'm gonna sit inside and avoid being eaten."

The caravan swayed and jostled as Pyro opened the door of the wagon and slammed it shut. Something like glass clinked overhead. He looked up just as a small, corked vial was falling through the opening of Staccato's loft. Pyro reached up and caught it before it hit the ground.

"Got it!"

A bit of light drew his eyes upwards. Several more vials rolled over the ledge. He snatched three, but the last one hit the ground with more force than the others. The cork dislodged from the neck. Pyro grabbed the vial, but it was too late. A golden trail of glitter leaked from the tube, swirling around Pyro's ankles and climbing into the air. An image formed in the mist. It was Staccato, seated on the edge of a bed beside a young woman with long, golden hair. She appeared angry with him.

"… When what you should have done, the only sane thing to do, was bring her here!"

"I am not discussing this again," said Staccato. "I refuse to keep defending my position—which should be an obvious one! Until the Land Lock breaks, Lydia shall not set foot in Voiler! It's too dangerous!"

"If you're so afraid of the Land Lock then why on earth would you let her get on a boat and cross five thousand miles of ocean?"

Pyro was beginning to understand. This woman must have been Staccato's wife, Evangeline, only it couldn't have been a memory, for Staccato was in the vision as he was now, his forty-eight-year-old self, and Evangeline had been dead for years.

"For the last time I did not let her! I didn't know! I thought she would go to England!"

They were inches apart. Evangeline narrowed her eyes and portioned her words out one at a time.

"Bring. Her. Home!"

Staccato raised his eyebrows and tightened his jaw. "It. Is. Too. Dangerous!"

Evangeline growled and threw her hands in the air. "Staccato!"

"Evangeline, you were not there that night! You were not there when the Land Lock was placed! You didn't see what I saw!" His head dropped, and there was a pained look in his eyes. "For heaven's sake, look what happened to Sonata!"

Evangeline's shoulders rolled forward. She looked down at her hands.

"Had you been the one who found her lying there, with her legs …" Staccato took a deep breath. "It was hard enough to watch Sonata go through it. Lydie and her children are a threat to the C.O.N., Evangeline! Heirs to the throne of Ursa. I could never put them in that kind of danger!"

"I understand," she finally confessed, her eyebrows knitted upwards.

"Lydia is safe now. They reached Ellis Island. What's more, they're just down the hall from Aunt Poppy."

"I suppose so."

Staccato brushed her hair from her face. "Come now, let's not sulk anymore."

"I'm not sulking."

Staccato cocked an eyebrow and smirked at her. He took her left hand and drew it towards him. Evangeline gave a warning grunt but Staccato did not listen.

"No," she grumbled as he kissed the back of her fingers. "No!" He kissed the back of her hand. "You can kiss me all you like but you'll not charm your way out of this one!"

Staccato flipped her arm over and hovered his lips over the underside of her wrist to give her a mermaid kiss. Mermaid kisses were a special kind of kiss that could only be given or received by mermaids, in which the recipient could feel a physical manifestation of all the love harbored for them by the giver. Each kiss was different, as the feelings would vary based on what it was like to be loved by the kisser. Pyro had never experienced one himself, but it was said to be one of the most beautiful sensations one could encounter.

Staccato froze and looked up at his wife expectantly, waiting for her protest. A flicker of a smirk was forming at the corner of her mouth. Staccato stifled an amused chuckle and kissed her soft skin.

Evangeline lifted a hand to her heart, her lips relaxing in an open expression as she felt all the strength of his affections rushing through her veins. For a moment, Evangeline looked as though she might cry. When the sensation had passed, she let out a squealing giggle. They threw back their heads and laughed as Staccato picked her up and swung her around in a circle.

Pyro raised his eyebrows. It was like seeing Scrooge at the end of *A Christmas Carol*. Never had he beheld Staccato so carefree and relaxed.

Pyro had become so absorbed in the vision that he was startled when the tube unceremoniously sucked the image back into its confines. Pyro corked the vial, and gathered the containers into his pocket. He scuttled up the ladder and popped his head over the ledge.

Staccato was lying on his back in deep sleep. His brow was furrowed and one arm was thrown over his head. In the other hand he clutched an open locket to his chest, picture-side down. Pyro raised his eyebrows. At times it seemed Staccato fluctuated between being an insomniac and a narcoleptic, and he always slept the most after returning from a trip to New York.

"Staccato?"

Staccato gave no response.

"*Oi!* Staccato!"

Staccato awoke with a sharp inhale. He rose up on his elbows, squinting irritably at Pyro.

"What? What is it? What do you want?" He hastily shut the locket and shoved it into his pocket.

Pyro held up one of the vials. "You dropped something."

Staccato's eyes stretched awake. "What?" He seized the vial.

Pyro laid the rest on the floor between them. "One of them popped open. It, uh, it had your wife in it, I think."

Staccato grabbed him by the shoulder and wrenched him forward. "Did anyone see it?"

"Just me. It was an accident. It fell from the loft."

Staccato released his grip. His chest rose as he sucked in a mouthful of air and exhaled. Pyro pulled himself up through the porthole and sat on the ledge.

"What are they exactly?"

Staccato passed his hand over his mouth. "Dreams. Visions." He checked the label of the vial that had broken apart. "Technically this was a recreation of a dream. For some reason I've never been able to preserve my visits with Evangeline. So I remake them in the form of visions." He looked back at Pyro. "Miraculous can communicate with the dead through dreams, you know. Somnium Orbatus, Dream of the Bereaved, or colloquially known as Widow's Dream, though it's not limited to dead spouses. One has a dream of the dead person in question, then enters a state of hypnagogia, a state between asleep and awake, and is able to meet with the deceased. It's proven quite helpful with rebel work at times."

"You mean because the dead can tell you things no one else can?"

He shook his head. "Well, not exactly. You see, the dead tell no tales. Meaning all help and information has to be given as a sort of clue. They can never give information outright, only lead you in the right direction."

"So, you still see a lot of your wife then?"

Staccato laid the vial aside. "In a manner of speaking."

A few moments of awkward silence passed between them before Pyro spoke again.

"Does it feel odd to interact with your wife while you continue to age?" He probably shouldn't have asked, but to his surprise Staccato didn't seem to mind.

"Actually, I can't explain why there is an age difference between my wife and me when I meet with her in my dreams." He removed the locket from his pocket and opened it, revealing a picture of Evangeline. "Normally in a widow's dream everyone appears roughly the same age, somewhere between twenty-five and thirty, myself included. Unless of course they were children at the time of their passing, in which case they continue to grow until they reach their prime. Then they stop."

Pyro stuck out his lower lip as though it were a casual conversation. "She's beautiful, by the way. Your wife, I mean."

"Thank you. She was." Staccato looked down at the floor and stiffened.

"Is that why you sleep so often then? To see your wife?"

"I sleep often?"

"It's noon. We've been parked for twenty minutes, and already you were dead asleep."

"Catching up on the sleep I've missed, I suppose."

"If you want, I'm sure one of us could drive the caravan the rest of the way. Give you a chance to rest."

Staccato grunted and stretched his arms over his head. "That won't be necessary."

"Mate, you've gotta rest more often."

Staccato opened his trunk and stowed the locket away before waving him aside. "Nonsense. As I've told you before, I have no needs." He clambered down the ladder. Just as Pyro was hopping down, Sonata opened the caravan door.

"Sonata, dear, there you are!" exclaimed Staccato. "I was just about to call everyone back. We best be on our way."

At the sight of Sonata, Pyro's shoulders zipped back. She had removed her outer shirt and tied it around her waist, wearing just her camisole and showcasing her lovely shoulders. Her hair had been swept up off her neck with a clip, and she was sweating slightly about the temples. Pyro could feel the blood inside his chest growing warm.

"How much longer do you think it will be?" she asked Staccato.

Staccato paused at the door, consulting his watch. "Oh, I'd say about three more hours." He shut the door behind him.

"Three more hours." Sonata cocked her hip and smiled at Pyro. "Just you, me, Skelter, and Melodious for the next three hours. I daresay this arrangement has made us all quite intimate."

"Yeah." Pyro swallowed and fumbled with his pockets. "Very intimate."

It was all he could do to keep his gaze from slipping down to her hips. He plopped down on his mattress. Sonata yawned.

"Who would have thought sitting around doing nothing could be so terribly exhausting!" She sat down beside him and laid her head in his lap. Pyro could feel his muscles tightening. His skin grew hot beneath her touch. It was a perfectly meaningless gesture on Sonata's part, as mermaids were a very physically affectionate people with less awareness of personal space than most. It wasn't uncommon for them to snuggle their friends in addition to their lovers. But for Pyro it was torture having her curls strewn across his lap, and the softness of her breath on his skin.

"Don't you just want to fall asleep?"

"Uh … yeah." Pyro's hands started towards her hair, then her shoulders, but he drew back. What was he supposed to do with his hands?

She yawned and stretched her arms over her head. "Wake me up when we get there."

"I just remembered I left something outside!" he burst out all at once. Pyro sprang from the mattress, practically knocking Sonata to the floor by accident, and shot out the door. He caught up with Staccato. "Mind if I join you up front?"

Staccato looked him over curiously. "As long as you're not too rambunctious."

Chapter 29:
The Grasshopper Inn

Khan Lau was a gritty, puddle-strewn city and the poster child for the importance of historical preservation. What could have been a charming, tourist-filled river town complete with sightseeing, cafes, and historical markers had been reduced to pox-infested alleyways, motels run by illegal potion traders, and old women hawking counterfeit charms and bottled sunshine.

The rain was coming down in sheets, and Staccato had been forced to pull out the awning over the driver's seat.

"I would avoid making eye contact if I were you," said Staccato to Pyro as they drove further into the city, "lest we be bombarded with traders and pushcarts."

Pyro said nothing but lowered his head and glanced at the passing gutters from the corner of his eye. As the sky grew darker beneath the storm clouds, one by one the turquoise archways began to glow. Errand boys as young as five or six dashed through the mud in their bare feet, their linen shirts pasted to the small of their backs with a glaze of sweat. On the counter of a soup vendor stand, a chorus of spotted mocking toads were engaged in a barber shop quartet rendition of *My Dragon-Eyed Gal*.

They pulled up to a moldering wooden building with a dangling sign in characters Pyro did not recognize.

"The Grasshopper Inn," translated Staccato. "This is where we'll be staying."

A man in a poncho and wide straw hat came shuffling out of the stables with a clipboard shoved under one arm and holding a lantern.

"Name?"

"Staccato Nimbus's Singing Circus."

The man wrote something on the clipboard and nodded before directing Staccato to drive into the barn. After dismounting, the company was led through a covered walkway to the front door. As they crowded outside the threshold with their luggage, Pyro thought he heard a low rumbling like thunder from beneath the porch. Skelter pointed beneath the stairs. A large barrel-chested beast with a head almost as wide as a bull lurked beneath the porch with the carcass of a raggedy bird-like creature wedged in its underbite.

"It's a foo dog," exclaimed Sonata as the creature sauntered past them and squeezed its ginormous head through the curtained door.

Pyro held the curtain aloft for the others. "Wonder where the other is." For they always came in pairs.

They did not have to wait long to find out, for inside its mate was sitting atop a pedestal beside the woman at the front desk. The lady's dense, curly hair was styled in a neat bouffant. She wore a pair of red tortoise-shell glasses that popped against her dark complexion, which was the color of sunflower seeds. At the sound of their footsteps she glanced up and smiled.

"Welcome to the Grasshopper Inn." Her eyes flicked over the guests with a knowing expression. "Something tells me you must be Mr. Nimbus and his singing circus."

Staccato set down his suitcase and tipped his hat. "You would be correct, Madame."

"Well, come on in and get yourself out of the cold." She opened the guest book. "If you'll just sign in here, I'll get your keys." She opened a drawer. "If you need anything at all, my name is Fina Pulvervass. My husband Typhon and I are the innkeepers here and can answer all your questions. I know it doesn't look like much, but we've really got a lovely establishment he—" Her eyes swelled as she spotted something behind Pyro's shoulder. Pyro turned to see the other foo dog sitting proudly in the corner, the dead creature still in its teeth.

"Shishi!" Mrs. Pulvervass grabbed a broom and marched out from behind the front desk. "What have I told you about bringing haíchi in the house!?" Just as she was winding up to smack the foo's haunches with the broom, Shishi spat the dead animal onto the floor, which resurrected itself all at once with a shake of its molting head. Mrs. Pulvervass gave a shriek and swung her broom at the haíchi as though it were a golf ball, pitching it back onto the porch where it hastily hopped away. She turned towards the stairs and cupped a hand over her mouth.

"Sal!" She winced apologetically at Staccato. "I am so sorry, Mr. Nimbus! My son has been teaching the foo dogs to scare off the haíchi … not that we have an infestation, mind you! It's just a preventative measure, you see—"

A long-limbed boy of about nine, wearing a linen tunic and trousers with a rice hat strapped over his back, appeared at the top of the steps. He was skinny, with a shaved head and large, open eyes that radiated all the youthful energy accustomed to a boy his age.

"Salamander Pulvervass, what did I tell you about letting the foo dogs bring dead haíchi inside?"

"How else am I supposed to keep track of their kills?"

"Why on earth do you need to keep track of such a thing?"

"It's all part of my business plan. Salamander Pulvervass's Extraordinary Extermination Services, guaranteed to rid your home of haichi, rats, and various vermin with the help of my magnificent foo dogs!"

Mrs. Pulvervass arched a suspicious eyebrow. "This wouldn't have anything to do with that new bicycle you've had your eye on it, would it?"

"So what if it does? It's the fastest way to get around the city for a boy my age."

"Well, I do not want Shishi or Chinchin bringing any more dead animals into my foyer. Is that understood?"

Sal dragged his feet down the steps and nodded. "Yes, ma'am."

She set her hands firmly on her hips and mustered a tired but warm smile. "My son. Sal, why don't you come down and introduce yourself to our guests?"

This was all Sal needed to give full vent to his enthusiasm. He raced down the remainder of the steps.

"Are you the circus that's come to stay with us?"

"This is Staccato Nimbus's Singing Circus," his mother explained.

Salamander grabbed Staccato's hand without the slightest hint of intimidation and yanked it up and down in a hearty shake. "Hi! I'm Sal!"

"Sal is your nickname," his mother corrected. "Give Mr. Nimbus a proper greeting."

"Why? It's too long to remember anyway! You said so yourself!"

Mrs. Pulvervass lowered her head with maternal authority. "It's the polite thing to do."

Sal gave a grievous sigh. "My name is Salamander Hephaestus Ignition Pulvervass the third."

Staccato chuckled. "That's quite a mouthful."

"I know!" Sal stretched his eyes open, making it seem as though he wholeheartedly agreed. "Ma says it's too much for most people to remember so it's better if I just go by Sal. But I wanna know, if she thinks it's too long of a name, then why'd she name me that in the first place?"

She placed a hand on his shoulder. "Names are a very important part of Fay culture. It's part of our heritage. I'm sure Mr. Nimbus could tell you all about it. The Cirque De Fay is an ancient Fay art form, you know."

Salamander turned to Staccato. "Do you have any igneous like me in your show?"

"That would be Mr. Anomaly."

Pyro thrust out his chest like the proud, fire-breathing rooster he was. "So, you're an igneous, eh? I might have known, with a name like 'Salamander.' That's a good strong dragon name, that is!"

"I guess, even if it is a bajillion letters long." Salamander's eyes narrowed with a curious smile. "'Anomaly.' That name sounds familiar. Are you from around here?"

Pyro swallowed. "Ophiuchus? Uh, no. Nope. Not from around here."

Mrs. Pulvervass smiled. "If you'll just follow me I'll show you to your rooms."

***

The next morning, Mrs. Pulvervass had prepared a delicious breakfast of fermented rice and pickled cockatrice eggs, which were known for a mildly spicy, sweet, creamy yolk. The inn had a well-kept garden, and so the table was overflowing with fresh fruits and vegetables, and there was plenty of coffee to go around. Pyro had always been partial to Taurrean food, especially Ophiuchus fair, for it had a reputation of being quite spicy, a staple for any igneous.

As Pyro headed down the stairs to join the others, his attention was drawn to the headline of the newspaper resting on the sideboard in the passage.

Other Hit with Deadly Pandemic

Pyro stopped and unfolded the paper.

Following the heels of Voiler's Febris outbreak, the Other appears to be experiencing a pandemic of their own. Spanish Influenza, a disease hitherto unknown to otherworldly citizens, has killed 12,000 people in the United States this month alone. Signs of infection are said to manifest as typical flu-like symptoms but rapidly develop into deadly pneumonia. Stranger still, the disease appears to be most lethal for young men and women in their twenties and thirties. Meanwhile, Voiler continues to deal with the non-lethal Febris outbreak that began in Virgo in January of this year. Reports of the disease have spread across every kingdom within our world and show no signs of dissipating.

Pyro snapped the paper shut and stared absentmindedly at the wall. Something felt off. Footsteps rounded the corner. Staccato nearly ran headlong into the igneous.

"For heaven's sake! Are you having a catatonic meltdown in the passageway?"

Pyro ignored this remark and handed him the paper. "Have you heard about this?"

Staccato set aside his coffee and scanned the text. "What? The Firebird sighting in Khan Lau?"

"No, no! Look at the headline!"

Staccato did as told. A crease appeared in his forehead.

Pyro stroked his beard. "Why does it feel like something sinister is going on here?"

"Perhaps because it is." He folded up the headline. "I was afraid something like this might happen."

"What do you mean?"

Staccato sighed and passed a hand over his mouth. "The Jar of Elijah does more than make the soil fertile and the flowers grow. It's a powerful magical artifact that an entire community relies on. When you upset a magic that powerful you run the risk of throwing the entire world off balance. Wars are waged, curses are manifested, and sometimes plagues are born."

"You mean like Spanish Influenza? But why is it only affecting the Other? Why not Voiler?"

"My guess is it already is affecting Voiler." He set the newspaper on the sideboard. "Something tells me this Spanish flu is really just an outbreak of Febris that's spread to the Other."

"But Febris doesn't kill people!"

"It doesn't kill *our* people. Either because Voilerians have built up a resistance, or because the otherworldly don't know how to treat it properly. My guess is it's a combination of both. One thing's for sure, the sooner we can get that Jar back the better."

Chapter 30:

All Hallows' Eve

Faina did not know what to make of the pandemic that was rapidly closing in on their city. On Christmas Eve, in the bloody sanctuary of her church, death introduced itself to Faina for the first time. And after she had met him once it seemed as though his face continued to reappear. Boys in the tenement building were shipped away to France and never returned. Classmates developed fevers and disappeared from their desks. It was as though a door had opened that could never be shut, and from it a tidal wave of mortality flowed.

But life does not cease to exist when the sun goes down, and between the whispers of death and fear the students distracted themselves with thoughts of Halloween pranks, candy, and costumes. Faina was particularly excited, for it was to be her first Halloween and the idea of dressing up in a costume embodied a certain glamor from her perspective. It was all she could talk about on their morning walks to school.

"I've written down all my costume ideas in a notebook I keep beneath my pillow," she chattered as she, Leo, Anya, Pasha, and Katya made their way across the avenue, pulling down her mask so they could hear her better.

Leo caught her and reached over to tug her mask back over her mouth.

"Faina, how many times do I gotta tell you? Keep the mask on! Uncle Matvei's orders."

Faina stamped her foot. "But how is anyone supposed to hear me with this thing covering my face?"

Leo scoffed and rolled his eyes. "Trust me, Faina, it takes a lot more than a flimsy piece of paper to plug up your big mouth."

The others turned away and snickered, but Faina ignored them, eager to continue their conversation.

"First I wanted to be a cat, but then Leo thought that might cause trouble for me at school, so then I thought perhaps something exciting like a lion tamer, and Leo could be my lion!"

Leo held up his hands as though Faina were already coming at him with a three-legged stool.

"Something tells me handing you a whip is a bad idea."

Faina placed her hands high on her hips.

"You'd have nothing to be afraid of so long as you were a good lion. But you won't have to worry about that anyway because last night I got an even better idea! I was going through another one of those pamphlets school sent home with us again about Meatless Mondays when it hit me: what if I dressed up as the Statue of Liberty?"

Anya gasped approvingly and placed her hands over her cheeks. "Oh, that's a wonderful idea!"

"Isn't it though? What do you think, Pasha? I could have a crown and a big torch that I hold up just like this!" She stopped to throw up her arm in her best Statue of Liberty imitation, and looked at Pasha expectantly. But Pasha appeared baffled.

"What is Halloween?"

Faina broke her pose to leap excitedly up and down.

"I forgot! This will be your first Halloween too! Oh, Pasha, it will be so much fun!"

"Everyone puts out scary decorations, and carves pumpkins, and plays pranks on all the old folks," explained Leo in a more subdued manner.

"And all the children dress up in costumes and people give them candy," Faina finished for him. "It's a wonderful American tradition!" She stated this last part as if she knew from personal experience.

Anya nudged her in the side. "Technically, it's an Irish tradition." She held her head high, proud of her mother's heritage.

Pasha simpered at them incredulously.

"They give you candy?"

"Yes, yes, silly!" Faina insisted impatiently, fearing that Pasha might not believe her. "You knock on the doors and you say 'trick-or-treat' and hold out a bag, and the adults give you candy!"

Pasha covered his eyes and snorted. "That is the silliest thing I've ever heard! You three are trying to play a joke on us."

Leo shoved his hands coolly into his pocket. "No, no, it's true."

Faina spun in a circle and pulled at her hair as though Pasha's disbelief was too much for her to handle.

"It is, Pasha! It's real! Just wait, everyone at school will be talking about it! And then you will see we are telling the truth!"

Katya modestly raised her hand, as though school were already in session.

"Pasha, I want to dress up and get candy! Can I dress up and get candy?"

Pasha laughed as he knelt down and let Katya hop onto his back.

"If our friends are telling the truth here, I don't see why not. What would you like to dress up as?"

Katya's voice bounced with Pasha's stride as they resumed walking down the sidewalk.

"I want to be a marshmallow!"

The party stopped, looked at each other once, then doubled over in hysterical laughter. Pasha nearly dropped his little sister on the pavement.

"A marshmallow?" echoed Faina. "Why do you want to be a marshmallow?"

"Because I like marshmallows," she replied as though it were a very reasonable idea.

Anya reached over and smoothed one of her curls. "Wouldn't you rather be a princess?"

Leo nodded along. "Or a puppy dog, or a fairy, or something?"

Katya chewed on her lower lip and tapped at one of her dimples as she turned it over in her mind.

"No. I want to be a marshmallow. What will you dress up as, Pasha?"

Pasha kicked a can into the street. "Gee, I don't know. Since this is the first I'm hearing of it I don't really have any ideas."

Faina hoisted her satchel farther up on her shoulders. "With how tall you are growing, you'd make an excellent Abraham Lincoln."

Pasha gave a short laugh. "Me? Abraham Lincoln?"

"Well, if you can be the next Vanderbilt, or the next Rockefeller, why not the next Abraham Lincoln?"

Pasha nodded with approval. "I like that idea! I'll give it some thought."

"Well, you better decide quick. The sooner you make up your mind the sooner we can start working on our costumes, and I can't wait to begin putting mine together!"

As they strode up to the school, a group of girls clustered around a bench took notice of Faina and started up a chant in her honor.

"Faina is a witch! Faina is a witch!"

Faina lowered her head, grinding her teeth together.

"What's all this about?" asked Leo, eyeing the girls defensively.

"They saw me with Aunt Poppy at the market. We were gathering ingredients for those cakes she keeps sending us."

"She's making another batch of cakes?"

Ever since the beginning of the month, Aunt Poppy had been bombarding the Chevalskys and the Dalkas with veritable pounds of a bright orange cake made of herbs, spices, lemon, and who knows what else. Pasha and Katya loved them, but according to their mother, her aunt used to make a cake just like it growing up, and she'd never cared for them.

"Not only that, but we just started studying the Salem Witch Trials last week. So every time the girls see me eating one at school they call it a Witch Cake."

Now Faina's enemies had an entire textbook's worth of material to reference. So far, Faina had been accused of dancing naked in the woods, cursing other students, and keeping snakes as pets which she could then control and order to bite people. Perhaps the most hurtful thing said of her was that she looked like a witch because of her distinct, rather large aquiline nose and long, black hair.

Leo drew her to his side before she could attack.

"I'm your big brother, let me handle this one, Domino."

Clearing his throat, he raised his voice over the chorus of shouting.

"Ladies! Ladies!" He bent over them with a condescending air. "What seems to be the problem here?"

Lena Kuznestov wrinkled her brow and jabbed a finger in Faina's direction.

"Your sister is the problem! She's a hussy and a witch!"

Leo leaned back and stroked his chin thoughtfully. "I see. Well, if Faina really is a witch—" he threw up his hands, "and I'm not saying she is—do you really think it's a good idea to make her angry?"

The other girls lowered their heads and crept back a step or two, but Lena planted her hands firmly on her hips.

"Why not? What's she gonna do about it?"

"Well, for starters she'll summon a million spiders to lay eggs in your hair! Or she could put a spell on you so that you always smelled like dog poop! And if you really make her mad she might just send the Spanish flu to come and infect all of you in your sleep!"

"She can't do that!"

Leo winced and doubled over. "Wait!" He pulled his mask down and faked a coughing fit. "I think I'm coming down with something!" He draped his hand dramatically across his forehead. "It's influenza!" And then he threw himself forward in a choking fit, deliberately hacking on the girls, who screamed and scattered about. Faina, Pasha, Anya, and Katya could hardly breathe for laughing so hard.

"Leontiy Spichkin!" One of the female teachers, Ms. Busby, had witnessed Leo's little prank, and unlike the others had not found it particularly funny. She crooked her finger with a stern grimace. Leo sighed and threw back his head.

"Better go see what my penalty is."

As he marched in her direction they could hear Ms. Busby scolding, "Do you realize that if a police officer had seen you engaging in such behavior you could be arrested?"

Pasha shrugged. "She's right, you know." It was impossible to ignore the countless fliers and advertisements pasted across the city, threatening citizens with arrest for public spitting, and for coughing or sneezing without covering one's face.

The bell rang and the group split up to report to their respective classrooms. Anya and Faina were sporting makeshift suffragette badges in shades of purple and green that morning to protest the recent defeat of the suffragette amendment in the Senate. It had been Anya's idea, who, despite her quiet and reserved nature, was quite an informed and opinionated child. Indeed, it was she who had introduced Faina to the suffragette movement in the first place, and Uncle Matvei encouraged their involvement.

When they passed through the front door where Ms. Ballard was standing, her pale hand reached out and ripped the badge from Faina's lapel. Faina staggered backwards, thinking for a moment that someone had just assaulted her. When her eyes registered Ms. Ballard standing over them crumpling the badge in her hand like a crushed rose, Faina stared up at her in shock, in part because Ms. Ballard herself was an active suffragette, and a militant one at that.

"What did she do wrong?" said Anya when it appeared Faina was too astonished for words. "There's nothing in the dress code that says we can't wear suffragette badges, we asked Ms. McWhorter ahead of time."

"We only wanted to show our support," Faina finally managed to get out.

"Temperance is a part of the suffrage movement." She squeezed the badge tighter. "If you don't support prohibition then you can't support women. Your family earns their living by turning men of honor into men of violence through the sale of liquor."

216

Faina felt her hands balling into fists. "That's not true at all! Alcohol has nothing to do with suffrage! And even if it did, we're children, not business owners!"

Ms. Ballard held up her finger to silence them. "Not another word. Get to class before I decide to keep you after school."

Tears of rage were building behind Faina's eyes. Anya unclipped her own badge and tugged Faina towards the hall.

"Come on, Faina. Let's go."

***

By the end of October, paper mâché skeletons dangled from fire escapes and twisted in the harbor breeze. Cardboard decals of stringy black cats with pumpkin orange eyes and mouths shivered their jagged spines in the windows of storefronts. Chimneys heaved their lungs and emitted a gray fog upon the rooftops of the tenement buildings that smelled of burnt leaves and supper roasting.

On Halloween night the dark came alive with the soles of children's shoes scuffing the sidewalk, a percussion of doors opening and closing, and a chorus of children shouting "Trick-or-Treat." Matvei and Lydia did not think it prudent to allow the children to go knocking on doors when they could be housing influenza patients, but fortunately, the Vavilovs, whose children attended school with the Chevalskys, Dalkas, and Spichkins, were hosting a Halloween party for their young neighbors.

Like the Dalkas, the Vavilovs were a successful and generous family, and had purchased enough sweets to ensure every treat bag was satisfactorily filled. Faina and Anya were happy to introduce the Chevalskys to a variety of American sweets neither had tasted before—Pasha's particular favorites being Hershey chocolate bars and a chocolate taffy called Tootsie Rolls, while the outer edges of Katya's lips were stained orange from consuming the marshmallow-like Circus Peanuts. When the party was over, and the four children had begun their gradual descent from their sugar high, Uncle Matvei sent Leo to escort the group safely home.

Katya was struggling to keep up at their heels. Her marshmallow costume had not been difficult to put together; it was merely an old bolster with holes cut out for her arms and head. Unfortunately, it seemed to hamper her walking and range of motion. Pasha had originally confided in Faina that he was worried Katya might get upset when no one could figure out what she was supposed to be, but they soon discovered that as long as Katya got candy she didn't really care one way or the other.

"How you holding up, little 'mallow?" teased Leo, pushing his simple black mask back over his hair.

Katya huffed and puffed on the sidewalk as she struggled to hoist her little sack over her shoulder.

"I'm okay, Leo."

But this was obviously not the case, and when Leo offered to carry her, Katya immediately took him up on his proposal.

Faina sashayed along in a mint-green tunic fashioned from an old bed sheet, pinned and swathed in various places. Together she and Anya had crafted a torch from an old wineglass painted green, with yellow tissue paper stuck in the bowl for the flames. On her head she wore a pointed crown over perfectly coiled curls. At every apartment they visited, Faina's Statue of Liberty costume was the highlight of the group.

Meanwhile, Pasha had decided to dress as Eddie Ainsmith—more commonly known as "Dorf," the Russian-American baseball player— complete with hat and Louisville Slugger, which he tied his bag of candy to like a hobo sack.

As they made their way up Allen Street with their bags sagging towards the ground, they noticed a crowd had gathered up ahead, and a police van was parked on the side of the street.

"What do you think happened there?" inquired Anya, looking more innocent than ever beneath the halo of her angel costume. Leo squinted his eyes in the darkness and shrugged.

"Probably just some kids caught egging another storefront."

"But there are lights flashing up ahead," observed Faina.

Anya continued to stare. "They look like … camera lights."

As they neared closer, Faina realized Anya was probably right. Shots of white were salvoing into the night one after the other, and gradually they became aware of several men in trench coats with notepads in their hands. Leo squinted his eyes.

"Those are reporters!"

"In that case it couldn't be just another Halloween prank." Faina took a curious step forward. "Something serious must have happened!"

Anya's knees turned inwards as she drew back in the other direction.

"Which is exactly why we should avoid it."

But Leo pressed a hand to her back and shooed her forward.

"Oh, come on, Anya. The police are already there, what's the worst that could happen?"

Poor Anya rolled her eyes as she was once again overruled by her reckless relatives, and shuffled close behind Faina. When they had traveled halfway down the block they were able to pick up pieces of what the reporters were shouting, chiefly the words: anarchist, Galleani, Palmer Raids, bomb.

When they had made it a few yards from the front of the tenement building, Pasha turned cautiously to Faina.

"You don't think there's been another explosion, do you? I mean, by the Galleanists."

But Faina barely heard him. With every step her surroundings grew more and more familiar, until at last her senses had become infected with dread.

"Faina, are you alright?" inquired Pasha.

But she was unable to answer, for just as they were coming upon the scene the police dragged Anastas's mother and father from the building in handcuffs. Mr. Sippenhaft was hysterical, shouting in German at the tops of his lungs.

"*Schwein! Drecksau!* You filthy pigs!" He spat upon the ground as they loaded him into the back of the van. Mrs. Sippenhaft proved to be a far greater difficulty as she kicked both legs and screamed, fell to the ground, clawed at the doorframe, and tried to bite the officers. Presently, a man walking his dog came up behind them, also drawn to the commotion.

"What seems to be the problem, Officer?"

The policeman shook his head and sighed. "Oh, just another pair of Galleanists trying to construct a bomb inside their tenement. Had plans to set it off near Wall Street. We caught up with a few of their buddies earlier. Took them down to the station. But it's nothing to worry about now, sir. Got it all taken care of. If they ain't facing deportation, the judge will have them up for the electric chair."

Standing off to the side with nothing to do but watch the humiliating spectacle unfold were Anastas and his two younger brothers, who both carried an empty pillowcase for a Halloween sack.

The second brother, Vadim, had a cape thrown over his shoulders and a little black mask. The youngest, Alexei, who was no more than seven, wore a pair of puppy dog ears. Poor Alexei was inconsolable and his sobs were so loud they partially drowned out the reporters. Vadim

219

was also struggling, now and again rubbing his fists into his eyes. But Anastas was stone-faced. He did not spare a tear but watched his parents with fire in his eyes.

"Why is that boy so sad?" asked Katya, her voice taking on a pitiful tremor.

But no one dared answer her. Leo put his hand on her head and held it against his shoulder to shield her from seeing any more.

"Come on guys, let's get out of here."

But Pasha did not move. Faina stopped and looked back at him. It was though Pasha was seeing Anastas with new eyes. For a brief moment the resentment he owed Anastas was eclipsed by a heavy feeling of pity and sympathy. Faina wanted to say something to Anastas, wanted to comfort him, but she could think of no words to erase his pain and humiliation.

As Anastas was watching the police load his mother into the van, he caught the group passing on the sidewalk staring, and his eyes fixed angrily on Pasha. Pasha opened and shut his mouth, as though hoping something useful would spring forth, but nothing came out. Faina could only stare pitifully. Leo tugged on her arm.

"Faina! Pasha! What are you doing? Let's go!"

She did not look back a second time. She let Leo lead them away, and together they rounded the corner onto Orchard Street. Katya was in tears.

Chapter 31:

Mums

Things began returning to normal once the trees started loosening their grip on their colorful foliage. The worst of the Influenza pandemic had died off with October's final breath, and people shed their paper masks to reveal hopeful smiles embedded in chapped cheeks.

Leo's chin fell to his chest as he looked down into the viewfinder of the camera which sat slightly below chest level. It was odd to gaze towards the ground and find the scene in front of him replacing the asphalt, almost as though there were an entirely different world residing inside the box. Just as he was bringing his finger down over the button, someone came up behind him and tapped him on the shoulder.

"Hello, Leo!"

The camera flipped in Leo's startled hands and bounced around once or twice before he secured it against his chest. He looked over his shoulder and blushed. It was Jazmin Zureiq, standing there with her intense brown eyes gazing into his and smiling.

"I wouldn't have pegged you as the easily startled type!" She giggled and covered her lips with her fingers, which were sheathed in a pair of hand-me-down gloves. "You don't remember me, do you? I'm Jazmin Zureiq. We met once during the summer. Your sister liked my sunflowers."

Leo rubbed the sweat from his palms on the sides of his jacket. "Are you kidding? Of course I remember you! I just—I didn't expect to see you here is all!"

Jazmin swaggered past the storefront he had been standing in front of. "You'll find I'm actually here quite often." She threw out her hands towards the name painted on the window, the same way Leo had when he mimicked the perfume ads.

Zureiq's Nursery and Floral Arrangements

Leo threw his hand over his eyes and laughed. "Oh! This is your family's flower shop!"

"We live in the apartment above. I saw you from the window."

"You'd think as a photographer my skills of observation would be keener." He knit his hands together and cracked his knuckles. "So, how's business these days?"

"Things have slowed down lately. We sold a lot of floral arrangements at the height of the pandemic … what with the funerals and such. We're glad it's winding down now of course, but we could really use a little business, preferably for a happier reason. I've seen your pictures in the school paper, by the way. I read your articles too. You really are very talented."

For once in his life the boy who always had an answer for everything didn't know what to say. He scratched nervously at the back of his head.

"Aw, gee, I uh, I don't know about that." He held up the Kodak. "The Brownie makes it pretty easy, after all." He cleared his throat. "I'm actually saving up for a folding camera, something a little more professional."

The light from the sun caught beneath the brim of Jazmin's hat and lit up her irises like two garnet gemstones.

"My goodness, they're already so magnificent! I can't imagine them looking any better than they already do."

Leo wiped absentmindedly at the lens of his camera with a cloth.

"Well, that's real nice of you to say." His eyes darted from the loose strands of wavy hair falling in front of her ears, to the corners of her plump lips. "So, uh, you said things were winding down at the shop now that the pandemic is over. You have any nice autumn arrangements?"

"Certainly! Mums are especially nice this time of year. At the moment we have more than we know what to do with! It would be nice if we could pull in a little more business just to get rid of them."

Leo stroked his chin thoughtfully. "Is that so? Well, how would you feel about an advertisement in the school paper?"

Jazmin's mouth fell open as her mind opened to the possibility. "Gee, I don't know. How much would it cost?"

"How much would it cost?" Leo echoed, snickering. "It's a school paper, silly, it wouldn't cost you a dime."

Jazmin giggled and shook her head in self-admonishment.

"Picture it," he offered, throwing out his hand as though they were both looking at a vast, bucolic landscape. "We'll put up a big old picture of the storefront, the windows chock full of, uh, Mumps—"

"Mums," she corrected him, trying not to laugh.

Leo tossed his hand comically, "Same thing. Then we do a couple of close-ups, maybe with a pumpkin or two in the background, one with you and those pretty hands of yours."

Jazmin covered her mouth as a pinkish hue crept over her nose and cheeks.

"We'll do an article all about how Zureiq's Flower Shop is the number one place to get the perfect blossoms for your fall centerpiece, that Mums are the must-have item on your Thanksgiving table this year! Looks great next to the turkey! Kids love 'em! Helps with the seasonal allergies, all that kinda stuff."

Jazmin shook her head with an arch expression as she stifled another bout of laughter. "My, my, Leo! If things don't work out for you as a photographer, you'd make a wonderful salesman!"

Leo threw back his head and laughed. "Well, my mother did always say I had a flair for the dramatic. But then, the apple doesn't fall far from the tree."

"I'll speak to my father about your idea. I just know he'll love it! Anything to pick things up!"

Leo smoothed the collar of his jacket. "Yeah, just let me know and we can set a date for a photoshoot. My uncle owns the *Opa!* on Orchard Street."

Once she thanked him and returned back inside, Leo felt as though his chest had filled up with hot air. He ran his hands through his bangs and leaned back against the brick wall with a feeling of giddiness.

Chapter 32:

The Black Pavilion

Pyro kept the hood of his waterproof cloak pulled low over his brow as he trudged through the muddy back alleys of the Black Pavilion, the black market district in Khan Lau. They had each been assigned a specific task with the goal of locating Kha Fang's headquarters. Melodious was to speak with the local monks, Staccato was to gather information from the authorities, Sonata was to converse with Mrs. Pulvervass, and Skelter was to use his skills of stealth to spy on a local fruit vendor that was rumored to have a direct trade with the Jade Bone. But Pyro had been sent straight into the belly of the beast.

He reached into his pocket and took out a tin of Cherry Bombs, a chewing candy made with burning bush sap. They were such a notoriously sticky sweet they had managed to earn their own urban legend during Pyro's boyhood, touting that anyone who ate more than four at a time would get their mouths glued shut. While the rumor was plausible—it was made with burning bush sap after all—Pyro had refused to believe it. And after accepting a dare from Sparky Hoguera, Pyro had to have his mouth pried open by a caim.

Pyro popped one of the red, taffy-like balls into his mouth and returned the tin to his pocket. Many of the Primal hustlers in Khan Lau took to chewing illegal, highly addictive yogao leaves as a form of recreation, and Pyro wanted to add to his credibility without jeopardizing his health.

He crossed the broken and cracked stones of the street to a decaying tavern with a sign that read "Madame Green's". A turquoise cord with a crescent-shaped charm known as the Lunar Crest had been tied about the right-hand column. Historically, the Lunar Crest had been used to bring good fortune, but the invading Primals had re-appropriated the charm to identify dens where illegal drugs were sold, most notably sopor and yogao.

An old sylph man covered in graying thorns was squatting by the threshold. He was clearly suffering from a bad case of ligneus, a disease common to elderly sylphs where parts of the flesh become permanently wooden, causing the joints to stiffen and the flesh to become bark. He stretched out his arm across the entrance, allowing it to grow and evolve into a branch until at last he had barricaded the door.

"Password?"

Pyro could not help but notice that he had moss growing from his left nostril, and he could see from the state of his teeth that he was a yogao addict. He reached into his pocket and tossed the man a sack of change. The sylph pulled at the leather drawstring and squinted inside. He retracted his spiny arm from the door.

"You may enter."

Inside, the bar was dark and reeked of rot and drugs. He elbowed his way to the counter.

"Bruiser on the rocks, no ferōx."

The woman at the counter grabbed a coffin-shaped bottle from the shelf and poured a plum-colored liquid into a glass of ice. Pyro took her to be Madame Green, for her ensemble was overly embellished with the hue. She perfectly fit the description of a stereotypical mistress of a sopor house. She had over-accessorized with local ephemera: a trailing dress, braided earrings, and long, painted nails, but she stood out as a Draconian with her overly symmetrical face and eerily pristine features.

Despite the fact that Ophiuchus was constantly blamed and criticized for the emergence of sopor, it was the invading Primals who had introduced the illegal drug to Ophiuchus during their occupation, and the locals resented the Draconians for desecrating their culture.

As Pyro was sliding his money towards her fingers he slipped his palm over Madame Green's hand and leaned towards her ear.

"I hear you buy philters here." Philters was slang for love potion. He wondered if any of the others would've known to use such lingo.

A dimple materialized at the corner of her mouth. "Warm hands."

"Runs in the bloodline." Pyro summoned a flame to the tip of his tongue and licked his teeth with a wicked smile.

"You selling?"

Pyro pulled down the corner of his collar to reveal a vial on a string around his neck. It was a fake of course, but that didn't matter.

"For the right price."

"Upstairs on the right. Room with the beaded curtains. Wait for me there."

"Excellent."

He threw back his Bruiser and headed up the green carpeted steps, feeling at home for once in his work. It was easier to pretend here amongst the hustlers and gangsters and their illegal potions than it was to perform before the C.O.N. and turn a blind eye to their battered slaves.

The wallpaper was graffitied with a variety of runes and curses, and there was a mysterious cloud of pink swirling smoke hanging around one of the lanterns on the ceiling that most likely indicated an infestation of Mab Flies, a bug known for causing obsessive dreams of love and infatuation, and whose nectar was often used in the making of love potions.

"I told you, no one gets to Kha Fang unless they go through me," bellowed an angry voice from a room on the left.

Pyro tiptoed towards the door and leaned his ear against the wall.

"Listen," said another voice. "I know what Kha Fang is keeping locked up in that hideout of yours."

Pyro held his breath. He could hardly believe his luck.

"You know nothing," spat the first voice.

"Who do you think you're kidding? You got ophidians bringing you genuine Virgonian artifacts. Instead of sopor fiends we've got collectors coming in and out of the Black Pavilion. I know what Kha Fang's been up to, and so does Madame Green. We want in on the action. So, unless you want the authorities to know about the little professor you're holding hostage, I'd show me a little more respect. There's been a price on your head for sometime now. I wonder, how much will the bounty hunters pay for the infamous Boss Raksha?"

There was a crashing noise and then a moan as one of the men was hurled across the room. Pyro could hear choking, and then all went silent.

"You ain't telling nobody nothing," said Raksha.

Footsteps neared the threshold. Pyro sailed across the hall to the door with the beads and hid inside. He could hear the door opening, and the sound of Raksha passing down the hall. Pyro peeked his head out just in time to see the back of a large man hurrying down the stairs.

"Hey, can I get a sanguine on the rocks?"

Pyro retreated back behind the beaded curtains. He had to find out what Madame Green knew. He observed his surroundings. He appeared to be in some sort of chintzy smoking room. Silk cushions with fraying tassels littered the dingy floor, which was encased in a layer of ash.

By his foot was a discarded tray topped with what was known as a dragon pot, a miniature portable fire pit fashioned from a cauldron most often used to roast river prawns and eels. Situated at each corner of the room was a tall, narrow vase made from clear glass, of which Pyro could discern no purpose. The room might have been rather comfortable had it not been for the myriads of questionable stains amongst the silk and satin.

The beaded curtains made a second appearance in a raised wooden canopy with gilded accents and an embroidered mattress at the center of the room. Pyro pushed the tray aside with the toe of his boot and approached the bed. The front was flanked by pierced lattice panels painted to look like red lacquer. Below the mattress was a sort of porch with a step-up to the bed. Curious, Pyro wandered onto the platform and eyed the beaded drapes hanging on either side of the pallet. He reached out a hand.

The strands of beads curled upwards and snapped like a whip, springing to life. Before Pyro could react they circled around his wrists and ankles, ensnaring him to the bed. Pyro sucked in a gust of air and released a stream of fire from his lips, but the fire seemed to disappear from his mouth entirely and instead materialized in the four glass jars at each corner of the room. It was some form of enchantment.

High-heeled shoes clicked outside the door and approached the bed. Madame Green loomed over him with a knife and a pair of tongs. She had two men at her side.

"It's been a while since an igneous has wandered into my bar. You know the Black Pavilion will pay one hundred fifty thousand hands for an ignition gland." She turned to the men. "Hold his head back."

A pair of rough hands reached under his chin and jerked his head back, exposing the front of his neck.

"*Oi*! Let go!" Pyro kicked and flailed as a set of fingers clamped down on his mouth.

"Don't struggle now." Madame Green pinched the tongs open and closed. "Besides, it'll grow back."

A clamor echoed up the passage from downstairs. The man dropped Pyro's head. A cacophony of angry voices was mounting below.

"Intruder! Wait until I get my hands on him, the little petal-grubber!"

There was a sound like glass bottles being thrown at a wall and shattering. Madame Green drew back with a huff.

"What's going on down there?"

The voices were growing louder. Footsteps stampeded up the stairs and past the door. Madame Green and her two cronies flew out into the hallway, leaving Pyro tied up beneath the canopy.

"Acantho! What are you doing?"

"Snatch him! String him up by his ankles, the little briar!" Pyro recognized the wizened old voice of the doorman.

"Who?"

"The little boy! He gave me false coins!"

"You greedy idiot! You were taking bribes again, weren't you? It's no more than you deserve, you old fool!"

Pyro tugged at his restraints but they refused to come free. He would likely need some sort of password.

"Well? What are you two standing around for?" She must have been addressing her associates. "Go find him!"

She returned to the bedside. Pyro wasted no time. Taking advantage of the length of his cords, he looped the excess beads around her neck.

"You live, I live. Say the word to let me go."

"What word?"

Pyro pulled tighter. "Don't play games with me!"

She clapped her hands three times. "Red opals!"

The beads slackened. Pyro sprang off the bed and grabbed his chakras from their holsters.

"You made a mistake."

Madame Green rose up from the floor and scoffed.

"I run a tavern, mister, not a teahouse." She stretched out her arms and the roasting forks rose from the tray on the floor. Not only was she an ophidian but apparently a trained lilith as well. "I'm used to bar fights."

The roasting forks flew at Pyro's face. Pyro ducked as they whizzed past, embedding themselves in the wall. The crystals on the chandelier trembled and shot off the frame one at a time. They flung at Pyro's figure with such force they tore holes in the plaster. Pyro somersaulted across the room, and chucked his chakra at the spindly heel of her shoe, severing it clean off. Madame Green stumbled sideways onto the bed where the curtains snatched her up. Pyro hovered over her, his chakras lit.

"Suppose the password's no use if you can't clap your hands."

She spat at him. "Let me go!"

"Hold your horses now, it ain't that easy. You gotta answer my questions first."

"What questions?"

"What do you know about Dr. Desmond?" He tossed his chakra in the air, catching it before it hit her nose.

"You mean the professor from Virgo? She's being held hostage by Kha Fang and Boss Raksha."

"Where?"

"I don't know the location. Only that they've been holding her prisoner for the past year or so."

"Is Boss Raksha still here?"

"He left not long ago. Ordered a sanguine to go."

"Do you know where he was headed?"

"He didn't say."

"Where can I usually find him?"

"The fish market. He owns it. He lives in the old lighthouse."

Pyro reached into his pocket for the tin of Cherry Bombs. "You've been swell, Madame." He took a handful of the candy. "How about a sweet for your good behavior?" He stuffed the Cherry Bombs into her mouth.

Madame Green tried to open her mouth but it wouldn't budge. She squeaked angrily at Pyro.

Pyro threw back his head and laughed. "I hear the Black Pavilion sells teeth as well. You might be needing some by the time you get out."

As he approached the beaded door he stopped and gave them a suspicious poke. They swung lifelessly from the doorjamb. Pyro hurried through them all the same.

A soft thumping noise drew his eye to a door at the end of the passage. A loose doorknob was bobbing rhythmically in its brackets. Pyro ripped open the door and was met with a mounting tidal wave. He sprang up the wall and grabbed a beam in the ceiling as the water barreled down the hall in a slithery path.

That's not a tidal wave, thought Pyro. *That's a flood dragon!* As the tail trickled out the door, he spotted a familiar boy clinging to its back and yelling.

"Sal?"

Salamander and the flood dragon flowed down the stairs leaving a waterlogged Acantho in their path. Pyro let go of the beam, and vaulted over the railing. The dragon surfed across the bar in a watery stream, gathering up bottle caps and change in its wake. Pyro grabbed a leftover river prawn from an abandoned plate and seized an empty bottle from the counter. He jumped atop a table and whistled.

"*Oi*! Dragon!" The dragon turned. Pyro waved the river prawn and dropped it into the bottle. "Come and get it!"

The flood dragon sped towards him in a wavy line, whipping its tail back and forth. It dove nose-first into the neck of the bottle, liquefying and shrinking to fill the container. As it wriggled itself inside, Salamander fell to the floor. When the last bit of its tail disappeared into the container, Pyro corked the bottle and gave a shake. To the untrained eye it was simply a container of shimmery water, though now and again a pair of eyes would materialize and blink.

The remaining patrons, sopping wet with their drinks on the floor, scowled at Pyro. Acantho limped to the top of the stairs.

"Seize them both!"

Pyro grabbed Salamander by the back of the neck and shoved him under his arm.

"You're an igneous, right?"

"Yeah."

"Perfect."

He grabbed one of his chakras, lit it with his arm, and chucked it at the collection of alcohol displayed behind the bar. The counter went up in a fiery explosion. Pyro raced out the door, catching the chakra with his back turned. With Salamander still tucked under his arm, he sprinted as fast as he could until they at last reached the border of the Black Pavilion. Pyro ducked into a temple garden and hid inside an empty gazebo. He sat Sal down on the bannister with a stern look in his eyes.

"What were you doing in the Black Pavilion?"

Salamander crossed his arms over his chest. "I could ask you the same question!"

"I'm an adult, thank you very much! You on the other hand had no business being inside that bar!"

"I was there on a business venture."

"A business venture?"

"I need investors for my latest project, a hydro-powered booby trap for mega pests like mammoths, dragons, and bashe. I already have a prototype in my backyard. I call it 'Salamander's Sensational Snare!'"

Pyro looked him over doubtfully. "You're going to catch a bashe? A thirty-foot snake with teeth as big as you are?"

"I will with my Sensational Snare!"

"And what on earth would someone in the Black Pavilion want with an exterminator?"

"You saw the flood dragon, right? Haíchi are the least of their problems!" He held up the bottle with the flood dragon inside. "Wait until my customers see this! They'll be lining up at the door!"

Pyro snatched the bottle out of his hands. "Surely, you could find just as much business in a safer part of the city."

"Yeah, but the Black Pavilion's where the real money's at. They say gangsters are full of cash, and not just any kind of cash, I'm talking about that gambling money, son! The big bucks! These guys give out hundred hands as tips!"

"Kid, I hate to break it to you, but when these fellas are tipping hundred hands it ain't to exterminators." He sucked his teeth. "I'd ask if your mother knows where you've been but I think I already know the answer to that."

Sal removed his hat and fanned himself with the brim, looking exceptionally sly.

"Well, you still haven't said what you were doing here. The only reason anybody goes to the Black Pavilion is to look for trouble." He paused and lowered his chin. "Or money. But you don't strike me as a businessman." He gasped. "Wait a minute! I know why you're here! I've read all about this kinda stuff in books!" He put his elbow over his face as though he were some masked crusader from a melodrama. "You're seeking revenge on the kingpin who murdered your family!"

"Wrong."

"Well, it's either that or you're on some kinda secret undercover mission to rescue someone. I know you're not just here to put on some fancy circus show because nobody ever wants to come here; it's out in the middle of nowhere! And you can't be here to trade in the Black Pavilion because you have a princess with you, and you're the former prince of Aries who used to rescue children for the Saighdeoir! I recognized you from the papers."

Pyro roped his hand around his mouth and hissed. "Shhhh! Not so loud!" When he was convinced no one had heard he loosened his grip on Sal's mouth.

"My dad is a detective you know," whispered Sal. "That's how we ended up in Khan Lau in the first place. We're really from Pleione, but my dad got transferred here to monitor the local gang activity. So, you could say I'm kind of an expert on this stuff."

"Sal, your dad is a detective?"

"Yep! Detective Typhon Pulvervass, Malediction Investigator and Gang Intelligence Operative."

"Malediction? Your dad works with hex trafficking?"

"Hex trafficking, curse breaking, the illegal manufacturing of love potions, you name it."

Pyro stepped back and pinched his chin. The kid had them all figured out. He rubbed his hands over his forehead and drew a deep breath.

"Do you think your dad would know where I could find Kha Fang?"

Sal leaned back with a smug grin that filled his dimpled cheeks. "You're doing undercover work, aren't you?"

"Look, I could get in big trouble for saying any of this."

"But you haven't said anything." Salamander winked, and Pyro couldn't help but be amused.

"Listen." Sal looked once over each shoulder and leaned in closer. "I can tell you where Kha Fang is. They say he stores all his contraband in the old Tian Shi Yuan Trading Company warehouse on the river. You know where that is, right?"

"Yeah, I know where that is."

"But listen …" He placed a hand on Pyro's shoulder with the attitude of a thirty-year-old. "You can't just walk up and knock on the door. First, you gotta meet with Boss Raksha. No one gets to Kha Fang without going through Boss Raksha first."

"So I've heard. They say I can find him at the old lighthouse in the fish market. Do you know where that is?"

"It's right outside the warehouse. He lives there. You just gotta walk up to him and—this part is really important—you have to say, 'I need to see someone about a kissing loach.' And you gotta say it just like that."

"Why? What's a kissing loach?"

Sal stared back at him with eyes half shut in a sarcastic expression. "It's a code for selling illegal magic. How long did you say you've been working undercover? A kissing loach is one of the rarest fish in the world; they don't sell it at the fish market, so he'll know what you mean."

Chapter 33:
The Orphan Asylum

The orphanage on the Bowery smelled of damp sheets and damp cardboard walls, and of rusted tin mugs and heavily starched bed linens. It sounded like threadbare shoelaces being drawn too tightly through their gray grommets, the clunky heels of the house matron scraping the weathered floor. There were shrieking infants, sobbing children, rulers snapping over bare skin. All in all it wasn't much different from home, except that here there was less freedom.

Because they were older, Anastas and Vadim were placed in a dormitory separate from Alexei, who was struggling the most since their parents' arrest. Every night, just when they were settling into their thin mattresses with the cringing iron bed frames, Vadim would get up the courage to whisper to his brother.

"Anastas, what are we gonna do?"

And every night Anastas would make one reply. "We're not staying here."

He had barely spoken since the arrest, and his brothers were afraid to approach him. He had not shed a tear for his parents. He sat in silent corners alone, unblinking, with his elbows on his knees or on a desk, and his hands knit in front of his mouth. His spine was as rigid as an ironwood switch. He did not flinch at loud noises or sudden movements. It was as though the very heat from his impassioned bitterness had fossilized his exterior like rhyolite.

One evening as they sat down to their supper on the long wooden bench of the cafeteria table, eating their portions in silence, Alexei began to cry. At first neither Vadim nor Anastas said anything. But when the boy was not immediately tended to his tears grew fat, and his cries grew louder. Finally Anastas snapped his hand across his brother's wrist.

"Stop it! Stop crying! Do you wanna get in trouble?"

"I wanna go home!"

"You can't, there's no one there! And it's no use crying for Ma and Pa because they're the ones who put us here!"

Exhausted of Anastas's ill temper and sullen moping, Vadim slammed his fork down.

"Well, who's gonna be the one to get us out? Huh?"

Anastas glared at his brother in stony silence, but Vadim was not intimidated.

"You said we won't stay here. So what are you gonna do?"

Anastas exhaled heavily through his nose and, breaking off his gaze with his brother, stabbed his fork into a piece of meat.

"I'm working on it."

"What's to work on? It's simple, isn't it? We gotta go to the Bowery Butchers."

Anastas rolled his eyes and pushed back his plate in annoyance.

"Go to the Bowery Butchers," he snarled. "Forget the Bowery Butchers! The Butchers are the ones who provided Ma and Pa with the nitroglycerin for the explosives! They're every bit to blame for us being here as our parents!"

"Who cares if they gave them the nitroglycerin? After Angela's parents got arrested her uncle made arrangements with the Bowery Butchers to make sure she would be taken care of. I hear they've put her in a cathouse."

Anastas froze. A chill ran down his spine. Angela Bartoletti was a schoolmate of their's, only twelve years old. He rubbed the space between his eyebrows with his thumb and forefinger.

"Do you even know what a cathouse is, dummy?"

"Of course," shot Vadim defensively. "It's a boardinghouse for girls."

Anastas groaned into the back of his sleeve as he closed his eyes and tried not to imagine what poor Angela might be going through at that moment. He shoved the heel of his hand up against his forehead and cringed.

"What?" Vadim blinked his innocent eyes.

Anastas turned so that one eye was showing and scowled at his brother.

"You're an idiot."

"Fine, let's see you come up with a better idea!"

"I'm gonna join the Breadwinners. I hear there's big money to be made in street fighting."

"But Ma and Pa hated the Breadwinners!"

"Good. Even better! Let them see what becomes of their boys now they've abandoned them for their own glory. All I need is a stable job and then I can pay for board at the children's lodging house on Duane Street. We won't get separated, and we won't have to suffer this prison."

"But you're only twelve! What makes you think they'll take you?"

"I'm strong." Anastas pounded his fist against the table as though trying to prove it. "They made an exception for Grusha Garin. Once they see me they'll make an exception, too. Besides, they don't have to know the truth."

Anastas felt a pair of eyes narrowing on him hawklike from across the room. A housemother, her lips drawn tight with reprimand, was headed their way. She must have overheard them. Anastas's eyes channeled into a scowl of defiance. She stopped short of the table, her dry hands folded together. She looked down at Anastas.

"You have a visitor."

Anastas was so surprised that his seemingly permanent glower fell from his lips.

"Me?"

"Yes, you." Without further explanation she demanded that he come along. Anastas surreptitiously set his bowl of mashed potatoes on Alexei's plate when the housemother's back was turned, and allowed her to escort him towards the front office. Through the blinds he could see a pair of red galoshes. For the first time in weeks Anastas actually gave something of a smile. It was Faina!

The housemother opened the door. She recited some sort of condescending instruction, but Anastas didn't hear her; he was waiting for her to shut the door.

"Do you understand, Master Sippenhaft?" she finished.

Anastas gave a surprisingly courteous nod, prompting the woman to raise her eyebrows. Even Faina seemed to look him over with curiosity. Finally, the housemother shut the door. Without even thinking, Anastas pulled Faina up from the chair and roped her into a hug so tight he lifted her up on her toes. No sooner had he done this than he became aware of his actions and quickly set her down, backing away and shoving his hands in his pockets. Faina looked bewildered.

"How did you find me?" he asked, forcing a frown back into his features.

"It took some asking around, but we finally managed to track you down through the police station."

"We?"

Faina opened her mouth, then closed it again. "My family and I."

Recalling how Faina had stood on the sidewalk with Pasha and watched as his parents were arrested, Anastas turned away from her and stared out the window.

"Come to laugh at me?"

"Of course not! Why would I do that?"

"You and Chevalsky seemed to enjoy watching my parents get arrested."

She reached out and put a hand on his arm. "Anastas, we were not there to make fun of you."

Anastas screwed his head around to gaze darkly into her face. "Pasha wouldn't stop staring me down!"

Faina drew back and rubbed the side of her cheek with her hand. "He wasn't staring at you to be mean, he was staring because he was sad for you."

"I don't need his pity!"

Faina groaned and covered her eyes with her hand. "Would you rather he have been gloating?"

Anastas ground his teeth together and forced his head away from her. He did not know the answer to her question. Faina rummaged in the inside of her coat.

"His little sister wanted Alexei and Vadim to have this."

Anastas turned around. She was holding two very full brown paper bags. Anastas surveyed her up and down questioningly.

"She saw that their bags were empty and felt bad that they missed out on trick-or-treating, so she wanted to give them some of her own."

Anastas had a funny deflating feeling inside his chest and over his shoulders, as though he couldn't quite stand up straight. He lowered his head. Faina stared at him with an expectant look in her eyes and shook the bags.

"What? You don't believe me? Or you just don't want to because it's Pasha's little sister?"

Anastas chewed on his lower lip and conceded to take the bags. He had to admit she was pretty gutsy to visit him in an orphanage during an influenza outbreak.

"Little girls are always nice, I guess." He shrugged. "At least up until a certain point."

"Katya is a very nice little girl. When she saw Alexei was crying she sobbed all the way home."

At the mention of such an idea, Anastas could not help but snicker a little. Faina's face softened. She smiled, drawing his attention to the happy sprinkle of freckles across her full cheeks. She looked very pretty in her coat and hat.

"Tell her we said thanks." His smile was creeping further up his cheeks, and he had to duck his head to keep it concealed. "And that Alexei and Vadim were really happy."

He could see from the way she was eyeing him that she had seen the full extent of his grin, but Faina had a way of looking at him that made him feel less embarrassed.

"Didn't you want to go trick-or-treating?"

Anastas scoffed as he rubbed the space behind his neck. "I'm too old for that kinda kid stuff."

"How old are you anyway?"

"Twelve. Turned twelve two months ago. The twentieth."

Faina tugged playfully on his sleeve. "Why didn't you tell me when your birthday was?"

Anastas raised a comical eyebrow. She was always wanting to know little things about people. It was strange, but funny in a way.

"Why does it matter?"

"Because then I could have told you happy birthday!"

Anastas snorted, he couldn't help himself. "You are so strange."

They laughed as they sat down on the patchy sofa together. As he took her in with his eyes he began to notice the little changes in her. She was taller now. Bits of her were growing older. Not only did she look different but her English was clearer now, and he could find pieces of the city embedded in her accent. Faina lowered her eyes, and folded her hands in her lap.

"I'm sorry about your parents."

"Don't be. I don't care about them."

There was an awkward pause as Faina rocked back in her seat.

"Are they treating you well? Pasha says that the orphan asylums aren't always—"

Anastas cringed and squeezed his fists as she once again mentioned Pasha.

"What does Pasha know about the orphan asylums? Do you have to keep mentioning Chevalsky?"

Faina glared at him, offended. "Pasha is my friend and my neighbor. He's part of my life, just like Uncle Matvei, just like Leo. He's bound to come up!"

"You don't mention your uncle or your brother half as much as you mention Pasha. What's so great about him anyhow?"

"For starters, he is kind, and funny, and smart. Just like you!"

Anastas swayed back, dumbfounded. Kind? Funny? Smart, of course, but no one had ever used the words "kind and funny" to describe Anastas. *He* wouldn't have even used those words. She went on.

"You're just prejudiced against Pasha because his father was a baron, and if you hadn't been prejudiced in the first place there wouldn't be this row between you!"

Anastas could feel his shoulders locking and his eyes sliding to stare at the opposite wall. Before he knew it, Faina had gotten to her feet.

"I am leaving. I did not come here to argue with you."

Anastas snapped to attention. He reached out for her arm.

"Faina—"

But her hand was already on the knob.

"Pasha Chevalsky is my friend, and if you can't accept that then we can't be friends either."

And before he could stop her she had slammed the door in his face. Anastas stood there staring at the wood grain for several seconds, then slowly he sank back into the sofa with his head in his hands.

Chapter 34:

The Tian Shi Yuan Trading Company

Pyro looked down at the set of directions Sal had written for him on a piece of paper.

"Well, this is the place."

The rain pounded noisily against the tin roof of the dilapidated warehouse, causing the curvy wood to swell as it leaked down the exterior walls. The caravan was parked off the road and was well hidden behind the thick shrubbery.

"And you think Dr. Desmond is inside?" asked Sonata, pulling her coat tighter about her.

Pyro shoved the paper inside his pocket. "Seems the most likely place to me." He turned to Staccato. "You got your decoys?"

Staccato held up the box of vials he had been keeping in his pocket. "All here. The Black Pavilion will pay a handsome price for visions forged by a miraculous."

"And still more when they find out which miraculous forged them," added Melodious.

Sonata bit nervously at her lip. "Is it really safe for him to go as himself? Wouldn't it be better to use a fake name?"

Staccato shrugged. "If anything it will make me more credible to the C.O.N. to make them think I've been selling to illegal hex dealers. Now, do you and Melodious remember the signals?"

"If either of us has a vision of a blue bat then we're to ready the caravan because you'll be coming out soon," recited Sonata. "If, on the other hand, we have a vision of a green butterfly we're to flee immediately."

"Precisely." Staccato turned up his collar. "Are we ready, boys?"

Skelter threw him a thumbs up while Pyro nodded. The three of them headed to the lighthouse and pulled the bell. An enormous man with a long, tapering mustache ripped open the door. Pyro immediately recognized Boss Raksha by his silhouette. There was a bit of food stuck to his facial hair suggesting they had interrupted his dinner, and he didn't look too happy about it.

"Ah, Boss Raksha," said Staccato, his voice unwavering. "I need to see someone about a Kissing Loach."

"Who are you?"

"I am Sir Staccato Nimbus. Miraculous. These are my associates, but you needn't bother with their names." He pulled the box of decoys from his pocket and lowered his voice. "We're looking to make a trade."

Boss Raksha held the box close to his eye and peeked under the lid. His irritation subsided but he lost none of his suspicion.

"And what are you hoping to trade these for?"

"Depends on what you have."

"We have hexes, Mr. Nimbus, and various forms of dark magic. Tell me, what does a former Ecliptic Council representative want with illegal maledictions?"

Staccato scoffed. "You really mean to tell me that I'm the first former government official to deal in illegal maledictions?"

Boss Raksha gave the barest hint of a smile. "Very good." He held up a finger. "Give me one moment." He shut the door for a minute and reappeared with a lantern and a raincoat. "Follow me."

He led them down a gravel path to the loading bay of the warehouse where a myriad of boxes labeled "Dangerous" or "Toxic" littered the docks.

"Did these just arrive?" inquired Staccato.

"All the way from Capricorn." Boss Raksha shined a light on one of the crates. "Explosives."

Something crunched beneath Pyro's feet. He looked down. It was a human femur. Something gurgled from the darkened culvert. Boss Raksha held up the lantern. Behind the grate was a bashe, an enormous thirty-foot snake with a head the size of a dinner table. Its scales rippled in shades of orange and gold, and a mane of spines flared out from its neck.

"You want your bone?"

Boss Raksha reached down, grabbed the femur from underneath Pyro's foot, and chucked it through the grates. The bashe snapped it up between sword-like fangs and sank back into the shadows.

"You keep a bashe?" asked Pyro.

"Every business needs a mascot." He held up a small flute that hung from a chain around his neck, which Pyro assumed he used to call the beast. "Plus, it helps get rid of the evidence."

"Evidence of what?"

Instead of answering, he just threw back his head and laughed.

They followed him up a flight of stairs and down a narrow passage to an office with a cracked window.

240

Boss Raksha grabbed the handle. "I'll let him know you're here." He shut the door behind him, leaving them in the hall to wait.

Pyro squinted down the length of the shadowy corridor. "Where do you suppose they're keeping her?"

"Patience." Staccato shook out the moisture from his hat. "We don't have enough information to go running off just yet."

"What if we don't get enough information?"

"Let me do the talking and everything will be fine."

Skelter nodded in agreement with Staccato. Boss Raksha reappeared, holding the door open for them.

"You may see Kha Fang now."

They passed through the anteroom and were ushered into a shabby office overlooking the floor of the warehouse. It seemed an incongruent setup to say the least. The chairs were plush and fine; a silk carpet had been thrown over the moldering floor; a record from the Voilerian opera *The King's Undoing* was playing on a phonograph in the corner. And yet there were holes in the baseboard, and tears in the wallpaper, and a musty smell radiating from the wood. The high-backed chair behind the desk was turned away from them as they entered, but they could see a pale hand resting on the arm and swaying to the music.

"Come in, Mr. Nimbus," said a husky voice.

The chair swiveled round. Kha Fang's pale face was almost mask-like, with florid lips and skin free of pores. One of his eyebrows rested higher than the other in a bent position so that he maintained a constant expression of sarcasm. He had a glass of human blood in one hand, and the substance was leaking from the corner of his mouth. He set down his cup and smiled at them, his fangs hanging over his lips.

"What brings a famous miraculous like yourself to our grubby little corner of the world?" He gestured for Staccato to take the chair opposite him.

"What brings anyone here? Money, materialism."

Kha Fang ran his eyes down the front of Staccato's shirt. He used his fingers—which were fitted with diamond-studded nail guards—to comb through his waist-length hair.

"The Soter's former advisor in need of capital?"

"I'm afraid the Land Lock put all my savings under water."

Kha Fang twirled a lock of hair around his finger. "I should think the Soters would be ashamed to discover their beloved family pet selling weapons to the C.O.N."

"Survival has no shame, Mr. Fang. And to be honest, I couldn't care less what people think of me. Now are we going to stand around making jokes all day?" He tossed the box on the desk. "Or are we going to talk business?"

Kha Fang slid one of his nail guards under the lid and lifted it up. The light of the vials cast purple shadows on his colorless cheeks.

"Nightmares," explained Staccato. "Perfect for psychological torture."

Kha Fang held one to the light. "You made these?"

"I did."

He smiled and tapped it with the back of his nail. "Nightmares crafted by the most powerful miraculous of our time. A valuable commodity indeed!" He opened a drawer and produced a porcelain bowl. "Do they contain any additives?" He uncorked the vial and poured its contents into the container.

"Just a bit of glout as a preservative, but that's all. No caligo or other artificial mood killers, the darkness is completely natural."

Kha Fang whipped a stirrer back and forth through the substance. "One hundred percent organic nightmares!" The foggy liquid clung to the stirrer as he removed it, dripping like black gunk. "How much are you asking? Forty? Sixty?"

"Actually, I was hoping to do a trade."

He set the bowl aside. "What did you have in mind?"

"My sources tell me you've acquired some Virgonian artifacts as of late."

"You've an interest in ancient artifacts?"

"I've many interests."

Kha Fang poured the nightmare back into the vial and handed the case back to Staccato. "Well, if you'll just follow me, I'm sure we can find something that might spark your interest."

They followed him down the stairs to the warehouse floor. Boss Raksha had two underlings bring forth a crate packed with various heirlooms wrapped in brown paper.

"I have a feeling you'll find this piece particularly intriguing." Kha Fang removed a long, slender bundle from the crate and peeled back the wrapping. "It belonged to the miraculous Zuma Tepictoton in the third empire."

The staff had been crafted from a pine bough and painted in bright, vivid hues of turquoise, lapis, and coral. The head was some form

242

of sun disc and had a teal feather fastened to the handle with a string of leather. He handed it to Staccato, who held it to the light.

"Beautiful." He ran the feather between his fingers. "I take it the plume is from a collo swallow?"

"Yes! I believe so!"

"Well, then. I'm afraid it can't have belonged to Zuma Tepictoton, for he adorned all his staffs with the plume of an eñolia, a bird native to the valley region." He handed him back the staff.

Kha Fang appeared completely taken aback. "Mr. Nimbus, these artifacts were taken directly from the Virgonian Institute for Enchanted Archaeology. I assure you, it's completely authentic."

Staccato whipped out a handkerchief and set about polishing the head of his own staff in a rather bored manner. "Mr. Kha, I doubt you're aware of this, but I minored in Virgonian Ancient History at Mankib Fay University. Now either you've made a mistake or you're trying to shortchange me."

Kha Fang dressed himself with a desperate, pleading smile. "I can assure you, I am doing no such thing."

"Very well. I'll make a deal with you. If you can prove to me that's an authentic staff belonging to Zuma Tepictoton, I'll throw in three more nightmares."

Pyro could see the figurative dollar signs forming in Kha Fang's eyes. He turned to Boss Raksha.

"Fetch Dr. Desmond."

A moment later, he returned with a petite, young seraph whose spectacles appeared too large for her face. Her wings were chained in a vice and she had a big fluffy bow around her collar. Kha Fang waved her forward.

"May I introduce Dr. Desmond from the Virgonian Institute for Enchanted Archaeology."

Staccato acknowledged her with a bow of his head, while Pyro and Skelter remained silent.

"Dr. Desmond, would you please authenticate this staff of Zuma Tepictoton for our friend here?"

Skelter shifted from side to side, looking fidgety. After a minute or two of twiddling, he removed a thread from his pocket and set about making the sign of the Pleiades. Pyro watched the two thugs for any sign of recognition. He wondered how often Cat's Cradle had been used as a form of communication between rebels, and how long it would be before the C.O.N. figured it out.

"I was just saying to Mr. Kha here, that this couldn't have belonged to Zuma Tepictoton, as the feather is that of a collo bird."

Dr. Desmond pinched her eyebrows together incredulously. "A collo bird?" Then her eyes registered the thread in Skelter's hand. She cleared her throat. "I'm afraid you're mistaken, Mr. Nimbus. That plume is one hundred percent authentic eñolia." She looked down at the floor. "I catalogued it myself."

"Are you quite sure? I was under the impression that all collo plumage was violet hued."

Staccato slipped his hand behind his back and conjured a vision of a purple frog in his palm for Pyro and Skelter to see. It was a code. Before arriving, they had gone over several strategies for attack and assigned each a code name. The goal was to silence Kha Fang and Boss Raksha before they could call for backup.

Pyro cleared his throat. "Mind if I take a smoke break?"

Staccato pretended to be annoyed with this interruption and looked to Kha Fang for some sort of confirmation.

"You may."

Pyro slipped his cigarette case out of his pocket. "Thanks." He started for the door.

Just as he was passing Kha Fang, he reached into the inner folds of his raincoat and grabbed his chakras. Pyro jumped and hook-kicked the back of Raksha's knees. He flung a chakra at Kha Fang, who slipped out of its path just in time. Boss Raksha fell to the ground.

Skelter grabbed Dr. Desmond and towed her to safety behind a large stack of crates. Staccato took up both staffs, prepared to defend himself as Kha Fang's jaw began to stretch open. He bobbed at Staccato like a cobra. Staccato struck him in the side of the head.

Meanwhile Pyro had Boss Raksha in a chokehold, but he was too light for someone of Raksha's size. The man staggered to his feet, clawing at Pyro's bicep. Pyro's skin grew hot as he summoned a fire up through his arm, but Raksha wrenched forward, throwing Pyro over his head. Pyro's back slammed against the floor. The ground shook as Raksha barreled towards him, gun drawn.

Skelter raced after him with the crowbar used to open the crate and struck him in the head. Raksha turned and fired at Skelter. Skelter scurried up a mountain of crates, dodging him entirely.

"Pyro!"

Pyro turned around. Kha Fang had Staccato on his back and was clawing at his throat. He could just conjure enough force to keep the ophidian from fully enclosing his fingers around his neck, but Kha Fang was putting up a tremendous fight. Pyro took the other chakra and threw it at Kha Fang. The blade cut across both forearms. Kha Fang gave a screech and was forced to let go.

Skelter continued to climb when his foot went through the top of a crate, causing an avalanche of boxes. The shooting ceased. A package labeled with a skull crashed at Pyro's feet. A cloud of shattered glass and purple smoke rose up around him. Pyro limped out of the smog coughing and waving his hand, but he appeared to be unharmed.

With his powers, Staccato threw Kha Fang across the room. Kha Fang made a weak attempt to rise before collapsing to the floor. He was finished. He had lost too much blood. Raksha continued to shoot at Skelter, who was hopping from crate to crate.

The door was kicked aside and a series of foot soldiers filed into the room and began shooting. Staccato had just enough time to conjure a vision of a green butterfly to Melodious and Sonata before a soldier fired at his back. Staccato jumped and swung his staff in an arc towards the floor. A transparent wave of fire rose up from the ground and raced towards their attackers. Thinking it was real, and that Staccato were some kind of igneous, the men fell back and shielded themselves. With a wave of his hand Staccato forced the guns from their grips and tossed them out the window overlooking the river, breaking the glass in the process.

Pyro was about to throw another chakra when he felt a sharp pain clip his shoulder. He turned and rolled out of the way as a lackey fired another round in his wake. Staccato had missed one.

"Scared yet?" asked the mobster.

"A little bit, yeah." Pyro froze. He had been planning to say "Not a chance," but somehow the words had come out completely the opposite. As the soldier pointed the gun, Pyro kicked the firearm out of his hand and ducked behind a set of crates.

Staccato was surrounded on all sides. Still armed with both staffs, he kept them pointed in opposite directions. One lackey tried to attack him from behind, while another made a move to strike his face. Staccato jabbed the end of one staff into the abdomen of the attacker behind him, and kicked the groin of the one in front. With a burst of energy he sent them flying in all directions.

245

A tidal wave of broken glass sailed across the room as the remaining shards of the window broke apart. The caravan tore through the warehouse with Sonata and Melodious at the helm. The front right wheel collided with the head of Pyro's attacker, killing him instantly.

"Sonata!" Staccato thundered as he whipped his staff across the head of a foot soldier. "What are you doing here?"

"Rescuing you, obviously! Now hop inside!"

Boss Raksha stumbled back and swore. He'd run out of bullets. Skelter ran over the row of boxes, shoving over as many crates as he could. Foot soldiers scattered to get out of the way as a box of hexes and jinxes broke apart in an ominous cloud.

"Skelter! Careful!" scolded Staccato. "You don't know what's in those boxes!"

Two of the crates collided with each other on the way down, causing them to burst open midair, showering everyone with vials of microhexes. When the dust had cleared three of the soldiers were walking backwards, the other two were hopping around on their hands and feet likes frogs, the pegasi's wings had shriveled to the size of dragonflies, Boss Raksha had sprouted a pair of antlers, and Melodious had shrunk to around five foot seven. Sonata ran towards him. "Melodious!"

When he turned around to face her, Sonata gasped. His mustache had completely vanished. The gray had disappeared from his hair, and he appeared to be about twelve years old. Boss Raksha charged at Sonata, antlers first, but Melodious grabbed him by the prongs and flung him into the wall like a rag doll. He may have been a child, but he had lost none of his Herculean strength.

Sonata breathed a sigh of relief. "Who could have seen that coming?"

"I could," piped Pyro involuntarily.

Sonata eyed him suspiciously.

While the three soldiers walking backwards were flailing around, disoriented, Pyro ran at them. With one smooth kick he easily knocked the first one over. As the other two tried to get away he slammed their heads together, knocking them out cold. He looked around.

"Where's Staccato?"

Dr. Desmond peeked out from behind her hiding place and pointed at something scurrying on the floor.

"There!"

A hedgehog was running around in circles in the place where the box had fallen. Pyro leapt over the broken crates and grabbed the hedgehog before anyone could harm him. Staccato wriggled around in his grasp and flailed his fluffy arms.

"My staff! Get my staff!"

Skelter jumped down from the tower of crates and grabbed it just as the final two thugs were leaping his way. They sprang up from their haunches, hands outstretched for the staff. Skelter took them out with one swift swing.

A shrill whistle drew their attention to the place where Boss Raksha lay bleeding. He was blowing on the flute around his neck.

"No!" Pyro pitched his chakra, severing the chain and knocking the instrument from his lips.

"It's too late now!" Boss Raksha threw back his head and laughed until he took his final breath and died.

"What is he talking about?" demanded Melodious in his newly adenoidal voice.

"The bashe! He's called the bashe!"

Sonata swung open the door and motioned to Dr. Desmond. "Quick, get inside!"

She looked wistfully back at the crate of Virgonian heirlooms. "But the artifacts!"

Staccato waved his paw towards Melodious. "Grab the box! We don't have much time!"

A low hissing echoed down the hall.

"We can't fly," observed Pyro. "The pegasi's wings shrunk. How are we gonna get out?"

"There's only one way." Staccato indicated to the passage just as the bashe was entering. The great serpent reared its head and fluffed the spine around its neck.

"Sonata," barked Staccato. "Take the reins! Melodious, get inside the caravan and get Dr. Desmond out of those chains! Skelter, join Sonata up front!"

"What about me?" asked Pyro.

"Put me on your shoulder."

"On my shoulder? Wouldn't my shirt pocket be safer?"

Staccato tried to cross his arms but they were far too short. "If you dare try to put me in your pocket—"

The bashe whipped its tail at Pyro, sending him flying across the room. Pyro winced as he fell on his injured arm.

"Never mind! Put me in the pocket!" Staccato scurried up to his shirt pocket and clambered inside. "You need your hands."

The caravan veered around to the far end of the warehouse, putting as much distance between the wagon and the bashe as possible.

"Here's the plan," began Staccato. "I'll conjure a hallucination to distract him, and you attack with your chakras."

"Don't you need your staff?"

"Not in this case." He paused. "You can do this. Keep telling yourself this will all be over soon, and we'll be sitting in the back of the caravan sharing that Grave's Popcorn tin we bought in Alrezida."

"Yeah, Skelter and I finished it off when you weren't looking." He was going to lie and say it tipped over and spilled during a rough flight but for some reason he just couldn't.

"What?"

The snake charged towards them with a speed that belied that of a sidewinder. Red sparks shot out from Staccato's paws until they took on the form of fish swimming past the bashe's nose. The bashe turned and sniffed at it.

Pyro wrenched back his good arm and tossed the chakra at its head, but he only managed to sever one of the spines.

"What was that?" snapped Staccato.

"A chakra." Pyro bunched up his mouth. What was going on inside his brain?

"No! No! No! I mean, that was terrible!"

"I can't help it! My arm's injured, and I'm left-handed!"

The bashe dove for them, snapping open its jaws. Pyro leapt over its back and made a run for the window, drawing it away from the door. He waved his good arm at Sonata.

"Go! Go! Go!"

Sonata cracked the reins, and the pegasi zoomed off down the passage. Staccato conjured another vision, this time of fireworks, to keep the bashe from following.

"*Oi!*" Pyro hollered. "Come on, you big, ugly worm!"

The bashe turned and narrowed its eyes before going after them a second time. Pyro blasted a stream of fire at the bashe's head. The bashe swerved and hissed.

"Pyro, do you really think it's a good idea to try and stand your ground with a thirty-foot serpent?"

He hadn't planned on answering, but the words forced themselves out of his mouth.

"No! Actually, I don't!"

"Well, then get moving! What are you—Pyro, no more chakras!"

Pyro tossed the disc again, grazing the bashe's snout. Staccato tugged angrily on the material of his shirt.

"Do you ever listen to me?"

"Rarely."

"I beg your pardon!"

"I'm sorry! I'm sorry! I think I've been hit with some kind of hex that's making me brutally honest!"

The bashe dipped down for another strike. Pyro ducked and climbed atop a pile of crates. The bashe slammed its tail at the base of the boxes. The heap rocked forward. Pyro jumped off the stack, grabbed hold of a pendant lamp, and swung himself out the window. They landed in a muddy patch in the loading bay where the rain continued to pour. It was a good thing Pyro was still wearing his raincoat.

Pyro was just about to jump to his feet when the bashe stuck its head out the window and hissed. It plunged forward, jaws open. Pyro rolled to the left. It struck again. He rolled to the right and raced back down to the entry.

"You've come full circle," bristled Staccato.

"Well, why didn't you tell me where I was going?"

"Do I look like I know this place any better than you?"

"Yes!"

"And how is that?"

"Because you're old and snooty!"

"I'm forty-eight! I hardly have my foot in the grave!"

The bashe plowed through a pile of barrels and raced towards them. Pyro hurled a fireball in its direction.

"Pyro, wait! Those are explosives, remember?"

But it was too late. The bashe drew back as the first crate combusted. The blast continued down the line like dominoes. Pyro crouched down with his hands over his head, shielding them from any shrapnel. When the explosion subsided, Pyro carefully lifted his head.

"Did you kill it?" Staccato managed to sputter through coughs.

The water below the dock rippled. The bashe exploded out of the river, its head looming above the flickering flames.

"Apparently not."

"We just have to stay calm," advised Staccato.

"I can't stay calm!"

"Yes, you can! You're capable of keeping your head! Remember how well you did at the performance in Spica? What did you do then to keep calm?"

Pyro knew what was coming next. He tried biting his tongue but it was no use.

"Alcohol."

"See, now—What?"

A force struck Pyro under the arms. His feet left the ground. He was flying through the air. He looked up.

"Dr. Desmond!"

Dr. Desmond flapped her wings. "Hang on!"

Pyro couldn't help but be impressed that this tiny woman was able to lift him, but then sylphs were naturally stronger than other Fay races. The bashe sprang up like a coil, snapping its jaws at them like a cat after a dragonfly. But Dr. Desmond was fast. She zipped over the trees, keeping an eye on the path below. They came to a fork in the river.

"There's the caravan!" Pyro pointed to a spot near the bank. "Why aren't they moving?"

Dr. Desmond dropped down, depositing Staccato and Pyro on the ground.

"Come on, Scheherazade!" Sonata snapped the reins. "Pull harder!"

The pegasi were straining against their harnesses, while Skelter and Melodious tried to lead Scheherazade by the bridle.

"What's going on?" asked Pyro.

"The caravan is stuck!" Sonata hopped out of the driver's seat. "Skelter, you take the reins. Melodious, maybe we can push."

Sonata bent over and braced her hands against the back of the wagon, her hair damp and looking especially pretty as it fell around her face. Pyro froze with his thumbs in his belt loops.

"Pyro!" Staccato barked. "Don't just stand there! What are you doing?"

Ashamed, Pyro immediately looked away as he became aware of himself. "Having a gawk at your goddaughter."

Staccato climbed onto his shoulder. "Why?"

Pyro ground his teeth together but couldn't stop. "Because she's a right knockout!"

Trees and branches snapped in the distance followed by a loud splash. Pyro slammed his good shoulder against the wagon, trying to push. The bashe shot out of the water, its head thrown back with rage. Startled, Melodious threw the back of the wagon upward and plowed it forward like a wheelbarrow. Sonata and Pyro fell face-forward in the mud. Fortunately, Staccato had scurried to Pyro's head to avoid being crushed. Dr. Desmond swooped down and tossed them into the wagon before joining Skelter at the reins. Pyro landed on Sonata's arm.

Staccato scurried out of Pyro's hair.

"I'm going to direct Skelter!"

Just as he was approaching the rope ladder, Cello emerged from Sonata's berth looking as though he might pounce on Staccato any moment. Staccato grabbed Cello forcefully by the whiskers and looked him in the eye.

"Swipe at me and I swear I will turn you into a tea kettle!"

Cello seemed to have understood, for he immediately turned and scampered back to the berth. Staccato scurried up the side of the rope ladder to the loft and out the hatch.

"Why didn't you tell us it was coming?" demanded Sonata, pushing Pyro off. "Hasn't the Saighdeoir taught you anything?"

"It taught me a lot of—"

"You can't just zone out while fighting off a thirty-foot snake!"

"Yes, I know—"

"You have to pay attention! You lured that thing out of the warehouse, and yet you didn't bother to tell us? What were you thinking? Why were you just standing there?"

Pyro could feel his face turning red. He grabbed fistfuls of his hair and spoke through gritted teeth. His volume built as he tried to resist. "Because I was having a look at you!"

Sonata gaped back at him in shock.

"Because you're a gorgeous woman with a smashing figure," he went on. "You're an out-of-this-world, stunning, completely enchanting, downright Venus, and I am wildly, helplessly, desperately attracted to you! And every time you try hugging on me and getting all touchy I can't handle it, because all I wanna do is grab you and kiss your perfect lips, and I'm terrified you're gonna sense it because you're an empath!"

Through the open door, Pyro could see the bashe sliding into the river. The moment its belly hit the water it immediately began to pick up speed.

"Melodious!" Pyro scrambled to the opening. "Drop the wagon! We'll go faster!"

Melodious let go and jumped inside. The caravan hit the ground just as they were driving over a large rock. Pyro was thrown out of the vehicle. One of the door hinges caught at a tear in his pants, and he was dragged through the mud. The bashe spotted Pyro and slithered back on land. Sonata and Melodious each took a leg and pulled him inside as the bashe was striking.

Pyro scurried up to the loft.

"What are you doing?" Sonata called after him.

"Well, I gotta do something, don't I?" He climbed onto the roof.

"Blast him with your fire power!" hollered Melodious from down below.

"I'm not sure the woods are the best place to do that!"

"Take the bridge!" Staccato yelled at Skelter. "Go to the city! It won't follow us into urban territory!"

Pyro threw himself prostrate and held fast to the ledge of the hatch as Skelter took a sharp left turn.

"The arm's down!" shrieked Dr. Desmond.

Pyro jumped down into the driver's seat, and blasted the bridge's barrier with a stream of fiery breath. It disintegrated into ashes. The caravan tore over the bridge and down the road. But the bashe didn't stop. It raced out of the water and followed them into the city.

Pyro peeked over the ledge. "It's not stopping!"

They were coming up on the Grasshopper Inn now. Salamander was standing on the porch with his foo dogs.

"Mr. Anomaly! Mr. Nimbus!"

"Sal!" Pyro cupped a hand over his mouth. "Call for help!"

The door opened and Mr. Pulvervass appeared on the threshold with a rifle.

"Pull into the barn!"

Skelter steered the pegasi towards the empty stables while Mr. Pulvervass shot at the bashe. As they pulled in, Salamander and the foo dogs ran ahead of them into the loft.

"Sal! No!" hollered Pyro. "What are you doing?"

The bashe burst through the barn with a terrible hiss. Shishi and Chinchin ran at the beast, roaring and growling. The bashe drew back like a cornered cat. But before it could get away, Salamander pulled a lever, and the barn door snapped shut. He was standing behind what appeared to be an old cannon with a makeshift vent at the top. A gigantic net shot out of the mouth, trapping the bashe once and for all.

Pyro stood and gaped at the captured beast. "The Sensational Snare!"

Salamander patted the cannon and grinned. "I told you I could do it!"

Chapter 35:
Dr. Desmond

The company and Dr. Desmond sat shivering in the parlor with towels and blankets thrown about their shoulders. They'd cut off the sleeve where Pyro was injured and placed him in a tourniquet, but it had yet to be properly tended to, and the company was eager to leave Khan Lau lest the Jade Bone trace them back to the Grasshopper. Mrs. Pulvervass entered with a tea tray.

"Virtue's Tongue," she explained, handing Pyro a mug of something warm and minty. "An incredibly rare, incredibly expensive microhex that renders the victim incapable of lying." She shook her head. "I can't imagine the Jade Bone will be pleased to have lost such a commodity. This should take care of it though."

Pyro looked down at the swirling green substance. "What is it?"

"Bandit's Brew, a counter charm invented by pirates in the 1600s to avoid the gallows."

She turned to Melodious. "As for you, young man. You should be back to normal by morning. However, you may experience rapid-onset puberty until then."

"And there isn't anything you can do for me?" said Staccato from his place on the coffee table.

"I'm afraid not. But you should be back to your old self when you wake up tomorrow." She handed him a thimbleful of tea.

"You appear to know a lot about healing, and reversing hexes," observed Sonata.

Mrs. Pulvervass beamed with pride. "I was a caim's aid during the Treason Wars." She lowered herself into her chair with a girlish titter. "That's how I met Typhon."

"You know, Staccato," Pyro leaned forward on both elbows. "I think I like you better this way. You're much fluffier."

"I am not fluffy!" He waddled to the edge of the table. "Now somebody hand me my staff!"

"How you gonna hold it?"

Skelter handed Pyro the staff to give to Staccato.

"Just hold it right there, like that," Staccato instructed. He thrust out his paws. "Now turn it clockwise."

The staff shrank.

"Keep doing it … and … stop!"

The staff was now about the size of a pencil, but still very thick, so when Pyro handed it to Staccato he promptly fell over. He reached out to set him right.

"No, no! I can do it." Staccato reached his arms out, looking as though he were trying to touch his toes, but he couldn't seem to maneuver around his hedgehog belly. Pyro stared at him with a wry grin.

"You sure?"

"Yes, yes!" He tried again, grunting all the while. "Alright, fine! I need you to push me up!"

"I thought you had no needs."

"Will you just do it?"

Pyro did as told but not without laughing first. Salamander and the foo dogs entered through the parlor door, followed by Detective Pulvervass.

"Did you speak with the sergeant?" asked Mrs. Pulvervass.

"They're sending someone over to pick up the bashe, after which it will be released into its natural habitat, far from civilization." He smiled and sat down in the chair beside his wife. "So, you're undercover rebels?"

Sonata smiled and set her tea aside. "I'm afraid the cat's out of the bag."

"Well, you've done the police force a tremendous service by getting rid of Kha Fang and Boss Raksha."

"I'm afraid it's not the whole of the Jade Bone."

"Doesn't matter. Kha Fang was their most powerful leader, and has had a terrible grip on the city for the past decade. If there's anything we can do to aid you on your mission, please don't hesitate to ask."

Pyro chuckled and looked pointedly at Sal. "You've already done so much. That's a talented boy you've got there, Detective Pulvervass. If I were him, I wouldn't settle for exterminator. He'd make a fine assisier." An assisier being someone who catches, tames, and trains magical creatures for rehabilitation and captivity.

"If ever we get out of Ophiuchus, perhaps he will be one day. But what about this Jar business Staccato was telling us about? Is there anything we can do to help you there?"

"That's why we had to find Dr. Desmond." Sonata eyed the doctor, who was sitting on the stool near the fire. "The C.O.N. is on the move, and she's the only one who can help us trace their route, enabling us to intercept the Jar."

"I'm afraid I don't know their exact course—" started Dr. Desmond.

"But you know the instructions for carrying the Jar, right?" Pyro scooted his chair closer. "If we know the rules then we might be able to make an educated guess."

Dr. Desmond nodded. "Does anyone have a piece of paper and a pencil? You might want to write this down."

Mrs. Pulvervass fetched a notebook and pen from the secretary and handed them to Sonata.

"Would you like us to leave?"

Staccato waved his paw. "It's fine. You're involved now."

Dr. Desmond removed her glasses and sat up tall. "Are you familiar with the law of the seven ambassadors?"

Staccato nodded. "We figured that might be the case with the Jar."

"It must be carried by one member from every Fay race."

"Otherwise it's completely immobile?" asked Pyro.

"For the most part. One might be able to carry it with six, but make no mistake, it would be incredibly difficult. When traveling on foot it can only be moved at night. If traveling by river, one must always move with the current. When traveling through the woods the Jar cannot cross loam. If you come across a cemetery, don't read the tombstones and absolutely do not step on any graves. If the Jar grows unexpectedly heavy, stop where you are and fill it with water. Walk away and come back after an hour. If the water has turned to olive oil then empty the Jar and carry on. If the water has turned to blood then choose a different path. If you hear whispering from the Jar, it's best to listen. You must carry the Jar with your dominant hand or both hands, never your non-dominant hand alone."

There was a long silence which followed. Pyro raised an eyebrow. "That's it?"

"It's enough to make a significant impact on their route, believe it or not," said Melodious.

Staccato set aside his thimble. "They can't be moving very fast if they're traveling by foot. I bet you anything they plan to travel by the Caput. After all, it flows towards Draco. But we can discuss all that once we're back at Feifior. I think it's high time we get cleaned up and ready for bed. Sonata, don't forget you still need to take care of Pyro's arm."

Pyro lowered his head as he felt his cheeks flush.

"Is that really necessary? It's stopped bleeding!"

"Only because of how tightly that bandage is wound. We can't have you waking up covered in blood in the middle of the night."

***

Pyro sat in the chair in the corner of his room, waiting for Sonata. There was a soft knock at the door.

"It's open."

Sonata entered with a first-aid kit in hand. Pyro propped his fist under his chin and looked the other way, unable to handle the embarrassment. Sonata cleared her throat and sat in the chair beside him.

"Alright, soldier," she slipped a towel under his arm and began untying the bandage. "Let's have a look at that arm."

Pyro said nothing, only closed his eyes. He felt a measure of blood trickle from his wound.

"Now, Pyro, don't be like that."

"Be like what?" he muttered, propping his chin on his fist and covering his mouth.

"You've nothing to be embarrassed about."

"I don't?"

"I only mean that it's perfectly natural to find people attractive—"

She was cut off by Pyro's miserable groan.

"Oh, do stop making that dreadful noise and listen to me!" She began sopping up the blood with a damp cloth. "In my culture, we're quite used to knowing what people are feeling, whether they say anything or not. And so we take other people's emotions very seriously. I'm not going to laugh at you, or make fun of you. Attraction is inborn. And you were under a hex. You couldn't help saying what you said." She reached for the antiseptic. "And besides, we're young, we work in close proximity. You think I haven't caught myself staring at you from time to time?"

Pyro raised his head up, wincing at the strong smell. "What?"

Sonata poured the antiseptic on a cotton ball and shrugged. "You're an attractive man, Pyro. I can't help noticing that." She pushed her hair back from her forehead and cleared her throat. "As I said, perfectly natural. Just an impulse."

Pyro stared back at her in amazement. A bashful smile spread across her lips.

"You can't begin to know how flattered I am …"

Pyro cringed. *Flattered?* The phrase brought to mind images of awkward rejections and unrequited affections. Could a more degrading adjective have existed? Sonata must have caught his embarrassment, for she quickly explained herself.

"For the longest time after the incident, I worried that no one would ever think of me that way."

Pyro drew back and made a face. "What?"

"I was young." She gaped at the floor, appearing half embarrassed by her confession. "At the age when boys first begin to notice you. I feared without my legs no one would ever notice me."

It was easy to see how a girl of fifteen could harbor such anxieties, and Pyro understood. His eyes drifted over her comely features, lingering on the pursed shape of her ample lips that looked as though they had been fashioned for kissing.

"But, surely you don't worry about that now."

Sonata tossed her head in a clear effort to appear self-assured. "Of course not! I was but a girl then."

Pyro bit back an amused smile. "Clearly, you didn't know men very well."

Sonata lowered her head with a frown. "Or perhaps the opposite is true."

"Your legs are one of the most attractive things about you. When someone sees your prosthetics and they know your story, then they know most everything they need to know about Sonata Soter: that she's brave, selfless, strong, and can stick it to the Cobra. And if any man has a problem with that it's because he can't stand not being the toughest person in the room."

Sonata froze, staring at him, her eyes equal parts tenderness and intensity. Bit by bit her hand moved to her heart. When she said no more, Pyro gave an awkward chuckle.

"You gonna be okay?"

Without warning, Sonata leaned forward and kissed Pyro on the cheek. Her lips triggered a full-on hot flash across his skin, threatening to turn his freckles pink.

"That's the nicest thing anyone has ever said to me." She squeezed his hand. "You're a wonderful friend, Pyro."

Pyro shrugged, struggling to appear casual. "Just being honest."

When she had finished cleaning the injury, she leaned back with a capitulating sigh. "I'm afraid it's going to have to be sewn up."

"What?" Pyro shuddered. "Can't you just heal it up? Just a bit?"

"It's beyond my capability." She reached into the first-aid kit and removed a needle. "You're going to have to let me stitch—"

"No!" Pyro shielded himself with his arm, accidentally elbowing the needle out of Sonata's hand. When he realized what he had done, he stared back at her with his hand over his mouth. Sonata gave him a knowing look.

"You're afraid of needles."

"I'm not overly fond of them, no."

"Because of the tattoo gun?"

Pyro closed his eyes and instinctively covered the scar on his arm, as he recalled the night his brother had been killed, when he and his younger sister had been taken hostage by the C.O.N. He could still hear the whirring of the drill buzzing in his child ears. They had forced his head under water, torturing him until he gave up his birth name, the secret name Fay gave to their children to protect them from evil. Then they had tattooed it onto his arm to humiliate him. After his rescue, he had been so ashamed that he'd burnt the tattoo off with his own fire.

Pyro crossed his arms and nodded. She ran the cloth over the bullet graze a second time.

"Funny, isn't it? What sticks with you and what doesn't. Fire doesn't bother you. Water doesn't bother you even though it's been used to hurt you several times. But needles set you on edge."

Pyro pulled away. "*Oi*, you ever been forcibly tattooed?"

"I'm not making fun of you." Her voice was sincere and soothing. "It's perfectly understandable why those things would bother you." She gave him a nudge. "You do realize I can render you unconscious, don't you?"

Pyro stared back at her uncomprehendingly. Sonata smirked.

"While I stitch you up, so you don't feel any pain."

Pyro narrowed his eyes, unsure if he fully believed her. "You mean I won't wake up the moment you impale my flesh with that miniature javelin?"

"Not if you submit."

Pyro bunched his lips, then reluctantly uncrossed his arms. "Fine. Let's do that then."

"Excellent." She stood and waved him towards the bed. "We might as well get you comfortable first."

Pyro sat on the mattress, Sonata behind him. Pyro jumped as he felt her hands crawling over his shoulders and drawing him backwards. He twisted around.

"What are you doing?" His face was bright red.

"It'll be easier if you're comfortable." She crooked her finger towards her lap, tilting her head to one side.

Pyro swallowed. Was she flirting with him? "Okay." He allowed her to pull his head into her lap.

"Relaxed?"

Pyro frowned up at her biting her lip in that infectious manner. He was tempted by the thought of grabbing her and kissing her, his fingers tangling through her hair as he pulled her against him, showing her just how beautiful he thought she was. He pushed the thought away and nodded his head. She slid her hands down the sides of his neck. Pyro shuddered and instinctively reached up to stop her but managed to get a hold of himself.

"Cotton sheets are what get me." She forced a half-hearted giggle. "There were cotton sheets in the bed I awoke in after my legs were amputated. People must think I'm quite the diva when I say I prefer silk or satin." She turned away and hooked a curl behind her ear. "Blades don't bother me. I wasn't awake for that part anyway. Thunderstorms relax me. I'm not claustrophobic." A little self-deprecating smile filled her lips. "But cotton sheets give me nightmares."

"Don't look so embarrassed. You can't help it." He smiled playfully. "Besides, no one's gonna bat an eye at a princess who likes silk sheets."

Sonata smiled, this time for real. "I suppose you're right." She placed her fingers on his artery. "Now close your eyes."

Pyro didn't remember falling asleep, or any dreams that followed, but he soon found himself waking up to Sonata gently tapping his cheek.

"I'm just now putting on the bandage."

Pyro groaned and rolled his head towards her. The gauze was wrapped twice around his bicep.

"The stitches are nice and tight. Would you like to see?" She reached for a hand mirror.

Pyro squeezed his eyes shut and groaned. "If it's all the same to you, I'm not sure I want to see my arm looking like the tops of my shoes."

Sonata lowered her chin and laughed, putting the mirror away. "I'll finish the bandage then."

The effects of her natural anesthetic were quite heady and had yet to wear off, leaving Pyro feeling somewhat less inhibited than before.

"How could you ever have doubted anyone would think you're beautiful?"

The color in Sonata's cheeks rose. She cast her eyes downwards, looking exceptionally shy for once. "You'll only think me silly."

"Would I? Really?"

She paused with the gauze in hand, then pushed her hair away from her face. "I suppose I thought all people would see when they looked at me was a tragedy. Someone limited. Like a broken China doll."

Pyro sat up. He removed the gauze and scissors from her grasp and set them aside. Sonata froze, the confusion on her face evident. He turned towards her, grabbing her hands.

"You wanna know what comes to mind when I look at you?" His voice was soft and tender.

Before she could stop him, he cupped his hand to her cheek, letting its fullness fill his palm. He leaned forward, pressing his forehead against hers and closing his eyes. He tested the waters with a kiss below her left eye. Her lips parted slightly. He allowed his hand to fall to her neck. Sonata's breath hitched in her throat. He filled the gap between her lips with his own, kissing her softly, then more fervently as she leaned into his chest. Her hands slid over his shoulders, squeezing his muscles. Without warning, Sonata jumped into his arms, forcing him to stagger backwards as she returned his kisses with passionate enthusiasm, not limiting herself to his lips but kissing his cheeks, his chin, his forehead.

They drew away with ragged breaths, their foreheads resting together. Pyro sat back on the bed, still holding her in his arms. Her eyes met his with an apprehension he hadn't registered before.

"You alright?" He could barely get his brain to form the words.

She nodded, still trying to catch her breath. She pressed her lips against his, obliterating any lingering verbal integrity he still possessed. Pyro felt her fingers on his neck, and then, out of nowhere, he blacked out.

When Pyro awoke the next morning, he was lying beneath the covers of his bed fully clothed with the exception of his shoes. He held out his arm. It had been fully bandaged with clean white gauze. His fingers rose to his mouth as he recalled the touch of Sonata's lips on his.

Had it all been a dream? He looked back at the bedside table for the time. A note in Sonata's handwriting was folded neatly beside the clock.

Dear Pyro,

I wanted to apologize for last night. It turns out, I was hit by a curse yesterday—a love potion, to be specific—only I didn't discover it until after our encounter. I would appreciate it if you didn't share this with anybody. I'm sure you understand.

-Sonata

Pyro stared at the note and scratched his face. It was a clever attempt at a lie, but Pyro knew better. In order for a love potion to be effective it had to be customized for an individual to serve as the object of one's pseudo-affections. One could not simply be hit with a random love potion and fall in love with the first person they laid eyes on. So what about Pyro had scared Sonata away? Why had she forced him to pass out, and then left?

Chapter 36:

Faina Rebels

It might as well have been spring for all the lightness that was in the air. The collective fever of the city was finally breaking. The reported cases of influenza had fallen into the low hundreds. Libraries began circulating books once more; theaters opened their doors. Where once the world grew darker every day, now joy flowed in abundance, for no sooner had the pandemic begun to wane than it was announced that after two years of fighting overseas the doughboys would finally be returning home.

There is something warm and comforting in rejoicing over a blessing that is not your own. Though Faina herself had no relatives enlisted in the war, she had always been an empathetic child and was not immune to the infectious celebration of her neighbors.

Jazmin and Syreeta Zureiq had an older brother fighting in France, as did Dmitry Vavilov, and Kate Carmichael's father had fought in the Meuse-Argonne Offensive. And though Faina could not explain it, this happiness was as potent as her own personal victories, and it hung over Orchard Street like a fragrant cloud.

Still, there was a considerable degree of grief accompanying the armistice as well. While Dmitry and Syreeta's brothers had survived, Edita and Sergei Maslow lost their father. Mariangela Romano had a similar story. Yuri Mishkin's father would be returning home without the use of his legs and would struggle to find work. But Faina knew there was beauty to be found even in pain. She watched as the acidic sting of loss ate through calcified walls of anger. Families were putting aside their differences to mourn together. People were seeing each other as people. The lens of class and money, it seemed, was beginning to fissure.

For this reason, the continued harassment Faina experienced from her classmates became all the more disruptive to her sense of peace. When it became clear that her teacher would make no attempt to put an end to the bullying, Faina could not help but feel that her justice had been grossly violated. And that strong little mind began to grow hot and restless once more.

As Faina and Anya strolled into school one morning, a girl named Ethel Walsh stopped them outside their classroom with a mocking sneer.

"So, are the rumors true?"

Faina narrowed her eyes. "Which one?"

"That you have a big, hairy witch's mark on your chest!" The girls flanking her right and left giggled into their palms. Anya's mouth dropped open in horror.

"What?"

"Lena Kuznestov said she saw it when you took off your dress in the girls' locker room!"

Faina slammed her foot down and leaned threateningly into the girl's mean, catty face.

"Lena Kuznestov is a liar!"

The warning bell sounded overhead, and Faina was forced to abandon the altercation with a sharp, foreboding glare.

"Anyone who listens to Lena is a moron starved for entertainment. Why don't you try cracking open a book sometime to fill that empty head of yours!"

She rushed into the classroom, yanking Anya in after her.

"I'm sorry that happened, Faina." Anya put her arm around her cousin's shoulder, and Faina leaned her head into her neck. Unfortunately, it did little to soothe the burn.

As Faina crossed to her desk, she picked up a harsh strain of whispers coming from the gathering assembled at Lena's desk.

"I'm telling you, it's huge!"

"What did it look like?"

"Like a big, hairy, purple wart! It was oozing and everything!"

The girls made faces and gagging noises as Faina took her seat. In a desperate attempt to pull her attention away, Faina began bouncing her foot up and down.

"I heard she visited Anastas Sippenhaft in the boys' home."

"Hussy!"

Syreeta turned awkwardly in the seat in front of her and scanned Faina over for something to talk about.

"Your dress is very pretty today." She smiled at her brightly. "I have always loved velvet dresses."

Faina ran her hands over her skirt. "Thank you! I have always liked them too. You should wear one. Your hair would look so pretty with a dark green—"

But Faina could still hear her tormentors at her back.

"My mother says if she keeps carrying on the way she does she's going to end up in a cathouse just like Angela Bartoletti."

None of them could hold back their squeals and snorts at such a scandalous suggestion. Faina's heart dropped like a stone in her chest. A scarlet wave flushed over her cheeks and ears as she lowered her head, hurt and embarrassed. The percussion of her teacher's heels was welcome music to Faina's ears.

"Alright, girls! Settle down!"

Faina fixed her eyes on the front of the room. She watched the soft powdery decay of the chalk against the slate.

"Do you think she showed Anastas her witch's mark?" It was all the girls could do to keep from exploding with laughter.

A sort of heat collected in Faina's knees and she sprang from her chair. Suddenly, she was standing on her desk screaming at Lena and her comrades.

"Liar! You're a liar! Lena Kuznestov is a big liar!"

Horrified, Ms. Ballard slammed her chalk down on the tray. "Miss Spichkin, get down at once!" But no one cared to pay her any attention. Faina continued on.

"Anastas is my friend, and he just lost his parents! That's why I visited him at the boys' home! Aunt Poppy is not a witch, she's just a nice old lady who doesn't always remember things! She can't help it! And I am not a witch! I haven't cursed anyone! I don't dance naked in the moonlight! And I don't have a witch's mark! You're the one with a witch's mark!"

"Miss Spichkin!" Ms. Ballard repeated. "If you don't get down from that desk this instant—" But she was never given the chance to finish. Lena's eyebrows stretched up her forehead with an incredulous smile.

"I have a witch's mark?"

"Yes! You!"

Lena scoffed. "Where is it then?"

Faina pointed at her head. "It's right there! That giant thing that sits atop your neck that never shuts up!"

The classroom roared with uncontrollable laughter. Flushing with anger, Lena threw back her chair and got to her feet.

"If you don't have a witch's mark then prove it! Prove to everyone that you don't have a big, hairy, puss-filled witch's mark on your chest!" She stuck her nose in the air triumphantly, fooled into believing she had settled the matter. But Lena had underestimated this bold little girl, and no one could have predicted what happened next.

Faina flashed her an obliging, ladylike smile.

"Alright, I will!"

Without hesitation Faina lifted her dress and camisole all the way up to her neck.

Ms. Ballard went as white as a sheet. "MISS SPICHKIN!"

A chorus of scandalized shrieks pierced the air. Hands flew up over open mouths. Faina dropped her dress with a smug little grin, and smoothed out the wrinkles with a dainty hand. Just as she was about to jump down from the desk, a sharp hand reeking of rosewater broke across her cheek with stinging pain. A trickle of blood fell from the corner of her mouth. Faina looked up. Ms. Ballard had slapped her. She had a paddle in her left hand and was reaching for her collar with talon-like fingers.

Faina's lips curled up over her teeth, and much to her own surprise, she drew her own hand back and returned the blow.

A collective gasp rose up around them. But Faina hardly noticed. She could not stop herself now. Ms. Ballard dragged her from the desk and, using the paddle, struck her lower back with such force, Faina could feel the bruise immediately welling up on her skin. A hit on her thigh tore a rip in her stockings and weakened Faina's knees. Anya's chair scraped the floor as she jumped to her feet.

"Stop it! She's bleeding!"

Ms. Ballard grabbed Faina by the chin, pinching her cheeks, and deliberately sinking her nails into her skin.

"You are nothing but trash! You hear me? Trash!"

Faina stared up at her defiantly. A growl rose up in her throat. As Ms. Ballard was coming in for another strike, Faina snatched the paddle and whipped it back across Ms. Ballard's face. Ms. Ballard's glasses flew across the room and bounced off the wall.

As Ms. Ballard was reeling from shock, Faina grabbed her belongings and bolted out the door.

Chapter 37:
Thanksgiving

Balancing her heavy dish of homemade *zakuski*—Russian hors d'oeuvres—on her knee, Lydia reached up to knock on the door of the Dalkas' apartment. No sooner had she lifted her hand than she caught a glimpse of Katya's fingers sneaking their way towards the edge of her dish.

"Katerina, *nyet*!" Lydia swayed as she batted her daughter's hand away. Pasha craned his head over the stack of baking pans he was carrying.

"Katya, you'll spoil your appetite."

Katya bounced on her heels, making the scratchy white crinoline beneath her dress swing.

"Just one little bite of salmon?"

"It's Thanksgiving, you are going to want every little bite. Mr. Schultz says in America, Thanksgiving is the biggest dinner of the year, and afterwards you are so full you have to lie down and take a nap. Now be a good girl and knock on the door for Mama."

All sorts of noises were leaking out from behind the door. An Irving Berlin record spooled and snapped in the Victrola. Fragrant butter splattered and sizzled against a hot frying pan, and Leo and Faina bickered back and forth.

"Faina, you klutz! You nearly set the tablecloth on fire! Don't touch the candles!"

"I didn't touch them! I didn't even look at them! Anya, tell Leo I didn't touch the candles!"

As usual, Anya's passive voice was drowned out by the rowdy clash of the unruly siblings. Faina squealed.

"Agh! Uncle Matvei! Uncle Matvei! Leo tried to pour a glass of water on my head!"

"Because you need to cool off! Ow! Uncle Matvei, she tried to hit me!"

"Because you tried to pour a glass of water on my head! I spent the entire night in curlers just so I could look nice for Thanksgiving! Do you know how uncomfortable it is to sleep in curlers?"

Lydia was about to ask Katya to knock on the door a second time when the most alien clamor Lydia could have imagined erupted through the walls. Mr. Dalka's voice boomed overhead like Zeus, blustering in Russian phrases his poor daughter couldn't understand.

"*Chort vos mi!*" Devil take me. "Everyone, quiet! We are not animals! This is supposed to be a special occasion! We are going to sit down and have a nice Thanksgiving with our neighbors like civilized people! Is that understood?"

It was as though the rebellion had been blasted out of Leo's and Faina's voices.

"*Da*, Uncle Matvei."

Someone sat down in a chair scraped out from beneath the table. The pan hissed once more as a piece of meat was dropped into a skillet.

"Faina, stay in your chair. Leontiy, finish setting the table. Anya, dear, check the temperature on the turkey."

Katya was raising her fist a second time when they heard Leo comment, "And no flashing anyone, Faina."

Mr. Dalka made a grunting noise that Lydia assumed was to be taken as a threat.

The door swung open. Mr. Dalka stood on the threshold with his warm, generous smile and his long arms thrown open.

"Happy Thanksgiving! Mrs. Chevalsky, let me get that for you!" He bustled to relieve her of the heavy tray. "Come in, come in! You are just in time! Dinner is almost ready. That is quite a heavy load you are carrying, Pasha, my boy. Leontiy, come help Pasha!"

Lydia glanced around at the homey apartment with its well-thought-out decorations. A velvet runner the shade of marigolds was laid out across the piano. Red candles glowed inside their coppery holders. Paper rustled as her elbow brushed past a homemade garland of leaves.

"My, my! Everything looks so wonderful!"

Faina was at her skirts in a moment.

"Do you like the garland, Mama Lydia?" Faina had taken to calling Mrs. Chevalsky "Mama Lydia" lately, as Pasha had begun calling Mr. Dalka "Uncle Matvei." "Anya and I made it ourselves!"

Lydia ran her fingers affectionately through the child's soft black hair. "Yes, darling, it is very beautiful. Did you make it at school?" As soon as the words left her mouth, Lydia bit her lip. How could she be so tactless? Behind Faina, Mr. Dalka's eyes were searching desperately for a place to rest. But Faina was unfazed.

"Oh, I got expelled from school a couple of weeks ago. Uncle Matvei says I don't have to go back. And Anya switched classrooms."

There was a clamor from around the kitchen wall as Leo slammed a fork down on a plate.

"Faina! You can't go around telling people you were expelled from school!"

Faina stomped her foot angrily. "Why not? It's the truth!"

Leo's head swerved around the corner so fast his floppy bangs pasted to his forehead.

"It's not something you're supposed to be proud of!"

Faina swept her nose into the air with dignity. "I don't care! I hated school! I'm glad I never have to go back, and I don't care who knows it!"

Leo practically yanked the silverware drawer from its socket, his voice bitter with sarcasm.

"That's right! Look at you! Living the American Dream. Reputation ruined by the age of nine. A fourth grade dropout. It's everything Mama and Papa dreamed for you!"

"Leo!" Uncle Matvei finally snapped.

Leo's head dropped slightly to his chest as he straightened himself.

"I'm sorry, Uncle," he mumbled. But the way Leo glanced up at Matvei from underneath his bangs told Lydia he was not that sorry.

"Your sister is not a dropout, we are simply continuing her education at home, just as people have been doing since the dawn of time."

In an attempt to repair the damage she had caused, Lydia cleared her throat.

"Forgive me, Mr. Dalka. I wasn't thinking."

Mr. Dalka shooed Leo back into the kitchen and turned towards Lydia with a smile.

"There is nothing to forgive. Come, sit down." He pulled out a chair for her at the table.

In no time at all a colorful tapestry of food was set on the lace tablecloth. Glittering red beets bled over jade fans of cabbage and carrot buttons. Velvety gravy sluiced over soft pillows of warm, fluffy potatoes, and pink shards of fragrant turkey shimmied from the bone at the slightest gesture of the carving knife. The food was blessed, and the two families began their feast.

As they ate, Mr. Dalka suggested they each go around the table and say what they were thankful for. The gesture began with Katya, who was all too eager to share.

"I am thankful that we finally get to eat!" She stuffed a mushroom into the side of her mouth. "Thanksgiving is the best holiday ever!"

Lydia leaned forward and patted her daughter's lap. "Don't speak with your mouth full, darling."

Katya hastily chewed and swallowed. "Sorry, Mama." She turned to Anya who was sitting on her left. "Your turn, Anya! What are you thankful for?"

As usual, Anya's eyes lowered to her plate and her shoulders drew up around her ears as she smiled timidly.

"I am thankful that the war is finally over, and all our friends and neighbors will be coming back home soon. Though I will miss all the work with the Red Cross."

Everyone made a fuss over how sweet and thoughtful the child was.

"Mrs. Dozier said our Anya had a real talent when it came to volunteering," extolled Leo. "Who knows, she might make a swell nurse someday."

Anya's eyes lit up dreamily. "I sure hope so!"

When it was Leo's turn, he looked down at his plate, a smile tugging at one side of his mouth.

"I'm thankful to be alive, and to have my little sister safe. Most of all I'm thankful for Uncle Matvei, who took us in and gave us a home."

Lydia was not at all astonished when she saw Mr. Dalka had tears in his eyes. Everyone turned their attention to Faina who sat up in her chair, swinging her legs.

"I am thankful I don't have to go back to school anymore." She stabbed a spiteful glare at her brother who heaved an irascible sigh. Mr. Dalka lowered his voice.

"Faina, darling, perhaps let's not talk about school anymore. What else are you thankful for?"

"Well, that's easy, of course! I'm thankful for my family, and Pasha, and Katya, and Mama Lydia!" She gracelessly roped her arms around Pasha's neck and pulled him into a close hug, almost forcing his elbow into the bowl of mashed potatoes.

"Easy, Faina, easy!" Leo set aside the bowl.

Lydia watched her son giggle with delight as Faina mussed his hair with her crushing embrace.

"How sweet of you, Faina. We are so thankful to have you and your family as our friends and neighbors."

270

"Yes!" Pasha swayed as Faina released him. "There is so much for us to be thankful for this year: none of us caught influenza, and the war is finally over. But I'm most thankful for our new home in America, for the Dalkas, and for my best friend, Faina. New York wouldn't be home without her."

Lydia exchanged a furtive smile with Mr. Dalka. Once they had finished going around, Lydia remarked that the flowers centered on the table were the most beautiful chrysanthemums she'd ever seen.

"You really think so?" rejoined Mr. Dalka. "They are lovely, aren't they? Leo picked them up. Where was it you purchased them again, Leontiy?"

Perhaps it was the glow of the sun setting just outside the window or the dim ebb of the red candles, but it looked as though Leo's cheeks had suddenly grown very pink.

"It was, uh, um—"

"It was from Jazmin Zureiq," taunted Faina.

Leo's head snapped up. "Put a sock in it, Faina!"

"Leo is in love with Jazmin!"

"I am not!"

"Well, it's nothing to be embarrassed about, Leo. Not like when you were sweet on Mama Lydia."

By now Lydia felt so sorry for Leo that she hastily began shoveling food into her mouth in an attempt to look as though she hadn't been paying attention. Before anyone could stop him, Leo whipped his napkin out of his lap and lashed it at Faina's head. Mr. Dalka grabbed his wrist and wrenched it back.

"*Nyet*! Leontiy, what did we talk about earlier?"

"She started it!"

Faina was about to stick her tongue out, but Pasha hastily put his hand over her mouth. Lydia changed the subject.

"Leo, the photographs you took of Pasha and Katya came out so lovely! You really are a talented photographer! Tell me, do you have any plans to make a career out of photography? I just know you would be a great success!"

Leo turned from his sister. "Oh! Gee, thanks, Mrs. Chevalsky! You really think so?"

She flashed him her sweetest and most sincere smile. "I know so!"

271

"Well, I have been thinking of selling portraits lately. Uncle Matvei thought it might be a good idea to put up an advertisement in the store for Christmas."

Uncle Matvei wiped at his mouth with his napkin and hastened to swallow. "We have a little space in the back room that might work as a temporary studio. After all, people might like to include a photograph or two with their Christmas cards."

Lydia leaned forward in her chair. "Ah, so you like portraiture?"

Leo shrugged. "Eh, it pays well. My dream job would be in photojournalism."

"Leo likes that famous Danish photographer," explained Faina, matter-of-factly. "Jacob Reeves."

"Not Reeves, *Riis*."

"I'm afraid I'm not quite familiar with his work," confessed Lydia. "What is it that he is famous for?"

Uncle Matvei craned back in his chair and gestured to the room around them. "Buildings like this for starters."

"If you can imagine," Leo elaborated, "the quality of life around these parts used to be a lot worse."

"People were living in rooms without windows, buildings without air shafts. Not like this complex which has a courtyard and up-to-date plumbing. There was such a lack of light and fresh air that in the summertime infants were dying from the heat.

"Jacob Riis used photography to bring attention to the situation, and people wanted to do something about it."

Uncle Matvei wiped his mouth with his napkin. "And when the state passed the New York Tenement House Act, Jacob Riis's photographs were used as reference."

Leo's practiced manners fell away, and he became uncontrollably animated. His eyes were as vivacious as a child opening them for the first time.

"Jacob Riis not only used his art to move people, but he actually changed the law with his photography! He used his art to makes people's lives better! Boy, if I could do something as amazing as that then I may have a life worth living."

Lydia dipped her chin towards him approvingly. "What a wonderfully noble ambition! I'm certainly eager to see you succeed. To think one day I will be able to tell people that my children were photographed by Leo Spichkin when he was just starting out!"

Uncle Matvei's mustache twitched as he threw back his head and laughed. "I believe it is safe to say, Mrs. Chevalsky, that we dine with five highly important figures tonight. We have Pasha Chevalsky, future millionaire and philanthropist. We have Miss Faina Spichkin, Broadway's next big star. Leo, the progressive reformer who's going to change the world with his photography. Anya, the next Florence Nightingale." Matvei folded his hands in his lap and smiled teasingly at Katya. "And what about Miss Katerina? Hmm? What unparalleled talent shall you astonish us with when you grow up?"

It was clear from the way Katya confidently adjusted herself in her seat that she had already given the answer some thought.

"I want to paint pictures just like Mama."

"I had no idea you were a painter, Mrs. Chevalsky!" Uncle Matvei set down his glass of wine.

Lydia's head dropped as she recalled mournfully the feel of a paintbrush in her hands. "I was, back when I had time."

Faina dug her fork into her potatoes. "Don't worry, Mama Lydia. When Pasha becomes a rich philanthropist, I am sure you will have all the time in the world to paint. I bet he'll even build you a nice studio to work in."

The thought brought a smile to her lips. "You are so right, my dear." She smoothed her napkin over her lap. "Faina, I must say your English is coming along beautifully! Your pronunciation has improved quite nicely."

Matvei cut into a bit of turkey and chuckled. "All that practice is starting to pay off, isn't it, *Faishka?*"

Faina grinned. "It sure is. Pretty soon I will be like Leo and sound just like a New Yorker!"

Leo glanced up from his plate, unable to keep from snickering in amusement. "Well, you better catch up. Pasha's not far behind me. The other day I heard him say, 'yooz guys.'"

While everyone tittered away, Faina examined her uncle with curiosity.

"Uncle Matvei, if you've lived here so long why don't you know how to sound like a New Yorker?"

Uncle Matvei wiped his mustache with his napkin and leaned back in his chair with a sly tilt of his eyes. "Who says I don't?" Matvei sat up straight and pulled his chair closer. He cleared his throat once and, as if by magic, transformed into a different character. "Hey, yoo! Little gwirl, wid the black hair! Get ova' here, I gotta question for yooz," he shouted, scrunching up his mouth like a street salesman and adjusting his waistcoat.

No one at the table could keep from bursting out laughing. Faina got up from her chair and inched forward, giggling all the way.

"Yes?"

Uncle Matvei pointed a finger at the end of her nose. "Howsabout you and me start our own Vaudeville act, huh?"

Faina covered her face and doubled over with laughter, as her uncle roped her into his lap and dipped her upside down.

"How's about it, gwirlie? Yoo stick wid me an' we could travel da world!"

"Okay, okay," Faina squealed, wiggling to an upright position. "I believe you!"

"Are you sure?" he teased, tickling her.

"Yes! Yes! You sound just like Al Smith!"

Satisfied, Mr. Dalka put her right again and stamped her cheek with a kiss before letting her return to her seat. Faina was rounding the corner when she tripped and bumped into the table leg, almost knocking over one of the candlesticks. The taper swayed dangerously before Leo reached across the table and set it firmly back in place.

"What is it with you and fire?" he sniped authoritatively.

Faina plopped back into her chair. "It was an accident!"

"Yeah, yeah, you can write that on my tombstone. Here lies Leo Spichkin, his sister set the apartment on fire but it's okay because it was an accident!"

Uncle Matvei snapped his fingers discreetly under the table to catch their attention, but they paid him no mind. Lydia gestured to a photograph on the wall above Faina's head.

"Are those your parents, dearest?"

"Yes! Yes!" Faina scurried excitedly around in her seat and got on her knees so she could point to the photograph. "That is Mama and Papa!"

Leo yanked the bottom of her skirt.

"Sit down, silly, you don't have to point. She can see it!"

"What a lovely couple," extolled Lydia. "Leo, you look so like your father."

Leo sat a little taller, a smile tugging at the corner of his lips. "Thank you, ma'am."

"Wasn't Mama beautiful?" Faina dragged the word out almost as though it caused her pain. "She was so lovely, just like you, Mama Lydia! I wish you could have seen her. She had the most beautiful hair! Papa always said that when he and Mama first met he was so taken by her long raven hair that he thought she was an angel."

"How sweet. Tell me, how did your parents meet?"

At once Lydia realized this was not the right question to ask as Leo and Matvei jumped to attention.

"Mama found Papa passed out naked in the snow."

Katya squeaked and nearly fell out of her chair from laughing. Pasha covered his mouth with his napkin to hide his amusement.

"Faina!" Leo tore around in his seat. "You can't tell that story!"

But Faina was smiling just as much as Katya, completely unaware of the problem.

"Why not? It's a funny story!"

"A funny *family* story, yes, but it's completely inappropriate in front of guests!"

Mr. Dalka rubbed a hand across his forehead. "Faina, your brother is right." Turning to Lydia, he smoothed his mustache and managed a weak smile. "It's not like it sounds. You see, my brother-in-law was backpacking through the Urals and ran into a band of ruffians who robbed him and left him for dead."

"I don't know why anyone would go backpacking through the Urals in March," wondered Faina aloud. "Everyone knows it's freezing."

Leo silenced her with a stern look.

"He was a foreigner," Mr. Dalka went on. "An Irishman. Anyway, it's a wonder he was still alive when he was discovered. He'd been out there for hours, and yet he had no symptoms of hypothermia."

Lydia clicked her tongue. "My goodness, no wonder he thought your sister was an angel."

"She saved his life. Came back and alerted the family. We took him back to our house. We were living in the mountains at the time. We called a doctor and let him stay overnight. Would you believe when the man awoke he hardly spoke a stitch of Russian? Imagine coming all the way to Russia with plans of touring the Urals and hardly being able to speak the language! Fortunately, I had just finished studying English. I had plans to come to America. That's how we were able to communicate."

"And your sister? Did she know English as well?"

275

Mr. Dalka leaned back in his chair and laughed. "Ariadne? No, she was not as interested in learning English as I was."

"But how did they manage to communicate?"

"Through me at first, then Adrian began picking up a little more. It was odd, they almost seemed to have their own way of understanding each other." Mr. Dalka screwed up his eyes and rubbed his chin as he recalled the memory. "They were funny to watch. They'd act things out, point at things, botch phrases, get frustrated with one another and then burst into laughter. They would have such fun trying to figure out what the other was saying. I'm not even sure either of them had worked out the language barrier completely by the time they got married. And yet somehow they understood one another."

"Because they were meant for each other," insisted Faina who, after a long period of silence, had finally found her way back into the conversation. "They didn't have to speak the same language to know who they were."

As Lydia glanced back at the couple in the picture she found this easy to believe. Something about the way they were holding each other reminded her of two trees that had grown together. Even their names fit together: Adrian and Ariadne.

She was about to ask Mr. Dalka how he and his wife had met, when a blazing stream of fire ignited atop the turkey out of nowhere. Katya gave a squeal. Everyone lurched away, waving their arms and shielding their faces. Leo leapt up from his seat.

"Faina, what did you do?"

No one could have predicted Anya's reaction; she reeled around almost accusingly. "What are you talking about? Faina didn't move an inch! Your arm knocked the candle!"

"It doesn't matter who started it!" Matvei scrambled to his feet. "Just put it out! Leo, hand me that towel!"

Faina's hand enclosed around a decanter of clear liquid. "Don't worry, I'll fix it!"

Lydia's eyes swelled with horror. "No, Faina, that's vodka!"

Faina swung the container forward. The liquid poured over the turkey in a long, silvery arc. Leo grabbed his sister by the waist, jerking her back. The fire fountained towards the ceiling in a flat, fizzy wall of white-hot light. The remaining vodka splashed backwards over Leo's and Faina's heads. The flames circled back and washed over the pair in a ring of light.

Then it was over. Chalky smoke curled and pushed outwards in a fan. To everyone's astonishment, Faina and Leo stood there clutching each other, completely unharmed, as though it had been a horrifying magic trick.

Pasha grabbed the real pitcher of water from the sideboard and hurled it over the leftover flames. The sound of sprinkling water jolted Leo and Faina back to attention. They shivered and turned to each other in disbelief. They hadn't so much as a scorch mark on their clothing. Lydia covered her mouth and steadied herself against the back of the chair. Mr. Dalka's knees shook as he staggered towards his niece and nephew, his arms outstretched.

"*Slava Bogu!*" Praise God. "Oh, my children!"

Pasha pulled out a chair for Leo as the boy began to shake and fell to a seat with Faina crying in his arms.

"I'm sorry, Leo," she wailed.

Leo held her tightly to his chest as Uncle Matvei and Anya enclosed their arms around them. "It's okay, it was an accident."

Lydia shook her head incredulously. "I believe we just witnessed a miracle."

Pasha knit his brows together. "How did the fire even start?"

"It wasn't Faina," insisted Anya. "I know it wasn't. I saw her. She didn't move."

Leo hung his head in shame. "It had to have been me! It must have been!"

"It couldn't have been," said Anya. "All the candles are still standing, and your sleeve didn't catch fire."

Mr. Dalka leaned over the table and looked down into the pan. "Perhaps it was the grease?"

Lydia took a step forward and examined the dish herself. Unless the turkey had been unusually hot or sitting atop a heat source she didn't see how the bird could've gone up in flames. Still, it was the best explanation so far. She supposed it didn't matter, so long as Faina and Leo were safe.

Fortunately, the remainder of the feast was unscathed, and by then everyone had had their fill of turkey, so it wasn't a complete waste.

The Chevalskys gladly lent their hand in the recovery of the evening. Lydia helped Faina wash up so she no longer smelled of vodka, Katya assisted by opening all the windows to help air out the apartment, and Pasha aided with the dishes.

Before they knew it, everyone was settling down in a sleepy state of contentment. Leo had fallen asleep on the rug in front of the radiator with one arm thrown over his head and his mouth hanging slightly open. Anya and Faina had drifted off on the sofa while listening to the victrola, and Pasha and Katya were cuddled together in one armchair. Lydia and Matvei surveyed the endearing picture from the table where they sat and drank coffee.

"Look at them," laughed Mr. Dalka, "you'd never suspect a couple of hours ago they nearly burnt down the building."

Lydia snickered into her coffee. "One thing is for sure, they'll never be short on stories when they grow up."

"That's true." He stroked his mustache with his thumb and forefinger. "I'm sorry your first American Thanksgiving was so … disastrous."

Lydia craned her head back and laughed as she patted Mr. Dalka's hand.

"I believe the word you are looking for is 'adventurous.'"

Chapter 38:
Scarred for Life

"I was hoping Leo would stay with us, not drop us off." Faina kicked at a snowdrift with the toe of her boot as they neared the end of their walk down Fifth Avenue. "Oh! Look at that one!" She stopped and pointed to a mansion with a wreath six feet in diameter hanging from the wrought-iron gate.

The luxury mansions and townhouses of Fifth Avenue were regular stops for Leo on his deliveries, especially during festive seasons of the year, and Pasha and Faina had begged Leo to take them along on his route so they could ooh and aah at the expensive trees sparkling through the windows of the manors. When they were finished they were to meet him an hour later at Turtle Pond in Central Park.

"I hardly get to see him anymore between working for the school paper, gymnastics team, the Breadwinners, and now his deliveries for Uncle Matvei." She shoved her hands into her pockets and sighed. "He barely has any time for himself these days."

"I don't suppose he ever got around to walking out with Jazmin Zureiq, did he?" asked Pasha.

"Not that I know of. But Jazmin's parents would never have approved anyway, not with Leo's Breadwinner connections."

As they came to the end of their journey, Pasha gestured to the row of ritzy residences.

"Which one would you want to live in?"

Faina folded her hands behind her back and swayed ladylike down the sidewalk, appraising the elaborate houses like chocolates in a box. She lingered at the entrance of a limestone mansion built in the French Gothic style. The cozy shade of the exterior reminded her of the pages in an old book. She raised her finger and pointed to the gated double doors.

"That one!"

Pasha gazed up at the house with admiration. "That's the one I'll buy for you then."

"What?" Faina giggled.

"Someday I'm going to buy you that house."

"Why would you do that?"

"Because you want it."

Faina stared down at her feet with a blushing smile. She wanted nothing more than to kiss him right then and there. But she couldn't make it that easy.

"Will that be your wedding gift to me then?"

Faina whirled around to assess the state she had put him in. Pasha's face had grown so predictably scarlet that it was competing with the poinsettias for brightest color against the snow, and a smile was jamming its way into his cheeks so that his eyes were squinted.

"Does that mean you want to marry me after all?"

Faina fluttered her eyelashes to the best of her ability and edged towards him with her daintiest swagger. "It sure sounds that way, doesn't it?"

Pasha squeezed his eyes shut, hardly able to contain himself. "Does that mean you want to kiss me now?"

Faina giggled and placed one hand over his eyes. "Close your eyes."

Pasha obeyed without question. Faina stood back and watched as he struggled to relax his face. When she had kept him waiting long enough, she pulled his cap down over his eyes and yelled, "Tag! You're it!" before running down the sidewalk.

She was lucky Pasha was a good sport. They chased each other into the park. With all their energetic horseplay they managed to make it to Turtle Pond fifteen minutes early. The van was already waiting.

"Leo won't be expecting us for another fifteen minutes." Faina bent down and gathered a snowball into her open hand. "Let's sneak up on him!"

While Pasha was still rolling the powder (he had yet to master the art of the snowball), Faina ran ahead with three already piled in the crook of her arm. She could hardly control her giggles as she jogged around to the driver's side and yanked open the door. Faina wound back her arm. But Leo wasn't there.

She lowered her hand and stared curiously at the open seat. She heard movement from the back. He must have gotten up to rearrange the inventory. Faina hurried to the rear of the van and swung the hatch open.

"Hey, Leo!" As her vision adjusted to the dark she dropped her snowball in surprise.

Two figures were fused together in a mass on top of the crates. One of them was Leo, the other she couldn't quite see, but it looked like a girl sitting in his lap. They appeared to be kissing … but the girl's head was turned away from Leo, and his face was buried somewhere under her mass of hair above the shoulder.

It was Jazmin Zureiq, and Leo looked as though he were eating her head! Faina dropped her snowballs and let out an ear-piercing shriek. Leo jerked up so suddenly his head hit the roof.

"Faina! What are you doing?"

But Faina wasn't listening, she was too busy sprinting back the way she came. By now Pasha had his arms full of snowballs and was making his way towards the van at a ridiculously sluggish pace for ambushing someone.

"Pasha! Pasha!" Faina grabbed his elbow and towed him back in the opposite direction.

"Faina, what's the matter?"

"Just run! Keep running!"

Pasha leaned back with all his weight, forcing Faina to stop. "What on earth has gotten into you?"

Faina doubled over her knees, trying to catch her breath. "Leo … in the van … I saw … I saw …"

Pasha tossed his remaining snowballs into the air, utterly exasperated. "You saw what?"

Faina gagged and made a display of wagging her head and sticking out her tongue. "Leo and Jazmin! Together! In the van! They had their paws all over each other!" She gagged a second time and stamped in a circle.

Pasha put a hand over his mouth as he chuckled. "Is that all?"

But Faina was inconsolable. She took Pasha by the shoulders and shook him.

"Don't you understand? Five minutes ago I was an innocent child! I had a mind of purity!"

"You? Really?"

"And now it's tarnished!" She pulled at her hair. "Tarnished forever! Do you know what I saw in there?" She bent over him with crazed eyes and pointed to the side of her head. "He had his tongue inside her ear, Pasha! *Her ear*!"

"Faina!"

Pasha and Faina both jumped at the clamor of Leo's voice. If his face had been any redder the snow would've melted, and in fact, Faina could've sworn she saw puddles forming under her brother's feet. She let out a yell and scurried behind a tree leaving Pasha to stand awkwardly on the sidewalk.

"Pasha," Leo barked, "catch her!"

But Pasha backed away submissively with his hands thrown up. Weary of running, Faina grabbed a hold of a branch and was just hoisting herself into the tree when Leo seized her by the ankles and started pulling. Faina clung to the branch like a threatened opossum.

"You are sick, Leo! Sick!"

"Put a sock in it and let go," he demanded.

"No!" She tried to kick at him but his grip was too tight. Finally, he gave her one solid yank and they both went flying backwards into the snow. Before Faina could escape, he roped his arm around her waist.

"I told you no sooner than an hour!"

"So you could put your hands all over your girlfriend!"

Leo slammed his hand over her mouth. "Calm down! We were just kissing!" Faina bit his finger, causing Leo to recoil and yelp.

"You've destroyed my innocence!"

"I highly doubt that!"

With his arms still secured around her, Leo sat up and slammed her into the ground like a pro wrestler. He held her down by her wrists.

"Listen! You can't tell anyone about this! Do you hear me? Jazmin could get in huge trouble!"

"Let me guess, because her parents don't approve? I told you that would happen, but you didn't listen to me! You had to be stupid!"

Leo drew back suddenly and kicked the snow. "Yeah, alright, fine! I had to be stupid! But could you just do me this favor and not tell anybody?" Leo sighed and cradled his head in his hands.

Slowly, Faina drew herself up to a sitting position. Leo's shoulders were pulled in and locked like a stressed cat. Behind his hand, his forehead was wrinkled in a knot. She softened her voice.

"Glad you're finally beginning to see things my way."

Leo did not say anything. He remained bent over his knees with his fingers inching towards his hairline.

"As long as you don't do anything stupid—more stupid, I mean— I'm not going to say anything. And Pasha won't either. Right, Pasha?"

Pasha peeked around the trunk of the tree to throw them a thumbs up. Gradually, Leo lifted his head. He looked Faina up and down, then nodded.

"Thank you." He reached over to pat Faina's shoulder, then helped her to her feet. "Come on. We gotta drop Jazmin off at her aunt's."

Faina groaned and bent over her knees. "You mean we have to sit in the car with her and pretend like nothing happened?"

Leo nudged her forward. "It's only five minutes away. Relax."

"Easy for you to say!" She turned around and beckoned for Pasha to pick up the pace. Leo placed a hand on each of their shoulders and guided them back towards the fountain.

"Yeah, yeah. Look, if you're good sports about it we'll stop by the drugstore on the way home, and I'll buy you both sundaes."

Chapter 39:

Delusions

Lydia's head wrenched back as the blistering wind ripped the shawl from her head and scourged her hair. Her fingers, stiff with cold, fumbled clumsily as she worked to put it right again and bowed forward beneath the squall. She turned up the stoop of their tenement building and hastened inside. The door sucked shut behind her with a bang. Lydia fell against the wall, utterly relieved. The children in number six squealed past her on the landing with renewed jubilation. She laughed softly to herself as she remembered that tomorrow was the first day of Christmas vacation.

The thought of Pasha and Katya racing excitedly around the tenement spurred her up the stairs in a delighted dash. The fragrance of cloves boiling with meat welcomed Lydia as she raced down the hall and swung open the door.

"Can it be my two angels are finally home for Christmas?"

Pasha and Katya were standing at the stove, Pasha looking very official with his apron and spoon, while Katya stood barefoot on a stool gleefully nibbling a mushroom. At the sight of their mother the spoon was dropped and the mushroom promptly gobbled.

"Mama!" They flocked to her side, wrapping their arms around her waist.

"We've been waiting for you all evening!" said Katya, burying her face into her mother's shoulder. Lydia kissed the inside of her wrists and laughed.

"Did you do anything special at school since it was your last day?"

"No, not really."

Pasha nudged her in the side. "What are you talking about, *Katenka*? Don't you want to show Mama the Christmas angel you made?"

Katya's hands flew to her cheeks. "Oh, yes! Mama, you must see the angel I knitted today in school. Teacher said it was one of the loveliest angels she had ever seen!"

Katya soared to her book satchel and began fishing through an entire assortment of peculiar treasures in search of her ornament. She was always fond of gleaning strange objects from the sidewalk, and so far she'd produced a pinecone, a broken watch face, a house slipper, a glass ointment bottle, and a pigeon feather. Lydia knelt cautiously beside her daughter and smiled gently.

"Katerina, dearest, perhaps it is time we clean out your book satchel. We can always take your trinkets and put them in a special box."

"Okay! Let me just get the rest out."

Lydia shrieked suddenly as Katya yanked out a snakeskin and laid it in her mother's lap.

"Don't worry," Katya beamed. "The snake isn't there anymore."

Lydia put a hand to her heart to steady her breathing as Pasha, trying not to laugh, reached forward and removed the snakeskin for his mother.

"Katya, darling … Where? … Where did you even find this?" She glanced curiously over her shoulder at the cityscape filling up the window. The incongruity was lost on Katya.

"On the sidewalk."

Lydia opened her mouth to say something, then decided it was better not to—in fact, it was just better not to think about it.

"There is an empty shoebox under our bed. Why don't you take your collection and put it in there, and when you get back you can show me your Christmas angel."

"Okay, Mama!" She reached for the snakeskin, but Pasha drew it back.

"Sweetheart, why don't you let your brother take care of that. You wouldn't want it to break, would you?"

Katya eyed her suspiciously for a moment. Lydia resisted the urge to sigh and instead forced a smile. There was rarely any use in lying to Katya, but how could she keep such a horrid thing in the apartment?

Finally, Katya nodded and took the remainder of her assembly into the bedroom. When the door had been shut, Lydia rubbed the bridge of her nose with her thumb and forefinger and motioned to Pasha.

"*Patulya*, throw that thing away, will you?"

"She's going to know what you did with it."

Lydia propped her elbow on the arm of the sofa and ran her fingers worriedly through her hair. "I know …"

"Well, it's like she said. The snake is gone."

"But there could be eggs left behind in it!"

Pasha looked down at the skin and smirked. "Ma, you know it doesn't work that way."

Lydia managed a weak laugh and reached out to caress her son's face. "Alright, you caught me."

"Maybe we could keep it in a tin. You know, something more secure."

She scratched the end of his nose playfully with her finger. "That's a wonderful idea, Pasha. There's one in the kitchen hanging above the stove that I don't use anymore."

Pasha nodded and disappeared behind the dividing wall to fulfill his mother's wishes. "Our reports are in the front pocket of my satchel," he called out to her. "I put Katya's in there so it wouldn't get ruined by all her other stuff."

Lydia chuckled to herself. "Good idea." She reached down into Pasha's tidy book bag and retrieved the two folded envelopes. She opened Pasha's first. Her eyes lit up at once.

Pasha is an excellent student with a deep-seeded passion for academia. He excels at nearly every subject presented to him, but shows particular aptitude when it comes to language. It is clear this boy has a bright future ahead of him, and would do well at a university. It has been a pleasure supervising this young man's education. —M. Schultz

Lydia felt her eyes welling up with tears. When she lowered the letter, Pasha was peering timidly around the edge of the wall. Lydia threw out her arms.

"Come here, you silly thing!" She staggered to her knees and wrapped him in a snug embrace, kissing every spare inch of his cheeks she could get to. "I am so proud of you, Pavlo!"

Pasha laughed as she pulled him down to the floor and sat him in her lap. She brushed his bangs back from his forehead and looked him over. Already his face was beginning to look less childish, but his eyes remained as big and round as ever.

"You're going to accomplish everything you set out to do. I know you will." She kissed his forehead one more time. "You're my good boy, *Patulya*."

Pasha laid his head against her shoulder. "I love you, *Mamochka*."

Lydia held him tighter and let his hair brush against her nose. "I love you too." After sitting in silence for a moment, Lydia recalled the second envelope in her hand.

"Have you read Katya's yet?"

"No. I thought you should."

Lydia eyed the envelope warily. She had been dreading this for some time. A month ago, Lydia had had a meeting with Katya's teacher to discuss her daughter's odd behavior, which bordered on delusional. Katya often claimed to have seen things that were simply not possible, from angels flying around the city, to people living in the trees in Central Park.

As she was ripping open the envelope, Katya returned from the bedroom and sat down at her knee. With one hand, Lydia fingered her daughter's curls and read inside her head.

Dear Mrs. Chevalsky,

I hope this letter finds you well. I am sorry to report that Katerina continues to exhibit strange behaviors. I write this not as a criticism of her character, for she is a dear, sweet child who is eager to please, but out of concern for her well-being. I believe it would be best if we meet again before the new semester to discuss our options, and possibly have her evaluated. — B. Thompson

Tears gushed over Lydia's fingers as she placed a hand over her mouth. Evaluated? Evaluated for what? What could this possible mean? Where moments before she had wept from joy, she was now crying from stabbing grief. Pasha, who was as sensitive to the subtle shifts in her moods as a weathervane, stiffened with alertness. He leaned over her shoulder and scanned the contents. Katya's head fell between her shoulders, and she nibbled at the tips of her fingers.

"What's the matter, Mama? Didn't I do well like Pasha?"

Lydia crushed the letter with her fist, and forced a smile into her cheeks.

"*Da, Rybka*! You did so well, my sweet girl!" She bent forward and kissed the top of her head. Lydia stumbled to her feet and made for the bedroom door.

"Mama will be right back," she hollered over her shoulder, striving to keep her voice steady. "Pasha, go in the kitchen and get you and your sister a cookie from the jar. Have as many as you want."

She bolted the door behind her and threw herself on top of the bed, burying her face in the pillow so that no one could catch her sobs. Scenes from her childhood flew through her brain like shards of a broken window. She could remember so many impossible things: herds of unicorns stampeding through the woods, enchanted books that made you disappear when you read them, singing toads, and most of all, Papa's magic. How he moved things without touching them. After Papa died there was no one to reconcile Lydia's fantastic childhood with reality. She told herself she must have hit her head at some point, for it was all she could remember.

But now Katya saw them too. She saw things that weren't real. Whatever it was that caused Lydia to distort her own childhood was living inside her, and Katya had inherited it. Lydia lifted her head as an apologetic knock sounded on her door.

"Mama," urged Pasha from the other side. "I think something is wrong with Katya's eyes."

Chapter 40:
Pyro's Big Idea

Pyro yanked the door shut, struggling against the strength of the howling wind.

"Tongs and torches!" He collapsed on the threshold and tugged off his boots. "It's a blizzard alright!"

It was December. The company had been back at Feifior for some time now with little news about the Jar of Elijah. Rather than return to Spica, Dr. Desmond was staying with relatives in Ascella where it was deemed safer, enabling her to help Thayer track down the C.O.N. Dozens of Saighdeoir soldiers were stationed across Ophiuchus and Libra, but there was little to report. Though Pyro had been thoroughly reprimanded for his confession about the alcohol in Virgo, Staccato had not fired him, but kept a close eye on his behavior from there on out.

Pyro shed his coat and handed it to the footman before poking his head into the parlor. Melodious was seated at the piano playing Christmas carols while Skelter accompanied him on the violin. Sometimes it seemed music was the only real way for Melodious and Skelter to communicate with each other, and the songs that spun from their respective instruments sounded almost conversational at times.

"Well, aren't you two festive?" teased Pyro as he passed.

Skelter smiled and winked, but neither of them said anything. Across the room, Sonata was sitting in her wheelchair before the fire with Cello in her lap, busy with a sampler. Overall, she had been merciful following the incident in Khan Lau, and there was no awkward tension between them. Still, Pyro had not lost his attraction to Sonata, and her rejection continued to sting.

"I noticed another burn mark in the wainscoting in the west wing this morning," she said as he plopped down in the armchair beside her. "Another battle with the dry bellows?"

Pyro snickered. "Guilty."

Sonata shook her head in amusement. "How ever do you igneous manage to avoid burning down your house when even a simple cold turns you into a walking inferno?"

"That's nothing. You should see us when our powers first activate. Why, I remember when I was about fifteen or sixteen waking up every morning with scorch marks on my pillow!"

Sonata was aghast. "Scorch marks on your pillow?"

"Yeah. It's awful. You start mouth breathing when you fall asleep, then you start snoring. You get sinus trouble, sore throat, and heartburn. Food melts in your hands all the time. And then there's the night sweats, and… Oh! The spice cravings are terrible! I once drank all the juice from a can of pickled jalapeños. And you can't go anywhere near a match or else it's likely to fountain into a blowtorch."

Sonata stuck out her lip in surprise. "And I thought adolescence was bad for the rest of us." She went on dipping her needle in and out of the sampler.

"Can I ask you something?" Pyro leaned over the arm of his chair. "If you have those fancy prosthetics, how come you still use a wheelchair?"

She shrugged. "No artificial limb is without its problems. A prosthetic is still a prosthetic, and mine have given me a real problem with sciatica. The chair helps me recover." She shifted around in her seat and winced.

"Staccato says you began aerial ballet as a form of rehabilitation." He glanced down at her wheels. "Doesn't it help with the pain any?"

"Exercise of any kind is bound to help some, but it was mostly to strengthen my muscles." Cello rose and arched his back before jumping off Sonata's lap and settling on the hearth.

"You know," began Pyro, "when I arrived at Alveare I had no idea you'd lost your legs."

"What?" Sonata looked askance. "You really didn't know?"

"No. Not until you showed us your routine."

To Pyro's surprise she threw back her head and laughed, showcasing her lovely neck. "Well, that must have been quite a shock when I removed my prosthetic."

Pyro felt the corners of his lips tugging upward. Despite her refined manners, there was an unaffected genuineness about Sonata that could not be buried behind trained protocol.

"A little."

"I'm quite used to it now. If it had never happened then Staccato would never have had a reason to invent my prosthetics, and hundreds of people would never be able to walk again."

Pyro could have sworn he felt a physical force pulling him towards Sonata. His thoughts were a continual repetition of the word *Wow*.

"What made you go after Samael in the first place?"

"I had an opportunity no one else had. He didn't know I was there." She put down her sampler and stared pensively at the wall. "When you have a chance like that, you have to take it, don't you?"

She turned to him for confirmation, her eyes almost doe-like. Pyro stared back at her in perfect admiration.

"You didn't have to. That's what makes it selfless. No one would have blamed you if you had done nothing."

Sonata looked down with a sheepish smile before finding his gaze once more. For a moment they smiled at each other, their cheeks growing warm, and Pyro had to wonder if just maybe Sonata really did have feelings for him.

Pyro was just about to say something when a familiar figure drew his attention to the hallway. It was Private Hogarth Hickory, his old buddy from the Saighdeoir, and he was headed for the door. Pyro raced out into the passage.

"*Oi*! Ol' Hickory Sticks! Is that you?"

The sylph turned with a familiar chuckle. "Pyro Anomaly! Why, you old hearth winder!" He looped his arm around Pyro's neck and ground his fist into his hair. "I heard you'd been staying at Feifior, but I figured you'd be back home with your folks by now."

"Nope! Still here." He straightened. "What are you doing here anyway?"

He held up an empty envelope. "Official Saighdeoir business. Just delivering a report to King Thayer. Sobek's regiment was spotted making their way up the Caput." Hickory stopped and looked past Pyro with an intimidated expression. "Your Highness." He bowed.

Pyro looked over his shoulder. Sonata had rolled into the hallway.

"Good afternoon, Private Hickory." She turned her attention to Pyro. "I'm supposed to help Mei decorate cookies. You're welcome to join us if you like. We would enjoy your company." She smiled and rolled down the hall.

Hickory nudged Pyro in the side. "So, the princess enjoys your company?"

"She's just a friend. We grew up together, remember?"

"Ah, a childhood romance!"

"Oh, go on you old twig!" He gave him a playful punch.

"If I remember correctly, she's just your type."

"Yeah—I mean—ugh!" Pyro shook his head in embarrassment. "Look, it ain't going anywhere, okay?"

Hickory shrugged. "Why not? You're a prince by birth, aren't you?"

"I'm not sure princesses go for men with a past."

"Don't be so dramatic. A man's gotta sow his wild oats. It ain't nothing new."

Pyro tried not to appear downcast, but it bled through into his posture.

"She's made it pretty clear she wants nothing to do with me in that way."

He held up his hand, showing off a new gold band. "Hey, if it can happen to me, it can happen to you."

"What? You got married?"

Hickory threw back his head and laughed.

"Why you cheeky, old smokestack! When did this happen?"

"A week ago. It was a quiet affair. Courthouse marriage."

"What's her name?"

"Mary. And oh boy, I gotta tell you, buddy. I ain't never been so happy. She's the center of my world." He laid a hand on Pyro's shoulder. "Don't sell yourself short. You deserve to be happy."

Pyro rubbed the side of his arm. "Since when do any of us ever get what we deserve?"

"Chin up, Pyro. It'll get better." He made to open the door.

"You sure you can't stay longer?" Pyro gestured to the storm raging outside the window. "At least to wait for the weather to die down a bit?"

Hickory shook his head. "I can't. I'm needed back at Fort Halix."

Outside, the wind howled against the glass. "Boy, things must really be urgent for you to have to travel in this weather."

Hickory lowered his head. "Well, I haven't told you what's happened." He looked over his shoulder and lead Pyro to an alcove. "The Saighdeoir attacked Sobek's unit."

Pyro's adrenaline surged. "What?"

"They've managed to drive them into the Boötes."

"The Boötes?" Pyro glanced out the window. "It's December."

"We had to slow them down. At the rate they were traveling on the Caput they would've reached Draco within a week."

"But now the ambassadors have to carry the Jar on foot."

"Not if we're able to stop them."

"Can you stop them?"

Hickory paused and passed a hand over his mouth. His expression was pained. "It's not easy. This storm front has extended as far as Ursa."

"What does Thayer plan to do?"

"He wants to keep them there." He held up his hands before Pyro could protest. "If they cut through Lake Hercules they'll be in enemy-occupied territory again, and our chances of stopping them before they reach Draco will be impossible."

"But if you wait until you *can* reach them, innocents will freeze to death!"

Hickory sighed and shrugged. "It's a difficult situation."

Pyro stood stroking his beard and scowling at the floor. Suddenly, a thought struck him. He patted Hickory on the shoulder.

"It's been great talking to you, Hickory." He ran off down the hall. "And congratulations on the marriage!"

"Where are you going in such a hurry?"

"I've got to speak with Thayer!"

Pyro was relieved to find the cherries on the wallpaper already green when he entered the antechamber of Thayer's office. He beat his fist against the door.

"Thayer!"

Thayer opened the door and stared at Pyro as though he were mentally disturbed.

"What in the seven seas is the matter?"

Pyro pushed past him into the study, nearly tripping over Seaweed's tail. "We need to talk. It's urgent."

Thayer offered him a chair but Pyro ignored it and went straight to the point.

"Private Hickory says the Saighdeoir has chased Sobek's unit into the Boötes."

Thayer settled himself before the fire and tousled Seaweed's floppy ears. "They did."

"And you have them surrounded at the base of the mountain on all sides?"

"They won't be going anywhere anytime soon."

Pyro raked his fingers through his hair and sighed irritably. "And the Saighdeoir can't pursue them into the mountains?"

"Not until the storm passes." He shifted and crossed one leg over the other. "I see where you're headed with this, Pyro. I know you're upset. You work in rescue and recovery after all, and there are seven innocent people on that mountain, one of which is a child." His nostrils flared. "I don't like it either. But we don't have much of a choice. I take it Private Hickory explained to you why we can't let them slip into Lake Hercules. We'll have no chance of stopping them before they hit Draco."

"But that's just it. What if you don't need to stop them from reaching Draco?"

Instead of protest, Thayer merely twirled the end of his mustache around his finger and leaned back with thoughtful curiosity.

"I'm listening."

"The chances of you stopping Sobek's unit from reaching Draco are already slim to none, unless you want to let a bunch of hostages freeze to death. You won't be able to march the Saighdeoir straight into enemy territory without a considerable amount of resistance. This mission doesn't require brute force, it requires finesse, cunning. In other words, you need undercover agents."

"You want to take on Sobek's unit yourself?"

"Hear me out. When the Jar arrives in Draco, it will be a big victory for the C.O.N. And what do you do after a big victory? You have a big celebration, a festival or whatever. And what do festivals need? Live entertainment."

Thayer's mouth curled with a furtive smile. "I like where this is going, Pyro. I must admit, you've put an awful lot of thought into this. But there's one problem. It would be impossible for the five of you to carry the Jar alone."

"I've thought of that, and I have a solution." He braced the back of the chair opposite his godfather. "We'll recruit more Saighdeoir soldiers into the act."

Thayer frowned. "We've already tried that, remember? It didn't work out."

"It didn't work out because you hired a dance teacher to instruct a bunch of seasoned soldiers, when what you need is a drill sergeant with a knowledge of aerial dance. In short, me."

Thayer narrowed his eyes. "A drill sergeant in tights." Slowly, he nodded and let out a chuckle. "I love it!"

"I know how to communicate with soldiers. I promise you, I can make them take this seriously."

Thayer stood and stretched his arms over his head. "I think you've got something there, Pyro, my boy." He crossed to the chalkboard behind his desk and scribbled out a message. *Kemberling, send Mr. Nimbus to my study.*

After a moment the writing faded and was replaced with the words, *Yes, Your Majesty.*

Thayer took out a pen and a sheet of paper. "Just tell me what you think you'll need, and I'll try to get it for you."

Satisfied, Pyro collapsed to a chair and propped his feet on the hearth. "For starters, I want seven soldiers of every Fay race, and throw in some women this time. Let's see, we'll want Major Scampi, she'd be a shoo-in for acrobatics, and Captain Van Amstel … Ooh! Do you know Kim?"

Chapter 41:
In Flew Enza

Lydia's hands trembled beneath the light of the lamp as she fumbled with the starchy pages of the book the doctor had recommended.

An inherited illness resulting from a build-up of excess copper in the tissues ... can affect both the liver and brain ... symptoms of brain damage include psychotic hallucinations, false memories, speaking of things that aren't there ... Individuals suffering from Wilson's Disease may also develop a type of sunflower cataract known as the Kayser-Fleischer Ring, a goldish-brown discoloration wreathing the cornea.

Lydia lowered the book and glanced up at the mirror hanging on the wall. She peeked over her shoulder at the children lying asleep on the sofa. It was Sunday and she'd had the day off. Most of it had been spent trying to explain to Katya the circumstances of her illness without frightening her. The rest had been devoted to trying to understand it herself. She had yet to meet with Katya's teacher, but she knew from the diagnoses that the school would want Lydia to continue Katya's education at home.

Not wanting to disturb the children, Lydia got quietly up from the chair and tiptoed to the mirror. She leaned forward and stretched her eyes open. The book said it was a hereditary disease, and Lydia remained convinced it was she who had passed it off to Katya. She dropped her fingers from her eyes and sighed. How could one identify a brown ring around their eyes if the eyes were already brown? She put her fingers to her temples and sighed. Her body was overwhelmingly tired, but then the news from the doctor had taken quite a lot out of her. She rubbed at her lower back.

Just as she was returning to her chair, Pasha lifted his head and rubbed his eyes. Lydia smirked as she watched him turn this way and that.

"Well, hello there, sleepyhead."

Pasha let his head fall back on the arm of the couch. "Hello, Mama." He yawned and rolled off the side of the sofa to his knees. Lydia shook her head and laughed.

"Are you sure you're ready to wake up?"

Pasha nodded as he crawled forward on all fours and planted his head on her knee. She ran her hands through the little curl of hair at the base of his neck, brushing it in opposite directions and twining it around her finger.

"What are you reading?" His voice was muffled by her skirts.

Her smile faded as she closed the volume and set it on the side table. "The book the doctor gave me for Katya."

Pasha turned and looked at her innocently. "Mama, you don't really believe Katya is ill, do you?"

"Why wouldn't I, *Patulya*?"

Pasha raised up and rubbed his hands nervously over his legs. "Well, because *you're* not ill. All those things you saw when you were a little girl, the unicorns, the angels … Katya is just like you! She couldn't be delusional because you're not delusional! You just see things other people can't."

Lydia felt sick. Her chest seemed empty of air. She covered one side of her face with her hand and propped her elbow on the arm of the chair.

"Pasha, forget I ever said any of that, please." She could hear the stress in her own voice. Pasha rocked back on his heels and smiled.

"But Mama, you and Katya aren't crazy!" He giggled and tugged playfully on her skirts. Lydia's temper snapped inside her like a severed rubber band. She slammed her palms on her knees and lunged forward.

"I said never speak of it again!" The words shot out of her like a javelin, grating and sharp. Pasha fell back on his rear as though her voice had physically pushed him.

Lydia immediately regretted what she had done. Pasha's mouth hung slack, and his cheeks colored with pink splotches as he stared up at his mother, blindsided, hurt, and embarrassed.

She knew he meant no harm, but it was imperative he understood the danger of repeating her words. It was her own fault for telling him those stories in the first place. Even if it was for their own safety, Lydia couldn't help but feel as though she had betrayed Pasha. Pasha, her sweet boy, her helper. Pasha, who was always putting everyone's needs ahead of his own. Pasha, whose greatest aspiration in life was to become wealthy enough to take care of all the people he loved.

Lydia sank back into the chair and covered her eyes. There was an aching throb in her joints. As she drew her hand across her brow, beads of sweat transferred to her fingertips. Pasha eyed her with caution.

"Mama," he said more quietly than before, "are you feeling well?" He crept closer. His forehead drew up with concern. "You're pale."

A plunging feeling entered Lydia's heart. Before she could stop him, Pasha placed a hand over her forehead.

"Mama, you're burning up!"

Chapter 42:

Magic and Thieves

Pasha's head throbbed against the frilly pillows of Faina's bed as he lay in a stiff ball. A half-empty glass of water sat upon the nightstand for him to drink. The door opened, and Faina pattered towards the bed in her stocking feet. Pasha didn't feel up to turning around so he played opossum. Faina wasn't fooled. She sat on the end of the bed in complete silence.

Curious, Pasha peeked open one puffy eye. Her hands were folded in her lap, and her eyes trained on her shoes. When she noticed Pasha watching her she reached out and put a comforting hand on his leg, but said nothing.

"You're quiet," he observed.

Faina shrugged. "Would it make you feel better if I talked?"

"No."

"Do you want me to leave? I know sometimes people would rather be by themselves when they're sad."

"No." Pasha stared at her for a moment, surprised by his answer. Normally, he would've preferred the solitude, but there was something oddly comforting about Faina's presence.

"Then I'll stay right here."

Pasha felt his tongue go dry. His head rolled slowly to the side, allowing him a view of his mother's bedroom window. The light was faint behind the curtains. It seemed that it ought to have been brighter.

"Papa told me to look after her. I should be with her to take care of her." He fought against the tremor in his lip. "I should—" He winced until the burning tears squeezed down his cheeks like lemon juice.

Faina scooted closer and grabbed his hand. When he looked up again she was staring down at him with eyes that did more than watch. He rubbed at his tears until his skin felt raw, and took a deep breath.

"Sorry. I bet I look like a real wimp, crying like a baby."

Faina shook her head, possessed by a calmness he didn't know she had. "No. I think it's beautiful."

Pasha lifted his head, confused. "Crying? You think crying is beautiful?"

Faina turned her eyes sheepishly towards the ground and shrugged. "Yeah. I mean, it's nothing to be ashamed of. It just means you love someone very much."

"But boys aren't supposed to cry."

Faina threw up her shoulders in a manner that showed how ridiculous she thought that was.

"Well, you're a boy and you're crying. Why do you think boys aren't supposed to cry?"

"Because they have to be strong for their family. If Katya sees me crying she might get scared. She'll think something bad has happened."

"Something bad *has* happened. Your mother has influenza, and you have every right to cry about it. Leo cries in front of me, and so does Uncle Matvei. And I've never once thought less of them for it, or gotten scared because of it. In fact, I think it makes me love them more."

Pasha's tears were so thick he was forced to sit up so he could breathe.

"Crying doesn't take away from who you are as a man. It makes you more human." Faina squeezed his hand tighter. "I'm going to look after you, Pasha. I'm going to stay right here beside you, and I'm going to take care of you." She bent forward. "I'm going to teach you something. From now on this is how we will make promises to each other. Do you remember the *bezprizornye*, the children in Russia who make their living off the streets? My brother once told me that they had a way of pledging their loyalty to one another. They take hands like this." She clasped Pasha's left hand, and raised her right hand in the air. "And they say, 'May I,' and then you say your name, 'never enjoy liberty if I ever forsake' then you say the other person's name. You don't have to say liberty if you don't want to, you can come up with your own thing to say. They call it Thieves' Honor. And if you do break your promise the only way you can redeem yourself is by letting the other person punish you any way they want."

She raised her right hand in the air once more while clasping his left hand with hers. "May I, Faina Adrianovna Spichkin, never enjoy liberty if I ever forsake Pasha Ruslanovitch Chevalsky. Now you do it."

Pasha sniffed and sat up. "May I, Pasha Ruslanovitch Chevalsky, be struck by lightning if I ever forsake Faina Adrianovna Spichkin."

There came a knock at the front door.

"Faina, my hands are covered in flour," Anya called from the kitchen.

"Coming!"

Faina dashed out the bedroom. Pasha listened as the doorknob turned.

"Faina, my dear!" It was Aunt Poppy. "Where is your uncle, I must speak to him at once."

"He isn't here just now, Aunt Poppy. He's speaking with Mrs. Chevalsky's nurse at the moment. But I'm sure he will be back soon."

"It is true then that Mrs. Chevalsky is ill?"

Pasha looked up at the door. What was Aunt Poppy's interest in his mother? He tiptoed to the hallway.

"I'm afraid so, ma'am," Faina explained. "She has influenza."

"Then I must insist I remain here until your uncle has returned."

Pasha was just about to peer around the corner when Uncle Matvei burst clumsily through the front door, accidentally bumping Aunt Poppy.

"Oh, Aunt Poppy! I am so sorry! Do forgive me, my dear woman!"

"Nonsense, Matvei! No apology is needed. Your head is in your heart, as it should be in times such as these."

"So you've heard about Mrs. Chevalsky then?"

"That is why I am here." There was a moment of silence in which Pasha could imagine Aunt Poppy's owlish eyes sweeping meaningfully across the apartment. Uncle Matvei cleared his throat.

"Faina, why don't you join your brother downstairs? Or better yet, check up on Pasha. Anya, take Katya to your room for a moment."

The floorboards creaked, and Pasha scuttled behind Faina's bedroom door to listen. He waited for Anya to pass. Before he knew what was happening, Faina popped her head around the frame and hid behind it with him.

"Scoot over, I want to listen too!"

Had it not been for the circumstances, Pasha might have laughed. A scolding for eavesdropping was never something he had to fear from Faina. Together they put their ears to the crack.

"Now then," Aunt Poppy began when she was certain the room was empty, "I insist that you allow my doctor to take a look at the poor woman."

Pasha and Faina exchanged curious glances. Aunt Poppy might have been a regular good fairy when it came to clearing up sinuses with cake and making tea that smelled like the ocean, but could she really cure Pasha's mother of a disease that had already claimed 30,000 lives in New York City alone?

"That's awfully kind of you, Aunt Poppy, but—"

"My nephew shall cover the expenses, Matvei. There's no reason to deny me."

"Your generosity is inspiring, Aunt Poppy, truly, but—"

"How is my doctor superior to these learned butchers you rely upon so faithfully? I cannot tell you, Matvei, only show you, if you give me a chance!"

"Aunt Poppy, I would gladly give your physician a chance, but it's not really up to me who treats Mrs. Chevalsky. You'll have to take it up with Mrs. Chevalsky herself."

Aunt Poppy made a noise as though she were about to say more, then stopped.

"This is true."

"How about this," suggested Uncle Matvei, "why don't I just go back to the apartment and ask her?"

There was a shuffling noise as Aunt Poppy made her way to the sofa. "Good idea. In the meantime I intend to stay right here until you return. I must have my answer at once, Matvei. The woman's life depends upon it. You may not believe me now. But tomorrow morning you will see."

There was a slight uneasiness in Uncle Matvei's voice as he replied, "Very well, Madame. I'll be right back."

No sooner had the footfall of Uncle Matvei's long-legged stride died away than Aunt Poppy called out, "You may come out of the closet now, Pasha and Faina."

Pasha and Faina stared at each other wide-eyed and slipped out into the hallway. Aunt Poppy was sitting with her back turned and her walking stick propped against the side table. As Pasha and Faina took their seats, Anya appeared from the kitchen.

"Ah, Anya!" Aunt Poppy settled into the fluffy cushions like a bird in her nest. "I'll take a cup of tea, please. No sugar, just cream."

Anya hesitated for a moment in the doorway, then sighed and returned to the kitchen. The three of them sat in absolute silence. Pasha and Faina stared expectantly at Aunt Poppy, hoping she would explain herself any minute, but she merely smiled and tapped her fingers on her knees. Pasha could hardly stand it.

"Aunt Poppy, what's going on? Why do you want your doctor to take a look at my mother?"

Aunt Poppy swiveled around with such astonishment one might have thought Pasha had uttered a curse word.

"Because I want her to live! Don't you?"

"Of course I do! But how's your doctor any different from a regular doctor? How will he save my mother?"

By now Aunt Poppy had grown thoroughly impatient. Her elbows poked out from her sides like ruffled feathers, and she fidgeted to and fro.

"With magic, of course!"

Pasha's shoulders felt as though they were pulling him towards the ground. "I was afraid you would say that."

He rose miserably from the chair and turned back towards the bedroom. But Aunt Poppy grabbed a hold of his arm.

"You are afraid?"

Pasha shook his head glumly from side to side. "No, just disappointed."

"Disappointed about magic? Why, that makes about as much sense as being disappointed it's your birthday, or that your mother made chocolate cake, or that school was cancelled because of snow! You are a smart boy, Pasha. What has caused you to feel this way?"

"Magic isn't real." A part of him felt bad for saying it. He knew it wasn't right to utter such things in front of a poor, sick, old woman whose aged brain made her believe all sorts of things. But he was too tired to behave properly just now.

Aunt Poppy did not fly into an outrage, nor did she protest. She only steadied her eyes on his and, taking him by both hands, gently guided him closer.

"I see. So, if it were up to you, you would rather not have your mother examined by my magic doctor?"

Pasha's shoulders tensed. "I didn't say that!"

Little by little the wrinkles surrounding Aunt Poppy's eyes stretched with amusement. "So you are not quite the skeptic you claim to be."

Pasha's chin dropped to his chest. His cheeks tingled with warmth. "It can't be a very good thing to believe in magic because my sister had to leave school for saying she believed in mermaids. The doctor said she has brain damage. Mama told me never to speak of it."

Aunt Poppy's eyes glazed over as though she were all too familiar with Pasha's dilemma. "Ah, yes. In this world it can be dangerous to believe in things other people do not. But if you fall prey to the ways of the world you will rob the magic of having any power in your life. Pasha, there are three things magic needs to survive: faith, hope, and love. You must have faith magic exists. You must have hope to keep believing in magic even when you are persecuted for it. And you must have love so the magic can be used for the good of everyone." She pinched his chin affectionately and, smiling, tilted her head so low her glasses slid down the bridge of her steep nose. "Now, you certainly aren't lacking love, that much is clear. And you have a lot of hope invested in your future, Mr. King of New York. But you could do with a little faith."

"But how do I get faith?"

Aunt Poppy sat him down on the ottoman and squeezed his hands tighter. "Well, you can start by repeating after me. I believe all things work for good."

Pasha raised an eyebrow. "All things?"

Aunt Poppy nodded. "All things."

"Even the bad?"

"Even the bad. Now are you going to say it or not?"

Pasha looked down at his shoes and sighed. "I believe all things work for good."

"I believe in miracles."

Again Pasha repeated her, and found the courage to look into her eyes. "I believe in miracles."

"And finally," Aunt Poppy's voice fell to a whisper, "I believe in magic."

Pasha hesitated, feeling his tongue curl up inside his mouth. "I … believe in magic."

The handle on the front door turned. Uncle Matvei peered around the corner.

"Mrs. Chevalsky has accepted your offer."

Aunt Poppy said no more but reached for her walking stick.

Chapter 43:
Febris

Staccato burst through Aunt Poppy's door, not realizing Ink, one of her cats, had been standing on the other side, sending him flying across the room.

"How's Lydie? How's my girl? When can I see her?"

Aunt Poppy had been sitting quietly in her chair with her knitting needles. She had hardly flinched when Staccato bombarded her apartment. She raised her eyebrows.

"You're going to see her, are you? Does that mean when she pulls through you're going to take her back with you?"

Staccato shut the door behind him and, removing his hat, ran a handkerchief over his damp forehead.

"I can't think about that now. I just want to see my girl. She doesn't have to know I'm in the room." He reached into his collar and held up the ambiguous as tears began falling down his face. "I just have to see her, please."

Aunt Poppy drew a long sigh. She set aside her needles and got up.

"Don't you fret now." She placed a hand on his elbow. "It's a case of Febris. That's all. Meaning we know how to treat it."

"We know how to treat it *before* it progresses into pneumonia! I don't understand! How could she have contracted it? Weren't you giving them those Sun Cakes?"

Aunt Poppy sighed. "Apparently, she is no fonder of Sun Cakes now than she was as a child, or at least that's what Pasha told me."

"She didn't eat one? Not a single one?"

"If she had she wouldn't be in this state. She's just like her father. Always refusing to take his medicine." She reached up and pinched his cheek. "But don't you fret. She has a caim looking after her now. Things are going to get better, you'll see."

Unable to handle any more pressure, Staccato collapsed into a dining chair and buried his head in his arms on the table. He felt Aunt Poppy slide her arm around his shoulders, chuckling.

"*Lyubov moya,*" my love, "if you broke down like this more often you might not be so tense all the time."

Staccato wiped at his tears and sniffed. "How can you joke when my only child has a disease that has killed thousands of people in the city alone?"

Aunt Poppy pinched his chin as though he were five years old. "Because I know things other people in this city do not, and so do you." She let go. "We will go see her now." She turned towards the door but Staccato grabbed a hold of her sleeve.

"But what will you tell the caim? I'm a well-known figure to other Voilerians. If I ask to see Lydia they'll suspect something!"

"You have a point. I will ask to see Lydia alone, and I will let you in through the window."

Staccato let go of her sleeve and nodded. Without another word, Aunt Poppy slipped out the door. Staccato couldn't bear sitting idle at the table for very long. In less than a minute he was on his feet rushing to the window that looked out on the courtyard. He peeled back the thin curtain and stared directly at Lydia's window. The drapes were shut and faintly illuminated by a dim lamp.

When eight minutes had passed, Aunt Poppy appeared at the window. Staccato was out on the fire escape in a flash, willing the air around him to ripple and change so that his figure was almost unnoticeable. He ran down the ladder into the passage, and bounded up the fire escape leading to his daughter's room. When he knocked on the glass where his aunt was staring, she jumped with fright.

"Sorry," Staccato whispered, confident that she could hear him through the cheap material. Aunt Poppy rolled her eyes and slid open the window.

"You can take off that ridiculous necklace."

Staccato's faint features rematerialized. "Why? Did you take off yours?"

"No. But she is too delirious to know the difference."

Staccato clambered over the windowsill and immediately understood what she meant. Lydia lay on her back, her lips pale and dry. Her complexion had turned silvery and damp, like a fish. Wisps of her dark hair clung to her skin in sticky, humid swirls near her temples and forehead. Staccato covered his mouth with a sharp inhale. Poppy grabbed hold of his arm.

"It's not as bad as it looks. The caim says it will take a few hours for her body to flush out the toxins. It all has to come to the surface."

Staccato swallowed and nodded his head. He understood. Without taking his eyes off Lydia he reached up and removed the ambiguous from around his neck. With gentle footsteps, he approached the bed.

Lydia gave a soft moan in her sleep. He lowered himself onto the edge of the mattress, taking note of the way her eyelashes lay across the tops of her cheeks. He reached out and cupped her face, caressing the feverish skin. Lydia's eyes fluttered open.

For a moment, Staccato was overcome with fear as she stared up at him. He was completely exposed.

"Papa, I knew you'd come."

Staccato's fingers rose nervously to his collar. Poppy had said she was delirious, and yet she seemed lucid.

"Of course you did, Lydie dear."

She shut her eyes again. "Ruslan will be so happy to meet you finally."

Staccato sighed and tucked the covers up around her shoulders. "I should be very glad to meet him too."

"And the children, Papa!" She coughed slightly. "You must see my children!"

"Shhh." He brushed her hair from her forehead as she opened her eyes again to look at him. "I have seen them, my darling. They are so extraordinarily beautiful." He lifted her chin. "Just like you. Now, you must rest, my dear. Pasha and Katya are eager to get back to you. And I'll be here looking after you until then."

Lydia nodded, drifting off with her head in his hand. Staccato could not help but recall the very first time she had fallen asleep in his arms, when she was just an infant.

"Yes, Papa. Only …" Her eyes fluttered with sleep. "Only you must promise to kiss Mama and me before you leave this time."

Staccato felt as though his heart were being sucked down towards the floor.

"With all my heart."

Chapter 44:
The Eighteenth Amendment

January settled over New York in pale crystal sheets with thin, rimy temperatures. The windows remained in a perpetual frost. Engines chilled overnight, and the cars which normally spun slush from the asphalt sat motionless by the curb. The steady stream of water sapping from the gutters gradually thinned and stiffened until it too hung suspended in indefinite dormancy, an icy monument to warmer, greener days.

Because of Aunt Poppy's special doctor, Lydia recovered. She remembered little of her treatment or most of her illness, but much thanks was given to Aunt Poppy, though Lydia never had the opportunity to thank her in person. And though there was much joy and gratitude for Lydia's restoration, the jubilation ceased upon the discovery that due to her illness, Lydia had been let go from her job, and was having no luck finding a new one.

Leo knew Pasha had been hoping things would pick up once Christmas was over, but this was not the case. It was already difficult enough to find a decent-paying job as a poor immigrant, let alone a single mother in a suffering economy, but it wasn't long before Mrs. Chevalsky came face to face with another hurdle: she was Russian. During the war every German was an ally of the Kaiser. Now that it was over, every Russian was a communist.

Two tenants were arrested for suspected Bolshevik sympathies: one for speaking Russian over the telephone, the other for encouraging his fellow steel mill workers to unionize. The latter was now awaiting deportation.

Not even Uncle Matvei was immune to the mania rapidly spreading over the country. Though the numbers were still far from abysmal, business had been declining somewhat. With the end of the war, work at the Junior Red Cross had slowed, causing Anya to mope about aimlessly. Wandering through the house one might have been tempted to salute every doll and stuffed animal for their service, for Anya had bandaged every single one out of sheer boredom.

Meanwhile Pasha and Faina frightened everyone when they simultaneously came down with a fever and body aches one afternoon, only to break out in scarlet polka-dotted rashes a couple of hours later. It was chickenpox. To prevent Katya from catching the disease (for she had never had chickenpox, as opposed to Leo and Anya), Uncle Matvei allowed Pasha to stay with them until he was well again, enabling Mrs. Chevalsky to continue looking for work. Never had two invalids had more fun. As Leo put it, "They never shut up."

Once the scratching commenced, Aunt Poppy was standing by with one of her mysterious home remedies that numbed the skin to prevent itching. It was so effective Pasha and Faina couldn't keep their hands out of the mason jar it had arrived in. One thing led to another and the next thing the pair of mischief makers knew they had gotten it in their mouths.

When Leo passed by the open door and spied the two punching each other in the jaw and giggling, he was beyond alarmed.

"What do you two think you're doing?"

Pasha and Faina could hardly contain their laughter.

"Aunt Poppy's medicine made our mouths numb," explained Faina. "And now we can punch each other without getting hurt. See?" She turned and punched Pasha so hard in the teeth that he fell backwards.

Leo let out a cry of shock and fell beside Pasha, helping him back into a sitting position. To his surprise, Pasha was still grinning and laughing, albeit with blood running down his lip. Leo pulled out a handkerchief and blotted the blood from Pasha's mouth. Faina had knocked one of his eye teeth crooked. Leo pinched the bridge of his nose between his fingers and growled.

"What is wrong with you two? Did your brains fall out of your ears?"

Faina shrugged her shoulders. "It doesn't hurt."

"Well, it's going to! That medicine doesn't last forever you know, and you two have been sitting here coldcocking each other like a couple of idiots! Faina, you knocked Pasha's tooth sideways!"

Needless to say in a couple of hours they were sorely regretting their decision. Not only did they have to put up with itchy red blots but they now had several black and blue ones as well. After that they made considerably less noise. Fortunately, Mrs. Chevalsky was not angry with Uncle Matvei that it had happened, but she did punish Pasha for being thoughtless and striking a girl.

One particularly frigid morning, Leo awoke to find Faina curled up in his bed for the third time that month. Though Uncle Matvei kept the apartment well heated, next to the window was still not a good place to keep warm in the winter. He didn't say anything but quietly got up to dress. Faina grunted and thrust her hand out grumpily.

Leo's eyes glazed over as he stared down at her hand with a raised eyebrow. "What are you doing?"

"Don't leave me, I'll freeze to death! That's the rules of the tundra."

Leo scoffed and tossed a pillow over her head as he moved towards the bathroom to brush his teeth. "In Siberia you never griped about the cold. We move to New York and you might as well be from the desert! Besides, how can you be freezing? I was sweating all night!"

Faina merely grunted and burrowed back under the comforter like some hibernating creature. When Leo went back to check on her he found Faina stuffing her feet into the pillowcase where his head had been laying.

"What do you think you're doing?" he demanded from the doorway, his mouth full of toothpaste.

Faina's voice was muffled beneath the covers. "My feet are freezing!"

Leo made his way back to the sink and called over his shoulder. "Well, take them out. I don't want your feet where I lay my head every night!" Leo spat, then twisted the rusty faucet until a fountain of frigid water poured from the spout. When he had finished rinsing his mouth, he made his way back to their room and snatched the pillow from Faina's feet.

"How about I stick them up your nose?" she joked, playfully kicking at his face.

"Ew!" Leo laughed and shoved her away. "Alright, Domino-Face, that's enough." He tucked the blanket around her ankles.

"Leo, are you going to do anything about your snoring anytime soon?"

Leo looked at her in surprise. "Snoring? Since when do I snore?"

Faina rolled her eyes. "It started last week and hasn't stopped! Every time I look over at you your mouth is hanging open."

Leo put a hand to his lips. That would explain why he had been waking up with his mouth so dry lately. Just as he was about to say more, a terrible shouting noise roared up through the ventilation shaft.

"Chort voz mi! Etogo ne mozhet byt!"

Faina sat bolt upright and looked questioningly at Leo. Rarely did Uncle Matvei shout with such aggression. They flew up from the bed and dashed down the stairwell.

When they reached the landing, Anya was already ahead of them, her book satchel busted open at the foot of the steps. A headline was sprawled across the store counter, and Uncle Matvei was bent over it like a wild, predatory animal. Fearing that Uncle Matvei might startle her, Leo nudged Anya behind his back and took two cautious steps forward.

"What's wrong, Uncle Matvei?" But Uncle Matvei was too distraught to hear him, or even notice he was there. Leo peered over his shoulder at the headline.

U.S. is Voted Dry
36th State Ratifies Dry Amendment

Leo edged back cautiously, his eyes wide with disbelief. "They really did it. They actually managed to pass prohibition."

Uncle Matvei jumped at the sound of Leo's voice. "Leo? What are you doing down here? Shouldn't you be getting ready for school?"

"I—I came down to check on you. I heard you—"

Before he could finish there was a frenzied knock at the window. Leo turned to find Mrs. Chevalsky peering through the glass with her shawl clutched tightly about her face, her eyes swelling with concern. Without having to be told, Anya and Faina raced to the door to let the woman inside.

"Why, Matvei Dalka, whatever is the matter?" She must have been on her way to look for another factory job, for her hair and hands were exceptionally neat, and she was wearing her best hat.

Uncle Matvei turned to Anya, Leo, and Faina. "You three go on back upstairs. Everything is fine."

Faina was the first to protest. "But Uncle Matvei—"

"No buts!"

Faina and Anya turned back towards the stairwell, but Leo remained.

"I already saw the headline," he said in a lowered voice.

Uncle Matvei sighed and gave a curt nod. "Very well. You can stay."

At the sight of Uncle Matvei's pale face, Mrs. Chevalsky put a hand to her lips. "Matvei, you look positively ill! Are you well?"

Leo pulled out a chair for Uncle Matvei as his legs began to buckle. "It is all over the headlines. Nebraska just became the thirty-sixth state to ratify prohibition. Starting a year from now there's going to be a national ban on the sale of alcohol." Uncle Matvei tried to hide his tears from Leo by covering his eyes but it was no use. "Don't these harpies down at the Temperance League realize what they have done? They've taken away my livelihood! The bread from my children's mouths! And right as we were about to open our second location in Midtown! I had to get a twelve-thousand-dollar loan from the bank just to pay for the expenses! How will I ever repay them now?"

When Leo caught Mrs. Chevalsky's eye, he was flabbergasted to find the hint of a smile hiding at the corners of her mouth. Removing her handkerchief from her pocket, she bent low over Uncle Matvei as though trying to console a distraught child who had upset himself over something silly.

"Now, Matvei, I am surprised at you, letting yourself get worked up like this! Why, you're not thinking clearly!"

She bade Uncle Matvei to sit up straight. Uncle Matvei sniffed, causing his carefully groomed mustache to twitch and bristle.

"Wh—what do you mean? If I can't sell liquor how can I continue to manage a liquor store? How can I continue to make a profit?"

Mrs. Chevalsky leaned back from him with her hands on her hips, so that she appeared taller than she really was.

"You really don't know?" She swiveled around and reached for a bottle of *Kvass* from the shelf. She laid it carefully in front of him on the counter. "Tell me what this is."

Uncle Matvei waved his hand as though it didn't matter. "*Kvass.*"

"I see. And how much alcohol is in this bottle of *Kvass*?"

Uncle Matvei froze as he dabbed at the corners of his eyes. "Less than one percent! No more than a bottle of vinegar."

Mrs. Chevalsky nodded her head. "Exactly. And what product is responsible for making you the successful business owner you are today?"

Uncle Matvei sat a little taller, his voice growing more even. "*Kvass*!"

Lydia beamed. "What is your number-one bestselling product?"

"*Kvass*!" Gradually, the storm of red gently sloughed away from Uncle Matvei's face. He drew his hand across his forehead, then laughed. "I don't know what I allowed myself to get so worked up for! It will be no different from wartime Prohibition! After all, they're not going to put a ban on beer and wine!"

"Yeah, that's right," agreed Leo. "You'll only be cutting your inventory by a tiny bit."

"And there's no reason why you should have to close your Midtown location," touted Mrs. Chevalsky. "Though if you did, you would still have a year to pay back the bank. In the meantime, just imagine how great the demand for alcohol will be! People will be wanting to stock up while they can. I would imagine this year alone you'll earn enough to open twelve new locations!" Mrs. Chevalsky chuckled and patted Uncle Matvei on the shoulder. "Dear Matvei, you better pour yourself a stiff one while you still can. You look like you could use it!"

Uncle Matvei shook his head and snickered. "That's not a bad idea!" He stretched his arms over his head, refreshed with a brighter perspective. "Thank you, Lydia, for helping me see things more clearly. Though I cannot say I won't miss a nice glass of vodka."

Mrs. Chevalsky scanned the front page. "I wouldn't be dismal just yet. It says here, there's no law against the private consumption of alcohol, only the sale. So as long as you know how to brew it, which you do, there's nothing to apologize for."

Leo sucked his teeth. "Boy, just imagine all the poor saps who don't know how to make their own alcohol!"

Uncle Matvei sighed pitifully. "They'll be a desperate lot, that's for sure! People are attached to their liquor. There's no telling what they'll pay to get it."

Leo leaned back against the counter. "Ain't that the truth! Prohibition!" He threw back his head and scoffed. "Now there's a law even a decent man wouldn't be ashamed of breaking!" No sooner had the words left his mouth than an idea struck him. Uncle Matvei was right. Starting one year from now, alcohol would be highly sought-after contraband! Instead of stealing from poor, honest, hardworking folks, he could just nab some stockpiled alcohol from wealthy snobs and make just as much money.

When Mrs. Chevalsky had departed, Uncle Matvei was surprised to find Leo still standing around.

"Leontiy, don't you have to get ready for school?"

But Leo was only half-listening. "Hm? I'm sorry, what did you say, Uncle Matvei?"

Uncle Matvei's right eyebrow rose by degrees as he closed in on his nephew suspiciously.

"Leo, what are you up to?"

Leo knit his hands sheepishly behind his back. "Oh, nothing."

Leo's grin felt too big for his face as he made his way back up the stairs. Finally, a law he didn't have to feel bad about breaking! It may have been one of the worst things to happen to America, but it could have easily been the best thing to have happened to Leo Spichkin.

Chapter 45:
Conviction

While Leo was back in school, Faina decided to be helpful and make the deliveries within walking distance herself. She still had her wagon and was happy to help Leo free up some time so he could work on his photography. Over the holidays he had managed to procure quite a profit for himself with his makeshift studio, and the demand had been good for Uncle Matvei's business. Now he was already getting requests for Easter portraits, months in advance. In Faina's mind, Leo's future as a photojournalist was already secure.

She was just about to turn onto Hester Street when a figure dashed around the corner and waved her down.

"Faina! Hey, wait up!"

Faina stopped and turned abruptly. "Anastas?"

She hardly recognized him for the jaunty bounce in his step, and the smile, wry as it was, creeping up one side of his face. He had grown taller since the last time she had seen him, and his shoulders appeared broad enough to walk upon.

"What? You don't recognize me?" He playfully punched her on the shoulder. Faina shook her head and laughed.

"Well, I haven't seen you since before Thanksgiving! Where have you been?"

He tossed his head to one side and shrugged. "Oh, around."

"You aren't at the boys' home anymore. They said you left. I've been worried sick about you."

For a moment, Anastas's ears looked pink. But then it was considerably frigid outside, and he never did wrap up properly. He waved an airy hand, which also seemed to have grown bigger.

"You worried for nothing. I got me a place near the Bowery."

Faina shoved her hands on her hips and arched an incredulous eyebrow. "Now see here, Anastas Sippenhaft, just what are you trying to pull? You can't have a place near the Bowery! You're only twelve years old!"

He hooked his thumbs behind his braces and thrust his chest out like an enormous lion displaying its powerful muscles. "Klokov made up an arrangement."

A bell rang in Faina's memory. Klokov … where had she heard that name before? Her eyes dilated.

"You mean—"

"I take it your brother didn't tell you? I joined the Breadwinners."

Faina's face brightened. "Oh! So you are an associate like Leo?"

Anastas's shoulders sank. "An associate?" He seemed downright offended. He rolled up his sleeves and held out his fists, showcasing the purple bruises on his knuckles. "I'm a street fighter. They call me 'the Russian Rogue.'"

Faina would've laughed had she not been so disturbed. A street fighter? Weren't those the boys who they tied to a post and whipped?

"D—did they—"

"Did they flog me?" Anastas threw back his head and scoffed. "Oh, yeah! Twenty lashes. They locked my hands in a vice and everything." He reached up to his collar and undid the top two buttons.

Faina glanced around nervously, wondering if anyone was watching, unsure of how to react. As she bent slightly so she could see better, Anastas pulled back the neck of his shirt so that part of his shoulder was visible. She could just make out the jagged, enflamed tips of three long gashes. Without thinking, she reached out and ran her finger along the edge. Anastas flinched. Faina drew back, startled and somewhat embarrassed.

"Does it hurt?"

For a moment Anastas's face petrified into his old stony countenance.

"No." He straightened himself and buttoned his shirt back up. "They're deep, ain't they?" The way he talked one might have been fooled into thinking it was a tattoo.

"Pretty deep … I thought you had to be fourteen to become a street fighter."

"Normally you do, but Klokov made an exception for me on account of how strong I am." He stretched his arms over his head and flexed his muscles. "So, what do you think?"

Faina eyed him up and down, hoping any moment he would say it had all been a joke.

"I wish you hadn't done it."

Anastas's arms fell to his sides like crumbling pillars. "You … what?"

"Why couldn't you have just gotten a job at a shop or a factory? Or shined shoes even!"

Anastas was beginning to resemble his old self as his eyebrows lowered, and a sneer tore into his mouth.

"Shine shoes? You really do see me as nothing, don't you?"

Faina rolled her eyes. "Don't start that. What I mean to say is there are a million things I would rather see you do than get hurt. Working for the Breadwinners is a dangerous business!"

"But it's perfectly alright for your brother!"

"Leo is an associate! Not a member! Why did you have to become a street fighter? There are plenty of other jobs you could've taken without ripping your back open!"

"You wouldn't understand! You don't have two little brothers to support! Your uncle is rich!"

Faina charged towards him until she was standing on her tiptoes. "My uncle worked for everything he has!"

"You're beginning to sound like Chevalsky!"

"What's wrong with that? Do you hate people just because their situations are different than yours? Just because they see things differently than you do? How do you stand it?"

Anastas stared down at Faina with such quiet ferocity that for a moment she began to feel afraid. At last, he turned his head and spat upon the sidewalk. Without another word, he pivoted on his heel and walked away. Without thinking, Faina chased after him.

"All I meant is that I don't want you getting hurt! Nobody wants to see the people they care about getting slashed to bits, whatever the reason!"

Anastas froze in the middle of the sidewalk. Bit by bit he turned his head to glance at her over his shoulder.

"Why did you do it?" she pleaded breathlessly.

"I told you," he kicked at a pebble on the pavement. "I have my little brothers to care for." He turned and strode casually toward her.

"But your parents hated the Breadwinners." As soon as the words departed her lips she knew she had made a mistake. "Please don't take that the wrong way!"

Anastas scrubbed his fingers violently through his hair as though something had stung his scalp. "For the last time, I am not my parents! It's high time everyone learned that! My parents cared more about politics than their own children. They chose martyrdom over family. Why would I want to follow in their footsteps?"

"But what about anarchy? What about the cause? You had that in common, didn't you?"

Anastas narrowed his eyes and gave her a once-over. "What's it to you? You're not an anarchist."

Faina sat herself on the edge of the stoop where he was standing, determined to have a grown-up conversation with him.

"I'm only curious is all. Does joining the Breadwinners mean you're giving up anarchy? I mean, once you're a Breadwinner you're a Breadwinner for life. Desertion is punishable by death. You've sold your freedom to a mob of gangsters. You'll have no choice but to follow their rules. That goes against everything you believe in!"

Anastas paused and leaned against the brick wall with his eyes fixated on the toes of his boots.

"When a man has children it ain't about him anymore, whether he likes it or not. There are mouths to feed, and he can't just run off and chase his dreams. He can't, but that's what most of them do. That's what my old man did, he and my ma. They landed themselves behind bars. Now, I'm the oldest in my family, which means I'm a man with mouths to feed. And if I'm a man of my word, if I really believe in what I say, then I ain't got much choice. It ain't about me anymore, Faina. Anarchism is the belief that human beings don't need a higher power to force them to be good. Goodness is in our nature, and mankind *is* capable of living by an honor system. For those very reasons I gotta face the responsibilities my parents didn't. I gotta do what's right. Street fighting for the Breadwinners will get me a lot farther in life than something as simple as shining shoes, and I'll be able to give my brothers the stability we never had."

Faina was in absolute awe. She knew Anastas was smart, and she knew deep down inside he was a good person, but never had she expected such maturity to come from someone she thought to be so incurably petty. At twelve years old, Anastas was sacrificing his childhood for the sake of those who depended on him. He had chosen to become a man before he ever should have had to.

Faina got up from the stoop and, standing beneath Anastas's proud, blocky chin, hugged her arms around his shoulders.

"You're a very brave young man, Anastas Sippenhaft. There aren't many people as noble as you."

For the first second or two Anastas felt stiff in her arms, but after a moment he began to soften and finally, to Faina's astonishment, returned the hug, pulling her close to his chest.

Chapter 46:

Absence

Ever since Faina had been banned from school, Pasha had been forced to associate more with his male playmates. In a way he was glad to have a chance to make friends with other boys, but he still struggled to find common ground between them.

Out of all the children in his class he found Sergei and Yuri to be the most like him. Like Pasha, Sergei was the son of a widow, and he, too had a sickly younger sister. And Yuri's father had lost the use of his legs during the war, making it difficult to care for seven children. And like Pasha, both boys felt a heavy sense of responsibility towards their families.

One day in late January, Pasha happened to be walking home with Yuri. With his busy schedule Leo did not often have the opportunity to accompany Pasha home anymore, and Anya was helping tutor younger students after class.

"Have you heard from Sergei lately?" Pasha asked as they crossed from one sidewalk to the other. Ordinarily, Sergei would have walked home with them, but he hadn't returned after Christmas vacation. "Do you know why he hasn't been at school? He didn't get the flu, did he?"

Yuri sniffed and wiped his nose with the back of his sleeve. "Nah, it's nothing like that. I caught up with him at the fishmonger over the weekend. Things ain't been too good at home. He had to drop out of school to help his folks. He's tried to find a job but there ain't a lot available. In fact, things are so bad he was thinking …"

Yuri stopped and stared down at his shoes. Pasha waited anxiously for him to continue. Yuri wasn't exactly the type to stop and think about what he was saying. Words usually just flew out of his mouth with little consideration.

"Yeah? What was he thinking?"

Yuri frowned, then shook his head. "Nothing. Forget I mentioned it."

Pasha wasn't one to press a person past their comfort zone, but this was different. Yuri rarely chose to be silent about anything, and his reluctance to speak hinted at a much larger problem.

"Yuri, if Sergei is in trouble then we should try our best to help him. Tell me what Sergei said."

Yuri slowed to a stop and lifted his cap to comb his fingers through his greasy, strawberry hair. "He said he was thinking of becoming a street fighter for the Breadwinners."

Pasha scrutinized Yuri with grave eyes. He knew about the Breadwinners from Leo and the boys at school. Lately, the older boys in his class had taken to spending their weekends at the Foxhole, the Breadwinner's home base on the Bowery, which had a bar and a restaurant. Many went there to watch the street fights, or else to take their sweethearts dancing on the top floor, and they often came home with hair-raising stories.

According to Pytor Ivashin (who was a street fighter himself), becoming a street fighter wasn't like becoming an associate. Unlike associates, street fighters had to become members and could never leave service. Not only did they have to fight three times a week but they also had to steal things to sell on the black market. And unlike the associates, a street fighter had a quota to fill or else they would be flogged.

But that wasn't the worst part. To gain admission into the Breadwinners, you had to pass an initiation. There were three stages. In the first stage you were blindfolded and made to endure a gang beating. In the second stage you had to strip down to your underwear and submerge yourself in a tub of freezing water for ten minutes. Afterward, you were made to stand against the wall while other members pelted chunks of ice at you. The third stage was brutal. If you managed to pass the first two tests, you were handcuffed shirtless to a pole, and whipped twenty times. As long as you didn't faint, or act like a baby, you were in. You were in for life.

Pasha pinched his brows together. "You really think they would accept Sergei?"

Yuri shrugged. "They don't just accept anybody. My neighbor is a foot soldier for the Breadwinners, but he started out as a street fighter. He says Klokov wants young boys between the ages of fourteen and twenty who are trying to take care of their family. Boys who will grow into men who put their wife and children first. I'd say Sergei fits the bill perfectly."

"But if Sergei joins the Breadwinners he'll be throwing his life away! Leo says once you're a member you're a member for life. And if you try to leave, they kill you."

"I know, I know. But what can he do? His family is pretty bad off."

They continued walking, and were silent for some time, but Pasha could not move past the subject.

"If a street fighter can't be any older than twenty, and they have to serve the Breadwinners for the rest of their life, what do they do when they're all grown up?"

"Whatever Klokov tells them to do. If the boss wants someone to disappear they make him disappear. You know the Butcher man who was hassling Mr. Dalka?"

"Faina told me about him."

"What do you think happened to him?"

"They chased him out of town, didn't they?"

They stopped. Part of Pasha was expecting Yuri to laugh at him. But Yuri didn't do that. He simply shook his head, and for once seemed utterly expressionless.

"They found his head in the driver's seat of his car parked outside a bakery. There was a crust of bread stuffed into his mouth. Nobody's sure what they did with the rest of him. My uncle worked in the barbershop next door and was there when the head was discovered."

Pasha found himself shivering in the bare patch of sunshine that he happened to be standing in. "Do you think Leo knows that?"

"If he didn't before he's bound to now."

"Knowing Leo, it's doubtful he knew Klokov would kill the Butcher man. Otherwise, he probably wouldn't have done it." Pasha straightened himself and looked Yuri squarely in the eye. "We can't let Sergei sell himself like that. Are things really that bad that he feels like he has no other way out?"

"His sister has polio. Kid's gonna need leg braces and everything."

Pasha sighed. "Surely, there must be some place willing to hire him."

"Your Ma find a new job yet?"

"No."

Yuri threw up his shoulders as though to say, *Well, there you have it.*

The next day, Yuri did not show up at school.

Chapter 47:

Thin Ice

When the weekend finally arrived, Faina could not have been more grateful, that much was true. On Saturday morning, Pasha awoke to find her banging on his window with a pair of ice skates thrown over her shoulder.

"Come on, Pasha! Get the lead out, it's Saturday!"

Pasha flopped back on his pillows, grumbling. "Exactly, it's Saturday, which means I get at least one more hour of sleep."

Faina pressed her hands against the glass like a disappointed puppy. "Aw, come on, Pasha! I've been waiting for this all week!"

Still rubbing his eyes, Pasha sat up and lifted the window hatch. In tumbled Faina, soaking the sheets with bits of ice crumbling from her boots and hat. Pasha tugged the tam off her head and tossed it onto the empty chair. Then he helped her remove her coat and draped it over the bedpost. Once that was done, he pulled the covers up over his head and lay back down. Faina stared at him dumbfounded.

"Aren't you gonna get up?"

"No."

"Then why did you let me inside?"

"To make you be quiet."

Faina laughed as she grabbed a pillow and whacked him in the back of the head. "You should've known it takes a lot more than that to shut me up!"

Pasha giggled as he reached up from the covers and yanked a lock of her hair, and before they knew it they were engaged in a vigorous game of horseplay.

The door swung open and Pasha's mother stood on the threshold. Pasha pushed Faina back and threw the covers over her.

"Morning, Ma!"

Lydia leaned slyly over her cup of coffee and smiled. "Good morning, *Patulya*! Pasha, do you think you could stop by the drugstore late this afternoon and pick up Katya's prescription? I'm applying for a job today on Fifth and West, and I expect it may take a while."

Fifth and West? Unless she was applying for a position in service she had to be pulling his leg or straight-out lying, and yet neither was likely.

"Fifth and West? What kind of job is it?"

"It's an art gallery, darling." Her eyelashes seemed to bat with pride as she said this. "The Jameson-Wells Gallery for European Art."

Had it not been for the fact that Pasha was hiding Faina under the covers, he would've leapt up and given his mother a hug.

"Wow, that's great, Ma! How did you manage to snag an interview?" For it did seem rather unlikely that a fancy art gallery would be willing to hire a poor, struggling, immigrant single mother with a thick Russian accent.

"I have a friend from my old job at the factory whose sister happens to be Madame Wells's lady's maid. It turns out Madame Wells wants to open a gallery to showcase her collection of Russian Fine Art, and she's looking for a curator with a knowledge and understanding of the content."

Pasha bit his lip and, still smiling, softened his voice by degrees. "But Mama, don't you need a degree to be an art curator?"

Lydia gave a furtive shrug as she leaned coolly against the doorframe and took another sip of coffee. "Well, it helped that Ms. O'Hara mentioned I was a baroness."

"A *former* baroness."

Lydia waved her hand. "What does it matter so long as I have secured the interview? I am hoping once they have a chance to meet me they will overlook the details."

"Well, I'm sure they'll love you, Ma. I'll pick up Katya's prescription."

"Thank you, darling. Faina dear, will you be joining us for breakfast?"

Faina poked her head out from beneath the covers at the end of the bed. "No thank you, Mama Lydia. I already ate."

"Very well then." She waltzed over to Faina and kissed her cheek.

Pasha scratched his head. "What gave us away?"

Lydia retrieved the tam sitting in the empty chair and hung it from the bedpost with Faina's coat. "Not that I mind, of course." She flashed them a wink and departed.

When Pasha's mother was well on the other side of the tenement, Faina met Pasha's eyes with a look of astonishment.

"Anyone else's mother would've thrown me out the window! You never get in trouble for anything, do you?"

Pasha propped his arms beneath his head as he lay back. "Of course not, I'm the perfect son."

Faina responded with another pillow to the face. Pasha snorted as he scrambled to get a hold of the cushion.

"Alright, that's enough, crazy!"

As Pasha listened to the pan sizzling on the stove, he saw the cheeky grin evaporate from Faina's face as she lowered her voice.

"Pasha, does your mama really have an interview with the owner of a priceless art collection?"

Pasha could see from the way she fiddled with her shoestring to avoid meeting his eye that Faina was doubtful anything would come of it. He threw up his shoulders.

"That's what she said."

Faina's mouth hung open for a moment as though she couldn't decide whether or not she should say more.

"Didn't Madame Wells want to know how Ms. O'Hara knew your mother? I mean, Ms. O'Hara is a lady's maid. Wouldn't it seem strange for her to know a baroness?"

Pasha gathered his knees to his chest and hunched his shoulders. "People in service come across all sorts of upper-class people. That's who they work for, after all. It's not unheard of that Ms. O'Hara knows a baroness."

"But a baroness looking for employment? That sounds a little peculiar, don't you think? Most of the white emigres, if they came to America at all, are hiding out in Brighton Beach waiting for the fall of the Soviet—"

Eager to put an end to the conversation, Pasha cut her off with a forced smile. "This is America, Faina. People remake themselves all the time."

Neither of them said any more about it.

***

Pasha curled his toes inside his skates as he sat on the damp, icy bench and watched Faina tie his laces. He couldn't help but feel a little embarrassed, but Faina had insisted on tying them herself.

"You have to wrap it three times around the ankle," she kept jabbering, "or else they'll feel too loose. Mine always do whenever Leo ties them, and I always tell him …"

His eyes brushed over the frosty horizon where a hundred blades were shaving heaps of ice right off the top of the lake as they skated along. Pasha couldn't help but imagine those thin, keen knives on the bottoms of his shoes slicing right through the ice and cutting a perfect

Pasha-shaped hole to fall into and drown. Having never experienced snow growing up, he had never been ice skating, and the prospect was terrifying.

"Is that tight enough, Pasha?" Faina inquired, sitting back and admiring the bow she had tied. Before Pasha could answer, Anastas and his brothers came stomping down the hill with their skates thrown over their shoulders.

"Geez, Chevalsky, don't you know how to tie your own shoelaces?"

When Pasha first heard Anastas had been allowed to enlist in the Breadwinners early due to his size, he had thought this especially ridiculous. Now that he saw him in person he immediately believed it. His form was taking on the subtleties of a boy becoming a man. He was taller, broader, and even his voice had begun to deepen. Pasha wanted to respond but found himself so embarrassed by his childish voice that he thought better of it and decided to ignore Anastas.

"Hey, Chevalsky!" Anastas cupped his hand over his mouth. "I'm talking to you! Didn't you hear?"

Finally, Faina pursed her lips and turned to glare at Anastas with her hands on her hips.

"You know he does, Anastas. Why don't you quit your bullying and come sit down with us?"

Pasha flashed her a scowl. He was aware of Faina's uncanny ability to befriend nearly anyone, but he would never understand what possessed her to put up with Anastas of all people.

Anastas hesitated and stared at Faina. Just when Pasha thought he might shut up and walk away, Anya returned with Katya from the skate rental.

"Well, it took long enough but they finally found a pair small enough to fit Katya's little feet," Anya explained, taking a seat beside Faina and placing Katya on the bench next to her brother. She patted Katya's knee. "You must be Cinderella!"

Alexei tugged on Anastas's sleeve.

"Anastas, Katya is here! Please, let's go sit with them! Please!"

For once in their lives, Pasha and Anastas seemed to share the same sentiment. Their eyes met with surprise and disapproval. Anastas opened his mouth to say something, but Katya took notice of Alexei and elbowed Pasha in the side.

"Pasha, look! It's the little boy who I gave my candy to!"

With a roll of his eyes, Anastas nudged Alexei forward and the three made their way down to the place where the little group was sitting. First Alexei threw his arms around Faina's neck and gave her an affectionate squeeze, then his knees turned inwards as he summoned the courage to face Katya, who sat smiling and swinging her legs back and forth.

Pasha steeled his jaw as he scrutinized Anastas's youngest brother from head to toe. For the most part, he was a healthier, brighter version of Anastas, unlike Vadim who had inherited their mother's horsey features. *Far better*, Pasha thought, *if he did look like Vadim than Anastas, then I might like him more.*

Anastas gave Alexei a hard push that appeared to have been rougher than he intended. "Don't you have something to say, Alexei?"

Alexei's plump, pouty cheeks glowed pinker as he lowered his chin and smiled.

"Thank you for the candy you sent us last Halloween."

Katya blinked her long eyelashes and pulled her lips into an even wider grin.

"You're welcome! Did you like it?"

Alexei seemed to relax a little as his knees turned back to a front-facing position.

"Yeah, it was delicious."

The snow crunched behind them as Leo and Jazmin came striding up to the bench, each with a cup of hot chocolate. They were walking fairly close to each other but did not hold hands for fear of someone spotting them. At the sight of Anastas and his brothers gathered peacefully with Pasha and his sister, Leo ground to a halt and raised an eyebrow.

Pasha watched as Alexei forced his shoulders back and looked his sister directly in the eye.

"You're the prettiest girl I have ever seen!"

Anya, Faina, and Jazmin looked as though they had just discovered a nest of baby bunnies.

"Alright," barked Anastas, grabbing Alexei by the wrist. "That's enough. Let's go."

Pasha got to his feet and swung Katya's skates over his shoulder. "Come on, Katya, we'll find somewhere else to put your skates on."

That was when Leo threw up his hands and stepped between them. "Now, wait a minute, you two! Where are your manners? Anastas, bring your little brother back here!"

Anastas stopped cold in his heavy tracks and turned. Pasha was not sure how he would react to receiving orders from Leo. His eyes glazed over as he turned to face him, then slowly towed his little brother back towards the bench. Leo nodded his head towards Pasha.

"Sit your sister back down."

Still red in the face, Pasha did as told. Anastas sneered disdainfully at Leo as he looked him over from head to boot.

"I'm not sure what you mean. Our mother taught us it was impolite to intrude."

Katya shook her head. "You're not intruding."

Anastas regarded her carefully before responding in a low, swift voice. "Your brother seems to think otherwise."

Pasha thrust his shoulders back. "Well, that was awfully forward of Alexei."

"That's rich coming from you, Casanova!"

"And what exactly do you mean by that?"

Leo stepped between them and pushed on their chests.

"Hey! Enough already! Cut it out! Look, what's the matter with Alexei and Katya being friends, huh? Or are you two gonna drag your families into your feud?"

Pasha and Anastas reluctantly met each other's eyes. As usual, Pasha was the first to relent.

"Alright, fine. Let them play together. What does it matter?"

Anastas glanced off to the side and nodded. "Fine."

Anastas and Vadim planted themselves angrily on the bench adjacent, while the others remained at their post. Katya and Alexei bridged the gap in between, talking and giggling as young children are apt to do. Pasha continued to scowl at his shoes.

"Don't be angry, Pasha." Jazmin winked and nudged his shoulder. "You've read *Romeo and Juliet*, haven't you?"

Pasha wanted to say, "Yes, and they both end up dead in the end," but this seemed rather tactless when Jazmin and Leo were living out their own version of the Shakespearean drama. With their laces secured tightly around their ankles, the group edged towards the ice. Pasha kept his head held high on the off chance that Anastas might be watching, but his hand was firmly gripped around Faina's forearm as he stepped out on the frozen lake. Faina smiled encouragingly.

"See? That wasn't so bad, was it?"

Pasha raised his foot and pushed off with the toe of his skate. His feet swiveled and turned. Leo gracefully skirted around him and halted with an audible scraping sound.

"It's easier if you push off from the sides of your skates. Like this, see?" Leo turned out his left foot and shoved himself forward, then repeated the action with the right, propelling himself in a smooth, even line. Pasha gave it a try, and was relieved to find his movement much more stable. Gradually, he built up the courage to let go of Faina's arm.

"There you go!"

Jazmin smiled and clapped her hands. "You're doing excellent, Pasha!"

Anya shook Katya's hand. "You wanna give it a try?"

Always eager to try something new, Katya followed her brother's example, and soon picked up on the rhythm.

Up ahead, the Sippenhafts were filing onto the lake one by one. Anastas poked a fresh cigarette between his lips and exhaled a cloud of smoke.

"That doesn't look safe." Leo swiveled around and began skating backwards.

"Didn't you say that boy was only twelve?" Pasha gathered from Jazmin's tone that she wouldn't have believed it if Leo hadn't told her so.

"Look at them," Faina whispered to Pasha in a conspiratorial tone. "She could have at least brought a friend, then they might not look so obvious!"

Pasha couldn't help but notice that other students Leo and Jazmin's age were staring at them curiously as they skated by. The difference in their complexions alone was enough to draw attention from complete strangers, even though Syrians had been declared legally white ten years ago, making Leo's relationship with her completely legal. Pasha shrugged.

"Maybe she doesn't have anyone she can confide in."

"There's her little sister." Anya popped her head between them. Katya had already abandoned her, clearly a natural. "Syreeta knows all about it, and she would never say a word. If she had brought her along they could've said they were taking us for a play date."

Pasha snickered. "Maybe you two should write an instruction manual. 'How Not to Get Caught: A Guide for Secret Lovers.'"

"I think it's romantic." Anya swung her arms dreamily, her scarf trailing behind her. "Even if they are breaking the rules."

Faina grabbed the tail and gathered it back around her neck before someone could trip.

"Well, sure, it's romantic! I'd love for things to work out between Jazmin and Leo."

Pasha was surprised. "Really? You would?"

"Of course I would!" Her eyes darted warily at her brother's back, and her smile began to fade. "It's just … sometimes I worry about what's going to happen if Jazmin's parents don't change their mind about them being together."

"Besides getting in trouble, what's the worst that could happen?"

"You've read *Romeo and Juliet*, right?"

Anya threw back her head and laughed. "Faina, you aren't saying they'd commit suicide, are you?"

"Of course not! That's not what I meant at all. Only that there are a lot of risks people are willing to take when they're in love, and Leo doesn't always think before he acts. I meant it when I said he needs me to keep him from making stupid decisions."

Faina was being uncharacteristically cryptic. Whatever it was she was suggesting was not meant for shock value, but was a real concern in her mind.

Leo was a yard or two ahead of them now, his shiny hair sticking out from beneath his cap. What would someone like Leo, the golden boy, the overachiever, the wisecracker, be willing to jeopardize for a high-school romance?

"I'm surprised he came at all," Pasha remarked. "Hasn't he been sick?"

According to Faina, Leo had had a recurring cold all winter, complete with sore throat.

"I think at this point he's just trying to muscle through it. The doctor is starting to think he needs his tonsils removed."

Up ahead, Alexei turned around and headed for Katya.

"Got the hang of it yet?"

Katya watched her feet gliding beneath her. "I think so!"

Alexei reached out his arm. "Wanna hold my hand?"

"Okay!"

Pasha cringed as the miniature Anastas took Katya by both hands and towed her forward while he skated backwards.

"We can go faster this way."

Katya squealed with delight as they swept past Pasha, Anya, and Faina.

"Look, Pasha! Look how fast we're going!"

As Pasha turned to watch his sister, he noticed a familiar face amongst the crowd gathered on the banks.

"Hey, isn't that Jazmin's brother Jasar?"

Anya looked to where his eyes were pointed. "Uh-oh."

"It is!" Faina let go of Pasha's arm. "We better tell them before he spots them!" Faina skated off towards her brother and his girlfriend. "Leo! Leo, hang on a second!" She reached out to grab his scarf but Leo and Jazmin took off in a race before she could catch him.

Anya made a groaning noise. "Great, that won't grab anyone's attention."

Leo and Jazmin were both skilled skaters with a shared love of competition. They wove in and out of the crowds with stunning grace and alacrity.

"I'm going to beat you, Leo!"

"Oh, I don't think so!"

Pasha cupped a hand over his mouth. "Do you think you can catch up with them, Faina?"

"I can try!" Faina dug her skates deeper into the ice, and took off in their wake. Anya craned her head, still searching the crowd.

"I can't see him anymore."

"You don't think he spotted them, do you?"

Anya cased the lake with her eyes. "If he did, we'll probably find out in a moment."

Leo and Jazmin were three quarters of the way around the lake by now, and weren't far behind Pasha and Anya. Meanwhile, Katya and Alexei were in their own little bubble.

"Have you ever fallen before?" Katya stared down at his skates in amazement as they swiveled back and forth in perfect synchronization.

"Oh, yeah! Loads of times! It's a lot of fun!"

"Fun? How can it be fun? Doesn't it hurt?"

"Not if you know how to do it right. When you feel yourself start to fall, you gotta bend your knees and then drop on your side. That way you don't have as far to fall, and instead of hurting yourself you slide all the way across the ice! Here, I'll show you."

Alexei let go of Katya's hand and took off in a dash towards his brothers.

Leo and Jazmin had just completed their circuit and were drifting towards the inside edge of the crowd, Faina close behind them. When Alexei had gained enough speed, he bent his legs and dropped sideways at an angle. Alexei skidded and spun past his brothers towards the center of the lake just as Leo and Jazmin were closing in.

Anya grabbed a hold of Pasha's shoulder and pointed to a figure pushing off from the bank.

"There he is!"

Faina skated past them, her hands fanned over her mouth like a megaphone. "Leo! Jazmin's brother! Two o'clock!"

Leo froze and wrenched his head back towards his sister. "What?"

Pasha gasped as Leo careened towards Alexei. Anastas saw what was about to happen and bolted after his brother. Leo threw himself down on the ice. Anastas shoved Alexei out of the way. The boys collided with such force that Anastas's cigarette flew out of his mouth and was pinned under the heel of Leo's hand.

What followed went down in Manhattan history as an urban legend, passed on from grandparent to grandchild through the generations, and is still discussed to this very day. An arc of flames flowed in Leo's path like a swell of ocean water, so that it almost looked like Leo had fire coming out of his hands. The crowd gasped and screamed under the rainbow of spitting sparks. Anastas and Leo sailed forward for a few yards and drifted to a stop. Pasha had never seen anything like it before.

A sheaf of thin vapors was rising up in their wake. Leo scrambled to an upright position. To the horror of all who were watching, Leo's blade was covered in blood. A red cloud was blossoming on the trousers above Anastas's left knee. Leo's jaw went slack. He reached towards Anastas and mouthed what Pasha was sure was an apology, but Anastas jerked away with a scowl.

Jazmin glided towards them, her gloved hand covering her open mouth. Pasha thought he heard a branch snap. It must have been a rather thick branch, for the sound carried across the lake. Then came a second snap. Pasha looked back over his shoulder at the bank. That's when it happened. Jazmin gave a little screech. Pasha turned in time to see the ice

331

splitting open and Jazmin dropping between the frosted shards. Everyone scrambled for the shore.

"Come on!" Anya pulled Pasha towards the shore, grabbing Katya in the process.

"Jazmin!" Jasar was racing to get to her. Leo fumbled to his feet like a newborn giraffe and staggered towards the broken ice.

"Leo, no!" Faina showed no signs of returning to land, but stood in place, shouting at her brother to come back. Anya stamped her foot.

"Faina! What are you doing? Get back here!"

Leo and Jasar were already kneeling at the precarious edge of the hole, while several other gentlemen rushed to their aid. They each grabbed one of Jazmin's arms. Anya jumped from the top of the snowbank onto the ice, determined to retrieve her cousin. She latched onto Faina's wrist and tried towing her back to land.

"Anya! No! I'm not leaving Leo!"

"You're not helping him either, not by standing here waiting to be next!"

Jazmin was dragged out of the water, coughing and sputtering, her clothes pinned to her skin. Anya and Faina returned to land. Someone from the skate rental was already kneeling beside Anastas with a first-aid kit.

Jasar gathered Jazmin in his arms and carried her to a bench. Several Good Samaritans were offering their coats and scarves to help Jazmin warm while someone called an ambulance. When Leo tried to help undo Jazmin's skates, Jasar turned to him, nostrils flared, and shouted something at him in Syrian. He flung his arm away, indicating for Leo to leave. Leo's chin hung towards his chest as he backed away, heartbroken.

Chapter 48:

Foreigners

By the time Pasha and Katya reached the front door of the apartment, they could already smell supper boiling on the stove. It was an absolute pleasure to inhale the aroma of a meal prepared by the expert hands of their mother after such a chaotic day. Eager to hear how his mother's interview had gone, Pasha grabbed a hold of the knob and swung the door open.

"Ma, we're home!" He swept off his cap and tossed it on the hook by the wall. "You won't believe what happened today!" He didn't bother to untie his shoes but yanked them off while balancing on the opposing foot, almost tripping in the process.

He dashed headfirst through the cloud of steam billowing up in the kitchen with his arms outstretched for his mother. His hands found her arms first, and he pressed his face against her shoulder. The worn canvas of her apron was warm from the stove. She cupped one hand against the back of his head and held him tight.

"There's my darling boy." Her voice was somewhat hoarse.

She sniffled once, and put down the knife she was using to reach up and touch her face. Pasha eyed the cutting board over his shoulder, hoping to find onions. It was clear she had been crying for a long period of time. The deep creases of her eyes were puffier than usual, and the whites were split with red veins.

"*Mamochka* is sad!" Katya observed from the chair by the door, still struggling to get her boots off.

"What happened, Ma?" asked Pasha.

Mama looped her fingers under his palm and, taking it to her lips, kissed the ridge of his knuckles with a weak smile.

"Go help your sister with her boots, and I'll tell you all about it."

Pasha nodded his head swiftly. "*Da*, Mama." He set about helping Katya.

"I didn't get the job," she said simply, picking up the knife again and sinking it into a head of cabbage.

Pasha unbuckled Katya's wellington boots and began working his fingers through the laces of her canvas shoes she was wearing underneath.

"Why not? Had they already hired someone?" He was trying to sound positive, but he already knew the reason. He watched the corners of her lips twitch as she lowered her eyebrows.

"It's quite funny actually." She ripped off another chunk of cabbage and let her knife fall into the flesh with a heavy thud. "I was brought before Madame Wells. I smiled and introduced myself. The moment I was done speaking, she took one look at her maid and said, 'You didn't tell me she was Russian.'"

Pasha was so surprised he dropped Katya's shoes on the floor. "They didn't hire you because you're Russian?"

"That is why."

"But it's a Russian art collection!"

Lydia scoffed as she lifted the cutting board from the counter and scraped the vegetables into the pot. "Madame Wells isn't the cleverest hen in the coop, nor the most accepting."

With her feet freed, Katya hopped down from the chair and ran along, but Pasha remained kneeling on the floor. The factories weren't taking anyone on. Mama had tried to find work in shops but was repeatedly turned away due to her accent. She said she had enough saved up to last them until summertime, but Pasha was finding that difficult to believe.

***

Later that night, Pasha lay staring at the stack of books piled on his dresser. He thought of Sergei, and Yuri, and the countless other boys who had been forced to drop out of school to help their families. He thought about the Breadwinners. If Sergei had quit school earlier, would his family still have become so desperate that he had to turn to Klokov?

He turned over and covered his face with his pillow. As he managed to quiet his brain, he became aware of a faint whispering noise. He sat up in bed and listened. It was his mother. He strained his ear, searching for a second voice, but there was none. Who was she talking to?

Pasha peeled back the covers, tiptoed across the frosty floorboards to his bedroom door, and carefully nudged it open. He could hear her more clearly now, clearing her throat and then enunciating in a bright voice.

"Hello, I am Lydia Chevalsky." She dragged the word "hello" out as though she were trying to get more air behind the vowels. She stopped for a moment and then repeated the phrase again. "Hello, I am Lydia Chevalsky." Parts of her voice were stabilizing but she just couldn't get the subtle flow of music out of the "D," the part that sounded like a drop of water.

Pasha stepped out into the hall. She was standing in front of the mirror near the front door with a dictionary in her right hand. Her breath fractured with an exhausted exhale. With her eyes covered she tried again.

"Hello, I'm Lydia Kingsley." She was using her maiden name, her father's name.

The floorboards creaked beneath Pasha's weight, and Mama looked straight at him.

"Ma?"

She smoothed her hands over her hair and cleared her throat. "What is it, my love? Did I wake you?"

"No."

They stared at each other in silence before Mama pulled the cord of her dressing gown tighter and edged forward.

"Can't you sleep?" She held out her arms to him. "Come, sit with me. Let me hold you." She lowered herself onto the sofa as Pasha came and curled up beside her. "What is troubling you, *Patulya*?"

Pasha rested his head against her shoulder while she wrapped one arm around him.

"Mama, I was thinking maybe I could get a job. You know, to help out."

She traced her nails through his hair and pulled him closer. "Nonsense! You should be focusing on your studies. Remember what Mr. Schultz said? He thinks you could get into a university."

Pasha wondered whether or not she was aware he was the only ten-year-old on Orchard Street to not have a job to help the family.

"Everyone else at school has a job."

He could feel the smile in her lips as she kissed the side of his head. "But not everyone has a sick little sister to look after when they get home."

"Sergei's little sister has polio, and he has two other little brothers. And Yuri's family has seven children he has to help out with, and his father's in a wheelchair."

He watched the muscles in her neck tighten. "What about Faina?"

"Ma, Faina helps Uncle Matvei in the shop, and makes deliveries, and sweeps the building, and helps collect the rent. But Faina doesn't count anyway. Her family's rich."

Mama said nothing but continued stroking her fingers though his hair.

"I just want to help out before things get bad."

Lydia leaned back and covered her eyes. After a moment, she sat up and faced him. "Okay. How's this? We'll wait and see where we are in a month, and if things aren't any better, then we will discuss the possibility of you getting an after-school job. How does that sound?"

She placed one finger beneath his chin and tilted his head up to look at her. Pasha felt his spine unlatch knob by knob, like dominoes.

"That sounds like a good idea."

She pressed her lips against his forehead. "Does that put that brilliant mind of yours at ease?"

"It does."

"Good." She placed her hands on either side of his head and tousled his hair. "Don't you worry about how we're going to make ends meet, that's my job. The best thing you can do for Mama right now is go to school and learn as much as you can."

Chapter 49:

No Good Thug

Leo counted the last of the change, placed it in the drawer of the cash register, and locked it shut. It had been a long day of deliveries but he was thankful to have so much money to count. As he craned his head back to check the time on the clock hanging above the counter, he rubbed his neck. The minute hand was just lining up with the thirtieth mark. Seven thirty. Jazmin would have finished dinner an hour ago.

Though Uncle Matvei knew all about the ice skating incident and that Jazmin had fallen through the ice, he was not aware Jazmin had been there on account of Leo, and neither Leo, nor Faina, nor even Anya had any plans to enlighten him.

He hadn't spoken to Jazmin since the incident. Jasar had discovered their little secret, and yet what proof did he have? How did he know he and Jazmin weren't just friends? Would it be so bad if they were just friends? But then why would Jazmin have lied about going ice skating? He would find out tonight.

Leo checked his wallet, then threw on his coat. "I'm going out, Uncle Matvei!"

Uncle Matvei's voice echoed as he made his way up the back hall, dusting the front of his apron with his large hands. "I take it the deliveries went well then?"

Leo brushed his fingers through his bangs a couple times before sliding on his cap.

"Yeah, earned about twenty-five dollars in tips, so I'd say that's pretty good."

Uncle Matvei smiled and ran a wet rag over the top of the counter. "Excellent! I am glad to hear it."

Before Leo could reach for the door handle, Uncle Matvei slung the rag over his shoulder and crossed his arms over his chest.

"So Valentine's Day is next week. If you're looking for something to send your sweetheart they're having a special on sweets at the bakery."

Leo crept closer to the door. "I haven't got any sweethearts, Uncle Matvei."

Uncle Matvei was cordial as usual but refused to let the subject drop. "What about Jazmin Zureiq?"

Leo felt his shoulders sink. He rubbed his hands over his eyes and exhaled through his nose. Uncle Matvei beckoned him back.

"Come here, my boy. You're not in trouble."

Leo dragged his feet across the floor and slumped over the counter with the brim of his cap covering his eyes.

"Did Faina say anything?" He didn't really believe she would give him away, but she was the first person who came to mind.

"Jazmin's father came by today. He wasn't angry, in fact, he was very polite. He wishes for Jazmin to focus on her studies right now."

"What he really means is he doesn't want her hanging around me."

Uncle Matvei was silent for a long while, then he uncrossed his arms and rested his hands on the edge of the register. "Leo, we must respect her family's wishes."

Leo scratched at a spot of dried *Kvass* near the jar of wine corks. "What about her wishes?"

"Jazmin is a young girl, Leontiy. Just as you are still a boy. Until you are grown and can make decisions for yourself there are rules you must obey."

Leo felt a seed of disappointment rooting between his eyes. "Do you disapprove then? You know, because … we're different."

"Do I disapprove of you and Miss Zureiq?" He stepped back from the counter as though Leo had challenged his honor. "Certainly not! This is America after all, a modern country, and we are modern people!" He leaned forward and placed a hand on Leo's shoulder. "You know if it were up to me only, I would gladly welcome Miss Zureiq to our table. But we must also consider Jazmin's family and how they feel about the situation."

The pressure was building in Leo's chest until finally he threw up his hands in exasperation.

"I don't understand! It's not illegal for us to be together, you know! I checked!"

Uncle Matvei hesitated, then held up his hand. "Leo, it's nothing to do with race."

"It's not like I come from a bad family, right? I mean, you're a successful business owner! You own this whole building!"

"It has nothing to do with status."

Leo smacked his hands on the counter. "Well, what is it then?"

"It's the Breadwinners, Leo." Uncle Matvei shrank back, as though he regretted telling Leo the truth. "You have a criminal record, Leontiy. Now, we know you're caught in this situation with no way out, but you have to look at it from their perspective. Jasar is a war hero. Her parents are business owners too. They're just trying to protect their daughter's reputation."

Leo curled forward. His face burned. "You mean, I'm no good?"

Uncle Matvei pinched his eyes shut and swallowed, wishing he had taken a different approach. He lifted Leo's chin up.

"They don't know you, Leo. And they don't know your situation. If they did, maybe things would have turned out differently. But this is the reality. You have a year left, and then all this will be over and you can move on. Let Jazmin go."

Leo gazed up at his uncle with helpless eyes. He opened his mouth to explain that he loved Jazmin, but thought better of it, and sighed instead. His chest was aching.

"You are quite popular, Leo," Uncle Matvei went on. "You are smart, accomplished, funny. There are plenty of girls out there. You'll find another one. Besides, you are only sixteen. You have your future to look forward to. You can't let yourself be distracted by a pretty face now, can you?"

Leo shed his coat and draped it listlessly over one arm. He never had any trouble speaking loudly, but as he turned and slogged towards the back staircase he could only manage a thin, hushed, "No, Uncle."

Chapter 50:

Fifth-Grade Dropout

When Lydia finally consented to let Pasha get an after-school job, he had no such luck finding any. Employers who didn't turn him away based on his heritage were obliged to hire boys who didn't have to worry about getting home to finish schoolwork. When all Lydia could scrape together for dinner was cabbage and potatoes in a thin broth boiled from leftover fish bones, she was forced to face reality.

Mr. Schultz had been very understanding about the whole ordeal, but it did little to ease Pasha's sense of loss. He wandered through the city before heading home, trying to pull himself together. As he trudged through the Five Points neighborhood his eyes snagged on a Help Wanted sign in the window of a hardware store. He'd tried nearly every shop in the Lower East Side. Why not try one outside his neighborhood? Pasha hastily brushed his bangs to the side and gathered up the courage to walk inside.

No one was at the counter, but there was a silver bell sitting near the cash register with a sign that read, "Ring for service." Pasha reached across the surface and tapped the little button softly. A man cleared his throat from the back room, progressing into a series of hacking coughs. The floorboards creaked as the manager appeared in the doorway. He was a tall, thin, balding man with long limbs and a flat cap. He took one look at Pasha and released an impatient sigh. Pasha cast his eyes towards his feet.

"Excuse me, sir. I noticed the Help Wanted sign in the window and was wondering if I could apply."

"You talking to me or your shoes?"

Pasha felt his cheeks redden as he forced himself to look into the man's face. He had a natural scowl and looked most intimidating standing there with his hands bracing the countertop.

"You, sir."

"What's your availability?"

"Anytime."

The man leaned back and placed his hands on his hips. "You go to school?"

"No, sir. I had to drop out to help my family."

"You did, eh?" He rubbed at his bare chin. "Well, you wouldn't be the first. You ever had a job before?"

"No, sir. But I'm a fast learner, and I don't mind taking orders."

The man reached behind the register for a pen and a piece of paper. "That's what I like to hear. How old are you anyway?"

"Eleven."

The man nodded approvingly as he jotted down Pasha's information on a piece of paper. When he was finished he stopped and looked up.

"Can you read and write?"

"Of course."

But the man didn't seem convinced. He retrieved a newspaper from the top of the radio, and laid the front page on the counter.

"What does this say?"

Pasha looked down at the newspaper and read the headline aloud. *"The Red Menace is Real."* Below was a cartoon of a large hairy man wearing a pointy hat with a red star.

The manager shook his head. "Damn commies. I tell ya, they let any more Russians into this country and we'll all be getting threats in our mailboxes."

Pasha rocked back on his heels and swallowed. Now he remembered why he hadn't applied to any shops outside his neighborhood. The man hadn't figured out Pasha was Russian. When he had put away the newspaper, he drummed his hands on the tabletop, looking a little friendlier than before.

"So, you got a name or what?"

"Paul," Pasha blurted out, using the English translation of his name.

"Paul what?"

"Che—" Pasha slowed. He was so nervous he hadn't stopped to think about his last name. "Che … perd. Shepherd. Paul Shepherd."

For the first time in the interview, the manager smiled. "Paul Shepherd … now that's an American name!" He thrust out his hand. "Nice to meet you, Mr. Shepherd."

Trying not to appear too relieved, Pasha grabbed it and shook. The man tipped his cap.

"I'm Henry McCady. You got yourself a job, kid."

Pasha's mouth fell open with a gasp. "You really mean it?"

The man stood back and tucked his hands in his pockets. "I do. Be here tomorrow morning at seven and we'll start your training."

Chapter 51:
Forgetting

Sonata stood leaning against a pile of mats in the gymnasium watching Pyro dismiss practice for the day. They'd been training the new recruits for a few weeks now, and her amazement had yet to wear off. There were now forty-nine performers, split into three groups: aerialists who were taught by Pyro and Sonata, tightrope walkers who were taught by Skelter with the help of a translator, and marksmen taught by Melodious.

"*Oi*, Private Fernando," Pyro barked at an igneous who was chatting up a sylph hired as an aerialist. "Next time, I wanna see less flirting with Carrion and more tightrope walking. You keep gawking at her that way you'll fall right off the high wire. Understand? Practice dismissed."

Pyro turned and approached Sonata with a smile. "Well, Sonny," he stood next to her. "What do you think?"

Sonata gaped at the bustling auditorium. "I simply can't get over it. In just a few short months, you've managed to accomplish what none of us could."

"And what's that?"

She gestured to the well-organized soldiers packing up their bags for the day. "Forty-nine new recruits! All members of the Saighdeoir at one point or another, and they're absolutely perfect!"

Pyro shrugged. "Ah, you just gotta know how to communicate with them is all."

"And it helps that you had some idea of who would be best suited for the job." She indicated towards an igneous headed for the door. "That Captain Brush might be as skilled a knife-thrower as Melodious himself."

Pyro chuckled. "Yeah, ol' 'Brushfire' once blasted an ophidian off a balcony from forty yards away with nothing but some gasoline and a lead pipe! And Private Cooper? Next to Staff Sergeant Graham he's one of the highest fliers of the third sylph division."

"I wish we had come to you ages ago!" She was about to say more when a tall, statuesque sylph with cascades of blooming wisteria growing through her hair approached Pyro with a friendly wave.

"We tackling Jar tactics tomorrow, Pyro?"

Sonata sniffed. Calling him by his first name seemed awfully familiar. They must have known each other well.

Pyro looked up with an enthusiastic smile. "Hiya, Ivy!"

Sonata examined the sylph from the corner of her eye. She looked to be somewhere around Pyro's age and was rather striking, with a natural green blush to her cheeks, and a sprinkling of shiny gold freckles across the bridge of her nose.

"Let's see." Pyro looked down at his clipboard, something Sonata would never have dreamed of him owning, let alone using. "Yes. You're with Unit B."

"But Zinnia is in Unit B, and I thought you couldn't have two of the same Fay in a unit."

He ran his finger down the page. "According to my notes, Zinnia is in Unit J. But we can sort it out tomorrow."

Sonata's eyes bulged as Ivy played with the charm dangling from her neck as though to deliberately draw more attention to her décolletage.

"Excellent." She paused with a calculated expression of bashfulness. "I, uh, also wanted to ask you about some of my routine. I'm afraid I'm having a rather difficult time with some of the partner moves and was wondering if perhaps you could help me with my form after practice one day. Just you and me, that is. I wouldn't want to distract you from the others."

Sonata's eyebrows rose steadily up her forehead. It was all she could do to keep from rolling her eyes. She trained her attention on Pyro, waiting for his reaction.

"Ah, no need for all that," he answered without hesitation. "Sonata can give you some pointers tomorrow when we go over your number with Captain Redman."

"Oh." Her smile shrank. "Okay then. In that case, I guess I'll see you tomorrow." Her fingers fluttered in a little wave as she turned to leave.

"See you then!" He didn't even bother to look up from his clipboard.

Sonata waited until the girl was out of earshot before pretending to examine her nails and asking casually, "You, uh, know her well?"

Pyro looked up from his clipboard with an innocent expression. "Who? Ivy?" He tossed his shoulders. "She's just a friend."

"Well, I think little Miss Petals has a crush on you."

"Then she's barking up the wrong tree." He glanced back at her suspiciously.

Sonata edged clumsily towards the silk and forced a laugh. "Pun intended?"

It took Pyro a moment to catch on, but when he did he laughed. "It wasn't, actually." He followed her to the mats.

"I'm surprised," she remarked, trying to sound offhand. "She's very beautiful."

"Is she?"

Pyro appeared so genuinely clueless to Ivy's charms that Sonata could only stare back at him in surprise. When she did not reply, he simply sucked his teeth and shrugged.

"Ain't really my type, I suppose."

Sonata's eyes skittered off to the right as she recalled Pyro's words to her in Khan Lau: *You're an out-of-this-world, stunning, completely enchanting, downright Venus, and I am wildly, helplessly, desperately attracted to you!*

"That strategy you came up with is brilliant, by the way." She took hold of either side of the silk and leaned forward. "Creating units with one of each race so they can trade off carrying the Jar."

"You really think so?"

When she looked up, Pyro was closer to her than she realized. He backed away with an awkward smile.

"I do." She hoisted herself up and sat down in the crook of the loop. "You're a brilliant strategist."

"I only wish you could come."

Sonata groaned and flipped upside down. "Don't remind me."

"Why aren't you and Staccato going again?"

"Because according to him it's unnecessary. Which is hard to argue when we now have forty-nine extra performers, all of whom are experienced Saighdeoir soldiers. According to Staccato, we've done our duty. Why endanger our lives if we don't have to? Still, at the very least the pay would be nice. It'd help him with his aunt's bills, anyway."

Pyro shuffled towards her with his hands in his pockets. "Well, I'm sorry to hear you can't go. I know how much it meant to you."

"It's alright. Just give Samael a swift kick for me."

Pyro chuckled. "Will do."

She glanced up at him and instinctively bit her lip. His hair was tousled from practice which made the smirk he always wore somehow even more playful and attractive. The simple undershirt he wore for practice exposed the smooth skin of his muscular shoulders. She didn't know why, but she suddenly had the urge to begin smoothing a stray curl over her neck.

"Have you ever gone stargazing in the foothills?"

Pyro looked up at her with genuine surprise. "Hm?"

Sonata waved a hand, trying to hide her embarrassment. "I'm sure you have, seeing as you've spent so much time in Sagittarius." She cleared her throat. "They say in late winter you can often see meteor showers. Perhaps when you return from your mission—"

"I won't be returning to Sagittarius after the mission," he said slowly, continuing to stare at her in confusion.

Sonata's mouth fell open. She could feel her energy draining as she struggled to get her words out. "You … you're not returning?"

Pyro rubbed awkwardly at the back of his neck. "My two years are almost up. I'll be returning to the Saighdeoir after this mission."

Sonata snapped her mouth shut and forced a polite smile. "Right. Of course you will. So silly of me to think you'd be staying on as a … what's the phrase you always use? 'A spangly circus performer.'"

Pyro tried to ease her with a warm simper. "Can't say it hasn't been fun. But we all gotta move on at some point. I suppose when the Land Lock ends you'll go back to being a queen-in-training again."

At the mention of returning to her old life, Sonata's heart felt as though it were sagging inside her chest.

"What's wrong?" he asked, taking notice of the shift in her mood.

Sonata rolled down off the silks, feeling quite heavy all of a sudden. "Nothing."

Pyro stared back at her awkwardly, waiting for some sort of explanation.

"It's just …" She pushed back her hair. "Sometimes I forget I'm going to be queen one day … or even that I'm a princess at all. What with everything that's been going on these past few years. My life is completely different now."

The gymnasium was empty. Their voices echoed off the high walls.

"Makes sense." Pyro took a tentative step forward. "And that bothers you?"

"It used to. But now, I understand something I didn't before." She turned and faced him. "Things are changing. Even if the Land Lock breaks, life is never going to be the same again. I used to think that if I wanted to be queen there were things I couldn't have. But I know now that's not true."

They stared at each other in silence for a moment, then Sonata flowed towards him with urgent, pleading steps.

"Pyro, is there really nothing that might make you stay?"

Pyro swallowed. "I can't say there weren't times when I was tempted." His gaze fell from her mouth to her neck.

"And what about now?" Her eyes met his. "There's nothing that could tempt you to stay now?" She took another step towards him, her head tilted to the side and her lips hanging partly open.

Pyro's voice grew stiff and quiet. "No. I don't think so."

"Not even stargazing in the foothills?" She reached for his hand.

Pyro stared down at the small space between their feet and swallowed. "You once said we were two of a kind. That what we want more than anything is to take down the C.O.N. For you that means staying here and doing undercover work. For me, that means returning to the Saighdeoir." He let her hand drop.

Sonata stepped back, her eyes filled with disappointment. "I'm sorry I lied to you about the love potion." She could feel her cheeks coloring with shades of regret. "I suppose it's too late now."

Pyro shook his head. "Don't be sorry. You made the right choice." He turned away and began gathering his belongings. "You reminded me that I can't allow myself to get distracted. Not if I want to make something of my life."

"You don't think there's value in a life spent with someone who loves you?"

Pyro froze and stared at her. Realizing what she had done, Sonata immediately began to backtrack.

"I mean, everyone settles down eventually. Someone is bound to fall in love with you at some point, don't you think?"

Bit by bit, Pyro straightened. He looked her in the eye. "My purpose in life is to serve the Saighdeoir. It's what I'm good at it. It's what I was made for. I'm not cut out for love."

Sonata opened her mouth to say more but the growing warmth in her cheeks stopped her. Unable to look at him, she excused herself and ran out of the gymnasium.

Chapter 52:
Fired

Pasha hummed quietly to himself as he dragged the broom behind the counter of the hardware store. Sheets of summer rain were spraying down the storefront. It had been a slow morning so far, but Pasha was glad to have an opportunity to tidy up. Several months had passed since he was first hired, and although his mother would've much preferred him presenting her with report cards every two weeks, she was proud of his paychecks all the same. Working for Mr. McCady had not been easy at first, and would've intimidated most children, but Pasha had a way of winning people over, and Mr. McCady respected hard work. Though his manners were no less rough, and his smile remained scarce, he trusted Pasha. That being said, Mr. McCady's ill-tempered ways appeared trivial compared to his anti-Russian sentiments. Pasha hoped that in time, Mr. McCady would come to respect him enough that he could be open about where he came from. However, it soon became clear after Pasha's employment that his manager's comment about Russian immigrants had not been a throwaway remark, but a passionate manifesto.

Overall, Mr. McCady was a taciturn man. He seldom gave verbal answers to simple questions, but preferred to communicate through a series of grunts, nods, and spits, and he regarded most questions as stupid anyway.

If one wished to carry on a conversation with Mr. McCady, one had to bring up the headlines. The man's opinions had the volume and endurance of a soapbox preacher in a red-light district. Once he got started, he could prattle on for hours about Washington, the Palmer Raids, and the Russian Revolution. There were times when Pasha longed to escape to the back and turn on the chainsaw just to drown out the ranting.

What bothered Pasha most was that all Mr. McCady's hatred of Russians appeared to be centered on his dislike of communism, and yet Pasha, who was Russian, also opposed communism. Because of Mr. McCady's strong feelings, Pasha remained in a constant state of anxiety, terrified that his boss might one day figure out his true identity. And yet, he never seemed to suspect a thing.

By now, Pasha's American accent was immaculate; what's more, he was quite eloquent for his age and station. He was careful to utter native expressions low under his breath if he uttered them at all, and when he was anxious he made a conscious effort not to relapse into

Russian or Ukrainian. Still, it was easier all around to just say little. And soon he too found himself communicating with grunts and nods.

Pasha emptied the dustbin into the wastebasket and returned the broom to the corner behind the counter. He was about to dust the cash register when a woman with a shawl around her head sprinted past the window. Thunder rumbled as she fought against the wind to open the door with one hand.

As Pasha raced from behind the counter to help her, he realized she had a baby in one arm. The woman was so thoroughly soaked from the rain she almost slipped in her own puddle as she staggered over the threshold.

It was not often that they received female customers, and a hardware store seemed the last place a person would be hurrying to with a baby in a rainstorm. When Pasha had managed to shut the door, the woman, who was no more than twenty, turned to him with frenzied eyes.

"*Ne mogli by vy mne pomoch', pozhaluysta?*" Can you help me, please?

Pasha stared stupidly at the woman as adrenaline spilled into his veins. He glanced nervously over his shoulder. Mr. McCady was in the back. The woman knit her eyebrows and tried again in English.

"Help, please?"

Pasha swallowed once, trying to take a deep breath. "What can I help you with?"

The woman hesitated with wide, uncomprehending eyes.

"Nester *Ulitsa*." Nester Street. She held up her child. "My baby, *on bolen*!" He is sick.

Pasha understood at once. She was looking for *Hester* Street, but in the Cyrillic alphabet H made the N sound. Pasha looked over his shoulder once more to see if Mr. McCady had heard them. Nothing stirred. He returned his attention to the woman and lowered his voice.

"You are looking for Hester Street," he explained in Russian. "Go down two more blocks, then turn right." He peered over her elbow at the soft, cherubic face of the baby who was covered in dried remnants of what looked like strawberry jelly. "What's wrong with him?"

The woman, trying not to tear up, indicated to the garnet-colored splotches on his cheeks.

"My little sister was supposed to be watching him while I took a bath. When I got done he had broken out in this rash."

Pasha held up a finger. "One second."

He slipped behind the counter and wet a handkerchief under the sink with warm water.

"I think this might help. My little sister has had the same problem before."

The woman turned the child so that Pasha could see him better. Pasha dabbed at the red splotches on the baby's face. The dried goo rolled into sticky balls and stuck to the handkerchief. Pasha smiled and held up the cloth for the young woman to see.

"It's jelly."

The woman let out a relieved gasp, then burst out laughing.

Pasha giggled. "He must have found his way into the kitchen when your sister wasn't looking."

The woman shook her head with a self-admonishing simper. "You certainly are a clever little boy. What is your name?"

"Pasha Chevalsky."

"Pasha Chevalsky," she repeated. "You have been a big help to me today, Pasha. Thank you so much!"

She turned to leave but the rain had yet to lighten up, and Pasha hated to see her get soaked again.

"Here, take my umbrella." He removed it from the stand by the door.

The woman waved her hand. "Nonsense! You will need it when you go home."

"I can always borrow one from my boss."

The woman clicked her tongue, impressed. "Such a gentleman you are! How about I come back to return it when the rain stops?"

"That'd be swell." He held open the door for her, and opened the umbrella.

With her free hand she patted his head. "Thank you so much, my little friend!"

He waved goodbye and watched the woman and her baby disappear up the street. Pasha shut the door and turned back around. Mr. McCady was leaning against the wall with his arms crossed and his lips pulled tight. Pasha's hand jumped to his chest.

"Mr. McCady—!"

Mr. McCady bent his head and spat on the floor Pasha had just finished sweeping.

"Get out."

Pasha's mouth fell open. He felt his knees begin to shake, but he stumbled forward all the same, a pleading look in his eye.

"But why?"

"I don't tolerate dishonesty."

"But Mr. McCady, when was I dishonest?"

Mr. McCady gave an impatient exhale. "You didn't tell me you were Russian."

"You didn't ask—"

"Never mind that," retorted Mr. McCady, his voice climbing over Pasha's. "I can't have commies running my store!"

Pasha could feel the tears rising up to the waterline of his eyes. "But Mr. McCady, I'm not a communist! The Bolsheviks killed my father! That's why my family came here! I love this country as much as you d—"

Mr. McCady thrust his finger at the door. "Didn't you hear me, kid? I said get out!"

"Mr. McCady, please! I really need this job—"

Mr. McCady darted towards him with a violent gesture. "GET OUT!"

Knees trembling, Pasha dashed out the door in tears. He didn't stop running until he reached the end of the street. Pasha doubled over and winced at the pain in his chest. Rain sluiced down the end of his nose. As he gasped for air, his breath came out in a hoarse, rasping wheeze. Pasha looked up at his surroundings, feeling lightheaded. He had to get home. Ignoring his pain, Pasha began jogging down the sidewalk, trying to keep close to the buildings so the awnings would keep him dry.

Chapter 53:
Broke and Blind

Staccato braced his umbrella against the heavy wind as he made his way up Orchard Street. The weather had chased everyone inside and the sidewalks were empty, affording him a greater opportunity to grumble to himself.

He had just returned from the VIPA, the Voilerian Immigration Protection Agency, where he had been forced to pay a fine of two thousand dollars to prevent Aunt Poppy from being deported after she had been arrested yet again. Truth be told, he was tempted to let them do it; she'd caused enough trouble for him in New York City. But then there would be no one to keep an eye on Lydia and the children, and settling her back into Voiler under such circumstances would hardly be a minor inconvenience.

As he crossed to the next block, he noticed a small, huddled figure draped against the bannister of the stoop across the street. There was no awning to take shelter under, and whoever it was had clearly resolved to get sopping wet. Curious, Staccato squinted his eyes. It was a boy ten to eleven years of age. He showed no signs of movement. There was something familiar about the long legs and the lanky form. Staccato dashed across the street without hesitation. It was Pasha.

As he drew nearer, he could see Pasha's mouth was hanging open slightly. Staccato knelt down on the pavement and tapped his cheek.

"Pasha?" All thought or care for blowing his cover evaporated at once. Pasha's head rolled to the side lifelessly. "Pasha, can you hear me?"

He held his hand near his grandson's open mouth. He was breathing. He grabbed a hold of Pasha's wrist and checked his pulse. He appeared to have fainted. A soft moan came from the back of Pasha's throat. His head turned slightly. His eyes fluttered open and shut.

"Are you alright?" Staccato held the umbrella over him.

Pasha's eyes darted about wildly. It had been years since Staccato had been so close to Pasha, since he'd had the pleasure of looking his grandson directly in the face. So much had changed since then. His neck had grown longer and thinner. His heavy eyebrows were becoming more defined, and his front teeth seemed rather large. Staccato held the umbrella over him, trying not to let his emotions overwhelm him.

"Can you hear me?"

Pasha began hyperventilating to such a degree he was practically choking. Trying to swallow, Pasha nodded his head. Though his eyes were directed in Staccato's general vicinity his gaze remained unanchored. Staccato's brow gathered into a knot.

"You can't see me, can you?"

Pasha squeezed his eyes shut. A whimper escaped his throat as he shook his head back and forth.

"It's alright, it's alright." Staccato's voice was hushed and calm, though on the inside he felt as though he himself might start to hyperventilate. "Did you hit your head?"

"I don't know, sir. I was walking home, and all of a sudden everything went black." He reached out and grabbed Staccato's arm, desperate for help. "Please, sir, I don't know how to get home."

"Shhh. Don't worry, we'll get you home and get you safe. What was the last thing you did before losing your vision? Did you eat something? Look into a bright light? Were you feeling sick?"

"I was getting fired, sir … for—for speaking Russian. My boss didn't know I was Russian." The muscles in his face contracted, and he covered his eyes in embarrassment. "I'm sorry, sir. My family just really needs the money."

Staccato's mouth hinged open. He wanted nothing more than to hug his grandson close, to tell him everything was going to be fine, that he would take care of everything. But he couldn't. Pasha's hands shook. It was acute anxiety. He was familiar with the symptoms. It was genetic. Aunt Poppy's sister had experienced fainting followed by vision loss as a symptom, and he himself had suffered an attack once as a child. Still, it needed to be confirmed by a doctor.

"Can you stand?" Staccato tried helping him to his feet, but it was clear Pasha's legs were still weak. "I think I'm going to have to carry you. Is that alright? We're only a few steps away from Mr. Dalka's." He stopped himself. "You know Mr. Dalka, don't you? Perhaps he can telephone an ambulance."

"Yes, sir. He's my best friend's uncle. I don't mind if you carry me."

"Alright. Hang onto my neck." Staccato hoisted Pasha into his arms.

"Wait … are you Ms. Potemkin's nephew?"

Staccato grimaced. He might as well admit it. "Yes."

"Leo told me you had an English accent."

"He did, did he?" He carried on down the sidewalk. "Well, you may call me Mr. K. Now, you'll be happy to know you were on the right track. Mr. Dalka's building is right at the end of the street here."

He was speed walking now. *Opa!* came closer in his field of vision. Lightning fissured through the clouds with a timpani of thunder. A figure coming down the opposite direction opened the front door.

"Leo!" Staccato bellowed over the thunder.

Leo looked up and ran towards them. "What happened? What's wrong?"

The boy bent over Pasha, his eyes filled with concern. Staccato explained what Pasha had told him, and Leo helped him through the door. Mr. Dalka scurried out from behind the counter.

"What's all this?"

"Call an ambulance." Staccato sat him on the counter. "He can't see."

Leo got to the phone before his uncle. Mr. Dalka began examining Pasha's eyes.

"You'll want to be sure, of course, but it may just be anxiety," Staccato explained. "It runs in our family." Staccato paused, his eyes bulging.

"Aunt Poppy has a similar condition?" Uncle Matvei grabbed the pendant light over the counter and shined it into Pasha's eyes. Staccato exhaled.

"Uh, no, not Poppy, her sister. So we're rather familiar with the symptoms."

"Do you think a tablespoon of wine might help?"

"Perhaps something a little stronger. Try brandy."

Pasha's pupil flickered slightly at the shine of the light. Staccato closed his eyes, feeling that he too needed a tablespoon—or ten—of brandy. It was a good sign. Leo hung up the phone.

"They're on their way right now."

"Good." Mr. Dalka poured the brandy into a tablespoon and fed it to Pasha. "How long were you out in the rain?"

Pasha swallowed. "I don't know. I don't remember much."

"It was a good thing Mr. K was there to rescue you!"

Staccato watched Pasha's every move in desperation. Soon they heard sirens in the distance. Staccato stayed with them until Pasha was loaded into the back of the van, Matvei accompanying him. Leo was instructed to stay behind and look after the store. Staccato stood beneath the awning and stared after the vehicle until it had rounded the corner.

Why couldn't I stay? he thought to himself. *After all, he doesn't know who I really am. He visits Aunt Poppy and yet he doesn't even know she's his real aunt.* He sighed. It was imprudent. Impractical. Dangerous. That's how mistakes were made.

"You'll let us know how he gets on?"

Leo straightened his cap and sniffed. "Of course!" He craned his head forward and looked at Staccato curiously. "You alright, Mr. K?"

"Hm? Yes! Yes! I'm quite alright, Leo, thank you." It was high time he was back at the train station and returning home to Voiler. He cleared his throat and turned back towards the sidewalk. "Like I said, do let us know how he gets on."

***

By the time Staccato received word from Aunt Poppy he was back at Feifior, lying down. At supper he had hardly touched his food. Sonata naturally sensed something was wrong, but he refused to say anything lest she follow him around for the next twenty-four hours smothering him with her pitying glances and forcing him to talk about his feelings. He needed solitude. He needed to reflect.

The calling glass pulsed on the bedside table. Staccato jumped up and seized it by the handle.

"How is he?"

The dim light of Aunt Poppy's apartment filled the reflection. "Pasha is going to be fine. He is home now and his sight has been fully restored. It was as you suspected. The attack was brought on by acute anxiety." She sighed. "It seems a shame for him to have had to go to the hospital to confirm what we already suspected, but better to be safe, of course."

Staccato bent over his knees, his jaw clenched tight. "How bad was the bill?"

"Criminal."

Staccato let out a long exhale. Poppy continued.

"They have been hit with much hardship. Lydia still has not been able to find a job, as you know. You'll want to send them what you can. I can easily find a way to hide it in the—"

"I can't send it!" His head snapped up with a scowl.

"What do you mean you can't send it?"

Staccato felt his knuckles tightening around the handle of the calling glass. He slid a hand over his face, trying to keep his tone as controlled as possible.

"How much money do you think I have, Aunt? My savings are under water too, you know."

Aunt Poppy wrinkled her nose. "You're working, aren't you? Paid by the nobility as a matter of fact!"

"They're not in an ideal position either. Everyone has been affected by the Land Lock! Cassiopeia and Scorpius were home to two of Voiler's largest federal reserves, meaning their joint rules, Aries and Sagittarius, have little access!"

Aunt Poppy's voice was wavering somewhere between desperate and angry.

"Well, it's not as though you're making house payments! Where is it all going?"

Staccato blinked in surprise. "Well, I'm making somebody's house payments!" He leaned forward, a deep crease forming between his eyebrows. "Not to mention I have a disabled goddaughter to care for!"

"Sonata is a thriving young woman!"

"She has a physical disability!"

"Didn't you just get a bonus?"

"Well, yes, Aunt! I did! And I could have used that to help Lydia, but do you know where it went instead?"

The fire in her eyes shrank and died. The truth had finally registered. Staccato knew better than to twist the knife, but he was angry, angry for his daughter and grandchildren, angry for Sonata, and angry for himself.

"There are consequences to your actions! The last of my paycheck went directly to your fine! Which means I have no money to give to my daughter. Someone who really needs it!"

Aunt Poppy's hand shook over her open mouth. "What have I done?" Tears filled her eyes.

Staccato stared at her in stony silence. He had nothing left to say to her. He pressed his hand to the glass, and Aunt Poppy disappeared. His mother would have been horrified at him for snubbing his aunt in such a way, and a part of him was ashamed. But he couldn't face her right now.

Staccato hid the calling glass in a drawer and exited the room. He made his way towards Thayer's study on the upper floor. He did not have to wait long in the antechamber, for Thayer had just finished a meeting with the general of the Saighdeoir.

"Staccato Nimbus!" Thayer closed the door behind him and offered Staccato a chair. "What can I do for you today?"

"I've changed my mind. I'd like to assist with the mission to retrieve the Jar."

Chapter 54:
Volstead

October 28, 1919

"The American people have said that they do not want any liquor sold, and they have said it emphatically by passing almost unanimously the constitutional amendment." These were the words spoken by Judiciary Chairman Andrew Volstead of Minnesota in the defense of the new Volstead Act which was passed earlier this afternoon by Congress, overriding President Wilson's veto of the National Prohibition Act.

The twenty-five-page piece of legislation determines the penalties of violating Prohibition laws as well as specifying what constitutes "intoxicating liquor." Here at the New York Daily we've broken down the law for the convenience of our readers.

It is Legal to ...
Consume liquor in the privacy of your own home or at the home of a friend.
Keep a stock of liquor in your private residence. A private residence is defined as any place you live permanently. You may have more than one.
Store liquor for the sole use of family and neighbors, not for profit.

Alcohol may be manufactured, sold, or transported for medicinal, scientific, or sacramental purposes with a government permit.

It is Illegal to ...
Carry a flask.
Gift someone a bottle of alcohol, or receive alcohol as a gift.
Consume or transport liquor to restaurants, hotels, or public property.
Buy or sell recipes for homemade liquor.
Store liquor outside your private residence.
Manufacture intoxicating beverages in your own home.

Intoxicating liquor is defined as any beverage with an alcohol content above one half of one percent. This includes beer and wine.

Chapter 55:

Performing for the Cobra

Apophis Manor was one of those stone, dungeon-like affairs that are often the subject of lithographs in serial gothic novels. The expanse of rocky valley below made the castle seem taller than it actually was, and the bottomless shadows gave off a sort of dizzying effect if you stood too close to the edge. To one side lay a cold and unforgiving sea that roiled beneath the glacial wind. It was the first place you'd expect to find a family of blood drinkers, and yet the last place they themselves would have chosen to be.

"I reckon this is about the most soul-crushing place I've ever been," remarked Pyro as they pulled up to the manor.

"I take it you've never been to Crux then," said Captain Brush.

"What makes Crux so much worse than Apophis Manor?" asked a sylph named Holly with evergreen branches growing from her head. She was still new to the Saighdeoir and had much to learn.

"Do you recall how Scorpius tried setting up several military clinics in Therion to deal with the Fury outbreak in the '80s?" said Pyro.

Holly shook her head.

"After so much resistance, Scorpius was forced to abandon the clinics and get out of Therion. Now the C.O.N. uses the abandoned facilities as a prison camp to torture their victims for information. They say it's miserable."

The steep and broken road to the manor had been hard enough to navigate on its own, but the ice had made it nearly impossible. As a result, the performers had to be taken up in intervals in a sleigh. The interior of the manor was little more accommodating, as there remained a constant chill to the old place even without the help of the harsh winds. The archways were low-slung, heavy things made of dark wood, weighted down with clunky, overwrought motifs reminiscent of an old monastery. The passages were heavily incensed, and the thick tapestries seemed to smother out the already dim light of the dusty chandeliers.

To put it plainly, Apophis Manor had all the warmth and invitation of a crime scene. For one knew instinctively upon crossing the threshold that many bad things had happened there, and many more were likely to happen again.

The antechamber to the throne room had been made over to serve as a sort of backstage, complete with partitions and dressing screens. Food was served in the throne room, and despite the utter lack of appetite their surroundings inspired, the company was obligated to mingle. For many of the new performers who had never been exposed to a Primal celebration, it was a difficult adjustment. When Private Weedley demurred at an hors d'oeuvre offered by a footman, Major Periculum could not help but mock her.

"All you Fay are so squeamish about our cuisine. Go on, we haven't poisoned it or anything." He made a show of slurping the blood from his glass and allowing it to drip down the corner of his mouth.

Pyro was contemplating sneaking back to the antechamber when a hand pulled him from the crowd and behind a tapestry.

"Madame Raíz?"

Lavanda had pinned him against the wall with a frantic look in her eyes. "You came back?"

"Of course we came back. Did you think we would abandon you for good?"

She withdrew her hands and looked down at the ground. "We lost all hope once we reached Lake Hercules." Her eyes met his. "You shouldn't be here."

"Meaning we should have just given up?"

"It is dangerous! You cannot expect to get out with the Jar alive!"

"Doesn't mean we won't try. Where are they keeping it?"

She paused and took a deep breath. "The room next to the antechamber."

Pyro couldn't have been more pleased with their fortune. "Perfect. Thank you."

He slipped out from behind the tapestry and made his way over to Staccato, who was looming near the exit with an exceptionally moody demeanor. It was clear he did not want to be there, and Pyro felt sorry for him.

"Have you seen the wallpaper in the room next to the antechamber?"

Staccato pretended to check his watch, a signal that he had understood Pyro. "Why? Is it very ugly?" He shoved it back into his pocket. "You'll have to excuse me, I need to have a word with Captain Brush."

Seated in a row of chairs at the base of the throne were the ambassadors. The C.O.N. had at least had the decency to dress them in proper clothing; in fact, they had been adorned in finery just for the occasion, but they were noticeably careworn and tired. Cassia and Fuerza had both lost a tremendous amount of weight, and Cassia had had little to lose to begin with.

Sonata bumped Pyro with her hip. "How are you feeling?" She was wearing the costume from their saignant number, which had been specially requested by Samael. No doubt as a means to humiliate her. After Sonata's revelation that day in the gymnasium, Pyro had been afraid things would be awkward between the two. Fortunately, Sonata had behaved as though it had never happened, though he still caught her staring at him regretfully when she thought he wasn't looking.

It would never work out, he repeatedly had to remind himself. *You aren't cut out for serious relationships. You're needed in the Saighdeoir. This is what you wanted, remember?*

Pyro swept his eyes across the crowd of raucous Primals, slinging their glasses of blood as they toasted their new victory.

"I'm alright."

"You're certain?" A dimple appeared at the corner of her smirk. "I worry about you."

"You worry about everyone."

"Speaking of worrying …" She nodded to the ambassadors. "Those poor souls."

Pyro lowered his voice. "Just remember. It's almost over."

Fuerza caught sight of Sonata watching her and clapped her hands. "*Princessa!*" She bolted out of her chair and came running towards them, Cassia in her wake.

"*¡Hola*, Fuerza!" She pulled the child close and wrapped her in a tight hug.

When Cassia caught up to her she appeared considerably winded.

"Surely, they won't mind that much, Ms. King," said Sonata. "They're too caught up in their celebration. If you exert yourself much further I fear you'll be out of commission for some time."

Cassia nodded and steadied a hand to her heart. She caught Skelter eyeing a plate of miniature turnovers with a brightly colored savory filling.

"Don't worry, they're safe to eat," she assured him. "I prepared them myself."

Sonata lowered her voice. "They have you working in the kitchens?"

Cassia shrugged. "They can't let us have too much rest now, can they?"

Pyro glanced back at some of the more questionable dishes laid out on the banquet tables. "They aren't making you prepare … Primal delicacies, are they?" Meaning dishes requiring human parts.

"Fortunately, no, but only because we have no experience preparing it." She leaned back and tossed her head. "But, uh … I just wanted to let you know that it's nice to see some familiar faces." She drew the red cord out of her pocket and began weaving her fingers in and out. "It's been so long, and yet it seems like it was only yesterday." She continued to extemporize until the design was finished. It was the sign of the chapel, the symbol of sanctuary and safety.

Pyro looked her straight in the eye and nodded. This seemed to be the answer she was looking for.

"We better let you get ready for your performance." She and Fuerza bade them farewell and returned to their seats.

An attendant ophidian with platinum hair and delicate features known as Xylophis called out over the crowd.

"Everyone stand for the arrival of the Cobra."

Chairs were pushed back as the crowd staggered to its feet and the doors were thrust aside. Cobra Samael made an angelic figure gliding down the aisle to a subdued and melodic march in his trailing robes of fur-lined velvet. Pyro had never seen the Cobra up close before, and was surprised by how innocent he appeared. He had massive doe eyes, high cheekbones, and dark hair that flowed behind him like a veil. An attendant helped him to his throne, a grotesque design fashioned after a breeding tangle of serpents.

"My friends," he declared when the music had stopped. "Our hour has come at last."

To say the crowd cheered would be a poor description indeed, as it was much more like a series of bestial drunken growling, snarling, and screeching with the intent of cheering.

"Today we welcome a mighty gift into our kingdom. A symbol of victory over our enemies. With the Jar of Elijah, the soil of this country will at last be awakened. A bounty shall spring forth, and Draco will rise to prosperity. Let our enemies squander in shadow, let them know the sting of famine! For we have suffered long. We were fenced in, caged, stifled by a complex system of virtues designed to control us, when in reality we were born with the truth inside us. Instinct is our virtue. There is no such thing as a wrong instinct. This is a lie we have been conditioned to believe. Whether it is violent, greedy, or covetous, you have a right to pursue your happiness and satisfaction. Immorality is myth. And soon the world will be liberated."

While the Primals continued clapping and hollering, Pyro and the rest of the performers slipped away into the antechamber to prepare for the performance. Grateful to not have to listen to any more of Samael's speech, Pyro sat down on a trunk and waited for the show to begin. Each unit was already lined up together. The show had been ordered so that the first to perform was the last unit to be called upon to help move the Jar, ensuring that there would be no interruptions. When the first notes of the overture began, Sonata dispatched Unit A.

Pyro stood by the door biting his nails, desperate to supervise, but it was his job to keep watch while Staccato accompanied them, using his magic to help them move about unnoticed. It took one unit to move the Jar into the antechamber in fifteen minutes. Meanwhile, Unit B went about replacing it with a decoy expertly designed by Dr. Desmond. When Pyro saw the artifact for the first time, he was astounded that they were able to move it so quickly. The vessel was ponderously large and made of solid bronze.

"You could fit a full-grown man in there!" he whispered to Skelter. "Blazes, I bet you could fit Melodious in there!"

Skelter braced his hands against the Jar and tried pushing it to gauge how heavy it was. It didn't budge.

"Let me try!" Pyro bent forward and tried giving it a shove. It might as well have been cemented to the floor. "Crikey! Dr. Desmond wasn't joking!"

Skelter gestured for him to move out of the way as a large box was brought forth, the kind normally used for carrying set equipment. Designing the box had been the trickiest part of all, for it had to be built in a way that enabled a unit to carry the Jar according to the instructions without drawing attention to themselves. To accommodate the instructions, seven handles had been added to the box, making it appear almost casket-like.

"Alright, everyone," said Private Fernando, the appointed leader of Unit A. "On the count of three." They each took hold of the poles. "One … two … three!" They lifted the Jar into the box as though it were cotton candy.

Staccato checked his pocket watch and receded from the door. "Pyro, Sonata, you're up next."

Pyro took a deep breath and took several steps back from the Jar. He felt a hand on his shoulder.

"I guess this is our last performance together," said Sonata.

An unexpected heaviness seeped into Pyro's chest as he realized she was right. He offered a weak smile.

"I suppose you're right."

She grabbed his hand and squeezed. "Let's make it our best performance yet."

Pyro squeezed back, struggling to push down his melancholy. "Deal!"

By now, Pyro had performed so many times he felt nothing when he walked onto the stage and took Sonata's arm. The dance had become muscle memory. When he crocheted his arm through the silks and lifted himself into the air, it felt completely natural. At one point he was even able to observe his audience. Samael wore a look of utter surprise when Pyro performed a move known as the Bird of Paradise, in which Pyro was practically doing the splits upside down. When the number was over and Pyro and Sonata returned to the antechamber, the first two units had been dismissed to make their way to the escape route. By the time the performance had ended, only three units remained.

Pyro, along with the other leftover recruits, returned to the throne room where the celebration continued. While Pyro sampled one of Cassia's turnovers, he was shocked to find the Cobra himself gliding towards him. If it wasn't for Skelter poking him in the back, he would have forgotten altogether to bow.

"Now, there's something I never thought I'd see," Samael observed casually.

"What's that, Your Majesty?"

"An Anomaly bowing down before an ophidian. It's about time."

Pyro cringed. He wished now that he had ignored Skelter.

Samael's pale blue eyes slithered towards Sonata. "And the Princess."

Everyone held their collective breath as they awaited Samael's reaction.

"Well, there's no point in adding insult to injury. I see now that the loss of your legs has sufficiently humbled you." He reached forward and lifted her chin. "Suffering chastens pride. You've been made all the better for it, my dear."

Pyro's fists were trembling; it was all he could do to keep from lighting Samael's face on fire.

Samael folded his elegant hands in front of him. "This is quite an aristocratic little troupe you have, Mr. Nimbus."

Staccato was faring little better than Pyro and had to swallow before he could get himself to speak. "I suppose you're correct. But then, I have friends in high places."

"Yes, I can see that." He stood silently taking them all in for a moment or two more, before sighing and drawing away. "Well, we certainly appreciated your little performance. Lucien was right. It truly is like nothing we've ever seen." He turned and made his way back to the throne.

Soon it was time for the big ceremony, where the Jar would be anointed over Draco. Complete silence was called for as Xylophis made the announcement.

"Bring forth the Jar of Elijah!"

Pyro held his breath. Beside him, Sonata looped her arm around his and gave him a nervous squeeze. Pyro swept his eyes across the throne room. There was a sylph and a miraculous staged at each corner. Staccato was partnered with Sergeant Espinoza. The ambassadors filed through the entrance, carrying the Jar aloft on poles threaded through the handles.

A mound of Virgonian clay was poured onto the floor and spread with a shovel. Gently, the Jar was placed upon the heap, and the poles carefully removed. The ambassadors were then arranged in a circle around the pot. They were made to present their right arm. Pyro started as Samael drew a ceremonial knife from his sheath, but Sonata pulled him back. Cassia leaned over and whispered something to Fuerza with a calm expression as the child trembled.

Across the room, Lavanda swallowed and furrowed her brow. One by one, their palms were cut. They turned and extended their hands over the Jar, watering the bronze with drops of their own blood. Samael made a violent motion for them to back away. The room was still.

A cloud of vapor rose up from the bowl, quickly followed by another. The engravings and inscriptions etched into the bronze became luminous, and glowed with turquoise light. The dust piled beneath the vessel at once stirred to life. It swept upwards in a spiraling arc above the mouth of the Jar. The floor began to shake beneath them.

Cassia pressed Fuerza close to her chest as the crowd murmured, their voices tinged with worry. Something long and lithe slithered over the lip of the vessel. A robust, green vine. Lush buds materialized along the muscular tendril and opened their fronds, revealing soft, voluminous petals in bright hues. The crowd cheered as a full tree rose up out of the jar and blossomed there in the middle of the throne room.

Pyro watched as one by one the pairs of miraculous and sylphs took turns slipping into the crowd to disappear into the antechamber. He wondered if anyone had noticed. Two of the ambassadors, the mermaid and the seraph, had already vanished from the throng.

Amongst the overjoyed countenances, Colonel Lucien's cynical glare stood out with obvious contrast. He rubbed his thumb and forefinger over his beard. Lavanda must have noticed for she suddenly seemed very eager to pull him away towards the bar. But he held up his hand in a swift motion to stop her. He would not so much as look at her. As Samael began another speech, Pyro observed Lucien flagging down his main attendant. Pyro exchanged nervous glances with Skelter. Melodious braced a hand on both their shoulders.

"Now is the time to move."

Pyro reached a surreptitious hand into his pocket and retrieved the mermaid's breath he had been given prior to arriving. When there was a break in the Cobra's address, Xylophis pulled him aside.

"Someone needs to grab Madame Raíz," whispered Pyro.

Melodious hardly moved his jaw as he spoke. "You're right."

"I can do it."

Melodious nodded. "Go then."

Pyro slipped backwards through the crowd and ran along the edge of the wall, while Samael made another announcement.

"Ladies and gentlemen, if you will please stand by for another quick procedure, the festivities will continue in just a moment."

Colonel Lucien knelt down beside the Jar with a studied air. He ran his finger along the lip.

Pyro pushed through the crowd towards Lavanda. "Madame Raíz!"

Lavanda turned with a hand on her heart.

"You're needed in the antechamber."

There was a resounding clang as Colonel Lucien sprang up and kicked the Jar over on its side. The crowd gasped. Pyro swallowed. They were found out. The Jar should never have been so easily moved without the aid of the ambassadors, not even with the colonel's superior ophidian strength. Pyro grabbed Lavanda by the wrist. They dashed out the nearest exit into the hallway, leaving the commotion behind them. Pyro reached into his pocket for another olive.

"Here, take this." He laid it in her palm.

"What? Why?"

"For your escape. We need to get to the west tower."

Lavanda looked back over her shoulder. "But the antechamber is the other way!"

"We're not going back to the antechamber." They ground to a halt as two large shadows appeared on the opposite wall.

"Are you telling me you marched halfway across Voiler for the past year carrying a forgery?" Samael thundered.

"Quick, hide!" Lavanda pulled him into a side room and shut the door.

"Of course not, Your Majesty," insisted the colonel. They could still hear the conversation taking place outside.

"Then what exactly are you suggesting?"

"That the Jars were switched."

"On the way here?"

"No. Today. This evening."

A long silence followed in which Pyro could feel the understanding surfacing to Samael's radiant blue eyes.

"Xylophis," said Samael in a cool, even voice.

"Yes, Your Majesty?"

"Have Mr. Nimbus come out here please."

Pyro passed a hand over his face and bit his knuckles.

"What should we do?" inquired Lavanda.

Pyro made his way over to the window and opened the latch. He looked out towards the sea. There was movement on the horizon. They may yet be able to pull this off.

"Nothing yet." He dropped down to the floor in front of the door and looked underneath the crack. Footsteps echoed down the hall as Staccato was brought forth. Pyro could just see the bases of the guards' spears. They had already taken him into custody.

"Where's the Jar?" demanded Samael.

"Until just moments ago I had thought it was sitting in the middle of the throne room like everyone el—"

There was a sound like a hand striking flesh.

"Don't lie to me!" boomed Samael.

"Sire," came the stray voice of an attendant. "The antechamber is empty! All the performers are gone!"

"Gone?" Pyro watched Samael's shadow turn towards the opposite passage. "Search the manor! And the grounds! Don't let them get away!" He turned back to Staccato. "Arrest him!" There was a clanking noise as they handcuffed Staccato's wrists. Staccato's staff clattered to the floor and rolled to Samael's feet.

"You're going to tell us everything you know!" The Cobra grabbed the staff. Pyro could hear it slicing through the air, then a cry as Staccato was struck. He scrambled to his feet and guided Lavanda away from the door.

"Stay here. If I don't come back, you need to get to the west tower!"

He seized his chakras and threw open the door with an angry cry. He flung the discs at the guards, taking them both out in one move. The chakras ricocheted back towards Samael but he wove out of the way. Samael. Staccato lay on the ground, bleeding from his temple. Samael turned with a wicked smile.

"Ah, the little prince!"

Colonel Lucien removed a pair of khopesh swords from his back, while Samael stretched his jaws open to twice the size of his head. His fangs lengthened. The stench of blood tinged his breath the way alcohol does a drunkard's. Pyro retrieved his chakras just as the colonel was bringing one of the blades down over his head. Pyro blocked him with the chakra. Lucien stabbed with the other blade. Pyro blocked him again and kneed him in the abdomen. Lucien stumbled back.

Meanwhile, Staccato had managed to rise to his knees. His handcuffs were shaking but remained locked.

"Did you think we'd put you in any old pair of chains?" scoffed Samael.

Lucien sprang at Pyro, lifting himself twelve feet off the ground. Pyro flung the chakra and missed. He grabbed Lucien by the right hand but was unable to properly block the left. The blade cut across his bicep. Pyro gave a cry.

Samael lunged at Pyro. Staccato ran at him with his staff, knocking the Cobra off his feet. Staccato stabbed his staff into the floor, causing the ground to shake. The room melted around them. Pyro backed away, clutching his arm. He had been sucked inside one of Staccato's illusions.

The white tiles remained on the floor, but the black disappeared in the void, making it look as though he were stranded on a disjointed bridge of white diamonds. Pyro braced himself. He daren't move. He jumped as a sound like a roaring tiger echoed over his head. Lucien flew towards him, fangs unsheathed, his khopesh extended. Pyro lifted his arms and lit his body on fire. Lucien knocked him to the ground but immediately withdrew, burned by the flames. Pyro felt his body flickering. He wouldn't be able to sustain it for much longer.

The floor folded beneath them. Pyro and Lucien were cast into the darkness, falling without end, when suddenly Pyro saw himself staring up at the ceiling. Was the vision over? He took a deep breath. Something whistled past his ear. The khopesh embedded itself in the tile next to his head. Pyro gasped. Lucien loomed over him, his jaws unhinged. As he was about to clamp down on Pyro's throat, something wrenched him back.

Lucien gave a yelp. Green vines were emerging from Lavanda's skirts, and one had lassoed itself tightly around Lucien's neck. He clawed at his throat, gagging and croaking. Lavanda dragged him towards her with a tremendous grunt, her eyes livened with years of resentment. She bent over him, grinding the heel of her shoe into his chest.

"This is the end, Lucien," she hissed, as spit flew from her lips.

He reached out for her one final time as the vines wrenched tighter. Lucien's soul departed from his body unremarkably, and with little ceremony. When she was sure he was dead, she withdrew her limbs and gave him a final kick. Pyro staggered to his feet.

"Where's Staccato and Samael?"

"I don't know." Her hands were shaking. "When I stepped out into the hall they were gone."

Pyro squeezed the space between his eyebrows. They were running out of time. His duty was to the hostages. They had to come first, and Staccato would have told him the same. He grabbed Lavanda by the hand.

"Come on, we don't have much time. Did you eat the olive?"

"Yes!"

They sped down the corridor and up a flight of stairs.

"Hey!" A guard skittered onto the landing, blocking their path. Pyro reached for his chakras, but Sonata came swinging down from the ceiling on a tapestry, a trident slung over her back. She kicked the guard in the side of the head. The sentry flew down the stairs.

"Sonata, what are you still doing here?" sputtered Pyro.

"Same as you! Helping everyone escape!"

They mounted the steps as four more soldiers soared down the passage. Pyro lowered his head and blew into his hands until a fireball had formed. Winding back his arm, he chucked it in their path. One of the guards on the left drew back as his robes caught fire. Pyro's breath was cut short as an ophidian soldier plowed into him with unbelievable speed, pinning him to the ground and clawing his face. Nearby, Sonata let out a squeal of pain.

"Sonata!" Pyro could not see what was going on, but was frantic. He opened his mouth and blew a torrent of fire into his attacker's face. The guard scrambled away, writhing on the ground and clutching his skin.

Sonata was balancing on one leg, blood gushing from her lip. The other leg lay on the ground. The soldier gave a triumphant laugh. But Sonata stabbed her trident into the floor, swung herself in an arc, and landed her foot in her attacker's abdomen. She grabbed her missing leg and, with great force, brought it down over his head, rendering him unconscious.

Meanwhile, Lavanda appeared to have poisoned her assailant with some sort of venomous plant of her own creation. She held Sonata up while Pyro hastily helped her to reattach her leg. Together, they ran to the galley overlooking the passage which led to the west tower. It was crawling with soldiers.

"There's more!" shouted one of the guards, pointing in their direction.

"What should we do?" exclaimed Sonata.

Pyro directed them through a side door. "This way! I've got an idea!"

They filed into the room and barred the door. Pyro unlatched the window.

"We're gonna have to climb."

Sonata stuck her head out the window and looked up the steep wall. "Climb? That's impossible!"

Lavanda pushed them aside. "Not with me." Vines materialized out the top of her head, weaving through her hair and up the roof until they had coiled around a chimney. She tore the stalk from her scalp and handed the slackened end to Pyro. "Put her on your back. We'll go much quicker."

"But you're lighter," Sonata protested.

"I can grow vines out of my body to pull myself. It doesn't matter."

Pyro bent down and allowed Sonata to clamber onto his back. Lavanda waved him out the window. "You go first."

"Are you sure?"

"Yes, I'm certain. Just hurry!"

Pyro latched onto a thick, robust vine with both hands. Sonata let out a little groan.

"I gotcha, Sonny. Just don't look down." He began scrambling up the wall towards the roof.

Lavanda snaked another set of vines up the tiles, and towed herself up as though she were being lifted by wires. When they reached the roof, Sonata was eager to get her feet on the ground.

"It's still slippery," Pyro warned. "Don't let go of me!"

Sonata bowed her head against the blast of wind. "Where are we going?"

"To the top of the western tower."

"We're almost there!"

When they reached the crest of the roof, Pyro stood and smiled. The ocean had risen several leagues and was flooding the courtyard below. In the near distance they could see their fellow performers collected on the roof of the west tower. A series of jade banners stamped with scorpions rose up from the sea like the masts of sunken ships rising from a watery grave. A jade light emanated from beneath the glassy, rolling surface, so that the waves glowed like green lanterns. Between the gusts of powerful wind, Pyro could just pick up the faintest stains of music.

"What's going on?" Lavanda clutched the roof. "Everything's flooded!" She narrowed her eyes. "Is that the Sting?"

Pyro threw back his head and laughed. "It sure is! An entire legion of Scorpius's finest soldiers here for a rescue!"

Lavanda's hand flew to the charm around her neck. "That's why you wanted me to take the mermaid's breath!"

A unit of performers consisting of seven members, one of each Fay race, was carrying the Jar towards the edge. Pyro pointed.

"Look! We're just in time to see it go!"

Lavanda shook her head. "See what go? Is that the Jar?"

They could just make out their chant over the high wind. "One … two … three!"

They cast the Jar into the sea where it promptly sank beneath the waves.

"One thing the instructions didn't warn against," explained Pyro, "was underwater voyage, where the ophidians can't interfere. According to Dr. Desmond, the only stipulation is that it must be carried by seven mermaids."

One by one, the performers began taking turns jumping from the west tower. Pyro stood and whistled to one of the seraphs flying overhead.

"*Oi*! We need a lift here!"

Sergeant Graham, a seraph with wavy dark hair and rounded cheekbones, spotted them from afar and began making her way over. Lavanda was still baffled.

"But what about Sonata? She cannot jump in the sea! Not with the Land Lock in place!"

"There are other arrangements in place for our landlocked mermaids." He shielded his eyes against the bright moonlight. "Hiya, Sergeant Graham! We're in need of a lift."

Sergeant Graham saluted and reached for Lavanda. "Three lifts coming right up!"

Before Sergeant Graham could pick her up, Lavanda turned and kissed each of their cheeks. "God bless you both!" She allowed herself to be carried away to the sea.

Sonata turned to Pyro with a relieved smile. "We did it!"

But Pyro could not be relieved. Not when they didn't have Staccato. "Sonny, I have some bad news—"

The tiles rattled beneath them as a tremendous force landed on the roof behind them. Samael had leapt from the neighboring tower, and was now rising up before them, his jaws unhinged, his robes saturated in blood. His eyes narrowed on Sonata.

"It's high time I finished off the rest of you, Princess. How about we start with one of your arms?"

A tremor of flames ran down Pyro's arms as he grabbed the crest of the roof and ignited a barrier of fire between them. Samael merely laughed and tossed his hair over his shoulder. The tiles gave another tremble as he shot into the air, his body stretching over their heads and landing on the other side. Pyro pitched his chakra at the place where Samael stood. The shingle gave way causing him to slip, but Samael pulled himself up until he was scrambling towards them on all fours, his jaws snapping.

They had no choice but to scuttle to their feet. Sonata stabbed her trident at Samael's figure, puncturing the back of his hand. Samael drew back with a howl before backhanding her across the roof. Sonata tumbled backwards, sliding down the incline. Pyro grabbed her by the ankles and hoisted her into his arms just as Sergeant Graham was returning.

"Take her!" He lifted Sonata up towards Sergeant Graham. "Take the princess!"

"Pyro, no!" Sonata reached back for him.

"I'm not leaving you behind! Now go!"

Sergeant Graham carried her into the air. Pyro reached for his chakras just as Samael collided against him. Pyro slid backwards off the roof.

"Pyro!" He could hear Sonata screaming. "Pyro! No!"

But Pyro grabbed hold of the eaves with one hand at the last minute. He swung himself from eave to eave, trying to put distance between himself and Samael. When he thought he had gone far enough, Pyro climbed back over the roof. All was silent save for the wind whistling through the air. Then, a force grabbed him from behind and turned him round. A hand clamped down over his throat. Samael lifted him into the air. Pyro struggled to free himself, clawing at Samael's hands. He would've lit up but he could not do so without oxygen. His boots kicked at the empty air as Samael held him over the side of the roof and grinned.

Over Samael's shoulder, Pyro could see the shape of a sylph, Captain Dudley, heading his way. Pyro tried not to smile as Samael let go, allowing Pyro to fall through the air. Almost immediately, he was caught by his friend. As they lighted back into the atmosphere, Pyro laughed at the enraged expression carved into Samael's features, and waved goodbye mockingly.

Chapter 56:

Pyro Returns

Pyro stood on the platform of the train station outside of Fort Corapinym, flicking his cigarette ashes into the smoky morning air. Following their escape from Apophis Manor, the company had stayed there several days while rounding up a search team and investigating leads. a task force continued to search for Staccato. When nothing turned up, the others had been forced to return to Ascella where they continued to wait for news.

As for Pyro, he had a one-way ticket to Fort Halix. It had been an emotional farewell, even more so due to Staccato's absence. But Pyro believed the best way to help Staccato was by returning to the Saighdeoir and assisting in the search from there.

Further down the platform, a man and a woman were exchanging tearful kisses as they parted ways, prompting a series of unwanted thoughts about Sonata to flood his conscious.

She had come to see him in his room at Fort Halix just before his departure. She'd been so quiet he hadn't even heard her approach. He'd merely looked up to find her leaning against the door frame, the morning sun cascading around her as though it were a spotlight.

"So, I guess this is goodbye then." On her lips she wore a sad little smile, though Pyro suspected it had not been meant to look sad.

He was already wearing his coat and had his hat in his left hand. "I guess so." He didn't know what else to say.

Sonata smirked. "I suppose it had to come sooner or later."

Pyro glanced around the bare room awkwardly. "You can come in, you know. You don't have to keep standing there."

She shifted uncomfortably from one foot to the other. "You look as though you were just leaving."

"Well, I was … but—"

Sonata shook her head. "I don't want to hold you up." She moved away from the frame, allowing him to pass. As Pyro brushed past her, he stopped and turned.

"I really enjoyed getting to see you again, you know." The hall was rather cramped, forcing them to stand closer together than they normally would have.

"I enjoyed getting to see you, too. I'm very happy for you, Pyro. You've wanted this for so long."

A moment passed before he realized what she was referring to. "You—Oh! Returning to the Saighdeoir. Yeah. More than anything." Even he noticed the uncertainty in his own voice. They stared at each other in silence, before Sonata smiled and tossed her head towards the door.

"Well, you better get a move on. The car is waiting for you."

Pyro nodded and doffed his hat. "Goodbye, Sonny." And not sure what else to do, he reached out and gave her hand one last squeeze.

Pyro hardened his face and forced himself to look away from the couple. He'd made his decision, even had his things from Ascella shipped ahead of him, so he couldn't change his mind.

As he was checking his watch, the train pulled into the depot. A hand reached out and grabbed his shoulder.

"Finally coming home, I see," said the familiar voice of Hickory.

Pyro turned around and smirked. "So, we meet again!"

Hickory set down his valise and chuckled. "Thayer told me you would be returning to the Saighdeoir soon. I take it everything went well with the mission?"

Pyro sighed and turned up his collar. "Can't say everything went perfectly. I mean, the Jar is currently on its way back to Virgo, and the pandemic in the Other is finally coming to a close. But I'm afraid we lost someone along the way."

Hickory frowned and bowed his head. "I heard about Mr. Nimbus. I'm so sorry for your loss."

At the word "loss" Pyro felt a twinge of anger that had nothing to do with Hickory. "Don't be sorry yet! They're still searching for him!"

Hickory began to open his mouth but stopped and bit his lip instead. Pyro furrowed his brow.

"What? What do you know that I don't?"

Hickory sighed and shook his head. "I'm sorry to be the one to have to tell you this, but the Saighdeoir is giving up the search for Staccato. They believe he's dead."

"Dead?" Pyro's muscles seized with adrenaline. "That's ridiculous! He can't be dead! He's too valuable! The C.O.N. would never do away with him so quickly! What about Crux? Haven't they searched Crux?"

"Pyro, be realistic for a moment. How could they search Crux?"

"The Sting has infiltrated Crux on a number of occasions!"

"That was before the Land Lock, when the mermaids were able to walk on land and sea. In their present state the Sting can't set foot on shore. Sure, they may have been able to flood the courtyard of Apophis Manor, but flooding Crux for a search and rescue would risk drowning countless prisoners!"

But Pyro wouldn't let it go. "Nonsense! There has to be a way!"

The shrill sigh of the train whistle cut through the air, agitating Pyro further. Hickory pulled his hat down low over his brow and grabbed his suitcase.

"We better get a move on if we don't want to miss the train."

But Pyro took a step back, shaking his head all the while. "I gotta go back."

"Go back?"

Pyro ran back to the ticket booth, calling over his shoulder. "Sorry, Hickory! I'm afraid you're gonna be traveling solo!" He slapped his wallet on the counter of the window and braced the ledge with both hands. "When's the next train to Ascella?"

***

Pyro flung himself out of the taxi and tripped across Feifior's gravel courtyard beneath a moonless sky.

"Mr. Anomaly," sputtered the butler as Pyro burst through the front door. "What brings you back to Feifior?"

"Can't talk now, Kemberling." He didn't even bother to remove his hat and coat. "I need to speak with Thayer!"

"I'm afraid His Majesty and the family have gone out for the evening—"

But Pyro wasn't listening. It was late. *The household will have just finished supper*, he reasoned. Pyro sped down the hallway and burst through the drawing room door. A lone figure hid behind a newspaper.

"Thayer!" Pyro exclaimed. "We need to talk!"

The paper lowered to reveal not Thayer, but a startled-looking Skelter. The moment his eyes registered Pyro, he threw down his reading and stood looking as though he might shout Pyro's name any moment. Before anything could be said, the door opened again.

"Pyro?" Melodious stood on the threshold, anxiously clutching the handle.

"It's me, Mel."

Melodious's bristly mustache stretched as he broke into a grin. "You came back!" He was at Pyro's side in moments, plucking him up off the ground and encasing him in a bone-crushing hug. "Oh, my friend, how good it is to hear your voice again!"

Pyro wriggled around in Melodious's grip, trying to free up some space in his lungs.

"Yeah, I missed you too, Preacher Man. Where's Thayer? I need to speak to him immediately. It's about Staccato."

Melodious gently set him down. "He and the family are having dinner with his cousin, Lady Urbina, that is except for the two princes—"

The door creaked open behind them once more. Pyro turned to find Sonata standing there clutching a tissue, staring at him with red eyes.

"Pyro?"

Melodious moved aside. Pyro stepped forward and removed his hat.

"Hello, Sonny."

Sonata sniffed, her gaze muddied with confusion. "What are you doing here?"

"I changed my mind."

Unlike the others, Sonata did not smile. She did not run to embrace him. Grief had her firmly in its grasp, and it wasn't letting go anytime soon.

"Changed your mind?"

"When I heard about Staccato, I knew I had to come back."

At the mention of her godfather, the corners of Sonata's lips forced themselves downward and fresh tears collected beneath her eyes. Pyro rushed to her side, bracing her shoulders with both hands.

"Hey, listen. Staccato is not dead. Do you hear me? We're gonna find him, and we're gonna bring him home."

"But the Saighdeoir has already declared him dead—"

"What do they know? Look, I've found dozens of missing people. Even got a medal for it. Staccato once pulled all his resources together to save my sorry hide even though I'd done nothing to deserve it. Well, I have resources too! And I'm gonna use them to find Staccato if it's the last thing I do!"

Sonata gazed up at him, her expression difficult to read. At last she sighed.

"Took you long enough!"

Chapter 57:

Cleopatra and the Roman

"All hail Cleopatra!" the owner of the drugstore called from her doorway with a friendly wave.

Faina dropped her head and smiled as she made her way towards the Bowery. "Thanks, Mrs. Rogers!"

The fierce late-December breeze hissed in Faina's face, making the beads of her headdress click together. Peggy Pensky was having an Egyptian-themed New Year's Eve party at her father's restaurant on Elizabeth Street, and everyone was expected to come in costume.

It was a welcome invitation. Things had been dreadfully dreary around the apartment. After the Volstead Act had declared any beverage containing one half of one percent alcohol or more as intoxicating, Uncle Matvei had been forced to shut down his brewery for good. There was to be no beer, no wine, nothing remotely alcoholic. It was the final nail in the coffin for the business which had rocketed her uncle to success. All around the country people would be partying as though the night had no end, but for the Dalka household the mood was far from celebratory, and it did not help that the anniversary of her parents' death had occurred only a week ago. Faina would be happy to forget their troubles if only for a night.

Faina had not lost her enthusiasm for dressing up in fabulous costumes, and she was not about to let their newfound money trouble stop her from attending a glamorous party. Fortunately, creativity was something she and Anya were never short on. For their Egyptian-inspired ensembles, the two had made bracelets from gold paper, beaded headdresses from broken strands of jewelry sewed to fabric headbands, and tassels from embroidery thread.

With the money she'd saved, Faina took things a step further and bought a pot of lip rouge and eyeliner. Anya chose to abstain from face paint but didn't mind helping Faina hide the cosmetics from her father. When Faina had looked in the mirror that evening, it was the first time in ages she'd felt pretty. Her thick hair fell in coils around her shoulders, the black liner appeared to elongate her lashes, and the dark rouge gave her lips definition, endowing her with a more mature look.

If Uncle Matvei had seen her he would never have let her leave the apartment, especially not alone, but Pasha wasn't coming until later, and Anya had to finish babysitting before she could leave. Leo was supposed to escort her to the party but he'd never made an appearance.

After fifteen minutes of waiting, Faina had grown impatient and snuck down the fire escape on her own.

She would be fooling herself if she thought her brother wouldn't mind her walking down the Bowery alone at night, but Faina didn't care. In all likelihood he had snuck off to be with Jazmin somewhere and had lost track of time. If he didn't want Faina embarking on her journey alone then he should have kept a better eye on the clock. Besides, she'd been to the Bowery plenty of times during the day. She was no stranger to rough talk, or shocking sights. It wasn't as though she was going to faint in the middle of the sidewalk.

As the streetlights grew dimmer, the crowds congregating on the pavement grew noisier. Broken beer bottles crunched under her shoes. Faina raised an eyebrow as she stepped around the odorous puddles. Nobody even tried to hide their alcohol.

A trio of drunks swaggered her way, belting out familiar tunes and replacing the lyrics with dirty words. Faina moved to the far edge of the sidewalk and ducked her head inside her collar, hoping to escape their notice. But her hopes were dashed as a whistle pierced her ears.

"Hey, Cleopatra, how's about you let me be your Mark Antony?"

Faina blushed. Didn't they realize how young she was? She glanced at her reflection in a storefront. She supposed the makeup did make her appear older. Something about the whole interaction made her want to pull her coat tighter about her and keep her head down.

The flicker of fear burning in her sternum surprised Faina as she took off in a jog. Any more rude commentary was lost in the distance beneath the clip-clop of her heels. She scanned the road for a familiar face, someone to attach herself to. She had been a fool not to heed Leo's instructions!

The shadows fumbled as someone moved through the alleyway and knocked into a trashcan. Faina swerved sideways, nearly tripping over her own feet. She was about to cross the street, when a broad hand enclosed around her arm like a leghold trap. Faina let out a yell.

"Hey, hey, calm down! It's only me!"

Faina spun around to face her attacker and let out a sigh of relief. It was Anastas, looking sturdier than ever in a shearling leather jacket. Faina steadied a hand over her heart and let out a slow but relieved laugh.

"Thank goodness, it's just you! I thought you were some kinda prowler or something!"

Anastas let go and chuckled. "Nah, just your old pal." He tossed his head towards the alley. "I live in the apartment upstairs. The Breadwinners own the laundromat on the first floor."

Faina nodded her head approvingly but kept her eyes on Anastas. Something about his gait seemed a little unstable as he leaned against the wall of the airshaft.

"Where's Alexei and Vadim?"

"Went over to Brooklyn. I imagine they'll be back sooner or later."

"It must be nice that Vadim is old enough now to keep an eye on Alexei. Gives you more time to yourself." She smiled politely but Anastas wasn't really listening. His eyes, which were looking a little bloodshot, dragged over her.

"Well, aren't you gonna show me your costume? You're obviously going to the party over at Peggy's. Let's have a look."

Faina hesitated for a split second. Something felt off. It was clear Anastas had been drinking, but then it was only Anastas, not a stranger. What harm could he do her? Faina glowed with pride as she slid her coat partially off her shoulders and showed off the tassels she'd sewn onto an old cotton dress. Anastas raised his eyebrows with obvious pleasure and popped a cigarette between his teeth.

"Very nice." He removed a box of matches from his pocket and scraped out a flame. Faina had hoped he would quit after the ice skating incident, but she'd had no such luck. She watched the filter turn bright orange and crumble away. "Them Romans better watch out. Take your coat off, I want the full picture." He pushed off the wall and circled around her, stumbling slightly as he went.

Again, Faina ignored the sinking in her chest. She peeled off her jacket and folded it over her elbow, shivering. Anastas came to a halt over her shoulder. From the corner of her eye, she watched him take a drag from the cigarette.

"You smoke a lot for a thirteen-year-old."

"Don't be such a prude, Faina."

Several moments of silence passed. Faina sucked her breath impatiently and threw out her hands, indicating the costume.

"Well, do you like it?"

Anastas exhaled a thin gray cloud down the back of her neck. "I do."

Faina tensed and waved the smoke away from her hair. Anastas edged around to her front.

"I, uh, especially like this part." He reached up and flicked one of her tassel earrings. "Very nice."

Faina drew back at once, pulling her coat to her chest. "What are you doing?"

Anastas shoved his free hand into his pocket and snorted. "What? Don't tell me that's not the look you were going for?"

Faina's eyebrows drew together as she pulled the coat further up to her chin.

"Of course not! I'm just a kid! Why would you think that?"

"Well, you're wearing all that makeup, for starters. And you ain't that much of a kid." Anastas slid closer until he had her against the wall. "Come on, Faina, you can act as high and mighty as you want but you ain't exactly a nun!" He held his cigarette towards her. "How 'bout a cigarette?"

Faina glared up at him defiantly. "No, thank you!"

He drew another mouthful of smoke and, leaning into her, exhaled it into her face. Terrified, Faina pushed her arms up and shoved him away.

"Get your nasty cigarettes away from me!"

But Anastas pushed right back into her, snickering, and chucking her under the chin.

"I love it when you get that little pout on your face. Come on, just a little puff." He pinched her cheeks and tried to force the cigarette between her lips. Faina's heart jammed into her throat. Her breathing quickened as she wriggled away, appalled, and smacked the cigarette so hard it fell out of Anastas's hand.

"I said no!" She was practically screaming now. Anastas straightened. He took one look at the cigarette lying damp in a puddle and gave an amused simper.

"Alright, alright. Geez! I can take a hint."

Faina jammed her arms through her coat sleeves and fumbled with the buttons.

"That wasn't a hint, it was an order!"

"Can't say I take too kindly to those."

Faina wrenched towards the opening of the alley to leave but Anastas drew her back, pinned her against the wall and kissed her on the cheek. His arms dropped down to his side. Faina gaped at him in frozen disbelief. When nothing else happened, Anastas stared down at her expectantly.

"Well?"

Faina threw up her shoulders. "Well what?"

"Aren't you gonna kiss me back?"

Faina's voice was a harsh whisper. Her anger had surpassed yelling.

"No. No, I'm not going to kiss you back!"

Shadows fell beneath his eyes as he lowered his chin and glared at her. "Why not? You kissed all those other boys."

"I didn't want to kiss all those other boys! Why doesn't anyone understand that?"

"At least you know me!"

Adrenaline blossomed inside her chest as she stomped forward, her fingers curling into fists.

"Which is exactly why I don't want to kiss you! You're a brute!"

Anastas peeled back his lips. "I see how it is. After all these years I'm still not good enough for you, am I? You're too good to be my girl!"

He was beginning to scare her now. Faina drew a deep breath and ducked under his arm, but Anastas snatched her by the hips and pulled her backwards.

"Come on, Faina, I know you want me to kiss you!"

Faina twisted around and batted at his face. "I said n—"

Her words were cut short as Anastas grabbed her shoulders and slammed her savagely against the wall. His breath burned with the chemical smell of liquor as he lowered his face to hers.

"Let me go!" she screamed, trying to kick at him, but Anastas stepped on her feet. "Get off! Get off!"

"Back off, trash!" ordered a feminine voice at the end of the alleyway. Anya grabbed the lid off a trashcan and hurled it at Anastas's head.

Drunken and startled, Anastas jumped and reeled backwards, freeing Faina once and for all. At the sight of little Anya glowering at the end of the passage, Anastas threw back his head and let out a hoarse cackle.

"All you micks are alike, you know that?" He stabbed a glance at Faina. "Both of ya! Like little rat terriers, always thinking you're bigger than you really are!"

Anya plucked an empty bottle from the pavement by the neck and smashed the bottom against the wall. "Don't forget, we can bite!"

Faina was in absolute awe. She could see the well-defined muscles in Anya's arms as she drew back her shoulders in an intimidating stance. Anastas remained unimpressed.

"What are you gonna do? Tell Leo?"

Anya plowed forward in three long strides, holding the jagged end of the bottle aloft like a shining sword.

"I don't have to tell Leo!" Spit flew from her mouth. "The only person I have to tell is Klokov. Or are you so drunk you've forgotten the consequences of breaking your oath to the Breadwinners?"

Faina shivered and bolted around Anastas's frozen figure to Anya's side, who remained warrior-like as she backed them out of the alleyway.

"If I were you I'd turn around, crawl back into that hole you call a front door, and stay there the rest of the night!"

Anastas could harden his face as much as he wanted but he still wouldn't be able to mask the tremulous expression of utter helplessness knotting his brow. He had committed a capital offense. He'd attacked a young woman, and for that he could die. He would die if Anya chose to tell. Faina laid her hand on Anya's elbow. There was heat rising up from her skin through her coat.

"Let's go," Faina whispered. "We've made our point, now let's go."

Anya grabbed her hand and, with her eyes still on Anastas, escorted Faina out of the passage. The moment they were out of sight, they sprinted arm in arm toward the Foxhole. Once the building was in sight they pulled off in front of a darkened stoop to catch their breath. Faina doubled over, grasping the railing, and burst into sobs. Black puddles glared into her vision as the eyeliner moistened and smeared. Still heaving, Anya plodded towards her and wrapped her in a comforting hug.

"Here." She pulled a handkerchief from her pocket. "Take this before you ruin your makeup. Where's Leo? Did you take off without him?"

Faina nodded her head and rubbed the handkerchief beneath her eyes. "He never showed up. Anya, don't tell Leo what happened. If you do, he'll tell Klokov." She looked down at her dress. A smear of red lipstick had managed to find its way onto the white fabric in all the chaos. She couldn't stop staring at it for some reason.

Anya wet her lips and stared off into the distance. Her eyes didn't want to settle anywhere in particular. "Are you sure you don't want to tell Klokov?"

Faina leaned against the wall, hugging herself. "Anastas broke his most sacred rule. The punishment is death. As much as I'd like to see him get punished, I don't want to be responsible for his death."

Anya crossed her arms and massaged her fingers over her left eye. "He's what, thirteen? You really think Klokov is going to murder someone his age?"

"These are thugs we're talking about, Anya. I don't think they make exceptions." She winced and let out another whimper. "Besides, if I do that, everyone will say it was my fault! That I was asking for it by walking down the Bowery on my own with my face painted! My reputation can't survive another blow like that."

Anya sat back on the bannister and tucked her feet beneath her. "Let's at least tell Leo so he can beat the daylight out of him."

"Anya, you know Leo will tell. You know he will!" Faina ducked her head inside her collar. She was ashamed and frustrated. "This is all my fault. Maybe I was asking for it. I deserved this, didn't I?"

Anya knelt down beside her and squeezed her hand. "Of course not! Don't you dare think like that! You did nothing wrong!" She sighed and let her shoulders fall. "Let's go home."

Faina sniffed and tossed her hand up dismissively. "I don't want you to miss the party."

Anya brushed a stray hair from Faina's forehead and squeezed her arm. "Faina, I don't mind. You've been hurt. I'm worried about you."

"If we go home, Uncle Matvei will know something is wrong. And if Leo's back, he'll definitely figure it out." She sopped up the last of the dampness with the handkerchief and forced a smile. "Besides, I think I'd feel a lot safer in a room full of people than I would walking back just the two of us. And if we go to the party, Pasha can escort us home."

"I see your point." Anya hoisted Faina up by the elbow. "Well, if you're sure …"

"I'm sure." Faina brushed the dirt from her knees and steeled her shoulders.

Chapter 58:
A Full Moon

When Leo returned home, Uncle Matvei informed him that Faina had already left for the party, presumably with Pasha. In a way, Leo was relieved; if Faina was already at the party then he wouldn't have to go. Pasha could escort her back, and he could spend the rest of the evening at home. Still, he felt bad for losing track of time. One thing was for sure though, Faina would never let him forget it.

Leo lay on his bed hugging a pillow to his chest, feeling too heavy to do little else. Every gesture made him painfully aware of the weight of his flesh dragging behind his bones, and he craved sleep in a way he hadn't before. He hadn't even bothered to turn on the lights.

"Leo, aren't you going to eat?" Uncle Matvei called from the kitchen.

Leo could smell the butter coating the crispy skin of the halibut all the way from his bedroom. His stomach growled. He rubbed the back of his neck. It wasn't easy for Leo to pass up food, especially good food.

"Uh, yeah!" He hesitated for a moment, then rolled off the mattress. "Yeah, I'm coming, Uncle Matvei."

He smoothed the back of his hair and made his way tentatively towards the kitchen. Uncle Matvei slipped off his oven mitts and hung them over the stove.

"What's wrong with you? You've been back in your room ever since you got home. Your throat's not hurting again, is it?"

Leo hunched his shoulders and pulled out a chair. "No. Nothing's wrong."

"Tired?" Uncle Matvei chuckled and sat down beside him.

Leo nodded so that his bangs flopped against his eyes and poured himself a glass of water. The moment his food touched his plate, he immediately began shoving it into his mouth. Uncle Matvei paused with his fork lifted halfway to his lips and stared at Leo in confusion.

"Son, are you feeling okay?"

Leo froze with his mouth full of mashed potatoes. Uncle Matvei was catching on. He knew he should have skipped dinner and muddled through. But it was too late now. He swallowed his bite and tried to sit up straight.

"Yeah. What makes you think I don't feel well?"

"It's just, you seem a little … down."

Leo's eyes slid instinctively towards his shoes. He had thought he was rather good at hiding his emotions. Perhaps he was wrong.

"Didn't you have fun with your friends?" he pressed further.

Leo jammed a smile into his cheeks and turned up the brightness in his voice. "Oh, yeah! I had a swell time! That's why I came home so late. You know what they say about how time flies."

Uncle Matvei's eyes glazed over skeptically. "Right." After a moment, he set aside his fork and cleared his throat. "I miss them too, Leo."

Leo paused and looked up at his uncle's pitying eyes. Uncle Matvei's brow furrowed.

"I know it's hard for you this time of year."

Leo forced his eyes away, afraid that if he looked at his uncle's sympathetic stare a moment longer, he would burst into tears. To his relief the front door opened at that very moment, and Faina and Anya appeared over the threshold. Uncle Matvei pushed his chair back and stretched his arms over his head.

"Well, well, if it isn't the queens of the Nile!"

Anya took one look at the pair sitting at the table and raised an eyebrow.

"Why are you eating dinner so late?"

"Why are you back so early?"

Anya looked back at the clock and set her purse down on the sofa. "It's nine forty-five. I'd say what you two are doing is by far stranger than returning from a party before midnight, even if it is New Year's Eve."

Uncle Matvei took his napkin and wiped the crumbs from his mustache. "I got caught up doing inventory while I waited for Leo to get home. It was nine when I finally put the fish in the oven."

Leo waited patiently for Faina to go off on him, but she didn't. Instead she went straight to the bathroom. Uncle Matvei's eyes bounced from Leo to the place where Faina had been standing.

"What's the matter with everyone tonight?"

Anya tossed up her shoulders and set about removing her coat and hat. "Maybe it's a full moon. They say it throws everything off."

Uncle Matvei tilted his chair back on two legs and folded his lips over his teeth, trying to remove a bit of food stuck between his incisors. "The full moon isn't until next week, *lapochka.*"

385

Leo glanced over at Anya. Her shoulders were drawn up as though she were keenly aware of her father watching her put away her belongings.

"Well, close enough. You can hardly tell the difference by looking anyway."

Leo squinted his eyes. Anya was hiding something. He listened to the bathroom door open and close and caught a brief glimpse of Faina slipping into the bedroom and closing the door. Leo hastened to clean his plate and rinse off his dishes. The moment he was free, he barged into their room without knocking, hoping to provoke his sister's nerves, but Faina was already in bed with the covers pulled up to her chin and the lights off.

Leo didn't bother feeling his way towards his bedside lamp. Without hesitating, he reached over and flipped on the overhead light. Faina winced and tossed a pillow over her face, but she didn't snap at him. She didn't complain. Leo was at a loss.

"What's wrong with you?"

Faina opened her eyes and rolled onto her back. "What?"

Leo plopped down on the edge of the bed and leaned towards her on his elbow. "It's New Year's Eve, and you're already in bed. Meanwhile, that party's got a good three hours left."

"Oh." Faina shut her eyes and let her head fall to the side. "I'm under the weather, that's all."

The verve was sapped from her eyes. She had lost her spirits. Leo would have accepted this explanation if it hadn't been for Anya's behavior. It didn't matter how earnest her motives were, Anya was the worst secret keeper on the whole block. She certainly kept them all honest.

When Leo looked up again, he was surprised to find Faina staring at him with her brow furrowed. "What about you?"

Leo snorted and pushed himself into an upright position. "What about me?"

"You seem … kinda sad."

Alarmed, Leo got up from the bed and crossed to the dresser. "How on earth could you pick up on that? You've only seen me for two minutes!"

He pretended to be fooling with a stack of books, but he kept his eye on her from the mirror.

"Just a feeling." She rolled back onto her side and hugged her pillow to her body.

Leo wanted her to say more, then he would've believed she was okay. A dark fear was rising up in his chest, and he didn't even know what it was. All he could feel was worry for her. He flipped the lamp on and switched off the overhead light. The blanket sheltering Faina rose and fell with slow, heavy breaths. He crept close to her bedside and laid his hand on her arm.

"I'm sorry I was late. I should've been keeping an eye on the clock."

Her voice was muffled by the covers. "It's okay."

She didn't ask where he was. She didn't ask why he was late. She didn't accuse him of being with Jazmin. Leo coughed and took a step back, afraid he might give himself away, afraid Faina would find out what he'd really been up to that night.

"Goodnight, Checker-Face."

He pivoted on his heel.

"Love you, Leo."

Leo smiled and, turning back around, kissed her on the head.

***

"Leo, wait!" pleaded Anya, hurrying after him down the hallway. "You haven't heard the rest of the story!"

Leo nearly kicked down the door as he marched into the room he shared with Faina, and pulled the covers back from her head.

"What happened?" he demanded.

Faina stared up at him with disoriented eyes. "What?"

He grabbed her chin and turned her head, examining her for injuries.

"Leo, what are you doing?"

He grabbed her hands and pushed up the sleeves of her nightgown. "Are you hurt? Did he hurt you?"

Leo watched her gaze dart to the doorway where Anya stood gaping at Leo with an uneasy expression. Faina groaned and, covering her eyes, flopped back on the pillows.

"Hey!" Leo patted her cheek lightly with the back of his hand. "Did you hear me? Huh? What did Anastas do last night?"

Faina refused to remove her hands from her eyes as the tears flowed over her fingers.

"Leo, I don't want to make things worse! Everyone will say it's my fault! And besides, I don't want to be responsible for anyone's death!"

Confused, Leo grabbed hold of her wrists and pried her hands away. "What are you talking about?"

"If Klokov finds out he'll kill Anastas!"

Leo felt as though someone had reached inside his chest and twisted his heart in the opposite direction. What Anastas had done to his sister was worthy of death by Breadwinner standards, which could mean only one thing. Faina's hand flew up over her mouth as she became aware of the implications of her words.

"I'LL KILL HIM!" Expletives flew from Leo's mouth like missiles.

Faina and Anya flew towards him, grabbing his arms and trying to get him to lower his voice, but Leo was already drawing a warpath towards the door.

"Leontiy!" barked Uncle Matvei as the stairway door slammed open and shut. "What on earth is going on?"

Uncle Matvei rounded the corner, his mustache twitching with shock, but Leo continued to rave.

"The Sippenhaft boy took advantage of Faina!"

It was Uncle Matvei's turn to grow pale now. He staggered backwards. "*Mozhet il tak byt'*?" Can it be? He gave vent to a robust, heart-wrenching wail. "*Moya devushka! Moya bednaya devushka!*" My poor girl!

"No! Listen!" said Faina in Russian, getting out of bed and pulling on her uncle's arm. "Anastas threw me against a wall because I wouldn't kiss him, but Anya showed up before anything else happened."

"Look," Leo pointed a finger in her face, "you need to tell us everything that happened! And if you don't I *will* tell Klokov!"

Faina had no choice now. Sobbing, she told them everything. How Anastas had been drinking, how he had tried to jam a cigarette in her mouth, and how scared she had been.

"But Leo, please, you can't tell!" she pleaded when she had finished. "If you tell anyone it will only hurt my reputation more! They'll say I was asking for it by putting on makeup and going out alone!"

Leo passed a hand over his face and growled under his breath. He understood where Faina was coming from.

"*Moya Faina, tol'ko rebenok!*" My Faina, she's only a baby, Uncle Matvei continued to wail.

Sighing, Leo got up and made his way towards the door. "I won't tell Klokov."

Faina ran after him and grabbed hold of his sleeve. "Leo, I mean it! Do you promise?"

Leo turned and faced her. "I won't have to. By the time I'm finished with him, Anastas Sippenhaft will never bother you again."

Faina willingly let go of her brother's sleeve. Leo slipped down the stairs and into the street with great purpose. His teeth clenched until his ears hurt. He should have been there last night like he said he would. Leo kicked a nearby trashcan, frightening several passersby off the sidewalk. What would their father have said?

Leo arrived at the Foxhole in half the amount of time it should have taken to walk there. Anastas was standing outside, laughing with a few of the other Breadwinners over their late-morning cigarettes. Leo plowed through the gathering with clenched fists.

"What's the big idea, Spichkin?" jeered Anastas.

Leo struck him so hard across the jaw his cigarette split in two. No one made a move to defend him, instead they oohed, and backed up a few feet to make room for the show.

Anastas clutched his jaw in astonishment. But Leo would give him no time to recover. He grabbed Anastas by the scruff of his hair and slammed his face against the brick wall. A few of the boys clapped. Anastas swayed dangerously, looking as though he would black out. Leo wound his leg back and kicked him forward. Anastas went flying onto his hands and knees. Leo circled in front of him, toying with his victim.

"Get up!" he ordered, cursing. But the moment Anastas tried to raise up, Leo kicked him back down again. He spread out his arms in a mocking gesture. "Didn't you hear me, you piece of garbage?" He kicked a pile of rubble in Anastas's face. "I said get up!"

Anastas's face had turned scarlet with rage now. He fumbled to his feet and hurled himself at Leo. Under normal circumstances, Leo might not have been able to hold him off, for Anastas was built like a full-grown man, and Leo was quite small, but adrenaline had possessed his body, and in one swift move Leo was able to put Anastas in a headlock and wrestle him to the ground. Pinning Anastas with his knees, Leo pummeled Anastas repeatedly in the face until bruises began appearing on contact. Having satisfactorily avenged his sister, Leo pinched Anastas's mouth and leaned down so that only he could hear.

"If you ever touch my sister again, if you so much as acknowledge her existence in the street, I will tell Klokov everything. I will order your execution as a personal favor to myself. So if I were you I'd do everything in my power to get on my good side." He spat on his face. "Now apologize."

"I'm sorry," mumbled Anastas.

"What's that?" Leo squeezed harder.

"I'm sorry!"

"Louder!"

"I'm sorry!" shouted Anastas so that he spat blood.

Leo let go, gave the boy's face an open-handed slap, and got up to leave. With his wrath satiated, a new sort of intensity was washing over him. His hands trembled violently, and for a second he felt as though his knees would give out.

Leo veered down the stairs of a vacant building that was under construction, then into the undercroft. Away from the eyes of the city, Leo gave vent to a wild, animal cry and punched his fist through a wall of plaster. A burning sensation came over his hands. He stood gazing at the hole his passions had torn. A smoky smell filled his nostrils. The edges were blackened, almost as though they were charred. Leo scratched at the frayed plaster. It crumbled into ash.

Chapter 59:

Imprisoned

The moment Staccato opened his eyes, he immediately shut them again. The floor seemed to rotate beneath him. He clutched the surface he was lying on. His fingers brushed against a sheet. Something wasn't right, or perhaps it was—though there seemed little reason for things to be so. A pillow rested against his cheek. He moved his leg. A thin blanket brushed over his ankles.

Staccato opened his eyes a second time, ignoring the wave of dizziness that flushed through his sinuses. He was lying facedown on a bed set low to the floor. He pushed himself to a sitting position and placed a hand over his eyes. The gesture had proved more than his body could tolerate.

He surveyed his surroundings. The room was wholly unfamiliar. The walls and floor were of rough, gray stone, like something one might find in a dungeon. The space was roughly eight feet in length and five feet in width, sparsely decorated, with little more than the bed and a moldering chest of drawers in the corner.

Staccato braced himself against the wall and rose. The floor was almost painfully frigid against his bare feet. All his outer clothing had been removed with the exception of his trousers, though his belt was gone. He had only a long-sleeved thermal undershirt to warm his upper body.

As his eyes adjusted to the dim light, he became aware of a narrow door sitting adjacent to the bed. It was only partially closed. Staccato reached for the handle and stuck his head in. It was a small bathroom, complete with shower and mirror. He looked down at the industrial sink. A cup with a toothbrush sat on the corner.

Staccato blinked in confusion. Perhaps he had been rescued after all, though he could not begin to place his surroundings. Logically speaking, he should have found himself back in Ascella if he had managed to be found. But wherever he was, it certainly was not Feifior. Perhaps if he peeked into the hall he might be able to find someone with information. He looked about the room in search of his shirt, but there were no clothes lying about to be found. He eyed the mildewed dresser warily. He almost hoped they wouldn't be in there. He tugged at the handles with two fingers, but the drawer was empty. He checked the bottom drawer but it was no different. He pulled the blanket from the bed and wrapped it over his shoulders like a robe.

He turned the doorknob. It was locked. Staccato's hand dropped lifelessly by his side. Dread awakened his dulled senses. He stepped back and tried turning the doorknob with his powers. An instantaneous flare of unbearable pain, like intense frostbite, seized his muscles. Staccato stumbled back with a cry, clutching his arm.

"I wouldn't do that if I were you," came the disembodied voice of the Cobra.

Staccato stumbled back against the wall, still reeling from the pain, and searching for the source of Samael's voice. "What have you done to me?"

"All I can say is that you won't be needing your powers during your stay. Can't have you escaping now, can we?" He snickered. "Your performance was captivating, by the way. I must say, you almost had me fooled."

Staccato snorted. "Almost? You were gloating a great deal for someone who had it all figured out."

The silence which followed was deadly yet satisfying. But Samael did not take lightly to having his intelligence insulted.

"Pride cometh before the fall, Staccato. We're none of us immune to the old adage, something I would advise you to remember in your position. I'll admit I had my doubts about whether or not it was possible to trap the most powerful miraculous in Voiler, but then everyone has their weakness. And it appears yours is weakness itself."

Staccato cradled his head in his hand, overcome with dizziness once more.

"What do you mean?"

"A weapon is only as good as the person who wields it. The sword and spear are comforting companions to carry in the dark, but they're useless unless one has his wits about him." He paused, an audible smile leaking into his voice. "I'm afraid you don't look so good, Staccato. Perhaps you should eat something."

When Staccato looked up again a full plate of sumptuous food sat on the surface of the dresser, accompanied by a chalice of fragrant, red wine. The place was lousy with dark magic. He wasn't even certain it was really there. Staccato gave a weak scoff.

"You're going to have to do better than that."

"I wouldn't be so suspicious if I were you. You've consumed nothing during your stay so far, yet your senses are corrupt."

Staccato staggered towards the bedpost, feeling weaker by the second.

"Whatever drug you've administered is bound to wear off eventually. This is merely an attempt to issue a second dose."

He climbed onto the bed, reaching for the narrow window ledge just below the seam of the ceiling.

"We're not far from Fort Corapinym, you know. I must say I'm surprised you're willing to risk the Saighdeoir showing up on your doorstep." He peered through the icy bars and, much to his surprise, was met with a gray horizon of foggy ocean.

"I'm afraid the Saighdeoir is not something you or I have to worry about, Staccato."

Staccato narrowed his eyes, desperate to identify a familiar landscape. He could just make out the distinct shape of curved gables stacked one on top of the other. It was the unmistakable skyline of Scorpius. And if Staccato was looking out at Scorpius with an ocean between them, there was only one place he could be.

"Welcome to Crux, Mr. Nimbus."

Chapter 60:
No Turning Back

Faina sat on her bed huddled over the paper heart she had made, nervously biting at the tip of her pencil. It was a frilly valentine complete with lace border and fluffy bow. She'd even managed to draw a halfway-decent picture of a cat in the lower right-hand corner. Carefully, she scribbled Pasha's name, followed by "Love, Faina."

"Faina," called Anya from outside the door. "Papa's leaving for the bank! I'm going downstairs to look after the counter!"

"Okay! Thanks for letting me know!"

Faina stared down at her work, trying to acquaint herself with the reality of what she had written. She imagined handing it to Pasha. What would he do? Would he think she meant it just as friends? When she examined it closer it looked rather juvenile, after all Pasha would be turning twelve just before Valentine's Day. Maybe she shouldn't send it at all. She had one week to make a decision.

As Pasha rapidly took on the appearance of a young adolescent as opposed to a boy, Faina had found herself more and more attracted to him. He had shot up the way a sunflower might, seemingly overnight and with such height he had a tendency to bend forward. His forehead broke out frequently, but it seldom showed for his bangs covered a great deal of it. And his eyebrows were now so thick they appeared almost bushy. His face had thinned and set somewhat, and his shoulders had broadened with his new frame. All these changes, whether good or bad, called Faina's attention to the features which she had always favored in him: his large, brown eyes and his sweet, genuine smile.

But there was a drawback to their new found maturity, one that she had not foreseen. She couldn't remember the last time he had asked to kiss her, and he never asked her to marry him anymore. He had grown out of it, she supposed, which was only natural. But was it possible he had grown out of his crush as well? Now that they were older, Faina had little interest in playing hard to get, and would have happily kissed Pasha if he asked. All the baiting in the world could not get him to admit he had feelings for her. It was now Faina's turn to pursue Pasha, before it was too late.

Leo's measured footsteps echoed in the hallway. Faina hastily slid the valentine into the back of her book and pretended to be reading. The door opened and Leo entered.

"Hey, Leo! How was school?"

"Fine. Nothing exciting to report."

Faina couldn't help but notice that he seemed unusually sullen, flat even.

"Is something wrong?"

He plopped down on the bed and eyed her suspiciously. "No. Why would anything be wrong?" He tossed his backpack aside.

The bag slumped over, partially spilling its contents onto the floor. Faina immediately got down on the floor to help her brother collect his belongings. A small, velvet box had stopped just short of the dust ruffle on her bed. Faina stared down at it with curiosity. It looked like something one might house new jewelry in.

Leo appeared not to have noticed its disappearance. Faina hid the box behind her knee and handed him a folder that had fallen on the floor.

"Thanks." He was so moody he didn't even bother to look at her as he took it.

Faina waited until Leo had settled onto the bed and opened his textbook before turning her back on him and examining the box. Carefully, she picked it up and turned it over in her hand. She recognized the gold embossed seal as belonging to a jewelry store on Stanton. Faina's mouth collapsed into a suspicious frown. She flipped open the box. Inside was a diamond ring that could only have been purchased with Leo's bootlegging money. The gem was circular in shape and only slightly smaller than a dime.

Faina's mouth hinged open in shock. She looked back at her brother, aged seventeen, with his skinny neck, and stubble-free chin, and her pulse trilled beneath her skin. She leapt to her feet and, taking a pillow from her bed, hurled it at Leo's face. Leo threw up his hands.

"Ow! What was—" He froze when he saw what Faina held in her hands.

"Leo, what's this?" She held the box up. When he didn't answer, she stamped her foot and repeated herself. "What's this?"

"It's none of your business, that's what it is!" He got up and snatched at the box but Faina was too quick for him. She ducked under his arm and ran to the door.

"You've been sneaking around with Jazmin again!"

"So what? I wouldn't have to if her father would just give me a chance!"

"And you think marrying her is going to change that? Leo, you are seventeen! You can't get married at seventeen! Why would you even want to?"

Leo hunched his shoulders. "Who says that's an engagement ring?"

"If it's not an engagement ring then why are you hiding it?"

Leo made to grab it again but Faina dodged him.

"I wasn't hiding it, I just don't want to lose it!"

Faina placed her hand on the doorknob. "In that case, you wouldn't mind me telling Uncle Matvei about—"

"No!" Leo cut her off. There was a wild look about him now. He smoothed his hair back in an unsuccessful attempt to appear calm. "Look, you're too young to understand! Okay?"

"And you're too young to get married! Besides, it's illegal! You have to have parental consent to get married before you turn eighteen."

"Not in New Jersey!"

"You've lost your mind! Uncle Matvei's going to have a cow!"

Leo shook his fists, but quickly composed himself. "Faina, I love Jazmin. When two people love each other they get married."

"So get married in a year!"

Leo tightened his lips and held up his hand as though the gesture would somehow keep him from flying off the handle. "I can't wait a year."

Faina could hardly stand his lack of reason a moment longer. She stamped her foot, raising her voice to new heights now. "Why not?"

"Because I just can't!"

Weary of arguing, Faina turned towards the door and cupped a hand over her mouth. "Anya!"

Leo flung his hands over his head in exasperation, hushing her until spit sprayed from his mouth.

"Shhh! Shut up! Shut up!" Leo twisted his arm around her neck, fastening her in a headlock. Faina tried to cry out but he slapped a hand over her mouth.

"Listen to me, big mouth! I got a reason for everything. So get off my back!"

Unable to stand being trapped any longer, Faina stuck her tongue out and licked his palm. Leo jumped back in disgust, dropping her on the floor, and wiping his hand on the knees of his trousers.

"Ugh, what is wrong with you?"

Faina scurried up off the floor and jabbed an accusing finger at his face. "You're barely out of school yet! You don't even have a real job! Why would you run off and marry Jazmin?"

Leo slid his fingers through his hair and let out a desperate groan. Faina watched him with a raised eyebrow as he crouched down on his knees and lowered his voice.

"Because I *have* to marry Jazmin! Don't you get it, smarty-pants?"

Faina leaned back on her elbows and rolled her eyes. "Oh, that's right, because you're sooooo in love you can't wait a year like a normal person!"

Leo reached forward and yanked her hair so hard she let out an involuntary cry.

"No! You're not paying attention! Look at me!" He forced her head around by the chin and drilled into her eyes with an intensity she rarely witnessed from him. "Even if I didn't want to marry Jazmin, which I do, I *have* to marry Jazmin."

Faina stared at him uncomprehendingly for a moment. Then it dawned on her.

"You didn't." Her voice was one harsh, disparaging hiss. "Leo, you didn't!" She backed away from him, shaking her head and narrowing her eyes. Leo closed his eyes and rubbed a hand down the side of his face.

"Faina, listen, you can't tell anyone, not yet—"

"I knew this would happen! I knew it from day one!"

Leo gaped at her, his eyebrows lowered. "What do you mean you knew?"

Faina threw her hands up. "Typical Leo, always assuming everything's going to turn out perfect, because why wouldn't it for someone so amazing?"

"What are you talking about?"

"You're an airhead! A pretty boy! You're so used to being popular, and having things go your way, that it's made you completely naive! When the Bolsheviks were executing people in Yekaterinburg, all you did was wave your hand and say everything was going to be fine! And then Mama and Papa were killed! After you became an associate for the Breadwinners you were completely shocked that Jazmin's parents thought you were a two-bit hood! Her family was never going to approve of you, but you couldn't accept that because you live in a complete fantasy world!"

Leo ground his teeth together and hunched forward. "So I should be like you? Moping around all the time when things go wrong? Complaining about how no one understands? Being a complete drama queen, and making people uncomfortable all the time with your brutal honesty? Honestly, what's so wrong with being optimistic?"

"This isn't about me, it's about you! What you did was selfish!" She ripped another pillow off her bed and bashed it over his head with such force she knocked him onto the floor. "Did you ever stop and think about what might happen to Jazmin? You don't know what it's like getting names hurled at you every day! Being bullied by adults you've never even met! I never wanna hear one word about how I got kicked out of school ever again!"

Leo shielded himself with his arm and held up his hand in surrender. "Hey, hey, I'm trying to do the right thing, aren't I? I'm doing this so she *won't* be ruined!"

Faina twisted the pillowcase in her fist as though it were Leo's own neck. "How stupid do you think people are? She's seventeen! If she marries you and pops out a baby nine months later people are gonna know why!"

Leo put a finger to his lips and hissed. "Would you keep it down? And do you gotta be so blunt about everything?"

"You know I'm right!"

Leo turned on his side, his head in his hands. "Yeah, I know."

Faina took a step back. "The night of the party … that's why you were late! You told me you were with friends, but really you were just—"

Leo looked up at her with openly apologetic eyes, looking small and weak for once.

"I'm sorry, Faina. I know you don't believe me but I am sorry. I shoulda known you would've gone off by yourself when I didn't show up. But I was too caught up doing what I wasn't supposed to be doing. And because of that you got hurt, and Jazmin … Well, I guess I hurt Jazmin too." He jerked his head down as his lower lip began to tremble. "I hurt her future, but I'm trying to fix it! I'm gonna fix it the only way I know how."

Faina bent towards him. Her hand found its way over her heart. She reached out and pulled his head against her side and held it there.

"Hey, Jazmin isn't the first girl to have a pea in the pod before she's shackled, certainly not in this part of town. But you know what? Jazmin is lucky, because she's got something most of those other girls don't have. She's got someone willing to do right by her. And more than that, she's got a beau who actually loves her. And if you ask me, that's all it takes to get a happy ending."

Leo sniffed and scrubbed at his eyes with his sleeves, unable to stop the tears. Faina sat down on her bed.

"As for what happened to me …" She sighed and glanced down at her feet. "I should have listened to you."

"Faina, what happened to you wasn't your fault."

"Well, it wasn't your's either. You couldn't have predicted that."

"Still …" Leo's voice was strained and hoarse. "I'm supposed to be there to defend you."

"Well, you did. Or have you forgotten about the black eye you gave him?" She took a handful of his hair and ruffled it. "Leo, if you still have that ring, does that mean Jazmin's told you the news, and you didn't ask her to marry you on the spot?"

Leo sat up and dried his eyes. "No, I asked her already. I just didn't have the ring on me, is all. I was gonna take it to her this evening. I've had it for months."

Faina narrowed her eyes. "If you didn't know Jazmin was pregnant until today, why did you want to run off and marry her before?"

A blush germinated across his cheeks and nose. "Because I thought it was the right thing to do anyway." He shifted awkwardly. "That's what Pa would've wanted me to do … if anything did happen, then we'd already be married."

"But you still love her, right?"

"I'm crazy about her." Leo gave her a weak smile. "You think I would've gone through all this trouble of sneaking around if I didn't?"

Faina's eyes glazed over as a wry smile appeared on her lips. "Is that what people do when they're in love? Get in a lot of trouble?"

Leo laughed. "If you're like me and you ain't too careful."

Faina gestured for him to sit down on the bed beside her.

"So, I'm assuming she said yes?"

"Yeah, she said yes." Leo lowered himself to a seat. "That doesn't mean her parents are gonna approve though."

"Under the circumstances I don't think you have to worry about them saying no, but I wouldn't expect them to be happy about it. Does anyone else know?"

"Jazmin may have told one of her sisters."

"When are you gonna tell Uncle Matvei?"

Leo took a long breath and let his hands drop. "Guess I better do it soon. It'll be worse if he has to find out from someone else, or if Mr. Zureiq shows up at our door."

Faina flopped onto her side and watched the sun wash streaks of scarlet through his hair. It was hard to imagine how Uncle Matvei would react.

"If you want, I can be with you when you tell him. You know, for moral support."

Leo smirked and reached up over his shoulder to pat her hand. "Thanks."

Chapter 61:
The Stalker

Lydia sat at the vanity backstage, watching the dancers apply powder to their décolletage, knees, and ankles of all places. The air reeked of cold cream, cheap perfume, and Marlboros. Lydia kept her trench coat pulled tightly about her neck, avoiding her own reflection. No matter how many times she wiped her face clean, she knew her skin was stained with rouge. She may not have been a dancer, but that didn't stop the owners of the speakeasy from making her dress like one.

Lydia had not anticipated what an opportunity Prohibition might be for someone as desperate as her. When she had failed to land a job by Christmas, the illicit offer had seemed like a godsend. After all, there were so many worse illegal activities she could be doing to get by. Furthermore, she only had to work nights, allowing her an unprecedented amount of time with her children during the day. But it did not come without costs.

Ethel, a fellow waitress, appeared in the doorway, her cigarette hanging out the corner of her mouth. Lydia wrung the lapels of her coat with both hands.

"Is he gone?"

Ethel plucked the cigarette from her heavy lips with two fingers and blew into the air.

"Dina says she saw Piyakov step out fifteen minutes ago, but he never came back. I imagine he got tired of waiting on you and decided to go home."

"Thank goodness."

Ethel swaggered towards the vanity in her skinny heels and leaned against the counter.

"You know if he tries anything funny the manager will have him out on his ear."

"I'm afraid that does little to help me outside the club."

"Blanche says he followed you home last week. That true?"

"Last week, the week before … He's done it three times now!" Her pulse beat faster against the inside of her wrist. "Last time he stayed in the courtyard for a whole hour after I went inside."

Ethel's penciled-on eyebrows quickly rose to her hairline. "Sounds like you need to find yourself a man!"

"A man?" Lydia snorted. "That is the last thing I need!"

"Not just any man! I mean a big, hardboiled johnny. A protector. Someone all muscled up and brawny."

Lydia packed the remainder of her belongings into her purse and stood.

"Yes, well, perhaps I'll run into one between caring for my two children and serving cocktails to perverts. Take care, Ethel." She turned and headed for the door.

"Buh-bye, doll! Stay safe!"

Lydia braced herself against the bitter wind that flooded the fire escape. The door banged shut behind her as she pulled her coat tighter. Her gloved fingers braced the railing, too thin to shield her from the freezing burn of steel.

She made her way onto the street. The crowds had thinned since the club closed, and she couldn't decide if the quiet comforted or unnerved her. Ice glazed the pavement like hardened frosting. As she turned up Orchard Street the echo of her footsteps seemed to duplicate. She glanced over her shoulder. No one was there.

She pressed onward, ducking her chin into her collar. The footsteps continued. She looked again. Several paces behind her was a male figure with an unkempt, slouching silhouette. Above the shrill wind she could hear him singing a lewd song. It was Piyakov.

Lydia dashed to the opposite side of the street. She jogged around the corner, not caring that her scarf had fallen away. When she made it to her destination, she turned around in search of her pursuer. She had lost him. Lydia leaned against the wall of the neighboring tenement building, her hand pressed over her chest. Surely, he would grow tired of chasing her home every night when he failed to get what he wanted.

She turned and headed for her own apartment building. Lydia's fingers reached for the railing of the front steps. A hand shot out and grabbed her forearm. Lydia let out a cry. Piyakov wrenched her towards him, his breath moist and saturated with foamy, fermented beer.

"You enjoy playing hard to get, don't you, *lapochka*?" He pulled her close, but Lydia rammed the toe of her shoe into his shin. He drew back and let go.

Lydia didn't bother with the door key. She ran straight for the courtyard and scurried under the fire escape. She jumped and grabbed hold of the ladder, pumping her legs in an attempt to pull it to the ground. Just as it was giving way, Piyakov grabbed her around the waist, and pried her from the rungs.

Desperate for help, Lydia screamed and writhed, but even when inebriated Piyakov was strong. He clutched her tighter. Lydia's stomach turned as his calloused hand pressed over her lips. Refusing to be overcome, she bit down on his fingers. Piyakov dropped her on the pavement. Lydia landed hard. She could feel a bruise welling up on her lower back.

"Ma!" Lydia looked up. Pasha was leaning over the fire escape with horrified eyes.

Piyakov grabbed her by the hair and hoisted her back into his arms.

"*Svolotch*!" A bell rang as the door of *Opa!* tore open and slammed shut.

With an angry war cry, Matvei barreled into the courtyard armed with a Louisville Slugger. Piyakov stumbled back in alarm. In a display of intimidation, Matvei struck a nearby trashcan with all the power his hand could muster, blasting it onto the sidewalk.

"Hey!" Leo vaulted over the bannister of the fire escape, swinging down from the landing with one hand. He jumped to the ground and pointed a handgun in Piyakov's face.

Leo didn't even have to utter a threat. Piyakov turned and ran off into the misty night, disappearing behind a cloud of snow. Leo sheathed his gun in the waistband of his pajama pants. Matvei stared down at the boy with wide, incredulous eyes. For a brief moment their gazes met.

Lydia fell back against the wall with a wail of horror. Matvei and Leo each took an elbow and helped her into the shop. Through her tears, Lydia could see Pasha standing at the edge of the fire escape. His hand dangled lifelessly by his side, his mouth stretched open in shock.

Chapter 62:
Man of the House

Pasha removed the wooden spoon from the pot and laid it on the trivet.

"Dinner's ready, Katya."

He turned down the dial of the stove and removed his apron. Mama was resting before she returned to work. He'd begged her not to return after last night's ordeal, but what choice did she have? Pasha tiptoed back to his mother's room to wake her. After knocking twice with no answer, Pasha gently pushed open the door.

"Mama?"

At the sight of his mother, Pasha immediately blushed and shut the door. Lydia had been asleep with her back towards the entry, wearing only her drawers. Her soft, clean skin was marred with a black-and-yellow bruise on her lower back measuring about the same width as a grown man's hand. A melted icepack lay on the floor, as though it had been kicked off the bed. Pasha crossed to the sitting room where Katya played, trying to forget the sight of his mother stretched out in her underwear, but no matter what he could not erase the massive bruise staining her skin, like mold on an otherwise pristine piece of bread. He placed a hand on Katya's shoulder.

"*Katenka*, can you go wake Mama and tell her it's time to eat?"

Katya happily obliged, and he went about setting the table. Moments later, his mother emerged fully clothed. An enormous shiner had materialized above her left eye.

"Ma!" Pasha's words came out in a breath.

Lydia made no pretenses as she sat down at the table. "Oh, *Patulya*, darling, don't make such a face, I'm trying to forget it's even there."

As she scooted her chair, she winced and put a hand to her lower back. Pasha continued to stare at her in shock.

"He hit you in the head!"

Lydia picked up her spoon and thrust it into the broth. "No. That's where my head collided with the ladder of the fire escape." She shoveled a spoonful into her mouth. "Thank you for making dinner, Pasha, dear. It's wonderful as always." She waved him towards the spot next to her. "Now sit down and eat before it gets cold."

Pasha carefully pulled out his chair, eyeing her all the while. As Lydia reached for a glass of water, her sleeve fell back exposing the hand-shaped bruises on her forearm. Pasha's eyes nearly left his skull. Lydia placed her hand on his.

"I'm fine, Pasha. There's no use getting upset. It's all over now."

"But it could happen again—"

"Pasha, there is nothing you can do about it, sweetheart. So, what's the use of working yourself up? Hm?"

"I don't understand. Why can't we call the police?"

Lydia shut her eyes and exhaled as though steeling herself for a difficult conversation.

"Because I work at a speakeasy. Do you know what a speakeasy is?"

"It's a place that sells illegal alcohol."

"That's right. If we called the police they'd want to know why I was out late at night by myself. If they found out I was working at a speakeasy I could get in a lot of trouble, and so would all the people I work with. I'm not the only one in need of a job you know."

Pasha frowned and stared dismally down at his soup.

She lowered her voice. "I have a gun. Okay? Your mama knows how to defend herself. She's no stranger to hard times."

Pasha bent his head forward in defeat. Katya was staring worriedly at the shiner on their mother's forehead. Lydia clicked her tongue.

"Come now, both of you, eat your supper."

Pasha tore off a bite of his bread but he could hardly bring himself to chew. The last words his father had shared with him before he died kept repeating in his mind: *You are the man of the house now, Pavlo. You must take care of your mother and sister.*

***

At ten o'clock in the evening, long after Katya had fallen asleep, Pasha snuck out his window, determined to do what needed to be done. The city grew louder as he reached the Bowery, where thirsty faces lurked under the dusty tracks of the El Train in search of a good time. Pasha had never been to the Foxhole, but he recognized it from Leo's stories, and the odd gang symbol painted over the doorway. Overhead, young women in short, flashy dresses leaned over the balcony.

After staring blankly at the entrance for some time, Pasha drew a deep breath and opened the door. He was immediately overcome with the sharp, dry smell of spirits, blood, and body odor. Stratus clouds of pale, brown tobacco smoke perfumed the air. A beautifully crafted bar wound almost the entire length of the room, complete with a polished brass rail, and just about every bottle of liquor Pasha had ever heard of. The space was enormous, and yet every spare corner was crowded with sweaty, overheated men.

At the center of the room beneath an overcrowded awning of drooling spectators was a raised platform where two brawny boys, both about sixteen, battled each other in their undershirts, banging their fists against each other's heads. When one finally went down, a deafening bell clamored overhead, and a short, boulder-like bald man waddled into the ring to declare the winner. As he lifted the victor's fist over his head, and placed a load of bread in his free hand, the light flickered in his right eye—or at least, what Pasha had thought was his right eye. It was actually a Russian kopeck, situated in the vacant socket with the eagle side facing outwards. Pasha swallowed. This was Klokov; this was the man Pasha had come to see.

When the excitement of the victory began to wane, the spectators began crawling back towards the bar and billiards. Klokov took his place at the bar with his back turned, laughing and cutting up with a few of the street fighters. Up until that point, no one had noticed Pasha. But as he timidly neared Klokov's imposing figure, people turned their heads, including the boys Klokov was conversing with, one of which was unfortunately Anastas.

Pasha caught Sergei looking up from a game of pool. The boy froze.

Pasha cleared his throat. "Excuse me, Mr. Klokov?"

The area around them grew silent as Klokov turned and snatched the cigar from his lips. His single eye scrutinized Pasha from head to foot. He must have been accustomed to young boys approaching him in such a manner, for instead of dismissing Pasha, he said in a short, gravelly voice, "What can I do for you, boy?"

Pasha felt his mouth grow dry. Once he said it there was no going back.

"I—I'd like to become a Breadwinner, please."

Already the amused grin was growing on Anastas's face. "You? A Breadwinner?"

Klokov merely smiled. "A new recruit, eh?"

"Sure you didn't get lost looking for your mother?" Anastas elbowed the boy sitting next to him. "I hear she's working on the Bowery these days."

Pasha shot him a single, fiery glance, but Klokov ignored him altogether.

"I'm assuming you're interested in street fighting. How old are you, kid?"

"I just turned twelve." As the last word departed his lips his voice cracked, sending the older boys into fits of hysterics.

Anastas slapped the counter and chortled. "He even still sounds like a baby!"

Klokov inhaled his cigar. "Normally, I don't let anyone in under fourteen." He tilted his head, sizing Pasha up.

"I hear you make exceptions."

A smirk tugged at the corner of Klokov's mouth.

"I do, on occasion."

Anastas watched the exchange with his mouth hanging open in disbelief.

"Oh, come on! We still talking about this? He ain't Breadwinner material!" Anastas hopped down off the stool and grabbed Pasha by the chin, turning his head so that Klokov could see a scar just below Pasha's ear.

"You see that scar, right there? That's my handiwork!"

Pasha wrenched his head away, his cheeks burning with indignation. "Don't flatter yourself! The cut's from the chain-link fence. All you did was push me up against it."

"Give it a rest, Anastas!" Pasha turned round to see Yuri making his way through the crowd. "Everyone knows you don't want Pasha becoming a Breadwinner because you're afraid he'll lick you like he did in the fourth grade!"

Anastas turned on Yuri with a vengeance in his eyes.

"If I were you, Mishkin, I'd shut that mouth of yours. Or do you want any more of your teeth knocked out like last week?"

Weary of Anastas's interruptions, Klokov sneered and waved him towards his seat.

"Rogue, sit down, why don't you? Show some respect!"

At Klokov's command, Anastas did as told, though it was clear from his expression he wasn't happy about it. Klokov turned to Pasha with an apologetic expression.

"It takes guts to come in here and ask to be a Breadwinner. That in itself is worthy of honor." He scratched the side of his face. "However, you are a little on the scrawny side."

407

"Most people consider me tall for my age."

"You are, and I have no doubt you'll grow more in time. But it ain't just your height I'm referring to. You're thin. You ain't got a lot of bulk."

"Which makes me quick."

Klokov suppressed a chuckle. "That ain't exactly how it works." He paused, appraising his cigar. "But tell me, why is it you're interested in becoming a Breadwinner?"

Pasha hardly paused for a breath as he recounted his story. How his mother had ended up working in a speakeasy, how a man at the bar began stalking her.

"If I become a Breadwinner then my mother will never have to work at a speakeasy again."

Time seemed to tick by in a slow measure as Pasha watched Klokov suck thoughtfully on his cigar, a cloud of smoke wreathing his head.

"Where is this speakeasy where your mother works?"

"It's called the Panther, over on Canal Street. She doesn't know I'm here."

Klokov chuckled and shook his head. "I bet she doesn't. What's her name?"

Pasha hesitated, wondering what on earth he could want her name for. "Lydia Chevalsky."

"And this man, do you know his name?"

"Johann Piyakov."

"I know Piyakov."

He beckoned two of his underlings closer, and whispered something in a low voice. The two men nodded and left. Pasha didn't know what to say, but Klokov simply leaned back and puffed on his cigar.

"I'll have two men keep an eye on your mother for the rest of the night. No harm will come to you or her. Now, tell me, are you familiar with our initiation rituals?"

Pasha's eyes widened. He couldn't believe it. He was actually being considered!

"Somewhat."

"We start out with a blindfolded gang beating." By the casualty of his voice one might have thought Klokov were reciting an advertisement for a family-owned bakery. "You know what a gang beating is?"

Pasha nodded his head as Klokov went on to describe the three phases of initiation.

"For the next nine or so years you will spend your time street fighting three to five times a week. On those days you will be required to either steal or bootleg and report back with your goods at sundown. The products you acquire will then be sold in the Paddock, or the black market, to help support the brotherhood."

"Does that mean when I grow up I have to be a—" Pasha could not think of the correct term. Thug? Gangster? Mobster? They all sounded too offensive.

"A foot soldier?" Klokov shook his head. "We're a diverse family here. We got Breadwinners all over the country, in places I bet you didn't even know about. We got lawyers, musicians—one of the best street fighters we ever had is now a chef at the Waldorf Astoria. We even got police officers." He turned and snuffed out his cigar in the nearby ashtray. "You see, kid, contrary to what you may have been taught, we 'thugs,' as we're called, are living the American dream, taking hold of the promises that brought us to this country in the first place. It's kids like you, hardworking, immigrant bucks, that are the reason the Breadwinners exist at all. To help people, *our people*, make a better life, the life they were promised when they came to these shores."

Pasha felt a wave of relief rush over him. He wouldn't be sacrificing a normal life. There was still hope. Why, being a Breadwinner sounded no different than being an alumnus.

"So, what do you say, kid? You in?"

"I'm in!"

A broad smile unraveled across Klokov's jowls. "How soon can you start the first stage of your initiation? I understand if you need to schedule a time when your Ma's less likely to find out what you're up to."

"I can start tonight."

Klokov's eyes widened in pleasant surprise. "Very well then." He got up and motioned for the nearest street fighters to follow him. "To the Crucible."

The moment the party began moving towards the basement, Sergei rushed up to Pasha.

"Pasha, you sure you wanna do this?"

Before Pasha could answer, Yuri was on his other side staring at Sergei in disbelief.

"Shhh! What do you think you're doing? You wanna get him blacklisted? He can't back out now!"

"The first trial hasn't started yet. There's still time!"

But Pasha shook his head. "I don't need any more time. I know what I want."

He moved to follow Klokov, but Sergei stopped him with an outstretched hand. "You think you know what you want. But there's no going back after—"

"Broadshanks," barked Klokov, calling Sergei by his street-fighter name, "you can congratulate him later, you're slowing him down."

Pasha slipped Sergei a pleading look. "You had to do this too, once. Now I have to do it."

Chapter 63:
Selling One's Soul

"Come on, Leo, get a wiggle on!" Faina pranced down the sidewalk, swinging her basket.

The snowfall had thinned somewhat, and the sidewalks reeked of salt that crunched beneath the treads of Faina's wellington boots. Behind her, Leo groaned.

"Faina, slow down! Why do you always have to be so perky in the morning?"

"Aw, quit your griping! You could use the fresh air! Besides, if you don't hurry up all the good chickens are gonna be taken, and Jazmin wouldn't like that!"

Leo and Jazmin had only been married a week and were now living in the apartment directly above the Dalkas at half the price, thanks to the graciousness of Uncle Matvei. Though Jazmin's family had not been pleased with the situation, they were grateful that Leo was willing to do right by her, and had finally managed to come around in the end.

Leo ground to a halt as Faina stopped in front of the Waidelich's fruit cart to examine an apple.

"I tell you what!" He rolled his neck. "These pregnancy cravings are killing me!"

"Don't worry, Leo." Faina turned around and patted his stomach. "I'm sure the baby will be here soon. I think I can feel it kicking!"

Leo flashed her a sarcastic smile. "Alright, wise guy."

Faina slipped the money into the girl's hand. "Thank you, Katherine!"

"Men." She snorted, and continued down the sidewalk. "Woman has to carry his baby for nine months, but guess which one's doing all the griping?"

"Hey, you try to find …" He paused to consult his list. "Tahini and ba—ha … baharat."

Faina tossed him one of her apples. "Little Syria. Or you can go to Brooklyn."

Leo stared at her in disbelief. "Why can't I just pick it up from Mr. Cuppenheimer's?"

"It's a Syrian dish. You ain't gonna find Middle Eastern spices in a shop owned by Germans. How long have you lived in New York City now? Clearly, you need to expand your horizons!"

He hurried to catch up with her and roped an arm around her shoulder. "You're a lifesaver, Checker-Face! How can I ever repay you?"

"Give me the naming rights to your firstborn child."

Leo chuckled and took a bite of his apple. "Nice try."

Just as Faina was sinking her teeth into the crisp skin of her fruit, she spied Pasha's duck-tail cowlick from amongst the crowd gathered about the fishmonger's.

"Hey, look! There's Pasha!" Shoving the apple into her basket, she took off in a mad dash to catch up with him. "Pasha! Wait up!"

She could hear Leo whining in her wake. "Not again, Faina! Slow down!"

Faina grabbed hold of his shoulders with both hands. Pasha gave a cry and stumbled backwards clutching his ribs. His cap was pulled down low over his forehead.

"What's wrong?" Faina rushed forward to examine him for injuries. "Are you alright? I didn't mean to hurt you!"

"I'm fine, Faina."

As he held up his hand to ward her off, Faina noticed a blackish welt on the back of his palm.

"Pasha, your hand!" She grabbed him by the wrist before he could take it away. "What happened?"

Pasha turned away, his chin still tucked to his chest. "I, uh, accidentally smashed it in a doorway."

Faina narrowed her eyes. He was clearly being evasive. "Why are you acting so strange?"

"I don't know what you're talking about."

"Yes, you do! You won't look at me!" She inched closer. "Is it because you're mad? I didn't mean to hurt you!"

"No, that's not it at all!"

As Pasha backed away, he collided with a man passing through the crowd, bumping him forward and knocking the hat from his own head. A black bruise was creeping down from the bottom of his eye to the corner of his mouth. There was an open cut on the left side of his forehead.

Faina pulled down his scarf, revealing the lower half of his face. A scab was forming beneath his nose.

For a fleeting moment, Faina felt as though her heart had been plunged into darkness.

"Pasha." Her voice was hardly above a whisper. "You didn't. Tell me you didn't!"

Pasha retrieved his cap and looked down at his feet. "Didn't what?"

Faina craned her head back, the tears welling up in her eyes. "I knew you were asking too many questions about the Breadwinners lately!"

"I had to do it, Faina!" Pasha wrung his cap with both hands. "What other choice did I have?"

But Faina was already headed in the opposite direction. "Leo! Leo!"

Leo was shuffling along, only a few yards away. "What? What are you shouting for?"

"Pasha's sold himself to the devil!"

Leo looked as he often did when he was about to scold Faina for being overly dramatic. "What on earth are you talking about?"

She towed him back to where Pasha was standing with both hands shoved deep in his pockets.

"He went to Klokov and enlisted in the Breadwinners! Leo, you have to do something! You can't let them do this to him!"

Pasha looked up at them with mournful eyes, exposing his gray bruises to the sunlight. Leo seemed frozen. The wind railed against his back until finally he spoke.

"They already put you through the first stage, didn't they?"

Pasha said nothing but nodded his head. Leo passed a hand over his eyes, looking greatly distressed.

"Then there's nothing I can do."

Faina drew back in consternation. "What do you mean there's nothing you can do? You're one of Klokov's favorites, aren't you?"

"It ain't that simple, okay?" He pasted his hand over his mouth and shook his head. "If I try to get him out of it, or if—Heaven forbid—he fails the initiation, he'll be worse off than before."

"They'll really blacklist him?"

"Even if Klokov decided not to blacklist him, the city will. It's an unspoken rule, I've seen it happen before. There ain't a single business in all five boroughs that would give him the time of day, or anywhere in Jersey for that matter."

Pasha eyed Leo with wariness. "You've seen kids fail the initiation before?"

413

"Oh, yeah. Loads of times. You remember my friend Myer Jannowitz? Why do you think he left New York? They pockmarked his whole family!"

Faina put a hand to her head and swallowed. Myer Jannowitz was a pretty big fella, and a tough egg at that. She looked back at Pasha with his gentle eyes and thin, wiry frame. If Myer Jannowitz couldn't make it through the initiation, what chance would Pasha stand?

"I can't do this, can I?" said Pasha, suddenly growing anxious. "I'll never make it, just look at me!"

"You don't know that yet." Leo sighed and licked his lips. "There's nothing I can do to get you out of this. But that doesn't mean I can't help you get through it."

Faina clutched her brother's arm. "But Leo, you have to get him out of it! Pasha's not a street fighter! Even if he does pass the initiation, he'll never be able to keep up with all those other boys!"

"Geez, Faina!" Leo scoffed in surprise. "He's standing right there you know!"

"I didn't mean physically capable! Regardless of Pasha's strength or size it's just not in him to be violent. Sure, he can throw a punch if he gets worked up, we've seen him do it before. But he can't stay like that all that time. It'd tear him apart."

"Look, we don't know what Pasha's capable of, alright? Street fighting is like anything else, it's something you gotta learn to get good at. As for the initiation, there are ways to get around it."

"You mean not go through it at all?" Pasha looked hopeful for a moment.

"I mean to survive it. To pass. Look, we'll get through this, alright? Your Ma know anything about this?"

"You kidding? Of course not! And she can't know until it's all over!" He sighed and turned away. "Hopefully she'll never find out."

"That's asking a lot." Faina slipped a hand under his chin to examine his injuries. "How you gonna hide those bruises you got now?"

Pasha hunched his shoulders. "Why do you think I'm out here?"

"You can't avoid your mother every time you get injured. That's impossible!"

Leo checked his watch. "Alright, look. There's a barber shop that does black-eye service on Mulberry. I got a few hours to spare. Let's take you down to Tony and get you fixed up. I'll pay for everything, okay?"

"Really?" Pasha hung his head. "You don't have to do that, you know."

Leo put his arm around Pasha and shepherded him forward. "Don't worry about it. You got a rough road ahead of you, kid. I won't sugarcoat it. But we'll get through this together."

Faina hurried alongside. "So that's it then? There's really no way out?"

Pasha looked down at his feet almost apologetically. Faina could hardly stand it. She imagined herself grabbing him and kissing him, telling him how brave he was. Instead she nudged his forearm.

"Hey. What you looking so guilty for?" She slipped her hand silently into his palm. "I get it, alright? And I'll be with you every step of the way, I promise. Thieves' Honor! Right, Leo?"

Leo bounced his chin up and snickered. "Thieves' Honor!"

Pasha's eyes ran from one to the other as he gave into a weary smile.

"Thieves' Honor."

Chapter 64:

Hazed

Pasha stared at his reflection in the cold, silver flask as he sat across from Leo in his bedroom.

"Go on," Leo encouraged him. "The sooner you get it down the sooner it will kick in."

Pasha flicked open the top. The dry odor of alcohol seemed overwhelming.

"Just think of it as taking cough medicine."

Pasha raised his eyebrows. "That's a lot of cough medicine."

"You get used to it." It wasn't the first time Leo had used that phrase in an attempt to acclimate Pasha to something outside his nature. He raised the flask to his lips and took a swig, trying not to let it touch his tongue. The whiskey felt warm and almost smoky as it rolled down the back of his esophagus. The heat flushed through his veins with such intensity that he couldn't help but cough.

A cold breeze swathed the back of his neck as his bedroom window opened.

"Sorry I'm late." Faina scrambled over the windowsill and flopped on the mattress.

Pasha could hardly greet her for coughing.

"What's wrong, Pasha?" Faina's sharp eyes narrowed on the flask in his hand. She seized the container and faced Leo with a vicious growl. "You're giving him whiskey? Have you lost your mind?"

"Calm down, Faina! We've got an hour until his initiation."

"So you're getting him all liquored up? He's twelve!"

Leo snatched the vessel and replaced it in Pasha's hands.

"Do you have any idea what he's about to go through? They're gonna hurt him, Faina! They're gonna hurt him bad!"

Pasha hastened to swallow. "Not so loud, you'll wake Katya!"

Leo lowered his voice. "What do you take me for? You really think I would just hand a kid a bottle of whiskey for kicks and giggles? We're just gonna give him a little to calm him down, so he doesn't feel as much pain. That's all I know to do. You got any better ideas? Or would you rather him get the full brunt of the experience to satisfy your principles?"

Pasha listened to the exchange as though it were happening to someone else. He felt weightless, like a balloon bouncing aimlessly against the ceiling.

At some point Faina turned to him with a pitying expression. "I'm coming with you."

"Faina, you can't." Leo sighed and rubbed his eyes, weary of arguing. "Klokov will never let you."

"Then Klokov can kick me out himself."

Pasha wrapped his fingers around hers, remembering what it was like to stand witness to his own father's suffering, how it still woke him up at night.

"I don't want you to have to see that."

"You mean violence? Since when am I so delicate?" She leaned closer, her knees turned towards him. "I'm not like that. The thought of you having to face this alone bothers me more than blood on your back. I'm not leaving you."

***

They entered the Foxhole through a side door that led directly to the cellar, avoiding the pitiful stares and anxious glances of the late-night crowd. It was a maze of cavernous, empty rooms, spiral staircases, and wrought-iron parapets. As they traveled deeper below the building, Pasha could just make out an aged Victrola scratching out a sultry melody in the distance.

A far-off cry of agony echoed down the tunnel. Faina jumped and grabbed her brother's arm.

"I told you not to come down here." Leo pulled her head against his chest to muffle the sound.

Pasha swallowed and looked down at the floor. Dried blood stained the concrete.

"You alright?" Leo grabbed his shoulder.

"Yeah." Pasha took a deep breath. "Yeah, I'm fine."

Leo held out his flask. "You want another swig?"

With trembling hands, Pasha reached for the whiskey and drained it into his throat. He noticed Leo staring at him. There was a sense of despair in his eyes, almost as though he himself had done something wrong. Pasha capped the flask and handed it back to him, wiping his mouth on his sleeve.

"Come on, kid." Leo patted his back. "It's almost over."

Klokov was waiting for them at the bottom of the steps in the former distillery room. He was dressed in one of his finest charcoal suits, with a silk tie knotted about his invisible neck. At the sound of their footsteps, he smiled and threw out his arms in a welcoming gesture.

"Pavlo Ruslanovitch Chevalsky! Today is the day you become a man!"

A splintered wooden post loomed behind him, cemented to the floor. It was six or eight feet tall, and had six metal vices at varying heights. Several places in the wood had grown soft and pulpy from an excess of bodily fluids.

A group of boys, mostly around Leo's age, was standing by, stripped down to their undershirts. The tallest held the whip in his hand.

Faina gave a whimper at Pasha's shoulder. He spun around and grabbed her by the hand. Her face wrinkled in a sob.

"You can't do this to him!"

"Faina, shhh, it's okay." Pasha hooked his arm around her and pressed her cheek to his chest. "Calm down."

"No! I won't let you go through with it!" She wrenched away from him and rushed towards Klokov with pleading hands. "Please, Mr. Klokov! Don't do this to him! Please let him go! Please!"

Klokov knit his eyebrows together and looked up at Leo with abject disapproval.

"I'm surprised at you, Leo! Bringing your little sister down here! What were you thinking?"

"I'm sorry, Klokov." Leo grabbed Faina by the shoulders and drew her back. "Faina, you have to let it go. Pasha's gonna be fine."

Klokov snapped his fingers at one of the boys. "Moneyrider, escort Miss Spichkin to the top floor please, and have the waiter bring her a cup of tea, and anything else she wants."

As Moneyrider moved aside, Pasha's eyes snagged on a familiar face. Anastas stepped forward, cracking his knuckles.

"We gonna get started soon?"

At the sound of Anastas's voice, Faina dug her heels into the ground. "What's he doing here?"

Moneyrider moved to stop her, but Faina ran back down the stairs and pointed a finger at Anastas. "This boy is nothing but a bully! He's only here so he can hurt Pasha! He doesn't give a fig about chivalry or any of the rules of the Breadwinners!"

Embarrassed, Leo grabbed hold of Faina and turned her back towards the stairs.

"Faina, that's enough. You're causing trouble."

"He shouldn't be here, Leo! You know I'm right!"

Pasha watched as Leo lowered his lips to her ear. "I won't let him hurt Pasha, okay? If I need to, I'll talk to Klokov about it."

Placated, Faina finally gave in and allowed Moneyrider to lead her away.

Pasha could hardly unbutton his shirt for the way his fingers shook. It didn't help that Anastas was watching him intensely, savoring each little symptom of fear. The other boys were quiet, respectful, sympathetic, even. But Anastas bounced about the room boasting and cursing in a way Pasha had never seen before. It was as though it energized him, this violence.

A boy Pasha recognized as Leo's friend, Trifecta, offered to take Pasha's shed clothes, and stored them away where they'd be protected from any blood. Leo, too, shed his shirt and vest so that he could be close to Pasha during the process to encourage and comfort him.

Pasha crossed his arms over his bare chest and shivered. He turned to Klokov in anticipation. Klokov nodded. With his head down, Pasha approached the whipping post. Trifecta unlocked the cuffs that were level with Pasha's gaze.

Pasha leaned forward and hugged the beam with his elbows, obediently placing his wrists in the vice. The steel had a rough, rusted texture against his skin, and Trifecta had to adjust it several sizes to fit Pasha's scrawny wrists.

With Pasha's nose pressed against the wood, his senses were overwhelmed with the salty aroma of dried blood. His thoughts drifted towards images of the butcher's with its scarlet-stained countertops, and red-tinted drains on the floor. He began to shake. He felt a hand on his shoulder. His eyes fluttered open. He was face to face with Leo.

"I'll be right here the whole time, okay? Just keep your eyes on me. I'll be right here with you."

Pasha nodded, a lump swelling in his throat. "I need you to pinch me." He kept his voice at a whisper. "Otherwise I'm gonna cry."

"It's okay to cry. There aren't any rules against crying, but try to keep it quiet. Don't start wailing or anything. If you have to make a noise, yell but don't scream. You know what I mean?"

"Yeah, I know what you mean."

"Growl if you want. You can even curse. They just want you to prove you can take it like a man. No begging, no asking for pauses or time-outs. If you ask them to stop you'll be disqualified."

Pasha could hear Klokov clapping his hands behind him. "Are we ready?"

Leo looked at Pasha for confirmation. Pasha nodded.

"We're ready." Leo began to back away. "Just remember why you're doing this. Keep thinking about that. I'm right here."

Pasha squeezed his eyes shut and tried to concentrate on how soft the wood felt against his forehead.

"God help me," he chanted under his breath. "Please, God be with m—"

Pasha's head was thrown back as the first strike was administered. A guttural moan knocked from his lungs. The skin on his back burned and smarted. He could already feel a welt forming.

"One," Moneyrider called out.

Hardly a second passed before Moneyrider issued the second blow.

"Two!"

The second was far worse than the first, and Pasha had to bite his lip to keep from crying out.

"Three! … Four! … Five!" With every blow, Pasha's naked spine twisted and recoiled. Raw shards of wood poked and drew red scratches along his chest as he writhed against the whipping post, feeling like he was on fire.

"Seven! … Eight! … Nine!"

"You're doing it all wrong!" The sound of Anastas's brash, arrogant voice was about as pleasant as a drum set being dropped from the ledge of a five-story building. "You ain't even breaking the skin!"

"Hey!" exclaimed Moneyrider.

Pasha had no idea what was going on. The leather straps of the whip tore into his skin with incomparable force, one strike following the other. Pasha was helpless against the anguished cry that escaped his lungs. He could feel his skin ripping open. Faint dabs of his own blood sprinkled his neck and shoulders like heavy rain. It was as though he were being mauled by a tiger.

"Hey!" Leo's voice was deafening as it thundered across the vaulted ceilings and reverberated down the surrounding tunnels. Pasha could just make out the reflection of the events in the glass doors on the opposite wall. Leo grabbed Anastas by the wrist, pried the whip from his grasp, and backhanded him so hard Anastas tripped backwards.

"That's enough outta you, Rogue," Klokov snapped, smacking Anastas in the back of the head. "Get out!"

Anastas lowered his head and scowled, but he didn't dare look Leo in the face. Without another word, Anastas disappeared through the passage.

Moneyrider cussed and spat on the floor. "Shouldn't have been here in the first place."

By now Pasha could feel the blood trickling down his lower back and past the waistband of his trousers. The numbness that had developed after so many repetitive strikes was wearing away, and he could feel his skin beginning to throb.

He heard Klokov whisper to Moneyrider, "Rogue is right though, you gotta break the skin more."

The thought of more strikes like Anastas's made Pasha gasp for air. Leo clapped his hands and rubbed them together.

"More than halfway there, Pasha! Only nine more to go!"

Pasha swallowed the dry lump in his throat and nodded his head before Moneyrider resumed.

"Twelve! … Thirteen! … Fourteen!"

Bitter tears dragged down Pasha's cheeks as he dug his nails into the wood. But Moneyrider went fast, and he was soon announcing the victorious final number.

"Twenty!"

Pasha felt his entire body go limp. Were it not for the braces he would have collapsed on the floor in a fit of relief. Pasha felt Leo's broad hand cupping his cheek and lifting up his head.

"You did it, Pasha!" His mouth was stretched in a wide grin. "You're done! You got through it! It's over!"

Klokov snapped his fingers. "Alright, bring in the brine."

In his disoriented state, Pasha couldn't be sure he had heard Klokov correctly. "What?"

Leo's forehead contorted in confusion. "Brine?"

Leo was blocking the reflected view Pasha had in the door, so he could not see what was taking place behind him. But the moment he saw Leo's face he knew it wasn't good. Leo opened his mouth as though to stop them, but it was too late.

Pasha's nose was overwhelmed with a brackish, almost rotting odor. He heard the water slosh over his shoulder. It was like being struck with a tidal wave of flames. Pasha roared with inconsolable torment. His limbs jerked and his body contorted. He rose up on his toes. He bit his lip until blood trickled over his teeth. He rammed his forehead into the pole.

Leo was dumbfounded. Clearly, he had not been aware of the brining stage, and neither had Pasha. He stepped back in awe as Moneyrider hurried to unlock Pasha from the stocks. Leo caught him before he could fall to the floor.

"Okay," he whispered into his ear. "We're going to do this as fast as we can so we can get you home, alright? So keep gritting your teeth."

Pasha nodded, still chewing on his lower lip in an attempt to keep from groaning. All he could think about was reaching back and digging his nails into his skin to numb the pain. Moneyrider nudged Leo's arm.

"I'll get Faina."

Leo helped Pasha kneel down at Klokov's feet. In his hand he held a sacramental wafer.

"Open your mouth, son."

Pasha did as told, trembling and wheezing. Klokov placed the wafer on his tongue.

"Pavlo Ruslanovitch Chevalsky, you are now a member of the *Malchiki*, the Breadwinners. May you always have meat on your table, your cellars filled with salt, and your mouths filled with bread. May you prosper. May your family never go hungry. May your sons grow up strong, and your daughters secure. You may eat."

Pasha closed his mouth and swallowed as Klokov stepped back.

"Rise, Pavlo Chevalsky. For today you are a man. You've passed the test, my boy. You'll have a month to recover, then we'll arrange your first fight where you'll be christened. Now go home and rest. The boys will help you rinse off."

The other Breadwinners helped him beneath a spout on the wall. Pasha stared down at the drain as Leo put his hands on his shoulders.

"Just hang on to me, okay?" Trifecta turned on the faucet. Cooling liquid spilled over Pasha's ragged spine, rearranging the motes and flooding Pasha with renewed pain.

"Give it a minute, hang on." Leo lightly smacked his cheek, trying to keep him awake.

After a minute or two of standing beneath the running water, the sting of the salt subsided somewhat, though the marks of the lash continued to torment him.

Trifecta handed Leo Pasha's clothes, but there was no way he could put them on while the injuries were still bleeding. He handed Leo a towel.

"Wrap this around him, and then throw his coat on over that."

Pasha was barely listening. He was leaning up against the wall with one hand pressed over his eyes and was sinking his teeth into the other. Trifecta's voice seemed to move in and out, despite the fact that he was standing still.

"Leo," Trifecta said in a lowered voice, "you need to get him outta here quick. If he faints he'll be automatically disqualified. Go home and finish cleaning him up, then give him laudanum for the pain."

Pasha groaned as Leo wrapped the towel around his torso like a bandage.

"Almost done, pal." He pulled Pasha's arms through his jacket. A feminine cry echoed from the top of the stairs. It was Faina.

"*Moya Patulya*!" She slapped Moneyrider's chest. "You butchered him!" She ran down the steps and threw her arms around Pasha's neck. Pasha gasped in pain.

Leo grabbed her by the wrist and tugged her away. "Easy, Faina!" He lowered his voice. "We have to get out of here now!"

Leo yanked Pasha to his feet and practically dragged him down the passage. Pasha was hardly aware of himself. They reached the alleyway in what felt like seconds. Leo slammed the door behind them.

"Alright, now you can scream all you want."

Pasha's mouth wrenched open as he took in a mouthful of air and shouted. He threw his hands up over his face, digging his fingers through his hair, desperate to make the burning stop. Unable to control himself, he reached back into his collar, clawing at his skin.

Faina froze, gaping at him in horror. Leo tried to grab hold of Pasha's hands.

"Would snow help? You want me to get you some snow?"

Distraught with pain, Pasha wound back his foot and kicked a trashcan across the alleyway. Leo pulled him back by the collar and lifted the bottom of his coat over his head.

"Okay, okay, hold on! Here's some snow!"

Upon the immediate contact of the ice, Pasha's skin burned with such intensity he felt as though it would shrivel into leather and fall off his bones. Faina was shouting.

"Wait! Leo! Stop! Stop!" She grabbed hold of his jacket and towed him back with all the force she could muster. "They salted the pavement! I think you might be making it worse!"

Pasha never caught what followed. He blacked out almost instantly.

Chapter 65:

Wait and Hope

Staccato's muscles ached. After the first week and a half of his imprisonment in Crux, he had succumbed to the intense hunger gnawing away at his stomach and taken part in his daily rations. Samael had not been lying; whatever was causing his weakness and lethargy was not being administered by food, or if it was, it wasn't the only way it was entering his system.

The C.O.N. wanted him alive. There were things they wanted to know. What had they done with the Jar? Who else was working undercover? They came often, timing their visits at irregular intervals to further disorient Staccato. They beat him, whipped him, and drank his blood. He frequently misled them just to buy some relief. But they were never fooled for long, and their last encounter had resulted in a severely injured leg.

His greatest comfort was his dreams where he could meet with his mother, and sometimes Evangeline, only Evangeline never came. Time and again he had seen her in his dreams, and yet they had never entered a state of hypnagogia. But it mattered little, for he had resigned himself to his fate. He would be with Evangeline soon.

"Don't lose hope," his mother had said to him in his last Widow's Dream.

They were young there in his vision. Not just his mother but Staccato as well. When restored to youth, they looked nearly indistinguishable from each other, though his mother's hair was dark like Lydia's. She always wore the same outfit every dream: a full, seaside bustle gown with gray stripes and an oversized hat. In life it had been a gift from Calliope's mother, and she cherished it so that she was known to wear it long after it had gone out of fashion.

"I don't think of it as losing hope, *Maman*," was his response. "I've been ready to go for a long time now."

They were in Pisces, side by side on the beach, a blanket spread out beneath them.

"You think you have nothing to live for?"

"Does it matter if I do?" The breeze blew his bangs into his eyes, and he quickly pushed them back. "This is it, *Maman*. I can't save myself this time, and I don't expect anyone else to either." He leaned forward and cradled his head in his hands. "It's alright. I'm not bitter. All I would have wanted is to see Lydia one last time … and my grandchildren." He rubbed his hands over his eyes, trying not to give in to the tears. "They don't even know who I am."

There was silence for some time, and then his mother sighed. "'All human wisdom is contained in these two words—Wait and hope.'"

Staccato lifted his head. "*The Count of Monte Cristo*."

"Your favorite." She smirked and smoothed her skirt. "You always wanted to be just like Edmund Dantes."

Staccato gave a bitter scoff. "Well, I certainly feel like Dantes now. Trapped in the Château d'If." Staccato froze. He turned and stared at his mother who stared back with a knowing smile. "*Maman*, you're brilliant!"

Staccato was torn from his dream by the sound of a door slamming against the wall with a loud bang. A cold hand grabbed him roughly by the collar and hurled him out of bed. Staccato gasped with pain and clutched his injured leg.

"I've had it with your false information, Staccato." Samael's shadow grew long in the moonlight.

Staccato did not have the energy nor the inclination to respond. Samael grabbed him by the collar once more and slammed his head into the dresser. Staccato fell to the floor in a daze.

"You can't do this forever!" Samael leaned over him, his fangs unsheathed. "Well?" He slapped at Staccato's face. "Speak! I grow weary of your silence!"

Staccato had no intention of obliging him, but as he lay bleeding on the floor, he noticed he was not shivering. For once the concrete seemed bearable to touch.

"It's warm."

Samael turned away with an impatient sneer,; apparently he had been hoping for something more exciting.

"The crematorium is broken. We can't seem to turn the heat down. It just so happens your room sits directly below it."

"Crematorium?" Staccato tried to sit up but his muscles wouldn't allow it. "You burn the bodies of dead prisoners?"

"We have to get rid of them somehow."

"I'm surprised you bother. I would've thought you just ate them."

Samael pursed his lips together. "You expect us to dine on the bodies of emaciated, infected prisoners? And I suppose you enjoy the occasional roadkill!" He peered out the window, the moonlight catching in his pale eyes and shrinking his pupils. "A minor inconvenience. The mermaids can deal with the bodies for the time being." A dark grin came over his features. Staccato's stomach turned.

"Why are you still here? Wouldn't you rather be in Capricorn, trading weapons with the Sultana?"

Samael smirked. "You don't enjoy our visits?" He scratched at the back of his neck. "Let's just say I have a personal interest in you."

Staccato narrowed his eyes. Something was different about Samael tonight. It was difficult to put his finger on, but his skin was looking rather dull, and he distinctly recalled his eyes having been more vibrant in the past.

"Which is another way of saying you don't believe your underlings are competent enough to deal with me."

Samael jabbed the end of his walking stick into Staccato's neck. "Would you trust children with your valuables?" He nudged Staccato's arm with the toe of his boot. "I knew it was too good to be true. The former advisor of two kings turned traitor? You're full of surprises, Mr. Nimbus. Unfortunately for you, I don't like surprises. So if you value your legs, your arms, your skull, your peace of mind—you'd better come out with the truth." And with that he turned and left.

Staccato remained on the floor, staring up at the door in shock. It was by far the mildest encounter with Samael he'd had so far. What sort of game was he playing?

Chapter 66:
Busted

Paper crinkled as Leo bent towards the doorknob, juggling two large bags of groceries in his arms. An apple was jammed into his mouth like a suckling pig. When he tried to turn the handle, the right bag began to slip. He floundered to catch it before it hit the floor.

"Come on, Jazmin," he grumbled through his teeth, trying to knock by gently tapping the door with his foot. "Jaz? Can you open the door please?"

His gaze drew towards their neighbor's door. Mrs. Feinman was standing on the threshold with a cup of coffee, gawking at him suspiciously.

"Good morning, Mrs. Feinman!" he greeted her, the apple still wedged between his teeth. Mrs. Feinman quickly shut the door.

Leo growled under his breath. "Thanks for the help." He leaned against the door. At that moment, Jazmin opened it, and Leo tripped forward.

"What on earth are you doing?" She caught Leo by the chest before he could fall over, and took one of the grocery bags.

"I didn't have a free hand."

Jazmin plucked the apple from his mouth and kissed him. "Why didn't you just set them on the ground?"

"Uh …"

Jazmin giggled and corked his mouth with the apple again. "You're taking on too much, Leontiy. You didn't have to go to the market for me, you know."

He put the bag on the table and slipped the apple into his jacket pocket. "You had morning sickness."

Jazmin waved a hand and began putting away the groceries. "I didn't mind waiting until it passed. Besides, you haven't been feeling well either. You slept with your mouth open all night last night. How are your sinuses?"

"They've been worse." Leo wrapped his arms around her from behind. "Actually, I'm starting to get a little heartburn lately. How about you? How are you feeling now?"

"Much better." She patted his hand and turned around to face him. "Leo, have you been smoking in bed when I'm not around?"

Leo raised an eyebrow. "No, why?"

"When I woke up this morning there was ash all over your pillow. That's the second time this week."

Leo shrugged his shoulders, unable to come up with an explanation. "I don't know what to tell you."

Jazmin shook her head and crossed over to the sink where she began rinsing some carrots. "Well, maybe make sure you wash your hands after your evening cigarette from now on." She shook the water from the leafy tops. "Oh, before I forget, your uncle is looking for you."

"Oh, yeah?"

"He wants to see you right away." She turned and leaned against the counter with her arms crossed. "So, what did you do?"

Leo's eyebrows stretched up his forehead. "What did I do?"

"You heard me, what did you do?"

Leo chuckled and removed the coffee tin from the paper bag. "I didn't do anything that I know of." He placed it next to the grinder.

"That's not what your uncle seems to think."

"He's mad?"

"Sure seemed like it."

"Huh." He pivoted towards the door. "Well, I guess I better go see what it is then."

Leo found the store empty of patrons as usual these days, but was surprised to see no one at the counter. Shrugging, Leo slipped through the door, and made his way to the back room.

"Uncle Matvei?"

"In here, Leo."

Leo winced. Jazmin had been right; he didn't sound too happy. But surely it had nothing to do with him. He was too caught up in married life to have caused his uncle any trouble.

All oblivion of his own transgressions vanished when he saw Mrs. Chevalsky sitting in front of Uncle Matvei's desk, dabbing at her eyes with a handkerchief. Pasha was perched glumly on the stool beside her. Faina looked as though she had been deliberately placed next to her uncle where he could keep a strict eye on the girl. Leo cleared his throat.

"You wanted to see me, Uncle?"

If Uncle Matvei's eyebrows had sat any lower they would've obscured his vision. He jabbed an authoritative finger in the direction of the bed perpendicular to his desk.

"Sit."

Leo immediately did as told. Uncle Matvei folded his hands together.

"I think you know why you are here, Leontiy."

Leo opened and closed his mouth several times before he could find the right words.

"Okay, I know what this looks like, but I didn't help Pasha join the Breadwinners, not exac—"

Uncle Matvei's voice climbed in volume, appalled by Leo's denial. "Oh, you didn't, did you? Because from what I understand you coached him through his initiation, you helped him hide his injuries from his mother, and you and your sister have been giving him laudanum to help with his pain!"

"It wasn't like that," insisted Pasha. "Leo and Faina didn't do anything wrong! They didn't start helping me until after I began my initiation, when it was too late for me to back out! All they did was help me avoid getting blacklisted!"

"Yeah!" Leo leaned forward. "He went through the gang beating and freezing water entirely on his own! We had no idea he had gone to the Breadwinners, and if we did we would have stopped him!"

"Exactly!" Faina nodded her head emphatically.

"We would have told you! You know how the rules work, Uncle. Once you start your initiation you can't back out, not unless you want every door in the city slammed in your face!"

Uncle Matvei banged his fist on the table. "As opposed to now that he has successfully completed his initiation, in which backing out will get him killed!"

Lydia gave a terrified sob into her handkerchief. Uncle Matvei glanced back at her with a guilty expression before returning his attention to Leo and continuing angrily.

"There is absolutely no reason why the two of you shouldn't have involved us!"

Faina bowed her head. "Pasha didn't want us to upset Mama Lydia when there was nothing she could do about it."

Uncle Matvei's eyes looked as though they would float out of their sockets.

"Young lady, I don't care if Saint Michael himself showed up in Pasha's room and handed him a sealed scroll commanding him to join the Breadwinners! He is twelve!" If there had been any customers up front, they would have run out the door in fear. He pointed a finger at each of them, moving like the hands of a clock.

"He is twelve! You are twelve! And you, sir," he speared his finger towards Leo, "you may have a wife upstairs, and a child on the way, but you are still only seventeen!"

"Even if we couldn't have negotiated Pasha's freedom," sniffed Lydia, looking up from her handkerchief, "it still would have been better for you to inform one of us at once." Her lips curved downwards. "Maybe we could have come up with an alternative."

Leo's lips parted in a frown as he realized Mrs. Chevalsky and his uncle were right. Even if they hadn't been able to spare Pasha, it would have been far better for everyone to face the situation together as a family. Instead they'd put their three juvenile brains together and what solution had they arrived at? Liquoring Pasha up before the final stage of his initiation.

Faina bent her head forward and whimpered, the tears running down her cheeks.

"I'm so sorry, Mama Lydia! I should have thought about it more! If I thought coming to you would have stopped Pasha from becoming a Breadwinner or getting blackballed then I would have told you! I was just too stupid to realize it!"

Leo pushed his fingers through his bangs, his face growing red with shame.

"I'm sorry too, ma'am. What we did was irresponsible, and wrong." He rubbed his forehead and slumped down in his chair.

Uncle Matvei exhaled so heavily his mustache shuddered. He covered his eyes, and then covered his head, strained for words.

"I want so badly to say there is something I can do to get him out of it, Lydia … but I know there is nothing." He paused and pinched the space between his eyebrows. "I'm not saying this to scare you, only to advise you not to attempt it. I know the Breadwinners seem small, but the truth is, there are few places you can go in this country to escape their reach. They have allies, they have spies. But just because Pasha is a Breadwinner doesn't mean his future is limited to the life of a thug."

Lydia furrowed her brow. "Doesn't it?"

"The way I see it, if he does well there may be hope for him. There are a lot of normal people out there, you know, with ties to gangs. He doesn't have to grow up to be a foot soldier."

Lydia wiped her eyes, a bitter expression lining her features. "Does well? At street fighting?"

Footsteps echoed down the hall. "Papa? Did you know no one's at the counter?" Anya peered her head around the doorframe. The moment her eyes registered the gathering, her eyebrows knit together cynically. "What's going on now?"

Uncle Matvei drew back, surprised by her cheek. "A small crisis, *Annushka*, darling. I appreciate you letting me know about the counter, but I've put up the closed sign while we sort out this issue."

"Is that all you're going to say about it?"

Everyone stiffened. Even Mrs. Chevalsky's tears appeared to freeze as she looked up from her handkerchief. Angry red splotches were forming across Anya's cheeks.

"I may be quiet, but I'm not stupid, and I'm not fragile! I've had it with being left out! Every time there's some sort of family crisis it's always, 'Anya, be a lamb and make some tea,' 'Anya, go fetch so-and-so a handkerchief.' What's happened now that you're trying to shelter me from?"

Everyone looked down at their laps. Faina was the first to rise to her cousin's challenge, sitting up and clearing her throat.

"Pasha joined the Breadwinners. Leo and I have been helping him recover from his initiation in secret."

"And no one thought to consult me?" She stared them down impatiently. "Junior Red Cross volunteer, going on three years now! Just how exactly have you been treating his injuries?"

Faina glanced away awkwardly. "With laudanum."

"Laudanum?" Anya faced her with a hard stare. "That's it? How often are you changing his bandages?"

"Uh, whenever … whenever they get too dirty."

"That's how people get infections! You need to be changing his bandages at least twice a day!" Without warning she tore around Pasha and, much to his surprise, yanked his shirttail up over his shoulders.

Pasha's entire face went red, but he appeared too afraid to stop Anya.

"Just as I suspected!" Anya let his shirttail fall back down over his back. "Filthy! They should be changed immediately! And with a good, strong antiseptic!"

Lydia raised her hand timidly, leaning towards Anya with hopeful curiosity. "Can you show us how, Anya, dear?"

432

Anya crossed her arms over her chest. "Certainly. Not only that, but I can get you proper medication from my Junior Red Cross leader for free." She faced her father. "What good has come from keeping secrets in this family? You with the extortionist, Leo with Jazmin, Faina with Anastas, and now this!" She turned to Pasha, her voice softened. "How long did they give you before you have to fight?"

"A month and a half."

Anya nodded her head with a somber expression. "Sounds about right. As long as the wounds aren't infected it should take four to six weeks to heal."

Uncle Matvei lifted his chin from his hand. "That's quite a lot of time until the boy begins." His eyes fixed on Lydia. "Perhaps we train him."

"Train him?"

"You know, teach him how to fight, help him build some muscle!"

Faina arched an eyebrow. "Do you know how to fight, Uncle Matvei?"

Uncle Matvei straightened his tie. "Oh, my dear girl! I was a regular Jack Dempsey in my day! Why, they used to call me *Bogomol*!"

Leo snorted. "The praying mantis?"

Uncle Matvei held his fists up. "Because of my speed and agility, of course!" He hopped back and forth like a grasshopper, accidentally bumping his hip against the desk. Pasha giggled in spite of himself, and Lydia's full lips actually showed traces of a smile.

"Well," began Leo, sheepishly scratching at his head, "whatever Uncle Matvei doesn't teach him, I can … that is, unless you think I've helped enough already."

Mrs. Chevalsky offered Leo a gentle smile. "I would appreciate that, Leo."

"Anya is right." Uncle Matvei rubbed at his sore hip. "We need to face this together …" He reached forward and took hold of Lydia's hands. "Like the little patchwork family we are. We're going to help Pasha in any way we can. We'll have Anya see to his injuries, and Leo and I will build up his strength."

"And what about me?" piped Faina.

Uncle Matvei turned to snicker at her. "Well, as Pasha's best friend I'd say you have the most important role of all, *moya pteechka.*" My little bird.

Pasha looked up at her and smirked. "Someone's gotta keep my spirits up."

Chapter 67:
Ophiomormous

The morning following Staccato's encounter with Samael, he was awakened by a noticeable increase in the discomfort of his mattress. He reached under the pallet, feeling more alive than he had in weeks. The possibility of escape had had a revitalizing effect on him, and for the first time he was able to push through some of his pain.

A fleeting memory from the previous night's sleep breezed through his thoughts. He had the vaguest recollection of Evangeline entering his dreams, and the beginning of what seemed like a Widow's Dream, only it was over as soon as it began. He could remember only that she had placed her hand on his neck as she gazed down lovingly at him, and nothing more.

Staccato froze with his hand halfway off the bed. Should he really be so excited at the idea of an escape? How was he going to pull off a getaway like Edmund Dantes in *The Count of Monte Cristo*? Did *Maman* mean for him to convince his captors that he was dead? It would be nigh impossible.

He felt under the mattress. His hand enclosed around something thin and wooden. He felt the slick ebony pressing into his palm. It couldn't be. Ignoring his weakness, Staccato sat up and peeled up the corner of the pallet. His staff was laid upon the frame as though it had been there all along. But of course it hadn't.

He let the mattress drop, terrified that someone might walk in and see it. He lay back with a hand over his eyes. How had it gotten there? Could a fellow prisoner have managed to sneak it inside in the middle of the night? Or was there a double agent in his midst? He looked twice at the door, then snuck his hand beneath the mattress again and held it tightly. Staccato had been rare in that he never needed a staff to extend his powers, rather he needed a staff to control and subdue them. But now that he was weak, was it possible it would work the other way?

He focused on the empty cup atop the dresser. He reached out his arm. He felt his muscles tensing. The cup gave a twitch, then a shudder, then levitated off the table. Staccato felt his arm straining. He dropped his hand. The cup clattered to the floor. He would need to recover somewhat first.

If he wanted to escape he needed more information. But he wasn't strong enough yet to venture out on his own. If only he had a fellow inmate, someone to do the groundwork for him. That's when it hit him.

He wondered … would it still work? After all, it required far less effort than moving things telekinetically. He grabbed the staff once more. He closed his eyes.

Please work. He felt the wood bend, felt the smooth ebony grow textured and scaly. He opened his eyes and smiled. Ophiomormous: the act of a miraculous transforming a staff into a snake. The serpent coiled around his wrist. Staccato let his hand drop to the floor. It slithered in the direction of the vent. Staccato shut his eyes, willing it to slip through the bars and into the darkness. He allowed his muscles to relax and his eyes to roll back. His consciousness was replaced with the perspective of his staff as it slunk through the shadows.

A violet-hued light glared in the distance. The snake crept closer. An odd wailing sound echoed through the ribs of the shaft. It was a peculiar, otherworldly noise, somewhere between crying and singing. As the serpent neared, he began to make out the shapes. There were four lights, not just one, and they were emanating from a human skull. It had been situated in a makeshift nest of sorts concocted from thorny branches pasted together with what appeared to be congealed blood and bits of human hair. It was black magic, though nothing he recognized.

There was no way of knowing how to break it, not off the top of his head anyhow. He thought back to the principles of curse breaking he had learned as a boy, the most basic of which was Circulo Sheva, an ophiomormous application often used to crack minor spells and ward off bad energy. The serpent had to circle the object seven times for seven days while the miraculous chanted. But could it work in a place like Crux? A prison so potent with evil it was nearly tangible? There was only one way to find out.

For days no one came to his cell. The broken furnace continued to warm the room, and Staccato continued his Circulo Sheva. Already he could feel a difference in the air. He wasn't quite so dizzy, and although he was weak from his injuries and the conditions of his cell, he was able to move with considerably more strength than before.

He kept the serpent inside the vents at all times as a precaution, enabling him to spy on his captors, listen to their conversations, and take note of the prison layout.

"You haven't paid a visit to the miraculous in some time," he heard a servant remark to Samael once.

"I am afraid I cannot risk it with my condition at present."

"You are ill, Your Majesty?"

"Don't be ridiculous. Just a bout of ecdysis is all."

Now he knew why Samael had been looking so dull lately, and why their last encounter had been so mild. All ophidians shed their skin every two months. It was said to be quite debilitating, as the eyes would grow cloudy resulting in temporary vision loss. Not that this was as great of a disadvantage as it would have been for non-ophidians—for their heightened senses made it easy to function without their sight—but the skin would become irritated.

"The weather conditions here don't exactly favor shedding," Samael went on. "It's far too cold."

"Why not return to the mainland? We can deal with the miraculous on our own."

"Absolutely not! He's too clever, and can't be trusted with just anybody. I have made him my personal responsibility." He sniffed at the air. "What is that horrid smell?"

"In truth, it could be any number of things, Your Majesty. It isn't the most savory of places, our establishment."

"It smells like—" He paused. When he spoke again his voice was dry and ominous. "Tell me you fools have had the sense to move the bodies that were in the crematorium."

A long silence followed. "That was never discussed, Your Majesty."

"'Never discussed?'" There was a crash as Samael threw the servant against the wall. "You idiots! Why do you think we keep the morgue so cold?"

"It keeps the bodies from rotting," the servant managed to croak.

There was a flurry of noise as Samael dropped him to the ground. "Go down to the morgue and bring back several body bags—"

"But they're already in body bags—"

"And probably leaking! I want you to take the bodies in the old bags—do not remove them—but put them, spoiled bags and all, inside the new ones, and dispose of them like all the others!"

Staccato followed the servant's path through the ventilation, making note of the direction so he would remember where to go later. Fortunately for him, it wasn't far. A plan was forming in his mind.

On the seventh day, he had yet to receive another visit from Samael, and the light of the skull was waning. After one final rotation it split like a spoiled egg. A single black vapor rose from the fracture with a faint scream. Staccato gasped as though an enormous weight had been lifted off his chest. He sat up. Awed by the lightness of his movements, he flexed his hand in amazement. Now was the time to act. He would not risk another visit from Samael, especially not after his absence had enabled him to recover somewhat from his previous injuries. After another beating he might not have the physical capability to get away.

He had the serpent return to the cell and transformed it back into his staff. Using the rod as a sort of crutch, he made his way to the bathroom. He extended his hand towards the shower head, building up pressure in the pipes until at last it burst in a giant flood. He hobbled his way back towards the bed and waited. It wasn't long before the train of water was seeping out the door.

Footsteps came running down the hallway. When the door swung open, Staccato was ready. He wrenched his victim through the door and threw him against the wall with such might that he was rendered unconscious. Staccato leaned over him. Using his telekinesis, he lifted the orderly onto the bed and removed his outer clothing. He slipped the robe and veil on over his own attire. It was deceptively warm and would help to disguise his face. Though he was not likely to get very far with his leg in the shape it was.

He hid the ophidian beneath the sheets and slipped out the door. The passage was wide and dimly lit with kerosene lamps. He repeated the directions to the morgue inside his head. "Left, right, left and down the stairs."

A door opened down the hall. Staccato froze and made himself small against the wall. With a wave of his hand, he blended into the brick. A guard came barreling around the corner, swearing and spitting at the film of water advancing down the corridor. Staccato held his breath as the guard passed. The man stopped two feet from the place where Staccato was standing. His heart sank as the hulking form veered around.

"I smell deceitful blood."

His eyes rolled over into black chasms, his jaw unhinging. Without revealing himself, Staccato blasted the guard onto his backside. The ophidian scrambled to his feet. As he let out the first notes of a wild cry, Staccato thrust his staff over the ophidian's head and forced his vocal cords to constrict. The guard went silent. Staccato turned his attention to the lamp nearest the guard's head, filling it with pressure until it exploded in a sprinkling of glass shards, cutting his attacker's face.

Were it not for his leg, Staccato would have run, but he had no choice but to finish him off without drawing anyone's attention. With a wave of his staff, the iron sconces came alive and twisted around the ophidian's neck. Staccato whipped the crown end of his staff against the guard's temple, knocking him out cold.

He knew he had little time to waste. He hobbled on until he came to the stairwell. He found the morgue unguarded and unlocked. From there it was easy. Struggling to ignore the presence of several inanimate bodies around him, he lay down amongst the pile by the door waiting to be carted away. Staccato slipped into an empty body bag and closed it up using his powers. For a moment, he thought he could detect smoke, and he couldn't help but wonder if by breaking the kerosene lamp he had started a fire without realizing it. It had all happened rather quickly.

It was ten minutes before anyone came to collect the bodies. Staccato lay as stiffly as possible, clutching his staff close to his body. He winced when he was loaded onto the cart, his leg aching.

Soon he was being wheeled down a passage. Through the material he could vaguely see the hooded figures carrying him away.

"You don't suppose the tunnel is flooded, do you?" said the first one.

"Weather hasn't been that bad yet."

Someone held open the door for them. Rushing water echoed all around. The surface they traveled upon grew rough.

"See? It hasn't even reached the bridge yet."

Staccato continued to squint through the material. It appeared as though they were traveling through a cave with a raging river beneath them. At last, gray light began to filter between the threads. The fragrance of the ocean almost brought tears to his eyes. They were rolled to the edge of a precipice. Staccato swallowed and pinched his eyes shut. He reminded himself to think of Edmund Dantes, and how heroic his adventures had seemed to him as a child. A lever was pulled, and the surface of the cart tilted upwards. Staccato slid forward into the bottomless air and was plunged into the water.

Chapter 68:

Bargaining with the Devil

Lydia hugged her coat tighter about her chest as she strode down the Bowery in her best hat, her hair clean and soft. Above her the tracks of the El Train trembled with invasive, overpowering noise, filling the air with black dust. She crossed the street towards the three-story, brown brick building with the arched windows. So this was the Foxhole. It was certainly nicer than she'd imagined, from the outside anyway.

Lydia fearlessly tugged open the heavy doors. It wasn't terribly crowded, being the middle of the day, but the men who were there stopped and stared as she entered the hazy, brown light. Uncertain of how to proceed, she locked eyes with the mustached bartender and approached him with large, aggressive strides.

"Excuse me." She removed her gloves one finger at a time. "Do you know where I might find Mr. Klokov?"

The bartender pointed to a table across the room surrounded by towers of wooden crates. The others gaped at her in curiosity as she swaggered, head held high, towards the stocky figure swathed in a cloud of his own cigar smoke.

"Excuse me, Mr. Klokov?"

A squat, fleshy skull breached the fog like the crest of a full moon. He took one look at Lydia with his single, beady eye and bowed his head respectfully.

"What can I do for you, Madame?" He put out his cigar and folded his broad hands on the tabletop. His manners were surprisingly genteel for an experienced thug.

"My name is Lydia Chevalsky. I've come to discuss a personal matter involving my son. Is there any way we can speak in private?"

At the mention of her name, Klokov's eye glazed over with a knowing expression.

"Certainly."

Lydia blinked at him with wide eyes as he rose and politely gestured to a hallway at the back of the room.

"Right this way, Mrs. Chevalsky."

Lydia was speechless as she followed him back to his private office. Perhaps this would be easier than she thought. Klokov held open the door for her. The room was rather nice, with an oversized mahogany desk, Persian rug, and fully stocked sidebar.

Klokov offered her a seat in one of the pristine velvet armchairs across from his desk. Lydia's eyes wandered through the authors on his crowded bookshelf: Tolstoy, Dostoevsky, Pushkin. He certainly was well read.

"May I get you anything? Tea? Water? Whiskey?"

"No, thank you."

"Very well then." He lowered himself into his chair with a long exhale. "So, you're Mr. Chevalsky's mother. You must be very proud. That's a fine young buck you got there."

"Yes, thank you, I am proud of him." She hastened through the formalities. "I wanted to discuss—"

Klokov held up his hand. "I get it, you're here to negotiate the terms of your son's release from my services."

Lydia's face brightened. "Yes! As a matter of fact, that's exactly why I have come!"

"Then you know I can't help you."

"You can't?"

"As I'm sure your son explained to you, membership with the Breadwinners isn't a monthly subscription sorta deal. Once you're a Breadwinner—"

Lydia rolled her eyes. "'You're a Breadwinner for life. Desertion is punishable by death.'"

Klokov raised his hairless brows, impressed. "So you're familiar with the code!"

"What I am familiar with, Mr. Klokov, are the ways of the world. The Breadwinners are far from unique. There are many like you out there, making your code of honor somewhat predictable."

Klokov stroked his chin in a philosophical manner. "You sound as though you speak from experience."

"Becoming orphaned at sixteen gives you quite an education. The point is, I know how these things work. Your laws are hardly final."

"Mrs. Chevalsky," Klokov interrupted her. "If by any chance your son has changed his mind about entering into my services, there is still time for him to back out."

"There is?"

"Sure, with one caveat. He backs out now, I'm afraid you may find your situation to be worse off than before."

"You mean to blacklist us?"

Klokov turned his head left and right, as though searching for another person in the room.

"Me? If it were up to me, every buck who couldn't make the cut would walk outta here without a single blight on their reputation. It's the public who are less forgiving."

Lydia was straining not to grit her teeth. "I am no fool."

"I'm sure you aren't, which is why I would encourage you not to have young Pavlo welch on our agreement. It's not honorable, not respectable. Young boys like Master Chevalsky must learn the value of an agreement if our people are ever to be taken seriously. That is the purpose of this brotherhood: to preserve the honor of our community by raising boys to be men."

"An honorable pursuit indeed, were it not for your narrow definition of what constitutes manhood."

Klokov gaped amusedly at her. "My narrow definition of manhood?" He snickered. "And pray tell what is it about my definition of masculinity that you find so limited?"

"You engage these boys in humiliating and often dangerous rituals to prove their worth, teaching them that their identity as a man is dependent on physical strength alone. You encourage violence not only in your initiation process, but in your ruthless manner of street fighting. It would be far more constructive, at the very least, to teach them a more structured form of fighting, such as boxing or wrestling, which fosters discipline, and patience. You have them steal daily from others to supply your black market with inventory, and threaten to flog them if for any reason they show up empty-handed. And despite this enormous stress you burden these lads with, you deny them the right to any sort of emotional expression besides anger, because despair would be too weak."

"It is only natural that you should find my methods somewhat brutal, Mrs. Chevalsky. You are a woman, after all; it would be unnatural if you didn't. But a man knows that trials build character. I'm not asking that all my boys be Apollon." He chuckled. "If I were, I wouldn't have allowed your son admittance. But I do ask that they be tough, that they be the best they can be. So, yes, I encourage hand-to-hand combat. I find the lawless nature of street fighting allows my boys the freedom to learn problem solving in a way that best suits their strengths, whether that's physical prowess, speed, agility, or even mental toughness.

"I discourage tears, but so do the majority of men when it comes to rearing their sons. As for stealing, what else would you have me do?

We live in a city with corrupt law enforcement, and even more corrupt politicians—I should know, I got half of them working for me. To win you gotta play their game, and every last opponent out there is cheating. The rules are there, they're just unspoken, therefore you ain't breaking any."

But Lydia shook her head. "You can't teach boys honor and integrity while having them thieve at the same time."

Klokov smirked at her. "Sounds as though you're suggesting that all law is honorable and has integrity. Not something I'd expect from a woman wise to the ways of the street. Now who is the narrow-minded one?"

"Of course not. But having escaped a revolution which advocates the eradication of all wealth, and the genocide of the upper and middle class—a movement which might not have existed were it not for the intolerance and indifference exhibited by the Tsar—I am not fond of extremes. You cannot argue that your disregard for the law borders dangerously on the drastic." She turned her attention to his bookshelf. "Is not *Crime and Punishment* a warning against the dangers of living by a self-tailored brand of integrity? Of disregarding the law?"

Klokov shrugged. "Must I agree with all the themes to enjoy it? Self-sacrifice, responsibility for one's actions … these are what define a man."

"Are not gentleness and compassion also valued characteristics in a man?" posed Lydia, practically raising up in her seat. "They are there in your books! Does not Dostoevsky end his novel by emphasizing the importance of love? And what about *War and Peace*? Does it not teach us that men of harmony are just as valuable as men of valor? That the philosopher is every bit as important as the soldier? Is not the character of Pierre just as admirable as the character of Andrei?"

Klokov stared back at her, impressed. "You're quite well-read for someone who was orphaned at sixteen."

"I could say the same of you. My father instilled a love books in me before he died." Klokov threw up his hands in capitulation. "Look, we can argue philosophy all day. If your boy wants out then he has a month and a half to walk away with his life."

Lydia laid a hand against her heart and took a deep breath. "I would rather beg on the streets of Memphis than allow my son to be a prisoner in New York City."

"That's great. But it's not up to you."

Lydia gawked hopelessly at the mob boss with her mouth slightly open. At length, she lowered her head and swallowed. The thought of her desperation made her head fuzzy with fear. Lydia squeezed her eyes shut. She would never get through it if she allowed her emotions to get in the way. She forced her head up.

"Alright."

"What?"

"It's as you say. To win you must play their game, and every opponent is cheating." She reached behind her head and removed her decorative comb, letting down her soft, full hair.

Klokov's voice softened. "What are you doing?"

She leaned forward with her elbow on his desk, forcing down the dark feelings inside of her. "Playing the game, Mr. Klokov. 'The rules are there, they're just unspoken.'"

She slid the comb to him across the desk. Klokov picked it up and held it to the light with an examining eye.

"I underestimated you, Mrs. Chevalsky. You really are wise to the ways of the world. And I'm all the more sorry for it." He dropped the comb on the desk and slid it back to her. "Your son flayed open his back, trusting that I would keep the creeps away from his ma." He leaned forward, his eyebrows pinched together. "We may seem like a bunch of mindless, barbaric, uneducated thugs to you, Mrs. Chevalsky. And, yes, I am a criminal, but I have my convictions. Would you like to know another reason why the Breadwinners deal in street fights? Because next to bootlegging it happens to be our most lucrative business. The money we make in street fighting means we don't have to rely on prostitution, drugs, or arming radicals. My boys know that if they raise a hand to a woman, if they take advantage of a female in any way …" He mimed putting a gun to his temple and pulling the trigger. "They're dead. I don't care if they're twelve, sixteen, or twenty. We don't endorse that kind of behavior.

"You shame your son with that kinda performance. You think you're the first mother to come into my office begging for her son's discharge?" He scoffed. "I've heard it all before." He rose and made his way towards the exit. "Take all the time you need to make yourself decent. I wouldn't want my men thinking anything untoward about their colleague's mother." Klokov disappeared into the hallway and closed the door behind him.

Hurt, humiliated, and ashamed, Lydia gave vent to a desperate sob as she strived to put her hair back exactly as it was before.

Chapter 69:
Uncharted

PYRO -(STOP)-
    MIDNIGHT, FEBRUARY 28TH, CRUX SET ABLAZE AND
NEARLY BURNT TO GROUND -(STOP)- FIRE ENGULFED
THIRD OF FORMER SCORPION CLINIC WHERE PRISONERS
HELD -(STOP)- WITNESSED BY OVER FORTY MERMAIDS -
(STOP)- FIRE CAUSED BY ESCAPED PRISONER -(STOP)-
MANY ARE SAYING IT WAS STACCATO NIMBUS
    PRINCESS KOI KASAGO

Pyro lowered the telegram and stared at the opposite wall.

"Well?" said Thayer, who was sitting patiently behind his desk. "What does it say?"

"They think Staccato escaped." He folded the paper and slipped it into his pocket.

Outside Thayer's study, the collected snow was forming a thick crust on the windowsill, limiting the shine of moonlight that filtered through the glass. Seaweed was stretched out on the warm stones of the hearth, soaking up the heat and wheezing softly.

"That's good news, isn't it?"

Pyro passed a hand over his beard. "I don't know. What do you think?"

Thayer hesitated at first, reluctant to disappoint Pyro, but eventually gave in with a sigh.

"If he really did escape, where could he have realistically escaped to? He can't be with the mermaids because we would know. It's unlikely he made it all the way to Scorpius's shores, and if he did it's flooded with Primals. He could've gone to Therion but I doubt he would've lasted amongst the Furies. The fact of the matter is, there aren't many places to go."

Pyro turned away and swallowed. He understood what Thayer was saying, but the idea that Staccato could have escaped was so encouraging it seemed impossible to give up just yet.

"You're sure there's nowhere else he could've ended up? An island perhaps?"

Thayer reached for the globe at the edge of his desk and turned it with his scarred finger.

"The only islands I know of are either under Primal occupation or belong to Therion."

Pyro exhaled and crossed his arms.

"I can send out a search party through Scorpius territory if you like," Thayer added.

"Do that." Pyro turned to the door. "Let me know if you find anything."

Too restless to return to his room, Pyro wandered aimlessly through the palace. Was it possible Staccato had gotten hold of some mermaid's breath and was hiding underwater? Or had found a vivarium that was still intact? What if he had made it to shore somewhere only to be killed by Furies or Primals? The thought froze Pyro mid-stride. He couldn't allow himself to think about it.

Now that he had stopped, Pyro became aware of his surroundings for the first time. He was standing in the Great Hall before the singed tapestry, practically eye-level with the faceless Tripp Cortair. Pyro fingered the burn mark where his head should've been, surprised it hadn't crumbled away into ash years ago. Pyro had been only twelve when his case of the dry bellows had caused him to accidentally burn through the tapestry, and since forgotten what the pirate captain had originally looked like. On the outer edges of the charred spot were the remnants of a raven ponytail. The sleeves of his shirt were rolled up exposing a series of tattoos. Pyro followed the trail of inky mermaids, tropical birds, and thorny flowers to a pale spot on the inside of the captain's wrist.

Pyro narrowed his eyes and leaned in for a better look. Last time he had examined the tapestry he hadn't noticed the mark, but perhaps he had been too busy goggling at Sonata. It wasn't a tattoo, but a burn. It appeared Captain Tripp Cortair had been branded for piracy like so many others of his profession. At least, that's what Pyro assumed. The mark was unique after all, and Pyro recognized the symbol as being a Scorpion character.

Cortair must have spent a lot of time in Scorpius, he thought to himself. An idea struck him. Pyro dropped his hands down by his sides. He backed away from the tapestry and dashed upstairs to the library.

The hour was late, and the room was predictably empty. Pyro fumbled with the dial on a lamp, eager to get at the shelves and find what he was looking for. He wound his way through the history section and began snatching every book he could find on Captain Cortair. Once his arms were sufficiently full, he made his way gracelessly to the table before the empty hearth, and began ravenously pouring through the volumes. It wasn't long before his search turned fruitful.

For over a hundred years, no one knew where Captain Cortair stashed his loot, he read from the largest tome. *It wasn't until 1887 that famed archaeologist Koto Yosai discovered an uncharted island in the Sea of Scorpius where Captain Cortair was known to pillage. The island, which the pirates referred to as Iwakishi, boasted an abundance of artifacts dating back to the time of Captain Cortair, including a correspondence between the Captain and the daughter of a spice merchant in Antares. It is theorized that the reason the island remained hidden for so long was its lack of accessibility, as it is heavily surrounded by rocks, and is plagued with rough waters for three quarters of the year.*

Pyro couldn't believe what he was reading. He eagerly flipped to the map on the following page and rooted out the isle that had gone unspotted for years. It was small, infinitesimal even, and it was easy to believe how so many cartographers had overlooked it in the past. Pyro ran his finger in a straight line from the small island to Crux. The distance was not short; in fact, the island seemed to be equidistant from Scorpius, Crux, and Therion. But it was close enough that one could plausibly have swum it if he had to. True, the choppy current might have been difficult to navigate, but a single person swimming could have easily avoided the rocks where a ship could not.

Pyro slammed the book closed. This had to be it. It was the only explanation. If Staccato was alive, he was staying on the Isle of Iwakishi.

Chapter 70:
The Stallion

Faina sat on the stool behind the register and watched her uncle stock the last jar of pickles. It was March. Under normal circumstances, Faina would have been excited for February to pass away. But her happiness was overshadowed by the advent of Pasha's inaugural fight.

Faina turned to Anya, who was leaning on her elbows and drumming her fingers on the counter.

"Did you check his wounds one last time?"

Anya nodded. "All healed. Though there will be some scarring."

"How bad?"

"The worst will be the one running from his left shoulder towards his flank. It's left a huge gash. The others might fade with time."

Faina felt her face turning red as she thought of Anastas. Pasha had told her how he'd taken the whip from Moneyrider's hand.

"Relax, Faina." Jazmin emerged from the back room, tying her apron. "Worrying isn't going to change the outcome."

Anya flexed her eyebrows. "Not necessarily. Worrying can help you prepare for the unexpected."

Uncle Matvei shot Anya a look, and she hastily withdrew from the conversation. The bell over the door pealed as Leo entered blowing into his hands and rubbing them together.

"Well?" The stool rocked violently forward as Faina shot up. "Who is he fighting?"

Leo removed his hat and shook his head. "It ain't what we hoped for. He's up against Sergei."

"*Da pomozhet nam Bog!*" God help us, cried Uncle Matvei, lifting his hands to the heavens.

"No!" Faina melted onto her elbows and covered her face with her hands.

Jazmin's eyes flickered between the two. "Sergei? Isn't that the boy nearly as big as Anastas?"

"Not only that," said Anya, "but Sergei is a close friend of Pasha's."

"And that's bad because …?"

"Because Pasha doesn't want to hurt anyone," explained Leo. "Especially not his friend. Pasha puts up his best fight when he's angry."

"So?" Jazmin sat down behind the counter. "Even better. Sergei will go easy on him."

"Sergei would be a fool to take a dive. Klokov may only have one eye, but he ain't blind. He knows a faker when he sees one. And in Pasha's case you can bet he'll be keeping an extra close eye on him. Everyone is expecting him to fail."

Faina braced the counter. "You don't think he'll fail, do you, Leo?"

Leo shook his head. "Pasha's just as capable as any boy up there. He may be skinny, but he has the skill, he has the technique, now all he needs is the conviction."

Uncle Matvei drew up quickly. "Alright, here they come. Now remember, we need to be as supportive as possible! No gloom and doom, got it?"

The four nodded their heads obediently.

"You really think Mrs. Chevalsky should be tagging along?" murmured Leo as Pasha and his mother approached the door. "It's a rough crowd."

Uncle Matvei threw up his shoulders. "I tried to dissuade her but she insisted."

The bell jingled and Uncle Matvei was all smiles. "There he is! Today's the big day!" He spread his arms out wide as he ushered Pasha forward. Faina looked him over. The boy looked positively green.

"Pasha just dropped Katya off with Mrs. Potemkin," said Lydia.

"Ah, how is Aunt Poppy?" said Uncle Matvei a bit too enthusiastically.

"Better now that she knows she's not going to jail again," muttered Anya.

Lydia turned her head. "What was that?"

Leo quickly slipped in front of Anya. "Nothing! Are we all ready to go?"

Everyone, save for Jazmin—who had agreed to man the shop—finished slipping on their coats and departed out the shop door.

They must have made a peculiar sight, the odd constellation of a family crossing the Bowery as though it were a Sunday stroll through the park. Outside the entrance of the Foxhole, the pavement reverberated with jazz beneath their feet. Faina looked up at her uncle. He had stopped in front of the double doors with a cold, hard stare. Leo was the only one brave enough to open it. He gave Pasha a hearty slap between the shoulders.

"Come on, kid." A brass tuba wailed eerily over a crowd of swaying beers. "Go get 'em."

Faina's eyes dilated as they crossed the threshold into a world of masculine odors and greasy fingerprints. They turned their attention to the ring. A boy Leo's age sailed over the edge of the platform. Faina covered her mouth as the young fighter collided with the circular table at Lydia's elbow, catapulting the empty beer bottles into the air, and landing on the concrete. Horrified, Lydia moved to help the boy up, but Leo held her back.

"Don't help him. You'll be doing more harm than good."

Somehow the boy managed to peel himself off the dirty floor, but the winner had already been declared. Faina's hand stayed pasted over her lips.

"Faina?" Pasha tugged his elbow away from her. "Faina, you're hurting my arm."

"Oh, sorry."

"Well, well, well!" Klokov made his way towards them, rubbing his hands together in anticipation. "Look who it is! The man of the hour!"

The starchy, fermented heat oozing from the crowd must have gotten to Mama Lydia for her face was quite red, and she turned her head away. Klokov laid a porky hand on Pasha's shoulder.

"Today's your big day, my buck!" His eye roved upwards and a smile split his wobbly cheeks. "I see you've brought the whole family! Leontiy, my boy! Good to see you!" When he went to greet Uncle Matvei, Klokov removed his hat in a gesture of profound respect and thrust out his hand. "Mr. Dalka, it's an honor to make your acquaintance."

Uncle Matvei was at a loss. His smile was pleasant but somewhat forced as he shook Klokov's hand.

The crowd was just beginning to settle, and for the first time since arriving, Faina's ears ceased ringing.

"Well?" Klokov raised his eyebrows. "You ready, kid?"

Pasha shrugged off his coat and handed Faina his cap. "As ready as I'll ever be, I guess."

"You're up against Broadshanks." Klokov began ushering him away.

They gathered to one side of the arena towards the front of the crowd. Mrs. Chevalsky was bouncing on her toes and fanning herself. Faina took her hand and patted it.

"It's alright, Mama Lydia. Pasha is gonna do swell!"

"I hope you are right, my darling … or at least, I think I do."

"Now don't start that again." Uncle Matvei removed his hat and waved it towards his own splotchy face. "You'll make yourself sick. What's done is done. We'll just have to make the best of it."

"Hey, Faina! Leo! Anya!" hollered a familiar, adenoidal voice. Faina turned to spy Yuri Mishkin trotting their way. He tipped his hat to Uncle Matvei. "Mr. Dalka." Faina's mouth fell open when she saw the enormous shiner mushrooming from his left eye.

"Yuri! Your eye!"

Yuri shrugged as though it were no big deal. "Oh, yeah. Got it in a fight with Mudlark." He turned towards Pasha's mother in surprise. "Oh, hi, Mrs. Chevalsky! Didn't expect to see you here!"

By now Lydia couldn't have looked worse if she tried. Her eyes bulged at the sight of her son's young friend battered and bruised.

"Yuri Mishkin? Is that you?"

Yuri grinned, displaying his abundance of crooked teeth saturated in blood.

"Long time no see."

Lydia's shoulders rose as she gasped. "Darling, have you seen your mouth?" She plunged her hand into her coat for a handkerchief.

"Yeah, I just finished up a fight with Steel Beast about an hour ago." He stuck out his chest and grinned. "You should see how he turned out!"

Without hesitating, Lydia began dabbing at his teeth as though he were her own child.

"Who?"

"Steel Beast."

Lydia shook her head disapprovingly. "Is that a boy or a racehorse?"

Uncle Matvei coughed into his fist. "Not sure there's a difference."

Yuri jerked his thumb towards a boy who appeared to be just shy of turning a man. Lydia's mouth twisted in shock.

"You fought him?"

"Yep! He's the second-highest ranked out of the eighteen-year-olds!"

"How old are you?!"

"Fourteen!"

Lydia threw up her hands and stared desperately at Uncle Matvei as though he could somehow explain it all away. But poor Uncle Matvei could only shrug and bite his nails. Yuri rocked back on his heels.

"What can I say? I'm strong for my age." He flexed his arm. "What do you say, Mrs. C.? Wanna feel some real guns?"

Yuri bowed forward as Leo socked him in the back of the head.

"Ow! Geez! Lighten up!"

But Leo snatched the back of his collar and hurled him in the opposite direction. "Get lost, Yuri!"

Lydia pivoted around and faced Matvei with wild eyes. "Eighteen!"

Uncle Matvei placed his hand on her shoulder. "Lydia, calm down."

But Lydia wiggled free, raising her finger high in the air. "No, my son cannot fight eighteen-year-olds, he's only twelve!"

"Lydia, the boy will be fine! You just have to accept it, there's nothing we can do!"

"No! Not my boy! Not my son! I refuse to let this happen!" With a violent twist she yanked herself away from Matvei with every intention of fetching Pasha and dragging him home.

"Lydia, no!"

Everyone jumped into action, grabbing an arm, a bit of coat, an elbow.

"Let me go!"

"Mrs. Chevalsky," Leo cut in, staring intensely into her eyes. "With all due respect, we know you love Pasha. He's your son. And you want what's best for him, you want what's best for his future. But if you try to stop this now, they will hurt him."

Lydia froze, her eyes locked with Leo's. Faina watched them with pity. The regret in her brother's voice was almost tangible.

"You saw what they did to his back. That's nothing. I've seen it before. I know this isn't what you wanted for your son. This isn't what any of these boys' parents wanted when they came to this country. But it's where we are now. And we gotta make the best of it."

Lydia knit her eyebrows together as she shook her head. "You don't understand, *Leonka*. You're not …" She stopped.

Leo slipped her a weak smile. "A parent? I am, Mrs. Chevalsky … at least, I'm about to be. We're all fighting for the future. You came here to make a better life for your children. And well, they're alive, aren't they? Who knows, maybe Pasha's children will have it better because of what he's doing now. That's what I'd like to think. That's what I tell myself every time I have to pick a lock or go on the lam."

Bit by bit, Lydia's body began to slacken. They let go of her. Uncle Matvei offered her his handkerchief as she lowered her head and sniffed.

"Would you rather wait outside? Leo can escort you home if you—"

"No." Lydia shook her head and dabbed at her eyes. "No, I'll be fine." She lifted her chin high.

"Ladies and gentlemen!" roared Klokov from the center of the arena. "It is an honor to host you all on such a momentous occasion! Today we welcome a new inductee. Here he is, twelve years old, standing in at five foot eight and a half, and 122 pounds …"

Already there were snickers running through the crowd.

"Pasha Chevalsky!"

Klokov stepped aside as Pasha made his way to the top of the stairs. He'd been stripped down to his undershirt. Faina instinctively cast her eyes down, even though she'd seen him wearing less when she was tending to his wounds. Something about the throng of inebriated men stomping and shouting made it feel indecent, and she wondered if modest Pasha was at all embarrassed.

Klokov held up his hands, signaling for the crowd to hush. "Most of you know the rules, but for those of you who are new with us, allow me to go over the protocol once more. If Master Pavlo here manages to put up a good fight his first round, he's in. Whereupon he shall be dubbed with his new name and added to the official roster." Klokov gestured to a chalkboard over the bar tattooed with names that sounded more at home in a paddock than an arena.

"And now, who shall it be to challenge our boy here? You know him, you love him! Standing at five foot ten and weighing 168 pounds, why, it's none other than fourteen-year-old Sergei 'Broadshanks' Maslow!"

The crowd hooted and applauded as the platform shook with the heavy tread of Sergei's boots.

A tremor ran along Lydia's shoulders. "You have got to be joking!"

Pasha's mouth hinged open. He spun and looked questioningly at the crowd. Faina swerved towards Leo in a fury.

"You didn't tell him he was up against Sergei, did you?"

"Why would I? It would only have made things worse!"

"How? He could've been preparing himself!"

"I didn't want to mess up his adrenaline! This way he'll still be fired up!"

"Hush, you two!" Anya poked her head between them. "What's the point in arguing about it now?"

Klokov ascended the platform and sprinkled the customary salt onto the mat. Pasha stood with his feet shoulder-width apart, flexing his fingers, and fixing his eyes on his opponent.

Sergei was built for fighting. Not only was he bigger and taller, but his whole body was wide-set and broad like a brick wall. His torso was long, and his legs were thick and muscled. Even his fingers were about three times the width of Pasha's slender digits. Lydia had to grab hold of Matvei and Leo as the bell rang.

Sergei socked him so hard Pasha sailed backwards. Were it not for the length of his coltish legs, he would've fallen over. But somehow he managed to catch himself. Pasha put his hands up in an obligatory block but he couldn't have looked more out of place if he had been wearing a tutu. Sergei lunged towards his face, but in one swift move landed his fist in Pasha's abdomen instead. Pasha doubled over and gagged.

Uncle Matvei groaned. "He's falling for the distraction!"

Faina cupped her hands over her mouth, feeling foolishly helpless. "Come on, Pasha! You can do it!"

Leo covered his eyes with his hands. "No, no, no! Come on, kid! Punch his lights out! It's okay!"

But Pasha continued his strategy of defense only. Sergei bounced forward, wrapping his arm around Pasha's head and throwing him to the ground.

"You were right, Faina." Leo pinched the space between his eyebrows. "I should've told him he was fighting Sergei, that would've given me time to come up with some story about Sergei trash-talking him before—" Leo paused and looked up, his eyes unfocused.

Faina tugged on his sleeve. "What? What is it?"

"He's gotta get mad."

"Who's gotta get mad?"

Leo snapped his fingers. "That's it!"

"What's it? You aren't saying anything!"

Uncle Matvei eyed Leo suspiciously. "What are you onto, my boy?"

But Leo didn't answer; instead he covered his mouth with his hand and shouted in an altered voice.

"What a wuss! Would you look at this kid? He ain't got the guts to swat a fly!"

A few of the nearby customers slapped their legs and snorted.

"He looks like a baby! A scared little baby!"

Faina felt her face go red. With as much force as she could muster, she backhanded Leo's head and pinched his shoulder.

"What do you think you're doing? Traitor!"

Uncle Matvei grabbed Faina by the wrist and pulled her backwards. "Faina! Don't you ever hit your brother like that!"

"I'm trying to help him!" insisted Leo, rubbing his pink skin.

"Help him?" Faina sputtered. "How?"

Another customer chimed in. "What a chump! Go home, kid!"

Sergei had Pasha on his back now.

"Pasha puts up his best fight when he's angry," Leo reminded them. "What better way to motivate him than getting him all riled up?"

It was all Faina could do to keep from strangling him. "If that's how you think then you're going to be a terrible parent!"

"What were you thinking, Klokov? Send him home!" a sweaty bald man guffawed.

Sergei closed in on Pasha, poised to pin him to the ground.

"Look what you started!" hissed Faina.

A horse-faced man in the gallery leaned over the railing and spat. "Get a load of the nancy boy!"

Pasha's fist ascended through the air like Lazarus rising from the grave, smashing Sergei's nose in a spray of blood.

"Yes!" Faina squeaked, covering her mouth and jumping up and down.

Pasha wound back his knee and pounded his heel into Sergei's chest, propelling the boy backwards. Anya smacked Leo's arm.

"Well, what are you waiting for? Keep going!"

Leo hid his mouth behind his collar once more. "You sure that ain't a girl you got fighting up there?"

Faina gritted her teeth. Even if it was motivating Pasha, she couldn't stand the thought of his feelings getting hurt. But she didn't try to stop Leo.

Pasha hurled himself on top of Sergei, drumming his fists into his opponent's face. Faina chanced a glimpse at Lydia over her shoulder. She had dropped Uncle Matvei's handkerchief and was gawking with her mouth open. No one would have believed Pasha to have so much fury in him.

It went on like this for another full minute. When it was clear Sergei was not going to get back up, Klokov rang the bell.

"Pasha Chevalsky wins the fight!"

A shrill scream of victory sent everyone jumping out of the way. Faina turned in shock. It was Mama Lydia, jumping up and down and waving her handkerchief back and forth.

"He did it!" Tears of relief sprang from her eyes, as everyone flocked towards her to give her a hug and lay a comforting hand on her shoulder.

Just as Klokov was lifting Pasha's fist high in the air and placing a loaf of bread in his left hand, an angry voice rose up from the back of the gathering.

"Challenge!"

The throng of cheering hushed, and the crowd parted for Anastas to make his way to the stage.

"Challenge!" he continued to shout, his fist raised over his head.

Anya turned towards Leo. "What's happening? What's a challenge?"

Klokov threw back his head and stuck his thumbs in his pockets. "Ah, it seems we have a challenge from the Rogue!"

"Standard Breadwinner procedure," explained Leo. "If a new recruit wins his first fight other competitors can contest his induction by challenging the winner. Kinda like at a wedding."

"Clearly you haven't been to many weddings."

"You know what I mean, like 'speak now or forever hold your peace.'"

Klokov invited Anastas onto the stage and stood him across from Pasha.

"Do you, Anastas the Rogue Sippenhaft, find fault with the inclusion of Pasha Chevalsky into the sacred fraternity of the Breadwinners?" said Klokov, reciting from the designated protocol.

"I, Anastas the Rogue Sippenhaft, do not approve the inclusion of Pasha Chevalsky into the brotherhood."

"State your reasons."

"Because he's a—"

Faina missed the vulgar name beneath the volume of Uncle Matvei's shocked gasp, though she could easily guess from reading his lips.

Leo threw back his head and gave vent to a long, cynical laugh. Faina balled her hands into fists.

"I think that's enough now! He's already fired up in case you haven't noticed!"

Leo shook his head. "No, that's not what I'm laughing about."

"What are you laughing about then?"

Leo stroked the corners of his mouth and grinned. "This joker thinks he's so damn clever. He doesn't even realize he's shooting himself in the foot."

Faina wrinkled her nose in confusion. "Huh?"

"Knock his lights out, Pasha!" thundered Leo before Klokov had finished speaking.

Klokov chuckled awkwardly. "Woah, woah, hang on there, Leo. I haven't even rung the bell yet."

"Rip him to shreds, Pasha!" Anya snarled, beating her fists on the platform. Uncle Matvei placed a hand on her shoulder and pulled her back.

Klokov raised his eyebrows. "Alright then! Guess I better let you two at it!"

For the second time that evening Klokov ascended his perch. Anastas rubbed his hand over his fist.

"You know some of the fellas thought you and Broadshanks were unfairly matched for your first fight. But I disagree. I say you're both nancies. I'm here to give you a real challenge!"

Faina practically clawed at the boards of the platform. "The only real challenge will be stopping himself from knocking every last tooth out of your big mouth!"

Anastas jerked his chin up and looked down at Faina with disdain. "You let your girl fight your battles for you, Chevalsky? Tell you what, why don't you let her come up here and fight for you?"

"With pleasure!" The crowd burst into laughter as Faina tried to climb onto the stage, but the others were quick to hold her back.

"Or how about your Ma?" continued Anastas. "I know she wouldn't want anything happening to her precious baby boy!"

Pasha's fists were shaking now. Leo shook his head and snickered.

"Keep at it, Anastas."

"It's a good thing she has you around to keep her outta the whorehouse!"

The bell sounded. Anastas was still laughing when Pasha drove the full force of his fist into the side of his face. Anastas staggered sideways. The crowd gasped. Pasha struck again, this time from the other side.

Anastas lifted his hands up to block Pasha, his brows lowered. Pasha may have caught him off guard the first time, but Anastas was focused now. Pasha did not stop moving. Even when he wasn't throwing a hit he was shifting from place to place. Anastas watched him like a cobra ready to strike. He threw one hit but Pasha leaned away, perfectly dodging him, and slammed his foot into Anastas's leg. Faina's eyes widened, and a little blush spread across her cheeks. She had no idea Pasha had come so far. Anastas toppled over on his side but was back on his feet in seconds.

Pasha maintained a safe distance, striking when he could, but Anastas quickly caught on. He closed the distance, thrusting his arms out to grab Pasha around the midsection, but Pasha was too fast for him. He grabbed him by the wrist, pushed back and kneed him in the abdomen. Anastas released him, shuffling backwards. But something was off.

Leo covered his mouth. "Oh my gosh."

Faina snorted and chortled into the back of her hand. Anastas looked down. His trousers were down around his ankles. In the few seconds when Anastas was pulling away, Pasha had managed to debag him in front of the entire Foxhole. The crowd roared with laughter. Above them, Klokov shook his head and guffawed without hesitation.

Anastas's lips peeled slowly back over his teeth as he jerked his pants up. His veins trembled as they nursed the blood into his florid cheeks. He lowered his head like a bull ready to charge.

"You're dead, Chevalsky!" Anastas gave vent to an animal-like war cry and charged at Pasha.

Pasha leaned forward and widened his legs as though preparing to block him, but sidestepped at the last second, allowing Anastas to run himself right off the platform and onto the floor. Faina was laughing so hard she had to clutch the side of the stage for support. Even Uncle Matvei had to wipe a laughter-induced tear from his eye.

Klokov hastily rang the bell before Anastas could get up. In all honesty, he was probably doing the boy a favor. Still chortling, Klokov declared Pasha the winner yet again. With no one else willing to challenge Pasha's entry into the Breadwinners, he was awarded his street-fighter name: the Stallion. Though he had done a good job of hiding it, Faina saw Pasha cringe the moment it was uttered. It was rather cheesy, she had to admit, and was more suited to someone macho and loud. Overcome with adrenaline, Faina unintentionally shouted at the top of her lungs.

"I love you, Pasha!" But fortunately for her, she was drowned out by the roar of the crowd.

Chapter 71:

Iwakishi

Consciousness returned to Staccato like a painful shock. Weakened and faint, his body mourned the awakening, and his eyelids seemed to resist opening. Sharp pebbles poked at his cheek. The only symptom of life about him was the angry roar of the cold, gray ocean which had raked him through the rocky tide, and spat him out on the grainy shore.

His eyes fluttered, then snapped open. He had managed to make it to the Isle of Iwakishi, an island with a history of piracy equidistant from Scorpius, Crux, and Therion. With great effort he managed to push himself to a sitting position. Gravel fell from his face and left pitted imprints along his arm. His staff had been lying just above his head. With both hands he jammed it into the ground and tried getting to his feet.

Staccato threw back his head with an involuntary cry as he tried putting weight on his injured leg. He doubled over his rod, head sagging between his shoulders as he struggled to catch his breath. At length, he sighed and, gritting his teeth, continued to pull himself the rest of the way up.

Behind him the landscape swelled in a series of stony levels and crags brushed with thick blankets of velvety green grass at random intervals. Staccato knew his survival depended on shelter, and that the bluff housed an assemblage of caves and grottos. He looked down at his wounded leg. Perhaps he could make it by relying on his upper body strength.

Staccato hobbled with his staff to the bottom of the cliffside, limping along in search of a level starting point. Though he did not find a slope shallow enough to walk up, he was able to uncover an incline suitable enough for crawling. Staccato lay out on his belly and, hugging the rock, began to shinny his way up.

Finally, he was able to locate a cavity amongst the rocks thirty feet from the ground, capped with a layer of vegetation and flanked by a patch of grass on either side. Staccato scuttled over the ledge and laid himself out on the icy, stone rock. The wind lashed at his bare hands and face but Staccato had grown too numb to flinch. After resting for a moment or two, he looked out over the horizon and assessed his surroundings. His heart sank as he noted the shallow tide pooling around miles and miles of sharp stone.

It'll be weeks before anyone can reach me. If they could even find me.

As far as anyone knew, Staccato was still imprisoned. He was caught between an abandoned Scorpius, hostile Therion, and Crux. If he could summon the strength to make any sort of signal, he would be more likely to alert his enemies than a rescue.

As the reality of his circumstances began to weigh on him, Staccato grew more and more exhausted. So this was how he would meet his end: starving on the side of a mountain, freezing and immobilized, his daughter estranged from him, his grandchildren unaware of his existence, not even a friend to comfort him.

He dragged himself into the cave and lay down in the wet shadows. His memory lapsing from fatigue, he instinctively reached for the locket with Evangeline's photograph he kept in his loft inside the caravan. When he realized what he'd done, tears began welling in his eyes. He summoned a picture of Evangeline to his mind, her hair loose and shining around bare, sun-browned shoulders.

"I'll be with you soon, my love."

He closed his eyes, prepared to sleep. But a voice staid his consciousness.

"What are you doing here, Staccato?"

He felt a shadow fall over him, and two budding hands cupped his face. He was too weak to be surprised, or to rejoice for that matter. He did not have to open his eyes to know it was Mother Genesis.

"I've had enough."

"You've had enough?"

"I have nothing to live for. I'm ready to die."

"Look at me, Staccato Nimbus."

Staccato opened his eyes. She had taken the form of a cedar tree and had blossomed from a small shoot growing amongst the crags. Her body had lengthened, and her roots germinated, until she was able to reach inside the cave and loom over Staccato like a protective guardian. Her moss-colored eyes, set like emeralds in her wooden face, roved over his broken body, taking into account every scratch and bruise. She clucked her tongue and made a face.

"You do not trust me as you once did."

"We must all die eventually. I refuse to be a fool and deny my own fate."

Her lips coiled into a wry grin. "And what makes you think your time has come? You have much left to do, Staccato Nimbus, and much will be restored to you."

"Restored to me?"

A limb branched from her side, thickening and growing sturdier. It slipped under his neck, propping his head up.

"I will sustain you. I will care for you."

Buds of grass sprouted from the floor beneath them and turned the rough stone into a bed of soft earth. Two-thirds of the cave's opening she sealed shut with a thicket of roots and branches, shielding him from the harsh winds. For warmth, she wove together a heavy blanket of her own vines and covered him from his chin to his feet. She ran her hand down the side of his face.

"Sleep now. You shall eat when you wake."

A shroud of poppies and lavender had just begun to materialize from the ceiling as Staccato shut his eyes and descended into a deep, velvety state of restorative rest, permeated by dreams of Evangeline.

***

Staccato thought he had awoken when the earthy fragrance of radishes reached his nose. He opened his eyes. A harvest of apples, potatoes, berries, and tubers was piled in a corner near his head. A glowing light drew his eye towards a figure seated at his feet. It was Evangeline, sorting through a pile of apples and cleaning them off with the material of her skirt. He had entered a dream. Desperate to feel the consoling touch of his wife, he reached out and grabbed her hand so suddenly he startled her.

"Oh, my love," she cooed in a soothing tone the moment their eyes met. She crawled to his side and laid her hand against his cheek. Staccato tried to sit up but winced. She placed a finger to his lips.

"Shhh, don't get up now. You need your rest." She grabbed a clamshell from the shadows. "Here, drink some water. You're bound to be dehydrated."

"But this is a Widow's Dream. It won't make any difference."

Evangeline ignored the comment. She propped his head up and helped him to drink from the shell. The water was fresh and cold against the roof of his mouth. It had been so long since he'd had anything to drink that the first sip triggered a coughing fit.

"It's alright now." She patted his back and waited for the coughing to stop. As he moved, Staccato noticed a stiffness in his leg that hadn't been there before. Evangeline pulled back the blanket of vines so he could see. A splint of branches enveloped his leg from the knee down.

"We set your leg."

"We?" His voice was hoarse.

Evangeline sighed. With a hopeless expression she opened her mouth to explain but her body immediately began to flicker. Staccato waved his hand.

"You don't have to bother trying to explain. I know you can't." He rolled over, grunting from the effort, and laid his head in her lap. "The dead tell no tales."

She ran her hand down his back, and Staccato felt himself begin to relax once more.

"Mother Genesis shouldn't have bothered setting my leg. I'm a dead man either way."

"You're a fool if you really believe that."

"Evangeline, look out at the horizon. It's only March, and this is Iwakishi. It will be months before a ship can have safe passage through those waters. I won't last until then. And even if I could, how will anyone know I'm here?"

"Mother Genesis will ensure you have more than enough food to make it until then." She gestured to the walls surrounding them. "You have shelter. And when you're strong enough you can signal for help."

"Signal for help? The closest civilizations within reach have put a price on my head!"

"The closest?"

He huffed impatiently, knowing she was hinting at Scorpius. "With the Land Lock in place, what assistance could a water-bound mermaid kingdom offer me?"

She shrugged carelessly. "That's an excellent question. What assistance could they offer you, Staccato?"

Staccato pulled her hand close to his face and began stroking her fingers, as though doing so would help him think of a solution.

"If I had some sort of vessel I could send a message in a bottle. But I have nothing."

"You couldn't find something?"

"What could I possibly find on this uninhabited island? You aren't suggesting I craft some sort of container, are you? Because—"

He could see that Evangeline was just short of rolling her eyes. It irked her to not be able to share information at will. Had he been in her place he was sure he, too would have found it maddening.

"It wasn't always uninhabited, was it? Don't you remember the stories we used to read about? The tales you would tell me of Captain Tripp Cortair and the fifty mercenaries?"

A memory surfaced in Staccato's head. "It was a stopping point. The pirates used to stop here and stash their loot. Perhaps they left something behind I could use."

"Seems likely, doesn't it?" She patted his shoulder. "But for now, you must rest. You can't go roaming about the island with your leg in that state. You'll have to let it recover first." She stroked her fingers across his scalp and snickered.

"What is it?"

"By the time this is all over we'll know how many grays you've sprouted."

***

When Staccato awoke, the clamshell was lying near his head, empty.

Chapter 72:
How to Be a Hood

When Pasha first learned that he would be stealing in addition to street fighting, he had not anticipated thieving to be the more challenging of the two; the chief obstacle was his conscience. It was one thing to throw a punch in an arena where one was expected to fight, but to victimize another person by stealing? Pasha could hardly bear it.

And it was this very thought that plagued him most as he was running from the police down a street two days later, his hands completely empty. Pasha couldn't begin to describe the shame and embarrassment he felt as the cop chasing him blew on his whistle, ordering him to stop. He wasn't far behind now, and Pasha knew he wouldn't be able to keep up for much longer.

He turned up one street but the road was closed due to a crash, and the sidewalks were crowded with onlookers. Pasha ground to a halt, straining to catch his breath. He turned desperately in a circle, his hand over his chest. The whistle was growing closer. He'd been running so long, he could hardly get his legs to move. Pasha was at a complete and utter loss.

An unseen hand clamped down on his collar from behind, and Pasha was yanked into the back of a vehicle. The door slammed as Pasha was laid out across the back seat.

"What was that?!"

Pasha blinked in bewilderment as he found himself staring up at Leo. Leo's eyes dashed towards the window.

"Hold that thought."

He swiftly removed his coat and threw it over Pasha. Pasha heard the whistle pass by the car window, then fade away up the street. Leo peeled back the collar from Pasha's face.

"Well, what do you got?"

Pasha stared stupidly back at him. "What do I got?"

"Yeah, what'd you pinch?"

"I dropped it."

"You mean you went through all that trouble for nothing?"

Pasha's shoulders heaved as he looked down at his feet and frowned. "Looks like it."

Leo rubbed his hand over his face and leaned back against the seat. "Hot dog! I knew you had your reservations about fighting but you didn't tell me you couldn't steal!"

Pasha sat up. "How was I supposed to know? I've never stolen anything before." He paused and looked around. "Whose car is this, anyway?"

"I don't know. It was unlocked." He scratched under his cap. "First rule of the streets: there ain't no rules. You see an opportunity, you take it. You needed a place to hide. The door was unlocked." He looked at his watch. "Speaking of which, it's about time we skedaddled." He scooted out the back seat and held open the door for Pasha.

"But what if the car hadn't been empty?" Pasha stood and dusted the knees of his trousers. "I couldn't get around the crowd."

"Pasha, Pasha, Pasha." Leo pinched the space between his eyebrows. "You're going about this completely the wrong way. A big crowd is a thief's best friend. Why do you think there are so many of us in a place like New York City? You wanna disappear? Any thief worth his salt knows you gotta find yourself a big crowd of people."

"Yeah, but—"

Pasha turned around. Leo was gone.

"Leo?"

"Up here, kid!"

Pasha craned his head back. Leo was leaning over the fire escape from the second floor of the nearest building.

"Looks like you're gonna need someone to show you the ropes."

Pasha clambered up the ladder after him. "You can say that again."

Leo climbed over the ledge of the roof. "What were you trying to lift anyway?"

"A hubcap."

"A hubcap?" Leo tossed his head and laughed. "Starting kinda big, aren't we?"

Pasha swung his leg over the seam of the building. "They're valuable, aren't they?"

"Look, Pasha, you're making it way too hard on yourself." He crossed to the opposite side of the rooftop and stood on the ledge. "This is 1920!"

He threw up his hands and, in a swift hop, jumped off the roof and disappeared. Pasha raced to the edge and leaned over. Leo was laying on his back on a fire-escape landing with his feet kicked up on the railing.

"There's only one commodity you can steal that's guilt-free, an easy lift, and is worth hundreds of dollars. That's alcohol."

Leo somersaulted backwards, propelling himself through the cutout in the floor where the ladder was. He grabbed the ledge and swung his feet onto the bannister of the lower landing. From there he jumped across the airshaft, grabbing hold of a windowsill and planting his feet on a narrow concrete rim. With one final hop, he landed atop a dumpster, and stepped down onto the pavement. Leo rubbed his nose and sniffed.

"You coming or not?"

Pasha examined the alleyway with wide eyes. Leo made it look so easy. He climbed up on the ledge.

"You just gotta commit!" Leo stood watching him with his hands in his pockets. "Make a move and stick to it. Don't second-guess yourself halfway there."

Pasha drew a deep breath. He hopped down on the fire escape, slipped through the hole, and grabbed hold of the ledge. Gingerly, he balanced his feet on the railing. His eyes glided skeptically towards the opposite wall. He wouldn't have thought it possible had he not seen Leo do it first.

"If you fall, I'll catch you."

Pasha looked down at the ground. He wasn't terribly high up, and the wall was less than four feet away.

"Commit," Leo repeated.

Pasha narrowed his eyes on the windowsill. He bent his knees and, with one tremendous leap, cleared the divide and grabbed hold of the edge. His feet shuffled, hastily trying to gauge his footing.

"You catch on quick, Chevalsky!"

Eager to get down, Pasha let go of the window and fell backwards atop the dumpster. It was more surprising than painful. Leo helped him down.

"Don't sweat it. With my help you'll be sticking that landing in no time."

From there, Leo took Pasha uptown to the back alley of a ritzy Italian restaurant.

"You gotta go where the pickings are good," he explained between drags on his cigarette. "Plus, you're gonna feel a lot less guilty when you're not stealing from neighbors—hardworking, honest folk struggling to make a buck." He crouched down below the portal on the kitchen door and looked inside. "But these fat cats …" He motioned for Pasha to peer through the glass. "Tell me they don't got a little something extra to spare. They'll hardly miss it."

Pasha leaned carefully against the door. Inside was a vast kitchen with cooks scurrying about in pristine white coats and hats. Leo slipped his fingers under Pasha's chin and turned his head so that he was looking at an adjoining room in a secluded area of the kitchen. There was a floor-to-ceiling shelf stocked with glistening white towers of china.

"Now watch carefully," Leo whispered.

Pasha focused on the platters, wondering what on earth he was supposed to be looking for. A balding waiter with a pencil-thin mustache slipped through the kitchen door, and set his empty tray on the corner of the counter. From the inner folds of his jacket he produced a brass skeleton key roughly the length of Pasha's pinky finger. Pasha furrowed his brow.

"What's he doing?"

"Shhh, shhh! Just watch!"

Carefully, the waiter ran his hand along a front panel of the shelf. His fingers lingered on a decorative tile crowning the corner of the middle rack. Pasha stretched his eyes open as the waiter flipped up the tile revealing a small keyhole, and inserted the key into the lock. The shelf slid sideways, revealing a fully stocked wine cabinet.

"Wait, isn't it illegal to sell alcohol at a restaurant now?"

"We ain't the only one's breaking the law, kid. And the best part is we don't gotta worry about the police coming after us!" He pulled Pasha away from the door. "The key is confidence!" He threw Pasha a wink. "Follow my lead!"

Leo took one last peek through the window, glanced over his shoulder, then pushed his way into the kitchen. Pasha was left gawking at the swinging door.

"What?" Pasha looked over his shoulder, then looked back at the door. "What are we—? Leo!" The door burst open. Leo grabbed him by the wrist and towed him in after him.

"What are we doing?" Pasha ground his heels into the white tile.

"Would you relax?" He pulled Pasha into a coat closet. "Take off your coat and hat."

Pasha did as told. Leo did the same. When they were finished, Leo took their outer clothes and rolled them into a tight ball, handing it to Pasha. He turned towards the door and held up a finger.

"Wait right here."

Pasha had no choice but to obey. He stood rocking back on his heels while Leo disappeared. A moment later, Leo returned with a large tub used for collecting dishes. He placed the outer clothes in the container, and threw some freshly laundered black napkins on top. Pasha watched in bewilderment as he pulled two more from his back pocket.

"What are you gonna do with those?"

"Hold still." Leo wrapped the napkin lengthwise around Pasha's neck and made a neat bow tie. "It's a good thing we're both wearing white shirts today." He stepped back and framed Pasha with his hands as though he were about to snap a picture. "Perfect! Now it's my turn."

Pasha cocked his head curiously as Leo began making his own tie.

"But your vest is blue. Won't they notice?"

"Confidence, pal, confidence!" He finished off the knot. "You don't have to know what you're doing, you just have to look like you know what you're doing."

"Ain't that the truth!" scoffed Pasha. "How are you gonna get that key from that closet sommelier?"

Leo tossed Pasha an apron and beckoned him towards the exit. "Like I said, just follow my lead."

Pasha suppressed a groan and, still holding the tub, followed after his leader. Leo moved so fast Pasha could only assume he made it up as he went along. He nabbed a tray from the counter with a bowl of tomato soup, threw a towel over his arm, and glanced over his shoulder to make sure Pasha was following him. Silently and swiftly they slipped out into the dining room.

The waiter with the key was jotting down the orders of a couple on the opposite side of the room. Leo made a beeline for the table. Pasha watched as the waiter closed his notepad, clicked his pen, and bowed to the patrons. Just as he was turning on his heel, Leo feigned tripping, and dumped the bowl of tomato soup onto the front of the server's jacket.

The waiter threw up his hands in an outrage. "*Sciocco*!" You fool!

Striving to make his face as contrite as possible, Leo set aside the tray, and immediately set about dabbing the stain.

"*Mia culpa, signore*!" sang Leo in a fake Italian accent. He tossed the dirty towel into the tub, and reached for the man's collar. "Here, let me take that for you! I will have the stain out in a jiffy!"

The waiter sniffed irritably but consented to removing his jacket. "Lucky for you I have a spare!"

And with one burning look of intense hatred, he marched past Leo and back into the kitchen. Pasha gaped stupidly at Leo in disbelief. Leo smiled and winked. They headed off towards the kitchen.

470

"Keep an eye on the waiter." Leo slipped the key from the jacket pocket. "Tell me if he's coming this way."

Pasha watched as the waiter stomped furiously towards the bathroom to clean the sauce that had bled through to his shirt and shut the door.

"Coast is clear. Let's go!"

The boys hurried to the adjoining room with the secret door. Leo began feeling along the side of the shelf.

"Quick, which panel was it?"

"The middle one."

Leo flipped up the tile and slipped in the key. He pushed the door aside. "Alright, *Pavlushka*." They slid inside and shut the door behind them. "Start loading up!"

They set the tub down on the floor and began grabbing bottles two at a time. When the tub was sufficiently full, Leo threw their coats overtop the loot.

"Ready?"

Pasha lifted the tub and almost stumbled into the wall. "I think so!"

Leo glided the door open just a hair, and peeked through the crack. He threw Pasha a thumbs up. The door slithered along the track. Pasha kept his eyes on the back exit of the kitchen, eager to get far away from the restaurant. Just as Leo was turning to move the shelf back into place, the sommelier emerged from the bathroom. Pasha jumped to attention like a hare in an open meadow.

"You two! What do you think you are doing?"

"Act natural—" Leo growled through his teeth, but Pasha was already bolting for the back door.

"*Fermare*! *Lardo*!" Stop! Thief!

The cooks and waiters turned and started towards them. Pasha and Leo had no choice but to run now. A deafening crash sounded behind Pasha as Leo knocked an entire stockpot of soup onto the floor. Buttery broth flooded the already slick tile in a slippery, golden sheen. Their pursuers skidded in the fragrant sauce, grabbing hold of countertops and shelves for support.

Determined not to be had by a couple of hoods, the head waiter continued to charge across the kitchen. The moment his footing began to give way, he grabbed hold of a pot hanging from the ceiling. The pot skated down the rack like the handlebars of a zip line. Pasha tried to move but the puddle of soup had spread to the place where he stood. He balked at the sommelier like a deer in the headlights. The waiter dropped to his knees and sent Pasha flying backwards.

Pasha lifted the tub of alcohol over his head. Leo hastily nabbed it, and hopped atop the counter to avoid the muck. The waiter grabbed the counter and clambered over the surface.

Pasha glided to the corner piled with sacks of flour. Plunging his hand into the bag, he hurled a fistful of dust at the waiter's face. Temporarily blinded, the waiter flailed backwards with an angry cry. Pasha grabbed a rolling cart, stepped onto the lower platform and pushed off from the wall. Leo leapt off the counter and dove onto the dolly.

As they neared the exit, Leo kicked the door open with both feet. They scurried into the alleyway, Leo carrying the tub. Scarcely had they made it back onto the street, when the kitchen door swung open. The waiter barreled into the passage, saturated with flour, and reeking of butter and scallions. He looked very much like a dumpling about to be tossed in the frying pan.

"Come back here, *teppisti*!" Hoodlums!

Pasha and Leo quickened their pace.

"What are we gonna do now?" panted Pasha. "We can't run up the fire escape with all this!"

"I'm thinking, I'm thinking!"

A shrill whistle from the opposite side of the sidewalk froze Pasha where he stood.

"Oh, no."

While Pasha's eyes darted from rooftop to rooftop, desperately searching for an escape, Leo ground to an unexpected halt. Pasha staggered to a stop.

"What are you doing?"

"Hush! Act natural!" Leo leaned up against the wall with a solicitous smile. "Afternoon, officer! What seems to be the trouble?"

The waiter slowed just as the cop was putting away his whistle. One look at the police officer and his knees shivered like aspic. Now Pasha understood. If the cop saw what they had stolen, the entire restaurant would be shut down. The policeman jabbed his pen towards Leo and Pasha.

"These boys steal something from you, sir?"

"Steal?" gasped Leo. "Why, no, sir! We were just on our way to borrow some ice from the restaurant two doors over, just like Boss here ordered." He nodded towards the waiter. "Honest, we were!" He held out the tub. "You can take a look for yourself if you want!"

The waiter's mouth hinged open like a dead cod, then quickly righted itself into an oily grin. He clasped his sausagey fingers together.

"These boys? Steal?" He threw back his head and forced a laugh. "Why, of course not!" He wrapped his arm around Leo in a one-armed hug. "It is exactly as they say, officer! Only I was calling them back because I had a ladle I wanted returned to the chef there." He reached over and adjusted Pasha's tie like a doting father.

The police officer clicked his pen shut and nodded. "I see. Very well then." He tipped his hat and headed back to his post. "Sorry to have troubled you."

The moment the cop was out of earshot, the waiter ripped the napkin from Pasha's neck and stuck a finger in their faces.

"You boys win this time!" And with that, he turned on his heel and marched angrily back to the restaurant.

Chapter 73:
Because You're a Girl

While Pasha and Leo teamed up to steal, Faina became predictably bored. Gone were the days when she and Pasha could run their morning errands together. He was never home after lunch for a quick game of checkers or a trip to the library. Though Uncle Matvei was fond of her company, he could see she was growing restless, and her talkative nature increased twofold in the absence of her friend.

"It has everything, Uncle Matvei!" She leaned over the counter clutching the copy of *The Count of Monte Cristo*. "It's got bandits, and romance, and masquerades, and pirates, and villains with curly mustaches!"

Uncle Matvei chuckled as he swept the dust pile into the pan. "Sounds exciting."

Faina threw her head back in a dramatic display. "You have to read it!"

Uncle Matvei dumped the pan into the wastebasket. "I feel like I already have, *lapochka*."

Faina propped her chin on her fists in defeat. "It's not the same. You have to read it, then we can talk about it!"

Uncle Matvei patted her back and kissed her head. "Leave it on my bedside table. I'll try to read some tonight."

Faina hunched over her knees and sighed. He'd never get through it all. He hardly had enough time to assign her lessons these days, let alone read a massive adventure novel.

"Where did you get that anyway? It looks too worn to have come from the library. Some of the pages. are coming loose, and the spine is falling off."

"Aunt Poppy let me borrow it. She says it's her nephew's old copy." She turned the book around and pointed to the letters S.N. written on the inside cover.

Uncle Matvei scratched his head. "But her nephew's last name begins with a K."

"Oh." Faina shrugged. "I don't know what that's about."

"Has Pasha read it?"

Faina ran her finger over a loose thread in the spine. "No. He never has time anymore. Leo's his new best friend now."

"Now, *Faishka*, dear, you know that's not true." His face grew sober. "Pasha has responsibilities with the Breadwinners now." He brushed her hair over her shoulder. "Things … well, things might be a little different from now on. But that doesn't mean your friendship has changed. Pasha needs all the help he can get, you know that! And who better to help him than your brother?"

"I guess."

The bell over the door jingled. Leo entered, the entire right side of his face covered in what appeared to be blue paint. Faina stood.

"What on earth did you get yourselves into this time?"

"Knocked over a couple of ladders. They had paint on them."

"*Ey, seychas*!" Hey, now! exclaimed Uncle Matvei, rushing towards him with the rag. "I just cleaned the floors!" Uncle Matvei assaulted his face with the washcloth. "What is your wife going to do with you, huh?"

"She's used to it." Leo wriggled away. "Hey, Uncle Matvei, I was wondering if you had any more of those hot pickled radishes? Jazmin's been craving them like crazy."

Faina wrinkled her nose. "Hot pickled radishes?"

"It's the hormones."

"Maybe you can name your daughter Rapunzel."

Uncle Matvei ruffled her hair. "I just got another shipment. They're in the back."

"Thanks." Leo slipped past the curtain and down the back hall. Faina followed.

"Hey, Leo, what's the big idea with you hogging Pasha all the time?"

Leo rolled his eyes. "I'm not hogging your boyfriend, Faina. I'm helping him. You should be glad!" He rounded the corner into the stockroom.

"He's not my boyfriend!"

"Yeah, sure." He found the box labeled Petrov's Pickles and cut it open with his pocketknife.

"Can I help too?"

Curls of packing paper littered the floor as he plunged his hand into the crate. "Yeah, you can pick up the packing off the floor."

"Not with the pickles, smartypants! I wanna help you and Pasha!"

"What? You mean stealing?" Leo stuffed the jar under his arm. "No way!" He grabbed a box of Hostess cupcakes.

"Why not?"

"Because you're a girl." He pointed to a stack of saltines. "Are those crackers?"

Sighing, Faina grabbed a box and threw it on top of Leo's stack. "So?"

"So the Breadwinners don't allow girls." He began waddling back to the storefront.

"I'm not asking to be a Breadwinner, just to help you thieve!"

"Forget it, Faina. There's no way you could keep up!" He dropped his pickings down on the counter and made his way towards a shelf full of tinned goods.

Faina's mouth dropped open in disgusted offense. "What do you mean I couldn't keep up? How do you know?"

Leo grabbed an armful of canned tuna. Faina lifted an eyebrow.

"Which one of you is pregnant again?"

"You're not helping your case." He crossed back to the counter and dropped the cans. "Look, you're shorter, and weaker. You'd only slow us down."

Faina felt the adrenaline rise from the bottom of her chest to the top of her head.

"Weaker?"

Leo put a hand over his ear and winced. "And louder."

"Leontiy Spichkin, I oughta deck you one good! Just last year I knocked Pasha's tooth crooked on accident! And let's not forget my batting average!" She climbed up on the stool and leaned over the counter in Leo's face. "Not to mention I outran every one of those boys last week after hitting a home run! Pasha can't even pitch! And as for slow …" Faina put her leg up on the table. "These stems aren't just for looks, you know!"

Leo flailed backwards in disgust. "Ugh! Uncle Matvei, Faina's talking about her legs again!"

Uncle Matvei turned from his dusting on the opposite side of the store and scurried towards the counter.

"Faina Adrianovna! Put that away!" He shooed her leg back under the counter.

Leo grabbed a pen and ripped off the cap with his teeth. "I swear, you're raising a stripper." He grabbed the inventory sheet and wrote down his purchases.

"I am not going to be a stripper!" Faina turned to their uncle. "Uncle Matvei, Leo says I'm slower and weaker than he and Pasha."

"What?" Uncle Matvei was aghast. "Have you seen her play baseball?"

Leo sighed and, gathering up his goods, headed towards the door leading to the hallway. But Faina wasn't about to let him get away.

"Leo, you know none of that is true! Come on! Why can't you let me steal with you guys? I never get to see Pasha anymore! And it's boring without anyone to talk to!"

Leo stopped on the first landing of the stairs and turned towards her.

"Faina! Do you honestly think it's a good idea for you to go running around the city with us in your fluffy skirts and dresses stealing alcohol? Let it go! You're not coming with us!" And with that, he charged up the rest of the stairs.

Chapter 74:
One of the Boys

Pasha and Leo bounced along in the back of the line-six subway headed for Grand Central, all the while keeping a close eye on the man with the rolling trunk facing the aisle. He was a rough-looking gentleman with thick muscles, a salty beard, and somewhat bulging eyes that remained steadfastly rooted to the opposite wall of the car. They'd tracked him all the way from the American Seamen's Friend Society Sailors' Home and Institute, an outpost for sailors in West Village. Their fellow passengers appeared too preoccupied with their hurried, metropolitan existence to afford the trunk and its lumbering master the slightest suspicion. Had anyone on that car managed to surmise the slightest notion as to the worth of that valise, every thirst-ridden, alcohol-deprived, money-grubbing tongue would have salivated right through the leather!

"Can we go through the plan one more time?" muttered Pasha out the side of his mouth.

Leo sighed and pulled down the brim of his cap. "Again? Are you serious?"

"Come on, Leo! No one's listening to us anyway!"

"I got a better idea. Why don't you repeat it back to me?"

Pasha leaned forward with his elbows on his knees and groaned.

"After arriving in Grand Central, we follow the fella outside." He looked uncertainly up at Leo.

"Yeah, go on."

"A delivery van will be waiting to transfer the whis—*oof*!"

Leo elbowed him in the side so hard it nearly knocked the wind from his lungs.

"Not so loud!" He looked down at Pasha with a guilty expression. "Sorry, kid."

Perhaps if they had been stealing any other kind of whiskey—had it been medicinal, or Canadian, or even moonshine—Leo might not have been so paranoid. But this was Irish whiskey, and it had traveled an entire ocean at a high price to arrive safely and secretly at the St. Regis Hotel.

Pasha rubbed his ribs and winced. "A delivery van will be waiting to take it to the St. Regis. After the whiskey's been paid for, that's where you come in impersonating a prohibition agent, and demand they hand over the trunk."

"That's right! Easy as pie!"

Pasha tried to mask his anxiety by chewing on the inside of his lower lip, with little success.

"But, Leo, do you really think that's gonna work? I mean, aren't you kinda young to be a member of the Prohibition Bureau?"

"It's like I said, kid. They take any random fella off the street, hand him a badge and a gun, and say go out there and bust up the bootleggers."

"Anyone? Really?"

"Anyone! No experience required!"

Pasha shook his head in disbelief. "But surely they go through some kinda training, don't they?"

Leo shrugged. "Not much, I'm told. Why just last week one of these bureau agents up in the Finger Lakes got a little too trigger-happy and shot an innocent victim for taking a swig of root beer."

"Where'd you hear that?"

"My buddy, Jonathon."

Pasha froze. "Jonathon? Please don't tell me you mean Jonathon Boucher!"

Leo sucked his teeth and crossed his arms over his chest. "That's the one."

"Oh, come on, Leo!" The volume of Pasha's voice rose involuntarily. "You know he was probably saying that just to mess with you!"

"Calm down! I did my research, okay? Even if they haven't shot anybody, these prohis are essentially nobodies with a badge!"

"Yeah, a badge. A real, bona fide, government-issued badge of certification." He glanced pointedly in the direction of Leo's pocket where he'd stashed away a toy sheriff's badge. "Not a toy!"

"I'll only flash it for a second!"

"Aren't you a little worried you're being overly confident?"

"Overly confident?" Leo threw back his head and snorted. "In this game there ain't no such thing! What do I always tell you? You don't gotta know what you're doing—"

"You just gotta look like you know what you're doing." Pasha threw himself back against the seat and sighed. "I know, I know." It was a stupid philosophy, and yet he'd never been able to prove Leo wrong.

The train lurched to a stop. Pasha started to rise but Leo pulled him back down.

"Easy there, buddy, easy. Don't be hasty."

They waited for the doors to open. Pasha started towards the exit on the opposite end of the train nearest the man with the suitcase, but Leo towed him through the nearest portal.

"Don't make it obvious," he whispered, dragging him onto the platform.

"I just don't wanna lose him."

"Relax, relax. The key is to keep a level head."

They followed him up the ramp. As they made their way through the concourse, Pasha realized the value in Leo's advice, for the man was fairly easy to spot in a crowd. Outside, a van was waiting just as Leo had said. A well-groomed man, possibly a concierge, in a tailored coat and hat was standing by the passenger door with his hands folded behind his back. Overall, the exchange had been somewhat discreet, but Pasha couldn't help but feel that sending this man to deal with the rough-handed gangster was rather imprudent on the part of the St. Regis. He couldn't imagine under what circumstances these two men would ever cross paths save for the exchange of illegal goods.

Leo guided Pasha beneath a nearby awning where they could observe the scene without being watched themselves. The concierge held out his hand to greet the thug. The gangster took an awkward pause before giving the man a brief, hearty shake. Meanwhile the driver got out and opened up the back. Pasha took one step forward. Again, Leo yanked him back by the shoulder. Money was exchanged and, together, the driver and the thug lifted the trunk into the cab.

Leo smacked his shoulder.

"Get ready." He fished into his pocket for the fake badge.

The concierge tipped his hat, and the gangster disappeared into the crowd.

"Let's go!"

Pasha followed Leo up to the van, struggling to mimic his confident swagger.

"Hey! Yous two," Leo barked.

The driver and the concierge jerked around. They hadn't even shut the doors yet. Leo whipped out his wallet with the badge with the speed of a jaguar.

"Agent Dwayne Thompson with the New York Prohibition Bureau." He held up his other hand and snapped. "Hey!" He jabbed two fingers at his eyes. "Eyes here, fellas."

It was classic misdirection. He didn't even give them a chance to look at the badge before he was shoving it away. He gestured to Pasha.

"This is my partner, Agent Norman Hooper."

A bead of sweat was forming on the concierge's temple, and he looked as though he were in the early stages of a heart attack. The chauffeur, on the other hand, narrowed his eyes.

"Aren't you boys a little young to be prohibition agents?"

"Tell that to my ex-wife, you wet sack of horse manure. That observation was about as useful as a box of cornflakes in a tornado on a Sunday. I'd slap you if I thought it'd do you any good."

Pasha stood off to the side wanting as little involvement as possible in Leo's ridiculous charade. From where he stood he could see clearly into the back of the van where the others could not.

"I'm gonna need you fellas to show me what's inside the trunk."

The chauffeur wasn't backing down. "Yeah? Where's your warrant?"

"Law enforcement doesn't need a warrant to search a vehicle suspected of transporting illegal liquor," Pasha piped up, feeling useful for once, "as stated in the Volstead Act."

Pasha wasn't certain if Leo had prepared a response, but judging by the look of gratitude he flashed him afterwards, he had not.

"You heard the man! Don't you read the news, you no-good slimeball? Don't you bother to acquaint yourself with the law? Why, if I had an apple seed for every stupid thing that comes outta your mouth I'd have enough cyanide to kill myself so I don't have to listen to you anymore!"

A snapping sound drew his attention to the vehicle. Pasha did a double take as he realized the trunk was opening of its own accord. A hand pushed open the lid. Pasha scurried around to Leo's side of the van and cleared his throat.

"Le—Dwayne? Um, Dwayne?"

"One second, Hooper." Leo waved a finger in the chauffeur's face. "And another thing! What makes you so high and mighty that you think you can dress down an officer of the Prohibition Bureau?"

A figure emerged quietly from the back of the van, that of a tall, long-legged boy in a baggy jacket and brown flat cap. Pasha tugged harder on Leo's sleeve.

"Dwayne!"

"Let's just see what you got back here!" Leo marched around to the back of the van and flipped open the trunk.

"Aha!" Leo's face fell. The trunk was completely empty. Pasha covered his face with his hand. The other boy was already dashing up the street. Before Leo could shut the suitcase, the chauffeur ripped the wallet from his pocket and held it open, revealing the toy sheriff's badge.

"You boys do realize that impersonating law enforcement is a federal offense … or don't you bother to acquaint yourselves with the law?"

Leo snatched back his wallet and grabbed hold of Pasha's elbow. "Run!"

They took off down Forty-fifth, their pursuers chasing after them shouting for police.

"I don't understand," huffed Leo as they turned onto Madison Avenue. "What happened to the mash?"

"You wanna know what happened to the mash?" Pasha pointed to the back of a cable car that was just crossing. "Ask him!"

The boy was hanging from a pole in the rear.

"What?"

"While you were talking he just popped out of the trunk and walked off! He has the whiskey stashed in his jacket, I saw some!"

Whistles blew in their wake. Pasha turned and looked over his shoulder. A cop was sprinting up the sidewalk. He supposed since the suitcase was empty the chauffeur and the concierge had nothing to lose by setting the police on them.

"Well, I'll say this about the fella," huffed Leo, "he's sure got swell taste. I have a jacket exactly like that!" Leo paused and narrowed his eyes on the culprit. "Wait a second, that ain't no fella." Leo picked up his pace, determined to catch up to the cable car. "Faina!"

Faina turned and jumped, the light striking under the brim of her cap affording them a good look at her. Now Pasha saw it. The sprays of thick black hair sticking out from under the hat, a perfect aquiline nose, and freckles like a turned-over pepper shaker. She pushed through the crowd towards the front of the tram just as Leo was swinging himself onto the back.

Pasha picked up his pace and grabbed hold of the railing. Leo was already at the front.

"Where'd she go?"

Leo leaned out the side of the car. "She's headed for Central Park!" Before he could jump out after her, Pasha grabbed hold of his shoulder.

"Wait! What are you gonna do about the cop?"

They could still hear the shrill whistle chasing after them. "Stop! Stop the car!"

Pasha could see Leo was formulating a plan by the way his eyes darted about the car.

"Right." He pulled his cap down. "I'll ditch the cop, you go after Faina. I'll catch up with you in Central Park. I'll jump out first."

Leo swung himself back into the street and waved his cap. "Hey! Over here!"

Pasha sighed and got out at the next block. He wasn't sure what he was supposed to do with Faina; he certainly wasn't going to try and trap her like Leo would. Perhaps it was better that Leo had sent him after her. He spotted her entering the park through the plaza, so he headed for Gapstow Bridge where he could cut her off.

Not wishing to be seen as she approached, Pasha stood at the corner and waited, but the moment Faina spied Pasha, she ran right past the bridge and continued north.

"Faina!" He ran after her. "Hey! Faina, what are you running from me for?"

But she did not stop; in fact, she ran all the way to the carousel before she showed any signs of slowing down. Just as Pasha was staggering out from under the Playmate's Arch and up the incline, Leo came barreling down the adjacent path and hit Faina like a juggernaut.

"What do you think you're doing?"

He roped her in a headlock and dragged her back under the arch, Faina squealing all the way.

"Leo! Lighten up!" Pasha pried at his elbow. "You don't have to be so rough!"

Faina sprang back into an upright position like a cattail. Now that she was up close, Pasha could see the full getup. He didn't know how she had managed it, but she'd stolen a pair of Leo's trousers, along with his jacket.

"How did you get hold of my clothes?" demanded Leo.

"Clothesline." She turned and struck a pose. "And I gotta say, I think they look better on me than you!"

"They look fantastic on you!" blurted Pasha without thinking, unaccustomed to seeing a girl in something as formfitting as men's trousers. Leo flashed him a look.

"Give me that!" He ripped the jacket from her torso, making the bottles clank, and immediately gasped. Apparently, she had forgone the button-up in favor of one of Leo's thermal undershirts, leaving little to the imagination.

Leo draped the coat back over his sister like a magician trying to make a rabbit disappear.

"Why aren't you wearing a shirt?"

Faina stared back at him dumbfounded. "I am wearing a shirt."

"A real shirt! With buttons!"

Faina threw up her shoulders. "It was too small."

"So? Who do you think you're fooling? You can't let people see you like this!"

Pasha was still grinning like a complete idiot. "Why not?"

Leo turned and stuck his finger warningly in Pasha's face. "You're really asking for it, kid!"

Faina stamped her foot. "Fanny Brice dresses like this!"

"Fanny Brice wears a tuxedo in a cabaret show!" Leo pinched her shoulder. "This is real life! Not only that, but did you really stuff yourself inside some gangster's suitcase from West Village to Grand Central?"

"Obviously."

Leo's hands slid up his temples and into his hair. His eyes widened with a terrible realization.

"Faina, you could've suffocated! You could have died! You could have been caught and strangled to death by a member of the Irish mafia!"

She crossed her arms over her chest with a smug smile. "But I wasn't!"

Leo grabbed her by the wrist. "Come on!" He tugged her in the opposite direction.

"Where are we going?"

"I'm taking you home so you can change!"

"And then I can come back and steal with you guys, right?"

Leo ground to a halt. He turned to face her, his eyes wide with exasperation.

"No! Absolutely not! No! No! No!"

"Why not?" Faina was shouting now. "You saw me just now! I was every bit as good as you and Pasha! I stole fifteen bottles of Irish whiskey while you and Pasha were busy getting caught! It's not fair! You know I deserve to be here just as much as you do!"

"You need to be at home with Uncle Matvei!"

"Doing what?" There were tears in her eyes now. "Sitting at the counter talking about things nobody cares about? Going to the drugstore with my invisible friends? It won't interfere with my lessons, I promise!"

Leo craned his head back and pinched the space between his eyebrows. Faina kept going.

"You can't make me do anything. If you send me home, I'll just come back! I'll sabotage every last heist you come up with until you let me join in!"

Leo had heard enough. He hooked her under the arm and dragged her off towards Fifth Avenue.

"Oh, yeah? I'd like to see you try!"

***

Leo got his wish. Not only did they see her try but they saw her succeed time and time again. She circumvented them at every available opportunity. They'd break into drugstores only to find that Faina had snatched up every last bottle of medicinal whiskey on the shelves. They'd target restaurants and discover their quarry had taken security precautions after Faina had already paid them a visit. As for how they knew it was Faina undermining all their operations, she would always leave a red kiss stain at the scene of the crime as a sort of calling card in homage to her days as the Kissing Cat Burglar. Eventually, it got to the point where Klokov was beginning to notice a decline in Pasha's and Leo's productivity.

After several weeks, Leo burst into Faina's room without knocking and threw her a pair of sports knickers. Faina held them up with two fingers.

"What's this for?"

"Wear those under your dress whenever you tag along. No showing up in a pair of my trousers like some two-bit floozy! Got it?"

Faina turned towards him with a smug simper. "I knew you'd come around eventually."

Chapter 75:
Delmonico's

Time spent with the Breadwinners passed quickly at first. Fighting might not have grown on Pasha, but he learned to bear it, and it became easier. Not only did Uncle Matvei and Leo frequently school him on his technique, but the running around and climbing was making him stronger. Leo even showed him how to run up a wall. By the end of the summer he'd shot up another three inches, and now had several stretch marks accompanying his lash scars. However, he couldn't complain much, for his increase in size had helped him earn the rank of twelfth out of twenty-four street fighters.

On a swampy day in late August, when the air was soggy and burdensome, Pasha and Leo made their way to the Foxhole to turn in their goods to Klokov. It had yet to grow very crowded, and Sergei, Anastas, Yuri, and a couple of other street fighters were hanging around in their undershirts, fanning themselves with bits of old newspaper and slipping ice down their collars. Even Klokov had stripped down to his shirtfront in an attempt to beat the heat.

"I gotta hand it to you, boys," he said, thumbing through a stack of hundred-dollar bills. "You make an excellent team." He handed them both their pay. "Pleasure doing business with you, as always." He stood and rubbed at his lower back. "Pretty soon Chevalsky here will be on his own. But it's a good thing he had someone showing him the ropes his first year."

"Times up already, Spichkin?" asked Moneyrider. "Boy, time flies." He lit a cigarette.

Leo leaned against the counter and proudly lifted his chin. "Next week's my last week."

"Just in time for the baby, eh?" said Yuri. Before Leo could answer he turned on
Moneyrider. "What do you think you're doing? Don't smoke that over here!"

Moneyrider held the cigarette between his teeth and thrust out his arms. "Since when do you care?"

Yuri grabbed the electric fan sitting between them and turned it so that the hot smoke blew back in Moneyrider's face.

"Alright, alright," he coughed, waving his hands. "I get your point. It's too hot." He got up and headed for the alley door. Leo took his empty seat, and Pasha pulled up a stool from the bar.

"The whole thing couldn't have been timed any better," Leo admitted.

As Klokov passed, he laid a leather folder on the table. "Been meaning to get this back to you, Leo."

Sergei craned his head forward. "What is it?"

"My photography portfolio. Klokov asked to see it a month ago …" He turned sheepishly to Klokov. "Only, you never told me what you wanted it for."

Klokov slipped his hands into his pockets and smiled. "I was showing it to my buddy down at the *New York Evening Post*."

Leo grabbed the table as though he might fall over. "You what?"

"Said he liked what he saw. And he wants to meet you for a job interview September sixteenth down at Delmonico's."

"Delmonico's?" exclaimed Sergei, his eyes wide with fascination.

Yuri could hardly contain himself. "You mean that fancy joint where all the Wall Street fellas eat?"

Leo opened and shut his eyes several times, looking as though he might faint. "Delmon … a—a job interview?"

Klokov was beaming like a proud father. "You've been a loyal associate, Leontiy. You've served me faithfully for four years now just like we agreed. Now it's time for you to go and make something of yourself."

Leo might not have been one for teary displays, but for a moment Pasha was sure he was going to cry.

For the first time that evening Anastas perked up. "The *New York Evening Post* wants to hire this guy?" He hopped down off the barstool and swaggered towards the table. "Let me see this." He snatched up Leo's portfolio and paged through the files.

Pasha's insides burned with indignation, but the stub of a cigarette hanging from Anastas's mouth made him too nervous to try and take him by surprise, lest Leo's photographs be harmed somehow.

"I don't see what's so special." He snickered as he came across a picture of a German patriarch staring tearfully at his boarded-up liquor store. "You're telling me the *New York Evening Post* is interested in pictures of weepy old men?"

Leo reached up and snatched the photograph from Anastas's grip. "That man lost his entire business thanks to Prohibition!"

"What's that gotta do with the *Post*?"

Pasha felt his jaw tensing. "Haven't you ever heard of Jacob Riis?"

"Of course not, Pasha," teased Leo. "All Anastas ever reads is the *Subversive* and *Tijuana Bibles*."

Sergei and Yuri bent forward and chortled merrily. Anastas's eyebrows lowered together in a sharp point. The muscles in his neck seemed to bulge. He threw the portfolio down on the table.

"If I were you, Spichkin, I wouldn't get my hopes up."

Pasha stole a glance at Klokov, who was watching the exchange with an impartial eye, and his hands in his vest pockets. Trash talk was something he encouraged between the boys; it built character. But he did not like injustice, and usually ended up having to intervene where Anastas was concerned.

"And if I were you, Sippenhaft, I'd stick my head in kerosene and light a cigarette."

Pasha covered his mouth and sputtered while the boys let out a raucous laugh. Anastas slammed his fists on the table and leaned low into Leo's face.

"Go ahead, try to make something of yourself. But deep down everyone knows you're just cheap trash like the rest of us."

Leo leaned back in his chair and snickered. "Please, Anastas, if I tried half as hard at photography as you do at being a complete moron, I'd be Man Ray."

Anastas gave Leo one final vicious glare before turning and leaving, and in that brief moment Pasha discovered something profound, something he never expected. Anastas hated Leo far more than he would ever hate Pasha.

Chapter 76:
Old Associations

Anastas flicked the remains of his cigarette over the railing as he made his way across the Brooklyn Bridge in the pale shade of early evening. He was just returning from a visit with a girl he'd met on the third floor of the Landmark Tavern, whom he was walking out with. The relationship was nothing serious. She was an Italian, fifteen, and lived with her artist mother in a boardinghouse in Brooklyn Heights. Still, it was something to pass the time, and it was nice to have someone to talk to. Anastas may have considered himself a loner, but even he needed to be reminded that not everyone hated him.

He had just made it to the halfway point when he noticed a couple of hoods congregated beneath the lamplight on South Street below the bridge. Anastas slowed and narrowed his eyes. They weren't particularly big fellows, and their clothes were rather shabby compared to other gangsters.

Anastas drew back into the shadows. He was familiar with these thugs. He'd seen them before at his parents' secret meetings in east Harlem. Better to keep walking and steer clear of South Street. He was headed home anyway.

The promenade went on for a good distance, and fifteen minutes passed before Anastas made it back onto the street. He traveled up Center and took a right on Worth headed towards the Bowery. He turned the corner.

"I thought I smelled schnitzel down by the bridge earlier."

A fifteen-year-old with greasy hair was crossing his way in the opposite direction.

"What's new, Spike? Ain't you due back at the zoo by eleven?"

Spike, the son of his parents' friends, chuckled and shook Anastas's hand. "Good to see you again, Sippenhaft. We hardly ever cross paths these days!"

"Yeah, well, can you blame me? Breadwinners ain't exactly welcome amongst Butcher types."

Spike shrugged. "You did what you had to do." He punched Anastas's shoulder playfully. "Just so you know, you ain't got no hard feelings from me."

Anastas gave a gentle nod, his version of a smile. "I take it you joined up with the Butchers?"

Spike removed a pack of cigarettes from his pocket. "Not if I can help it." He offered the box to Anastas, who declined. "Seems like I'm the only bum around here opposed to making enemies."

"Then what were you doing with those thugs beneath the bridge?"

Spike stuck a cigarette between his teeth and shrugged. "Just being neighborly." He flicked his lighter over the tip and inhaled.

"Neighborly?"

"Don't look so cynical." He pocketed the lighter. "It pays a lot more to have friends in high places than picking a side. If you'd'a waited a bit longer before joining the Breadwinners you'd know that."

"Pays how?"

Spike glanced from one side of the street to the other before pinching Anastas's forearm and dragging him beneath a fire escape on Mott.

"Look, I like you, okay? And because I like you, I'm gonna share a bit of information with you. But you can't say nothing to any of your Breadwinner friends, you hear?" He looked over his shoulder one more time. "Don't venture below Chambers this Thursday, understand?"

"Why?"

"Never mind why, alright? Just stay in the neighborhood."

Anastas squinted. "They're targeting Wall Street again, aren't they?"

Spike straightened and lowered his cap down over his eyes. "I ain't said nothing."

Anastas grumbled and slid his hands into his pockets. "Do they really gotta do this?"

"Shhh! Keep your voice down!"

"I mean, since when has this ever worked? They never even hit their target. Instead other working-class people get caught in the crossfires! Like that time they went after the senator in Atlanta! And who was it who got hurt? The maid who opened the package! Took off both her hands! It's gotta stop!"

"Look, you don't gotta tell me twice. I ain't the one making threats!"

"Yeah? Well, you ain't doing nothing to stop them either."

Spike scoffed. "And you're telling me you are?"

Anastas turned and stared irritably at him. Spike took another drag.

"You really gonna turn them in to the police?"

Anastas took a deep breath and let his shoulders drop. "Nah. I ain't putting another working sap in jail."

"Then I'd appreciate it if you toned down the accusations a bit."

Anastas chuckled and shook his head. "You're a rat, Spike."

"One of the smartest rodents in the animal kingdom." Spike tipped his cap and headed off in the opposite direction. "And they own this city."

Anastas raked his fingers over his face and sighed. The anarchists were in serious need of some new leadership. How many failed attempts would it take for them to grow? How many of their own would have to suffer before they changed tactics? When he tried to think of a reason to wind up on Wall Street on Thursday he came up with nothing, and yet the date continued to stand out in his memory.

He was nearing his apartment building now. Anastas reached into his pocket and dug around for his keys. Up ahead Leo was emerging from the Foxhole. Anastas dropped his keys on the pavement. It wasn't he who had an appointment on Wall Street that day, but Leo. That was the day he would be meeting the journalist at Delmonico's for an interview.

Anastas snatched his keys off the ground. If the Gallianists were planning to cause trouble in the Financial District, the first place they'd target would be the J.P. Morgan building, five blocks away from Delmonico's. Furthermore, what were the odds that the demonstration and Leo's interview would occur at the same time?

Slim at best, he thought, turning into the alleyway where his apartment was located. He paused below the steps. That wasn't true. But what did he care? After all the times Spichkin had humiliated him, what did Anastas owe him? And he hadn't forgotten how badly Leo had assaulted him New Year's Day. He may have treated Faina poorly, but he had been drinking and would never have behaved in such a way sober. But wouldn't he have done the same if the tables were turned? If it had been Alexei who was hurt?

Leo was crossing towards his block now. Anastas hurried up the stairs, but stopped halfway. Leo crossed in front of his apartment.

"Hey, Spichkin!" Anastas raced down the stairs.

Leo took one look over his shoulder and continued walking.

"Spichkin!" He ran out to the sidewalk. "Hey! I'm talking to you!"

"So? I ain't listening!"

Anastas caught up with him in front of the barbershop. "Well, maybe you oughta start."

Leo turned and spat. "Since when do you got anything interesting to say?"

"Hey!" Anastas jumped in front of him and planted his feet firmly on the ground. "If you ditch the attitude for five minutes you might find you're interested in what I have to say. You think you can manage that?"

"Can I manage to ditch the attitude?" Leo pretended to think it over, then shrugged. "No, actually, I can't manage it. Because the deep-seeded disgust your face inspires in me is so overwhelmingly powerful that no human could resist it. Physicists study it at their universities. It is so far beyond my capabilities to refrain from insulting you that science cannot begin to explain such a phenomenon. I find it easier to respect a cockroach crawling on a piece of crap on the sidewalk than I do your ugly mug. Freud's Oedipal Complex is less disturbing than you. Were I to so much as smile in your direction, the Pope would declare it a sign of the End Times. Dogs would howl. The sun would grow dark. Men would rise up from their graves. And a fire would probably start under the city that burned for forty years. So not only is it beyond my capability to be nice to you, but for the sake of humanity itself I'm afraid I cannot ditch the attitude."

Anastas responded with two words, one of which was of the four-letter variety.

"I haven't forgotten what you did to my sister," warned Leo. "I never will. And I don't suggest you forget either."

Anastas was in an exceptionally obnoxious mood now. He eased back, grinning deviously.

"Oh, trust me, I think about her every night."

Anastas took off towards his apartment just as Leo was lunging for him. He ran up the stairs and locked the door behind him. Leo drummed his fists on the door.

"You stay away from her, you hear? Or I'll kick your teeth out of your head!"

Chapter 77:
Trinity

Faina had never seen Leo so up. And why shouldn't he be? He may have been a two-bit hood but unlike most boys in his position, Leo was about to leave all that behind. He had a baby on the way and a future on the horizon. He had married the girl of his dreams even if the circumstances had been less than ideal, he was making money hand over fist, and the career he'd always dreamed of was finally within his grasp.

It was almost comical to see the way Pasha looked up when her brother entered a room. To Pasha, not only was Leo the poster child of the American Dream, he was a ray of hope.

Thursday morning, Faina awakened to her bedroom door swinging open with a loud bang, and Leo plopping down at the foot of her mattress.

"Rise and shine, Domino!"

Faina winced and rubbed her eyes. "Did you hit your head and need me to write down the directions to your own apartment?"

Ignoring her quip, Leo reached into his pocket and counted out a considerable stack of money.

"Here, take this." He slapped it down on her stomach.

Faina stared at him in tired confusion. "Okay, now I know you've hit your head. What's all this for?"

Leo's mouth widened with a facetious grin. "A thank you would be nice."

"*Doveryay, no proveryay.*" Trust, but verify.

"I'm in a good mood, okay? Take this money, and you and Pasha go have lunch at Trinity Place while I'm having my interview. That is, unless you've robbed them too, in which case you might wanna head to a restaurant you haven't pilfered from. Why should I have all the fun?"

Faina glanced from the wad of bills to her brother in astonishment. Leo patted her knee.

"You two kids have helped me a lot the past year."

Faina smirked. "Pretty sure you've helped us more than we've helped you."

"Yeah?" He reached over and ruffled her hair. "Well, let me do this for you anyway." He kissed her head and headed for the door. "You'll wanna look nice. Use the morning to get ready. Meet Pasha and me at the Fulton Street Station right before the lunch hour. That way you can wish me good luck before my interview."

As Faina washed and dressed she couldn't stop fantasizing about what it would be like to see her brother's name printed on the front page of the *New York Evening Post* beneath a giant photograph he himself had taken. Leo was going to change the world. She truly believed it. He would make things better for immigrants living in the Lower East Side. Kids wouldn't have to go to the Breadwinners when their families fell on hard times; they would find real, high-paying jobs regardless of their names, languages, or backgrounds.

He'd get a house on Long Island, a classy, brick residence with a wrought-iron fence, and plenty of room for the baby to run around and play. And then Leo and Jazmin would have more children. Faina would be the crazy aunt to dozens of little nieces and nephews, and just like a forest mowed to the ground, their little family would grow back, larger and stronger than before.

She slipped her stockinged feet into her shoes and tied her bow. She twirled before the mirror, admiring the pleats of her red-and-cream-colored dress with the checkered windowpane pattern. Faina had always been told she looked striking in red, what with her raven-colored hair and dark eyes. She even put on her garnet ring. It was not a real garnet, of course, but Faina was not pretentious, even if she was, on occasion, a little flashy.

When it was time to leave, she kissed Uncle Matvei goodbye and headed off towards Fulton Station. The radio had forecasted rain, but as far as Faina could tell it was a mild day with just enough heat left over from the summer to be pleasant. With so many children having returned to school the streets remained relatively quiet and open during work hours.

She sauntered towards her destination with the pleasant feeling of entering a quiet room after being stuck in a noisy hall for too long. As she approached the corner of Orchard and Grand, she could have sworn she heard someone calling her name.

"Faina!"

Faina turned and spied Anastas of all people waving her down from the opposite sidewalk. Faina shivered. It had been nearly a year since the incident that had ended with Leo beating the stuffing out of Anastas. To see him acknowledging her now, to hear him calling her name as though nothing had transpired, made her stomach turn. Faina ducked her head and hastened across the crosswalk. But she could hear Anastas's steps pursuing her.

494

"Hey, Spichkin! Where you going?"

Faina stuck her hands in her pockets, refusing to answer.

"Spichkin! Speak! Talk to me!"

Faina's eyes widened. How he could possibly have the nerve to address her so forcefully and with such demand was beyond her comprehension.

"Where you going, huh? I said, where you going?"

Eager to get rid of him, she finally ground her heels into the asphalt. Perhaps if she made a big enough scene Anastas would grow embarrassed and leave her alone. She pivoted violently towards him.

"Go away!"

Anastas took a step back and threw up his hands. "You really hate me, don't you?"

Faina pinched her eyes closed and drew a breath. It was all a game, and Anastas was determined to get her to play.

"You must really want another beating from my brother."

"Look, I just wanna know where you're going. Okay?"

Faina's voice broke as it rose in pitch. "Why do you suddenly care? We haven't been friends for a year! What business is it of yours where I go and what I do?"

"It's just, you look awful nice for a day of pilfering and bootlegging. You got yourself a boyfriend or something?"

Faina lowered her head and glared at him. "You really are insane, aren't you?"

She turned and continued on her way. Anastas grabbed her by the arm. Faina jerked around with all her strength and slammed her open hand across Anastas's cheek.

"Let's get something straight here. You don't touch me! You don't look at me! You don't say a word to me!"

Anastas threw up his hands. "Look, just do me a favor and stay away from Wall Street today, okay?"

Faina dared towards him ready to knock him upside the head a second time with her purse.

"I can go wherever I want! Why should I do you any favors?"

"Will you just lis—"

"Excuse me, young lady," said an elderly, protective voice. Faina turned to see a kindly older gentleman in a flat cap staring warningly at Anastas. "Is this young man bothering you?"

Faina turned and smiled appreciatively at the old man. "Yes, sir. I'm afraid he won't stop harassing me."

By now the other street vendors and several other passersby had stopped to watch the pair. Anastas threw up his hands and swore. The man lifted his walking stick and jabbed it threateningly at Anastas's knees.

"Now, look here, boy. You have until the count of five to turn back up this street and vanish before I call the police."

Before the man could even enumerate his first number, Anastas spat on the ground and cursed. As he spun around in the opposite direction, he picked up his foot and slammed his heel into a nearby trashcan, kicking it several feet down the sidewalk.

Faina swallowed as her eyes threatened to fill with frightful tears. But she steeled her shoulders. She wouldn't let Anastas ruin her day. Faina generously thanked her rescuer, and went on her way.

Soon Faina was passing Dutch Street with its red-brick buildings and crow-stepped gables. Pasha and Leo were standing at the corner of Fulton just outside the subway entrance. Leo had never looked more dapper. He stood leaning against the hunter-green railing in a three-piece brown-worsted suit, his chestnut hair slicked smartly to the side beneath a straw boater. As a gift, Uncle Matvei had saved up and bought Leo a brand new leather portfolio with his name embossed on the cover in glittering gold letters. Leo tucked it protectively against his side with the label facing outwards. Pasha turned and, spying Faina, nudged Leo's side. Leo stretched his arm over his head and waved.

"Faina!"

Pride and excitement bubbled to Faina's lips in an enthusiastic grin. She raced down the sidewalk towards her brother.

"What do you think, kid?" He removed his hat and turned in a circle.

Faina stood back and stroked her chin. "Look at you, dapper dan! You clean up nice!"

"They say first impressions count for everything," observed Pasha.

Faina took each of their elbows as they headed down William Street.

"What I wanna know is, what are you gonna order at Delmonico's?"

"What am I gonna order?" Leo scratched at his chin and raised his eyebrows. "Gee, I never thought about it."

"You're telling me you're about to go to what is probably the ritziest steakhouse in all of Manhattan and you haven't given one thought as to what you're going to eat?"

Pasha chuckled. "Clearly, your priorities are out of order."

Leo rolled his eyes in a playful manner. "Oh, no doubt!"

"You could have eggs Benedict!" Faina prattled on. "Or beef Wellington, or—Oh! Do you think they have oysters? All the fanciest restaurants have oysters! Did you know Charles Dickens ate at Delmonico's?" She arched her head back and sighed. "I would give anything to sit at a table where Charles Dickens sat!"

Leo smirked at her with a playful fondness. "Maybe if I get this job we'll go visit his house someday." He kissed the side of her head.

They stopped at the corner of Broadway and Cedar. Leo turned towards Faina with his head bent as though presenting himself to a priest for a blessing.

"Well, this is it. One last chance to wish me good luck!"

Faina placed her hands on her hips, and drew herself up in a most regal manner.

"First, you must bow!"

Smirking, Leo took a knee. Faina held out her arm as though it were a saber and tapped both his shoulders.

"I bestow the greatest fortune and best of luck upon thee, Leontiy Adrianovitch Spichkin."

Leo looked up at her and squinted his eyes in the afternoon light. "May I rise now, Your Highness?"

Faina placed her finger to her lip as though she hadn't quite decided yet. "I suppose you may."

Leo got to his feet, but before he could dust the knees of his trousers, Faina wrapped her arms around him in a tight hug.

"You're gonna do great, *Leoshka*."

Leo patted her back. "Thanks, Domino-Face."

Pasha shook his hand and wished him luck one last time, and then Leo was on his way.

"How long do you think the interview will take?" asked Faina as she watched her brother disappear into the crowd.

"As long as it takes to eat a meal, I guess."

Faina scoffed and began walking in the direction of Trinity Place. "In that case, Leo will be done in no time."

"I don't know. If I had a big interview at Delmonico's I don't think I'd be able to get a bite down."

"Even if you were eating at Delmonico's?"

Pasha smiled. "I suppose I'd have to get over it, wouldn't I?"

"Only if you don't want to spend the rest of your life filled with regret."

When they reached Trinity Place, Pasha held open one of the heavy wooden doors for her. It was just short of the afternoon lunch rush, and there were two people ahead of them waiting to be seated. Faina didn't mind waiting. She was happy to pass the time admiring the finery. Outside, the bells of Trinity Church tolled the hour at a grand volume.

On the seventh bell, Faina's eyes slipped towards Pasha, who was quietly standing with his hands in his pockets, his eyes trained on the dining room. When he saw Faina looking, he smiled, his shoulders rolling forward slightly.

"You hungry?"

Sonorous thunder socked the room, swallowing up the clanking silverware and pleasant murmurs of the diners. The floor rocked beneath their feet. The walls shuddered. Faina's stomach turned as her body was sent into the air, along with everyone else in the room.

The next thing she knew, she was lying on her back. Above her the pendants in the chandelier were still swaying. She lifted her head and found that her right ear felt funny, muffled almost. An assortment of legs and shoes stampeded past her in a rush to the door, while several ladies gasped and whined. Pasha grabbed her shoulder.

"Faina! Are you alright?"

"There's smoke coming from Wall Street!" hollered a man, leaning out the door and gaping in the direction of Broadway.

Faina had always been an intuitive child. Logic was never a threat to her convictions, and it often bothered her when people shrugged off her premonitions as childish fancy. But in that moment, that bleak second that reeked of gunpowder and fear, Faina wished desperately that someone would prove her wrong.

She jumped up off the floor and bolted for the exit, pushing past the astounded men in their fancy suits until she felt the tainted air on her cheeks.

"Faina!" Pasha called after her.

As Faina turned and looked out at the street, she gasped. An umbrella of greasy, black smoke was wafting up the corner of Wall and Broad. Faina's gut drove her forward. She dashed down Cedar and cut the corner onto Broadway.

"Faina!" Pasha hollered, still trying to chase her down. "Faina, come back! It could be dangerous!"

Particles of ash and metallic debris caught in her hair as she rounded onto Wall Street. The paneless windows of the surrounding buildings had an odd, toothless look about them. Fire tore and clawed at curtains four stories up. Splinters of glass broke beneath the treads of her shoes.

The Morgan House, with its pale façade, shone through the black smoke. Faina's heels dug into the pavement. Her chest fell. Blackened and torn bodies carpeted the space between the J.P. Morgan Building and Federal Hall. Some were still moving, still moaning, embers clinging to their faces like charred kindling. Severed body parts lay amongst the hats and broken window pieces as casually as scraps of old newspaper.

As Faina staggered backwards, her shoe slipped on a shiny, papery material. She looked down. It was an 8x12 photograph of a suffragette march outside *Opa!*. In the picture she could see herself standing at the window. Faina gave an involuntary whimper.

A trail of photographs led to the opposite sidewalk. The leather portfolio lay splayed in the gutter, a peculiar-shaped hole burnt through the cover.

Pasha grabbed Faina's shoulder from behind with a warm, sweaty hand.

"Faina …" Pasha fell silent. His hand slipped from her shoulder.

Faina froze on the sidewalk, uncertain if the body lying on the corner in front of Federal Hall was really whom she thought it was. Her thoughts scolded her. *Why are you still standing here?* A pained groan rose up in her throat. She flung herself forward in a staggered run.

The features of the victim came into focus. Leo was laid out on his back with one hand clutching his chest. His legs were sticking out into the street. He must have been crossing the road when it happened.

"Leo!" Faina threw herself down on her knees and bent over her brother with panicked eyes.

Leo's jaw shook as he tried to open his mouth. His eyes stretched to their widest, exposing the full shape of his cool, blue irises. Faina scanned the front of his shirt. Dark red stains were seeping over a series of frayed holes in his vest. She traced her hand over his right arm and shifted it slightly so that she could see his side. Faina gasped. Three more jagged holes were burned just below his ribcage.

Faina could feel the edges of her mouth contorting. She bit down. A long, slow whimper escaped her. Something sharp poked at her knee. Faina looked down. The ground was covered with fragmented bits of iron.

Pasha knelt down on Leo's opposite side near his shoulder, his hand flat against his lips. Tears streamed over the back of his palm and leaked between his fingers.

Leo's shoulders trembled. His eyes squeezed shut as he cried out in pain.

Faina cupped his face with both hands. "Don't go, Leo!" Her voice was ragged and desperate.

His eyes met hers. His pupils focused on her. His face seemed to soften. She reached for his hand.

"Just hold my hand, Leo."

Leo locked his fingers with hers and squeezed. His shaking grew more violent. She could feel her dress growing wet with his blood. When she looked down, the white checkers of the fabric were flooded with red at the hem. Faina swallowed another sob, preparing herself.

Whistles cut through the clearing smoke. Policemen were flagging down cars to take people to the hospital. A young cop, probably not much older than Leo, was jogging their way. Faina combed Leo's bangs away from his forehead.

"They're coming to take you to the hospital."

Leo's eyes gradually closed. "I won't make it," he managed to get out.

"Leo, no! You have so much to live for! You can't go yet, you'll miss it!"

Leo turned his head towards her. Their eyes met. "I ain't missing a thing."

Then, he was gone.

Chapter 78:
A Little Piece Left Behind

Faina didn't know how she got through the funeral. Possession seemed the only rational explanation. All she could really remember was holding Pasha's hand, and the migraine that came afterwards.

The coroner had said Leo died from internal bleeding caused by shrapnel. Whomever had planted the bomb had packed iron sash weights around the dynamite just for the purpose of creating deadly shrapnel, which explained the bits of fragmented iron on the ground. But Leo's death had been unique, if not somewhat perplexing, in that he had not been burned despite his proximity to the explosion. Indeed, there had been victims within four feet of Leo whose bodies had been charred beyond recognition. And yet Leo had remained pristine, as though he were fireproof. But what use was there in trying to make sense of it all now? Either way, Leo had died.

When Faina recalled how Anastas had tried to warn her not to go near Wall Street the day Leo died, Faina was outraged. Convinced that Anastas had known about the bomb and purposely not warned her brother, Faina had physically attacked him in the middle of the Foxhole. It had taken several Breadwinners to pry her away, and when the scene was over everyone was convinced it was Anastas who had caused Leo's death.

After arriving home, Faina had slipped her shoes off at the door and thrown herself onto the bed. Pain pierced her on all sides like feedback from a microphone, deafening and too loud to ignore. She remembered how frightened she had been to be separated from Leo their first night in the city because he was the only thing left that was familiar to her. Now there was no one left. No one to remember their childhood, no one to remember their parents, or home. Faina was the sole keeper of the memories now, and it felt as though no one could ever understand her again.

Two days passed. Faina had yet to move from the bed, or even change her clothes. The grief could only be described as waking up and realizing it's still dark outside. You sit there blinking in the blackness feeling alone and utterly disoriented. The door would frequently open, and tentative footsteps would approach the bed. But Faina acknowledged nothing and no one, not even herself.

Once or twice Uncle Matvei knelt down at her bedside with food, begging her to eat, and fully intending to spoon-feed her if he had to. She recalled the voyage from Russia to America, how Leo had force-fed her potatoes while she grieved their parents, and the circularity of life repulsed her.

On the third day, Faina awoke to another round of frantic hissing outside her door. It was noon, and the sunshine made Faina vaguely nauseous. Footsteps again approached the bed. But they were different. Too light to be her uncle's, and too tentative to be Anya's. They stopped halfway across the room.

"Hello, Faina." It was Jazmin.

Faina did not respond. The mattress sank beneath the weight of Jazmin's belly as she lowered herself down beside Faina. Feminine fingers ran through her hair and removed it from her eyes in a soothing gesture. At her sister-in-law's touch, Faina's lungs instinctively drew in the air around her. It was the most Faina had felt physically since the funeral.

Jazmin's hands traveled down to the nape of her neck. She made a noise that could only be described as a concerned grunt. Faina knew her hair was probably shocking; the underside had an insufferable tendency to rat, and was a source of constant frustration for Faina. Jazmin released a long, pent-up breath and got up. A drawer opened and shut. The bed gave way once more as she returned.

Faina felt a slight tug on the lower part of her scalp. She shivered as Jazmin made a fist around the section of hair and held it away from her, exposing her skin to the rapidly cooling autumn air. The brush was loud as it raked through her coarse tresses, but Faina was too numb to wince.

Once that was done, Jazmin left for a period of time and returned with a soapy wash rag. She pressed it to Faina's cheek. The material was warm and soothing against her inflamed skin. She felt the cloth hook behind her ear and travel over her neck and shoulders, sloughing away the dirt of tears and grief. And then, for some reason, Jazmin stopped.

"Faina! Feel this!"

She reached for Faina's hand and placed it on her abdomen. At first, Faina felt nothing, and then a hard force thrusted against her palm from deep within Jazmin's womb. Faina's eyes stretched a little wider. The sunlight burned her eyes. She became aware of the cool air on her damp cheeks, and the stuffiness in her nose. Somewhere within her, Faina felt a light forming. She lifted her head, stimulated by the life reaching out to her. Faina propped herself up on her elbow, and placed her hand again on her sister-in-law's belly with curious intention. Again, there was that lightening pressure, the feeling of a hand pressed against hers.

Jazmin giggled. "It knows you already."

Faina looked from Jazmin's face to her stomach, then back again. The muscles at the corners of her mouth twitched. She whimpered, then gave vent to a sob. Jazmin reached out and brushed Faina's hair over her shoulders.

"It needs you, Faina. It needs their aunt. I gotta know I can count on you to always keep an eye out for them."

Faina took in a mouthful of breath, the kind one takes when waking from a nightmare. She still had her hand placed on Jazmin's stomach. It was as though she could feel Leo's life breezing past her as another was ushered in, a new life created from one already gone.

"I will be there." She knit her eyebrows together and sniffed. "I will be there for everything. I'll be there to tell it all about Leo."

Jazmin roped her arm around Faina and hugged her close. "Look how lucky we are that we still got a piece of him with us, huh?"

Faina nodded as Jazmin rocked her back and forth, letting her cry into her shirtfront.

Chapter 79:
Rescued

Pyro stood on the front steps of Feifior and watched the state car make its way up the long, winding drive. He stuck a cigarette between his smirking lips and shook his head as the car came near enough that he could just make out Staccato's silhouette in the back window. The front door was wrenched open behind him and Sonata, Melodious, and Skelter came fumbling over the threshold.

"Is it him? Is it really him?" Sonata squealed. Her breath gathered in a pale cloud at the end of her nose, which seemed out of place in the rich golden sunlight of the morning.

"I told you to set your alarm clocks early," Pyro chided.

It was all he could do to keep from blushing when he looked at her.

When Pyro had first received the news that Staccato had been found alive on the Isle of Iwakishi, he had gone straight to the conservatory to tell Sonata the good news. Since the disappearance of her godfather, Sonata drifted about in a never-ending cloud of despair, hardly looking up at people and rarely speaking, and Pyro had been dying to pull her out of it.

The moment the words departed his mouth, Sonata leapt up with a cry of joy.

"You mean it?"

"Yes!"

"He's alive!"

"Yes!"

"And you found him?"

Pyro could not help but laugh as she forced him to repeat himself yet again.

"Yes, that's what I keep trying to tell y—"

Before he could finish his sentence, Sonata threw herself against his chest, wrapped her arms around his neck and kissed him full on the lips. Pyro was too taken off guard to shut his eyes, and saw when Sonata's own eyes snapped open at the realization of what she'd done. Stumbling back in embarrassment, Sonata rushed to apologize.

"For—forgive me, I'm not sure where that came from."

Not wishing to humiliate her further with teasing, he dismissed her reaction with an awkward laugh.

"Don't apologize. You're just a little overwhelmed is all. I'd kiss me too! I mean —you know what I mean."

He didn't wish to make things awkward between them, but it was difficult to look at her without remembering it all.

Cold gravel crunched beneath the tires as the car pulled up before the castle. The light was still rippling across the back door as it opened, when Sonata leapt down the stairs and ran to greet her godfather.

"Staccato!"

Staccato stumbled against the door with a grunt as he was struck with the force of Sonata's embrace.

"There's my girl!"

"I thought you were dead!" Tears soaked into Staccato's jacket as she gave vent to her emotions.

"I'm safe now, dear. Everything is going to be just fine." He held her close to his chest, caressing her thick curls, and kissed the top of her head.

The others followed suit, with Melodious smiling and sniffling, and Skelter grinning broadly. But Pyro was slower to approach, taking his time as he wandered towards the gathering with his cigarette still lit.

"Blazes," he exclaimed, eyeing Staccato up and down. "You look rather spiffy for someone who's been stranded on an island."

True, Staccato had thinned somewhat, but his leg was healed, his beard neatly trimmed, and he bore no visible injuries. Staccato faced him with a wry smile.

"What were you expecting? A shriveled old man with his beard down to his knees?"

Pyro shrugged and flicked his cigarette butt onto the gravel. "I thought you'd at least have grown your hair out."

Staccato straightened his lapels and swept his nose into the air. "Well, I'm sorry to disappoint you, but I thought it bad form to return to you unkempt."

"How long did it get?"

"Wouldn't you like to know!"

Melodious waved them eagerly towards the front door. "Come! Thayer and the family are waiting to greet you in the Great Hall! They've prepared a feast in your honor!"

As they made their way through the halls, Staccato lagged behind with Pyro, his sarcastic smile softening. He cleared his throat.

"I want to thank you, Pyro. You saved my life. If it weren't for you who knows how long it would've taken them to find me … if they found me at all."

Pyro shrugged with an air of casualness, not wishing to get too emotional. "Well, I owed you one. Besides, it sounds like Mother Genesis had you well cared for. With her assistance you could've lasted months, years even!"

But Staccato remained sincere. "Even so." His eyes drifted to the ground as he struggled to grind out his sentiments. "The thing is, you were there when I needed you. And for that I am grateful."

It was rare to see Staccato in such a state of vulnerability, and Pyro could not help feeling honored that Staccato had lowered his guard for the sake of thanking him.

"I thought you had no needs," teased Pyro, in an attempt to put him at ease.

Staccato's eyes glazed over with an errant wit. "Well, I can't always be right now, can I?"

Pyro raised his eyebrows and snickered. "Can I tell the others you said that?"

"Absolutely not."

What followed was a feast to rival every Christmas, and every wedding ever celebrated at Feifior. The food seemed endless, and they knew it wouldn't be long before Staccato gained back the weight that he had lost on the island. There were cakes soaked in wine, fruits glazed with sugar, and thick cuts of meat coated with fragrant gravy. When the celebration ended, the revelers were forced to retire in a state of satisfied lethargy that comes with eating good food.

Pyro was headed back to his room when he met Sonata on the stairs.

"Pardon me, Sonny," he yawned as he began to maneuver his way around her, but Sonata pulled him back by his elbow. Pyro regarded her with a raised eyebrow. "What?"

"Now that Staccato has returned, you aren't planning on leaving again, are you?"

"No. Why?"

Sonata walked her fingers over his shoulders until she had wrapped her arms around his neck and pulled him in for a passionate kiss. For a moment, Pyro was lost in the feel of her lips and hummed with delight as though biting into a particularly satisfying piece of cake. But he soon regained himself, and pried his head away from hers.

"Oh, no, no, no!"

Sonata was all innocence. "What? What is it?"

"Now see here, missy, I am not falling for that again!"

Sonata frowned as though he were being rather dramatic. "Now, Pyro, if you'll just listen to me for a minute—"

"The first time this happened you knocked me out and ditched me, making up some feeble excuse about a love potion—"

"I told you, I was scared—"

"The second time you brushed it off as an accident—"

"You had rejected *me* by that point! I was merely salvaging my pride!"

"I'm beginning to think you only see me as a big—"

She cut him off with another kiss, pressing him against the wall and causing his eyes to roll back into his head. Pyro forced himself away again.

"Will you—"

She pecked his lips.

"Stop it! I can't focus with you kissing me like that!"

Sonata withdrew slightly, an amused smile crowning the corners of her lips. "You think I only see you as a flirtation?"

Pyro sighed and threw out his arms. "Well, what am I supposed to think?"

She grabbed his left arm. "Why don't you let me show you how I feel about you?"

Sonata pressed her lips to the tender flesh beneath the base of his palm. Pyro's entire body went limp as a tidal wave of Sonata's love flooded his veins, saturating his nerves with a warm, weightless sensation that was something between floating on your back in a pool of water and being satisfyingly drunk. He recalled how a mermaid's kiss could feel different from person to person, as the sensation was unique to how an individual loved. Sonata's love was a warm, nurturing passion that soothed and secured, folding around him like a thick blanket. When she pulled away, Pyro found that he was bracing the stair railing.

"Are you alright?" she asked after a moment.

Pyro steadied a hand on his chest, catching his breath, then grabbed her by the wrist and returned the gesture. Sonata's knees trembled as she fell against him in a swoon. Pyro withdrew in a panic. He had never given a mermaid kiss before. Her wrist was glowing with a blue-green light. Had he somehow hurt her?

"Sonata?" Thinking she had fainted, he shook her by the shoulders. "Sonny, are you alright?"

Sonata giggled, her head still buried in his chest. A door opened and shut on the floor below them. Pyro and Sonata huddled against the wall as footsteps passed, afraid of being discovered.

"You know," whispered Pyro, "if you—uh—want to continue this discussion somewhere more private, there's a secret passage behind the kelpie statue in the library."

Sonata sank her teeth into a mischievous grin, and practically yanked his arm off as she dragged him up the stairs.

"What are we waiting for? Let's go!"

Chapter 80:
The Baby

Faina sat at the register and twirled her chow mein absentmindedly around her chopstick. Behind her, Uncle Matvei was on the phone frantically engaged in sorting out the details of a missing order.

"No, I don't want the twenty-pound bags, just the ten-pound … Yes, I can hold."

Faina's hand crept towards her knitting. She had almost finished the blanket she had started for the baby. Uncle Matvei plucked a dumpling from the box with his own chopsticks and shoved it towards Faina's mouth.

"Eat, *malyshka*, eat!" Eat, baby, eat!

Faina nearly fell backwards trying to avoid her uncle's chopsticks.

"Uncle Matvei! I'm not a turkey!"

"You can work on that blanket later." The dumpling slipped from his chopsticks and Faina caught it in her bare hands.

"The baby is due any day now, I need to finish!" She wondered if Jazmin could be in labor that very moment without them knowing. Since Leo's death she had moved back in with her family where someone experienced could keep an eye on her.

"The baby will have plenty to keep it warm until you complete it. Until then I don't want to see you skipping any more meals. If you're that in need of a distraction, we can always work on your geography lessons."

Faina wrinkled her nose. "Not geography!"

"Then you better eat up!" He kissed the side of her head and picked up the mouthpiece again. "Yes, hello?"

Faina rolled her eyes and tore off a bite of the dumpling with her teeth. She set aside the chopsticks and reached for her needles. A wave of fatigue washed over her as she bent forward and placed the yarn in her lap. Her throat felt heavy when she breathed.

She wound the white thread around the needle. There was something comforting about the monotony of knitting that she'd never felt before. It was just enough to keep her busy without draining any more of her energy, and it was satisfying to watch the knitted seams grow longer, and longer overtime. She paused and took another bite of the dumpling with her fingers.

"Alright … thank you." Uncle Matvei hung up the phone and turned around to face Faina. Faina quickly dropped her yarn and dug her knitting needles into the chow mein. Uncle Matvei placed his hands on his hips.

"Nice try." He took the knitting from her lap and handed her the chopsticks.

The bell rang as someone entered. Faina didn't bother to look up but moved her lunch to one side and grabbed a napkin.

"Well, if it isn't Miss Syreeta," exclaimed Uncle Matvei in his usual friendly manner. "How is our expectant mother these days?"

Faina wrenched her head up. Jazmin's younger sister was hurrying to the counter. "The baby is on its way! The midwife is already at our tenement!"

"Really?" Faina jumped off the stool. "That's wonderful! When can we see her? How long will it take?"

Uncle Matvei placed his hands on Faina's shoulders and laughed. "Slow down, *Faishka*. These things take time, darling. They don't just pop out like biscuits. It could take until tomorrow."

"Tomorrow?" Faina groaned.

In her mind she could already see the baby bundled up in the new, white blanket she had knitted. She saw herself peeling back the covers to peer into the baby's face. Would it look like Leo? Or her? Or maybe even their parents? Would it be a boy or a girl? Would the baby be talented and competitive like Jazmin and Leo? Or was it possible that the baby would be like her?

Syreeta gave her a sympathetic laugh. "I promise we will call you as soon as the baby is born." She began backing out the door.

"Wait!" Faina grabbed her knitting from the counter and ran to give it to Syreeta. "It's not finished yet, but go ahead and give it to her now, so she knows I am thinking of her."

Syreeta grinned. "Would you like to give it to her yourself?"

Faina looked back at Uncle Matvei with hopeful eyes. Uncle Matvei smiled, relieved to see her spirits lifted for once.

"Go on, *solnyshka*. Just be back in time for the mid-afternoon crowd."

Faina was relieved to find Syreeta moving so fast as they made their way to Little Syria. The flower shop had not closed for the occasion, and the pair had to weave through customers to get to the steps leading to the apartment. The sitting room was already crowded with female family members, of which there were several, and Mrs. Zureiq barking instructions at each relative. At the sight of Faina she smiled.

"Ah! Faina, dear! What brings you here?"

Syreeta gestured to the unfinished blanket. "Faina wanted to give Jazmin this baby blanket for good luck, Mama."

Mrs. Zureiq waved towards one of the bedrooms in the back. "Go on back, my dear. She's not quite there yet. And I'm sure she'd appreciate a visit from you."

Syreeta led Faina to the bedroom where Jazmin was situated on one of the two beds shoved up against the wall. There was barely a foot of space between them. She was in her nightgown with the covers thrown off her bare legs and leaning towards the open window. Her forehead was damp with sweat, causing the fine hair around her temples to cling to her skin.

"Faina!" She smiled between heavy breaths and patted her tummy. "Baby Leo is on his way!" She patted the bed beside her and Faina sat down.

"Last chance. Is it a Zain or a Mina?" Zain being the name they had chosen for a boy, and Mina for a girl.

"Hmm." Jazmin shut her eyes and leaned her head back against the wall. "Zain."

"Well, I think it's a Mina." She scooted closer. "But if I'm wrong, I promise to buy you a milkshake as soon as you feel good enough!"

Jazmin bit her lip and chuckled. "Sounds like a plan." She winced and clutched her stomach.

"I won't keep you," said Faina. "You need your rest. But I wanted to give you the baby blanket I've been making to remind you that we're all thinking of you and praying for you." She placed the blanket in her hands. "I promise I'll finish it up after the baby is born."

Jazmin's face lit up as she held the blanket to the light. "Oh, Faina, it's beautiful!" She beckoned her forward and kissed her cheek. "Baby is going to love it very much."

"I'll let you get some rest now."

Jazmin squeezed her hand and winked. "Next time you see me it'll be with your little niece or nephew."

Faina beamed as she reached for the door. "I can't wait!"

***

The hours dragged by and still there was no news of the baby. Without her knitting Faina could hardly sit still when she returned to the store. Through dinner she was constantly jiggling her foot and playing with her food. And when it was time for bed she could only achieve a light, shallow sleep. So when the phone finally rang downstairs, Faina shot out of bed and raced down to the shop to hear the news.

"Hello?" She could hear Uncle Matvei's sleepy voice when she opened the door to the stairwell. She didn't even bother to throw on her robe or slippers, and nearly tripped down the steps in her excitement.

"What?" Uncle Matvei's voice was suddenly quite awake.

Faina jumped down the final step and raced around the corner to the counter. Uncle Matvei was staring at the mouthpiece with his lower lip hinged open. Faina froze. Uncle Matvei passed a hand over his mouth and winced.

"Oh, no, no, no." He sniffed.

Faina staggered closer, trying to catch what they were saying. Whatever had happened, surely everything would be fine. Surely. Uncle Matvei gave a whimper.

"Okay. I am so sorry. Please let us know if you need anything. We'll talk again in the morning." He bade them goodbye and hung up the phone. Uncle Matvei turned and flinched. He hadn't noticed Faina standing there. His expression was helpless.

"*Faishka*, dear …"

Faina staggered forward. Her face crumpled as a heavy feeling descended upon her.

"The baby? Is it alright?"

Uncle Matvei reached an arm out and pulled her to his side. She could feel him swallow as she laid her head against his chest. A premature sob escaped her throat. She knew without him saying more. They stood there, clinging to each other and weeping for some time.

"The child was stillborn," he finally managed to get out.

Faina clenched her fists and wailed into her uncle's embrace. Though Faina had come to be quite familiar with death over the years, she had yet to experience the loss of a new life, and its singular sting. It was as though the baby had never existed at all. A life hadn't just died, it had vanished.

Faina swallowed hard, determined to get her words out. "How is Jazmin?"

Uncle Matvei squeezed his eyes shut and exhaled through his nostrils. When he didn't answer, Faina pulled away to look up at him.

"Uncle Matvei?"

Uncle Matvei steadied his eyes on hers, taking the time to smooth her hair over her shoulder.

"Faina, Jazmin died giving birth."

Faina's legs began to shake. She stepped away from her uncle, feeling as though her skin were on fire. Her hands flew over her face as an unbearable pain entered her skull. Something deep inside her began to tear, and a wild, animalistic cry rose up in her lungs. Uncle Matvei grabbed her and brought her to his chest once more. With her throat aching, Faina began to feel lightheaded. She swayed against her uncle and passed out.

Chapter 81:
Catching Up

Staccato sat in the armchair of Aunt Poppy's apartment absolutely speechless, unable to comprehend everything she had just told him. After gaping at her in confusion for several seconds, he at last found his voice.

"I don't understand." He leaned back and ran a hand over his mouth. "You're telling me that in my absence, my daughter was forced to pick up an illegal waitressing job, was brutally attacked, and now Pasha has sold himself to a gang of thugs for her protection?"

Aunt Poppy nodded and sniffed. "I didn't know a thing about it until it was too late. They brought him to me after they had completed his initiation." She removed her glasses and dug her fingers into the corners of her eyes as though to physically push back the tears. "Oh, Staccato, it was awful. They slashed him to ribbons. There was one gash so deep I feared I would have to stitch him up."

Staccato stood and bit down on his finger, unable to sit any longer. "And he's healed now?"

Aunt Poppy dabbed at her eyes. "He is. Though Anya says there will be scars."

Staccato stared at Pasha's window through the glass. "And you really think there's nothing I can do?"

"I know there's nothing you can do."

"I can't pull what I did with the guard on Ellis Island and force this Klokov fellow to let him go?"

"It's not just Klokov you'd have to fool, dear, but practically all of Lower Manhattan. Pasha has been publicly recognized as a Breadwinner now. Even if you managed to trick Klokov into dismissing him he would be blacklisted."

Staccato pinched his eyes closed and tried to think. "I know what you're going to say." He paced across the room. "I want to bring them home, Aunt, I really do. But—"

Aunt Poppy sighed with an air of understanding. "It is a bigger risk than I first imagined."

Staccato stared back at her in surprise. Aunt Poppy wadded up her handkerchief in her fist and shrugged.

"Look at all you have been through. I could never have imagined it. It is a wonder you are alive at all." She wiped at her eyes and scoffed. "A blood nest. That's what you found in the ventilation that was making you so ill. It is an ancient curse used to weaken and disorient miraculous for long periods of time. I thought we'd seen the last of those during the Liberty Wars. Never would I have dreamed to come across one in my lifetime."

"Why?"

"It requires an abundance of dark magic to create a blood nest, more than one person can manifest. It takes a mass of people to produce that amount of sorcery, more than just a coven. A … culture, if you will. That you were able to destroy it with something as simple as Circulo Sheva is nothing short of a miracle." Her expression grew dark. "These are dangerous times we are living in, nephew. Something is about to happen. I can feel it."

Staccato did not dispute her. He'd seen the change with his own eyes.

"How did you manage to get hold of your staff while you were being held prisoner?" she asked him suddenly.

Staccato shrugged. "It's a mystery. I just happened to wake up one morning and find it under the mattress."

"Could it have been there the entire time?"

"How? The C.O.N. would never be so careless as to leave my staff with me in my cell!"

"Perhaps there is a double agent amongst them?"

Staccato exhaled. "Perhaps. I've thought of that."

They sat together for some time in silence, but Staccato could not get Lydia and her family off his mind. There had to be some sort of solution.

"There has to be a way to get them back to Voiler. But now that I have made myself an enemy of the C.O.N., I am a danger to my daughter and grandchildren by association. That certainly doesn't help things. We don't even have a place for them to stay." He sighed and curled his hands into fists. "And yet I can't just leave Pasha here, can I? Leave him to thieve and fight night after night! The boy's a prisoner!"

Aunt Poppy held up her hand. "Let's just wait and see how he fairs. There is big money to be made in street fighting. Perhaps he will do well."

"Do well at being a criminal?" The words made him scoff. The very idea seemed backwards. "It's hardly the life I would want for my grandson!"

Aunt Poppy shrugged. "You have two choices. And for once I'm not against either of them. There will be risks involved whatever you decide to do. But I don't think haste is in your best interest." She took him by the hand and pulled him close. "Remember what the song says? We are to pray for wisdom. To lean not on our own understanding but seek guidance."

He fell back in his chair and crumpled over his knees. "My poor boy. My poor, poor boy."

Chapter 82:
The Tombs

Pasha sat on the bench with his knees pulled to his chest and his head buried in his arms. He couldn't bear to face the reality that he was actually sitting inside a jail cell for attempted burglary. The shame was suffocating.

It seemed as though Leo's death had just happened when in reality six months had passed since the incident, and unlike Pasha, Klokov was not one to lose track of time. Pasha had struggled to fill his quotas ever since. Faina continued to grieve, as was natural, and would need time to heal. As a result, Pasha was left on his own. He'd never turned up at the Foxhole empty-handed but he often had little to show for his efforts. It was quickly becoming clear just how much he'd relied on Leo.

This newfound desperation ultimately drove him to a boardinghouse in Greenwich Village, where he made a clumsy attempt at a burglary. He really had no sense of what he was doing. He wasn't even sure if he would find any alcohol. He wound up climbing a tree and entering through an open window directly into the room of a middle-aged woman, who happened to be sitting on her bed. When he tried to climb back out, his suspenders got caught on a branch, and he was stuck between the window and the tree. Ultimately, he was seen by a total of ten witnesses. And when the police tried to get him down, he fell directly into a trashcan in the basement walkout. Needless to say it would be a long time before he could show his face in Greenwich Village again.

Up to that point, Pasha had never been arrested, but several of the other street fighters had, and depending on their age and if they were a first-time offender, they were usually taken to the nearest precinct, fingerprinted, and made to wait while an officer contacted a parent to come pick them up. Though it was certainly not ideal, it wasn't the most traumatizing event any of them had ever been through, and Pasha was only thirteen.

So, one can imagine his shock and terror when he was taken not to the local precinct but the Manhattan Detention Complex, better known as the Tombs. This was not a prison for troubled youths and petty thieves. The Tombs housed serious criminals—famous ones—including the former husband of Evelyn Nesbit—the millionaire Harry K. Thaw—who shot and murdered her lover, the architect Stanford White.

Someone tapped at the bars. Pasha looked up. An officer whom he had not seen before was standing there with a clipboard. He was a smaller gentleman with a kind face and brown complexion. His eyebrows were thick and heavy, and framed a pair of overly large, black eyes. His curly, black hair was just beginning to recede, and Pasha guessed that he was somewhere around thirty-five.

"I'm Officer Liebowitz. I'm here to get your particulars."

Pasha was confused. The man was smiling at him.

"Okay."

Liebowitz pulled a chair up to the cell. "You said your name was Sasha?"

"Pasha," he practically whispered.

"What was that?"

Pasha cleared his throat. "Pasha Chevalsky."

"Pasha!" He tapped the clipboard with his pencil and scribbled it in. "Small world!"

Pasha eyed him with uncertainty. "Your name is Pasha?"

"Pavel, to be exact, and at work I go by Paul. But my family calls me Pasha."

"Smart choice."

"Hm?"

Pasha felt his cheeks turning red. He hadn't meant to let the comment slip, but he was tired, and his brain wasn't working as it should.

"I said smart choice. I went by Paul once too to get a job. But my boss fired me when he caught me speaking Russian."

"Ah." Officer Liebowitz knit his eyebrows together and nodded. "Yeah, it ain't always easy. There are a lot of small-minded people out there. But they ain't all bad." He threw him a wink.

Pasha was intrigued by this officer. The other boys had made it sound like all cops were bullies who'd look for any excuse to arrest a Slav. Not only that, according to Yuri they were all Irish, but this man was a Slav himself.

"Date of birth?"

"February twelfth, 1908."

Officer Liebowitz peeked over his clipboard with a sly smile. "You planning on running for president someday?"

By now Pasha was so baffled by his behavior he didn't know how to respond.

"You got the same birthday as President Lincoln," he explained.

"Oh. Yeah. I learned that in school."

When Liebowitz had finished with the basic questions, he set aside his clipboard and scooted closer.

"Now, tell me, why were you trying to break into that boardinghouse, Pasha?"

Pasha dropped his head between his shoulders. He was sure he had seen the end of Officer Liebowitz's sunny behavior.

"You don't seem like a bad kid," said Liebowitz when Pasha didn't respond. "And to be honest, you didn't seem to know what you were doing either."

Pasha wound his shoelace around his finger and continued to stare at the ground.

"Let me ask you another question." He leaned forward with his elbows on his knees. "How'd you get those scars on your back?"

Pasha looked up at him curiously, but still did not answer. They must have seen his scars while searching him.

"It's okay, kid. I know you're a Breadwinner. You're not the first young man to come through here with lash marks. How's a kid like you get caught up in such a racket? Huh?"

"I was attacked by a dog. That's what the scars are from."

Officer Liebowitz looked unimpressed. "A dog, eh? You sure?"

Pasha leaned back into the corner and turned his head away from Officer Liebowitz, refusing to say anymore.

"What if I told you this stays completely off record?" Officer Liebowitz offered. "Would you tell me then?"

Pasha glanced back at him. "You promise?"

Liebowitz held up his right hand. "I promise."

Pasha lifted his head and sat up a little straighter. "Remember how I said I was fired?"

"Your family needed money?"

Pasha nodded. "My mom needed protection from a stalker."

"A stalker? Why didn't you just come to the police?"

Pasha immediately clammed up again. He'd said too much. Officer Liebowitz nodded as though Pasha had answered him anyway.

"I see. She … uh … she a call girl?"

Pasha slammed his fist on the bench. "No!"

Officer Liebowitz held up his hands in surrender. "Alright! Alright! I'm sorry, that … I shouldn't have said that. It's just, that happens a lot of times, especially in the immigrant community. A woman can't find work to feed her children, sometimes she has to resort to desperate things."

Pasha stared at him, allowing his shoulders to relax a little. "Well, that's not what happened."

"I'm sorry."

A long silence followed. Pasha couldn't figure out if Liebowitz was done asking questions or not. He just sat there with his arms crossed, tapping his foot.

"*Czy ty jesteś Polakiem?*"

Officer Liebowitz looked up in surprise, then laughed. "*Tak!*" Yes! "I am from Poland. Or my family was, originally. But I was born in Odessa. We came to America to escape the pogroms." He slipped him a mischievous smile. "I thought you were Russian."

"My mother is Russian. My father's family is Polish."

"Are you also Jewish?"

"My father."

"Ah! What synagogue does he attend?"

Pasha's face fell. "My father was killed by Bolsheviks."

"Oh. I'm terribly sorry." He looked as though he meant it too.

Pasha dropped his legs into a cross-legged position. "That's kinda how we ended up here. Been here for a few years now."

"I see." He cleared his throat and stood. "Well, I better go log this away. It's been nice talking to you, Pasha. You seem like a nice kid."

Pasha looked up at him curiously. "Even though I'm a Breadwinner?"

This made Officer Liebowitz smile. "Even though you're a Breadwinner." He came closer. "You might not always be a Breadwinner, you know."

Pasha looked down at the ground and scoffed. "Easy for you to say."

Officer Liebowitz gave him one final wink and left.

It was another hour before Pasha heard footsteps again, and by then he'd nearly fallen asleep. The footfall stopped in front of his cell. Pasha didn't dare look up, mortified by the thought that anyone might see him, even if it was only another criminal. A latch turned. The hinges wailed loudly as the door swung inward. Pasha peeked out from behind his hands. Officer Hayes, the officer who had arrested him, was standing on the threshold with his chin held high. He crooked his finger at Pasha.

Pasha snapped his head into an upright position and clutched the bench. "What is it?"

"You're going home, kid. Someone's here to pick you up."

Pasha flew up from the seat and ducked out the doorway with his head hanging towards his chest.

"Who is it?"

No sooner had Pasha asked than he caught a glimpse of Trifecta through the front-desk window. He was accompanied by Mudlark, the oldest street fighter to date, who had earned his name back when the Foxhole still hosted open-air matches once a week. It was said Mudlark always fought his best in an outside match after a good rain. Thank goodness they'd put a stop to those after automobile traffic began taking over the city.

"They paid my bail?"

Hayes took one glance at him from the corner of his eye and, deliberately ignoring him, walked on ahead of Pasha towards the exit. Pasha felt his cheeks flush. Of course they hadn't paid his bail. Probably all Klokov had to do was snap his fingers and Hayes did whatever he wanted. It obviously wasn't Liebowitz they had in their pocket.

Pasha wasn't quite sure what to expect when he was escorted out the front doors of the Tombs, but he wasn't anticipating two separate vehicles to be waiting for them in front of the sidewalk.

Mudlark patted his shoulder like some sort of protective older brother. "Klokov's waiting for you in the Cadillac." He and Trifecta turned in the direction of the Buick parked behind it. Pasha felt the color drain from his face. He caught Trifecta by the arm. "Wait, you mean you're not coming with us?"

Mudlark shook his head. "Boss says he wants to talk to you."

"Bu—but where is he taking me?"

Trifecta lowered his voice so Mudlark couldn't hear. "Relax, Pasha. He just wants to talk. He's gonna drop you off at your place after."

Pasha stared in horror at the back passenger window of the green Cadillac where Klokov was waiting for him. Klokov was going to drop him off at home? Wouldn't that depend on the manner of their conversation? Pasha had failed, he'd been arrested, put in the Tombs for heaven's sake! He was useless, utterly disposable. What purpose could he serve Klokov?

When Pasha looked back, he realized Mudlark and Trifecta were no longer beside him. He was a solitary figure trembling beneath the cold glare of the dim streetlamp. He gaped stupidly at the Cadillac, unable to make himself move. He'd seen this all before. He'd read about it in the papers. This was how mob bosses bumped off the underlings that had disappointed them, by tricking them into taking a little ride.

The light rippled as the back window was cranked down.

"Chevalsky!" The glass stopped short beneath Klokov's narrowed eye. "Get your hands outta your pockets and get in the car!"

Pasha jumped to attention and raced to the opposite passenger side. The driver, whom Pasha had not seen exit the vehicle, was standing there holding the door open. Klokov sat huddled in the far corner. There was a vulture-esque quality about him that evening, with his hairless skull cropping up from the excessive fluff of his fur coat, and his curved nose hanging over his collar. His fedora was inclined severely over his good eye, exposing the Russian kopeck to the pale orange shine of the lamp.

Before Pasha could hesitate, the driver shoved him inside and shut the door.

"So, you got caught, did ya?" Klokov removed his golden cigar case from his pocket.

"I'm so sorry, Klokov! It won't happen again, I prom—"

"Relax." He hovered his stubby fingers over the open case before plucking a fat, round stogie from the lineup and stabbing it between his lips. "You ain't the first of my bucks to wind up in the Tombs with a set of silver bracelets." Klokov chuckled and lit his cigar. "Not by a long shot."

The engine growled. Pasha was practically rocked out of his seat as the driver took off suddenly without warning.

"Just last year, Overland, Moneyrider, and Stride got pinched for packing heat in Bryant Park after pickpocketing some chump with his lady friend." He snickered. "Eighty-nine cents! That's all the sap was carrying! Boy, I would've loved to see the look on their faces!"

"I'm not in trouble then?"

The simper fell from Klokov's lips. "You ain't been doing so hot lately, kid." He took a drag and turned towards the window.

Pasha made no attempt to defend himself. It didn't seem wise to make excuses just now.

"At first, I told myself you were just grieving. You and Leo were close after all. It would take some time before you were back on your feet again. But six months have passed. You're bringing me less every week. Now you're getting arrested before you've even crossed the threshold!"

He propped his elbow on the armrest and stared thoughtfully at the back of the driver's seat. "I'm beginning to wonder just how dependent you were on Spichkin's talents."

Again, Pasha wasn't sure what to say. In his opinion, he had neither the guts nor the brains to pull off any sort of impressive sting operation. To admit it was cowardly, to deny it was bold. In the end he decided to change the subject.

"How about my fighting?" This seemed like a safe bet. So far, Pasha defied expectations with his skills in the ring. He was still far from exceptional, but he wasn't bad either, and he was amassing more and more bets every week.

Klokov pinched his lips together. "I gotta level with you, kid, if it weren't for your street fighting stats you'd be in hot water right now. You ain't no Jack Dempsey, but your slipping's faster than any boy I've put out there. And your palm strike's pretty decent too. Though I would still like to see a little more gusto when you throw a punch."

Pasha felt his shoulders settling back into a normal position. Perhaps he'd live to walk out of this Cadillac after all.

"But you gotta remember," Klokov continued, "you ain't gonna be a street fighter forever. The ring is only half the job. You read your Bible, son?"

Pasha balked at him in surprise. He'd never expected a seasoned mobster to be monitoring his Sunday school habits.

"Uh, sometimes."

"You familiar with James chapter two, verse seventeen?"

Pasha felt his eyes slink off to the side as he tried to think back. "'[1]Even so faith, if it has not works, is dead.'"

"Think of it this way, Stallion: when you joined the Breadwinners, you made a covenant with me. You vowed to serve and obey your master. In exchange for your fidelity, I delivered you from your enemies. The Paddock is my altar, your goods the sacrifice. But faith without works is dead. He who fails to provide an acceptable sacrifice is a faithless servant indeed. And in my kingdom there is no room for a faithless servant."

The car slowed as they pulled up before the courtyard splitting the tenement building where Pasha lived.

---

[1] King James Version (KJV)

Klokov pinched his shoulder and pulled Pasha close. "I want you to prove your faithfulness to me, Stallion." His breath reeked of alcohol, and even by the limited light of the gas lamp shining from the stoop, he could make out the brown tobacco stains on Klokov's teeth.

Pasha dropped his head and stared down at the leather interior. "Yes, sir."

Klokov waved his hand. "Sleep it off, kid. Tomorrow is a new day."

Pasha thanked him and exited the vehicle. As the Cadillac purred and zoomed away, a flurry of movement drew his eyes up the row of windows on Matvei's side of the building. Faina was watching him intently from behind the curtains. Pasha gave a half-hearted wave. Rather than return the gesture, Faina began mouthing questions through the glass as though Pasha were a master lip-reader.

Pasha gaped up at the window. "I can't read lips, Faina!"

Faina glared at him impatiently as he scrambled up the fire escape towards his bedroom. "I'll tell you about it in the morning!"

Pasha entered the tenement through his window and found his mother hunched over the table with her head in her hands.

"Hey, Ma."

The chair fell backwards against the wall as Lydia leapt to her feet.

"Pavlo!" She grabbed him and pulled him close to her chest. "You realize we have a front door." She slipped her hand under his chin and tilted his face towards hers. "What happened?"

Pasha pulled away and shed his coat. "Klokov made them let me go." He hung it on the rack.

"Yes, I know." Lydia fiddled with her fingers still looking distressed. "But how did you get arrested in the first place?"

Pasha's hands dropped to his sides. He remained with his back to her. "I got caught."

"Caught doing what?"

Pasha felt his shoulder blades tighten as though someone had wound him up with a key like a toy soldier.

"Doing what Breadwinners do." He reached into the breadbox and ripped off a hunk.

"Stealing?"

Pasha slammed the lid shut and grabbed a glass from the cabinet. "Yes, Ma! It's a rule! It's not like I have a choice!" He turned on the faucet and held the glass beneath the stream.

Lydia took a moment to shut her eyes and press her lips together. "Yes, Pasha, I am aware of that." She reached forward to place a hand on his shoulder. "You're not in trouble—"

Pasha twisted away from her. "Then why are we talking about it?"

Lydia's mouth fell open in surprise but she quickly recovered. "What's wrong with talking about it?"

"Because there's nothing to talk about! I broke into a house, I got caught, I went to jail, they let me go! This is my life now! What more is there to say?"

He dashed back to his room and slammed the door.

* * *

"He asked if you read the Bible?!" Faina was sitting cross-legged on her bedroom floor clutching a pillow to her chest.

It was the next morning, and much later than Pasha had anticipated having this conversation with her. When she hadn't shown up on the fire escape outside his bedroom that morning, Pasha had taken the liberty of knocking on her window. She hadn't even dressed yet.

Her eyes were heavily lined with gray shadows these days as though she weren't sleeping, her hair was noticeably more tangled, and there was little color in her face. Leo's blue jacket lay crumpled on the bed with the covers, and he often had glimpses of her through the window clinging to it the way a fawn huddles up to its mother. The blanket she had knitted for Zain—for the baby had indeed been a boy—sat folded on a shelf, unused. A minuscule speck of blood stained one side, but Faina kept it facedown where no one would see it.

One by one her freckles were fading like faint stars in the pale dawn. He had asked her if she wanted to sit outside, but Faina declined, saying it was too chilly.

"Yeah," Pasha continued. "And then he went on about how 'faith without works is dead,' and he's basically God, and the stuff I steal for the Paddock is like a sacrifice."

Faina swallowed her coffee and raised her eyebrows. "So, he's not religious, he just thinks very highly of himself."

"Apparently." Pasha grabbed hold of his ankles and rocked back on his tailbone. "What am I gonna do, Faina? If I don't step it up there's no telling what Klokov will do to me! I honestly thought I was being 'taken for a ride.'"

Faina plopped her chin in her hand and stared at him thoughtfully. "What were you trying to steal anyway?"

Pasha threw up his shoulders. "I don't know. It looked like a nice house, I figured they probably had some jewelry or something."

"You didn't even have a plan?"

"Well, I mean …" He scratched his head. "No."

Faina threw back her head and groaned. "Pasha, Pasha, Pasha …"

"Oh, what? Like you're so methodical, Miss Fly-by-the-Seat-of-Your-Pants?"

Faina got to her feet and approached her vanity. "Hey, I might not line up my shoes at the bottom of my closet like some people I know—"

Pasha's eyes glazed over. "You mean like everybody you know? Every normal, high-functioning individual you know?"

Ignoring his remark, she removed a notepad and pen from her drawer.

"But I know how to come up with a plan when I need one." She handed him the writing instruments and sat down across from him. "Take this down. First off, alcohol is where the real money is at."

"I know this already."

Faina waved her hand and lowered herself onto her stomach. "Good! Then you know what you're gonna steal. Now, we just gotta decide where you're gonna steal it."

"We've already hit up tons of restaurants and hotels. I can't go back there and do it again!"

"So, don't! There are plenty more where that came from!" She crawled forward, biting at the nail on her index finger with a secretive smile. "I hear the Yale Club has enough hooch to last out the decade!"

"You expect me to steal from the Yale Club?"

Faina rolled onto her back. "Why not?"

"Why not? Faina, do you hear yourself right now?"

Faina snatched up the pen and balanced it between her nose and upper lip.

"Of course I do, darling! I just love to hear the sound of my own voice, don't you?"

Pasha leaned over her with a smirk as Faina tried not to laugh. "You're a mess."

"And that's why you're so madly in love with me."

Pasha knew she was only joking, but it didn't stop the butterflies from stirring inside his ribcage.

"Probably." He set aside the notebook and bracketed her with his arms. "Hey, what would you say to a coke with peanuts? Bet the drugstore wouldn't be crowded right now."

The boldness evaporated from her face, and she rolled up to a sitting position.

"I don't think I'm in the mood right now."

Pasha drew back slightly. "Okay, well, how about lunch?"

Faina folded her hands in her lap and stared out the window. "I'm not hungry."

"Well, we don't have to eat. We could play catch, or go to Tin Pan Alley."

Faina said nothing but cast her eyes towards the ground.

Pasha sighed. "Okay, what's it gonna take to get you outside?"

"Outside? Pasha, this is March! It's fifty degrees outside!"

"So what? You're from Siberia! Faina, you've been stuck inside for six months now! You didn't even go ice skating this year!" He pointed to the cheval looking glass. "Look, I can barely see your freckles anymore!"

Faina crossed her arms, turning away from the mirror. "So? Isn't that a good thing?"

"No! Not for you! Not for the Faina I know!" He grabbed her hand.

Faina tugged away and hid her face behind her hair. "People hate freckles! That's why they try to get rid of them with lemon juice!"

"Well, I don't hate them! I love your freckles, and so do you! They're a part of you, you said so yourself, just like your father's!" He leaned sideways, peering around her hair so he could see her face. "They're pretty. But if they don't get some sunshine they're gonna die."

Faina's face softened for a moment. Their eyes met.

"I just want you to be happy again." His voice was weak with desperation.

Faina buried her face against the side of the mattress and winced. "We can't always have what we want." She sniffled. "I don't know how I'll ever be happy again."

Pasha couldn't help but feel utterly useless as he watched the tears roll down her cheeks. He couldn't stand to see her suffer.

"What can I do that would make you happy right this moment?"

Faina hesitated and then said in a quiet, uncertain voice, "Hold me?"

Pasha gaped at her in surprise before his voice came out in a hoarse whisper.

"Of course I'll hold you. I'll hold you for as long as you want."

Faina got up and sat on the bed. Pasha nervously followed her example.

"How—how do you want me to hold you?"

She positioned him so that he was sitting with his back propped up by the pillows, then she crawled next to him and laid her head on his chest.

"Like this. So I can hear your heart." She paused. "Is that okay?"

Pasha closed his arms around her. "Of course."

She settled into his arms and released a long-held breath. Everything was quiet. Pasha was stiff at first, afraid that she would notice the rapid drum of his heart her proximity inspired. After a while, he grew comfortable and began stroking Faina's hair until at last she fell asleep.

"Faina?" Pasha whispered, testing to see if she was really asleep. He ran his fingers through her hair. She didn't stir. Carefully, he bent down and kissed the top of her head. "I love you."

Faina continued to sleep.

Chapter 83:
The Yale Club

By the time Monday rolled around, Pasha was little better off than he was on Saturday. He'd taken into consideration what Faina had said, and had settled on infiltrating one of the restaurants in midtown to nab some liquor. There was only one problem: where were they keeping it? As he stood outside a fancy eatery on West Forty-fourth, he tried to put himself in Leo's shoes and come up with a plan.

But it wasn't that simple. Leo always gathered tips from other Breadwinners and friends he'd made around town. Everybody knew Leo, and he was a friend to all. Pasha released a sigh, lamenting his introverted nature. He had no connections, no confidence, and no partner.

The revolving door rotated and spat out a squat, foppish-looking gentleman walking a Pomeranian. Pasha could not help but stare at his moneyed morning suit, with pearl buttons of all things! As he waddled past, Pasha noticed his wallet hanging out of his jacket pocket.

Pasha narrowed his eyes suspiciously. It was almost too easy. It strained believability. He'd read of undercover cops baiting pickpockets in books, and judging by the state of the man's dress and the obvious angle at which his wallet was sticking out, it had to be a setup. He began to walk away.

But then again, that's only in stories. Pasha stopped. He'd never heard of anyone attempting this method in real life. He looked back over his shoulder. The man had stopped to light a cigarette. Pasha scratched the side of his face. He knew he had a habit of being paranoid, and thieving wasn't exactly an occupation that thrived on being overly cautious. He looked back at the restaurant. He had two choices.

Groaning, Pasha turned around and hightailed it after the gentleman. He kept his head down and his footsteps soft, trying to blend into the crowd. He reached out once but quickly drew back, afraid someone might be looking. He flexed his fist. He had to commit! He reached out a second time.

"You!" The man turned on Pasha, raising his walking stick in a threatening fashion.

Pasha gasped and, ducking under his swing, dashed up the sidewalk. The Pomeranian shrieked and snarled. With one swift tug she had managed to pull the leash out of her master's hands, freeing her to run after Pasha.

"Kill, Abby! Kill!"

Pasha pumped his legs as fast as they could carry him. He would've turned over a trashcan in an attempt to block the dog's path, but it was such a tiny thing he was afraid he might accidentally hurt it, not that it minded hurting him. He turned into a gated alleyway and scrambled over the wrought-iron fence. A police whistle rose up behind him. Pasha's lungs tightened. He was certain that if he was arrested this time Klokov wouldn't bother to bail him out.

He slipped through the bars on the other side of the alley, and was about to cross the street, when a large van came squealing down the asphalt and slammed on the breaks in front of him. The driver leaned out the window.

"Hop in, toots!" It was Faina in her uncle's delivery van, looking livelier than he'd seen her in months. "I got a fresh coat of rouge, and I'm champing at the bit!"

Pasha's mouth fell open like the flap of a mailbox. "Faina?"

She tossed her hair over her shoulder and rolled her eyes. "Well, it ain't Gaston Chevrolet!"

"Are you driving that van by yourself?"

Faina glared at him with record-breaking sarcasm. "No. I got a leprechaun hitting the gas pedal. Will you get in already before someone sees?!"

Pasha peeled around to the other side and hopped into the passenger seat.

"Faina, what do you think you're doing? You're thirteen!"

Faina shifted into gear and took off down the road. "You said I needed to get out more." She reached between the seats and tossed a duffel bag into his lap. "Here, put these on."

Pasha reached into the satchel and removed the nicest pair of Sunday clothes he owned.

"Are these my clothes?"

"Yeah, Katya let me raid your wardrobe. Oh, and I packed some pomade in the side pocket. You're gonna need it to slick back your hair."

Pasha narrowed his eyes. "Why?"

"So you'll blend in at the Yale Club."

"The Yale Club?" He grabbed hold of the dash, trying to steady himself as his words came out faster and louder. "Faina, we need to have a talk. I know I said you needed to get out more, but clearly I was wrong! Things haven't exactly been easy for you lately, and I think it may be affecting your judgement!"

Faina clenched the steering wheel and groaned. "Would you say that if it were Leo driving the car?" She sped up to beat a yellow light. A roadster slammed on its breaks and laid on the horn.

"No, because Leo had a *license*!" Pasha shouted the last word.

"Well, how else we gonna steal a truck's worth of alcohol?"

"You seriously want me to try and steal alcohol from the Yale Club?"

"You thought I was joking?"

"Yes! Yes, I thought you were joking, because that's ludicrous!"

Faina leaned back against the seat and grinned. "You know what they say, if it doesn't sound crazy, you ain't dreaming big enough!"

By the time they made it to Vanderbilt Avenue, Faina had somehow managed to convince Pasha to go through with the plan.

"At this point, I might as well accept that the normal part of my life is over," he griped as he pulled on his trousers in the cargo hold. He pitched violently forward as Faina swerved to change lanes.

"Try putting them on sitting down," she suggested.

Pasha's eyes bulged as he realized Faina was looking in the rearview mirror. "Hey! Hey! Hey!" He tossed his shirt at her head. "Don't look back here! I'm undressing!"

"I'm not! I gotta check the mirror before I move over! You're in the way! You want us to get rear-ended?" She turned off the blinker. "Your scars are healing up nicely by the way." Pasha growled and finished putting his pants on directly behind the driver's seat where she couldn't see him.

"And what are you gonna be doing the whole time I'm in there, huh?" He buckled his belt. "You know it's a men's-only club, don't you?"

"That's what the fatigues are for! I'm a delivery man!"

"Man?"

"They're baggy. I got a hat."

Pasha pulled his sweater over his head and scoffed. "A hat? That changes everything!"

"Do you always have to be so cynical?" She reached back and handed him a pair of glasses.

"What are these for?"

"To make you look smarter. You are portraying an Ivy League student, after all."

Pasha held them up in front of his eyes. They must have at one point been part of some costume, for the lenses had no effect on his vision.

"Don't you think they'll notice I'm a little small for my age?"

"I said you had to look smarter, not bigger." She pulled up to the sidewalk and threw the van into park.

"Here's the plan." She turned around in her seat to face him. "There's a bar in the main lounge as soon as you go into the lobby."

"In the lobby? Right where everyone can see?"

"It ain't illegal to drink alcohol, only sell it, remember? The Yale Club is a private institution. As long as they're serving previously owned alcohol to club members only, they're not breaking any laws, so there's no reason to hide it."

"And what's your plan for getting some of that alcohol into this van?"

"Easy. All you gotta do is go in there and pull the fire alarm. Everyone will come running out of the building, and that's when I run in with the dolly. Together you and I will load up as much alcohol as we can, throw a blanket over the top, and hightail it outta there."

Pasha stared back, awed by the simplicity of it. It seemed so obvious, and yet it was utterly genius.

"All I have to do is walk in there and pull the alarm?"

"Well, not exactly. If you enter through the front they may try to check your I.D. to confirm you're an alumni."

Pasha's eyes glazed over. "If I'm not entering through the front, where am I entering?"

Faina's mouth screwed up in a sheepish smile. Pasha sighed and leaned back against the wall. He drummed his fingers against his knee and thought for a moment.

"Where's the airshaft?"

Faina jerked her thumb over her shoulder. "East Forty-fourth."

"Okay." Pasha stood with a grunt.

"You think you can do it?"

"Yeah. I think so." He reached for the back door.

"Here!" Faina tossed him his coat and hat. "Put it on overtop, then take it off once you enter the building. That way no one will recognize you."

Pasha did as told and ventured onto the sidewalk. When no one was looking, he slipped in through one of the entrances of the adjoining office building. He referenced the directory hanging near the door, hoping to find a vacant office, but they were all occupied. Pasha continued down the hall towards the stairwell. Maybe he would come up with something along the way.

Footsteps echoed down the corridor. He could hear two men laughing and conversing on their way out the door. Pasha ducked into an alcove, fearing he looked too out of place to be seen in an office building.

"Shame Frank wasn't in the office this morning."

"Where'd that receptionist say he was again?"

"Uh, said he had to run down the street to get papers signed. If it weren't for our meeting I'd say we wait for him, but we better not keep Mr. Orzabal waiting."

"Say, when do you think we're gonna meet that lady friend of his, Ms. Dimbitzer?"

"You mean Barbara?"

Pasha watched from the shadows as one of the men threw a large, brown paper bag into the trash. Pasha was seized with a stroke of inspiration.

When he was certain the men were gone, Pasha rushed to the trashcan and fished out the bag. Fortunately, the sack wasn't too wrinkled, and the rolled-up paper inside made it just heavy enough to appear full. He checked the directory again. There was only one Frank listed: Frank Sheffield of Sheffield Realty on the fourth floor.

Pasha hurried up the stairs and turned the corner of the landing. His heart did a leap. The firm was situated on the side of the airshaft. It was too perfect. He could see the receptionist through the window, seated at her desk. She was a young woman, with short, brown hair and spectacles. A nameplate on the desk read Ms. Carmichael. Pasha entered and approached the desk with a friendly smile.

"I have a delivery for Mr. Sheffield."

Pasha peeked over her head at the office behind her. The nameplate read Frank Sheffield, and his desk was situated directly in front of a window leading out into the airshaft. The receptionist hardly glanced up from her paperwork.

"You can leave it here."

Pasha blanched. He had assumed she would tell him to leave it on *his* desk. No matter. Pasha cleared his throat.

"I was, uh, instructed to leave it in his office."

The receptionist set down her pen and looked up at him with a curious expression. Pasha was sure he was sweating, and he could feel his face going red. Deep down there was a part of him that just wanted to sit down in the chair and break down to this woman. That's when another idea hit him. Pasha bent his head low.

"Look, I, uh …" He paused, sighing and passing a hand over his features dramatically. "I apologize if this seems a little awkward." It took him no effort at all to produce a nervous laugh. "In fact, this is all really embarrassing, but there are some really personal items in here—"

"Wait, aren't you delivering bagels?"

Pasha looked down at the bag. He hadn't noticed the label that read Keener Bros. Bagels.

Pasha bit his lip and made a show of cringing. "The thing is, ma'am … these are not bagels. I was told to put them in this bag so as not to draw too much attention."

The receptionist's eyes bulged. "What is it?"

Pasha took a deep breath, taking advantage of his already existing anxiety. "It's from Ms. Dimbitzer." He pretended to fumble around in his pocket for a note. "She left a message. She said something like, 'In case you were wondering what I'm wearing, here's what I'm not. Love, Babs.'"

The receptionist rolled her eyes back into her head and sucked her teeth. "Why am I not surprised?"

"It's ladies'—"

"Say no more." She jerked her thumb over her shoulder. "Mr. Sheffield's office is directly behind me." She picked up the phone and dialed away at the numbers while Pasha hastily slid into the office and shut the door behind him. He could hear the receptionist chatting away into the phone.

"Yeah, Meredith? It's Kate. You'll never guess what the hussy's done now. Apparently, she's delivering her intimates to the office! I am this close to turning in my notice!"

Pasha wasted no time sliding out the window and onto the cement roof between the buildings. There was no fire escape outside the Yale Club but there was a ladder. Pasha gradually made his way up the side of the building until he found himself on the roof. Instead of finding the utility door, he found something better: the Yale Club had a popular rooftop restaurant known as the Rooftop Terrace, and the roof of the patio was situated directly below him. Pasha carefully lowered himself onto the covering, then swung onto the patio from there. It was still the off season, and so the establishment was empty.

He jiggled the door handle but it was, of course, locked. Pasha stood back and sighed. He had accepted early on that he was probably going to have to break a window, but it did nothing to ease his conscience. The doors were glass and hatched with a series of panels. By removing the panel nearest the door handle he would inflict the least amount of damage.

He removed the flathead screwdriver he always carried on heists from his pocket, and went to work removing the rubber beading. Once that was out, he had only to jiggle the flathead screwdriver between the glass and the frame to coax it out. He carefully leaned the panel up against the wall so as not to break it, and slipped his hand through the hole to unlock the handle. The door clicked. He tiptoed inside.

Pasha was surrounded by luxury he hadn't experienced since leaving Russia. Plush chairs of rich, velvety blue flanked every table, and crystal chandeliers glittered in the shadows of the high ceilings. Pasha removed his coat and hat and put on the pair of glasses. He slicked back his hair. He couldn't allow himself to be distracted. He pressed on towards the exit and out into the hallway in search of an elevator.

The top floor was mostly empty, and Pasha felt safe as he pressed the button to summon the lift. But his sense of security immediately evaporated the second the door opened and he was greeted by the operator. Perhaps it would have been better to take the stairs.

"Main lobby, please."

The operator simply nodded and pulled the lever, showing no signs of suspicion. When the doors opened again Pasha could hear soft murmurs of conversation floating from beyond the corridor. He walked out of the elevator and immediately collided with a broad, bulbous figure.

"Pardon me, son."

Pasha looked up. His eyes bulged. He was staring into the face of a corpulent, jovial man in his sixties with a familiar handlebar mustache. Pasha finally managed to clear his throat.

"No, no. My apologies, I, uh, I should have been paying more attention … sir."

The man smiled and tipped his hat as he approached the elevator. The operator gave him a respectful bow.

"Where to, Chief Justice Taft?"

"The library, if you please, Henry."

535

The doors of the elevator closed. Pasha cupped his hands over his mouth and exhaled. He had just broken into a building where a former U.S. president happened to be staying, and was about to commit a major theft. Pasha swallowed, tightened his shoulders, and marched himself through the velvet curtains into the lobby.

The coffered ceiling was tiled with a medallion pattern of white ornamental plaster. Relief tableaus crowned the floor-to-ceiling windows, each flanked by an ionic column. The bar was a masculine affair, carpeted in studded leather and dark wood. Pasha took his time loitering nearby, familiarizing himself with the arrangement and setup, before departing in search of a fire alarm and a place to hide. He soon located one outside in the corridor.

Pasha waited until the coast was clear, then he swiftly yanked down on the lever and ran into the bathroom, where he closed himself up in a stall and climbed onto the toilet tank to hide. He could hear the confused voices over the incessant drill of the bell. He checked his watch. They would have to time it so that they beat the fire department.

When two minutes had passed, he rushed back into the corridor where the last of the gentlemen were scuttling towards the exit.

Careful not to draw attention, Pasha snuck back into the lounge. He was just peering over the bar when a figure in gray fatigues popped up like a jack-in-the-box. Pasha jumped reflexively.

"Get a hold of yourself!" It was Faina, and she already had a full box of liquor in her arms. "It's only me!"

Pasha did a double take over his shoulder. "How did you get in here so fast?"

"At this point, can you honestly say you're surprised?" She gestured behind the bar. "Now hurry up and help me finish loading these. We don't have much time. What you can't fit on the dolly, stash in your clothes."

Pasha and Faina managed to transfer an impressive load onto the pushcart, and only stopped when they heard sirens in the distance. Faina threw the sheet over the goods and wheeled the carrier towards the corridor.

"Time to hit the road!"

A team of firefighters paraded through the door as they rounded the corner towards the exit. Pasha grabbed Faina by the shoulder and pulled her back behind a potted plant.

"What are we gonna do now?"

"Hide!" Faina pulled him into the elevator and pushed the button for the doors to close.

"Now what?"

"Umm …" Her mustache was beginning to peel off. "You got a match?"

"Yeah."

"Good! Go light something on fire!"

"Are you crazy? I'm not gonna light something on fire!"

"Why not? We pulled the fire alarm."

Pasha's eyes bulged. "Faina, that's arson! We could actually hurt somebody that way!"

"Oh, yeah, I guess you're right."

They each jumped as the doors slid open revealing a suspicious-looking firefighter.

"Hey!"

Faina grabbed one of the bottles from her jacket and tossed it to the firefighter, distracting him so she could shut the doors, and pulled the lever back. Pasha stumbled back against the wall in horror.

"What'd you do that for? You just gave us away! Now he knows what we're stealing!"

"Shhh! Calm down!"

But Pasha was apoplectic. "Calm down? How can I calm down? Do you even know how to operate that thing?"

"No—"

"You're going up! Why are you going up? You said there's only one entrance! What are we gonna do now?"

"If you pipe down, I'll figure it out!"

She pulled the switch back in the opposite direction.

"No, no, no!" Pasha waved her away from the handle. "Don't go back down!"

"Well, which way do you want me to go? I can't go up, I can't go down, there's only two directions you know!"

The elevator stopped and the doors opened upon the second floor as a series of firefighters skidded around the stairwell.

"There they go!"

"Close it! Close it!" shouted Faina. Pasha jabbed the button as she shifted the lever forward once again.

"There has to be another entrance!" He turned towards her with a look of desperation. "Someone had to get all this stuff into the building!"

Their eyes met with a synchronized flicker of genius. "The freight elevator!"

Faina tightened her grip on the lever. "But where is it?"

"I think I saw something that looked like a service entrance on the west side when I was climbing up the building."

When they had traveled some ways, Faina stopped the elevator. With hushed voices, they peeked out into the passage.

"Looks like the coast is clear," whispered Faina.

They pushed the dolly down the hallway, headed for the west side of the building. A bell rang. Pasha and Faina turned. The elevator on the opposite side of the corridor opened upon a flood of angry firefighters. Pasha and Faina gasped and skittered down the narrow, checkered passageway until they came across a long, empty corner with the service elevator tucked away in the shadows. Pasha threw the door open and pushed Faina inside. Faina yanked down on the lever, and the car traveled down.

The police cars were rounding the corner as Pasha and Faina exited the building, drawing the spectators' attention up the street. Pasha and Faina hurried towards the van and hastily began unloading the crates into the cab. Fortunately, no one outside the building had any reason to look for them.

As they were loading the last crate into the van, Pasha saw the police chief marching their way. Pasha shoved Faina around towards the driver's side.

"Go!"

The chief picked up his pace. "Hey! You two!"

Pasha grabbed the sheet that had been covering the boxes and ran at the officer, throwing it over his head and affording himself a chance to dive into the passenger's seat. He slammed the door.

"Drive, Faina, drive!"

Faina stepped on the gas, pinning Pasha to his seat. She veered around the firetruck, forcing people to move aside.

Faina pulled off her mustache. "I feel like I'm in a Charlie Chaplin film."

"Yeah, we're really living the dream," retorted Pasha sarcastically.

Faina swerved into oncoming traffic. Pasha clutched his chest.

"*Chort voz mi*, Faina!" Devil take me! "Do you think you could drive a little less conspicuously? A whole crowd of witnesses saw us fleeing the scene! They know what car to look for!"

"What about my driving is conspicuous? This is Manhattan, ain't it?"

The crates slammed against the opposite wall as she skidded around a corner.

"How about in a way that's not going to get us killed then? Or break the merchandise?"

Police sirens echoed a few blocks behind them. Pasha swallowed. "We gotta get rid of these boxes quick! And whatever you do, don't go back to *Opa!*"

"Where exactly do you expect me to go then?"

"Go to the Foxhole, pull into the loading bay. Looks like I'm gonna be making my delivery early."

With Faina's erratic driving, they somehow managed to make it to the Bowery in half the amount of time it should have taken. The loading bay was empty and Faina was able to pull in swiftly and smoothly. She threw the van into park and ducked down to the floorboards.

"This way no one will know you had help."

"Good idea." He jumped out the passenger side. "I'll be right back." He shut the door and dashed in through the side entrance.

"Klokov!" He was in such a rush to get rid of the stuff that he tossed all sense of decorum aside. "Klokov!"

He ran down the hallway where Klokov's office was located. The door opened, and a disgruntled Klokov stuck his head into the corridor. Pasha slowed to a halt and swallowed, praying he hadn't just interrupted a meeting.

"What do you think you're doing running up and down screaming like that?"

Pasha cleared his throat and tried to stand up straight. "I, uh, I brought my delivery a little early today, if that's alright with you. I need to get rid of it as quick as possible. I got a van out in the loading bay."

Klokov stuck his stubby neck out as though he were trying to hear better.

"You've got a van?"

"Uh huh."

"In the loading bay?"

"Yes, sir." At that moment sirens could be heard faintly down the Bowery. "And if it's all the same to you, sir, I'd like to get it out before the cops find me."

Klokov snapped at a nearby underling. "Open up the garage." He returned his attention to Pasha. "Go ahead and pull in."

Pasha practically sprinted back to the loading bay, and hurled himself into the van, accidentally stepping on Faina's arm.

"Ow!"

"Sorry, *Faishka*." He hurled the vehicle into reverse. "What would I do without you?"

"Go back to jail, that's what you'd do."

Chapter 84:

No Greater Love

Needless to say, Uncle Matvei kept a close eye on Faina the following week. Pasha managed to get by on his own in the wake of their glorious success, but he knew he could only ride that wave for so long.

Monday evening, before Pasha could even so much as open his mouth for an obligatory hello, Anastas slammed Saturday's headline beneath Klokov's shadow at the counter of the Paddock.

"See? What did I tell you?"

The scrap was ripped from the front page of the *New York Daily*, and it smelled of Anastas's stale pockets. The photograph gave a somewhat clear view of the driver of the delivery van. It was far from immaculate, but it was enough to deem Faina recognizable to anyone well acquainted with her.

Anastas jabbed his finger at the wrinkled newsprint. "He was relying on Spichkin the whole time! This proves it!"

Pasha froze. His eyes focused on Klokov, desperately trying to read him. Klokov lowered his head and squinted. The corners of his mouth twisted downwards in an irritated expression.

"Proves what? That she drove her uncle's delivery van?" He shoved the paper back at Anastas, his stubby fingers spread wide.

But Anastas was persistent. "This is man's work, you've said it yourself. The Breadwinners don't take in no women!"

Klokov was growing impatient. "Do you see me dragging her in here for an initiation?" He held up his hand. "Look, what do I care if Miss Spichkin wants to follow Chevalsky around town all day?" He pointed his pen at Pasha. "All I know is, while he brought in hundreds of dollars' worth of hooch last week, you showed up with fifty pounds of broken car parts."

Undeterred by the edge in Klokov's voice, Anastas leaned forward, angrily clutching the table with chapped hands.

"You don't get it, do you? She ain't just following him around!" He tapped his finger on the photo with exasperated emphasis. "She was the brains behind the operation! You know she used to be the Kissing Cat Burglar, right? You think Chevalsky could come up with something like that?"

Klokov raised his head in a long, slow drag to stare dully at Anastas. All at once he began to chuckle.

"Are you telling me that a thirteen-year-old girl was the mastermind behind stealing pounds and pounds of liquor from the Yale Club?" He threw back his head and roared with laughter. "In that case, maybe we *should* start letting girls join the Breadwinners!"

"He's using her as a crutch! The same way he did Leo! How is this any different?"

Weary of their conversation, Klokov stared up at Anastas with a tired expression. "Rogue, she's a girl. End of discussion."

Pasha shut his eyes and allowed his lungs to deflate.

Klokov appraised Pasha's inventory and paid him for his service. He muddled through his fight, this time against a boy called Overland, and achieved a narrow victory along with a minor hip sprain.

When Klokov laid the money in his hand, Pasha could not help but stare at it. It was extra cash, to be honest. They didn't really even need it. Pasha's income from the Paddock was more than enough to cover his family's weekly expenses. Without Faina's aid, would his paycheck even amount to half? Though he would never admit it for the sake of his own neck, Anastas was right. Pasha did rely on Faina, and what had she to gain from lending him a hand? Nothing. She had continued to assist him even after Leo's death, only to keep him alive. Meanwhile, her own family was struggling. Since Prohibition began the bank had raised their interest rates, making it nearly impossible for Uncle Matvei to pay back his loan, and for the first time he was forced to actually collect rent. Bit by bit their prosperity was dwindling, and yet Faina thought little of her own circumstances, going out of her way to improve Pasha's.

To say Pasha ran home would be a gross inaccuracy, for his injury made that quite impossible, but he did hurry back to the tenement with all the enthusiasm of Bob Cratchit on Christmas Eve. He bypassed the front door, and clambered up the fire escape to Faina's window. The curtains were pulled back and the room was empty. It occurred to him that perhaps they might be having dinner at that moment, but Anya pushed up her own window and stuck her head out to look at him.

"She's on the roof. She's grounded right now, so try to be sneaky about it."

Pasha nodded. "Thanks, Anya." He turned and made his way up the rest of the building. Faina was slumped dully against the ledge, staring out at the horizon and looking utterly dismal. There was a tear in her stockings, and the sole of her shoe was beginning to detach at the toe.

"Aren't you cold?" he asked without greeting her.

Faina jumped at the sound of another voice. "It's not so bad," she said, regaining her composure.

"Glad to see you're getting outside again."

She shrugged. "I'm not supposed to be. Uncle Matvei put me on restriction."

Pasha shoved his hands into his pockets and shuffled her way. "So I've heard." He leaned up against the ledge with his back to the city.

"Yeah, he didn't take too kindly to the police searching our tenement."

The only reason Pasha and Faina weren't sitting in a precinct at that moment was because no one could provide proof that Pasha and Faina had been the ones to steal the alcohol. The liquor, which the Yale Club was able to report stolen since it was legal private property, was already gone when the police showed up at their tenement. The van was back in the garage. All they had were eyewitness accounts.

Faina drew a long inhale through her nose, her expression wilting further. "He hates me."

Pasha drew his eyebrows together in disbelief. "Your uncle doesn't hate you! He loves you, Faina. He's just scared for your safety, is all."

"If Leo had done the same thing, Uncle Matvei wouldn't have batted an eye."

"Leo was older and contractually obligated to serve a street gang. You're not."

Faina turned and threw her arms out in a violent display of desperation. "If I had done nothing, what would've happened to you? Does anyone ever think about that?"

Pasha's head bent forward with shame. "I do." He reached into his pocket. "That's why I want you to have this." He produced what could've been described as a fistful of cash, only it was much larger than his fist, and placed it in her hand. "This is your half of the money."

Faina stared down at the cash with wide, bewildered eyes. "But I'm not a Breadwinner."

"Maybe not, but you earned it. The whole point of the Breadwinners is to help young men take care of their families." Without thinking, he took a step forward, closing the distance between them. "You're my family, Faina. I'm always gonna take care of you. You and everyone you love. Without you, and Leo, and Uncle Matvei, and Anya, I never would have made it through my initiation, and I would never have

543

lasted this long. You've sacrificed your safety and your reputation just to keep me alive. I owe you everything." He closed her fingers around the cash. "Use this to help your family. There will be more. Every week. Every paycheck I get, half will go to you."

Faina stared up at him, tenderness filling her eyes. "Pasha, you don't have to do this."

Pasha slipped her an easy smile, and smoothed a lock of her hair over her shoulder.

"I like taking care of the people I love." He winked and made his way back towards the fire escape.

"Love?" she called over the high-pitched wind. But Pasha didn't hear her.

Epilogue

Staccato sat in an armchair facing the window in the drawing room of Feifior, his face eclipsed by a newspaper. Beside him sat Melodious, diligently tuning his accordion and saying little. Skelter had gone out foraging for spring onions some time ago, and Pyro and Sonata were huddled up in the corner whispering and snorting at each other's jokes in a rather conspicuous manner.

"How much longer are we going to pretend we don't know?" muttered Melodious with an amused smirk.

Staccato turned the page and shook the wrinkles from his paper. "Not too much longer. They need to be made aware that someone's keeping an eye on them or there's no telling what they'll get up to."

Sonata stood and cleared her throat. "I think I'll go out for a walk in the gardens."

Staccato didn't bother looking up from his paper but replied with barely perceptible sarcasm, "Enjoy your stroll, dearest."

She did not seem to notice, for she left rather abruptly and without suspicion. Staccato and Melodious counted together under their breath.

"3 … 2 … 1 …"

Pyro stood with an exaggerated stretch. "I'm gonna go take Brash out for a ride."

Melodious snickered while Staccato shook his head.

"Oh, Pyro?" Staccato called, his tone slightly ominous.

Pyro froze halfway over the threshold and turned with a sheepish expression. Staccato lowered his paper and beckoned him closer. Pyro did as told. Melodious set aside his accordion and excused himself from the room. Staccato waited until the door had shut behind him to begin, leaving Pyro to cower nervously before his chair.

"You're quite a bit older than her."

Pyro raised an eyebrow. "Older than who?"

Staccato paused to stare him down for a moment, then continued. "Sonata is mature for her age. But I want you to keep that in mind."

Pyro looked over each shoulder as though to confirm they were the only two in the room.

"You can be assured I will treat Sonata with the utmost care and respect," he said in a lowered voice.

"I appreciate that." He hesitated. "Pyro, something we haven't discussed … I know with things the way they are right now, the Land Lock, and Sonata being separated from her parents, it's easy to forget that she is the sole heir to her father's throne. And one day, she's going to be queen. You, on the other hand, gave up your title—"

"And I'd give it up again to let Sonata be queen."

Staccato stopped and raised his eyebrows at this remark, clearly impressed with Pyro's devotion.

"I am pleased to hear you say that. However, you've shown quite a disdain for being addressed as 'Prince' in the years since. You do know that if you end up marrying you will have a title again."

"You can call me whatever you like. The only title I care about having is 'Sonata's man.' This isn't a casual relationship for me, Staccato. I love Sonata. I know you have reservations about your goddaughter's involvement with me because of my past, and I can't blame you for that. But I can promise you that Sonata will always come first—her safety, her happiness, and her wellbeing."

For a moment, Pyro thought he could detect the barest hint of a smile in Staccato's countenance.

"Very good. Then you have my blessing." Before Pyro could declare his joy, Staccato smoothed a hand over his beard. "But there are some ground rules." He paused and drew a deep breath before continuing. "I realize the two of you are responsible adults, and I can't force you to do—or not do—anything. However, I am in charge of this group, meaning I decide who stays and who goes, and may exercise that power whenever I please. I see little use in forcing a chaperone on you two, or depriving you of a solitary walk in the woods or being alone in a sitting room together. But I cannot abide sneaking off to each other's rooms, hiding in broom closets, or skulking off to the secret passage behind the kelpie statue in the library."

At the mention of the statue Pyro's face turned scarlet.

"In other words, I expect you to be a perfect gentleman, is that clear?"

Pyro gave a solemn nod. "You have nothing to worry about."

"Good." Staccato picked his newspaper back up. "You're free to go catch up with Sonata."

When Pyro did not immediately leave, Staccato flicked his eyes over the top of his reading curiously. Pyro was squinting at the headline.

"There's been another Firebird sighting?"

Staccato scoffed and shrugged. "Appears so. This time in New York City. I wouldn't give it much attention. The papers have been reporting Firebird sightings for the past twenty-eight years."

"Weren't you just in New York City?"

Staccato nodded. "I was. Why?"

Pyro shook his head and rubbed at his chin. "It's just, it seems like there's always a Firebird sighting wherever you are."

Staccato put down the paper and stared up at Pyro with quizzical eyes.

"Well," Pyro began to explain, "before New York it was spotted twice flying over the Sea of Scorpius near Iwakishi. And before that it was spotted while you were in Aquarius checking on your property. That was when we started training the new recruits. Then it was in New York again during one of your visits to your aunt. And again in Khan Lau." Pyro gestured to the newspaper. "Check if you don't believe me."

Staccato riffled through the pages until he found the article about the Firebird, and scanned through the paragraphs where previous sightings had been mentioned.

"Well, we can't be sure they were the same dates."

"They are," Pyro insisted. "Because I noticed every time it happened."

For a moment Staccato sat staring at the dates, absentmindedly stroking his beard. Then he folded up the paper and dismissed the idea with a shake of his head.

"Well, as I said, the papers have been predicting Firebird sightings for the past twenty-eight years. It's nothing but a coincidence." He set the paper on the table once more.

Pyro shrugged and made his way towards the exit. "If you say so."

The door slammed behind him, prompting Staccato to grind his teeth and sigh. He drummed his fingers on the arm of the chair. His eyes flicked temptingly back towards the paper. Unable to resist, he reached for the article but stopped himself with a particularly arrogant grimace.

"Firebird following me?" He scoffed. "Utter nonsense!"

To be continued in The Star Catcher …

Keep reading for a preview of The Star Catcher!

June 1924

"Why are we here?" Pasha sat at the lunch counter of Vavilov's drugstore with Sergei and Yuri staring dismally at the opposite wall.

Yuri scraped his spoon against his glass and spoke between mouthfuls. "Because it's hot, and when it's hot you eat ice cream."

"Could we not have gone somewhere else?" Pasha twirled the bottle cap of his untouched coke between his fingers. "Are you two trying to kill me?"

Yuri waved his hand as though Pasha were being dramatic, which, in a way, he was."Will you relax and drink your coke?"

In the bright light of the drugstore's windows, Pasha noticed for the first time that there were dark circles under Yuri's eyes. "You look exhausted."

"Mila has colic."

"I thought you said she was a peaceful baby."

"She was. But she's three weeks now. That's when colic symptoms start showing." He pushed the cherry around with the end of his straw. "Should probably go stay with Emma."

"What about her parents?" asked Sergei. "I can't imagine you'd get much sleep avoiding getting caught."

"It'd still be more than I get at home."

"Well, you look awful." Sergei shook his head. "If you don't get some sleep soon you're gonna get licked your next fight."

"Trust me. I can handle it. I worry more about my sisters. Lana said the foreman almost caught Maryusa falling asleep at the machine the other day."

Pasha put down his coke mid sip. "Maryusa's working? How old is she?"

"Seven."

Pasha wasn't sure what to say, but Yuri seemed to already know what he was thinking.

"Be glad you only have one little sibling."

Pasha took an awkward swig of his coke, and the conversation grew quiet. At length, he lowered his voice.

"Hey, did either of you get a message from Klokov to meet him in his office on the 26th for a special assignment?"

Yuri abandoned his glass and leaned in further. "I thought I was the only one."

"I got one too," added Sergei. "Any idea what it's about?"

Pasha shook his head. "Not a clue."

"Alls I know is, I better be getting paid for it," declared Yuri.

The door opened and a dark haired girl walked in holding hands with a boy. Pasha instinctively twitched.

"Will you cut it out?" Yuri practically shouted, finally losing his patience. "Faina and Dmitry ain't even—" Before Yuri could finish his sentence, they heard laughter on the stairwell leading to the flat overhead. Faina and Dmitry danced into the room, their fingers laced together and swinging between them.

"I hate you right now," muttered Pasha between clenched teeth.

Sergei gave him an apologetic pat on the back. "Sorry, Pasha. We should have listened to you."

Dmitry Vavilov was a handsome, pristine looking young man with smooth, perfectly parted blonde hair, and eyes so blue and bright you forgot he was wearing glasses. His hands were always immaculately clean and his teeth were perfectly aligned. Without so much as a glance about the room, he leaned in and kissed Faina squarely on the lips.

"I really hate you right now," Pasha hissed again.

Yuri dropped his spoon down inside his empty cup and rolled his eyes. "Relax. Don't act like such a baby." He started to raise his hand. "Hey, Faina!"

Pasha grabbed his hand and slammed it down on the counter. "Shut up! Don't call them over!"

"This is your chance to show Faina what she's missing! Give her a little side by side comparison!"

"What's to compare? Dmitry and I are exactly alike only he's better! He's actually better at being me than I am! I can't compete with a better version of myself!"

"Pasha, calm down," said Sergei. "You said it yourself, Faina's relationships never last."

"It's been two months, Sergei. Faina's never gone out with anyone this long before."

"So find someone else." The three turned to see Roan sitting at the end of the counter, who had apparently been listening to their conversation. "Listen, Pasha, to be honest, you're dodging a bullet. I've dated Faina, and she's a nice girl but she's completely starved for affection. No man needs a clingy broad. Not while you're young anyway."

Pasha drew back, trying not to look offended on Faina's behalf.

"Listen to the man," said Yuri, tossing his shoulders. "You're sixteen and you've been hung up on Faina for years. You've never even dated before! Have you even kissed a girl yet?"

Fortunately, Sergei stepped in before Pasha had to answer. "I think what Yuri is trying to say is maybe you should pursue someone else for awhile."

Pasha propped his elbow on the counter and held his chin up with his fist. "Like who?"

By now, Yuri was getting irritable with Pasha's pity party. "Oh, come on! I know Faina isn't the only girl you've ever been attracted to!"

"Nadia Berkowitz," answered Sergei, slyly indicating to the girl sitting at a table near the window.

"Shut up!" Pasha practically pulled his cap down over his face. "Don't tell him that!"

Yuri narrowed his eyes at Pasha with an incredulous scowl. "Boy, you really have a type, don't you?"

"What are you talking about? They look totally different!"

"They look just alike!"

"Oh, what? Because they both have dark hair?"

"They're built similar."

"I don't know, Yelena is kinda skinny," interjected Sergei.

Pasha enumerated their differences on his fingers. "Their noses are different, their eye color is different—"

"Alright, alright! Point is, if I saw them both from a distance I wouldn't be able to tell them apart."

"Pasha!" Faina had spotted him from across the room and waltzed towards him, dragging Dmitry behind her. "I didn't realize you were here!"

Dmitry greeted them with an all too enthusiastic grin and a friendly wave. "Hey, fellas!"

Pasha tried to smile but it felt more like he was baring his teeth. "Hey!"

"We were just finishing up," Sergei hastily explained in an attempt to save Pasha the heartache.

"Already?" Dmitry noted Pasha's mostly full bottle of soda. "You've hardly touched your coke. Does it taste alright?"

"Yeah, everything is fi—"

"I know what it needs," interrupted Faina. "It's missing a bag of peanuts."

Dmitry looked her askance, his arm fitted firmly around her shoulders. "Peanuts?"

"Mhm! Pasha and I like putting peanuts in our coke. It's even better if you add it to a float with vanilla ice cream."

"Oh, yeah! I have noticed you two doing that before! That's right!" It didn't even seem to bother him that Pasha and Faina had a special dish they shared.

"It was my idea to try it." Faina made a display of placing her hands on her hips with a sassy expression. "Another of my genius ideas."

"Yeah, sure, Huncamunca." Pasha froze the moment the name left his mouth. He hadn't meant to call her that.

"Huncamunca?" echoed Dmitry with an amused and curious simper.

Pasha stared down at the counter and fiddled with the coke bottle. There was no going back now.

"Yeah, that's uh, that's my nickname for Faina."

Again, Dmitry remained nonplussed, if not delighted. "Huncamunca! That's cute!" He squeezed Faina closer to his side. "Maybe I oughta start calling you that!"

Over my dead body, thought Pasha.

"Well, Faina and I better skedaddle. We've got tickets to a matinee." He pulled her away and waved goodbye. "You fellas enjoy! See you later!" The bell over the door rang as they departed.

Yuri stared at Pasha with his nose twisted up in disgust. "The hell's a Huncamunca?"